17

The Lees of Menokin

An Early American Love Story

a novel by

Suzanne Hadfield Semsch

Suzanne H Semsch (signature)

The Sept. 17, 1776 letter on cover, from Francis Lightfoot Lee to Thomas Jefferson, is used with the permission of The Historical Society of Pennsylvania (HSP), Gratz Collection.

Photograph of Menokin ruin, National Park Service
http://www.cr.nps.gov/history/online_books/declaration/site49.htm

Architectural drawing of Menokin House, c.1769,
by permission of The Virginia Historical Society

Dislaimer
The contents of this book are solely the responsibility of the author and have not been endorsed by any other publication, organization, or persons.

ISBN: 1-4392-4596-7
ISBN-13: 9781439245965
Library of Congress Control Number: 2009905980

Visit www.booksurge.com to order additional copies.

For Francis Lightfoot Lee
on the occasion of his 275th birthday,
October 14, 2009.

Francis Lightfoot Lee, 1734 - 1797
a Virginia Signer of America's Declaration of Independence
(Used with permission of the Independence Hall Association,
on the web at ushistory.org) by Ole Erekson,
Engraver, c1876, Library of Congress

Author's Note

What on earth, you may ask, prompted anyone to spend years of research in order to write a novel about an old ruin and a quiet unassuming man whose greatest known accomplishment, although he was in public life for almost thirty years, was to put his name to a famous piece of paper? Well, read on.

It began one day over thirty years ago in the mid-1970s when I was driving down a back road through Richmond County, Virginia, a road I had traveled many times before. On this particular day something made me stop and take a serious look at the historical marker along the road's edge. I knew it had been the home of a member of the famous Lee family, but that's all I knew. A narrow farm lane led along the side of a field and, feeling adventurous I turned  in, knowing I was probably guilty of trespassing. I came to an old shed and parked, proceeding warily on foot. Very soon the outline of a chimney appeared through the trees and I realized I was approaching whatever remained of Menokin House. My heart began to beat faster. There is no way to describe my excitement as I made that first tour of the abandoned 18th century ruin—at least a fourth of it destroyed with the roof caved in on one corner. It was completely overgrown by weeds, trees, and brush, yet colorful faces of daffodils and star-of-Bethlehem poked through on the hillside, signaling a welcome. It appeared that window-framing and interior paneling had been removed, and what remained was the shell of what once must have been a handsome plantation home. I imagined ghosts popping up at every turn, not to mention the possibility of snakes, which was very real indeed.

Fascinated, charmed, and captivated all at once, I wanted to know more, to learn about the people who had built this house and lived there. Long before the internet made such things simple, I began what turned into several years of serious research. In order to organize and keep track of events and the many political and family connections, I created extensive index files, one alphabetical, the other by date. I began my quest in the libraries and historical societies in Richmond, gathering and transcribing a collection of more than fifty of Francis Lee's letters, some of his brothers' many letters to him, as well as letters of other members of the Continental Congress. I contacted libraries across the country that were known to have collections which might be helpful; laboriously copied records from county and state deeds and wills; and made many more trips to the Menokin site (after seeking permission from the owner, who was said to roam the area with a shotgun to ward off trespassers!).

As I scoured countless books and references and poured over my pages and pages of notes, my passion for the task increased. The characters of Francis Lightfoot Lee and Rebecca Tayloe Lee began to take on reality and come alive for me. They began to walk and talk. I truly fell in love with dear Frank and his Becky, as you will no doubt discover within these pages. After completing the manuscript, sharing it with my writing group and a few family members and friends, I went on to write some short stories, several magazine articles, the military history chapter of Westmoreland County, Virginia's bicentennial book, another novel, and took on a new job as publications director at a private school. Then we moved across the state when my husband retired (for the second time). The Menokin story remained on the useless floppy disks of a KayPro computer and on a dog-eared paper copy in a box for over three decades. In early 2009, with encouragement from an old friend who had read it in its early stages, I decided to pull out the faded hardcopy for a review. So began an *affaire de cœur* all over again. You are looking at the result.

Prepare to travel back in time to the year 1768, when America was thirteen colonies ruled by England's King George III. During the next fifteen years while these colonies struggled in uncharted seas suffering untold hardships, losing battle after battle, before at last winning their freedom from Crown and Parliament, it is a certainty none of the participants knew how long or bitter the task would be. Yet once the Declaration of Independence was signed and delivered, there was no turning back. It was a long and bloody road they traveled from the time they first met as a revolutionary congress in 1775, until the peace treaty was signed in 1783 and thirteen very diverse colonies found themselves as one country—the United States of America. The Virginia Colony contributed more than its share to this epic effort, not only during the revolutionary beginnings, but in the fulfillment of the deed. In the forefront of the political fight were the Lee brothers of Stratford Plantation, one of whom was Francis Lightfoot Lee. Francis and his brother Richard Henry Lee (the most fearlessly determined politician of the six brothers) were among the fifty-six signers of that famous Declaration in 1776. Although Francis Lee was known as a calm, rather inconspicuous man, he was definitely associated with that "hot-headed group of radicals" in the 1760s and 70s Virginia House of Burgesses along with his brother Richard, Patrick Henry, George Mason, and Thomas Jefferson, among others. They were the "rabble-rousers" during the early days of unrest with England's rule.

This novel is Francis Lee's story. It begins with his adult life in the far western county of Loudoun on lands left to him in his father's legacy, where he was soon elected as a burgess to represent his county in the colonial capital of Williamsburg. Francis served many terms through the early revolutionary days in Virginia's House of Burgesses, first from Loudoun County, and later from Richmond County. This service was interrupted when he was elected to the Continental Congress, where he remained four long years away from home. Returning to Virginia, he was soon called to a term as senator in the newly formed state government. In 1787 he contributed to the eventual acceptance of the Constitution in his state while others, including his brother Richard opposed it, thinking it unfair to the south.

Equally important is the story of Francis Lee's delightfully poignant marriage and lifelong love affair with Rebecca Tayloe of Mount Airy Plantation. Her father provided them with 1,000 acres and built them the home they would give the Indian name for the surrounding hills, Menokin. The home soon became Frank Lee's refuge and the place where he was always happiest. The fact that Becky traveled with him to Philadelphia, remaining at his side throughout his four years in the Congress, is certainly testimony to her strength and devotion. Their contented, but sadly childless, existence was surely blessed when two of his brother William's young daughters came to live with them and grow up at Menokin House.

Although every one of Frank's five brothers came to be, at some time and in one way or another, vilified, criticized, or challenged for their actions or political positions, not one word of condemnation or scorn did I ever come across concerning Francis. He was occasionally deemed "quiet" or "lazy," even "weak" in one case, but he was liked and respected by all, so far as I could discover. He was named in a poem written by one of his many nieces as "the sweetest of all the Lees," to which I would have to agree.

Fictitious characters and situations are included in my narrative for the purpose of story telling—to breathe life into the personalities of Francis and Becky Lee, as well as to portray typical period backgrounds amidst a variety of actual events. Foremost among those characters who have no basis in fact are Martha Tutt, Francis's housekeeper at Loudoun farm; the slaves Ben, Berth, Isaac, Samuel, Pompey, Zeke, Zoey, Cris, Hector, and George; the overseers Joe Grimes and James West; Peter Hauck, the Pennsylvania soldier; Mrs. Bolton, the Baltimore landlady; Doctor Richter, the butcher-surgeon from New York; and the "disreputable" Rappahannock half-breed, Charles MacIntosh, among others. Becky's personal maid was indeed named Cate, and Landon Carter frequently mentioned his slave Nassau in his diary. These and others have all helped me tell the story of *The Lees of Menokin*, and their actions are products of my imagination. I hope that neither Francis nor Becky Lee would be too critical of my having added these individuals to their story. Perhaps, after all, their inclusion won't cause the reader to stray too far from the reality of their lives.

Menokin Today

Today's Menokin site is far different from when I first explored it. A foundation established in 1995 by Martin Kirwin King is thriving and growing in scope. The ruin has been sheltered by a roof, and parts of the walls have been reinforced. More than a thousand pieces of woodwork and trim removed in 1965 have been returned, and are now being preserved and selectively exhibited in the King Conservation and

Visitor's Center opened near the ruin in 2004. The Foundation's intent is to use Menokin—the house, site, and architectural fragments—as a lively teaching resource, perhaps without substantially restoring the house. The Menokin Foundation preserves and interprets Menokin to further the world's understanding of architectural conservation, archaeology, history, ecology, and other areas of the humanities.

The Foundation owns and manages the 500-acre property, more than half of which is in the Rappahannock River Valley National Wildlife Refuge; their vision is to inspire the public to be responsible stewards of the world's historic places. Their goal is to educate students of all ages on the conservation of cultural and natural resources by using Menokin and its surrounding acres of forest, wetlands, and shoreline as a teaching and learning center. To learn more, check out their website: www.menokin.org. or call (804) 333-1776 for membership details or to verify visiting hours.

It is my hope that this biographical novel, by enhancing and showcasing the lives of those who lived and loved within these 18th century walls, will aid the efforts of the Menokin Foundation in the preservation and study of what remains of Menokin House. May it also entertain and, perhaps, educate the reader.

– Suzanne Hadfield Semsch, August 2009

Menokin ruin, probably vintage 1960s (National Park Service, Littleton)

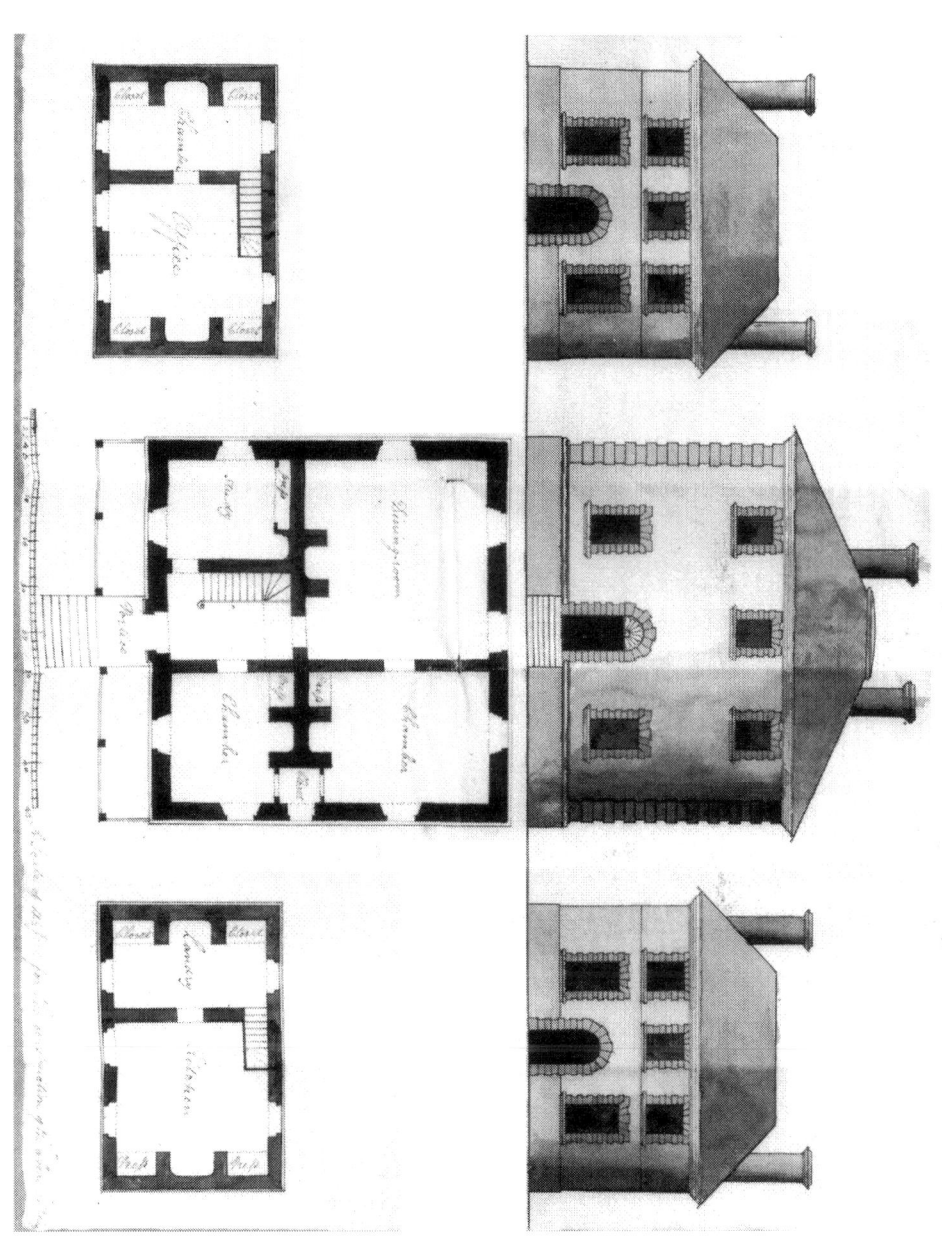

*Copy of an original 1769 architectural drawing of Menokin House.
(by permission of Virginia Historical Society, Richmond, VA)*

Contents

PART I
A VIRGINIA COURTSHIP
1768 – 1769

PART II
RICHMOND COUNTY
1770 – 1775

PART III
THE CONTINENTAL CONGRESS
1776 – 1779

PART IV
HOMECOMING
1780 – 1797

PART I
A VIRGINIA COURTSHIP
1768 – 1769

As opposed as the American colonists were to taxation without representation, they were even more opposed to any token representation in Parliament which England offered them.

> " ... *considering the utter impracticability of their {our} ever being fully and equally represented in Parliament, and the great expense that must unavoidably attend even a partial representation there, this House think that a taxation of their {our} constituents, even without their {our} consent, grievous as it is, would be preferable to any representation that could be admitted for them there.*"

Circular Letter,
Massachusetts House of Representatives
to the American Colonies
Boston, March 1768

The Burgesses

Williamsburg was not only sleepy, it was definitely provincial if compared to its sister seats of government such as Philadelphia, Boston, or New York. Those who came to govern here were, for the most part, unaware of this difference and for several months every year when the governor called the assembly to session, the tiny town bustled like an anthill on a warm spring day. During these two periods this small village in the colony of Virginia played at a sophistication that was not the least out of keeping with the charm of its European architecture nor the backgrounds of its visitors.

The village had begun to shake itself out as His Majesty's governing body once again burst upon its sleepy scene. For a week the travelers had straggled into town. Gates creaked on hinges, doors slammed, friends called to one another, and bedding aired in the yards. Candles glowed yellow-white in the windows at dusk. It all meant one thing. The burgesses were back. Travel-wrinkled and weary, from every corner of the Virginia Colony they rumbled into town by carriage, chariot, coach and horseback. A few sailed up the James or York Rivers from the Chesapeake Bay. From stately mansions along tidal waterways came Carters, Lees, Byrds, Blands, Beverleys, Wormeleys, Masons, Harrisons, and more, two from each county. A variegated hodgepodge of wives, children, pets, and slaves clamored in their wake. And gossip commenced at the Raleigh. It was definitely the place to bide time until the opening session.

It was late March 1768, the day before the first session was scheduled. By noon the shopkeepers realized there would be little profit while everyone was getting settled in and because of the unusual heat. Smiles, brought to their acquisitive English faces by the influx, faded as the hours passed. Although it wasn't even April, the temperature pushed as high as mid-July and then some for the second day, and those gathered in Virginia's little capital were feeling summer-time hot. No one was likely to venture upon the sweltering gritty streets longer than necessary. The merchants, shrugging to one another, settled down to wait. They would line their pockets soon enough—it was a twice yearly certainty.

Late that afternoon the elected burgess from Loudoun County rode into the village, tired and exhausted after his long journey, almost one hundred and seventy-five miles. Thinking the trip had never seemed so long, Francis Lightfoot Lee knew he had a peck of dirt lodged beneath his clothes. Every muscle ached. Saddle jounce could cause a man a mountain of discomfort, and he rubbed his backside, while perusing the room he'd call home for the next six or so weeks. He was waiting for Ben to unsaddle the horses and make some housekeeping arrangements. The Negro had been part of his life since childhood; keenly observant and helpful for the most part, Ben was also skilled at bargaining and easily bribed the lazy housemaid to make immediate preparations for Colonel Lee's bath. Francis never asked the particulars.

Confident, and following Ben's directions, he crossed the yard, boots crunching on the crushed shell of the walk, to enter the slatted door adjacent to the stable. He was stripped to his skin in barely a minute. Climbing over the wooden staves of the half-hogshead tub, he found the water tepid, but decided not to complain. The slave sloshed the grime of the journey out of his master's hair and scrubbed his back in silence. Francis went limp as the strong fingers eased the misery out of his aching shoulder blades. "Dear God," he groaned, "don't stop, Ben." It was probably the last time he'd have the stuffy little necessary to himself during the entire stay and he languished in full enjoyment of it. When the tenement filled up it would be a tussle to use the place at all.

A huge three-quarter moon above the tree tops grinned at him as he sauntered down the steps of the Ludwell tenement an hour later. A few wispy clouds flitted across its face. Wonderful. Just wonderful, Francis marveled, thinking what a fine place Williamsburg really was. Feeling remarkably refreshed, he thought he might be able to face his fellows after all, now that he was relieved of the tiresome soil of travel. He had no immediate cares, real or imagined, to spoil the prospects of good companionship. Tilting his head so as to keep an eye on the moon, and swinging his arms jauntily, Francis Lee headed for the Raleigh.

A hound in Randolph's stable yard bayed suspiciously as he passed. Curiosity sent him on the long way around to the tavern. He wondered who'd arrived and whom he might encounter during the evening. The night was balmy and he inhaled deep exaggerated breaths of warm air. Excitement lurked around every corner. He could feel it. Striding down Gloucester Street, he passed the shuttered silversmith and shoemaker's shops and paused to adjust the ruffled cravat at his throat, examining his reflection in the bubbled panes of the apothecary window. It didn't occur to Francis to recognize the brief stop as an act of vanity because he'd never considered himself to be vain. He was, however, always a bit nervous about these first night meetings with his fellow assemblymen after the half-year separations.

"Evenin', Mistah Frank." It was Lucas, Richard Henry Lee's manservant. The square-jawed black face peered intently at his master's younger brother in the moonlit street. Lucas always looked as though he knew what you were going to say before you got it out, and much of the time he did. Francis nodded, waiting.

"Massa Richard, he lodg'd at de inn." Lucas thumbed in the direction of the Red Lion, a building away. "De Missus a mite sickly. She stayed to home."

"Thank you, Lucas." It was disturbing to learn Anne wasn't well. He was more than passing fond of his brother's wife. "I'm sorry to hear about Mrs. Lee."

"Yas-suh," Lucas nodded in agreement. "Gone to de ord'nary he has. 'Bout a hour past, as I figgers it." Again the slave pointed, this time toward the Raleigh Tavern.

"I appreciate it, Lucas. Thank you. You have answered all my questions as usual."

The Negro beamed, stepping into the shadows to let his master's brother pass.

Once inside the tavern, Francis spotted Richard immediately. He was seated at their favorite corner table. It was an excellent spot they had discovered over the years, from which to view the comings and goings. The brothers hadn't seen each other in several months. Their pleasure would have been just as complete, however, had it been only days and they made no secret of it. They embraced, clapped one another on the back, and embraced again. For an hour they traded family news. Francis listened sadly to the trouble of Anne's recurring ague. The persistent chills and fevers had plagued her since before Christmas, her husband explained. When finally the conversation turned, it was to a subject always on Richard's mind and for which they had both come to Williamsburg. Richard's news was of the turmoil in the New York Colony and the letter sent from the Massachusetts Bay representatives.

"So it seems, Frank, as though barely having trampled the stamp tax monster, we're now faced with an arbitrary duty on paper, glass, lead, and tea—of all things—tea. I could scarce believe my ears when first I heard it. Patrick, by the by, should be here soon. He's got a copy of the Massachusetts letter from somewhere. He showed it to me this morning. His sources of information remain a mystery to me! At any rate, the Bostonians hope to oppose Parliament with a solidly united colonial front, and they'll need our help to do it."

Patrick Henry always knew ahead of everyone else just what outrages were being considered by the British government against her American colonies, and he made it his business to spread the word as quickly as possible, Francis noted, not for the first time.

"Speaking of Patrick, and in he walks," Richard said, catching sight of the burgess from Louisa. "Sir," he began, rising to his feet. "Join us. Frank and I are just sharing a cup after our separation. What will you have?"

"Nice to see you, friends. Are you sure I won't be intruding?" Patrick Henry paused, waiting for the agreeable nods that were forthcoming. "Then I shall do so, Gentlemen! It has been an exceedingly trying day. I'm bone tired."

"And I also," Francis offered. "Especially so. The journey was abominable."

Richard turned back to his brother. "What time did you arrive?"

"Oh, a couple of hours ago I should imagine. Long enough to have had a good scrub, thanks to Ben and his ingenuity!"

"Patrick, I was just telling Frank I saw you this morning. That you showed me a copy of the letter from Massachusetts Bay. But that's not what I was leading up to just now."

"What then?"

"There was a slave auction this afternoon. I was just wondering if either of you witnessed it?" Richard's intense eyes bored into his brother.

"No, but was this one any different? They're common enough. Not pleasant, but common enough."

An awkward silence ensued. Patrick Henry ordered a tankard of ale; the three fidgeted, waiting for the black serving man to leave the table. When he was gone, Richard continued. "It was an ugly thing today."

The other two shrugged. It always was. They would have preferred him not to talk about it and concentrated on their drinks.

Richard, ignoring their disinterest, pursued his subject. "There was a girl, good-looking, very young ... thirteen, fourteen at the most. They ... ah ... tore the few remaining shreds of clothing off her as she stood on the block ... beautiful nubile body she had ... " Richard paused, seemingly lost in thought.

"What are you leading up to, R.H.? For heaven's sake, spit it out, man." Francis leaned back in his chair, beginning to feel the relaxing effect of the rum. "You didn't buy her, did you?"

Patrick shot him a glance. He hadn't been with the Lee brothers often under this type of circumstance. Most frequently their contacts had been made in a strict atmosphere of business. Now he was uncertain what to expect and decided to wait for the outcome in silence.

Richard scorched them with a shriveling look. They obviously weren't in the mood to hear his lecture on the evils of humanity. But, damn it all, it had been a grueling experience. The wench had been so terrified or mortified or both, that she vomited a watery mucus all over the man who was examining her for purchase. The infuriated buyer had paid his money and ordered her ten lashes. "She was bought by one of our upstanding fellow burgesses, Gentlemen," Richard spit out scornfully. "For the purpose of pleasure, as he announced loudly to the crowd gathered there. It was a sickening performance all round," he declared, lowering his voice. "I merely wondered if either of you might have witnessed it. The gentleman, I might add, is a newcomer to the House."

Francis shook his head sympathetically. Every so often Richard set off on a tangent to abolish the inequities of slavery. Francis didn't disagree with the principles espoused, he just hoped this was not going to be one of those times. He was too tired this evening. Besides, Patrick might think they were trying to talk down to his level, which wouldn't be the case at all. But they had never been able to figure out his background, so it seemed best to steer clear of personal observations on social issues.

Patrick was staring at Richard with interest. He continued to discover things about the arrogant, self-assured delegate from Westmoreland County that fascinated him. The man owned countless slaves, yet he had this violent reaction to a public sale. "I didn't see it, Sir, but I believe I observed the hustling of the poor wench in question, on the corner, just a few minutes ago. They are selling her off for an hour of diversion at a time. I ... declined."

"My God! What is this colony coming to? What riff-raff are we allowing to be elected these days?" Richard moaned, signaling the innkeeper for more rum. He wished he'd never brought the subject up. "Frank?"

It was time to talk about something else and Francis knew it. "Times are changing, R.H. It's as simple as that." He shifted his chair to face Patrick. "Tell us what you know about the Massachusetts position. Richard says you have information."

The three talked until well past midnight. They were joined around ten by young Tom Jefferson who sat, rather stiffly, at the corner of the table, listening. It was only when the rum forced his tired eyelids to the halfway mark that Francis rose to break up the group, which had become congenial following Richard's brief burst of benevolence. The next day was Thursday. With the exception of Jefferson, who was not yet a burgess, the opening session of assembly would draw them together again at eleven.

"Adieu, my dear friends," Francis called over his shoulder. "The comfort of my bed beckons. I trust that on this trip perhaps, I'll find it free of lice!" Swaying slightly, he crossed the room suspecting he'd put too much rum and not enough food in his travel-weary stomach. He took the shortest route back to Nicholson Street, probably too pleasantly relaxed this time to be impressed by the moon.

༺◌༻

The following day the lawmakers took their places for the opening session. The lower chamber in the Virginia Capitol, meeting room of the House of Burgesses, provided somewhat minimum accommodations. The room was musty, stale with disuse; its occupants crowded together on stiff-backed benches. Soon all but the least sensitive among them became painfully aware of the sour scent of male bodies clothed in layers of woolen and silk garments. Virginia's elected body, answering writs of the royal governor, had met in this room or one similar to it for a century and a half. No less compelling than the governor's call was the clarion call of the social season. There would be parties, balls, and the theatre, not to mention the added spice of horse racing, matchmaking, high-stake gambling, and an overall brandied sort of fellowship. Wigs were freshly powdered and laces starched in gay preparation. Few established families resisted the temptation to groom a member to service in the Virginia House. Elected year after year, as the patriarch died or became too gouty to travel the wretched highways to Williamsburg, his son or grandson came to fill his seat. These families married and intermarried, and then again, until virtually every prominent name had crossed its blood lines with every other several times over. Powerful dynasties emerged, holdings expanded, and riches multiplied with each generation. The sun of prosperity beamed on Virginia's leaders as these wealthy self-acclaimed aristocrats ruled unchallenged in a green field of lush tobacco weed tended by African slaves.

Only recently had a thorny burr lodged under the complacent saddle of British America. Mother England, long an indolent parent, had begun to notice just how powerful the American barons in her thirteen colonies had become. Irritated, she demanded her share of the pot of gold, pressing a tax on stamps and legal paper from New York to Georgia. In each colony a few young firebrands sprang into action, spurring colonial apathy. Through their actions a reprieve from the Stamp Tax had been won. In Virginia, life continued as before. Except for one thing. The door to unrest had been unlocked. New alliances were formed, and agitated men had come to know one another and remained together, thinking and talking.

Francis sat, hands folded, as the opening formalities began and let his thoughts drift back to that time three years previously when he had been one of those restless young agitators. Was it the thrill of excitement that drew him? A youthful lark? A surge of patriotism inspired by his brother, Richard? He still didn't know the answer, only that he'd become caught up in it. With three of his brothers and over a hundred others he had ridden to enforce the resolutions signed at Leedstown. They had sought to enflame their neighbors with their own passionate feelings against arbitrary taxation. From the local merchants they demanded obedience. Ships were turned away. No hated taxes were to be paid on English paper in the Northern Neck. Not while the Sons of Liberty rode in Virginia as well as in New England. God, those were the days! They had really nailed old Ritchie, he remembered—his ship had bobbed unloaded on the Rappahannock for days.

Francis frequently felt he suffered more than he pleasured from his keen sense of smell. His nose twitched as he watched a lethargic fly buzz its way up a window pane. The heat, sweaty odors, and lengthy opening ceremony were beginning to squelch his excitement of the previous evening. He began to feel bored as he struggled to follow the speech of acting Governor and President of the Council John Blair, now being read in monotone by Speaker Randolph. Glancing to his left and right Francis knew he wasn't the only one to find the hour tedious. He saw that Dudley Digges had fallen asleep with his mouth open, while Mr. Page kept his eyes in focus by tracing small overlapping circles with a finger onto the fabric of his breeches. It was with some difficulty that he dragged his attention back to the proceedings, feeling again an impatience with the lengthy letter being read. Leaning toward his brother Richard, he murmured, "President Blair's concern for the settlers in the Indian Lands has taken enough time."

"Give him credit, Frank. He's on the spot as acting governor. I suspect there's nothing he'd like better than a permanent appointment to the post. He has to observe every formality."

"Damned if we don't perpetrate formalities in this place," Francis grumbled. "We'll drown in them one day if we aren't careful. As to Blair being appointed to Dinwiddie's chair, I don't imagine King George will choose a colonial at this stage, do you?"

Richard responded with a negative shake that did not wiggle a hair of his carefully powdered, tightly curled head.

Francis smirked, thinking it one of the more visible differences between them. His own hair, brushed back from his temples, hung loosely to his shoulders. Frequently he queued it with a narrow ribbon, but neither powder nor the wig, which he felt compelled to don upon occasion, were his idea of comfort. He wished he felt less impatience with this routine business. He knew it was necessary, yet his mind plunged ahead to important decisions they must make. With England heaping new injustices, they needed to respond with affirmative actions. Take a stand—as Massachusetts urged in the letter, or Parliament would squeeze from them a duty on paper, glass, lead and of all the rotten tricks, tea! This clearly was an attempt to achieve the same end as the Stamp Taxes by a fresh means. He was certain of it. However vague the difference between a stamp tax and a duty at the port, Parliament claimed it valid. The author and chief instigator of these duties was reputed to be Charles Townshend, said to be a brilliant speaker. It was true Townshend had convinced the British House and George III, that by earmarking duties collected at American ports to pay the salaries of the governors of the American colonies, the influence of the upstart colonials over their governors would be all but eliminated. The gall of the man to think they would stand idly by while he abused such a basic means of self-government! Tradition provided their right to hold the governor's purse strings. How could Townshend expect to reverse a thing like that without a fight?

Around the room Francis counted well over half of his fellow burgesses who would debate with their last breath that Townshend held evil sway over their beloved monarch, thus having *forced* His Highness reluctantly to the present position. Francis's worthy friend, Landon Carter from Richmond County, one of the wealthiest of the planters with eight working plantations, was a leading proponent of this view. While arguing consistently against the imposition of unfair taxes, Carter maintained the unerring belief that with changes in the British Ministry, complete unanimity could be reestablished. Most others of the staunchly conservative old guard held the same opinion. It was this cautious opposition that frustrated those of a more progressive turn of mind.

Sitting across from him, Francis observed Patrick Henry's dark and brooding expression. There sat the uncrowned king of the progressives, standing ahead of George Mason, Washington, Wythe, or even his own brother Richard. Francis had joined their ranks by his outspoken opposition to the Stamp Taxes. What an enigma is Patrick, he thought, puzzling how he and Richard had ever come to be allied with such a rebel. From the moment the man arrived in his simple parson's suit three years ago, a delegate from Louisa County, he had suffered ridicule for his wretched accent and lack of education. Yet as a speaker he was eloquent, and the latter charge was simply not true, just an ugly rumor. Francis knew Patrick's mind to be brilliant, active, constantly probing the political spectrum far beyond any save his brother's. The firmly entrenched House members, however, weren't about to allow this fiery upstart a piece of their cake. Who was he anyway, they asked? There had been sneering whispers over evening brandy cups. Catching the old boys off guard in the beginning had been a stroke of luck; Patrick had skillfully rammed through his bold Stamp Act Resolutions after many of them had left for home, and before the rest had a chance to stack the vote. His Resolves had squeaked past the House while outraged cries of "treason" resounded from the dome. What a *coup éclat*! No boredom that session. That was the utterly amazing thing about Patrick. When he addressed the House, minds snapped alert and heartbeats quickened. Whether they agreed with him or despised him, they all listened.

"Richard, do you think Randolph will address the Massa-chusetts letter today?" Francis whispered suddenly. The Massa-chusetts Bay Legislature in their open letter to all the colonies, requested support in retaliation to the Townshend Duties through *joint censure of Parliament and the Crown.* Considering it, Francis knew the falling out here would come over three words—"and the Crown." The letter further expressed the opinion that a mere token representation in Parliament, with which Britain thought to pacify them, was more unthinkable even than the unfair taxes without representation. That would be the rub. While many felt free to heap abuse on the comparative faceless-ness of Parliament, very few Virginians dared speak out against their royal leader. Richard was staring at him. "Well?" Francis asked.

"If he doesn't introduce it, he'll be drastically remiss!" he hissed under his breath.

"Indisputable, dear brother," Francis returned, irritated. Rich-ard had this annoying habit of acting much too superior at times. About once a year Francis recognized the possibility that were Richard not his brother he might not be quite so fond of him. "So, after he introduces it, do you think he'll appoint a committee to study the letter and recommend action, or do you think we'll have to push him to it?"

Richard Henry Lee, elder of the two by almost three years, was by far the most politically inclined. He continued to use every opportunity to stimulate Francis to follow in his public foot-steps. His efforts with brothers Philip and Thomas, both older, had proven less than dramatic; with brothers William and Arthur soon to return to England, it had become his habit to concentrate full attention on Francis. The Lees would not lose the stature gained by their illustrious father if Richard had any say in the matter. Enthused, he considered Francis's interest in the Massa-chusetts Bay letter. "Would you be prepared to lead the push, if it comes to that?" he probed.

"I think so," Francis nodded. "If all the colonies protest strongly, perhaps the Ministry will grasp the idea we intend to continue to levy our own taxes and dole out our governor's salaries when and how we see fit." He jabbed his brother with an elbow, directing their attention to the speaker's chair. The next item of business was coming up.

Peyton Randolph, a large man, full-faced and big boned, looked uncomfortable in his ruffled shirtfront and tightly buttoned waistcoat. Beads of moisture clung to his forehead beneath a heavy wig. He paused to dab at them before accepting the paper the clerk held out to him. "Gentlemen," he began, "I have here a letter, addressed to this august body by the esteemed House of Representatives of the Massachusetts Bay. It is my duty to introduce to you the contents and to present it as an item of record in this Assembly. I do so forthwith, and it shall be taken into consideration in due course." Randolph thus relieved himself of the burdensome task, hastily returning the document to the House clerk. He proceeded immediately with Orders to the Assembly. Not a word of the Massachusetts letter, which some among them were sure to label as treasonous, did he utter.

"I'll be damned! He's not even going to read it now, let alone appoint a committee to study it!" It was Richard's turn to be exasperated.

Francis chuckled. "No matter. He took the first step. The committee's appointment will no doubt come tomorrow. More time, and I am the more likely to be on it," he dropped casually.

Richard's head spun around. "What makes you think so?"

"I called on Colonel Landon this morning. I couldn't sleep thinking of what lay before us. He was delighted to have my company, I might add. He's an early riser, you know."

Landon Carter's personal habits were not of the least interest to Richard Henry Lee. "And?" he prompted impatiently.

Francis, ignoring an admonition from behind them to be quiet, said, "You know he favors me and he wields a mighty influence in conservative circles. We spoke of the protests to be written to London. I think we had a meeting of the minds although it took some fancy talking on my part, I can assure you."

"Your ploy had better work. If we don't have some free thinkers on that committee it will merely produce another job of wordy slop. Did Carter say he'd recommend your name? Or did you merely say you *wanted* to be on it?"

"My methods are more subtle. I flattered him shamelessly, tickled his ego you might say." His brown eyes twinkled.

Richard couldn't have been more pleased and, smiling at his brother, thought I'll make a politician out of this one yet, by the grace of God!

For the third time a disgruntled Benjamin Harrison turned a disapproving eye on the whispering Lee brothers. This time it silenced them.

From the speaker's stand Mr. Randolph continued, " ... and the following members shall be appointed to the Committee of Privileges and Election. Mr. Pendleton, Mr. Bland, Mr. Lemuel Riddick, Mr. Nicholas, Mr. William Digges, Mr. Benjamin Harrison, Mr. Dudley Digges, Mr. Page, Mr. Burwell, Mr. Francis Lightfoot Lee, and Mr. Blair." This was the Assembly's most powerful standing committee and Francis accepted his appointment with pleasure.

"Ordered," Peyton Randolph went on, "ordered, that Reverend Mr. Price be continued as House Chaplain, with morning prayers to be read each day at ten o'clock."

Francis wondered how many would appear for morning devotions with any regularity. It was normal for the anglican to read his prayers to a mere handful. The evenings would be filled with entertainments and gay carousing—late hours made for late risings.

The presentation of the Orders continued. As the afternoon wore on, the burgesses lolled in drowsy state, most only half listening. Several flies buzzed loudly in the upper windows, a sound that reminded Francis of home on a lazy summer afternoon. He let his thoughts wander to the Horsepen Tract, where he currently made his home in Loudoun County. *I hope Grimes has ordered the turning of the corn fields.* He speculated on the possibilities. *The fields should be ready to seed before my return. If it holds without a freak frost, this warm weather will bring in an early crop. Soon even the tobacco can go in the ground. Trouble with that overseer is that he holes up for a rousing drunk every time I leave the place. A hard worker when sober though, one of the best.* Grimes had promised his wages he'd keep hard at it this time. *Who could tell? He might just do it.* The Lee plantation under cultivation in Loudoun County was not a large one, especially in comparison to the home fields of Stratford, but these lands Francis inherited at his father's death eighteen years earlier, provided him with a comfortable life. It was home now, with the frontier town of Leesburg not far if he craved company. He had made a number of friends and acquaintances there in the ten years since leaving Westmoreland County. At first it had been difficult, a much less elegant way of life with virtually no social requirements or diversions. But in time it suited. His brothers nicknamed him "Loudoun" and chided him for his country ways. Especially Philip. Colonel Phil was a great one for ridicule. His eldest brother seemed to derive an immoderate glee from persistent nagging and petty jokes.

It was three o'clock before the motion to adjourn was seconded and the gavel pounded. The delegates would reassemble two days hence, Saturday, at eleven in the morning; committee work, however, would proceed immediately wherever possible. As they emerged by twos and threes into the bright afternoon, they found the air had cooled. A welcome breeze touched their damp faces and revived them, stirring thirst and hunger. Francis felt a surge of his usual vigor return as he strolled with Richard and Patrick. And with it, the anticipation he had known the night before returned also. He bragged to his companions, elaborating on his meeting with Colonel Landon Carter that morning. Dabney Carr from Louisa County and the young Jefferson from Albemarle, neither of whom had yet been elected burgesses, joined them. The group of young men had discovered they had much in common that set them apart from the older more conservative members of the House.

Bantering about nothing in particular, the five ambled down Duke of Gloucester Street. Patrick, not prone to participate in trivial conversation, kicked absentmindedly at pebbles in the road, only occasionally joining in the laughter. Carr swung his arm at all the low hanging branches, while Francis Lee rejoiced, knowing himself to be in the best of company. He had not the slightest intimation that before the walk was at an end, something would happen to alter the course of his life.

Tayloe's Garden

After walking a goodly distance they found themselves facing the symmetrical hulk of the College. The large facade stared boldly down the length of Duke of Gloucester Street at the mile-distant capitol building. The men were in good spirits, feeling light-hearted, as young men will when a spring evening comes on. Jefferson spoke, "I can't say I'm sorry my days in yonder hallowed halls are over. Yet ... I sometimes miss the old place." He stopped, studying the brick structure that was the College of William and Mary. "Credit should go to Mr. Wren for a most handsome design, I think."

"I've always thought of it as a bit bulky, Tom," Francis told him.

The younger man, red hair caught in the fading sunlight, looked down at the considerably shorter Francis. "No," he said. "Not at all. You see, he's balanced the proportions of it perfectly by the enormity of the rounded center opening ... not unlike the doors to a castle actually, topped by the massive cupola which overshadows even the powerful aspect of the twin chimneys. It's quite splendid, to my eye."

"Oh ... I see," Francis said, when in truth he did not.

Tom continued. "The design of public buildings has always fascinated me. The design of any building for that matter. Most of them are abominations."

"Our father held the same interest, didn't he, Richard?" Francis looked around for his brother and discovered the others had turned to go back, not listening. "Well," he answered himself, "he did. I think my father wrote his own epitaph when he left us our home at Stratford. Design of a public building would accomplish the same end, a thousand times over, allowing a man to leave quite a legacy, wouldn't it?"

"Yes, I've thought of that from time to time," Jefferson replied.

"What's keeping you two? We're hungry," Richard called.

"The special fare at the Raleigh is a beef steak pie," Patrick coaxed. "If we don't hurry, it will be sold out."

Dropping their discussion of Wren's building, Francis and Tom rejoined the others. The men turned a corner to vary their route, speculating who the next occupant of the governor's palace might be. Passing behind the courthouse, they crossed Market Square, deserted now. It was too early in the season for the produce sellers. The late afternoon was suddenly bathed in light. The sun, in a final surge of the day, glinted across the grass-green of leafing shrubs in Colonel John Tayloe's yard on Nicholson Street. The house where Francis had taken a room was next door but for a few outbuildings. Heady scents of spring wafted on the breeze. Francis inhaled, appreciating everything. A mockingbird held forth in a crab apple tree. The hum of honey bees trailing in and out of early pink blossoms vied with the bird song for his attention. Subtle enticement, he laughed to his friends, as he caught sight of a swirl of skirts in the Tayloe garden.

Ten years a burgess had afforded him many an opportunity to find joy in a Williamsburg spring. This year, warmer than usual, promised the same delights. Even knowing this, he was scarcely prepared for the curious premonition that touched him at that moment. Something he hadn't expected brought him up short; something he'd never been quite ready to bargain for. He stood rooted to the spot, leaden feet seemingly unable to detach themselves from the road. "Go on," he called, waving his companions away. "I'll be along in a minute." Although he'd eaten nothing since early morning when he'd been invited to share ham and biscuits at the Carter table, his hunger pangs seemed suddenly unimportant.

"Damned if Frank's not got himself intrigued by the Tayloe babes!" Carr taunted from the relative safety of his position as a married man.

"An old man after a spring frolic if you ask me," observed Patrick wryly.

"Like he told us, Gentlemen, he's easily enticed," quipped Tom. He felt more at ease joking about Mr. Lee since their conversation in front of the College. Jefferson and his brother-in-law, Dabney Carr, although not delegates, had spent the day in the capitol also. Seated in the visitors' gallery they had followed the proceedings. They were as tired and hungry as the others. The four moved off, leaving their bachelor friend to his own peculiar pursuits.

"We'll see a glass is filled for you, Loudoun, and save it till your thirst calls louder than a pretty skirt!" his brother chided in a rare moment of abandon.

Possessed of a unique ability to ignore that which was bothersome, Francis dismissed them as easily as he might a lost shilling. He lounged against a gate opposite the Tayloe garden. It was part of a property belonging to Philip Ludwell, as was the house in which he'd taken lodgings. Mr. Ludwell was his uncle, his mother's brother, and had removed to London some time prior to his death a year ago. Ludwell's several houses, now turned into rental tenements, were part of the large estate inherited by his daughters.

Francis fastened his gaze on three of the several Tayloe girls who had arrived with their parents to spend the season. Their gay nonsense captivated him. They were chasing a butterfly. Velvety blues and blacks caught a glimmer of sunlight as it led them a merry chase. Flitting back and forth, the butterfly winged to a mulberry bush, then a crepe myrtle. The girls danced after it.

Entranced by the swish of feminine apparel, Francis was drawn no less by the attractive symmetry of the garden. This was a lovely yard, skillfully laid out and set in an elaborate pattern of walks edged with small English box. A circular bed in the center awaited summer's herbs and marigolds; while fruit trees and flowering shrubs, fenced in by white pickets, lined the perimeter. Charming, he thought. Almost perfection. He would add a rose bed perhaps. A peal of girlish laughter rang sweet in his ears. Instantly, he recognized it as the source of his premonition.

As was only proper, the young ladies were paying him no heed. Even when several dogs penned behind the kitchen house set up a furious clamor, belatedly announcing an intruder to the neighborhood, they didn't raise their bobbing heads to greet the man they knew perfectly well to be Colonel Francis Lightfoot Lee of Westmoreland and Loudoun Counties. The trio settled on a marble bench and fell to whispering. Never once did they let on they were aware of the handsome gentleman in the fawn colored breeches and carefully tailored matching waistcoat who watched them.

Francis thought to leave, yet he lingered. It was bizarre but he found himself unable to tear his gaze from the well proportioned figure of what he took to be the eldest child. By process of elimination he tried to match her name with her face and age. Her movements were graceful, as natural as the flutterings of a young bird. Was she testing her wings, he wondered? Silly. Yet, she'd seemed to float across the lawn. Every motion intrigued him. He eliminated Elizabeth, for she had become Mrs. Edward Lloyd the previous year and moved to the Maryland Colony. Anne was shy, on the plump side and not nearly so delicate. That left only Rebecca, for the others were far too young. Could Becky have matured into such a lovely creature as this? When had he last seen her? Two years? No ... maybe longer. The visits to Tayloe's Mount Airy Plantation were always filled with chaotic confusion. Presenting a somewhat formidable posture to the world, Colonel

John Tayloe was known privately to be an overly indulgent father. He delighted in his brood of females and expected his wife to arrange for such unpleasant things as discipline. In addition to public service, the colonel was much involved in management of his vast personal affairs. The home plantation of Mount Airy, looming high above the Rappahannock River, and the Nicholson Street house, were but a small portion of his estate. Through inheritance and purchase he had acquired holdings in Virginia's western counties and beyond the Blue Ridge, as well as a large iron works in Baltimore. He supported a superb stable of thoroughbred horseflesh, and horse racing provided entertainment and excitement in his life.

Francis couldn't take his eyes off the beautiful child on the bench. Was it Becky? Her brownish hair sparkled with reddish highlights (or were they golden?) and grew in ringlets around a small well-shaped head. It was tied with a wide yellow ribbon. He found it attractive, but wondered how it would look if the lovely tresses could fall free around her shoulders. Then he remembered the ever present curiosity in her very green eyes. As a child she'd been surprisingly mature, as at the christening of Philip's Matilda five or six years back. Becky, chosen to be one of the godparents, had been pressed to perform in company with numerous aunts and uncles, all adults, and had carried it off superbly as he recalled. She had sought him out that day to accompany her to one of Stratford's chimney towers. Had he done so? He wasn't sure. He only remembered her asking. The two sets of four chimneys each, stacked formidably on the roof of his birthplace, always fascinated visitors. He was certain that forty years ago when his father designed the place he'd had that very thing in mind.

Entranced, Francis continued to watch the girl. He was intrigued by the sensation she stirred within him. There was no similarity to what he felt for Martha Tutt, even during their more intimate moments. A twinge of guilt nagged him. He remembered Martha's injured stare the day he'd set out for

Williamsburg. For the first time in their more than three year alliance, she'd asked to accompany him. He'd refused of course; Martha had no place in this part of his life. She knew that, had accepted it from the beginning. What made her force him to say it? The memory distressed him. Irritated, he shrugged it from his mind, thinking to deal with it later. What made him think of Martha anyway?

With a jolt he saw that Becky, if that was who it was, had left the others. It became obvious her sisters were trying hard not to notice him. As he wondered if he'd been caught in the act of snooping, he felt a light touch on his sleeve. Whirling suddenly he lost his balance, falling forward awkwardly. How comical, he berated himself, hastening to regain his footing. Feeling ridiculous, he found his face scarcely a foot from that of the object of his recent scrutiny. Dancing eyes met his own. No doubt remained as to her identity. Here before him stood a grown up Rebecca Tayloe. Her eyes were even more green than he had remembered, and a myriad of freckles spotted her nose, and she had breasts— fully developed. His heart pumped faster, his cheeks felt on fire.

"Hello, Colonel Lee," she said. "Are you waiting for someone?" Francis was relieved when she didn't wait for an answer. "I think I shall call you Francis. May I? We're cousins of a sort so I shouldn't have to continue on formality, should I? Do you agree? I know the others call you Frank, as Papa does, but I like the sound of Francis. To my mind, it suits you."

It was a fine name, the way she said it, he decided quickly. He'd never really liked it much before, but he nodded hesitantly. When had she managed to grow up?

She went on, "I'm sure you wouldn't approve of a young lady who approached a gentleman on the public roadway. Nor would my father. To save my reputation, please, won't you join us in the garden? Do you have time to spend a few minutes?" She glanced in the direction his companions had taken. "Or must you hurry to catch up with your friends?"

Her voice invited him while her eyes bewitched. The combination rendered him speechless. Where was his witty tongue? The velvet flatteries that usually came without effort now eluded him entirely. A rasping "Of course, I have plenty of time," was the best he could muster.

Becky took scant notice of his brief answer. She had worries of her own, thinking that her mother might be watching from a window. Taking the lead, she crossed the dusty street. The wooden gate creaked loudly on hinges left untended since the previous Williamsburg season. A hurried glance at the house told her that neither Miss Turnbull, their governess, nor her mother were looking out, but she knew she could be called at any moment.

Francis wondered why he hadn't heard the gate earlier. How had she left the garden? Giving him no chance to ponder it she indicated he was to sit on the bench. Aware he'd yet to utter one coherent phrase, he surveyed the area, noting the sisters had disappeared. He couldn't know that Anne and Eleanor Tayloe were behind him, concealed in the grape arbor, giggling as they awaited the first act. It was as exciting as any performance of Mrs. Osborne's Virginia Theater Company, they agreed, nudging each other. And the actors were not even pretending. Francis cleared his throat, begging his thoughts to arrange themselves and his voice to return. What was happening here? He liked to maintain an upper hand with women. But he was clearly not in command of this situation. What in God's name was the matter with him? He stole a glance at the creature next to him. Of course ... truth was, she was not a woman. Merely a girl. With the gamin face of a pixie. Merely that. His heart took to thumping again. She was young. Absurdly young. Even if he could dredge up his voice, what on earth would he find to say to her? *Audentes fortuna juvat*, he told himself, recalling his Latin. But a reminder that fortune favors the bold seemed ludicrous at this point. He suspected he'd lost all opportunity to appear bold.

Becky, showing off to her sisters that she was able to lure a gentleman into the garden, now began to suffer pangs of misgiving. There was the problem of conversation. It seemed he had nothing to say to start it off as he concentrated on the dusty tips of his fine buckled shoes. Perhaps he was wondering why he'd bothered to agree to the whim of such a foolish child as herself in the first place.

The silence lengthened until suddenly their sentences tumbled upon each other. Francis hooted, humored from his shyness, voice miraculously restored. To bolster his courage further, he dusted at his silk stockings, keeping his eyes off her face while he spoke. "I must apologize for remaining so long in front of your house that you thought it necessary to invite me to join you. It was behavior of the rudest sort and hardly worthy of a gentleman. Please forgive me."

When he looked up, a smile lit his face, drawing her instantly into his world. "No, oh no, it wasn't rude at all," she stammered. "It was obvious you were merely passing by, Mr. Lee ... ah ... Francis ... when I rudely detained you." She flashed her green eyes at him, laughing at her own boldness. "You may call me Becky if you'd like."

It was what he'd always called her, since she was a baby. "Yes, I should like that very much, Becky." Such interesting eyes she had. He quivered inside if he looked at them for more than a moment. "And now that we have re-introduced ourselves, I must ask you something. Did you catch the butterfly?"

The question caught her off guard. "No, but we weren't really trying to catch it. If you catch them, touch their wings, it rubs the powder off and they can't fly any longer. I wouldn't want that to happen. They're so lovely."

"I've never heard that, but I don't doubt it to be true. I've learned that nature's creatures don't adapt well to a captive existence." Did he sound priggish? Why, he wondered, am I so pleased to learn that she's gentle and sensitive? Why should it matter?

Becky noticed that when he appeared to concentrate, he drew his right eyebrow in an inward curve while the left remained in its natural pose. He really was even more handsome than she remembered. "Papa says I am so softhearted I wouldn't allow him to swat a fly if it bit his precious Yorick. And Yorick, you know, is the pride of his stable!" She laughed, tossing her head. "I never could stay around the yard when they kill a chicken for supper," she told him. "Annie likes to watch. She says the poor things flop all over the ground even after Cook wrings the heads off." She shuddered.

It seemed to Francis a logical reaction for such a uniquely feminine person. "I know your Papa to be a wise man in his observations, and therefore undoubtedly right ... about your being tenderhearted. I see it in your eyes," he said, feeling a little bolder and back on familiar ground. It pleased him that his words brought a blush to her cheeks and he took the opportunity to note the utter straightness of her back, the positive tilt of her head. Indeed this is no ordinary lass, suited merely for the bed and carrying on the name. She is spirited and exudes a rare confidence. She is willful too, I suspect. A certain amount of that was a good mix, he thought. It was entirely possible she'd planned their encounter today. He smiled at his own suspicious nature, but didn't dismiss the idea. Am I the unsuspecting fly drawn to the spider's web? Heedless of the sticky danger, watch how eagerly I approach! He had never felt so foolishly wonderful in the face of a new romance. But ... had he ever looked into pools of such deep green eyes he would be so willing to drown in?

Becky basked in his scrutiny. He was clearly taking an interest in her. She moved slightly on the bench, rearranging her skirts. "Your brother called you Loudoun," she remarked. "I never heard anyone call you that before."

Chuckling, because now he knew she'd been watching him before he started watching her, he explained. "I'm the only one in the family who has lived in Loudoun County. They tease me about residing in the out-lands and sometimes call me the family bumpkin. I suppose it's true in a way."

She was finding his easy humor infectious. She'd heard others say Francis Lee caused this reaction in the female sex—his two sisters, Hannah and Alice, had spoken of it. Both adored him. "I think it's rewarding when sisters and brothers can tease each other in good sport," she answered. "Don't you? It must mean they share an understanding ... a friendship to carry them through whatever trials may come upon them. That's important in a family. You know, I've always wished for a brother," she confessed wistfully. "I don't suppose I shall ever have one now."

Francis couldn't imagine why not. Lady Tayloe seemed to produce with clock-like regularity and showed no apparent signs of giving up yet. He'd lost track of how many sisters Becky had. In spite of that it seemed there was always the possibility for a boy late in the game. "Our sister Hannah used to swear that brothers were nothing but a bother and a nuisance. She was put to looking out for the lot of us, and we did nothing to make her job easy, I'm sorry to say. Quite the opposite actually. Especially William. I believe he was the hardest on her!"

Becky laughed. She remembered that William Lee could be a persistent tease. He was stiff, formal with adults, but when they were out of sight he took fiendish delight in chasing little girls to pull their hair or pinch their cheeks. But that was quite some time ago, she reminded herself. And William was a grown-up now himself.

A carriage drew their attention as it approached. Drawn by two handsome bays coming at a fast clip, it trailed a billowing dust cloud down Nicholson Street. "Here comes Mrs. Blair. They say she's hoping to move to the governor's palace." Becky glanced at Francis to see his reaction. "Surely the King won't appoint him. At least that's what Papa says ... that a colonial stands no chance in these times."

Francis nodded. He was thinking what a staunch monarchist John Tayloe was. Very much like Landon Carter. Only more so. Of course, Tayloe's position on the Council was a court appointment and it would hardly do for him to criticize openly. They watched as the carriage passed. Lady Blair sat, primly erect, glancing neither right nor left, intent on presenting a posture suitable to her station as wife of the Council's president. It was enough to cause Becky and Francis to exchange a muffled snicker. The boy on the high seat, hands tight on the reins, nodded almost imperceptibly in Becky's direction. His very black face glistened under the warmth of the impressive livery his master had provided for him.

"That's Isaac." A question in Francis's eyes prompted her to explain. "He comes to see our Catey as soon as we arrive in Williamsburg. I don't know how he manages it. Or what he tells them. But he comes. I've talked to him once or twice," she admitted. Then because Francis showed no sign of being offended, she added, "I plan on asking Papa to buy him, I think."

Something in her tone told him she had more to say on the subject. It was uncanny the effect her voice had on him. He waited, watching her eyes.

"Isaac told me once they chained him for two days. Ever since, when I knew he was with Catey in the room over the kitchen house and he stayed the night, I didn't tell Mama." It was a confession she had not made to anyone else. Having said it, she now realized in one swoop she'd admitted to a personal interest in the slaves, and a knowledge of the secret mysteries between male and female! As this came over her, her cheeks flamed a second time and she bowed her head, avoiding his eyes.

Francis smiled. Then, on a serious note, he wondered if she knew of the chains in slave ships, where two days was not much of a punishment. He studied her lowered head. What he saw was a deep forehead sloping to a small nose. Her mouth, some-what puckered in its natural pose, hid a luminous smile which she had cast in his direction any number of times. Her determi-nation showed in a rather prominent chin, a trait of the Platers, her mother's family. From the Tayloes she had inherited a barely noticeable slant to her lovely eyes. He wondered again if he could be falling under her spell—not an unpleasant prospect.

At this precise moment Becky's mother, Rebecca Tayloe, on her way downstairs, paused on the second story landing. Won-dering who Becky might be talking with, she recognized one of Thomas Lee's sons, quickly deciding it must be Francis. They seemed to be deeply involved in conversation, she thought, and why on earth were Ellie and Anne hiding behind the boxwood? Becky was obviously flirting ... and he certainly seemed to be enjoying it. Francis Lee was a gentleman and came from a most appropriate family ... but he was at least twice her age! It was then it occurred to her that she needed to have a serious talk with Becky about courting and marriage. Continuing down the steps she went in search of the governess, Miss Turnbull. It was time she called the girls in for music lesson.

The sun, now a blazing red-orange ball and sinking fast, threw long shadows across the garden, signaling that evening was ap-proaching. Francis wished the afternoon wouldn't end so soon. Not for the first time, it occurred to him that something of great significance was missing in his life. He had the alarming sensa-tion it was tantalizingly within his power to obtain—if he made the correct choices and uttered the magic words.

Then a commanding call shattered the tranquility of the gar-den causing them both to jump. "That's Miss Turnbull, our gov-erness. She wants us to come for music practice. I'm learning guitar now. Anne and Ellie are still on harpsichord." Holding out her hand as she rose, she said, "I hope you'll come again soon, Francis. I've ... had a lovely time. Will you think me bold when I tell you I'm usually here in the garden every afternoon?"

He held her hand, much longer than proper, savoring the remarkable thrill of her cool fingers. Could her hair possibly be as soft as it looked? Silk from a corn tassel or fuzz from a dandelion. She continued to stare at him. Nonplused, he imagined she was reading his thoughts. "My dear Becky, as it is my habit to stroll of an afternoon when the House adjourns, you have my solemn assurance that on future days I shall find Nicholson Street very much to my liking. Besides," he laughed, "I've rented a room next door in the Ludwell house."

"I know." He had that serious look in spite of the laughter, with one eyebrow down. He really meant it. He wants to see me again, too. She hadn't planned on telling him about yesterday. But that laugh of his made the garden seem intimate, existing for this day and this meeting only. "May I tell you something, Francis? It's another confession of sorts. But I think new friends must be honest with each other. I watched you last evening, when you rode in. I saw you send your serving man around and I waited until you went out back, to the bath house. Then it was too dark because you took a long time, and I couldn't see anymore." She ducked her head, but was determined to finish. "I had hoped to see what you'd look like after you dressed for the evening."

I'll be damned. So she had known I was here, he marveled. "That's wonderful. Just wonderful. I would have jumped the hedge and come to you, had I only known." They both laughed and he released her hand.

"Goodbye, Francis." And she was gone, running for the house. "Mama and Papa are having a party next week," she called. "You are certain to be invited!"

He continued to stand there, smiling at himself for feeling so like a school boy. Something he hadn't felt like for a long time. Anne and Eleanor loped past him, skirts held high. "Hullo, Colonel Lee," they chorused, their childish faces split in wide grins.

Now where in blazes had they been? From the look of things, all the Tayloe girls were growing up, he thought, taking a second look at Anne's rounded figure before the frame house blocked his view. Still afraid to believe his good fortune, he turned to leave. Familiar now with his scent, the dogs ignored him as he slammed the gate and headed in the direction of the Raleigh. Suddenly he stopped, changing his mind and retracing his steps to his lodgings. Arriving there, he ordered Ben to saddle Cameron, his dappled gelding, but turned down the slave's offer to accompany him. "No, no Ben, I'll not be needing you. I'm just taking a ride in the country."

In a few minutes Cameron was pounding down the Jamestown Road. Francis was not in any mood to listen to the teasing bound to come from Richard and the others, nor inclined to discuss the ramifications of the Massachusetts letter. That could wait. He remembered a little ordinary a couple of miles out. The Suckling Pig or some such name. He would eat there. He was starved. And he wanted nothing to interrupt the feelings brought on by the unexpected encounter with Becky Tayloe on what had turned out to be a most auspicious, even a superior day in the thirty-third year of his life.

Becky

The hours since she bid goodbye to Francis Lee crept slowly by, allowing Becky no time alone to think. Waiting, almost beside herself with impatience, she yearned for the moment when she could slip away to the chamber she shared with Anne and Ellie and relive the moments in the garden. As she prepared to excuse herself from table, her mother said quietly, "Becky, I should like to speak with you for a few minutes. Please join me in my chamber before you retire. I'll be up shortly."

"Did I do something wrong, Mama? Why ..."

"Oh no, my dear, it's a matter of a personal nature, you know, just a little talk between mother and daughter."

A short time later Rebecca Tayloe was seated at her dressing table, her maid removing the pins from her hair, when Becky knocked. Rebecca was remembering the time when she, herself, was young and courted by the dashing John Tayloe II from Virginia. She was eleven years younger than he and quite influenced by her father and mother, members of the wealthy Maryland Plater family. Both of them thought John would be a suitable match for her, as well as an excellent family connection. She had understood the choice really hadn't been hers to make and, while accepting this, she'd remained quite apprehensive in the beginning. Yet it had all worked out for the best.

They began married life in the original Tayloe home built by John's grandfather on the river's bank across the Rappahannock from the bustling shipping settlement of Hobbs' Hole. The years passed and John hired the building of their present home above the marshes and up the long hill—Mount Airy they named it.

When they moved there, now ten years past, they had four daughters, now there were three more. The move from Old House, as it came to be known, had brought changes to their lives. As their fortunes increased along with the size of their family, they hired a governess, and John's stable of horses increased also, so more stables were built. John had long been active in Richmond County politics; as an appointed member of the governor's council, he spent several months a year in Williamsburg; and this had prompted him in 1759 to purchase the Nicholson Street house where they were presently in residence. In her heart, without their ever having talked about it, Rebecca knew they'd both thought it important for their passel of females to have the exposure to society that the capital afforded, if they were to have an opportunity to make a proper marriage when the time came. "Becky, my child, do come in and sit by me," Rebecca said quietly, "I've been thinking about you today."

Lifting her nightdress slightly to sit on the floor, Becky settled at her mother's feet, crossing her legs and resting her elbows on her knees. She had no idea what was coming, and didn't particularly care, praying only that it would be short so she could be alone with her thoughts at last.

"You know, dear, now that you're sixteen you're going to have to start behaving like a young lady, not a tomboy. You must be very careful of your behavior when in the company of young gentlemen. Soon you'll be thinking about more serious things, a marriage perhaps ... but that's not to say that is what *they* will always have on their minds. I think what I'm trying to say is perhaps it's time to consider who might be a possible suitor ... as well as who might not."

Becky listened intently to this unexpected pronouncement. "Why, Mama, you sound as though you're afraid I might end up an old maid!"

"This is not a matter to be taken lightly, Becky. Please take what I'm saying seriously. Should you not make a selection yourself within a reasonable period, I expect there's little doubt your father will do it for you."

"Mama! Papa would never tell me I had to marry someone!"

Rebecca continued, saying that it was only because he *did* love her that he would concern himself with it. That he wanted the best for each of his daughters, a suitable family, a name to be proud of, a man with the means to spoil them. "Of course the right blood lines are important as well," she added.

"You mean blood lines, like for his horses?" Becky laughed. "Was it that way with you and Papa? Did your father choose him for you?"

"Well, yes I suppose so, in a way. It was both things. Fortunately, your father and I are well suited to one another. I've never regretted a single moment I've spent with him. But to answer your question. I suppose my papa did choose him for me, before I came to love him. Love came after. But it came. Sometimes, you know, it doesn't."

"Well, I can assure you my choice will be my own. Not anyone else's."

"That is the very reason I've brought the matter up. Knowing what a strong minded young lady you are, I knew you'd feel that way. When you're certain of who your choice might be, and I can't imagine you choosing anyone who would not be acceptable, don't hesitate to make your desires known to us. Promise me?"

They hugged each other. "How will I know if he's the right one?" Becky asked, remembering the time spent with Francis Lee.

"Oh, you'll know. It most likely will be someone with whom you're already acquainted. I don't expect he'll be a stranger to any of us."

⁊

Now the candles were finally snuffed. A scent of burnt wick drifted across the bed chamber. But for a patch of moonlight in the center of the quilt, the room fell into darkness.

"Tell me, Becky. What did he say? Do you like him?" Anne whispered, not wanting to wake Ellie, in the other bed.

"Mmm-hmm."

"Will you let him kiss you?"

Becky jabbed Anne's arm with her elbow. "Silly," she giggled. "I'm thinking about it. Now go to sleep."

Anne was not ready to give up. Where else could she learn about boys, men really, if not from her older sister. "He kept looking at you. I declare, he practically stared a hole through you. Like he'd never seen a girl before. What did he say?"

"Things. Nice things," Becky murmured, stretching, enjoying the feel of her body against the sheet. "I like his laugh, his laugh is truly marvelous."

"So when will you see him again? Will he become your beau? He's handsome I think. And I know he dances well because I've seen him do the reel. He dances circles around that stupid Wormeley Carter or fickle old Sam Thompson!"

"Oh, them. Who cares? Besides Samuel Thompson is sweet on my friend Betsy Blair. He hasn't even looked at anyone else since last winter," Becky agreed, trying to turn the conversation away from Francis.

"Well, I think Mr. Lee is very charming, and you could do a lot worse, Becky. I hope you're taking him seriously. I think he's the most exciting thing that has happened around here in ages!"

"Shh," Becky admonished. "You'll wake Ellie. We only got here last week. But I do agree with you about Mr. Lee ... Francis ... that it's exciting."

"So you *are* planning to see him again ... and allow him to squire you around Williamsburg this season?"

Becky lay silent, thinking, uncertain. "I don't know. I want him to, though. I most definitely want him to, Annie."

"Night, Becky," her sister whispered, satisfied that was all the information she was going to get, she rolled into a ball, pulling the quilt with her.

The house was quiet; soon Anne's breathing evened out. Becky squirmed until her pillow was pressed against the window sill. Looking across the lawn and the space between herself and the Ludwell house, she wondered if he was there. Would he be in his bed? Or still at the ordinary with his friends? Maybe if she stayed awake she'd see him return. It hardly seemed possible that only last evening, from this very spot, she'd watched him arrive. So much had happened since then. The moment he slid off that spotted horse yesterday, she recognized him. He'd looked so forlorn, limping to the door, beating the dust off his coat with that funny round country hat. She'd wanted to rush out, take his hand, and promise him he'd feel better soon. As soon as he had a cool drink, or a warm meal, or a book to read—she wondered if he liked *Tristram Shandy* or Shelton's novels? She'd kept watching, waiting, until he'd headed to the bath house, when she had to admit it was truly not proper for her to be so concerned with the personal activities of Colonel Lee. Yet she kept watching, thinking and wondering if he might really notice her this year. It wasn't sudden really, this thought. But now that she was sixteen ... that was old enough, wasn't it?

She'd known him all her life, grown up loving him. Not the way she found herself thinking of him now, but loving his quiet humor, his gentle voice and manner, his tender comfort when a knee was skinned or a dress torn. Wasn't that love?

The conversation in her parents' bed chamber an hour before came back to her—could it be that her mother had seen them in the garden? Was that what prompted her warnings? Pushing that aside for the moment she remembered her thoughts of a few days ago when, with the promise of parties, balls, and plays, she hadn't been able to stop thinking about who might be in town. It was then, for seemingly no reason, Francis Lee had come unbidden into her thoughts. Eavesdropping on Catey and Isaac one day she learned that Colonel Lee and some others would be renting rooms next door. Would that be Colonel Francis Lee from Stratford? she'd asked Catey later, in what she hoped was a casual tone. After that, all she had to do was watch for when he might arrive. The problem of how to capture his attention had remained unsolved until by a stroke of chance, Francis himself had provided the answer by strolling past the house at just the right moment.

Now, she thought, the short time spent with him in the garden was proof that he was indeed special. Being with him had seemed as natural as climbing on Papa's knee or kissing Mama goodnight. When he held her hand ... yes, he had actually held her hand, even longer than he had to, and said he'd probably be taking a walk tomorrow, she'd suddenly felt as though she'd always known it would be him. Could he possibly feel the same way? Was he even now thinking about her? "Please, God," she whispered, "if there's any way you can do it, make him be thinking about me." With that thought she punched her pillow into shape and lay back with her arms folded behind her head before tugging a corner of the quilt away from Anne.

Becky couldn't remember ever wanting for anything. Born into the wealth of a prominent family, her life to this point had been truly effortless; her responsibilities, other than obeying her parents, minimal. To six-year-old Becky, the move to Mount Airy, up the hill from Old House, had meant moving into the nursery, a goodly distance from her parents' room. Located in one of two large dependencies attached to the main house by long covered corridors, it isolated the older children. During brief periods each day they were summoned to the great house, but left otherwise to the care of a governess and several slave girls, they soon learned a double mode of behavior. In the presence of their parents they lowered their voices and didn't run or shout, because that way they could avoid being reprimanded by their mother, who desired them to be demure and ladylike. Returning to the nursery they could make all the noise they wanted, run and play and tussle with each other, knowing they'd seldom be disciplined. They soon came to enjoy their remote sanctuary.

Elizabeth, the eldest, was an assertive child and sometimes obstinate. Much like her mother, she was skilled in squeezing the last advantage from every circumstance. She talked back shamelessly to their governess. They called her Poor Miss Travers behind her back. That homespun young woman had from the beginning allowed herself to be outwitted and outmaneuvered by the precocious Tayloe girls. Spurred on by Elizabeth, they spent hilarious hours plotting new schemes to surprise and torment their keeper.

One evening at supper they truly humiliated the unsuspecting Travers. Elizabeth and Becky, innocence radiating from angelic up-turned faces, let it be known that their governess certainly did some funny things sometimes. Why, they had even seen her stuffing soft white cloth inside the upper part of her gown. "Why ever would she want to make her silly bumps look bigger?" Elizabeth inquired of her mother.

Rewarded by the purple flush on Miss Travers' pinched face, and before their mother could respond, Becky took the story further. "I saw her another time, too, peeking in the looking glass and she was stark neked, examining her ...."

"Rebecca!" commanded her mother. "You and Elizabeth are dismissed from table this very instant. You will apologize to Miss Travers and retire to your room."

The elder Tayloes had maintained wooden expressions through the episode but, later in the privacy of their chamber, they couldn't stop laughing. "By God, Rebe, those young fillies of ours have a sense of humor! What do you suppose Becky was about to say when you stopped her?"

"I'm afraid to guess, there's no telling," Rebecca howled and buried her face in the pillow to stifle her laughter. "They do seem intrigued of late with the anatomy. I saw three of them leaning over the paddock gate one day watching Yorick and the brood mare you had turned out with him. Nan called them away, but by then I'm sure there was little left to the imagination."

"Well, my dear, I've always said there's a lot to be learned from the horses, and probably from poor Travers for that matter. So the poor thing has underdeveloped bumps, hmm? I am eternally grateful, Rebe, that you're not in the same predicament. I'm very grateful for it." From the beginning, the physical relationship between them had been mutually gratifying. John Tayloe had never felt compelled to look elsewhere for his pleasure.

Miss Travers resigned her employ the following morning. Try as she might, Rebecca couldn't persuade her to stay. Her concern over the loss of a governess was heightened by the fact there were now six little girls sharing the nursery quarters. Where would she find someone willing to take on such a brood? In the end it took six months and, shortly after the arrival of Miss Lucy Turnbull, it was decided that Elizabeth and Becky would move into chambers in the great house. Music and dancing were included in their lessons. Becky had a fine clear voice, highly praised by their music teacher, while Elizabeth showed equal promise on the harpsichord.

The new governess, a spinster of twenty-eight, brooked no interference with discipline. She was masterful at ignoring a pout or temper tantrum. The sisters tried everything that had worked to annoy Travers, but Turnbull wouldn't break or give in. Nor even crack. As time went on she was clever enough to lead the willful Tayloe girls out of some of their spoiled ways. She instructed them in tatting and embroidery and, of course, the social graces. A tutor was employed to teach numbers and literature. Becky thought about how she always quizzed them on what they studied, and knew she'd never forget her admonitions about the travails facing them—a young woman entered the world under enough disadvantage without lacking an education as well, Miss Turnbull said frequently. To her credit, Becky thought it was from her governess she had learned a healthy loyalty and respect for family, and a strong acceptance of the role she was destined to play in the world—family name, position, and religious conviction were important. Unlike her mother, Miss Turnbull left out love and marriage, although she did stress the dangers of courting. Rules of acceptable social behavior were drilled into them. A lady was at all times polite, pleasant, demure in mixed company; if she flirted, she must know precisely when to cease, so as not to compromise her good name. A gentleman would not respect nor continue to court a promiscuous lady. Proper moral behavior was a must. Would Turnbull have thought her behavior toward Francis proper this afternoon? She had definitely flirted!

All these things passed through Becky's mind as she lay silently next to her sister on the day she had discovered that Francis Lightfoot Lee was someone she wanted to know better. Her thoughts drifted to other young men who'd paid her attentions during recent months, none so mature as Francis of course— the Carters, Corbins, Pages, and Turbervilles. They were all suitable by her mother's measuring stick but they seemed like boys, not grown men to be considered as possible husbands. They were sometimes fun to be with at dances and parties, but that was all. She'd allowed two of them to kiss her. The results were not memorable; the Corbin boy had wet lips and his teeth were too big. What would it be like to kiss Francis? It would surely be different because Francis himself was different and, being more than twice her age, he'd know how to do it. She felt a warm flush at the thought of his arms around her. Oh, yes, he'd know how to do it all right. She bet he'd make her wish she'd never heard of Turnbull's idea of proper behavior! Feeling a sudden strong desire to become a woman in every sense, a fully grown woman, to explore the wonders of what that might mean, Becky moved her hand until her fingers came in contact with Anne's arm. It was damp with sleep-warmth, and soft. There was a pleasant sensation just to feel it, yet it wasn't at all like touching Francis Lee.

But the sensation made her want to touch him again, to talk to him for as long as she wished without interruption, to share ideas and dreams with him and, yes, even to kiss him.

She wiggled around to get comfortable. Was that thunder she heard in the distance? Unusual in March, but then it had been so warm. Yawning, she was suddenly very sleepy. "I love you, Annie," she whispered. I guess I love just about everyone in the world right now, and everyone in the world must be asleep except me, she thought. Even Francis. Her last thought was that she was glad he'd substituted his tricorn for that silly farmer's hat. It suited him much better.

Francis

The storm blew over but a light drizzle began at dawn. Puzzled by his brother's disappearance the night before, Richard Henry rose early and sent his servant to fetch Francis. He'd learned that freeholders from Chesterfield, Henrico, and Dinwiddie Counties were preparing to petition against the Parliament's acts suspending legislative power in New York. He decided immediately that his own Westmoreland County wouldn't be upstaged. If others were going to protest this or the Townshend Duties by separate petition, then so would Westmoreland. And so would Loudoun County. If he could locate his wandering brother. Where in damnation was he anyway? He'd waited at the Raleigh until after midnight, thinking any minute Francis would turn up, but no such luck.

Swallowing his agitation, Richard began to scribble a preliminary draft of his petition. Soon Patrick Henry would arrive, and he expected Tom Jefferson and Dabney Carr to wander in before the morning was far advanced. Admiring Jefferson's youthful astuteness and agile flair with the pen, Patrick had already included him, along with his good friend Dabney, in their inner circle of confidants. They could certainly make use of Jefferson's talents.

❧

Richard's Lucas found Francis's Ben leaving the rear gate to the Tayloe house. Ben had delivered a message from his master to Miss Rebecca, and was in high spirits. Marse Frank sure was

43

worked up over this young filly, he told himself, as he almost bumped into Lucas.

"Massa Lee, he say fo Mistah Frank to come, soons he gits up, but dat soons he gits up bes' be now! Tell him to come straight away, hear?"

Lucas was his usual bossy self this morning, Ben noted wryly. He'd never cared much for Lucas, knowing he felt superior, being servant to the elder Lee brother. It irritated him, yet he didn't see much he could do about it.

"You heared me?" prodded Lucas. "Y'all bes' pay 'tention to what I say, nigger. I ain't foolin' 'bout what Massa Richard done ordered me t'say."

Ben scratched his head. "I'll pass de words, ol' man, but Marse Frank he done bin pow'ful busy dis mawnin'. He gots things on his mind." By denying a definite answer, he made a small point. By loitering on his return to his master's lodging, he could even claim a victory, A slave from birth, Ben learned at an early age to hoard scraps of power to the last morsel. He'd tell Marse Frank when he was ready, and that would be a while yet.

It turned out Francis wasn't in a hurry to respond to Richard's message either. His reason, however, was quite different. He couldn't stop wondering how Becky would respond to his hastily penned letter inviting himself to call on the Tayloe family at eight that very evening. The weather was his excuse, saying they might not be able to meet in the garden due to rain. Would she think him too forward pressing a second meeting so soon? How would she approach her parents? Would they think him too old to be penning messages to their daughter? Indeed he was quite preoccupied. Taking his time, he finished his morning tea thinking of Becky, and not the unfair acts of a faraway King and a heavy-handed Parliament that Richard surely had on his mind.

Ignoring the misty rain, he tread a careful path across the muddy roadway. Nicholson Street remained uncobbled, as did most others. Raindrops had washed the dust from a border of early jonquils on the corner. He paused, wondering what variety they were and saw that tiny pearls of moisture hung suspended from each petal. This served to remind him he must remember to seek a reliable ship's captain who could purchase bulbs from England for him in time for fall planting. Such arrangements would be made much easier after September when his brothers Arthur and William would be in London. Arthur was determined on a course of law, and William was looking forward to securing a position with the East India Company.

Now that he thought about it, there were other things he required from London, including eight or so sturdy hoes to replace those no longer repairable. Grimes had shown him the implements, worn out by constant work in Loudoun County's rocky soil, but also rusted through in many cases. Francis knew it was due to carelessness, but unless he chose to tramp the fields each evening in search of missing tools, he had no alternative but to accept the expense of new ones. It was also time to order fruit trees. He wanted a good strain for propagating. Apples thrived in the cool climate of the Catoctin foothills, and he looked forward to trying peaches, plums, and perhaps pears. A careful gardener, he preferred to allow one type of crop or tree to prove itself before embarking on a new venture. With but twenty-three working slaves on his Horsepen Tract, and four of these with child, he recognized his limitations. Figs. Figs were a possibility for his next experiment in grafting, he thought. Also, shoes for the slaves were needed. Ben had been promised a new coat before winter, and Martha hinted broadly for the blue china she'd seen advertised in a London paper. Twice she'd mentioned it, once before his brother Philip, Colonel Phil, arrived for a visit, and again one night as they lay abed. By purchasing the blue dishes he could apologize for his harsh words before he left last week. It seemed important that the unpleasantness be smoothed over. Memories of his mistress flitted through his thoughts as he sauntered past Bruton Church toward the capitol.

Martha Tutt was born of indentured servants. Having served their time and been thus relieved of indebtedness, they supported a large family by whatever means came their way. John Tutt, by all accounts trustworthy and sincere, was accepted in Leesburg as a hard working family man. Francis had hired him for five years to supervise the transport of his tobacco crop to a landing on the upper Potomac. Life's knocks left a mark on Tutt, however, as his family grew and his income did not. He became ill tempered and demanding of his children. When Francis had offered the position of housekeeper to his eldest daughter, she had accepted gratefully.

Martha welcomed her job as chatelaine and the independent comfort it afforded, and Francis was likewise pleased with how quickly she adapted to his household. As a bachelor, away from family for over six years, he had desperately needed a clever woman to manage things. He spent most waking hours attending his planting, reading, or socializing. Never one to turn down a party, at the slightest pretext he took frequent trips to visit one or another of his many relatives, leaving the fields to his overseer and the house to Old Berth, an elderly black woman of undetermined years. There were two young girls, daughters of Ben, who were in her care and helped with chores, their mother having died of chronic ill health soon after the move to Loudoun County. The arrangement under Berth left a good deal to be desired. Her idea of an appetizing meal was a pot of boiled greens and a chunk of fatback. Sometimes she would think to add a baked sweet potato.

Within a month after Martha's hire the household took on a glow. A curtain here, a chair or table rearranged there, black-eyed Susans winking from the sideboard and, at mealtime, a savory pudding or a meat pie. Daily miracles all. The changes sang out from every corner of the house.

Neither Francis nor Martha noticed when their relationship began to alter. They exchanged no furtive looks and conversations between them never contained subtle invitation. They respected each other and both wished to please the other. That was all. Yet, gradually, mutual respect had led down the path to mutual desire. It happened one evening when Francis rode in late from Leesburg, the county seat. Caught in a violent thunderstorm six miles from home, he struggled two hours over treacherous roads to reach the farm. Bone-chilled, drenched to the skin, he limped across the porch. His horse, terrified at a thunderclap, had spooked and unseated him. He felt fortunate to have arrived at all.

"I came within a breath of being left in the mud. But for Cameron's placid nature, I would have been. He just stood and waited for me to remount," he croaked to Martha as she helped him out of his dripping coat. Shivers began to rattle his thin frame.

"Berth," she shouted. "You, Berth! Get in here and help me with Mr. Francis. He's soaked clear to his bones. Fair drowned, he is." Together they scurried to pick up wet clothes behind him and to heat bricks to warm the bed linen. Ben was summoned to give a rub and start the circulation. An ague was certain to set in if the master was not warmed quickly. Broth, steamy and rich with the magic flavors from Martha's herb garden, was brought to him. Francis sipped and, feeling better with each spoonful, he relaxed gratefully under the flurry of attention. Somewhere in the middle of this activity and concern for his well-being, he became aware of Martha's tender touch. Closing his eyes slightly he imagined her hair to be shimmering, like a field of golden wheat in the sunlight. Squinting, he saw that the glow from the firelight behind her made it blaze even more brightly.

Ben banked a large log to the rear of the hearth, hoping he wouldn't be summoned until daybreak. He and Berth slipped unnoticed from the room as Francis watched the girl draw the window curtains. "Thank you, Martha. I'm sorry to be such a bother. I certainly made a wrong decision to ride into town today."

Martha, seeing the twinkle back in his eyes was satisfied of his recovery. Thinking he chose to dismiss her, she moved to the door. "Goodnight, Sir." She smiled, hesitating as something in his expression held her. "Would a glass of Madeira please you? They say it is warming when one is chilled."

Her concern thrilled him right down to the soles of his icy feet, and once again he was reminded of how fortunate he'd been in having hired her. "Wonderful! It would assure me of a good rest. But you must be tired and I'm unbelievably inconsiderate to prevail upon you further. Go to bed, Martha," he said gently.

"Oh, I don't mind," she said, thinking that she'd have walked all the way to Leesburg to get something if he wanted it. Shocked by this astonishing realization and feeling her face flush, she hurried from the room.

"Stay a while with me," Francis urged when she returned with the wine, not even certain why he said it. She handed him a glass of the amber liquid. "Just to keep me company," he added.

The request surprised her, yet she didn't question his motive and drawing up a chair to face the bed, she watched him as she waited for whatever he might say next.

Her face though not pretty in the accepted sense, he thought, was pleasant, and she had a happy easy-going way about her. "Thank you," he said after some time had passed, "for being here ... and ... well, being so helpful. I don't suppose I've ever properly thanked you, Martha, for the many things you've done since you came here."

She laughed self consciously. "You pay me." But his words warmed her as thoroughly as the wine warmed him.

"You know, I can't remember," Francis continued, "what it was like here before you came. It must have been grim indeed. We're all better off for your presence. The house slaves, the field hands ... but especially me. I don't even miss Stratford anymore. In fact, I rarely think of it. I used to actually be jealous that Colonel Phil lived in such grand comfort in our family home while I was relegated to this farmhouse."

Martha had no idea what his grand family estate might be like, but she couldn't imagine anything much grander than the rooms she polished and straightened daily. Still she welcomed the compliment. "Would you care for more wine, Mr. Francis?"

"Perhaps a small drop." Then, "Oh, not that small," he laughed, steadying the glass as she tipped the decanter a second time. Their hands touched briefly and, flustered, she allowed a few drops to spill on the coverlet.

"I was clumsy. I am sorry. I am so sorry." Tears welled in her eyes. After all his fine compliments he must think her careless indeed.

He silenced her apology by an amazing gesture. He touched his finger lightly to her lips. "There, there. It's nothing to be sorry for. It's not important," he whispered.

Martha blinked, and two tears rolled slowly down her cheeks. "You mustn't be so good to me. I ... I don't know what is expected of me when you're so kind." Confused, she stared at him, waiting.

Francis returned her stare. He churned inside, wondering how they had reached this crossroad. For a very long time they remained quiet, neither speaking, until their eyes seemed to finally reach a silent agreement. Martha didn't leave the room until after five o'clock. When she arose, the clouds had blown and the morning sky was streaked with red. The first cock crowed as she crept happily to her own room in the attic. From that time on she shared the luxurious feather bed with her employer, although her belongings remained upstairs.

There developed a strict sense of propriety between them. Martha, included at table with Francis from the beginning, continued this practice. But mealtimes remained formal and the familiar banter they sometimes engaged in when alone was absent. When there were guests she stayed out of sight until all doors were closed for the night. Then she would pad in bare feet to his bedside, to be gone again before daybreak. If the house slaves knew of the intimacy, none indicated it. If she called him anything more personal than Mr. Francis, no one heard it. Francis accepted Martha as his mistress in the same way he accepted her as keeper of his house. He was overjoyed at his good fortune and he thrived on the creature comforts a woman could bring to a man's empty home and to his lonely bed. But they shared little real companionship. They were from two entirely different worlds and in different worlds they remained.

Now, two hundred miles away on the rainy day in Williamsburg and remembering the blue china plates, he determined to order them. With luck they would arrive in time for Christmas. Shaking himself from his reverie, he thought to cross the street. A coach drew abreast and Landon Carter's face appeared. He ordered his servant to draw in the horses.

"Well, Francis," his voice boomed. "I see you are out early this morning. May I drop you somewhere?"

Francis didn't know why, but he was always happy to see the crotchety old man. "Good morning, Colonel. No indeed, I'm just on my way round to the Red Lion to see Richard. Mrs. Lee and the children aren't with him and he had no need to let a house this time." Pointing overhead, he added "The rain is so light I'm having a fine stroll in spite of it."

Carter frowned, pulling back inside the carriage. His aches and pains multiplied with even the thought of cloudy weather. "Francis, pray, I would have a word with you. Perhaps you will do me the honor of accompanying me on a short turn around the village whilst we talk?"

Francis briefly weighed the importance of Richard's summons against incurring the displeasure of his influential friend. Deciding quickly, he climbed into the coach. At Carter's nod the coachman flicked his whip and the horses high-stepped into a trot.

Landon Carter scrutinized his young friend. What was on Mr. Lee's nimble mind besides political matters, he wondered, to cause him to appear so jubilant on a rainy morning. "May I break into your thoughts, whatever they may be? I've heard you are most desirous of being named to the committee to draft the resolution to King George in support of our sister colonies." Letting his words sink in for a moment, he continued "However you didn't speak out on the subject clearly yesterday when we talked."

Francis wondered where Carter had gotten the information. He prickled with embarrassment, praying the colonel hadn't heard of what suddenly seemed brash boasting on his own part. "Well, yes Sir, I have hoped that if such a committee is formed that I shall be called to serve."

"Now that I hear this from your own lips rather than from the feeble course of gossip, perhaps I am able to be of help. I still have some influence, you know, in this House ... if not in my own," he grumbled, referring to the growing rift with his eldest son. Colonel Carter disapproved in almost every way of Robert Wormeley Carter, yet the two continued to share the comforts of Sabine Hall with their various offspring. Drawing himself erect, the colonel looked directly at his passenger. "Had you so informed me the other morning, in a simple statement as we enjoyed each other's leisure, I would possibly already have been able to secure the assignment for you. But as it is, the matter has been brought to me in a manner that can only be termed as second-hand."

Francis recognized it as a forward step in their relationship and one he would take pains to remember. "I can only say I'm sorry, Sir. I certainly should have been more forthwith. I can see that now." The coach was approaching the tavern where Richard was lodging. "Oh, here we are at the Red Lion now," he said, hoping to be let out.

Carter signaled the coachman and the carriage came to a stop. "Would you be free to join me this evening, Francis? There are many things happening in these colonies to provide us with much discussion. It is fundamental that we stand firm against the threats that would curtail our freedom as colonial citizens of the Crown. I would enjoy your company."

Any night but tonight, Francis thought. "I'm sorry, Colonel, but I must decline. Perhaps tomorrow? I've committed myself to calling at Colonel Tayloe's at eight."

"I see. Your friendship with our mutual friend would appear to be growing," Carter commented dryly.

Francis suspected Carter's testiness stemmed from an innately jealous nature and not from disapproval of Tayloe, for they were not only neighbors, but lifelong friends. "Well, Sir, as the plans have already been made I can only look forward to spending some other evening in your company. And thank you for the ride," he said jumping to the ground. "I'll look forward to the next time we meet!"

Carter allowed a wispy smile to cross his aristocratic face. "Remind me next time we do meet that I have a packet of corn seed for your kitchen garden. It is more tender than any I have developed yet."

"Wonderful. Adieu, dear Colonel." Waving, he turned quickly and in a few minutes had reached the second floor of the Red Lion. Hearing voices within, he guessed rightly that he was the last to arrive.

"Well, Brother. Come in. We are all gathered, awaiting your arrival. Not that we've been idle in your absence," Richard needled.

Ignoring the jibe, Francis greeted the others. The only one missing from their usual group, George Mason, was apparently not in Williamsburg this session. Tom Jefferson sat at a small writing desk, papers spread before him. Patrick Henry, consumed with nervous energy, returned to his pacing as soon as he shook Francis's hand. Richard and Dabney Carr had obviously been seated. Carr rose to draw up a chair for the latecomer. "We saw you arrive with Colonel Carter," he said, indicating the window.

"Yes, he gave me a ride. I ... it seems his purpose was to embarrass and put me in my place. And he succeeded. Somehow he heard of my conversation with you, R.H., boasting as it were of my confidence in his friendship. He chided me for not asking him straight out to use his influence to get me appointed to a certain committee. You all know which committee I speak of ... it has yet to be formed."

"There's always a lesson to be learned, Frank," Richard Henry declared. "Especially when one deals in the chancy game of politics. I rather suspect our friend Ben Harrison put the bug in Carter's ear. Harrison could probably scarcely wait to pass on what he gleaned from his eavesdropping on us during the session yesterday."

"That's right. I believe, now that I think of it, he waited until we finished the meaty part of our whispered conversation before he silenced us."

Dabney Carr interrupted the discourse between the Lee brothers by reminding them of the job at hand. "If you are named, Francis, to said as-yet-unformed committee to draft a disapproval of the recent acts put forth by our royal leader and his Parliament, then we must address ourselves to what it is we expect to accomplish by your appointment. Forget Harrison for the moment."

"Dabney is right. Gentlemen, let's get on with it," Richard Henry fumed. "We have here a beginning, a list of grievances we think should be included in any petition. And If we're going to do it, we should do it right, and once and for all include all our grievances, not just some of them. Never forget that we, as law abiding colonial citizens of His Majesty's government, have been prohibited from purchasing virtually any items from any source but our mother country. Therefore, for that country to then place a duty on what we must of necessity purchase from our own home country in order to live comfortably, is not only unjust, it is damned intolerable!"

Patrick Henry spoke up. "I am in absolute agreement. In addition I would remind us not to forget what else we've been hearing. If Britain actually retaliates against New York by suspending its legislature, that is an outrage that cannot be borne in silence. Today New York, I say, and tomorrow Virginia! Our displeasure with this has to be expressed in the resolution also, along with our support of the Massachusetts Bay grievances. Are we agreed?"

Heads nodded. Richard passed Francis a sheet of paper. "Read this. We drew it up last evening when, by the way, you were nowhere to be found. It's a separate petition we intend to present to the assembly tomorrow. I'll enter it as a protest from Westmoreland, to get things started. I'm sure I can get the necessary signatures this afternoon."

Francis saw quickly that the petition dealt with both New York and Massachusetts, the language was strong, and it ended with a tongue-in-cheek statement to the Crown that "such alarming actions on the part of Parliament would deprive His Majesty's British subjects in America of the means of showing loyalty to their most Gracious and Beloved Sovereign." Francis nodded in appreciation.

"I've heard that Amelia County freeholders are adding their names to the petition from Dinwiddie, Henrico, and Chesterfield," Thomas Jefferson told them.

"The more involvement, the better," approved Henry. "It will make it that much more difficult for the conservatives amongst us to push us to a lukewarm document. They'll have no choice but to bow to the majority."

The talk continued for several hours with precise wording being refined again and again. Francis exhibited even less than his usual interest and asked few questions. He barely contributed, turning frequently to gaze out the window at nothing. His thoughts kept straying to the Becky Tayloe he had met yesterday half child, half woman, something charming and fresh and wonderful in between. He wasn't sure he could wait for eight o'clock to see her again, to see if his memory served him right. Finally he sensed they had finished what they'd gathered to do and, once written in final form by Jefferson, and if he was named, the results of their efforts would be his to study and take to commitee.

"I think if you gentlemen will excuse me, I'll head for a meal. It's well past two I believe," he said to all, but to no one in particular. Everyone nodded.

Richard followed him to the hall. "Is something bothering you, Loudoun? You seem to have something on your mind."

Francis grinned. "I don't know what you mean, R.H., but I assure you if anything is worth the telling, you shall be the first to know." Clapping his brother on the shoulder, he bounded for the stairwell and took the steps two at a time. Turning at the bottom, he tipped his cocked tricorn in a salute. "Adieu," he laughed, thinking Richard's startled expression was worth a shilling at least!

Richard stood looking at the empty stairwell. He'd seen that twinkling in Loudoun's eyes on more than one occasion. Of course. So obvious. And so typical of poor dear Frank. He always had a love affair going, didn't he, and none of them ever serious. Remembering yesterday, the Tayloe garden, he said aloud, "Oh, no, surely not one of the Tayloe children?" How old were they anyway?

Francis stepped into a rain-dappled freshness. The rain had ceased and the sun was trying to overtake the clouds. A ravenous hunger came over him and he forgot his comrades might be watching from the window. Seeing no one about, he headed at a lope for the Raleigh. Hat in hand, leaping puddles in his path, he felt happy, and as carefree as a man could hope to be.

An Evening On Nicholson Street

A myrtle candle shown from a window in the Tayloe parlor signaling a welcome, as Francis approached at precisely one minute before eight. It was a long time since a young woman had given him such a case of jitters and he couldn't remember when he'd felt such a compelling desire to be on time. Dressed in his velvet waistcoat, forest green Martha called it when she folded it for packing, he was glad he'd ordered it in time from his London tailor for the trip to Williamsburg. He'd picked up the packet from Captain Dobbie in Leedstown on his way, never dreaming how important it would be to look his best once he arrived. His highly polished shoes made a thump on the wooden step as he took a deep breath before sounding the knocker. He glimpsed Lady Tayloe through the window as he brushed imaginary lint from his sleeve, and was ready with a smile when the door was opened and he was ushered into the sitting room.

"Ah, good evening, my dear Rebecca. How lovely you look this evening. I trust you'll not think I'm intruding by calling without invitation. I happened on young Becky as I passed yesterday and she suggested you and her father might enjoy my stopping by." When she made no immediate response, he continued, "I see that Williamsburg's spring agrees with you as usual." Perched on the edge of a fashionable corner-chair, a new design from a Baltimore cabinetmaker copied from England's Thomas Chippendale, Rebecca raised her eyes slowly from her needlepoint to smile at her guest, her expression holding no hint of what she really thought of his presence.

"How do you do, Colonel Lee ... my dear Francis?" She was quick to note the smile of an innocent boy that teased the corners of his mouth. It lit his eyes as he bent to kiss the hand she offered. The charm, the natural charm, it serves him well, she thought. His open face, the apparent desire always to be liked, and the gentle patient way he had with everyone he met, those were his greatest attributes. If a touch of vanity colored the whole, well, who would deny him that? She'd always been pleased to welcome Francis Lee into her home. That he was here at the invitation of Becky, however, was something different. ""Won't you sit down? John will join us in a few minutes. He told me you'd spoken to Becky about coming this evening."

"Yes, yes as I said. I happened to greet her as I was passing by." Wishing to change the subject, he said, "You do beautiful needlepoint. My mother would have been so envious. She wasn't terribly accomplished with it. But yours is truly magnificent." Did he sound foolish? Was his flattery too transparent? Why didn't the colonel hurry so there would be other conversation? And where was Becky? He was beginning to wish he hadn't come, when several of the girls burst into the room followed by their father.

The room soon filled with chatter and laughter. Francis and Becky greeted each other in a casual enough way, although Rebecca noticed the flush on both their faces. Francis settled in a chair next to John Tayloe and the two began to talk. Although he tried to ignore it, he sensed Lady Tayloe was studying him, listening to his every word.

Rebecca had accepted his compliments, considering them sincere enough. The Lees, she thought, produced gracious men and Francis was no doubt one of their most gallant. Not as elegant or forcefully virile as his handsome father perhaps; but then Thomas Lee had been blessed with a unique stature made so by his large build. Francis lacked that, yet he had something else. Was it the soulful look of his deepset eyes that made one look twice? Or his readiness with a smile and a soft compliment? Very attractive, no matter ... but was something going on between Francis and their sixteen-year-old daughter?

The evening progressed not unlike countless others he had spent with the Tayloe family over the years. Candlelight flickered from the sconces as slaves slid in and out on silent feet doing the bidding of the master. John Tayloe offered his best brandy served in silver cups, and the two men conversed, catching up on the news each had to share, with Tayloe as usual bragging about his promising crop of yearlings. Lady Tayloe clucked occasionally to the children, summoning Cate from the hall when they became too rowdy, with a tap of her mother-of-pearl fan on the arm of her chair. The older girls, Becky, Anne, and Ellie had prepared a musical program.

Francis found the performance much improved over former years, taking note especially of Becky's lovely clear voice, aware he mustn't appear to favor her by his applause, yet following her every movement. A glance in his direction from time to time let him know she felt his attention. Her green eyes sparkled as the pink and cream skirts swished and swirled around her, and Francis was certain he caught the scent of jasmine when she passed his chair. She was really quite the most lovely thing he'd ever seen, he thought, and then struggled to respond to the question her father had just put before him.

"I'm sorry, Sir ... I've been distracted by your daughters' program." Searching blindly for a new item of interest, his gaze fastened on the slave, Cate, who had just entered the room. Francis remembered what Becky had told him about Cate and Blair's Negro.

"I see you eyeing the slave," Tayloe said. "Handsome, isn't she? And she takes excellent care of my daughters, I might add."

"Ah, yes ... I expect she's a fine nursemaid," Francis stammered. At that precise moment, Baby Sarah, Sally they called her, bounded into his lap and threw her arms around his neck, freeing him of the need for further explanation.

Tayloe sipped his brandy and leveled his gaze above Sally's head directly at Francis. "I've recently made a gift of the wench to Becky. She has served all the girls, but Becky is particularly attached to her. I intend my daughter to have a handsome dowry," he added. He'd not missed his friend's inability to pay attention, nor his oldest daughter's pink cheeks and spirited excitement.

"Oh?" It was all Francis could manage. Sally had wriggled around in his lap until she faced him, and was absorbed in examination of the plush fabric of his waistcoat. He stroked her hair absently, as one would a purring kitten. A few years ago it had been Becky, not Sally, who snuggled there, he thought. "Your generosity is well known, so far as your daughters are concerned, Colonel." Although he wanted desperately to spend more time with Becky he had no desire to discuss dowries or marriage, either one. He'd avoided that pitfall thus far, for no reason he could pinpoint exactly and, with luck, intended to continue to do so at least for the foreseeable future. It had nothing to do with his desire to spend time with Becky, did it?

Tayloe caught the thread of reluctance in the words. Or perhaps in the lack of words. He knew Frank's reputation well enough. The man was a master at escaping the bonds of matrimony. Many considered Frank Lee an excellent catch in spite of the general knowledge that he had broken his share of maidenly hearts. Pleasant, witty, and good company, Frank knew how to listen and precisely when to flatter. His small build didn't detract in the least from his quality, and he was liked equally by both men and women. The same could not be said of many men, Tayloe mused. He'd been amazed when Becky brought him the news that Mr. Lee would call on them. She hadn't elaborated, but he could put the pieces together. He knew he'd be overjoyed to welcome Francis Lee as a son-in-law and wouldn't stand in his daughter's way if that's what she wanted. In fact when it came right down to it, given the chance, he would encourage it. "Well," he said, taking another tack, "since you mentioned Cate there, let me tell you a few things about her. She has quite a history."

Francis thought he saw a flicker of pain in her dark eyes as the colonel spoke of the slave as though she were deaf or not in the room. Was he actually being cruel telling her story in front of her ... or did he perhaps think it didn't matter because she belonged to him and therefore it was his right to treat her as he wished? He patched the story together as it went along, for Tayloe stated the facts only as he saw them to be true, and with little or no embellishment. It was a sad story indeed.

At the age of about ten the girl had been found wandering about in the woods near Mount Airy, lost and afraid, after having been reported missing by an overseer. Bruised and bloody, it became clear she had been raped. Her hands were still tied behind her back, her wrists raw with rope burn where she'd struggled to free them. Terrified black eyes in her small mulatto face stared out at a hostile world and she refused to speak or name her attacker. The elder Tayloes had agreed she should be allowed to recover away from the quarter, and she was taken to the nursery where she remained. There had been no complaint from her mother, who eventually admitted it was Cate's own half brother who had abused her. Taken in by Miss Turnbull, she was trained as a house servant and learned to wait on the Tayloe daughters and care for their clothes. She was permitted to share their playtimes and generally, their mealtimes. Scrawny and knobby-kneed, she uttered barely a word during her first year in the great house. Cate's attacker, who unwittingly had improved his sister's lot, was ordered twenty lashes, not enough to cause permanent injury, for he was strong and healthy, good breeding stock. Had Cate been a few years older at the time he took a fancy to her, the matter would undoubtedly have passed unnoticed by her master, Francis guessed.

As John Tayloe spoke, Francis filled in the details from his imagination and from what Becky had told him. Cate's fear of black men persisted even as her initial fear of white people vanished. She came to feel secure in her place in the household, her life safe and untroubled. Then one morning Isaac came to deliver a message to the house on Nicholson Street where he stopped first at the laundry to ask for Jacob, the colonel's man. Leaning over Cate's laundry tub he inquired if he might warm his hands by the fire. When she looked up she saw a tall, proud-looking man staring back at her. He was very black; unlike herself, no white blood mingled with the pure African in his veins. His eyes burned like two dark coals in a fine-featured face, and Cate felt no fear. Isaac returned many times during the next weeks and one day she took him by the hand and led him to her tiny room over the kitchen. It was broad daylight. While pans clattered, a stirring spoon thudded against the sides of a wooden bowl, and the cooks giggled below, Cate surrendered much more than her fear of men. They made love every chance they got after that. Then came the long separation, the long months of waiting at Mount Airy until the return to Williamsburg once more. In the family, no one but Becky was aware of the change in Cate's life.

"So you see, we have quite spoiled the wench, haven't we, Cate?" Tayloe chuckled, gulping down the remainder of his brandy. She might be a favorite but she was still a belonging, and it didn't hurt to remind her every so often, he thought, feeling the warmth of the brandy.

"Yas-suh, Massa," the mulatto responded dutifully.

Francis sensed pride in her attitude; by averting her gaze as well as by a natural dignity, she'd managed to convey a rebuff. She wasn't cowed by her master, nor stupid like many of them. Her eyes were bright and thoughtful, her brown skin gleamed in the soft light, and she moved with a precision born of confidence in her position among the other servants and in the family. And although it was clear she didn't like John Tayloe talking about her as he had just done, it seemed she'd learned to endure in silence. Francis had to admire the girl.

As they moved to the dining room for supper Tayloe changed the subject, asking how things were going on the Loudoun farm. Francis, seeing he was to be seated next to Becky, was happy for the chance to talk about what he'd accomplished on the western land. "I'm recently persuaded, Colonel, that a talented overseer is the key to a successful crop. As sure as we till the soil for tobacco and seed the corn in the spring, none of our endeavors can be productive if the overseer isn't patient with the ways of the Negro. He must watch them carefully, observe signs of illness, see to their rations and, while keeping them in line of course, treat them with at least a minimum of understanding, or they won't perform for him. I'm convinced it's that simple." Seeing Tayloe's raised eyebrow, he hurried to continue before being interrupted. "Oh, they'll turn out to the fields each morning, but only to avoid a thrashing. They'll find every means of shirking, especially if the overseer hasn't gained their confidence and respect. Believe me, I've seen it happen over and over again. Look at Landon Carter and my brother Philip, they have more able bodied slaves laid up with bloodied backs in a week than I would allow in six months! And if the poor creatures are not under the lash, they're settled somewhere on their backsides, a position they most dearly relish, I might add. And it is all because they are not under the orders of a decent overseer." Glancing at Becky, he thought he saw approval in her eyes.

Tayloe cleared his throat. He thrived on a good argument and this was a meaty subject, but Lee had pushed it too far. "Rubbish, man! The very nature of the beast is to be lazy. They must be prodded to work."

"Perhaps," Francis responded quickly, "Yet I feel certain, Sir, that the reason for my success on the Horsepen Tract is that Grimes sees it like I do. If given a chance to work under halfway decent conditions, the Negro will produce more, and create fewer problems. Beat them, starve them, treat them like animals, and no amount of divine weather or rich river bottom soil is going to produce a worthy crop. That's a fact."

"Well, your basic premise is sound, I suppose, but of course we must then acknowledge that blacks and whites are created the same. But ... can we do that? The reason we find black slavery a profitable form of labor in Virginia, as elsewhere, is because they do not require the same considerations as the indentured white. Education being one of these. So long as they cannot read or write, nor speak our language decently, their successive generations can be taught easily to do our bidding. It is the way, and that's the goal if we are to continue supplying most of the world with our fine tobacco leaf. Won't work with whites. Look at England. The serfs rattle the very doors of the middle classes! The entire system has broken down. Now what kind of a world is that?"

The passing of food and refilling of wine glasses went on around them as Francis continued, not ready to give up. "It seems to me that twenty well treated Negroes will raise you more hogsheads packed with larger, healthier leaf, than sixty harshly treated slaves can be expected to roll to the wharf from a larger acreage. You have to give a man some incentive, a reason to labor, if you will."

"Hmmph. Next thing you'll be advocating is that they be allowed to practice their voodoo and have their damned drums back," the colonel said, signaling Jacob for more smoked turkey. "On a large plantation it's not profitable nor possible to mollycoddle. In the first place, there are too many slaves to be watching out for all their ills. Some do sicken and die. The strong survive and have issue. That one, the brother of Cate I mentioned earlier, he's probably sired ten or twelve himself, and he's not a quarter of a century old yet. He's one of the strong ones. I don't think the overseer, whoever he may be, has a bloody thing to do with that basic fact. His task should be to get the most out of those who are strong and reproduce, with the least amount of expense and effort.

Pure and simple, eh? And the less a planter interferes with the methods, the better off they'll all be."

"Now John," his wife admonished sweetly from her end of the table, "You know we don't punish our slaves more than necessary. We don't under-feed them, nor do we deny them whatever medical treatments we're able to provide. They are taught the Holy Scripture. John is fortunate to have several stout overseers who are quite competent. He merely enjoys a good argument once in a while. As you know, Francis, whenever you two get into the subject of planting or politics, there will be spirited conversation." Rebecca turned then to her husband to ask him about their plans for the theatre season. "The first production, I've heard, is a comedy called *The Constant Couple*," Francis heard her saying as he took advantage of the chance to speak to Becky.

"These cold meats are delicious," he said quietly.

"Yes," she murmured. "Indeed they are. Cook knows just how to prepare them."

"I specially like the smoked tongue."

"Yes, I also."

"So which do you like best? The brandied peaches or the spiced pears?"

Testing a sample of each, Becky laughed at him, "Why, I do like them both equally well! Which is your favorite?"

Francis noted her teeth were uncommonly even. "I think I'm partial to the peaches. But figs are actually my favorite fruit." He could feel the effect of the brandy and the wine.

"Mine is strawberries," she said. Her eyes clung to him, caressing his cheek where Ben had shaved him so close not a hint of stubble shadowed his skin.

John Tayloe, glancing in their direction, had to look down to hide his amusement. Had he ever behaved so foolishly? Surely not ... yet thinking of days long gone, he looked past the silver bowl filled with daffodils and wild dogwood blossoms to the opposite end of the square table. His wife was still a beautiful woman. Between them, ranging in age from three to sixteen, sat six of their daughters, all save one. Catching Rebecca's eye in the candle's glow he thought he saw a question there. Did she, also, sense that soon they should prepare to lose a second one to marriage?

Soon Cate entered and after a whispered word to Lady Tayloe, summoned the younger girls to bed. In the silence that followed the goodnight kisses and chatter of little voices, Becky decided it was an opportune time to approach her father on the subject of Isaac.

"Papa?" she said, smiling at him. "I couldn't help listening to your conversation with Colonel Lee ... Francis ... earlier. You know, about the slaves and all?"

Tayloe nodded, wondering what was coming.

"I must confess, as much as I trust your judgement, I think Francis has stated a truth when he says a man treated considerately will work more diligently."

Her father frowned. "Now Becky, I don't truly disagree with Mr. Lee. I merely said that on a large plantation such as Mount Airy, that's not always possible, and to pamper the Negroes will not result in a good crop."

"But, Papa, what of house servants? Surely if you believe what you just said, there aren't so many of them, couldn't they receive more careful consideration?"

Perplexed but, more than that, irritated at his daughter's interference in a matter that didn't concern her, the colonel exhibited the reason he wasn't admired for his patience. "Don't beat around the bush with me, daughter! I'll not have it. Speak what's on your mind directly and get it over with."

"Yes, for goodness sake, Becky, do tell what you're hinting at," her mother encouraged, tired of slavery talk, which was never pleasant at best. Becky was acting very peculiar this evening. "We haven't mistreated our house slaves. You are quite aware of that."

Francis understood her goal instantly, and now spoke for her, fearing she'd lose her nerve. "If you permit me, I don't think Becky refers to any mistreatment, Madam. Rather, she's concerned with a circumstance existing at the present time of which you are perhaps unaware."

"Oh?" Rebecca's voice betrayed surprise at their guest's apparent knowledge of Tayloe affairs.

Impulsively, Becky reached for Francis's hand under the table and found it readily available. She squeezed it hard, gaining courage as well as a racing pulse from her bold gesture. "You see, Papa and Mama, it's about Catey. Over a year ago, it was winter before last, while here in Williamsburg, she became acquainted with a slave belonging to the Blairs. He is coachman for Lady Blair. His name is Isaac. What I wish to ask you, Papa, is will you buy him for Cate?"

"Buy him for Cate?" he croaked. "What for? I don't need any more Negroes. There are plenty of young bucks at Mount Airy for her if she wants a man." The wounded look on Becky's face caused him to go on. "Just how interested is she in this fellow Isaac anyway?"

"Very. She's very interested. She loves him."

"She *loves* him? But ... I don't understand how this happened. I am a sensible man, but I just don't understand how she even *knows* him."

Then everyone was talking at once. Questions and answers flew from one side of the table to the other, with Anne and Ellie joining in whenever they got the chance.

"We must allow them to marry, Papa," Becky finally managed above the other voices. "It would be sinful of you to keep them apart. Catey never even looked at another man before Isaac came along!"

"You always said you wouldn't separate families, John. And although they aren't a family at present, it sounds as though it could become one easily enough." Rebecca wasn't sure she should support the somewhat ridiculous request, except that it did seem curiously logical after all.

"Sir," Francis added, "the price would be a small one to pay. The fellow apparently knows horses and can manage them quite well."

Tayloe tapped his fork noisily against a pewter plate, a signal to all that the situation had gone far enough. Ellie ignored him. "But Papa," she persisted, "you've always said Cate gets special treatment because she takes such good care of us."

"And because of what happened to her when she was a little girl. You know, about the ra...well, the attack on her," Anne added.

"All right! All right, all of you!" he blurted. "Don't keep telling me what I have always said. It makes me livid. I'll speak to Blair about this young buck for my horses, and for Cate, hmm? But mind you, I don't promise a thing. It depends on his price." He laughed as he was swallowed in the arms and kisses of three daughters. Hell, he thought, I've been bested by a friend and a passel of damned females, and I may as well admit it.

For Becky's sake Francis was pleased. He was also relieved that Tayloe didn't relish the girl for himself. It was common enough practice. One could never be sure, no matter how well he knew a man, what his taste in women might include until it was put to the test.

At midnight Rebecca yawned, a signal to everyone that perhaps the evening should come to a close. Francis bid his farewells reluctantly. Becky followed him to the door.

"It's been a lovely evening," she said softly.

"Yes, indeed," he agreed, "one of the best, I should think."

They looked at each other. No one could see them now, for the hall was empty except for Jacob who waited patiently around the corner until he could bolt the door.

"Thank you for helping me, about Cate. I don't understand how you knew what I was going to ask before I said it, but you did."

"I just knew," he confessed, grinning. He didn't care if the silly smile spread all over his face now, it was just for her.

"I declare, Francis Lee, I don't know what on earth has happened to me the last two days. I feel like I own the world, the sun, moon, and stars, everything."

"I think I know what you mean," he said gently, touching her hair where it grew in a little curl beside her cheek. It was soft and silky and he twirled it around his finger, marveling at how very happy he felt at that moment.

"You do? However did you know?" she whispered, leaning closer.

"Because what has been happening to you, has happened to me also. I couldn't sleep last night thinking of you."

"Becky," her mother called. "Mr. Lee will think you have no manners, dallying in the doorway like that." Rebecca was sure of it now. Something was going on between them. But the difference in their ages ... had she pushed Becky too far, telling her it was time to think about marriage?

The two in the hallway smiled. From a long way off an owl hooted, a lonely night sound. "I'll send you a note in the morning," Francis promised, rattling the large bolt loudly so Lady Tayloe would know he was leaving.

"And meet me in the garden at four?"

"I'll be there even if I have to duck a committee meeting. They're usually boring anyway."

"Oh dear merciful Lord," she said, leaning weakly into the door as the latch clicked shut behind him, "I do believe I am in love."

"Yas'm, Miss Becky." A smile broke across Jacob's normally stoic face. "I 'spect you is at dat. You got all de signs!" He slammed the bolt into place, positive that Miss Becky's own happiness had something to do with her desire to improve Cate's. Whatever the reason, he blessed her for it.

A Touch of Weather

The March heat wave vanished from the Tidewater as quickly as it arrived, and early April basked in clear, cool days under an azure sky. Nights held crisp, topped with the million stars of heaven and the sliver of a quarter moon. The tiresome complaints of gout, croup, ague, colds and fevers seemed to evaporate on the heels of the unseasonable spell of heat. Francis found it, all things considered, a perfect time to play at love. If he had to thrash out government's frustrating complexities between times, that was all right, too.

A lengthy session riddled with problems was ahead for the lawmakers. Without a doubt the most important task was to decide what posture they should take against Britain in the face of new outrages. Petitions of every nature and consequence were introduced, many of them recommending strong language in support of the Massachusetts Bay and New York Colonies. On Saturday the letter from Massachusetts was read. Tempers flared and patience wore thin as the burgesses debated what to do but, the following Thursday, it was at last agreed they would prepare three documents. The first a Petition to His Majesty, the second a Memorial to the House of Lords, and lastly a Remonstrance to the House of Commons. Appointments were made to a committee charged with the task of preparing the documents, and Francis heard his name called. Second from the last on the list of eleven, he knew this would please Richard Henry. Silently he pledged a thank-you to Landon Carter. The old man hadn't let him down.

Of course there was other business before the assembly. Several laws about to expire had to be re-evaluated, and a lengthy time was spent arguing over whether to retain the wolf bounty in the western counties; Francis recommended against it. There were reports of fraudulent schemes to collect the reward by importing pelts from the wild lands farther west, he explained. He personally hadn't seen a wolf for months although he was frequently on the road. Yes, he admitted when questioned, they could occasionally still be heard at night. When the vote came, however, he went with the majority and the law remained on the books. He felt it unwise to be a poor loser and, seeing the way the wind blew, he bent with it on most issues even when he wished it to be otherwise.

Should taxes be raised to repair and straighten the abominable road system? John Henry presented a petition calling for surveys and studies, and wanted funding for the printing of a map. It was an elaborate plan, bound to take years and cost thousands of pounds. Francis was on the committee that proposed *"... said petition be referred to the consideration of the next session of Assembly."* Of course they all recognized it was a way of putting things off. Some had wanted to bury John Henry's road plan permanently, so they compromised by substituting *"referred to the next session,"* for *"rejected."* The final vote went with the amendment version. Too costly, they agreed, although their carriages would continue to bog down in the mud and they'd have to travel miles out of the way to reach many destinations in inclement weather.

As in most sessions of the assembly, there was haggling and personal bickering over the pronouncement of verdicts in countless disputes over the settlement of private estates, runaway slaves, stolen farm animals, and boundary lines. These were ever-present problems. Surprising no one, the burgesses voted money to pay their own salaries and to preserve the House journals of previous years. Curiously, funds were also allocated to repair the garden at the Williamsburg public gaol. Something must be provided for those poor souls incarcerated merely for debt or petty thievery, argued the burgess from Prince William County. It seemed this was an inexpensive way to prove their generosity to philanthropic causes.

Two weeks into the issues facing them, they came to the subject of how best to collect what was owed the colony from the estate of former Treasurer Robinson. Through the years Robinson had managed to embezzle over a hundred thousand pounds from the colonial treasury which he'd used to benefit himself as well as other wealthy planters.

"I wager you feel pretty smug every time Robinson's case is reviewed," Francis teased, as he and his brother left the burgess chamber together.

Ignoring the comment, Richard swung into stride, moving ahead.

Francis shifted his satchel to the other side and grabbed for his brother's arm. "I say, did you hear me? Hey, what's your damned hurry anyway?"

"I'm frightfully tired of the infernal subject, Frank, that's what. If they'd listened to me years ago, we wouldn't be wasting time now, trying to replenish our losses." Richard had almost brought about his own political ruin several years earlier by attacking Robinson and his cronies. His crusade had set him apart from the hard-line conservatives, a position he probably would have arrived at in any case, but fortunately he'd been proved right in the end. The old timers weren't inclined to forgive what they termed his 'audacity' but Richard seemed to thrive on the various impediments they continued to throw in his path. And he had Francis to smooth things out when he ruffled some feathers, which happened often.

Francis decided to drop the subject if Richard was going to grump about it. Pointing out the playbill in front of the Playhouse, "They're presenting *"Midsummer Night's Dream"* this evening," he announced, "and Lady Tayloe has consented to my escorting Becky. At first she said that she and the colonel would accompany us, but has now apparently decided that I'm to be trusted to return their daughter safely after the play and a late supper. Why don't you join us? I can easily pick up three tickets this afternoon instead of two. The change from political wrangling will do you good."

"Frank, how old is that child? It seems only yesterday she was learning to walk and talk! Aren't you rushing things a bit with her?"

"Actually, she's quite grown up now, and very lovely I might add. I'd like for you to meet her again and see for yourself."

"Hard to believe, but I'll have to take your word for it this time. I've promised to meet our friends for supper at the Raleigh again. But tell me, are you serious about the young Rebecca?"

"Serious?" Francis was not sure of the answer himself. He certainly wanted to spend time with her to discover what his true feelings might be. Smiling, he admitted, "Well, I guess a few more times alone with her should provide an answer. Perhaps if you joined us I would have the benefit of your opinion."

"Since when have you needed my opinion when it came to women, Loudoun?" Richard laughed, thinking again that Becky Tayloe was hardly a woman yet. Despite his interest in Frank's love life, he really wanted to talk privately and at further length with Dabney, Patrick, and especially the young Tom Jefferson. While some other tempers had begun to flare over the British demands, it was time to put fan to the fire and blow the tempest to a full blaze, he thought. They needed to stir the entire House to fever pitch and it would take all of them working behind the scenes to do it. "But you should be coming with me tonight, Frank, although I understand you've made other plans. There's so much we can do if we work together. and we're missing our dear friend George Mason as well."

"Yes, I'm also sorry George isn't here. And I'm sorry if I appear to be letting you down. It wasn't my intention to do so." As he spoke they passed under the sign of a peruke maker. "Singularly unattractive," Francis mumbled, although his brother had paused to examine what might be the latest English styles, which apparently featured very tight side curls.

Richard Henry stared at him, measuring the situation. "No," he said finally. "I think you're properly enough occupied, finding yourself a wife as it were. Every man deserves some time for that. Enjoy yourself."

And he was gone. Hurrying down the street, he disappeared into the Purdie-Dixon Office where the *Gazette* was published. Harness creaked and wheels on cobblestone rattled behind Francis. Abruptly aware he was standing in the middle of Gloucester Street, he jumped out of the way, deciding he should attend his afternoon's committee meeting after all. What had Richard said? Finding yourself a wife? Was that what everyone thought? A child passed, rolling a hoop. Sunlight bounced off reddish curls. Getting married meant the responsibility of fatherhood, a total commitment to the future, being tied down to one life, one person, a new family of one's own making. Was that where he was heading? It was a worrisome subject at best, he thought as he drew near once again to the capitol building. Enjoying the stretch of his calf muscles, he climbed the long steps to the second floor still deep in thought. Entering a room on the left, he found the committee assigned to consider the state of the Office of the Clerk of the House assembled around the huge oak table. It would be their final meeting. He arrived just in time to answer "present" when the chairman called his name.

≈

Laughter trailed through the floorboards and the weight of someone's body thumped into the mattress overhead as Francis dressed for the evening. "This place isn't maintained as it used to be, eh, Ben?" he said, surveying the cracked walls and peeling paint of the window moldings.

"No suh, 'deed it ain't." Ben unfolded a ruffled shirt, smoothing at the wrinkles of travel.

"No, not that one. It's the theatre tonight. Give me the new one, with the laced front."

"Yas suh!" The slave returned to the wardrobe. His wide mouth spread into a grin and his eyes rolled upward as he recognized the sounds from above. The rhythmic thud of heavy bed posts, strung together by rope springs needed no explanation. "Dat gen'lman ain't wastin' no time dis evenin', Mr. Frank. Dat negra gal just got dere!"

Francis sighed. "No, they don't even provide a covering on the floor to muffle the sounds of a man's passion. I wonder what's happened to the Persian carpets that used to grace these floors?" The house had been going downhill ever since his mother's Ludwell relatives had moved from Green Spring back to England. While in the Virginia Colony they had maintained not only the Green Spring plantation near Jamestown, but also the Ludwell properties in Williamsburg. But now that his uncle, Philip Ludwell, was dead, who knew what would happen to his holdings in the new world? Richard Henry was wise to have chosen rooms elsewhere he mused, glancing out the window ... however, it was certainly convenient to the Tayloe house ....

It was dusk, an hour before the play was to begin. Francis stopped for a word with the boy who brought the small chariot around from the Tayloe stable. This had been the colonel's suggestion, so that his daughter would not have to walk to the Playhouse. Looking up, he saw Becky in the window. She smiled and waved. He hoped she'd forgiven him for missing their afternoon date in the garden. Surely she was familiar enough with the demands politics could make to be understanding. If she appeared upset he could swing into the picnic idea for tomorrow. Otherwise he'd save this suggestion until they were at supper.

Jacob responded immediately to his knock. White teeth flashed in the man's face as he announced Miss Becky was ready and waiting. As Jacob left him Becky came down the staircase, pale green billowing around her. The gown caressed her figure, gently molding her shoulders and breasts in delicate lace. My God, she's beautiful, he thought, struck again by this revelation. He thought if he saw her a thousand times, the same feeling would come over him, rendering him powerless to resist her charms each time it happened. It was true. She seemed to have a strangle hold on his very senses.

Pausing uncertainly for a moment, she reached for his hand. "I waited for you this afternoon ... until five o'clock."

"I'm sorry, Becky. I felt compelled to attend a meeting. At first I thought to miss it, but ... well, something caused me to change my mind. Nothing to do with you of course. It's that I didn't want to appear to be shirking my duties." He pressed her fingers, thinking he felt her pulse beating under his thumb.

"I know. Papa told me he saw you returning to the capitol. He said there are many meetings in progress now and that you're serving on several committees."

"Would ... ?" he began, then stopped, searching the green eyes for something, a sign?

"Yes?" She knew he might kiss her, and her heart raced. He was watching her mouth.

The slightest tremor on her lips signaled they wanted the same thing as he bent toward her. At that moment the dogs set up a frantic barking and the mood was shattered. The loud baying continued, sure to alert the household, and they drew apart, suddenly feeling self-conscious. Lady Tayloe entered the hallway. Why were the dogs barking, she asked, instantly detecting the intimacy between them. Smiling, Becky and Francis bid a hasty farewell, anxious to be on their way so as not to have to answer her questions. Rebecca watched them out of sight and went immediately in search of her husband. It was time they had a serious talk about Becky and Frank Lee.

༄༅

Francis and Becky held hands in the darkened theater, and those seated behind noted that he frequently bent his head close to hers to whisper something in her ear. The two, however, seemed oblivious that their actions were causing some raised eyebrows and not a little speculation. Later, in the Raleigh dining room, they supped on batter fried oysters, York River crabs, spring asparagus, and spoon bread as they enjoyed a ruby port served in pewter cups. Seated in a room reserved for gentlemen accompanied by their ladies, they provided intrigue for several elderly theatre goers who delighted in watching as Frank Lee and the young Becky Tayloe laughed in gay abandon at each other's banter.

"I heard Mr. Lee has been seen frequently at the Tayloe house, now it's clear what his interest has been. Do you suppose her parents approve?" the wife of Stafford County's burgess whispered to her friend. Their husbands, deep in their own conversation, weren't listening.

"Why ever wouldn't they? He's much sought after. I should think they'd be delighted to marry off another daughter ... they have so many of them!"

"Well, I'll make a wager that Rebecca thinks he's too old for her. I can hardly wait to hint to her how well they seemed to be getting along tonight. They make a charming couple, don't they?"

Her friend nodded agreement. "If you ask me, a girl like that ... well, she needs an older man to keep her home where she belongs. She's quite spoiled, you know. Her father dotes on her, gives her everything she wants, I hear."

"Well, she's certainly making no secret of the fact that she has a serious interest in the handsome Francis Lee. Nor he in her, I might add. Even though he's almost old enough to be her father himself!"

Across the room Becky inclined her head slightly in the direction of the gossiping women. "I think they're talking about us," she said, turning to the serving man. "Oh, no thank you. I couldn't drink another drop. It was all very delicious." She waited while Francis accepted more wine. "Now what do you suppose they're saying about us?"

"I'm quite sure they are jealous."

"Jealous?"

"Yes, of how lovely you are, young and beautiful, when they can only claim to be gossipy, unattractive old biddies more interested in everyone's business but their own."

"Francis, how can you say that? You haven't even looked at them."

"I know. I don't have to. I don't care what they look like nor what they're saying. I'm only interested in looking at you."

Becky gave him a private kind of a smile as she remembered the moment in the hallway a few hours before. "Well, if they're jealous at all, and I'm not saying they are but, *if* they are, it must be because they won't be taking a picnic in the country tomorrow with Francis Lightfoot Lee!"

Draining his cup of wine, he reflected on her sparkling green eyes and wondered again how he was lucky enough to be sharing this evening with her. He must be the most fortunate burgess in Williamsburg tonight, he thought.

It was after midnight when Francis and Becky finally bid goodnight to the relieved and sleepy innkeeper. They stepped from the dry comfort of the ordinary into a downpour. Lightning flashed over the river in the distance and thunder rumbled another threat closer at hand. The cobblestone gutters of Gloucester Street ran full with water. The chariot was wet, inside and out, the poor horse chilled and forlorn, despite the fact the tavern servant brought it directly from the stable. The boy held the skittish mare's head so it wouldn't bolt if lightning struck again, as Francis helped Becky into the little carriage, then pulled himself up. Rain gusted into the open sides and the two huddled close on the seat, trying to stay dry. By the time they reached Nicholson Street, however, they were both drenched, and wasted no time between the stable yard and the house. Becky's bedraggled green skirts clung limply to her legs, and Francis fretted over the state of his velvet waistcoat. Lady Tayloe's candle sent a circle of light to guide them and Jacob was at the door, waiting.

"Missus, she waitin' to see you in her chamber, Miss Becky," he announced. "An' Cate she done fix't you some hot broth."

"It dasn't rain tomorrow and spoil our picnic, Francis," she called, watching his small, erect frame as he closed the gate and ran up the hill. For the second time tonight fate had conspired against the possibility of a kiss. Uncertain of what her mother wanted, she poked her way to the top of the stairs. She would let no amount of questioning dim her spirits. Knocking lightly, she entered her mother's chamber.

Wasting no time, "He's too old for you, Becky," Rebecca blurted, anxiety evidenced by the bright red splotch on each cheek. "Cate, get this child's clothing off and wrap her in something warm. She's dripping wet. And bring the broth, Cate. For goodness sake, get someone to bring the broth."

"I don't need any broth," Becky protested, as the once lovely gown was peeled over her head. Cate winked encouragement at her and disappeared to find a wrapper. Clad in her undergarments, she threw herself across her mother's bed. "Oh, Mama, I had such a divine evening! He was charming, witty, handsome, thoughtful ... and ..." her voice trailed off as she stretched her arms above her head, remembering his eyes on her mouth. Tomorrow, oh tomorrow he'd kiss her while on the picnic. She knew it for sure.

Rebecca observed her daughter's behavior with mounting dismay and steeled herself to be firm. "My dear, give me a chance to speak my heart. There is the obvious matter of your ages. Please, now pay attention. I speak only in your own interest.

Henry Corbin, rest his soul, was both your father's and Francis Lee's great-grandfather. They are of one generation, you of another." As she spoke she watched Becky, who twirled one foot in the air, not looking at her. "He is twice your age, Becky. Do you understand what that will mean in years to come?"

"What, Mama, what will it mean? It won't be one bit different than it is now ... except he'll still be older and I'll still be younger."

Rebecca paused, searching for a reason. She hadn't prepared herself to give specific examples why the age would make such a difference.

"See, you don't know a single thing dreadful or frightening enough to name! You're just trying to ruin my lovely evening, Mama, with your talk of future incompatibility. Why, how old were you when you married Papa?"

Rebecca sighed. The conversation was going in the wrong direction. "You know full well that I was fifteen."

"Well, there you are. I am sixteen."

"Becky, your father was merely twenty-six. We were close enough of an age. He was still a young man, while Francis is in his thirties and has undoubtedly experienced much more of life than your father had. And it's true, Mr. Lee does have a reputation of breaking young ladies' hearts. It's happened more than once, when everyone thought marriage was in the offing, Francis up and changed his mind. We don't want that to happen to you, my dear."

At that moment John Tayloe strode into the room. Working late over his account books, he'd heard voices, sounds of an argument, too. "Well, well, so you're home at last, my girl! And how was the play ... or did you perhaps find other elements of the evening of greater intrigue?" He could see immediately the casual approach was all wrong. Becky's expression was stormy. It was one of those times when he recognized too much of his own temper in this daughter.

Rebecca glared at her husband, wondering why he wasn't supporting her instead of making light of the situation. She thought they'd been in agreement as to how to handle this.

"Don't tease me, Papa!" Becky scowled, not wanting to feel angry when all she wanted was to hold onto the warmth that Francis made her feel and to shout to the world that she was wild, absolutely *wild* about him. "It's not kind to tease someone about a serious matter. Mama's trying to ruin everything with comments that are not true about how old Francis is. He's not old!"

Although John Tayloe ranted and raved with some frequency on various subjects, it was a rare occasion when he seriously reprimanded his girls. Whenever he did so, his tone remained measured and his voice low. But they never doubted what he was about, and they listened. "Becky, I must caution you not to be rude to your mother. I won't tolerate it. I shall have to ask you to apologize before we continue."

Becky bowed her head. "Yes, Papa. I'm sorry, Mama, I didn't mean to be rude."

"There now," her father continued, "Your mother's concern is only that you should be as happy in your marriage as she has been in hers. It's important that you listen to her, and then decide for yourself if the age difference is going to matter to you and Frank ... Mr. Lee. We have agreed with each other to accept your decision, haven't we, Rebe?" Turning to his wife he forced a reluctant nod from her before he went on. "So, you have considered marrying him, or am I assuming too much in thinking it may have gone that far?" he asked.

"Yes, Papa, I have thought about it." Dear Lord, please let Francis ask me now that I've said it aloud. Let him ask me tomorrow so we will have it settled between us. I can't be wrong that he feels the same way I do.

"The man comes from a fine family," her father went on. "His father, grandfather, and great-grandfather all served as members of the Council, and his older brother Philip serves on it now. The

Lees have been a powerful force in the colony and the Northern Neck for years. Francis himself is learning to be a good planter and, the Lord willing, may even make a tolerable politician one day. He's a kind and thoughtful man. I have no doubt he'll make a fine husband once he makes up his mind to settle down." He hoped he'd satisfied both wife and daughter. "So remember what we have said here tonight, Becky. We're both fond of Colonel Lee but, as you see, we have certain reservations about the chances for your continued happiness with one so much older than you."

"Dear child, I'm sorry to have upset you," her mother said, managing a wan smile. "Take your dreams and go to bed. But give some thought to the fact that Mr. Lee, while so very attractive now, is thirty-three years old, no longer a young man," she pleaded.

Becky pecked them each on the cheek, and fled. In the hall she paused to stare out the window at the downpour. "Dear Lord, make the storm go away. Don't let it ruin our picnic tomorrow. Please." As rain continued to beat on the glass, she hurried to her chamber where Cate was waiting with her wide-open comforting arms.

The Picnic

Becky and Francis rode on horseback in the direction of the James River. Rebecca Tayloe had reluctantly agreed to the excursion under the assumption that Willie, one of the young houseboys, would accompany them. She was mistaken. Becky, learning of her mother's plan, had bribed the gullible Willie to remain out of sight in a corner of the stable until he heard them returning. At first he refused, remembering Missus Tayloe's stern instructions, but an orange and a stick of licorice sealed the deal.

Alerting no one to his plan Francis, too, made arrangements to cover his absence. He left the House when the session broke for the members to present an address to the president in the Governor's Council chamber. It would be crowded, he knew, and he was unlikely to be missed until later. The break seemed a stroke of providence coming as it did at precisely twelve noon. The burgesses filed from the lower chamber in the wake of Speaker Randolph who led the way. Once in the hallway Francis turned left instead of right and, never glancing to see if he was observed, marched straight past the nodding doorkeeper into the sunshine. He expected Richard would berate him later. The House stood on the verge of supporting New York in demanding that the act suspending her legislature be withdrawn by Parliament. It could be a crucial day, but he felt sure his one vote wouldn't change the way it would go. Besides he'd done his share of supporting Patrick and Richard's petitions every chance he got. Today there were other things on his mind that were taking precedence over politics.

Last night's stormy weather had passed, and in its wake the earth was left lush and greening. A straw picnic hamper was tied to Francis's saddle. Blue ribbons whipping in the breeze, it bounced lightly against the gelding's shoulder. Becky held to the lead sitting her horse in style, her body in tune with each gait. A three-year-old out of Yorick, the bay had been a gift from her father when he found the horse didn't have the necessary size or stamina for racing. Riding some twenty to thirty feet ahead, she left Francis to follow. He soon found himself entranced watching the flow of girl and horse outlined against earth and sky. They rode in silence and he was content.

Heading south they left the town, soon coming upon field after field where slaves tilled the soil in preparation for the new tobacco crop. The sun had passed its zenith, yet the slanted rays burned warm, and the blacks worked almost naked. Muscled shoulders glistened with sweat as they raised and lowered their arms. In one field deep voices chanted a rhythmic song, keeping tune with the arc of the hoes. The words were a jumbled jargon, drawn from mixed tribal heritage and the white man's religion. The cadence was slow, mournful, yet at the same time almost proud, Becky thought. Gripping the horn of her sidesaddle, she turned to look behind Francis at the field they just passed. The tempo of the slave song drummed in her brain. She imagined the melancholy music long after the Negroes were lost to view. Eventually the road narrowed to a trail. Shiny dark-green laurel leaves brushed the horses' flanks, and the animals swished their tails at early season flies. Birds darted in and out of the bushes on either side as the distinctive chirp of cardinals, ahead and behind, alerted the woodland to the presence of intruders.

For a time they rode through pine woods where a thick carpet of brown needles padded the forest floor. Here they went side by side, horses at a walk. Inhaling the pungent, pleasing scent of pine, they laughed as gray squirrels raced helter-skelter trying to assess the danger. Once out of the dense forest, Becky again urged her mount ahead. Lilliput, she'd named her, after her father had turned the mare over to her. Before long a flock of sea birds flew over and she reined in the mare, waiting for Francis to catch up. The smell of salt water was on the breeze and she knew she'd never come this far. "Perhaps you should take the lead. I'm no longer sure of where we are," she told him.

"Glad we came?" he asked, inhaling the scent of the sea. "I love it on the river. Any river. It takes my breath away, knowing what's over the next rise. We're only going to Halfway Creek this time though because the James is too far. Follow me, my lady, and I'll show you paradise!"

The wind caught his hair as he crested the ridge and when he turned, the carefree jubilant look of a boy beckoned her. Her mother was wrong ... it was the buoyant grin of a young boy on his face. She had been waiting for it all her life. The answer was there in one luminous smile. What else did she need to know? Putting heel to the mare, she raced after him, up the ridge and down the hill to the creek's edge. She was forced to rein in sharply for he was dismounting.

"Francis! What are you doing? You look so funny." Her laughter startled a pair of herons standing long-legged in the shallows. They whirred suddenly into the air, coming to rest farther downstream.

"Fish," he said, wrinkling his nose. "Dead fish. They've got to be close." Walking ahead, he soon called out, "Ah-ha! As I suspected. Some clown has cleaned his catch here, leaving heads and bones to spoil our picnic." With the toe of his boot he poked at a bloated rock head. "No matter," he shrugged grandly, "a little atmosphere." Taking both horses by the bridles he skirted the fish skeletons and began to make his way down the creek line.

After they had gone some distance in this manner Becky asked, "Are you sure you know where we're going? We don't want to lose our way."

"Not a chance," he called over his shoulder. "I've been here many times."

She wanted to ask who he'd been with all those other times but thought better of it. Her mother was right about one thing. His experiences had begun long before she was even born. There were episodes of his life that were past, over, and she'd never be a part of them. She'd have to learn to accept that.

"What do you think about this spot?" he said stopping and looking around. "We can spread the cloth here and use that log for a table." When she nodded agreement he helped her down and, handing her the picnic basket, set about watering the horses before tethering them nearby.

Returning, he found Becky already unpacking their meal and noticed the cloth she had spread was of homespun, undoubtedly done on a loom at Mount Airy. Francis smiled, happy to see something not imported from England. It frequently worried him thinking of all the things they would have to do without if they continued to pursue a hard line toward the King and his parliament. Seeing Becky waiting for him to speak, he put aside such worries for the moment, noting the sliced pork and turkey, cheeses, boiled eggs, and ... even dried figs. "I'm famished. You remembered I like figs. Wonderful. And oranges, too? Where are those from?"

"Oh, Mama gets them sometimes from the merchant at Hobbs' Hole. They come in from the islands on the ships. These are the last two," she confided, placing the oranges side by side next to the figs, an action which somehow conveyed the thrill of forbidden fruit, he thought. "There was one other. I gave it to Willie so he wouldn't come with us."

"Willie?"

"A houseboy. He was supposed to come with us."

"Come with us. You mean here, today?"

"Mm-hmm," she smiled, mischief in her eyes. "Mama sent him to get a mule and follow us, but I hid outside in the bushes till he passed and grabbed him. I could tell he didn't want to come anyway, but they're all scared of Mama. I prob'ly didn't even have to give him the candy."

Francis burst into laughter. "Oh, Becky, you are truly an independent child at heart! And a nervy one ... defying your mother like that." He laughed until tears came to his eyes. Belatedly, he caught her expression.

She pouted, "I am *not* a child! Please don't call me a child, Francis. And would you want him to have followed us and, even now, be hovering in the background watching our every move and listening to our every word?"

"I'm sorry. I surely didn't mean to mock you." He searched the green eyes. And my dear girl, you may not know it yet, but you've made me very well aware of your womanly charms over the past few days. Quite aware indeed. "Actually I'm delighted you bribed the boy. Now am I forgiven for calling you a child? I didn't mean it, of course, it was just to tease you a bit for your youthful bravery in the face of so stern a task master as your mother."

Becky, reassured, smiled and offered him bread and cold meat. For the most part they ate in silence, avoiding each other's eyes. When she did look directly at him, she felt a curious excitement, a hunger almost, but akin to no other hunger she'd ever known. She could feel her heart beating and an unfamiliar prickly sensation in her spine. Eating slowly, she watched him devour the figs with exaggerated relish, a performance that made her giggle over his clowning. He peeled an orange and broke off segments to share with her, reaching to put them in her mouth, and she felt his fingers on her lip.

"This way your fingers won't get sticky, too," he explained. "We could pick up these things and walk down the shore if you'd like. The horses will be fine here."

Becky nodded, wondering what he was thinking. She stood, feeling funny inside, and spent a long time shaking out her skirts, waiting for the nervousness to pass. It certainly wasn't the first picnic he'd eaten alone with a girl, while for her this was a new experience being completely alone with a man, with no other human within sight or sound. She felt him watching her, waiting, and the jittery feeling came back stronger than before.

"I like your dress," he declared suddenly. "Pink is very becoming to you. Actually, if you would know the truth of it, every color is becoming on you, Becky. I've yet to see one that doesn't flatter." Then, reaching for her hand, he kept walking until they came to a grassy spot where they settled in an indentation on the edge of a slope above the wide creek. Francis set his waistcoat aside, together with her hat and shawl.

She knew it was time to say something and thought about how many things they didn't know about each other. Wanting to know more about his family and how he fit into it, she sensed this was a good time to start a conversation. "Tell me of your brothers and sisters. I know Philip is eldest and William the youngest, but I'm forever mixed up over the order of the middle ones."

Contented with whatever her mood demanded of him and, having sensed her unease during their meal, he responded enthusiastically. "Well, there you are, wrong already! Arthur is the baby, although now about twenty-eight I believe. He was only nine when Mother died, and then we lost Father the following year in '50. William and Arthur had a hard time of it, I'm afraid, what with Philip running a house for rather self-indulgent bachelors. Richard and Thomas too, were there at Stratford even after they married. Hannah, of course, had already married Gawin Corbin and moved to Peckatone. So, poor Alice, our serious little Alice, did her best to be a mother to all of us. Eventually, with William and Arthur both in London, she had enough of Colonel Phil one day and went to England herself."

"That was a brave thing for a young woman to do," Becky said soberly.

"None in my family have ever been called timid! And we do have relatives there. Alice went to the Ludwell's. Within two years she met and married Dr. Shippen and was on her way to a new life in Philadelphia." He picked up a clam shell, turning it in his hand. "One day I hope to visit there. In Philadelphia. But it's a goodly distance to travel."

"I wonder what it's like. Papa says it's quite different from life in Virginia. They don't have slaves, I know. Or at least most of them don't. I wonder how that would be?" Her expression was puzzled, in a face that had become pink from wind and sun.

"Put your bonnet on, Becky. Here let me tie it for you." His hands were gentle and not a bit clumsy. The little boy look skirted his eyes again, before he had the ribbons in a bow. "Your nose is red. And I believe I detect a smattering of freckles!"

"Honestly, do you see freckles? I hate them. And I don't much like this ridiculous sunshade either, but I guess it's one or the other, isn't it?" She flicked at the hat but left it in place. "But don't stop talking about Stratford. What were you doing, and the rest, while Alice was finding her Dr. Shippen?"

He took her hand again. The size of it seemed to fit perfectly within his own. Comfortable. "Before Alice left, I studied law with Richard and Thomas for about two years. Richard is a true intellectual you know. He's always been the best student among us, and he was always challenging us to study new things, to be inquisitive." The memory of those days caused him to pause for a full minute, and she wondered if he'd forgotten her, but when he was ready, he continued. "In time Thomas married Mary Aylett and moved to Stafford County, while Richard married her sister, Anne and, as you know, built Chantilly Plantation. It was after that, Alice left for London." Again he stopped, looking out across the water, lost in some private memory.

"And you?"

"Well, Philip had married Elizabeth Steptoe by that time and fancied himself quite the gentleman planter. I guess you could say I was in the way. He maneuvered me into accepting responsibility for my inheritance and settling myself in the wilds of

Loudoun County. Probably the best thing he ever did for me was to push me out on my own hook," Francis admitted, more to himself than to her. He'd never thought of it that way before, but it was obvious.

"You don't like Colonel Phil, do you?"

"Let's just say I'm more fond of my other siblings. It's always seemed to me that Philip takes much more than he gives, with everything and everyone. He's quite puffed with his importance. Actually arrogant at times and exceedingly demanding," he concluded.

"He is master of Stratford, Francis," she chided gently. "After all, that makes him a person of importance. So perhaps you should forgive him a few things."

"So was our father," he countered. "Yet he never acquired the reputation of a pompous ass!" The indelicacy of his language didn't occur to him. He felt that natural with her. It was almost as if they had talked this way, holding hands, many times and spoken of many things together. It was a most unusual feeling.

"Now tell me about Hannah." She had heard enough of Philip. "I know her husband died a fairly young man." It was well known in Richmond and Westmoreland Counties that the Widow Corbin had taken the handsome Dr. Richard Lingan Hall to live with her at Peckatone a year after the death of her husband. Their alliance had produced two children, yet the two remained unwed. "And I do know they say she's living in sin because she and Dr. Hall aren't married. I've heard she's been banned from the church because of it ... and has actually turned to the Baptists. Why don't they marry if they love each other?"

"Some say it is the estate. She loses two-thirds of it if she remarries, including Peckatone itself." He peered at the creek, considering how much to tell her, then quickly decided not to withhold anything. "I think there's more to it than that. Hannah left the Anglican church on her own and, yes, she's become a

Baptist. She despises and despairs of the corrupt practices she sees in our Church of England and its clergy. She scorns the double standard of priests who spout profundity on Sunday mornings, then spend the week behind the wine bottle and the gaming table. It's because the Baptists use our Anglican ritual for marriage, I think, that she refuses to take wedding vows with such a service." It had always made him sad that he'd never told Hannah he in truth agreed with much of her assessment of the clergy. He could never bring himself to express the disloyalty to his birth rite that such an admission would require of him, preferring instead to accept things as they were.

"Do you think there are many priests who have such failings?" She was thinking of Reverend Giberne of course.

"Some, I suppose. Young ladies are seldom aware of such goings-on," he said, making light of it.

"But you know, Francis, I've heard Papa say the Anabaptists are an evil threat to everything we believe in. He agrees, I'm sure, with Reverend Giberne that we should run them out of the county."

He shrugged. "A common enough attitude. There are too many in Loudoun County to run them anywhere. I expect there'll be more in Richmond County soon enough. Hannah makes no secret any longer of having joined the movement, and I hear it's spreading."

"What is it they say? Safety in numbers?"

"Then they should be perfectly safe in Loudoun. As are those odd Quakers. There are pockets of them, settled all around, but they keep to themselves. And in Leesburg, why, the place is overrun with the Scotch and Irish. A ruder, more bawdy populace can exist nowhere in the world. I am sure of it."

He didn't sound unhappy about it, she decided. "However do you get along, in such a place?" she asked.

"I'm used to them all, Becky. They are my friends and my neighbors. It's my home now," he answered simply.

She gave a small sigh as she heard the last. "Well. It's amazing that you can feel that way, when it's all so different than it is in this part of the colony where you grew up. But before you tell me more about what it's like in Loudoun, name your brothers and sisters for me, in order of age so I may get them straight once and for all."

"You're being mighty inquisitive this afternoon. Forcing me to reveal all the skeletons in the Lee closet, and now requesting their ages." But he was pleased by her interest. "Well, three have died ... that would be John, Lucy, and the first Richard. Of the living, we are Phil, Hannah, Tom, Richard, me, Alice, William, and Arthur." Listing them he wondered why he'd pondered the other day how many children Rebecca Tayloe had borne. His own mother had certainly outdone her.

"And here we Tayloes are," she smiled, "all girls ... Elizabeth, me, Anne, Eleanor, Polly, Kitty and Sally. It's strange, when you think about it, how families turn out. How many nieces and nephews have you? I know it's a lot, but I haven't any yet." She studied him as he drew his interesting eyebrows together.

"You are pushing me to the limit of my capacity. Let me see. Phil has the two you know, Matilda and Flora; Hannah has Martha by Corbin, and the two by Dr. Hall; Thomas, I think has three now; Richard's four you know; and Alice has little Anne and a son named after his paternal grandfather, Thomas Lee Shippen."

She kept count on her fingers. "That makes you fourteen times an uncle, Francis!"

"The way this family multiplies, there will no doubt be more, many more, I should expect."

Becky stole a timid glance at him from under the straw sunshade. "I hope the family does continue to grow. In certain cases anyway," she remarked, so softly he barely heard her.

Although he'd planned the move for several days, when it came it was spontaneous for both of them. Slowly, with great care he loosened the ribbons of the hat he had recently tied and, cupping her face in his two hands, he barely brushed her mouth with his lips. He held her slightly away from him while his brown eyes sought the depths of her green ones, and he saw invitation lurking there. Then his arms engulfed her and his kisses in the sunlight on the sand of the creek side were warm and very tender. She learned to kiss him back, allowing her mouth to become soft and searching, an imitation of what he taught her. Secluded thus from the world, protected from interruption, they explored the promise of new found intimacy. He twisted a lock of her hair around a finger, enthralled as before by its silky softness.

"You know something? I keep asking myself how I could be so lucky as to have you come into my life. How can I be so fortunate?"

Becky flushed with joy at his words, yet wondering if it could really be true, responded lightly, "Oh, I don't know ... maybe it's a reward for eating your porridge like a good boy and not talking back to your mama?"

"I'll have to teach you, my sassy miss, not to dash a gentleman's hopes when he's trying his best to tell you how much he admires you!" When he reached for her again he pulled her close. His lips were on her hair, her cheeks, her mouth, the hollow in her throat, and below. A great wave of desire seemed to overcome her. The body against her own taunted her, beckoned her, demanding her to seek pleasures unfamiliar. This rushing tide of passion hurried to overpower her, promising submission could only be sweet. Then, unbidden, a voice of caution told her it was not the time—stop. On the brink she wavered, knowing that beyond his caresses only a slender moment remained before she'd no longer care. The inner voice told her to tell him no. It was expected of her, she knew, but nothing had prepared her for how hard it would be to push him away when she yearned to hold him, kiss him again and again, give in to him, be one with him. Yet she must do it. Fixing her eyes on the heavens overhead so she didn't have to look at him, she placed her hands against his chest and pressing firmly withdrew from his embrace. Dizziness overcame her and she feared she might succumb to tears, a feminine wile she deplored. After that everything went wrong.

Francis flushed purple, mortified at her distress. He'd never meant things to go so far, but he'd been totally unprepared for her passionate response. It had thrown him off guard. Chagrined and angry with himself, he stood up. "I'm sorry," he croaked. "What a dunce I am. I've upset you and disgraced myself." Helping her to her feet, he added gently, "Come, it's time to go back anyway." He was suddenly painfully aware of her youth and inexperience, but could think of nothing to do but start walking. He felt drained, sunk in despair. He'd ruined everything. What an ass he was.

As they trudged in silence, Becky's anger built at every step. What had gone wrong? Why was he so quiet? They'd stopped in time, hadn't they? She'd permitted the kisses, the caresses and, she supposed, even encouraged them. He'd whispered such sweet words. It was more romantic than she ever could have imagined. Until now. Why didn't he profess his love for her? He'd had enough to say earlier! He could at least say he loved her. The sand became difficult to navigate, her feet damp and uncomfortable. By the time they reached the horses she knew he wasn't going to propose after all. She felt tricked, cheated by his silence. He'd led her to expect it was the reason for the picnic, so they could be alone to talk about the future. Or had he? Maybe it was something else he'd wanted all along. She didn't dare look at him. She just wanted to get away, to figure it all out.

She waited until he secured her left foot in the stirrup. Then, as he bent to pick up the picnic basket, she dug her heels into Lilliput, using the crop on the mare's flank. Her action had an amazing effect on Francis. Glancing back she saw that he remained planted in the sand, his mouth ridiculously ajar. Served him right, she thought.

"Becky, wait for me!"

Having steeled herself not to hesitate, she urged the mare to get a good head start so she could ride alone. She remembered the narrow path over the ridge that led back the way they had come. A clump of early blooming flags and a lone juniper tilting crazily out of the bank, alerted her to the spot. Francis was still far behind. Leaning forward, she aided the mare up the hill with her shift of weight. There was no worry when she lost sight of him because he would surely follow. She was glad she'd startled him, impressed him with her ability to be independent, and maybe even hurt him for daring to disappoint her. She'd done all that. It was written in that one glimpse of his face before she lashed down on the mare's hindquarter. But now ... now she began to wonder why she'd done it, lost her temper like that. In all the years she had known him, she'd never known Francis Lee to show one iota of temper. What must he be thinking of her? Her pride kept her going, moving ahead, maintaining the distance between them. She needed time between her rash action and her apology, and time in order for him to accept it. For it was becoming clear she must apologize.

There was another reason why she couldn't turn back nor wait for him, not just yet. It was much more obscure, undefined, but it hovered in her awareness of the afternoon. She'd learned the awesome joy of human contact. Mouth against mouth, flesh against flesh, desire matched to desire. That is, she learned it up to a point. Beyond that, the vast endless heaven or the deepest ocean could hold no greater mystery for her than exactly what would have happened between them had she not pushed Francis away. A bittersweet ache, an angry frustration of denial had plagued her all down the beach. It hadn't occurred to her to wonder how it might have felt to him. He was a man and knew about such things. While she ... while she what? Did she intend to spend their life together hiding behind the convenience of her immaturity every time something went wrong? Their life together ... there it was, tied all neatly in a package, waiting for them to open it, seek the treasures inside. By her foolishness had she destroyed all possibility of such a future?

Francis accepted the pace as she set it. This time he had little choice. At first, on the beach, he'd tried repeatedly to call her, feeling more foolish each time she ignored him. And no matter what Tayloe thought about the mare, his dappled gelding was no match for the fleet Lilliput. It was clear enough Becky did not wish to be near him anyway, so why even try to overtake her? By every thread of logic he should be irritated at her outburst, but somehow he wasn't. His heart ached for the both of them, for the insurmountable differences in age and those between man and woman that threatened to separate them. Her childishness surprised him. There was no denying that. Yet it surfaced at a time when he'd needed a sharp reminder of her youth. Moreover it put things in perspective. He had thought in recent days that he might be falling in love at last. There was a remarkable differ-ence between this and the usual lighthearted fling he'd bargained for in the past. And Martha, of course, well, that was different altogether.

Keeping Becky in sight, he was glad in a way to have the time to think. He recognized that he'd never been inclined to consider marriage seriously. Was it because the right woman had never been around at the right time? Or maybe, was it possible that he'd been waiting for Becky Tayloe to grow up? Such things did happen, he supposed, without a man even realizing it. Only once since his mother died had he felt anything for a woman akin to his idea of romantic love. And that had been born out of the search-ing, bumbling loneliness of boyhood. It was when Richard had brought his new wife, Anne Aylett, to live at Stratford. The scent of her rose water cologne drifting down the hallways, the ever present swish of silk and satin, her tinkling laughter from behind a chamber door that was closed to him—these things had set his head to reeling and kindled his first desire for sexual contact. She had guessed, of course. How could she have missed, he chuckled, the way he'd mooned around like a pup after a bitch in heat! God, he must have been insufferable in those days. And dear Anne. She'd been so kind and helpful, considerate of his feelings, very sweet, and never, never even once, did she encourage him in any way. She had simply tolerated him, knowing he would soon grow up. How a woman could be so lovely, so desirable, and yet so firmly remote, eluded his understanding to this day.

Anne had been right that his yearning for her would pass. Eventually he'd put his dreams away, moved to Loudoun County, and left his brother's wife in peace to raise her family. In time, as she'd known he would, he outgrew his youthful infatuation and they had become the best of friends. It came to him at that very instant that what he'd really wanted from his sister-in-law was affection. He had needed nurturing through the empty void in the years following the deaths of his parents—a gentle hand to lead him into the awesome, sometimes frightening world of men. And she'd given him just that, and no more. Not even when he had mistakenly confused her affection with his dreams of physical love, had she been anything but tender with him. It had taken this outburst of Becky's to help him understand clearly what had happened more than ten years ago. Amazing how the human brain worked, he thought.

Becky. It was all turned about the other way now. It was his turn to do the caring, the loving, the protecting and nurturing. He longed to sit her down, take her little-girl hands in his own where they fit so well, and explain it to her. All of it, and why he understood it all now. How, for him, it would be different this time, and it was right that it should be different. It would at last be a complete love affair, a total belonging, one to the other, for always. That's what he should have done today ... not kiss her into a state of confusion and panic.

Suddenly he knew! His laugh exploded on the forest as it came to him what had caused her spit of temper, her need to race down the beach at an almost full-out gallop. He saw her horse shy at the sudden burst of his laughter, but Becky kept her eyes straight ahead. It hadn't been his unruly passion at all that caused her anger. Of course. She was expecting something from him, had set a careful stage, and he'd overstepped his lines! But could he have done otherwise? Damn it all. Why was it so difficult for him to think of marriage? Had he been single too long? He had just finished having that long talk with himself, and now he was back on the stumbling block. What was the matter with him anyway, he wondered. What was he expecting would come of this alliance he had begun with Becky Tayloe? It was true, a world of experiences stood between them. He must seek ways to bridge the chasm, which had certainly widened today. Also, he had some affairs to settle. Martha for one, he owed her more than an explanation. Loudoun farm for another—he couldn't picture Becky as mistress of such a simple place. It was almost as impossible as trying to imagine her in Leesburg society. Yet, he knew he wanted her. Had it been wise to plan the picnic at all? Now besides wanting to be with her, he knew he loved her. And loving was proving to be painful indeed.

More than an hour passed. Becky slowed her pace, thankful they were through the wooded areas before the light faded. Once she heard him laugh and remembering the oranges, imagined him eating the other one. Wishing they were sharing it, she let her pride prevail and kept going. They weren't more that a mile or so from the village now, as she searched for a plan that would allow them to ride in together. She was ready to humble herself and beg his forgiveness. As they approached a dip in the land where there was a stream, she reined in the mare.

Francis had been expecting her to stop before it happened. No trace of daylight lingered, and the moon now hung low in the sky, behind the trees clustered near the water. He could barely distinguish her outline and he urged his mount forward fearful to have her out of sight.

"I'm here, Francis," she called timidly.

He caught a flash of the pink dress near the narrow creek where a streak of moonlight sparkled on the water. Jumping down, he was at her side in a single movement.

"I'm sorry," he began, so grateful to be near her again. He was ready to say what she wanted to hear, but she interrupted.

"No, I'm the one who is sorry. I behaved stupidly ... back there on the beach ... and after." She caught at his sleeve and rested her hands on his arms.

Love welled up inside him and he prayed his voice would hold. "I've never met a girl with whom I've felt it necessary to make amends after a spat. But today it matters very much." Unaware that his buttons pressed into her flesh, he felt her clinging to him. "Becky, I love you. I believe I have always loved you and always will."

She wondered if her knees might truly give way. He loved her. He had said so. Forever. Did anything else matter? She turned her face up to him, waiting. Very gently, he kissed her just once. Then he was explaining about his farm in Loudoun County.

"I haven't told you much about my house. It barely qualifies for a bachelor quarters, not suitable for a well bred young lady. The furnishings are very simple. There are no carpets on the floors, nor any decent china plates." He was begging her to understand that he needed time.

A night relation of the whip-poor-will trilled to its mate, and nearby the mysterious rustles of evening began in the brush. Francis was reminded of the time as he realized the day birds had long since fallen silent. "It must be after seven o'clock." A vision of a frantic Rebecca Tayloe came to mind. She'd probably discovered Willie holed up with his licorice by now. "Ye gods, woman," he cried, pushing Becky ahead of him. "To the horses. Ere I be banished from the House of Tayloe forever!"

She knew he was right. If her mother had discovered Willie wasn't with them, there'd be a price to pay. But she hesitated, turning back to him. "I love you too, Francis. With all my heart. I will never love anyone else."

He didn't have to ask if she'd ever said that to anyone before. He knew she hadn't and her words rang in his ears all the way to Nicholson Street.

∽

A week later he was on his way out of the capital city. In a few weeks he'd be home in Loudoun. First, he'd spend some time in Westmoreland County in order to attend a meeting of the floundering Mississippi Land Company. The Lee brothers all had money invested, and they must find a way to protect the venture. Current demands from England were designed to keep the Virginians out of the western lands and squelch the speculations there. This, more than the taxes, stood at the root of colonial unrest, thought Francis, as he traveled the familiar roads to the Northern Neck with Richard Henry. Well, at least the assembly had agreed to oppose Townshend's duty program. There had been plenty of compromise, but Virginia was now prepared to support the threat to her sister colonies. It had been a clear victory for the progressives.

By the second day on the road he was less concerned about such matters. Unlike Richard, who would brood for days on every detail of the assembly, he'd forget it quickly. His mind was almost constantly occupied with thoughts of Becky these days. It was clear he'd disappointed her by not seeking to establish a wedding date, but he needed time alone, away from her sweet persuasion, to put his house in order. He'd pacified her with the promise of letters, but now he wondered if he'd been right to leave before things were fully settled between them. Already, he found, he missed her fiercely.

Loudoun Farm

The meeting of the Mississippi Land Company produced no significant results. The Washingtons were there, George and Augustine, and Richard Henry, William, Arthur, and Francis Lee, as well as Henry Fitzhugh. They reaffirmed their commitments to one another and talked about ways to reinforce their demands that Mother England allow them to continue the land patents in the western counties. William and Arthur Lee promised to speak for their cause when they arrived in London.

After that the days stretched into a fortnight and beyond. Francis enjoyed himself and found he was in no hurry to leave Westmoreland. He spent lazy, happy days at Stratford with his two younger brothers. For once, no one complained about Colonel Phil's autocratic hospitality and, knowing he'd have no opportunity to be with William and Arthur again before they sailed for London at the end of summer, Francis was glad to be there.

Arthur seemed adamant about giving up his budding practice as a country doctor in Williamsburg. He'd become disillusioned in the treatment of the ill, he said, but Francis thought his brother was more than a little homesick for the sophistication of Europe and anxious to return to England. It was true, as Arthur pointed out, that by being present in London he might somehow be able to aid in the colonial battle against what the brothers had privately come to refer to as "the Mighty Oppressor." Being another admirer of Richard Henry's, Arthur also had turned more and more to the political world.

As for William, he was thoroughly disenchanted with the task of managing Stratford Plantation for Philip where, he said, he received no pay and precious little gratitude. He was excited about the opportunity to accompany Arthur and seek his fortune across the Atlantic. Although sad to think of them so far away, Francis understood they must make their own ways, as he had made his in Loudoun County. There was no longer a place for any of them at Stratford, sad to say, unless to pay a visit.

He spent a delightful day at Chantilly where he found Anne Lee recovered from her illness. Or at least she professed to be so. She'd left her bed, and was cheerfully back to spending the days in her garden, directing the servants, and tending her four children. Her coloring seemed wan to Francis, but she passed it off when he mentioned it. They had a good heart to heart about his intended marriage. Her approval was important to him and she gave it with no prompting, sending him on his way feeling all was right with his world. Or would be, as soon as he took the final step and made a formal proposal, setting the date. She'd laughed at him about that and called him "the reluctant suitor."

One morning he awoke to find the courtyard between the great house, the kitchen, and his father's law office, literally swarming with robins. Hundreds of robins. At breakfast Colonel Phil spoke to William about seeding flax and corn. It was a reminder it was mid-May and Francis knew he should linger no longer. There were many reasons that made it difficult to say adieu. It meant he'd be putting even more miles between himself and his love, it meant a farewell to his brothers for who knew how long, and it meant that at the end of his journey he'd have to face Martha. But it was planting time, he had a plantation to run, and it was time to head home to Loudoun farm.

☙

Many miles away that same day, Martha Tutt straightened slowly. She'd labored since noon and, although lower now, the sun still blazed in a bare sky. It was more than hot enough for

May, she thought, placing the balls of her fists square in the small of her back and pressing hard, hoping to relieve the knot of pain there. Before her the rows stretched neatly. Reward enough. She glanced to see how Berth fared on her side of the garden and saw the old Negress continued to work steadily, stopping now to wipe her homespun sleeve across a damp brow. Berth didn't work as did Martha, bending up and down to the ground. Rather, she squatted, bare dark toes clutching the moist earth, while pulling the basket of potato spuds behind her as she moved down the row. Fortunately, she and Berth had come to a mutual understanding early on, and each decided wisely to accept the other's capabilities and status. Mr. Francis had explained that although Martha was to direct the household, she was also to share in the chores with Berth, Cris and Zoey. She had soon broadened her own tasks to include the kitchen garden, for she dearly loved the out-of-doors where she found immense joy beginning with the planting, through the nurturing, even the weed pulling, to the ultimate pride of harvest.

One day, she recalled, after the intimacy with Mr. Francis had been established, he'd suggested perhaps the culture of vegetables was too much for her. Shrugging off his concern and continuing as before, she thought he might consider her toil in the hot sun with the old black woman a shade below her present station. She puzzled over that briefly but soon forgot to worry about it. Had she guessed that his fretting was based quite simply on his repugnance for the sometimes dirty, mud stained feet she brought to his bed, she wouldn't have dismissed his suggestion so easily, for it had become her life's ambition to please Mr. Francis in all things as best she could.

Today as she worked his garden she had other worries, serious worries; he'd be returning any day now, and she was going to have to tell him about Joe Grimes. Joe, who had come into her life so unexpectedly, at a time when she'd grown increasingly fearful of a shaky future as the mistress of Francis Lee. For several months she'd struggled with her choices, and when she asked Mr. Francis to allow her to accompany him to the capital, it had been a test—his indignant response was answer enough. He failed the test. It would always be the same, for so long as he needed her. He was never going to accept her on the same grounds as a lady of his own class. The boundaries were clear from the beginning, of course. The rules were there in this game they played, so why had she ever dared to hope otherwise?

Joe had always been there, since she'd come to Loudoun farm, and she'd suspected he made excuses to be around sometimes when she worked in the garden. The overseer would stand there, leaning against the sagging barn door and sometimes he talked to her, but mostly he just stood there, a tuft of straw tilted from the corner of his mouth, smiling and making her nervous. Then, one day shortly after Mr. Francis and Ben had left for Williamsburg, he'd up and said a whole lot.

"I'll not give you forever, Martha Tutt, to make up your mind. They's other chicks in the henhouse and other fillies in the field, you know. I believe you know I've been waitin' for you to pay me some mind, but you're always flouncing around so prim and proper like. It's taken me more than a year to get up the nerve to say this, and a half jug of rum to boot! I decided finally that you must be needin' some sweet-talk to make you notice me."

He had covered the distance between them in a few long strides before he went on, "Women like to be courted, I know. My mam told me they like to play coy for a while, before they give in. Do you reckon that's so?"

Martha had to laugh remembering how she'd answered him. "Well, I declare, Mr. Grimes. Some folks seem to think other folks are just here for the taking!" Visibly shaken, she'd told him to leave her alone. "If you ever plan on speaking to me again, you'd best plan on shaving that ugly face of yours and stop drinking!" She hadn't meant it as an invitation, but invitation is how he took it. He'd sauntered off saying something about doing just that. And he had.

True to his word, Joe had painfully scraped the beard from his chin every morning. He'd not touched the rum jug, not even for a sip. They began meeting in Francis Lee's simple parlor. How she ever had the courage to ask him there, she didn't know. But she'd come to crave Joe's company on the lonely nights. Certainly she didn't dare entertain him in her bed chamber over the kitchen, with all that such an invitation might imply. The parlor was the only place. She'd make it up to Mr. Francis somehow, her use of it in his absence.

Without fully realizing what was happening, Martha found herself feeling like a new person. Joe had more or less barged into her life—a great tenderhearted miracle of a man who adored her when she needed nothing so much as adoration. Yet, having held to the dream of Francis for so long, she was loath to part with it immediately. As she waited for his return she learned how to dangle Joe, by rationing her affection. He was like a giant bear, happy for whatever petting she might bestow upon him. Did he know of her alliance with Mr. Lee? She thought not. Each time they met, it became more important he shouldn't learn where she had slept for the past three years. Certainly she, herself, would never tell him.

As the days became weeks and then a month, Joe did many things for Martha. She could talk to him without the niggling worry they might not be laughing at the same thing, and never once did she have to consider whether or not her appearance pleased him. It did. He carved her an intricate little sea otter out of a piece of pine, and then a star fish. Martha had never seen the sea but she talked of its wonders every chance she got. Mr. Francis had read to her once from a book about the great oceans, and Joe told her wild and chilling tales of his voyage to the West Indies when he'd signed on as a deck sailor on a rum ship. She kept her wooden sea treasures where she could admire them daily, on top of the small iron-banded chest her mother had used to carry all her earthly possessions from the debtor's prison in Liverpool to the New World.

Joe did other things. One morning he cleaned out the smoke-house for her, and another day he weeded and tilled the late winter vegetable patch. Sometimes he brought her wildflowers or clumps of sweet smelling greenery he picked along the border of the fields.

The one thing he hadn't been able to do, perhaps because he didn't understand it was required of him, was to make her forget the master of the house. At night, alone in her bed, she dreamed of Francis. The summons of his boyish grin hovered always just above her head, mocking her. From these dreams she awoke clammy and exhausted. There were also daytime reminders of him. The scent of his pipe lingered for weeks in his study. If she stood for a few minutes staring at the cubby-holed desk, she could imagine the scratch of his quill as he posted his accounts or wrote his letters. A great letter writer, Mr. Francis was. Martha had aspired to read and write once herself, and he'd promised to teach her, but somehow he never got around to it. It was always tomorrow. This was another reason she reached the decision to give him one more chance. She'd never have another opportunity to learn to read.

Several times a day she scanned the road for signs of the dust cloud that would signal his return. He and Ben would ride in the eight or so miles from Leesburg. Though it was out of the way, she knew he'd stop there for a day or two, trading political news of the colony for local gossip. He was a highly respected man in the growing town—had been named a trustee of the county seat at its incorporation in 1758, and subsequently county lieutenant and justice of the peace. As county lieutenant he was accorded the honorary title of "colonel" as was the custom back east, he'd told her. Martha was wise enough to recognize that the owner-ship of many acres of land enhanced his importance, but knew in her heart they would have admired him anyway. No one disliked Mr. Francis. He always had a kind word for even the lowest field hand. She marveled sometimes that he found something to say to each of them. Kindness was a rare quality in the few gentlemen of her acquaintance, especially when it came to slaves and the indentured.

Early one clear morning, shortly after the sun was up, Joe Grimes prepared to set off for the distant acres. The plowing of the Horsepen Tract was accomplished and he must spend the next days supervising those lands farther from home. The plow and the hoes were loaded in the cart. He and the slaves wouldn't return until the task was finished, more than a week, he said, because it was a long distance and the slaves would be walking. Martha kissed him goodbye behind a corner of the woodshed, warning him to keep an eye open for trouble. She waved him out of sight, admiring the sheer hulk of him atop the roan, knowing she would miss him.

About an hour later she heard hoofbeats on the road. It could only be Mr. Francis. Glory be to God, she whispered to herself, Joe is safely out of the way!

Berth, too, had heard the sound. She broke into a wide grin and scurried to ready the tea things. "Marse Frank is a'comin'. He sho 'nuff is." Berth was fond of her master, as fond as it was possible to be of the man who owned you. He had saved her from a vicious lashing many years ago at Stratford, when he'd not been much more than a boy.

As the sound of the horses drew closer and Ben's voice called directions to a boy in the farmyard, Martha's heart thudded in her throat as she moved to the door. Steeling herself to issue a casual greeting, she knew it would be many hours before they'd be alone and she could face Mr. Francis with the choice she must make. Her fate would be in his hands.

Had Francis known her thoughts it would have saved him a great deal of anguish. For it was with trepidation he faced telling

Martha his news. He'd pondered how to go about it half the night then, in the morning on the road from Leesburg, had discarded all his previous ideas. Now, he planned after greetings to take to the fields for most of the day. After that he'd retire to his study to put his papers in order. This way he could avoid Martha until the other servants had retired. His original plan had been to call her immediately to his study, but that was too cold, too impersonal. He'd brought a small blue bowl for her dresser and some lengths of fabric, dimity and muslin, for a peace offering. He hoped she wouldn't think them a sort of payment. Or worse yet, a bribe. The last thing he wished to do was hurt her, but damn it all, he thought, what a situation he was in. There was no way to be tactful about turning the girl out of his bed! He would simply have to come straight out with it.

The door moved inward under his hand startling him. "Why Martha," he blurted. "Fancy your being right here to meet me. I never expected it. And Berth," he went on quickly, switching his attention to the old woman waiting to be noticed.

"Welcome home, Mr. Francis." Martha's voice sounded to her as though she had something stuck in her throat.

"Tea's a brewin', Marse Franak, tea's on," offered Berth.

"Well, fine. Wonderful. Just what I need before I inspect the fields, Berth. You never forget to look out for my comforts. How are you both?"

The wrinkled face beamed as Berth bobbed her turbaned head up and down in happy greeting. Martha fell silent thinking him even more remote than usual.

ᘐ

At the end of the day Francis retired as planned to the haven of his study. Here, Berth would serve him a quiet supper, he'd give the household a couple of hours to settle down, then go upstairs to face Martha. She would expect him around ten as had been their habit. Pushing the door firmly shut behind him he began to sort out his papers and the notes from the assembly. He might even delve into his account and crop books which he felt certain Grimes would have neglected. The overseer's abilities in this area were limited at best. Of course, there shouldn't have been too many expenses during his absence, not at this time of year, and only a few quit rents still due from January.

How unexpectedly enjoyable had been this first afternoon home, he thought. The fields, acre after acre of newly turned earth, were a thrilling sight to behold. Riding over the wooded hills, he had caught up with Grimes, whom he found asleep, the blacks nodding at their work. What was it he'd bragged to Tayloe about his methods? Yet, he couldn't bring himself to chastise the man, for all was in order on his farm, much better than he'd dared to hope for. Apparently Grimes had kept his promise to leave the spirits alone, which was nothing short of astounding in itself.

Next, he'd stopped to examine the apple orchard. The young trees smelled sweet, blossoms in full bloom. Everything was several weeks behind up here in the foothills. Calculating how much ground would require clearing in order to place two dozen fig trees, he estimated several days labor, hard labor. They'd have to cut pine and some hardwoods, grub the roots and dig deeply into the soil if the small figs were to flourish. Squinting against the sun, he recalled a treasured memory—the vision of his father, towering straight and strong, as he had appeared when he, too, had studied the land for clearing, or fretted over an insect or blight in fruit trees or a crop. Francis knew his own love of horticulture had come from the restless, acquisitive Thomas Lee who became, through his own determination, not only vastly wealthy, but also a great figure in the colony. Death alone had robbed this first master of Stratford Plantation of a permanent appointment to the Virginia governor's chair.

With a clarity that was still painful he remembered the day Thomas Lee died. Francis had been in the schoolroom with the younger children when the news was brought to them. Being sixteen he hadn't dared to cry. He'd waited in agony until the younger children were taken to the great house for supper. Lingering behind, he made his way to the orchard, for it was there that the binding together of this father and son had taken place. There he had spent precious hours alone with Thomas. They had touched, examined, and tasted the rich juicy apples, the succulent peaches, plums, and figs, the tangy persimmons. They had talked and laughed and come to know and respect one another. Francis had worshiped the giant of a man with the restless ways and the ever curious and searching nature, but he never got around to telling him that in so many words.

And it was there, in the dark privacy of his father's orchard, that he had cried. He remembered sobbing over and over again, "Father, why have you left us? Please, please don't leave us." He knew it was weak and foolish but he had been unable to stop, not for a long time. Both his parents would now be laid to rest beneath the earth in the Lee burial ground at Mount Pleasant, old Matholic. There was a new house there now, built for Thomas's nephew. Thomas himself had designed and supervised the construction. It was fitting he should be buried on Lee ancestral ground but Francis always wished his parents could have been put in the ground at Stratford where they belonged. No man had ever replaced Thomas Lee in his affections because his father had filled the role of idol, mentor, and friend.

Leaving his own orchard, Francis had ridden on to view the corn and tobacco fields, thinking that maybe Landon Carter had come close once or twice. As he checked on how deeply Grimes had ordered the fields turned, he thought now of the strange idiosyncrasies of Sabine Hall's master. It was Carter's opinion, and it made good sense to Francis, that many planters who realized poor crop production simply were not tilling the soil deeply enough between seedings. Or not allowing the dung to rot properly before applying it, so as not to burn the young plants. Carter was mightily opposed to the use of the newly invented plow, which he claimed when introduced in large numbers on a plantation only served to make the slaves lazy and do-nothings. He preferred to keep his blacks as busy as possible so they wouldn't degenerate into indolence, he said. Francis laughed aloud, recalling some of the foolish arguments they'd had over the use of carts and plows. If Carter had his whole way, there would be no mechanism at all on his acres. But grumbling all the while as he loved to do, he had bit by tiny bit given in on some counts.

Continuing to reminisce over the pleasures of an afternoon that had allowed him to view the fine condition of his farmlands, he supped on the stewed rabbit Berth had been taught by Martha to prepare. Martha's herbs must be what made it so good. Finishing his wine, he decided it was best to let his accounts wait until morning. Thinking once more of his father, he marveled over how different he, himself, was from the man who had sired him. There was one character trait of Thomas Lee's he certainly hadn't inherited, that of a bold nature—a nature that enabled a man to go anywhere, do anything, face any danger, and defend his actions against all comers. No, he didn't possess such a superior, determined will. Why, here he was at this very moment, faced with the ordeal of standing up to Martha, and the longer he put it off the more difficult grew the task. He'd give a great deal to be able to simply stride into his chamber, as he could well picture his father doing, and inform the wench it was time to pack her baggage and get out! He sighed, pushing his empty plate away, knowing that such would never be his way. He knew also that by tomorrow he'd be thankful it was not.

He climbed the stairs slowly, recognizing that for the second time in a very short while he found himself nervous and uncertain over a woman. He opened the door to his bed chamber ill prepared for what greeted him. Outlined by a single candle's glow Martha stood before him, her body clothed only in a gauzy nightdress. The filmy fabric revealed her breasts and the curve of hips beyond any need for imagination. A feeling of dismay wrenched at his stomach. Hurriedly, ignoring her anxious eyes, he crossed the room to the window where he frantically searched for words to begin his confession. Seeing her like this, it suddenly degenerated into a confession, an admission of having wronged her. He knew he couldn't think of it that way. It was madness. If he began feeling sorry for her he could never carry it off. He closed his eyes. After a moment he could picture Becky in that green dress, coming down the steps to meet him. And soon he was able to speak.

"Martha, I must talk to you. About a serious matter. There is something I must say to you."

"Wait!" she cried, staring at the coldness of his back. He must be disgusted with her attempt to entice him. "I've stood before you on many a night, and not been shamed. I shan't allow you t' shame me now. I am what you have wanted me to be and I ain't apologizin' for that. It'll be the last time, Mr. Francis Lee, the last time you will have t'see me thus. In a fortnight I'll be marryin' Joseph Grimes!" She was so distraught she hadn't noticed lapsing into the rough manner of speech she'd spent years trying to overcome. Now the words were out there was no way to retrieve them. She hadn't left the choice to him after all, she'd made it herself in the space of a few seconds. It was final and irrevocable as though she'd dropped a bucket into the well without tying the rope to it. She heard the final clatter and the inevitable plop at the bottom.

Incredulous, he stared at her, no longer seeing the seductive gown in his astonishment. A rosy glow of relief crept through him as the knowledge of what she said became a reality. "My God," he exclaimed. He slapped his knee and twirled in a circle. "My dear God in heaven, that is wonderful news! Martha, that is the most wonderful news." He laughed and danced her around the room.

Never had she seen him so foolishly relaxed, and it came to her how much of himself he hadn't shared with her. But it didn't matter any more, did it? It didn't matter at all.

"Come, come. We shall drink a toast, Martha, to your Joe and to my Rebecca. For you see, of all things, you'll never believe it, but that's what I wanted to tell you. I am also to be married!"

Only then was it clear. The strained homecoming, his obvious attempt to avoid her, his expression upon entering the chamber tonight, were all because he was going to marry some proper lady named Rebecca. Martha decided she was thankful she'd told him first as she watched him collect the Madeira decanter and two cups. He pulled her good-naturedly to the floor in front of the stone fireplace. No sooner were they seated, however, than he bounded to his feet again and, grabbing his dressing gown from the clothes press, thrust it at her.

"Here, put this on," he ordered. "You'll take a chill dressed like that with no fire set in the grate. And besides ... you're making me nervous." He felt better than he had all day. Why had he worried over it at all? Being honest was the best thing after all. "Martha, you are a gem," he announced, raising his wine cup to her.

They drank a toast, and then another, and still another. He told her of Becky and of Williamsburg, of Cate and Isaac, of William and Arthur, of Anne Lee's illness, and even of his burgess friends. She'd never heard him talk so freely nor so much. By the time it came her turn to tell him of Joe Grimes and what had happened while he was away, Francis had become quite intoxicated and thus failed to notice if her enthusiasm for her upcoming wedding was somewhat less than total. But, warmed by the wine and by his infectious good humor, Martha laughed with him, joining in the silly toasting.

"May my dear Becky forgive me for a lie!" Francis shouted abruptly. "I do have a carpet in my house! Look, I have a carpet. We're sitting on it."

Martha hadn't the least idea what he was raving about and he didn't bother to explain. But it seemed an hilariously funny joke, and they laughed together. And thus, until the wee hours sat Francis Lee, planter, and Martha Tutt, housekeeper; employer and employee, gentleman and daughter of indentured servant, lover and mistress drinking and laughing together for the last time. It was a fine farewell indeed, thought Francis. A fine farewell.

At last she said, "Go to bed, Mr. Francis, for you are quite tipsy."

When he tried to obey, he found his legs wobbly, unhinged from his body. She helped him, laughing and dizzy, to the bed. She undressed him and tucked the coverlet around him.

He grinned at her. "Would you like ..." he started to ask.

"No," she said firmly. Men were all the same when they'd been drinking, she decided.

Flat on his back, he stared at her for a moment. Then, seeing it wasn't Becky after all, "Sorry," he mumbled. "Not a good idea." His eyes closed and he fell immediately asleep, the snore of a contented man whistling loudly through his open mouth.

Martha brushed the soft brown hair back from his brow, waiting until his breathing became slow and even. Only then did she turn to leave. "Goodbye, Francis," she hiccuped, draining the last drops of wine from her cup. "May the Lord grant that she will satisfy."

Loudoun County hadn't changed in his absence. Not that he'd expected a change. Only once again, as in the beginning and each time he returned from elsewhere, he became sharply aware of its bawdy, brawling, unruly inhabitants; its fertile, lush and wide-open lands. It was a beautiful but untamed countryside. No denying that, he thought again, as he tried to envision it through the eyes of a newcomer. A newcomer like Becky.

Summer. Summer meant lovely, languid evenings during which the more pugnacious elements of the county seemed set on picking more fights and arguments with each other than they ever thought of during the winter. A wild bunch of Scotch-Irishmen headed the list of lawbreakers and kept the docket full on Leesburg's court days. The newly erected stocks around the corner on the Carolina Road were seldom empty. As the nights grew warmer, the ale and rum jugs were passed with more frequency around the slave quarters as well as the town ordinary. There was less sickness, although the stomach flux and diarrhea continued to plague many residents. Even the slaves grew fatter, for food was plenty. It was a time for a full belly at the end of each day, a time for wenching, and a time for praying that nature would do her part to produce the crops that would sustain them through another bitter winter. All fear of marauding wolf packs was forgotten; the predators had tracked to the Catoctins in search of cooler temperatures and easy game. As Frank Lee had said to his fellow burgesses, "There are a mighty few of them bothering in these parts nowadays anyway."

There continued much to do at Loudoun farm—heavily treed and shrub-covered lands to clear for an additional stand of tobacco, old fences to mend and new ones to build, last year's crop to pack into huge hogsheads to be hauled miles away to the upper Potomac, the land to be prepared for the fig orchard, and cattle, fowl, sheep and hogs to tend, shear, milk, breed, slaughter, cure and on and on and on. And the constant never ending hoeing, tilling, and weeding.

Martha and Joe were married just as she had forecast. On the wedding day, surprising everyone, Colonel Francis Lee appeared at John Tutt's tiny house on the outskirts of Leesburg to bestow his blessings.

Now, in addition to his overseer's chores, Joe was busy building a house for his bride. With Francis's permission they had located it above the creek in the lower pasture. Joe was set on completing the two rooms on the first floor by Christmas, and he worked like a man possessed. His son, he swore, would be born in the spring in the house his father built with his own two hands, and not in the stuffy crowded room over Colonel Lee's cook-house. Martha blossomed in face and figure, and wondered daily what she'd ever seen in Mr. Francis, when the nights with Joe had been what she craved all along. And she had a wedding band. She also had a fine set of white stoneware with an English country scene etched on each plate in brilliant blue, a wedding gift from her employer. They weren't the dishes she had longed for a year ago, but Francis had been lucky enough to purchase these from a family who gave up their stake in Leesburg and moved back east. A cup was missing and there were several chips, but Martha was more than satisfied.

For Francis, the days were busy ones. The court sessions took him frequently to Leesburg where many of the cases involved nothing but battery charges, yet they all required a hearing. Following one of the more humorous days he spent in court, he rode along the ridge of the Vestal's Gap Road headed for home. A paternity case, simple adultery, and it had taken an entire afternoon to settle it. What a waste of time, he thought. The last of the day's sunshine was warm on his back through the linen shirt, as he checked one more time to make sure his wig and waistcoat were secure behind the saddle. He felt compelled to set an example by wearing the uncomfortable wig in court, although he was the only one who did so.

In his satchel were two letters delivered to him by Nicholas Minor. They'd been put into Minor's hands by a traveler, who was paid by a ship's captain in Fredericksburg, to deliver them to be held for Colonel Lee. From the Northern Neck, they had been three or four weeks on the way. Knowing they were there, unopened, the contents still a mystery, was a treat.

He spurred Cameron to a gallop hoping to stir a breeze and loosened his ruffled shirt front as he rode, allowing air to billow under the stickiness of his armpits. The gelding picked up speed heading full out for the Goose Creek Crossing. The stream looked inviting and as the animal slowed at the top of the hill, Francis made up his mind to stop. He might as well waste a little more time. After he cooled off in the water, he would read his letters from Becky and Richard.

Throwing the reins over the animal's head, he allowed the horse to graze untethered, and having slipped quickly out of his clothes, plunged into the chilly water. When he stopped shivering, he splashed contentedly, floating on his back in the slow moving stream. The water rippled deliciously over his skin. A few years earlier he wouldn't have dared to place himself in such a disadvantaged position for fear of the French and Indian menace. He still carried a gun when he traveled the Loudoun roads but no longer felt that at any moment he might be called upon to use it. It was only the past year he had dared travel without Ben constantly at his side.

Envisioning Becky in this place, however, caused a frown to crease his forehead. She'd be tantalizing prey, on her horse or even in a chariot. Though the Indian raids were virtually a thing of the past, a certain lawless element roved the remote country. There were often reports of attacks by bandits and thieves. Yet he couldn't expect her to give up all social life, and there would surely be times when she might crave the company of the ladies in Leesburg. He knew she was accustomed to a freedom that wouldn't be possible here. Even a wish to spend an afternoon alone riding her mare on his own property would not be wise. Sending a slave to accompany her wouldn't be much protection either. He'd pondered the possibility of enlarging the house at Loudoun farm, or maybe building a new one. Now it came to him that a town house, built in the county seat of Leesburg, might be the answer.

With Grimes in charge at the farm, Francis himself could go back and forth as he deemed necessary. It was worth further consideration, he decided, relieved to have finally stumbled on a possible solution to what had become a dilemma.

After a while he climbed from the creek feeling refreshed, happy he'd stopped. Spreading his shirt on the grassy slope he lay down to dry in the sun, on his back, arms under his head. A red hawk swooped circles high above the tree tops. It reminded him of the eagles over the cliffs at Stratford. Stratford made him think of Richard, and he decided it was time to stop taunting himself and open his letters. He chose the one from Becky first. A reply, he dared to hope, to his suggestion he visit the Northern neck in the fall as soon as his crops were in. An excitement gripped him as he imagined her concentrating over the words, her lovely soft hair falling around her face as she bent over the paper. Lord, what he would give to hold her this very instant, he thought, suddenly aware of his own nakedness. Staring at the firm black lines of her precise penmanship, he wondered about the children who would be born to them. Who would they look like, and what would they be like? His thirty-three years prodded him to view the subject with some urgency. Although his body was healthy now, and sturdy, ready to sire any number of children, what would it be in ten years? Would his muscles begin to sag, his stomach grow flabby or protrude in a little pot like Carter's and Tayloe's did? Would his back become stiff, or even bent? Jarring thoughts. He turned back to the pages before him, puzzled that such things had never occurred to him before Becky.

"My dear friend," the letter read. *"I have many things on which to ponder as I gaze upon your recent letter. I received it only yesterday from the hands of Captain Richards, who personally delivered it into my keeping. It arrived almost twice as quickly as your last, for which fact I am most happy. However, letters from your Loudoun County take almost as long to arrive as those from England. Captain Richards swears it is not his fault. He says he picks up all packets on the Rappahannock from*

Fredericksburg, Port Royal and other points and delivers them straight-away to us at Hobbs' Hole. I suppose Mama is right, and that since Leesburg is a remote settlement, mail must depend on passing travelers on their way to the Carolinas."

So. Both Becky and Lady Tayloe had begun to worry about the long miles into Loudoun's wilderness. It heightened his own concern over her adjustment to the remoteness of it.

"I am pleased by your frequent and generous flatteries, dear Francis. Your letter gives me much to think about, as I am sure you knew it would. I have spoken to Mama and Papa in reference to your visit. We all agree that Mount Airy will welcome you. As to the question you say you are planning to ask me, I can only respond that I await your arrival with great anticipation."

Well, that was settled. He could forget his doubts that she might have changed her mind since April. Not that he'd considered that as a real possibility, but they were so far apart, and she was indeed very young.

"I had a letter from my friend Betsy Blair last week. She writes that a Baron de Botetourt has received the appointment as Governor of Virginia and will soon arrive from England. She did not mention, but I am sure she was disappointed the honor did not go to her father. She is to marry Samuel Thompson on March 16th next. Betsy said her mama has sent to London for a most exquisite wedding dress of the palest blue imaginable."

Reading between the lines, he grinned, thinking that Becky wanted so much to tell him what color she would like her own dress to be, but it wouldn't be proper for her to say, not before he had formally proposed and she had accepted. Funny, proud, enchantingly perfect little girl that she was. He hoped it would be green.

"Colonel Carter was here to visit Papa this very morning and when told of your proposed visit he seemed (for him) most pleased. He complained again about his wastrel son, Robert, who he says has now encouraged his brilliant grandson, young Landon of course, down the same paths

of playing and gaming his life away. The poor colonel is really quite beside himself. He went so far as to call Robert's wife Lady Fat. I think it is most unkind of him to call poor Winifred that. Do you agree?

"*Your brother Philip and family were here on Sunday last. Matilda and Flora are adorable. Everyone makes such a fuss over Matilda that she is quite spoiled. We go next week to your brother Richard Henry's at Chantilly for several days. The dancing master is to be there and we will all have lessons. I expect the Carters and Turbervilles will also come. And maybe the Washingtons. There is to be a fish feast at Stratford one day while we are in Westmoreland, and we are going for an outing on a boat. Do you miss all Potomac's delicious fish?*"

Now, just where did she think Loudoun was anyway? Did she think they had no fresh fish in these parts? Surely not. He had a lot to explain to her, he could see that.

"*I feel confident that a certain person will most assuredly answer yes to your mysterious question. I remain your affectionate friend and correspondent, Rebecca Tayloe.*"

A postscript was affixed below, in very small writing. "come quickly, my dearest," he read, his eyes misting, "lest I perish and blow away." He studied the words, willing himself to hear her voice as she might have whispered the thought before putting it to paper. It troubled him to realize that he couldn't truly remember what it sounded like.

The sun was dropping fast. and he decided to save Richard's letter for later. It was sure to be lengthy, full of politics and family news. Pulling on his soft linen drawers and then his breeches, he tucked his linen shirt inside. What a fool he was to ever have thought that marriage was only for other men.

The sweet smell of wild clover, its purple clumps mingled with golden daisies along the edge of his fences, greeted him as he neared the turn-off to the house. A captivating, heady scent of new mown hay was also on the evening breeze. Galloping down the lane past the three-foot-high corn, he knew the time was at hand to plan a wedding date.

Chantilly

It was three miles from Stratford to Chantilly. One brisk leaf-blown day in November, Francis turned his dappled gelding into the road. He needn't have bothered. The animal knew the way. There was nowhere else to go when one headed left out of Stratford's gate. The road trailed around until it arrived at a narrow ridge. This meant he had passed the halfway mark. Soon an open field came into view where nothing grew except tall grasses and the nodding heads of wild flowers. It occurred to him that the field, brightened as it now was by the season's last goldenrod and Michaelmas daisies, proclaimed louder than words how little of Richard's time was devoted to the role of planter. The area could easily and profitably have been seeded in tobacco. To his left he caught an occasional glimpse of Currioman Bay stretching away to the Potomac River.

Before he expected it, so engrossed was he in nature's bounty, the land dropped off sharply and ravines hugged the lane. Within a few minutes the panorama of house and river swept into view. No matter how many times he entered there, his mind never failed to note the scene's perfection. A slim twist of smoke spiraled from one of the chimneys. He imagined it to herald the welcome that awaited him.

"Ya-hoo! Uncle Frank! Hey everybody, it's Uncle Frank!" It was Ludwell, Richard and Anne's second son, who had spotted the visitor. He let out another whoop and within minutes the entire family crowded around. The four children pushed and shoved, each seeking his attention. He patted and hugged them each in turn, Thomas and Ludwell, Mary and little Hannah. Then he picked the girls up, and two sets of arms wrapped tightly around his neck as two soft sticky mouths smeared his cheeks.

"Who's been eating sweets?" he asked, trying to sound gruff. Mary and Hannah giggled.

"Well, it looks as though Uncle Frank is a mighty popular fellow around here." Richard directed a slave to stable his brother's horse, waiting his own turn at the affectionate greetings. When Francis set the children down the two men embraced warmly as always. "What you need, Loudoun, is a few wee ones of your own. 'Tis clear they adore you."

"Perhaps it won't be long before I have just that," he confided with a wink. "It's the reason for my visit to the Neck as a matter of fact."

"Well, I'm damned then, and here I thought you came only to see us. When all the while it's someone else you've got your mind on!" Richard was grateful to see Francis no matter what had spurred the visit. He really needed his brother at this moment.

Richard's attempt at lightness seemed to be hiding his true feelings. Francis glanced at the house. "Where's Anne?" The windows stared emptily back at him, a troubling sign.

"She ... can't leave her chamber."

"What do you mean? Is she still sick then?"

"I thought I wrote you she had another bad spell."

"But that was months ago. I had no idea she wasn't recovered. Is it serious? It sounds it."

Richard nodded, resignation in his eyes. "Dr. Dungan prescribes only complete rest now. The special foods, the herbs, the blood lettings, have all been to no avail. She vomits daily and suffers alternate chills and fevers. There's nothing ... nothing I can do ..." His voice trailed away.

"Good Lord, man, don't be absurd! Call in another physician. David Dungan is a capable doctor, I hear, but he can't know everything. What about Brockenbrough?"

Richard looked at him sadly. "Frank, before Arthur left he came almost every day to see her. He agrees with Dungan. We can do nothing now but wait. And the waiting is taking a toll on all of us. Until the moment of your arrival I hadn't seen the children excited nor laughing about anything in weeks. Your visit will make us all very happy."

"May I see her now?" He felt panicky as he made for the steps. Poor, poor Anne. Cursing under his breath, he said, "Why is it the very special ones must suffer the most?"

Outside the door to Anne's chamber Richard held him back momentarily. "I should warn you. She's a shadow of herself and lost much weight since last you saw her. Be prepared."

Francis hoped to keep the anxiety out of his eyes, but was appalled at sight of his sister-in-law, and was unable to hide his dismay. She was nothing more than bones with skin stretched tautly around the whole, holding it together. Deep purple hollows held her sunken eyes. The flesh drawn back from her mouth pulled her lips into a thin line. It wasn't Anne at all. But her smile when she recognized him rekindled the lifeless eyes, splashing a touch of the familiar across the mask of death her face had become.

"Frank," she said, reaching for his hand. "How good of you to come. You bring me great joy."

He prayed Richard would keep quiet about Becky being the reason for his visit. "Dear Anne. What can I say? Except how sorry I am ..." He gripped her hands tightly, vaguely aware that he was the one needing assurance.

Richard cleared his throat, thinking they'd forgotten his presence. "I'll make arrangements for refreshments to be brought up. You two can talk. I'll be back shortly."

"Let's celebrate, Richard. Do you think we might have some tea?" Anne asked, pulling her gaze from Francis to her husband.

Richard smiled. "Of course, my dear. A special treat for our special guest." Turning to his brother he explained, "We've vowed not to purchase any more of the stuff until Parliament removes the taxes."

"Oh?" said Francis, happy for another subject to think about. "Well, sounds like a splendid idea. The boycott, I mean. I wonder if others have thought of that? If the tea rots on the ships, the East India line will surely put pressure on the Crown to repeal the tax. I'll carry your plan to Richmond County and back to Leesburg," he decided promptly. He noticed that Anne's hairline had receded, and the hair itself was wispy and dull. How could Richard bear to see her this way day after day?

"Others are already doing exactly the same, Frank. It's not my idea. I'm surprised you hadn't heard of the plan."

Francis sighed. "Well, don't forget how isolated Loudoun is. Besides that, when I get home I become involved with the problems there. It seems far removed from current politics." He suppressed a smile seeing Richard's frown. "I didn't say I neglected them altogether, did I?"

As soon as Richard left the room, Anne turned to matters weighing heavily on her mind. "I'm so glad you've come, Frank. I need your help. You must promise to help me."

Wondering what she thought he could possibly do to help her, he nodded. "Anything at all I can do, I will. You know that."

"I haven't much time left on this earth. I suppose Richard has told you and of course you must be able to see it for yourself."

Again he nodded. No one would have had to tell him, it was true. Was she frightened, knowing death was coming, perhaps in a matter of weeks or even days?

"I'm not afraid," she said quietly, knowing the way his mind worked. "When it pleases the Lord to call me to His sweet salvation, I'll be ready. Forgive me the platitudes, but it does happen to one in time of crisis, I've found. My concern is for Richard. It will be impossible for him alone. With the children. They're so young and require much care. They need a mother's love and attention. Heaven knows, I haven't been able to be a proper mother for months. But more than just that, Richard will need someone for himself. Someone to whom he can turn when the frustrations of his politics exhaust him, wear him down. He has periods of the highest elation followed by the darkest despair. You'll see. It's then he needs someone to wait on him, nurse him, pamper him, and listen to him when he feels the world will not." The effort exhausted her and she sank into the pillows.

"He's always been like that, Anne. Rest, now you've tired yourself out."

Gathering what remained of her failing strength she began again, "Yes, but he's even more needy now. Much more so. I don't think you have any idea how really involved he's become in the state of our colonies. And how depressed when things don't go his way. I think he's a great man, Frank. I've always thought that, and now I believe he can do much for America. The trouble is, he feels it himself, and that makes him appear haughty ... and impatient. Others don't understand that it is merely his way. Sometimes they scoff at his ideas, more for the way he has presented them I think, than at the content of what he's trying to tell them. At those times of rejection, that's when he needs someone to take his hand." Closing her eyes, barely breathing, she fell silent.

The ache in his heart was unbearable. She looked so small and wasted, as though she might be shrinking away before his very eyes. "What would you have me do?' he whispered, thinking she might have fallen asleep.

"Encourage him to marry again. Provide the opportunity for him to meet the right woman if necessary, if he doesn't do it himself. He may resist. And in the meantime, stand behind him when he needs help, Frank. Please?"

Francis had no idea what to say. There were tears swimming in her eyes ready to brim over and he desperately wished to make her smile again. He decided to treat it lightly. "Now, Annie," he teased, knowing she loathed that version of her name, "he won't find a jewel like you around every crossroads, you know, and I suspect he's mighty spoiled and choosy, but we'll see what we can do. How about you just getting better? That would be ever so much easier." He squeezed her hand which still rested in his own. Seated on the edge of her high bed, his feet were propped on the padded stool beside it. While she talked he'd become aware of the faint stench of stale vomit. Was that what death smelled like?

"Yes," she said, seeming not to have heard him. "It has been a good marriage. For both of us. His strength has fortified our relationship, provided the rock on which we've built. But sometimes ... sometimes I think it's the strongest men who need the most love and assurance in order to go on. It's that way with my Richard."

Through the window, the familiar late fall gray of the great river stretched, but he couldn't see it through a haze of his own tears. He'd never been more aware of what Anne meant to him than at this moment. From the very beginning she'd been willing to share the affections of her new husband with all those who loved him. Francis had never felt left out. And it was from Anne that he learned what it was he would want in a wife, were he ever to marry. It had taken him a long time from the learning, to the finding of a perfect girl. He waited until the choked feeling subsided before he tried to speak. Thinking of Becky, he was able to smile weakly.

"Anne, when our father died I wasn't very old. It was a terrible blow to me, coming so soon after our mother's passing. I chose Richard as my hero, perhaps because we were closer of an age. I don't know. But I leaned on him for guidance and direction, rather than on Phil or Tom. I think you know how freely he gave of his time and his knowledge. His energies, dreams and ambitions have pretty well become my own. I know his vanities, his blasted impatience when things go wrong, and his sometimes arrogant temper. I can't begin to fill your shoes, and I'm not sure how soon I could speak to him about remarrying, but perhaps

I can carry a heavier load. Is that enough to bring you some peace? I do love him, and I believe in him. It's all I can offer." It seemed a mighty little, he thought, watching as she plucked nervously at the coverlet with her bony fingers.

It was enough for Anne. A sob heaved in her chest, but somehow she turned it miraculously into an enormous sigh. "Thank you, Frank. I just knew you'd understand. I've prayed everyday that you'd come ... before it was too late. My prayers are answered." Seeing Richard's face reappear, she sighed again, but this time with contentment. Without knowing it, he'd given her just enough time. "Now, tell me all about your plans with Becky. She was here with her family during the summer. We both think she's a lovely girl, just perfect for you," she said cheerfully.

"The children are clamoring to get at you, Loudoun." Richard had Lucas in tow with the tea board and a ruby red port. "They have made me promise you'll play with them when you're through with our repast. I'm afraid they'll wear you out if you're not careful."

"That's not likely. I've been fully broken in this year what with four days at Thomas's, and yesterday Matilda and Flora held me captive in the nursery for several hours. They certainly take after their mother. They have lovely, sweet dispositions. Spoiled, I suppose, but sweet nonetheless. And Philip does make a fuss over them!" He sipped his wine, watching Richard over the rim. "A delicious port, R.H. Phil hasn't changed a bit in his attitude toward our sister Hannah, has he? He kept trying to get me to admit what a scandal it is, but I managed to put him off. I can't find it in my heart to fault our poor sister. It upsets me when others do so."

Richard was wary. It was a subject he'd much rather not discuss. "It's difficult for me to accept what she's doing to the name of Lee ... for Philip, I expect it's nigh to impossible." Hurrying to change the subject, "How long did you remain at Stratford?" he asked.

Francis chuckled. "Well, actually only yesterday and this morning. That was enough of our good Colonel Phil's high-handed ways for me. I managed to liberate a few more of my books, however, and talked him into allowing me to take cuttings from some of Father's fig trees in the spring. I may purchase a horse from him if we can reach a price. Although I doubt it. I left Ben to look over the stock and check to see what Philip's stable hands have to say about certain mounts. I wouldn't put it past our dear brother to sell me a lame horse if he thought he could prove the ailment occurred after I accepted the animal."

Richard had always considered his younger brothers were too hard on Philip. He muttered an indistinguishable oath under his breath, but made no comment. It would accomplish nothing. Frank had made up his mind about Phil long ago.

Ignoring the scowl, Francis continued, "Well, what do you think of the appointment of our new Governor Botetourt? The *Gazette* painted a rather favorable picture, I thought."

"He seems popular with the conservatives, which makes me somewhat cautious. He arrived last month, you know. Poor Blair. I'm sorry in a way the honor wasn't given to him. At least he's one of our own."

Anne had finished a half cup of tea. "Richard, do you think I might rest now? I'm very tired, dear." The tea, like everything else, was not sitting well on her stomach.

The men stood to leave, mumbling apologies, embarrassed they had forgotten her. Francis guessed the exertion of her conversation with him to be at the root of her exhaustion.

The thud of a small body hit the door. Before they could cross the room, Hannah burst inside. Her apron pockets bulged and her baby face was flushed. "Can I bring my friends and sit with you, Mama?" she pleaded. "Ludwell's mean!"

"No, Hannah. Your mother must rest. Come now, we're just leaving." Richard reached for his daughter's hand, but she pulled away, backing toward the bed.

"We'll be quiet. Mama promised to tell us a story. And she already rested," she announced, her dark eyes defiant.

"Hannah, I said no. Now come, you know Mama isn't feeling well." Richard's voice had an unfamiliar edge to it. It was enough to send Hannah into a torrent of tears.

"Richard, I can ... " Anne began.

"I'll tell her a story. Hannah, will you come with Uncle Frank? I know a wonderful tale about a timid little elf who lived in the deep forest and drank his tea out of a lady-slipper."

"A lady's slipper?" asked Hannah, sniffling. "Really, Uncle Frank?"

"Really. Do you know what a lady-slipper is? Well, I'll tell you after you introduce me to your friends, peeking from your pocket. They must be shy, hiding in there." He grinned at Anne, who rewarded him with a look of gratitude.

As they left the room, Hannah pulled out a wooden horse with two legs missing, a grubby stuffed bear, and a cracked china doll from her voluminous pockets. "My friends," she offered hesitantly. Her brothers poked fun at her friends. "They may sit on your lap, Uncle Frank, while you tell the story, if you promise not to laugh at them."

"Wonderful. Wonderful," agreed her uncle, gathering the small wriggling body and her bedraggled companions into his arms. "They do have a certain ... uh ... charm about them, sweetheart. They look loved, I would have to say that." Then, seeing her anxious eyes, "I don't think they are the least bit funny. I like them," he announced firmly to the relieved little face, a miniature of Anne's.

❦

Francis was thankful he had stopped at Chantilly. The children, too young to understand the pall of death which hung over the household, yet knowing something was very wrong, took comfort in their uncle's presence and bounced around in normal fashion. They smothered him with affection as Richard had warned. The brothers made up for the months apart by hunting, walking, riding, and talking together. And he spent many quiet hours with Anne.

Although he was anxious to be on his way, almost from the moment he arrived, the urgency driving him had nothing to do with Anne, Richard or Chantilly. It was his own burning desire to be with Becky again. The closer the time came, the more impatient he was. He aimed to keep it under control somewhat longer, however, convinced that his visit brought cheer to Anne and companionship to Richard.

The house itself had always intrigued him; from the path atop the narrow lane between two deep ravines, to the inside furnishings, it was charming. Richard had sited the building on a large point of land above the Hollis Marsh and creek, and the view of Currioman Bay and the Potomac beyond was magnificent. Sometimes Francis wondered if his father had overlooked this spot in his search for the site for Stratford house. He had concluded that Thomas Lee must have preferred the grandeur of space rather than the smaller private paradise of the Chantilly lands. It was true his father had chosen a broad expanse of open view to the river and cleared his lands to complement the great brick mansion from every direction. He thought of Stratford as a dramatic fortress, but Chantilly was an exquisite home.

"*As much as I love Stratford,*" he wrote in the letter to let Becky know of his intention to arrive on Saturday next, "*I believe the setting of Chantilly would closely agree with my choice of a homesite. The gardens being small and intimate, immediately surrounded by untamed and glorious woodlands, give one a feeling of having discovered a small kingdom of sublimity in the midst of the natural wild order of things. The sense of isolation is complete, and I think grand. A most satisfying situation indeed.*"

He reread the letter, considering a tender line or two at the close as she had done. In a moment, discretion dictated such sentiments could better be whispered in person and he merely signed, *"Yours most affectionately, Francis."* It was customary to sign one's entire name, thus on other occasions he signed Francis Lightfoot Lee or sometimes Francis Light. Lee. Abbreviations were also in vogue, but it came to him that by the omission of his surname, he would impart a more intimate touch. Satisfied, he folded the page, waxed it, and pressed his seal in place. He called Ben and instructed him to deliver it in person to Miss Becky, and that he was to beg leave to remain in the quarter at Mount Airy. Francis himself would arrive in a few days. He'd also decided against the purchase of any of Philip Lee's horses, he informed the slave.

"Yas-suh, Marse Frank. I'll do just that right off." Anticipation stretched from ear to ear across the shiny black face.

"May I ask what is causing that smug look on your face, my man?" his master wanted to know. "Someone you want to see at Mount Airy, is there?"

Ben smiled, edging toward the door. "Oh, no Marse Frank. It ain't no woman. Not dis time. I jes' breathes easier when I git my bones out o' sight dat ol' Lucas, dat's all!" It was only half the truth. There was someone he wanted to see again. Cate. But only to look at her, because he knew she was Isaac's woman and he wouldn't interfere with that. He liked Isaac, and respected him, too. He was a fine young buck, and a smart and honest one. Nothing like the shifty, arrogant Lucas. But there was nothing wrong with hoping that maybe Isaac hadn't made it from Williamsburg to Richmond County after all, was there?

When Ben left, Francis finished reading the papers from Boston and Philadelphia. You could always read the news from around the world in Richard's study. After an hour he was ready to discuss the events in the other colonies, and found his brother studying a mixed flock of canvasbacks and mallards feeding in the marsh.

"Aren't they fascinating, Loudoun? Just look at that color. Green, blue, black, purple. I never tire of them. And I never cease to be amazed at the signal they receive from nature every fall, regardless the weather, that sends them winging here from the north, just about the time it becomes too cold for us to fish the river. There can be no place in the world with a more ready and delicious food supply."

For a change, Francis wasn't in the mood to explore the wonders of nature. He settled himself on the mossy bank. "Um-hmm. Wonderful."

"You sound absentminded enough about it."

"I was thinking of what I gleaned from your newspapers. The Ministry's seizure of Hancock's Liberty sloop, the British troops in Boston, clashes between the people and the soldiers ... it's all very disturbing. I'm afraid our northern neighbors have brought the wrath of England down on their own heads for sure this time. What do you hear from William and Arthur? I haven't heard from either since they sailed. It takes mail months to get out to Loudoun it seems. Have they said anything about what's really going on in the Parliament?"

"Arthur has made friends with the infamous John Wilkes, and do you know where Wilkes is now?"

Francis nodded. "I just read about it." Wilkes, a wealthy, arrogant rake and an outlawed member of Parliament with tremendous popular appeal, now languished in a prison cell. It was reported he'd turned it into a lavish political headquarters. He was incarcerated by order of a high court on a series of trumped-up charges, and all because he was adored by the people and had libeled the King. He was a Whig and a friend to America, hence Arthur Lee had sought him out immediately.

"Arthur apparently dines frequently with Wilkes in the Kings Bench Prison, and described the man's apartment there as quite comfortable and adequate, if you can believe it. He says people are constantly sending money and gifts to their hero Wilkes. Because of his countless connections in the government, Arthur thinks he can do much to aid our cause," Richard explained.

Francis smiled, finding it amusing. "From what I gather of it, Wilkes's personality bears scant resemblance to our brother's. I wonder how they manage to get along."

"I thought of that, too. Wilkes, with his series of torrid little love affairs, his flair for the bizarre as they say, and our morally timid brother would seem totally mismatched. But Arthur wants the Whig support. I pray that he gets it."

"You've trained him well, R.H. As you have all of us."

Richard shrugged, pleased with the compliment. "Arthur was never anything but an eager student."

Francis wondered if the implication was that he, or the others, were not, but decided to let it pass. "How about William? Is he also involved in this great political intrigue?"

Now Richard laughed. "Well, apparently, like you at the moment, he has other matters on his mind. Our brothers are staying at the Ludwell house, and it seems our William has designs on his cousin, Hannah Phillipa! It would be a promising match, don't you think? The girl has come into a good deal of money and property, including the merchant business in London, the houses in Williamsburg, and also Green Spring Plantation itself. There are only the three daughters, and it will be divided three ways I feel sure. Such a union would serve to ease William's financial plight as well as pleasure him."

William's financial plight, thought Francis, was primarily due to Colonel Phil's having not provided him with his full inheritance. Nor Arthur either. But there seemed no point in dredging that up again. "I think it sounds like good news. Maybe we can get two Lee bachelors married off in the same year," he joked.

"Then you've set the date?"

"No. I'm thinking of the spring, however. But I haven't asked her yet."

"What, for the date?"

"No. To marry me," he confessed.

"Good God, Frank, what can you be thinking? Women won't wait forever, you know. They can be the most impatient creatures under the sun. Especially when it comes to a man's stating his true intentions. They are fidgety, out of sorts, nervous as cats until they're certain they've trapped their prey. Believe me."

"I know. I know. I discovered that about Becky. A rather painful experience actually," he admitted, remembering the picnic. "But we've worked it out. She understands me, I think." His brown eyes twinkled. "And soon I shall put it all to rights in any case."

A thin mist had begun to rise from the creek. Hanging just above the water it had sent the ducks paddling into the reeds for the night. Francis was beginning to feel the damp ground through the seat of his breeches. He stood, leaning into a beech trunk, one foot braced behind him against the tree. "Arthur still wants to begin the study of law, I suppose," he asked, thinking it time to change the subject.

"Oh, yes, although I'm still distressed he couldn't find it in his plans to continue at his medical practice. I suppose I'll get over it, but I think that America needs the best of her sons to bring their worldly acquired knowledge home to roost. But Arthur wants to enter Lincoln's Inn, with a view to the Middle Temple in due course. At the end of all that time, the provincialism of Virginia may no longer appeal to him. That's my worry."

"Well, reconcile yourself with the hope that if he follows this path of his, he'll succeed and in the long run his talents may benefit our colonies much more than had he remained in medicine."

Richard sighed. "I suppose you may be right," he agreed, thinking how much they all admired Arthur. He had such a brilliant mind.

"Changing the subject back to Boston for a minute. It's an occupied city, is it not? There are shootings and injuries. The British seem to be parading shamelessly up and down the streets in their red coats and brass buttons, do they not? Why, it must be infuriating to be subjected to such a debasement! With the Massachusetts Assembly dissolved by Parliamentary order and a bastard local government operating in what can only be called an illegal manner ... why they're truly on a collision course I believe."

"Yes and who can blame them, Loudoun? The Bostonians are brave men. They exhibit a zeal I find sadly lacking in our own leaders. Virginians are in favor of patching up the wounds somehow, even if it means accepting some sort of abominable taxes that we've had no hand in setting!" His agitation was obvious. Richard had given this a great deal of thought.

"Well now, that surely can't be the case with Virginia as a whole, can it? I know it's not, R.H."

"Hear this, if you don't believe me. All my neighbors, Colonels Carter and Tayloe, Robert Carter of Nomini, our brother Phil, even Carter Braxton, are overjoyed at the prospect of our new English Governor Botetourt. Falling all over themselves to get down to Williamsburg to be presented. They maintain he'll miraculously steer us to a reconciliation with the Crown. I'm disgusted with the lot of them! They would capitulate without a fight."

"And how you love to do battle, my dear brother. A political fight is your meat and wine," said Francis, but not unkindly. "You know, there are two sides to the coin. Were we able to patch up our differences satisfactorily, with England returning to her former attitudes ... gentle persuasion, coaxing and occasional flattery, I think America, as a colonial entity, would continue to thrive. Just as we've always done." He paused, thinking. "On the other hand, I look around my own Loudoun County, and I do wonder. We have a population there of homesteaders. For years they've been moving in. Now, many eastern planters want to reclaim and cultivate those lands they've inherited, as I have done. The homesteaders will be forced out. Where do they go if

England restricts western expansion, such as our own land company seeks to establish? The Germans, the Quakers, the Irish and Scots ... why should they feel a loyalty or any ties to Britain anyway? And in Loudoun their votes are beginning to have loud voices. Some of them understand, but whether they know it yet or not, both their survival and their freedom are threatened. So ... I don't know. Perhaps I've talked myself around in a circle."

Richard stood up. Putting an arm easily around his brother's shoulder, he moved them toward the house. "Yes, a circle. It is that. But don't let youself make the mistake of following the wrong curve. The word liberty has only one meaning. The British constitution gives us the right to determine our own laws and taxes. We cannot, we will not, give up that right." He stopped, turning back to the marsh. "Enough! Shall we hunt in the morning?"

"Good plan," smiled Francis, scanning the weeds for ducks. "I can't see a single one at the moment, but they'll be back. We should get up early."

As they made their way up the hill, Richard reminded Francis of the plan he was forming for correspondence committees. "Besides John Dickinson, I've written to General Gladsden of South Carolina. There hasn't been time for a reply yet, but I'm confident he'll favor the idea. Keeping each other informed is of the utmost importance it seems to me. Arthur is writing to Samuel Adams in Boston, and I shall contact his cousin, John Adams. And Loudoun, I'm counting on you to do your share."

They climbed the steps to the hall of Chantilly. A crackling fire, and the smells of burning cedar and hot chocolate mingled to greet them as they entered. Incongruous somehow, that a house of death should smell so good, Francis mused. But for an entire afternoon they had managed, with no noticeable effort, to put Anne from their minds. She might as well be dead already. But she was not dead. Nor was she alive. Her life hung somewhere in a curious never-never land suspended, for God knew how long, between earthly concerns ... and whatever came after.

After they sipped the warm chocolate, devoured a delicious supper of crabs, venison, and late summer crabapples and shared several glasses of wine, it came to Francis. When you lost someone, it had to be that way. In order to preserve their own sanity it seemed they had all begun, hour by hour, to forget her. Soon it would be day by day, then week by week—until their grief passed and they scarcely thought of her at all, except as someone they had once loved dearly. Poor, dear Anne, lovely, sweet Anne, farewell.

Francis held up his cup to Lucas for more wine. "I'll set off tomorrow for Mount Airy as soon as we return from duck shooting," he announced abruptly. "It's time I was on my way."

Mount Airy

It was Friday morning and Francis was arriving a day early. He ached for those he left behind at Chantilly and agonized over the pain and suffering they had yet to go through, but he'd been glad to get away, put it behind him. Last night he had spent at Sabine Hall playing cards with Robert Carter, the colonel having been visiting in King and Queen County. Today he was in fine spirits. Alone on the road he hooted at the wind and almost wept for joy at the brilliant wonder of the dazzling blue sky. Within the hour he would surely hold his dear, sweet girl in his arms.

Cameron jogged into the courtyard presided over by the great stone creatures set to guard Mount Airy's circular entrance. Perched motionless on huge pedestals, a blank stare fixed on each of the two ageless faces, they kept a silent watch. Only they weren't lions. They were huge jardiniere-looking dogs, hunting dogs, he supposed. They were appropriate enough but, for the hundredth time he found himself thinking he really would like to see lions guarding the steps. It was one of the few things he found less than perfect at Mount Airy.

The family sat at breakfast in the elaborate dining room with the fine gilt-framed paintings of race horses on the walls. Silverware clattered, glasses clinked, and the drift of voices floated into the hall. Francis imagined them gathered around the table, as he wondered where Ben was, and if Jacob had announced his arrival. He had no plan for what he'd do when he first saw Becky. Would they have a private moment? What would she expect? His stomach churned as if to make butter out of the cream he'd had for breakfast.

Meanwhile, in the dining room, Jacob cleared his throat, seeking his master's attention. At John Tayloe's nod, the slave whispered of Mr. Lee's arrival. He was waiting in the great hall even now.

The colonel glanced past the younger girls, his eyes focusing on his second daughter. Picking at her food she was, no doubt about it. Not like her at all. Usually a good eater, that one, that's where she got her spunk. She ate well, rode a good horse, and knew her own mind. And since she'd made no complaints about not feeling well, whatever prompted her to slosh the porridge from side to side while gazing at the ceiling, could be caused by only one thing. Francis Lee's pending arrival. Tayloe was also aware, through a round-about series of conversations with Becky, that although the two had reached some sort of an agreement, France hadn't yet asked her to be his wife. This had to be what made her pensive, moody, and increasingly skittish as the day of his arrival had drawn closer—like a three-year-old filly with a stallion in the next paddock. He smiled to himself, enjoying the comparison. Suddenly he made up his mind.

"Becky," he called down the table. "My dear, would you be so kind as to check for my pipe? I seem to remember leaving it in the great hall, near the door perhaps, when I came in from hunting this morning."

"Of course, Papa," she said, blinking in surprise and wondering why he didn't send Jacob.

"John! You're not planning to smoke at table, are you? You know how I ..."

"Damn it, Rebe, allow a man some credit for good sense!"

Becky fled, happy to leave the unwanted meal, not caring whether her father smoked at table or not. It was a silly rule her mother had made up anyway.

"Yes, dear," she heard her mother's obedient reply as she left the room. "That child hasn't eaten a bite of food. Whatever is the matter with her this morning?"

"I think within a few minutes the answer to your question will walk through that doorway, my dear wife, a day ahead of when we were led to expect him."

This last was lost on Becky as she'd passed out of hearing. She saw Francis immediately. He had his back to her but she had no doubt who it was. Her first impulse was to run madly and throw her arms around him. That wouldn't be proper and she held herself back. "Hello," she managed to say, and he turned to find her watching him.

"Becky!" Had she grown even more beautiful? She looked older. They met in the center of the hall. Stopping a foot apart, they searched each other's eyes. There was no need for words. They discovered in silence, all over again, what they had learned six months before.

The wonder of his mouth was on hers. Oh Francis, I do so love your kisses. Please, please ask me to marry you. Then it will be proper for me to kiss you like this. There it was again. The nagging reminder of propriety. Ever so slowly she disengaged herself, establishing a few inches between them. They were so close in height, she had barely to look up to see his eyes. In a voice choked with emotion, she gasped, "I declare, Francis Lee, you've come all this way and not yet greeted my dear mama and papa."

Her eyes held laughter, and he laughed, too. "I had first to kiss the most lovely girl I ever met. A most satisfying embrace it was, I might add," he assured her. "Come," and he took her hand, leading the way to the dining room.

Becky knew her face must be scarlet. Who cared? Francis was here at last.

⤬

The midday meal was served as usual at three o'clock. Following an afternoon rest period, during which time Francis and John Tayloe smoked their pipes and conversed about nothing very substantive, Becky led Francis on a tour of the garden and out to the latticed arbor beyond the orangery. It was bare now, the wisteria vines beginning to shrivel, but the day was warm with the same cloudless sky of the morning. They spent a perfect two hours telling each other of the things that had transpired during their weeks apart. Francis expounded on Loudoun County, from its settlement and incorporation to the present day. Listening, she watched his face, the expressive eyebrows, the parallel lines that creased his forehead above them, and the little dents at the corners of his mouth that made it appear as though he was always smiling a bit. He usually was smiling. The dimples must have come to feel at home there, she decided, and so they stayed. How good to be together again, so incredibly good, she told herself as he talked.

Soon it was evening, too early yet for supper. They sat on Rebecca's favorite gold sofa, sent all the way from a fine cabinet-maker in Philadelphia when the new house was built. The family had gathered as usual in early evening in the great hall and were occupied with cards or sewing.

Except Anne, who plunked out a tune on the harpsichord, stealing glances at Becky and Francis. She thought Becky had been hatefully secretive this afternoon, refusing to tell anything about how things were progressing. Anne scowled at them behind their backs, watching Becky sitting there smugly, hogging all Mr. Lee's attention, and thinking that the way she batted her eyes at him was revolting.

"Yes, it's been a good year for my crops," Francis was saying. "We cut a healthy load of tobacco leaf in September, and will soon harvest the fall wheat and an acre of barley. I've got apples this year, Becky, as big as pumpkins!"

Her eyes widened.

"Well, almost," he laughed. "Red ones and yellow, and some green, for cooking. Four varieties."

"Well, I never. And to think I've been so worried that you lived in a wilderness. I guess I just haven't pictured it rightly."

He wondered how he was going to get around to what was on his mind. He'd let the chance slip past this afternoon and now they weren't alone. He detected a tenseness in Becky that he hadn't noticed earlier. They really needed some time alone, but how to arrange it without being obvious?

"We've talked about almost everything since this morning, haven't we?" she sighed. "Maybe you'd like to play backgammon. Do you enjoy the game?" she suggested.

Not fascinated with the idea, he agreed anyway. "Fine. Yes, I do like the game." Then, "Where shall we play?" His hopes raced to the possibility of the library.

"Pull that small table up next to the sofa, Becky," her mother suggested, as she searched through her yarns for the right shade of blue.

Francis glanced around the room. The colonel and Ellie were playing cards at the gaming table. Polly, Kitty, and Sally shuffled around on the floor with their dolls. He smiled weakly at Lady Tayloe, who appeared absorbed in her needlework. There was nothing to do but set up the game next to the sofa. Francis lined up the round markers and tossed the dice to see who would go first.

Anne began to hum softly. Then, in a clear tinkling voice which matched the instrument's tone, she started to sing, putting words to the tune she played. Everyone stopped what they were doing to listen.

"Would you wish to gain a lover, you must all your hopes conceal;
Men, inconstant, will discover, what our sex too oft reveal."

Becky, horrified, shot her sister a look of fury. It was a new song. The words had been printed in the *Gazette* a few weeks ago, and the girls had memorized them. Anne, remaining unconcerned by Becky's glare, continued:

"Virtue teaches wise discretion, fickle men are full of arts;
By a thoughtless, fond confession, they seduce and steal our hearts."

Francis tried to conceal a grin behind a studied concentration of his next move on the board. Becky recognizing his glee, flushed beet-red.

"Anne, dear," interrupted Rebecca's voice. "Do play something else. That is such an insipid little song, don't you think you could forego the last verse?"

Anne smiled wickedly, but obeyed her mother. She had already accomplished her purpose. It served Becky right for being so uppity about her old beau anyway.

Glancing at Becky, Francis guessed she might burst into tears at any moment. She fidgeted under his gaze, finally flouncing to her feet. "I don't believe I care to play this game any longer," she sniffed, taking uncertain steps to leave.

"Where are you going?" he asked under his breath.

"Upstairs. I shall come down for supper," she pouted, gaining control over her tears. "Certain people have made it very uncomfortable in this room." She stared at Anne, noticing her father was laughing behind his pipe smoke. Cruel, pitiless family!

Anne, still smiling, ducked her head and pounded into Johann Sebastian Bach. It was a piece Francis recognized. Arthur had hummed it frequently when he returned from his first trip to England. "Come here," he commanded quietly, hoping he sounded firm.

Becky's green eyes flashed. "What?"

"You heard me. I said, come here."

She faltered, not sure what to do. Then, taking a step, she stood in front of him.

"Now sit down. No, not there. Here, beside me." Pushing the backgammon table out of the way, he patted the gold damask next to him.

She sat where he indicated. He meant it.

"That's better. That's wonderful, in fact. Now Becky, look at me. Right in my eyes, like you did when we were on the picnic ... you do remember?" His voice had become soft, almost a whisper. No one could hear, not with Anne playing like that. "Do you feel anything?"

"Yes." It was a tiny response.

"Good. Wonderful," he said again. "Now listen carefully. You are not going upstairs. You are coming with me. We, you and I, are going to bid adieu, casually, to your parents and your sisters. We're going to step out on the veranda where the stars are shining and the moon is waiting. And then, my darling Becky, I'm going to tell you how very much I love you, and I will ask you to become my wife. I'm going to kiss you. So many times you won't be able to count, if you allow me to do so. Do you think your answer to all that is yes?" He was amazed at his own masterful tactics. He'd never felt so lordly nor in control of a situation.

She could only nod. The tears were back, burning hot on her eyelids, and she dabbed at them with the back of her hand.

"Then we shall not waste any more time. Come." He stood, ignoring the moist eyes.

"Francis," she whispered, "I don't believe I can do it. Not unless you hold my hand. I'm so happy that I fear I shall weep and make a fool of myself."

They sat on the veranda steps for some time, looking in the direction of the river. His arm was around her, encouraging her to lean against him which she did gladly.

"Tell me, what were the words to the last verse of that insipid little song, as your mother called it?" Francis asked.

Humming a few bars first, she sang:

"Shun, oh shun! their soft persuasion, let not tears your passion move;

But to embrace the first occasion, when convinc'd they truly love."

147

Turning to face him she wrapped her arms tightly around his neck, enfolding him in her woolen shawl. She kissed him then for a long time with her soft open mouth.

Later, when they noticed the wind come up, he said, "Shall we go inside? We have an announcement to make before supper is called." He kissed the tip of her nose.

"Indeed we do," Becky purred, linking her hand through his arm as they stood up. For the first time she began to understand what it was to feel possessive about another person. It felt better than she ever could have imagined.

◦◦◦

Although the intention to marry was announced to all, followed by hugs, good wishes, and toasts lasting until after midnight, Francis would follow tradition and seek formal approval from John Tayloe. He chose a quiet time early Sunday afternoon. They had just returned from services at Upper Lunenburg Church. On Sunday there were generally only two meals at Mount Airy, the second being most often served about five o'clock, so it seemed a good time. The two men relaxed, alone in the library, their pipes in hand.

"Giberne's sermons are getting shorter and shorter every week. It hardly seemed worth the trip this morning, did it? What's your opinion of our controversial Reverend Isaac Giberne, Frank?"

"I know little about him, to tell the truth. Only what I hear from Colonel Landon."

""Well, if that's the case, I'm sure Carter stressed his less desirable qualities, for he has little use for Mr. Giberne's fondness for gambling, eh?" laughed Tayloe.

"True enough. But he has no use for anyone's gaming, especially his own sons and grandsons. I've heard him say often enough that vice will be the ruination of his family."

"He could be right, you know," Tayloe agreed. "That crew of his really goes about it quite fiendishly I'm afraid. Their main interest in life seems to be the gambling, the cockfights, the horse races. They seem to have no regard for the money they lose either." Drawing on his pipe, he studied Francis, who seemed distracted as if he had other things on his mind. He easily surmised what that might be. Well, he had a surprise up his sleeve. "By the by, Frank, I was going to suggest we take a ride over the plantation this afternoon. I have some fine new riding steeds, Arabians. You'll enjoy the gaits I think. There's something I'd like to show you in the far quarter beyond the mill pond. I'll call to have the horses saddled and brought up."

They met Lady Tayloe in the hall. She reminded them that John Turberville and his lady would join them for dinner and not to be late. Smiling rather smugly, Francis thought, she bid them enjoy themselves.

The horses were as fine as promised. Their thoroughbred stride covered the fields with effortless speed as Tayloe led the way. After passing the mill they turned left, cantering along the creek line before slowing as they traveled forest trails floored with chestnut, beech, gum and maple leaves. Suddenly they came upon a widening of the stream where it flowed into a second, larger creek, and the marshy area was thick with cattails. "Rappahannock Creek," Tayloe called back. "And down there, near the river is our old house where my grandfather William settled. To the right we're heading toward a pond, a bay really, that's formed by the waters of Rappahannock Creek. Quite deep actually. I think it could even serve as a landing."

They rode on for perhaps two miles, sticking close to the creek bank, moving steadily to higher ground. Francis was excited at sight of the body of water Tayloe had described. He hadn't known of its existence before. It spread to a half-mile or more across. Here there were more cattails, and lily pads as well. Giant pines hugged the perimeter, and a large beaver dam humped its sticks along the far side. A startled stag bounded for the deep forest. Three does, at first hidden by the tall grasses, heard the alarm and followed the buck.

"Now there's a happy fellow for you!" Tayloe laughed.

"Beautiful. Just beautiful," Francis marveled, thinking how wild and pristine it was.

"I thought you might be impressed with the place. It's one of my favorite spots. It's difficult going from here, but I want to take you to the top of these hills where we get a view of the bay and the creeks leading to it. With a minimum of logging, you could even see the river, I think."

They dismounted at a point more than midway up a long incline and then continued uphill on foot to where the forest ended and a large clearing came into view. "Why, that's a perfect spot for a tobacco field, Colonel. Very little preparation would be required," Francis exclaimed.

"My sentiments precisely! I explored almost every inch of these acres a few months ago," Tayloe admitted. "Now walk back this way and see what I mean about the view."

Francis gazed across the lovely bay and beyond, to the marshes and creeks, all winding their way to the Rappahannock River. It was a long distance, miles in fact, but he thought between the trees he actually caught a glimpse of the river. Drawing a deep breath he stood quietly, absorbing the scene before him. It wasn't the same, yet somehow it reminded him of Chantilly. Perhaps it was the splendid feeling of isolation. "What is the area called? Does it have a name?" he asked.

"The Indian name for the hills is "Menokin." There's a creek branch near here we call by the same name, and the big creek you see down there is Rappahannock Creek, big enough almost to be a river itself."

"Menokin. I like that. Menokin." He rolled the word on his tongue. "A curious word. Kind of mysterious. Indian, you say?

I feel as though I'm standing on a very special piece of land." He scratched his head, tilting an eyebrow at the man he hoped would soon be his father-in-law.

"I think you are, my boy. By God, I hope to heaven you're standing on somewhere close to a thousand acres of very propitious property! Let's walk back to the horses and I'll tell you why I brought you up here to the Menokin Hills."

In the excitement of the beauty around him Francis had forgotten his reason for wanting to be alone with the colonel this afternoon. But considering Tayloe as his father-in-law brought it back to him. "Has Becky ever been here?" he said, thinking to ease the conversation around.

"Glad you mention her. As a matter of fact she hasn't seen this part of my lands so far as I know. I thought you might want to show it to her tomorrow if the weather holds nice."

"Well, certainly, we might do that," Francis nodded, somewhat surprised at the suggestion. "But actually, Sir, the reason I brought up her name, is that I've been waiting for an opportunity to state my intentions concerning our marriage. And to seek your permission ... and, of course, to listen to whatever advice you might wish to impart."

John Tayloe chuckled. "As the Lord is my witness, Frank, you know you have my permission! I'm delighted with the match. My dear wife as well, now that she's accustomed herself to the difference in your ages. We accept with pleasure your proposal for Becky's hand." Putting an arm around Francis's shoulders, he continued, "Besides your somewhat radical political leanings, we have only one small reservation. It concerns our daughter's comfort. We're most hopeful you'll accept our offer to build you and Becky a home ... on the land you've just surveyed." Pleased with himself, the big man waited.

Francis halted, a look of disbelief on his face. Realization of the purpose of the outing flooded his brain. It so overwhelmed him he found himself unable to respond.

"You don't have to answer me this minute," Tayloe assured him gruffly, feeling more than a little emotional himself. "Take some time. Bring Becky up here. Then make your mind up. I understand it will mean leaving the homestead you've established in Loudoun." He was beginning to feel disappointed in the hesitation he saw in his future son-in-law's eyes, but knew he must keep that to himself. Frank would come around, how could he possibly do otherwise?

∽

It took Francis three days to reach a decision. On each of these days he traveled the four or five miles, depending on the route taken, to the Menokin acres. Twice he took Becky with him. He saw two things in the offer on which to ponder, and discussed them both with her. The first, most obvious, was the Tayloes' desire to keep their daughter close to home; he judged their motives not entirely selfless, which meant the offer was not entirely generous. After consideration, however, he came to decide their motives were probably quite normal and not unreasonable. The second thing that disturbed him and bothered him far more, was the giving up of the life he had made for himself in Loudoun County—the place he'd carved for himself in the community, the lands he'd tamed from wilderness, the order he'd brought to the county court and, of course, his seat in the House of Burgesses. The law didn't require that a man must reside in the county he represented, however he was practical enough to know he wouldn't be re-elected if he moved.

Becky listened to it all and, despite her youth, was wise enough not to press him. For all her determined ways, she felt Francis must make this decision by himself. On the third morning he rode alone through the forest. The day was crisp and clear, following a frosty night. He arrived at the Menokin clearing and dismounted. Twigs snapped under his boots as he tramped the edges of the woodlands thinking this spot, as it was certainly cleared of original growth, must once have been an Indian village. He walked slowly around the area, peering in every direction trying to imagine men, women, children, and tepees, his mind racing through all the possibilities. Cameron, tethered on the far side, snorted occasionally or pawed the hard ground. Otherwise there was silence everywhere.

In an hour, the sun's warmth drew a steamy vapor to hover above the large clearing. By squinting his eyes, he had no trouble envisioning the area plowed and hoed in neat furrows. By pressing his imagination he saw the small green shoots of tobacco leaf begin to appear. Having traversed the length and width and breadth of the clearing several times, branching off into the trees any number of times, he returned to the forest's edge where he'd started. The season's first snow clouds were beginning to gather in the northern sky. All around him grew the Tidewater winter greens. He paused to admire the berry-laden holly, the spreading bushes of laurel, the pines and savin, the red cedar. Under his feet mingled with damp leaves lay a veritable carpet of acorns and chestnuts. Bending down he filled his hands with the nuts, letting them trickle through his fingers and bump to the ground. Then, gazing above, he stared at the towering heights of the lofty trees that had borne them. The oak leaves, now a rich russet brown, still clung stubbornly to the branches. They were always the last to give up. A woodpecker's sharp staccato drummed over his head. Invading the stillness, it jarred his aloneness. In that instant he knew. The relief of decision sent him bounding to his feet.

"Men-o-kin!" he shouted, dwelling on each syllable and loving the sound. "Do you hear me? Listen! I, Francis Lightfoot Lee, am yours! Your lands shall be my lands. And we shall call our house by your name ... Menokin!" His heart pounded as he waited ... and the echo that bounced back gave promise to his pronouncement.

Mid-December 1768 found the Northern Neck plantation countryside shrouded in white. The snow, heavier than normal, was piled six or more inches thick along the shores of the partially frozen rivers. Animal tracks crossed and recrossed the buried fields where no man had walked. The great houses despite thick walls were cold and drafty, and hundreds of logs a day were needed to keep the many fireplaces burning. In the slave quarters it was much worse. The cabins afforded very basic protection and the Negro families huddled within, venturing out only when forced. At Mount Airy excitement was building over the wedding and the plans for Menokin House. Until the snow came. Then the battle against the elements shadowed everything. Carts were sent daily to the forest to bring back wood. Sturdy shoes and boots were found to be in short supply and there were several cases of frostbite. An old mulatto man they called Doc Ephrim told them to plunge their feet in a bucket of melted snow for a while before attempting to warm them. It was a trick the Indians used, he said. The unfortunates howled in pain, but it seemed to work. Only one man lost a toe.

The third morning following the storm Francis rose early. Unable to sleep, he called to Ben to stir the fire. It had died to a few embers. When there was no response from the slave, he wrapped in a bed quilt and tended to the fire, grumbling. The next sensible thing seemed to be to get dressed before he froze, having been forced to part with the quilt in order to stoke the fire. Damn that Ben, he thought, where was he anyway? The water in the wash bowl had a film of ice on it. "By God, it's bloody cold this morning," Francis announced to the empty room. He wondered if that was why he hadn't slept well. Or had he had too much of John Tayloe's good punch last evening? No, it was something more disturbing that had made him restless during the night. A finger of fear tugged at the back of his thoughts. It continued to fret him as he pushed his arms into the heavy dark coat. Through the frosty pane in the south dependency he saw Ben hurrying across the courtyard from the kitchen house. What was the idiot doing out so early? And without seeing to the fire before he left. Ben's arms were empty even now, and there was only one log and a few pieces of kindling left.

The slave burst into the chamber as though pursued by a flock of demons, and crossed immediately to the fire. Stamping one foot and then the other, Ben blew on his fingers. "It's Cate, Marse Frank. She done had her baby. A girl, puny lookin', but breathin'." Ben was beside himself. In his excitement he almost forgot who he was talking to. "Dat Cate, she one hell-of-a fighter all right. She done had a bad time, a awful time. I help't Isaac keep de fires goin'. We was up de whole night."

Francis stared at his slave. He didn't know why the news should make him out of sorts, but it did. "Well, my fire nearly went out! That girl should be damned thankful she could give birth in the nursery chambers instead of out in the quarter," he grumped.

"Yas-suh, Marse Frank." The big black man turned, shaking his head in puzzlement. Marse Frank sure wasn't himself this morning. "I'll git some wood," he offered, heading for the door.

Immediately Francis was sorry for his impatience. He vowed to approach the remainder of the day with better temper. He certainly didn't want to subject Becky to such foul humor. Finishing up the sketches for the house should raise his spirits. The rough plan was to be sent to an architect as soon as they were certain what they wanted. Tayloe suggested several talented men; William Buckland had designed Mount Airy's interior and John Ariss had been recently in the county. But, of course, the colonel had said, they'd also require the services of a skilled housewright to carry out the plans once they were drawn. Francis knew this was partially what was at the root of his bad humor. Tayloe prodded, suggested, and interfered daily with his own ideas for Menokin House. Becky defended her father saying "Papa only wants to be sure we have a solid mansion, stone built, with two strong dependencies. Smaller than Mount Airy, but of similar design. The rest is up to us." But it hadn't been that way entirely.

Around noon Francis was alone in the library. Becky had gone to visit Cate and the new baby. Trying to keep warm, he finished off his second glass of Madeira. An idea had just come to him for a large wine cellar. It could be built right on the excavation site before the house went up. the ceiling would be vaulted as in the one in the Williamsburg Governor's Palace. It would be a room within a room, built to keep the cool away from the floorboards of the house above and the sleeping rooms of the house slaves next to it. It could have a full sized door that might be locked for security. He hurried to transmit his idea to paper. Of course the vault should be constructed of brick or stone. Brick would probably make it more simple to curve the ceiling; he'd discuss it with the architect as soon as he was chosen.

He raised his head, listening. It sounded like a visitor in the snowy yard. It must mean the roads were passable. Maybe tomorrow he could ride to Hickory Hill. He'd enjoyed the visit with John Turberville last month; the business venture John proposed bore further discussion, and he wanted to get a first hand look at the fulling mill that was underway. The more he considered it, the more he thought he might like to invest an interest in it.

The door to the library opened suddenly. Becky stood there. He started to beckon her to look at his plan for the wine cellar, then realized something was dreadfully wrong. When she didn't move from the doorway, he knew he was about to learn the reason for his morning's premonition.

"I'm so sorry, Francis. I wish I didn't have to tell you."

"What? Tell me what?"

"That was a servant from Sabine Hall. They received word from Chantilly yesterday. Your brother has sent you a letter." She crossed the room, handing it to him. "Mrs. Lee is dead."

Without speaking he pulled the wax off and opened the folded sheet, scanning the words quickly. "I've known it was coming.

I told you it would happen soon." The little wrinkles around his eyes twitched. "He wants me to go there. Richard needs me." He remembered vividly his promise to Anne. "I'll leave immediately."

"But Francis, the snow! The slave said it was drifted in spots and quite impossible. You must wait a few days. Richard certainly won't expect you yet."

"No, I can't wait. The Negro got through. So will I. I'll be ready in an hour. You're not to worry, do you understand? I'll be all right." He hurried from the hall leaving her and his dreams of a wine cellar in the library.

"Yes, darling. I'll try not to worry," she said to his disappearing back. "Not to worry at all." It was the first time she had called him by an endearment. Unplanned, it was as natural as sleeping or waking and she whispered it again into the empty hall ... darling.

He was gone a fortnight, but to Becky it seemed an eternity. The snow had melted and she ceased to have concern on that score, but he'd told her of his fondness for Anne Lee and how once he'd even fancied himself a little bit in love with his brother's wife. Becky guessed how difficult these days following her death must be for him. Searching his tired, sad eyes, she knew she'd been right. She led him to the orangery where they could be alone. As frequently happened in tidewater's Northern Neck the weather had reversed itself, teasing them with a mock spring day. The sun was warm and they settled on a stone bench, a robe tucked around their knees. They sat so close she felt the warmth of his thigh through the fabric of her skirts.

His arm was tight around her and she pressed her head into the curve of his shoulder. Francis was again impressed with how naturally the various parts of their bodies seemed to fit together. It was a good omen.

"It seemed forever you were gone. More like four weeks, not two. Was it an awful time, darling?" She had practiced saying the word in his absence.

He looked surprised. "I like it when you call me that."

"Then I shall do it often," she promised. "Tell me about what happened. Then your sadness will pass more quickly. I think people should talk about things that hurt them. It makes it easier to accept the bad things we can't change."

He was amazed at the wisdom from one so young, and it made him decide to share his heartbreak. "It was the very worst of times, Becky. Richard is devastated. He's a shadow of his former self. When I arrived the housekeeper told me he'd scarcely eaten nor slept in five days. He didn't want to talk much but I had him willing to eat before I left. And he was even beginning to recognize the children's loss and give them some comfort."

"Then it's a blessing you insisted on going there when you did, isn't it?"

"Yes, I had to go." He looked at her gratefully, knowing he couldn't have stood it if she chastised him about leaving in the snow. "We buried Anne in the burnt house field. That's our family ground, near the ruins of old Mount Pleasant. You can't imagine the thud as the first clods of frozen earth fell on the coffin. It was dreadful and so final." Staring blankly at the river, he remembered the sound. "She was a very special woman, and will be sorely missed by all who had the good fortune to know her..." His voice trailed away.

"I'm sorry, Francis. I am so sorry."

He forced a smile, realizing what a comfort it was to have someone of your own with whom to share life's sorrows and joys. "Well, it's time to put it behind us. She's in the hands of God." With a finger he raised her chin to look in her eyes. "What were you up to while I was away?"

"Do you really want to know?"

"I do. From now on I want to know everything about you."

Her eyes sparkled. "I selected the fabric for my wedding gown! Nan, our seamstress, has begun the cutting."

"Where in heaven's name did you get it so quickly?"

"Mama had it. It's the most beautiful pale green silk you ever laid your eyes on. She purchased it for draperies in the dining room but after a day of my pleading and carrying on she agreed to part with ten yards for my dress!"

"I'm so happy, my love, that you'll wear a green dress on our wedding day," he laughed. "It is exactly what I hoped for."

In an hour they were chilled and started back to the house. On the way, he told her of the day he spent at Hickory Hill with John Turberville after the funeral, and before heading back to Mount Airy. Hickory Hill was on the Nomini River in sight of Nomini Hall, Robert Carter's mansion. Robert was Colonel Landon's nephew and ran an exceedingly fine plantation. At the age of thirty he'd been named to the Governor's Council and was greatly respected. Hickory Hill, by comparison to its neighbor, was a modest house but Francis always enjoyed his visits there. Talk of the fulling mill had dominated the day.

"It's going to take considerable cash to furnish the machinery and get the place set up. Then of course, a fuller must be hired, and John thinks he's located just the fellow. He's from up north and is experienced in all phases of shearing, dyeing, and the main purpose of the mill, cleaning the wool. The process raises the nap of the fabric to the surface and the fibers are compacted and freed of all grease particles. I think it's time we encouraged such industry in Virginia. Now, let us hope we can convince every planter to invest in large flocks of sheep!"

"It sounds, darling, as though you have a mighty knowledge of the whole thing."

He was delighted to have impressed her. "Well I ought. I agreed to go into partnership with him."

∽

The season of Christmas was upon them. Boughs of pine and holly decorated the house. Fruits, hoarded in the cellar for the occasion were piled on the sideboards. In the evenings candles blazed in every room and guests came and went daily. Work, except in preparation for the holiday, virtually ceased on the plantation. Some of the older Negroes spent the days half drunk, and cockfights and gambling continued in the barn almost around the clock. The black children raced around the yard busy at their silly games, while the young Tayloe girls chased after them, overjoyed at several days freedom from lessons. The master was very lenient at Christmastime.

But on the eve of the celebration another death brought sadness to Becky and Francis. The girl child of the slave, Cate, died. Becky found Cate rocking back and forth, back and forth, next to the small wooden bed. Every so often she moaned, but there were no tears left to fall. The baby was stiff-looking and silent in the cradle. Becky wished she hadn't looked at it.

"Oh, Catey, it's so sad," she cried. "But you'll have other babies. I just know it."

Cate stared briefly at her mistress. She forgave her for not understanding. Miss Becky had never held a baby to her breast. "It won't make up fo' dis one," she replied.

In the morning the sounds of guns firing across the river to welcome the birth of the Savior reached Mount Airy. Becky found Cate still rocking near the child's cradle, even though the dead infant was no longer there. Isaac must have taken the tiny bundle away during the night, she thought. "See Catey? Today the guns fire for your little one. The infant Jesus has taken her to heaven and she sleeps on the whitest of clouds with all the angels to watch over her." But she hurried away, fearful the slave would see her chin quivering, her eyes uncertain and wet with tears.

A few days later Francis departed for Loudoun farm. He must settle his affairs so that he would be back for the spring wedding and the construction of the Menokin house. Becky stood beside him as he prepared to leave.

"We'll have no more sadness when next we meet, darling. Promise me that."

"I can safely promise you that will be the happiest time of my life, my love. Then we'll soon be looking forward to the births of our own beautiful babes."

"Hurry back, Francis," she whispered. "I do love you so ... and I can hardly wait."

He pondered her parting words as he rode away, wondering if he understood exactly what she had meant. He dared to hope that he did.

The Wedding

Becky awoke to the sound of voices in the courtyard, heard the stamp and snort of horses on the early morning air. Next to her Anne continued to sleep, rosy little girl cheeks buried in the heap of rumpled quilts she always hoarded. She hoped Francis didn't have this annoying habit. She laughed aloud, thinking it probably wouldn't matter if he did. Flushing at the thought of Francis in her bed, she pushed aside the bed curtains. Cate was at the window. Several months had passed since the loss of her baby and she, like everyone else, had been caught up in the flurry of wedding plans. What Becky didn't know was that she was pregnant again, and hadn't even told Isaac. She stood, hands on hips, bobbing her head in tune with the shouts below.

Becky was glad Cate's hair wasn't kinky like the others. It was always clean and hardly greasy at all. This morning she was dressed in a starched white apron with her head tied in a bright blue bandana. She looked fresh and bright as though the night had been good to her, Becky thought, trying to imagine Cate with Isaac's arms around her. What was it like, being married?

"Dey's goin' fo' turkeys, Miss Becky. I declare, if'n Mistah Lee don't look handsome dis mornin'. All dress't in a blue coat an' golden britches he is."

Becky shoved her aside, wild to peek. But Cate drew her mistress firmly away from the window. "T'ain't proper fo you to stan' in your nightdress, an' de gen'lmens below!"

"Oh pooh, Cate. They're not looking anyway."

"Yas-ma'm, dey is indeed. Mistah Lee he done waved to me already," she boasted.

"Mama says it's bad luck for me to see him on my wedding day. Do you believe that?" Becky asked, certain Cate would be on her side. It was not that Cate wasn't superstitious, just that she was superstitious about different things.

"Dat's jes' white folks talk. Ain't goin' make a speck o' diff'ence in de bed tonight, Miss Becky, w'ether you done seed him or not dis mornin'!"

Becky giggled. "Catey, you do know how to say the awfulest things! Mama'd just die if she heard you telling me such a thing."

The mulatto grinned. "Well, now ain't it de truth? Ain't it jes' de truth?" Her black eyes danced thinking of Isaac and last night. "You *is* plannin' on climbin' in bed wit him tonight, ain't you, Miss Becky?"

Becky sobered. She had thought of little else since Francis's return from the west. "Of course I am. You know I am. But, Cate, don't tease me about it, because I'm scared. I remember when you were scared once, too. Does it hurt?"

"Oh Miss Becky, I … no, it don't hurt a bit, not if'n you loves yo'r man. You do love Mistah Lee?"

"I do love him so very much. You know I do."

Cate nodded. She did know, and approved the choice her mistress had made. She'd observed a gentleness about Mr. Lee. His eyes were kind, and he never said cruel things or made ugly remarks to Ben or the Mount Airy servants. And he adored Miss Becky. That was written all over his face, visible for anyone to see. But most of all in his favor, he'd helped arrange the purchase of Isaac. "Now don' you worry none, Miss Becky. Mistah Lee, he ain't goin' hurt you no matter what. Why, I bets he goin' be so gent'l you'll think you's on a cloud, 'staid of de bed!" With this, Cate bustled away. She had to get the day's clothing organized.

Becky smiled nervously at her departing back, thinking that the day of her marriage had truly begun. How would it end? Leaning out the window she watched the men depart on the early morning hunt. The sun was barely up, a thin mist still hung over everything. A covey of quail startled from the brush, crossing in front of the horses. The men nodded to each other, finding it a good sign. Philip Lee was there, and Richard Henry. She spotted John Turberville and both Robert Carters, besides her father and Francis, before they urged their horses to a gallop and disappeared behind the trees that bordered the Mount Airy lane.

John Tayloe was in high spirits as he led the way up-river. His house was filled with guests and more would be arriving every hour. His tables were piled with food and drink; there were fish and crabs fresh caught from the Rappahannock, roast mutton, a calf had been slaughtered, hams were smoked and ready, fruits were there, both dried and brandied, and puddings, cakes, and breads. Rebe would see to it all. Nothing would be overlooked in the preparation of the wedding feast, so that Becky would have a day to long remember. And with luck they would bag a turkey or two. "They were setting the fires under the spits when we left, Frank. How many birds do you think we should try for?"

Francis was having a hard time keeping his mind on the business they were about. "Oh, I should think two, maybe three." All he wanted to do before the wedding was to escape for a few hours to Menokin, by himself. He began to plot how he might arrange just that. He'd had it on his mind for several days.

"I understand our brother Thomas may come for the celebration." Philip Lee sat his horse erectly, a man proud of himself and his steed. It was Richard to whom he spoke. "Even Hannah, according to Rebecca," he went on, sounding a bit miffed. The two brothers had dropped behind the other riders.

"So I've heard." Richard wasn't sure where Philip was going with this, so he decided to be blunt. "For Loudoun's sake, Phil, let's keep the peace today. It's his day, you know, not a time to air our family squabbles."

Philip sniffed, looking displeased. "Rest assured, I hadn't planned on making a public scene over our dear sister's indiscretions. Do you take me for a fool?"

The dogs had flushed something. Their baying echoed loudly across the countryside.

"Only a red fox!" Tayloe shouted. "I caught a glimpse of his brush." The grooms tore after the dogs, heading them back on the right trail.

"Mr. fox will live to see another day," Richard chuckled, glad for the diversion.

"Yes ... and as I was saying before the interruption by Tayloe's rather poorly trained hounds..."

"By God, Phil, did you not sleep well last night? You're certainly not in a festive humor today," Richard countered, beginning to wish he'd remained at Mount Airy to wait for Thomas.

"As a matter of fact, no. I didn't sleep well at all. Mrs. Lee was somewhat ... indisposed." The truth was Elizabeth spent the night on a chaise complaining his breathing kept her awake when she suffered one of her headaches. The headaches seemed to be more and more frequent, and he was beginning to suspect she used them to suit her own convenience. But it was Hannah's possible presence at the wedding which disturbed him at the moment, and he meant to get it off his chest. "Well, I think it's damned unfair of her to impose herself on a gathering of this nature with virtually everyone we know invited," he blustered, expecting Richard would know he was not referring to Elizabeth.

"Unfair? Why unfair? In poor taste maybe, but not unfair." To himself Richard thought Francis would most likely think it courageous, and would be delighted to see their sister.

"Humph! Well, I for one will be avoiding her should she come. You can be assured of that."

"Try to remember one thing, Phil, about Hannah. Her marriage to Gawin Corbin was probably forced on her. At the very least, we know it was abominably unhappy." Richard spurred his horse ahead leaving Philip to his grumblings and his sniffing. There were times he felt incredibly sorry for Hannah, and this was one of them.

The turkeys they shot were not large. Scrawny, half-grown birds, they were. Tayloe insisted on routing out five of them. Finally, he was satisfied and the party turned homeward. At the mill pond Francis allowed his horse to fall behind.

"Go on," he called. "I have a thing or two to check at Menokin." He knew his brothers were interested in seeing the place but he didn't invite them. There was time for that later, he thought, letting the forest swallow him. Arriving at what was to be the front of the house, he slipped the reins of his horse over a low branch and made his way around a pile of large oaks felled for timbers. Confident that he was indeed alone, he let out a loud "ya-hoo!" and dashed headlong to the foot of the hill, a distance of perhaps a quarter mile. Forgetting his light colored breeches he threw himself face down on the thick green moss of the creek bank and drank deeply of the clear water. Every inch of his being felt charged and alive. Life had never been so sweet. No doubts plagued him. He was in love, head over heels, as he had never been before. And would never be again. In the peace of Menokin's welcome silence he contemplated the joys of marital bliss that awaited him.

I will be sweet with her and oh, so tender. I'll be kind to her, and amiable. He chuckled, boasting of all he would be that night. I will not be excitable nor rush her if she's not ready. I'll be patient, considerate, loving, and thoughtful. And I won't make passionate love to her the moment we're alone. No indeed, I'll most definitely wait a proper few minutes at least.

"My friend," said Francis, poking at a curious looking beetle with a stick, "you clearly do not see what great things I be about. This very evening I am to be wed. I have come this morning to contemplate the terrace garden I will one day build for my beautiful bride." He watched as the beetle continued an endlessly patient struggle to make its way around the moving stick in its path.

In a while he tired of the game and began the long climb back to the house site. Pausing frequently, he surveyed the slope and angles of the hill. He'd already ordered seeds and bulbs from England, but the details of where to place them must be worked out carefully. Becky's terraces would be blanketed with jonquils and star-of-Bethlehem in the spring. Later they'd burst forth with the heady scent of lilac and the purplish pink blossoms of crepe myrtle. He wanted roses of every shade on the upper levels, and violets, ivy and periwinkle to grace the slopes. He had first thought to place some fruit trees, perhaps peach or cherry in an area of the terrace. Now he decided to keep all fruit orchards on the other side of the house. It was quite an undertaking and one that excited him greatly. He yearned suddenly to discuss the plans with his father, and wondered if Thomas Lee would approve of the layout he imagined. Of one thing he was certain, he would most surely have approved of the choice of Becky Tayloe for a wife.

Francis stopped a last time to look behind him. In some underbrush to his right he heard a rustle and decided it was worth investigating. A thick clump of last year's wild honeysuckle vine clustered around a level spot under a large beech tree. Circling the area he couldn't locate what had made the noise, but he came upon an opening in low-hanging branches barely large enough for him to pass through if he bent down. Once inside he discovered he could stand erect. To his amazement he found himself in a natural summer-house. Bushes and tree branches formed a sanctuary whose leafy green branches would form a sort of bower in a few weeks, allowing sunlight to filter in from above. The ground was covered with a lush grass that was flattened, probably by an animal seeking shelter, and wild violets were beginning to peek through. Maybe a doe and her fawn had wintered here.

He wondered how many other things he had yet to discover on his acres. There were years ahead of him during which he would search every corner, but he couldn't imagine finding anything as intriguing as the hidden bower he'd just stumbled upon.

⁓

Throughout the day carriages and chariots continued to arrive. Word of the romance had spread far and wide. There gathered Lees, Tayloes, Carters, Fitzhughs, Lloyds, and Corbins; also Turbervilles, Washingtons, Allertons, Jones, and Lewises, Parkers, Gaskins and Pages, many of whom traveled considerable distance to enjoy the festive occasion. The great house accepted the crowds of guests as graciously as did its host and hostess. Laughter and the shouts of children echoed from room to room. A group of musicians played in the great hall from noon until night. Isaac Giberne would perform the ceremony. Boughs of wild dogwood and laurel leaf decorated the small altar erected for the celebration of the vows, and a red plush kneeler had been borrowed from the church. For the moment, however, there was more interest centered around the enormous punch bowl in the dining room; John Tayloe's recipe for brandy punch was well known.

Richard Henry Lee had been waiting and watching for a long time for the green coach from Peckatone to bounce up the lane. He made his way down the steps behind the black grooms who were posted to meet arriving guests. The door to the coach was opened and Hannah Corbin appeared. Seeing Richard, his hand held out to her, she paused, her eyes misting. Then her chin came up, and he was very glad he'd decided to meet her. "I'll escort you inside, if I may, Hannah. Francis will be so pleased to see you," he said, taking her arm.

Hannah squeezed her brother's hand but didn't try to speak. There seemed no need. When they entered, Richard made a point of crossing slowly through each room regally nodding in every direction, as only Richard could do. Hannah followed his lead, wondering if she could ever have managed it alone. It wasn't that she'd become a recluse. Far from it. She and Richard Hall had many friends. There were her neighbors, and the Baptists, and others of Dr. Hall's acquaintances. But things had remained cool with her own family, and these were all relatives and close friends of the Lee and Tayloe families. The brother and sister approached a group of ladies clustered in a corner. Here, with a gracious bow, Richard Henry deposited his sister.

"Thank you, Richard. It was most thoughtful of you to meet me," Hannah said quietly.

After an uncomfortable pause, conversation resumed jerkily. The ladies hovered on the brink of including the newcomer to their group in their chatter. Inwardly Hannah seethed at their thinly veiled hypocrisy. Not a one of them brave enough to accept the man she loved on any but the prescribed grounds. If indeed any of them knew what love was. For the thousandth time she marveled that the passions she had known for Richard Lingan Hall had not diminished in seven years. The very thought of him made each new day a miracle. She wished she hadn't let him persuade her to come without him today. He'd argued it would be easier for her in company with so many of the Lees. But now she yearned for nothing so much as one glimpse of his deep blue eyes. What she saw there more than made up for the fact that their alliance had not been entirely accepted by her family. Lack of invitation to Stratford had certainly posed no hardship. She abhorred Philip's picayune ways and thought his treatment of their younger siblings following the deaths of their parents, utterly petty and outrageous. Yet she was never certain how Thomas, Richard and Francis felt. But she felt great fondness for them, and their opinions mattered to her. Today Richard had certainly given his acceptance. It was a great victory for the Widow Corbin.

At that moment she spotted Becky on the staircase. The girl seemed to float in the pale green of her silken gown. Hannah could see why Frank had chosen her above the others he might have taken for his bride. She was amazed to see the child making her way straight through the crowd in her own direction.

"I'm so happy you were able to come," Becky said warmly, taking Hannah's large hands in her own small ones.

Hannah studied her new sister-in-law for a moment, liking what she saw. "I was most pleased to have been invited, Miss Tayloe," she responded, smiling.

The smile brightened her entire face, Becky thought, and her eyes crinkled like Francis's did. "I should be most pleased if you'd call me Becky. I do hope when you come to visit Francis and me you will bring Doctor Hall with you. And the children also, for you'll always be welcome in our house." Although she meant this with all of her heart she said it now for the benefit of the eavesdropping women, as well as to reassure Hannah.

"Here comes Mr. Lee," someone exclaimed behind Becky. "Quick, hide or he'll see you before the vows are taken!"

Becky revolved slowly. She had no intention of hiding. She'd waited for days to have Francis see her in the new green dress. Once she saw him, however, she forgot her gown. She couldn't take her eyes off him. Watching his every step as he made his way through the crowd, she saw not his buff colored waistcoat and breeches, tailored to flatter the slender frame, nor the elegant trimming of gold braid and brass buttons, nor the elaborate buckles set with hundreds of glittering stones that held the breeches at his knees; nor did she notice that he wasn't wearing a wig as were so many others but, rather had chosen to have his hair brushed smoothly into a neat beribboned queue; what she saw was simply *her* Francis.

"You are beautiful!" he exclaimed, ignoring the lovely yards of softly gathered green silk that molded the girl he loved, and looking directly into her eyes.

"So are you," she whispered, feeling as though she might burst into tears at any moment. "Oh my darling, so are you!"

It seemed to Becky that the next hours flew past. Before she knew it, she could call herself Mrs. Lee. She supped for the first time as the wife of Francis Lee, and was toasted by all in the room. If the usual toasts to the King were fewer, only a few noticed it. When the dancing began she found herself safely in the arms of her new husband. She waved across the hall at her parents who looked, she thought, a bit sad. She supposed it was that way when one's children married, but quickly forgetting them, she turned back to Francis as they waited for a reel to be organized. The fiddlers tuned their instruments and everyone lined up.

"Happy?" he whispered.

"Oh, yes, and you?"

"More than I could have dreamed possible. Except it is quite possible I have had too much punch, and then the wine with dinner. I now find myself thirsty again and will probably need more when this dance is finished!"

"Is that all?" she laughed. "Well, it's your wedding eve. Drink what you will!"

Later she asked, "Francis, the children are conspiring against us and have threatened to put snakes and frogs in our chamber to frighten us. Do you think they'd dare?"

"My love, boys threaten such things but rarely do they carry out the threats. I remember doing the same myself. They can't even know which chamber is ours. So stop your worry." He wondered if she was worried about that time when they would finally be alone together. He was.

The punch quenched his thirst and felt warm as it went down. It so pleased him that he had a second, all in rather short order. His young cousin Harry Lee was repeating that bloody story about some hunt he'd been on recently. The punch seemed to be working inside him. He heard Harry's voice grow fainter and then louder. Feeling a bit light-headed, he thought it best to find a spot to sit down and headed for the library, but Becky waylaid him before he reached it.

If she noticed his woozy state she didn't comment. She simply took him by the arm and led him quickly to the back staircase. "Francis, hurry! I have permission from Mama and Papa to leave while everyone is dancing. Else we shall never get away. I doubt they'll even miss us for a while. Then they'll be too tipsy to even care. Go to our chamber, and I'll be along as soon as Cate helps me out of this dress."

He stared at her, barely comprehending. He reached a decision as they climbed the steps, realizing he couldn't take his new wife to bed while in his present state. It would ruin everything. What a fool he'd been to drink beyond his capacity. She had a right to expect more than he was prepared to give at the moment. In his present condition, he could barely walk, let alone ... "After consideration, careful consideration of the matter I think it appropriate that I ... uh ... not trouble you with my person tonight." He didn't know why it was funny, but he heard himself laughing. "I'm not very sober. Sleep well, my love." His tongue felt as though it had molasses stuck to it. Brushing her cheek with a kiss, he lost his balance briefly. Without a backward glance, for he couldn't bear to look at her face, he lurched down the hall. Alone in the chamber prepared for a night of nuptial bliss he collapsed fully clothed into the softness of the high four poster.

Becky, nearly in hysterics, found the astonished Cate. It took the slave five minutes to calm her enough to understand what had happened. "He doesn't want me, he's gone to bed alone!" Becky wailed.

Cate stared in disbelief. "I ain't never heard o' sech a thing." Trying to think, she wrapped her arms around her distraught mistress.

Becky suddenly remembered Anne. Anne would discover her here alone. "Miserable wretched man! How could he do such a thing to me? I hate him!"

Cate grabbed her by the shoulders. Pressing her fingers hard into the soft flesh, she shook, as hard as she was able. "Now you lissen to me. Stop dat. You no mo' hate him den you kin fly. Miss Becky, dey ain't no man what don' want his woman on his weddin' night. An' Mistah Lee, he not no diff'rnt den de rest. I don' know why he done sech a dumb thing, but we's got to fix it. Umm-hmm, we's goin' fix it," she declared. "He's prob'ly 'skeered he might hurt you, you bein' so young an' all." Humming, she began to loosen the dress, unfastening the countless tiny buttons down the front.

Becky stopped crying and stepped out of the gown as Cate untied the stays, giving her an immediate sense of relief. She began to pull the pins out of her hair, letting it fall loosely over her shoulders. "Are you sure?" she asked. "I want you to be sure."

"Mm-hmm," Cate answered, fingers flying. "You's goin' to him. Sit still so's I kin brush yo'r hair."

"Wash my face, Catey. Scrub the tears off. I want to look beautiful for him."

The long gown was made of soft white lawn. It tied under the bosom with a blue satin ribbon and lent her figure a fullness which pleased her. For a moment she stood before the looking glass. Running her fingers down her sides to smooth the nightdress, she felt the same tingle she'd experienced while dancing with Francis. She waited while Cate made sure the hall was empty then, in a rush to be with him, hurried to the chamber that had been prepared for them, turning at the door to wave a thank you to Cate.

Becky disappeared inside and Cate returned to fold the discarded wedding garments. Having completed her task she padded down the hall after her mistress. Outside the door she listened for a minute and, satisfied, settled down against the wall to sleep feeling quite pleased with herself.

Ben appeared in the upper hall and spying Cate, he approached warily. Talking to Cate, he had discovered, was usually disturbing. He looked at her every chance he got, but tried to avoid conversation when possible. She always managed to challenge him, making him somehow feel a fool. She was too damn smart for a gal, that's what. "What d' you think you's doin' here?" he demanded.

Annoyed, she whispered, "I 'spect de same thing you are, ol' man. Ain't no one gittin' pas' me to bother Miss Becky an' Mistah Lee dis night."

He'd expected a smart answer. "Well ... you kin go out t' Isaac now. I bin tendin' Marse Frank's bus'ness fo' as long's I 'member, an' I 'spect things goin' stay dat way." He gave her a fierce look. "An' b'sides, a gal ain't got t' sleep on the floor when ol' Ben's aroun'," he snapped, hoping that impressed her.

Cate, deciding there was no point in arguing, drew her heels under her and pushed to her feet. She'd much rather sleep with Isaac anyway. "Thanks, Ben." She moved toward the stairs, taking her time, not wanting him to think she intended to jump every time he felt like giving an order. She took her orders from Miss Becky and no one else.

Ben smiled from ear to ear at the sway of retreating hips. That Isaac was one lucky nigger. Yawning, he took her place against the wall.

The brief rest had helped Francis recover from the worst of his giddiness. Now he lay in a dejected state where he'd fallen on the bed. What a bloody fool he was. The noble gesture of an intoxicated idiot had left him miserable and alone on his wedding night. Where were all the tender scenes he'd dreamed of this morning on the Menokin hillside? He cursed himself for an utter buffoon and wondered irritably why Ben didn't come to help him undress. Then he heard the door open, but it wasn't Ben who entered.

"Darling?" She stopped just inside, waiting for a sign.

He couldn't believe his ears, nor his eyes when he saw the white gown. His weak knees were forgotten as the desire to hold her pushed all other thought from his mind. Lifting her lightly in his arms, he carried her to the bed, where he buried his face in her jasmine scented hair. "I'm sorry. Please forgive me. What have I ever done to make me worthy of you?"

"I love you, Francis. That's all that matters. I do love you so, even when you do crazy things like you did tonight."

"Are you afraid?" he whispered against her throat, wanting to forget what he'd done an hour before.

"A little ... I think."

"You mustn't be afraid."

"All right, I'm not afraid."

"I'm going to touch you, love. Here, and here," he felt her shiver beneath his fingers but it wasn't from fear. "And here. After a while it will make you want me, and when that happens, it won't hurt."

"I already want you, darling."

"I know. But this is wanting in a different way. You'll see." The punch, far from rendering him inept he discovered, had given him the courage he needed. But had he really needed it, after all? There were no tears, no holding back, and no shame on the part of either. Only tenderness, and joy in the give and take of their bodies as he led and she followed, in the discovery of love.

Much later Francis lay on his back, an arm outstretched. Becky put her head in the crook of his shoulder sighing with content-ment. "So this is what it's like to be married, Becky Lee," he said, trying out the sound of her new name. He loved the feel of her silky hair across his chest.

"I guess this is what it's like, Francis Lee. Tell me, what do you think of it?" she asked.

"Well, I ..."

"No, wait! Let me guess. I think I know what you're going to say."

"Oh, and what is that?"

"You'll first make that teasing half-smile, and twist your eye-brow just a tiny bit to show you're concentrating, then you'll say in a very droll fashion, 'wonderful ... wonderful', and of course all in a deep, very serious voice."

Francis smiled into the dimly lit room. "You think you know me pretty well, do you?" he laughed, pulling her even closer.

"Not too well yet, but I intend to spend a lifetime getting to know you ever so much better. Every inch of you."

"Well, I suggest you wait just a minute while I put out the candle before we continue the lesson, or we'll burn the house down." Dousing the wick quickly he returned to her and their love making began again. This time Becky knew what was expected of her; the miracle of love was no longer a dark mystery. When finally they slept, she curled so close to him it wasn't going to matter a whit if he hoarded the quilt or not.

PART II
RICHMOND COUNTY
1770 – 1775

"... never think that the collecting the Duty laid for the sole purpose of raising a revenue, in England or the Colonies makes any difference with regard to American claims, for since the Parliament of Great Britain in the first place obliges us to take from them what we consider as the conveniences or necessaries of life, if we have them at all—then to lay a Duty upon them is equally a tax not laid by our {own} representatives for the sole purpose of raising {a revenue}. I'm in a hurry to wait upon a Lady. Adieu."

Letter, F. L. Lee to Landon Carter
Mount Airy, April 9, 1771

On the Threshold

Francis and William Lee were married, just as Francis had predicted, within a short time of each other in 1769. The news of William's marriage to cousin Hannah Ludwell came in a letter from William himself. He was *"overjoyed at the full measure of his felicity,"* he wrote, *"at having taken unrivaled possession of the dear and amiable Miss Ludwell."* Sometimes William sounded as priggish as Arthur, Francis laughed, not meaning it in a critical way.

The main thrust of William's letter, it soon became apparent, was to convince Richard and Francis that he requested their assistance in the management of his wife's affairs in Virginia; as Robert Carter Nicholas, treasurer of the colony, had been named as one of the trustees of Philip Ludwell's estate, William had written to Mr. Nicholas that he was appointing his two brothers to look after his share. Due to the recent death of his wife's sister Fanny, the entire estate would be divided between the remaining daughters, Hannah and Mrs. Lucy Paradise. The Green Spring Plantation at Jamestown was to go to William and Hannah Lee.

What William was anxious to ensure was that the Williamsburg tenements go to the Paradises, while he should inherit the acreage contiguous with Green Spring. He was apparently aware that the condition of the tenements had been declining steadily and wanted no part in that situation; repairs would be expensive and a sale would be difficult to accomplish from England, thus he thought either alternative would bring little profit for his trouble in any case. It was clear that William intended his wife's inheritance to be a moneymaking proposition, and with the proper overseer he thought to make a handsome profit out of the Green

Spring Plantation. *"However,"* he wrote, *"as I am involved in setting up a new business plying the tobacco trade from the American colonies to London, plus attending to my duties as a new husband, I am prevented from journeying to Virginia. Will you or Richard make arrangements to attend the division of the estate in my behalf if you are notified by the trustees when it will take place?"*

It was clear he assumed they not only could, but would do so. The two brothers looked at each other as Francis finished reading. "Well, it sounds as though Arthur knew what was in the offing when he wrote you that William had developed an interest in Hannah Ludwell," he commented, folding the letter. "He's fortunate she's coming into an inheritance so quickly, I might add. It should set his new business on a proper path, eh?"

The men sat puffing their pipes in the chamber Francis and Becky had shared at Mount Airy since their wedding. Richard Henry continued to stare thoughtfully toward the Rappahannock and the bustling seaport of Hobbs' Hole where he supposed William's ships would be docking. There they would be loaded with rich Virginia tobacco leaf bound for the British market. Or, at least that was the idea. "I think our brother will require our help in more ways than the settlement of Philip Ludwell's estate, Frank," he finally remarked.

"Why? How do you mean?"

"It isn't easy to build up a new business. There's much competition for our tobacco on this river as well as on Potomac. William will need someone to drum up trade for him. I know he says he's busy writing letters to influential planters, but that won't be enough. He's going to need us, also. Mark my words."

Francis shrugged. "I shouldn't mind it, I don't suppose. Why, in my area of the Neck alone, I could probably sign up any number of hogsheads for him. And if he and his new bride handle the various requests for purchases made by the planters and their families to send back on the return trip, and do it satisfactorily, all should go well enough."

Richard drew on his pipe but made no comment, so Francis continued. "but I'm concerned that I might not be much help to him when it comes to the estate, tied as I am at present to the construction of Menokin House. I dislike the idea of being away for more than a day or two."

"Tell me, how is it coming? I apologize, Loudoun, I have quite forgotten to ask."

Smiling, Francis answered, "The ground has been cleared, leveled where necessary ... the foundation for the cellar is nearly complete, and they're making progress with the timbers." His eyes brightened as he explained, "The architect came from Baltimore to view the site and made some minor changes to our placement, and now a local man is hired, a Mr. Dobson, to supervise the work. We're pleased with how well things have gone so far. You know, depending on when the Ludwell estate is settled, I truly may not be able to leave. If we're at a crucial stage, it won't be possible for me to be away, and we're almost ready to begin work on my wine vault."

Richard wasn't fooled. "Knowing you as I do, I have a feeling that means you're not very interested in Ludwell's division of the estate. Am I right?"

"You know me too well," Francis responded grudgingly. "It seems to me William would do better to take it as it comes, rather than trying to influence the trustees. I fear Mr. Treasurer isn't going to care for being pressured."

"Well, since I'm on my way to the assembly, which will probably last the usual three or four weeks, I'll try to look the situation over. Perhaps Mr. Nicholas and I could ride to Jamestown to view the condition of the plantation. If not, there's no telling when I'd be free to travel there again either. Quite likely not until October or November when the House is again called to session."

Francis decided that settled the subject, at least for the present. "I'm feeling a few regrets that I won't be with you this session," he said. "In ten years I've become accustomed to the maneuvering, the excitement of verbal battle. I shall miss it, I think. And with Parliament calling for 'our American trouble-makers' as someone put it, to be sent to Britain for trial, I can well imagine tempers will be high."

"You're no more sorry that I, my dear Loudoun, over your resignation from elected office. I've come to depend on you ... in many ways. But you know that."

"Yes, I do know it." He hoped Richard wouldn't bring up the loss of Anne. In an attempt at lightness he said, "Actually you'll probably not miss me at all. I read in the *Gazette* where Tom Jefferson was elected in Albemarle. That will add more than a few brains and good ideas to your liberal side of the patriotic arguments!"

Richard laughed, knowing there was truth indeed in the statement. Francis was capable enough when pressed, and loyal beyond question, yet he could be a reluctant politician at times, while young Mr. Jefferson was anything but reluctant.

Work progressed slowly but satisfactorily on the house at Menokin. Yet, however it progressed it wouldn't have been rapid enough for Francis and Becky. He knew they both felt the same about it, and were desperately eager for the privacy of a home of their own. The carpenter hired to hew the huge oak timbers was a master builder. He would continue after the framing was completed to accomplish most of the joining work. Slaves had been trained to shape the rough clay from the river shore into stones and bricks which would be used for the nogging between the corner posts and studding in the interior walls. The exterior surface of Menokin was to be foot-thick sandstone blocks quarried up-river. The job of transporting the huge blocks from the landing would be slow and tedious and Francis was anxious to get it underway.

It was a hot morning and Becky sat cross-legged, calico skirts tucked around her, on a stack of squared timbers. Resting elbows on knees and chin on hands, she contemplated the scene. It was several weeks since she'd accompanied Francis to the site, and there was much going on today. Her mother frowned on her being there, admonishing that it wasn't the place for a young gentlewoman, what with all the physical labor, sweat, and vulgar language that surely was present. But today, watching her husband moving busily from man to man, encouraging, asking questions, and occasionally offering a suggestion, Becky smiled contentedly, thinking her mother quite old-fashioned.

A number of extra slaves were present, Francis told her, as two sections of the heavy timbers were to be raised and joined for a corner of the house frame. Ben and Isaac were among them. Using long sturdy pikes, they were helping to brace the large wooden frame as the carpenter shouted instructions. Francis, architectural drawings in hand, discussed a point with Mr. Dobson, the housewright. Apparently satisfied with the answer, he came to sit beside her.

"How exciting it is," she exclaimed, making room for him. "Just imagine, we're actually witnessing the very first wall of our very own house! It's marvelous. I'm so glad you brought me with you this morning, darling."

Francis reached for her hand. It slipped firmly into his own as it always did. It was no longer necessary to contemplate that curious phenomenon of giving himself to the married state—it was done. With simplicity and honesty he and this amazing girl had come together. Each of them opened as a vessel to receive the other's love to fill the emptiness that had been their separate selves. Had he ever doubted the rightness of it? Perhaps rather, he had known without knowing how completely it would absorb him. For despite what he'd told Richard about missing the assembly, it seemed he had time only for love these days. Worldly concerns fled before their togetherness as leaves before an autumn wind, he thought. Days were filled with giving, taking and sharing of thoughts and dreams; the nights with giving, taking and sharing their bodies. There was room for nothing else it seemed, nor did he desire more. Seeing a puzzlement in her green eyes, he explained, "I was just thinking ... about us, Becky."

"I was, too. Perhaps not so seriously as you were. I was just wondering where we are going to put ... us. Did you hear what I said about the wall going up?"

"Indeed I did. The wall of the right front corner, which will be the formal sitting room," he announced happily.

Disengaging her hand, she picked up the drawings from his lap, spreading them before her. A frown creased her brow. "Francis, I've been thinking. I know you have your heart set on that arrangement, but I wonder if we might just talk about it." Encouraged by his genial expression she went on, "It seems to me, as the room is smaller and therefore more suited to our personal needs, that we might use it for the family. A daytime nursery perhaps, and our sitting room in the evening. The larger room in the rear which opens to the dining room, could then become the formal parlor. What do you think?"

"Are you sure then, that such an arrangement would please you more than the other?"

Kissing him on the cheek, she said, "Most definitely." He smelled like the soap from his shaving mixed with clean summer sweat. Comfortable smells for a husband.

"Then so be it. And on the upper floor we shall take the large rear room overlooking the pond for our sleeping chamber. Right?"

"Yes, darling. Just right, and it will connect with the smaller front room, through the closet?" she wanted to know.

"I see no reason why it can't. I'll speak to Dobson about it." He guessed she planned to use this connecting room for the upstairs nursery. In a moment he was certain it was babies she had on her mind.

"Francis, when our children are older, the boys will sleep in the rooms over the dining room and study, while the girls can stay in the room that connects with ours. That should work out, don't you think?"

Francis shifted his position, feeling a twinge of something he couldn't identify. "Just how many of these various offspring are you planning for us to have?" Not waiting for an answer, he moved to help her down. "I must caution you, I intend to be quite jealous about sharing your attentions with them."

"Oh silly, by then you won't."

"What is that supposed to mean? By then I won't. Come, since the men are going to be busy with this part of the project for quite some time, let's find a quiet spot and have our picnic. I'll tell you how long I plan on demanding your full attentions, my love!"

"Good. I'm hungry. Let's go down the hill, near the creek. It'll be cooler there."

As they started through the trees over what would one day be a part of the cultivated terrace he was planning, he was reminded of his wedding day when he'd explored this same slope. The trees were in full leaf now, the shrubs and grasses deep green and lush. The skies were blue and the forest vibrated with the calls of hundreds of birds. He remembered the bower and thought they were close to it. Racing ahead, he disappeared. "Here I am. Becky," he called. "See if you can find me."

"I declare, Francis Lee, sometimes you are more little boy than man," she laughed, passing within a few feet of where he hid.

"You have gone past me," he warbled, teasing.

Turning in a circle, she said, "Well, where are you then? I can't see anything but laurel and honeysuckle."

"Wonderful, wonderful," whispered Francis, a plan forming in his mind. "Stop where you are. Now, turn to your right ... fine ... now five or six steps should do it. There you are. Now bend down a bit and you'll find me!"

Her surprised face appeared in the small opening. Lifting the branches for her, he leaned forward to plant a kiss on her open mouth. "Oh," she stammered. "How enchanting. A secret garden, and look! there are wild violets, darling. My favorite. However did you find this place? I couldn't see you at all."

"Not at all? You're sure?" When she nodded, he said, "Then we're truly alone. For the very first time since our wedding, Mrs. Lee, no one knows where we are and we're completely alone."

Awareness of his meaning registered in her eyes, and they held their arms out to each other. Their lovemaking was unhurried and lazy, in keeping with the hum of bees in the honeysuckle which hid them from the world. Serenaded by the songs of warblers in the giant pines and the methodical echo of a carpenter's adz, the slaves' hammers thumped in rhythm with their hearts. The ground was soft with thick sweet smelling grass, and leaves of the beech tree filtered the sun with an ever-changing pattern. Scents of earth and jasmine, shaving soap and summertime sweat mingled until they were indistinguishable. And everywhere there were violets.

When their love was spent they rested, gazing above them at patches of bright blue sky. For a long time neither said a word. Becky was first to break the silence. "Are you asleep?" she asked softly, not looking at him.

"Not quite," he murmured.

"Darling, do you know what I've been thinking? I think we should come here often. It's such a perfect spot ... for love ... and I'd like this to be where our baby is started." Still she avoided looking at him.

Raising himself on one elbow Francis turned her face so their eyes met. "Just love me, Becky, that's all I ask. And don't be anxious about bringing me a child. That will happen in its own time."

"I know. I do love you. How I love you! Can you ever know how much? And I want to bear your child, that's all. Wouldn't it be wonderful if it could be conceived at Menokin?" Did he understand how much she meant it? "But right now, I'm starved. For food!" she shrieked, as he grabbed for her again.

"My God," he roared, "we forgot our picnic!"

∽

Becky and Francis continued to visit the privacy of the bower during the warm months whenever it was possible. After a time her mother gave up trying to convince her daughter of the impropriety of a woman at the construction site. Becky had a mind of her own and, after all, she was married now. Sometimes she did insist that Cate should accompany her mistress. On such days, if Cate wondered where the couple disappeared during the middle of the day, she gave no indication of it. Curiosity, however, prompted her to watch and listen. By the second time she saw them wander hand in hand down the hillside, she had figured out the reason. And she heartily approved of the arrangement, she reported to Isaac when she returned to Mount Airy that evening. He laughed and took her to bed for their own lovemaking.

∽

It seemed to be the year for weddings. In addition to the marriages of the Lee brothers, Martha, daughter of Hannah Lee and Gawin Corbin, was wed to George Richard Turberville. This marriage meant that Martha was now the mistress of Peckatone House as provided in her father's will. It would probably mean that her mother, Dr. Hall, and their two children wouldn't remain comfortable there for long. There were also other Northern Neck weddings in the Washington, Fauntleroy, Bushrod, and Carter families. It was a very social summer. In mid-June Richard Henry surprised them all by his decision to marry, barely six months since Anne's death, a widow, Mrs. Anne Gaskins Pinchard.

Francis, upon hearing the news of his brother's impending marriage, was strangely disturbed although he wasn't certain why. It was what Anne had wanted for her bereaved husband, wasn't it?

"What do you think of Richard's marrying again so soon, Becky?" he asked, putting down his newspaper.

"I would say we should wish him every happiness. He needs a wife to care for those four children."

Francis was learning he could count on Becky to have a positive, as well as a practical, response to almost any situation. As one day when they discussed the House of Burgesses. He told her that the last session had been very exciting. "Resolutions of vast importance to our liberty were framed, resolutions that would have been unheard of last year. They were revolutionary enough to frustrate Botetourt enough to dissolve the assembly ... it's rare for the governor to do that, you know."

"Papa said there was more unity shown among the members than usual, but I don't think he entirely approved of some of the actions."

"Well, I was just reading in the *Gazette* that the unity among our burgesses can be attributed mostly to Parliament's act that threatens our right to trial in our own province! No man would stand a chance if he were tried in London with no friends, no witnesses present to defend him. What kind of justice would that be?"

"Do I detect the possibility that you're sorry you weren't there to sign your name to the petitions of protest, Mr. Lee?" She glanced at him over her needlework. Marriage had inspired her to improve her skills in this feminine art, and she was finding it quite pleasing.

"I suppose that *is* what I'm saying, if the truth be told, love. It seems more than ever that the cause of liberty needs her loyal sons to go to battle for what they hold dear. We can't continue to tolerate injustice or aggression. But here, in Richmond County, the freeholders would never vote me in. So, for the time being, I'm left on the outside."

"Then you've actually thought about putting your name up?" she asked directly.

"Well, I haven't considered it with any great urgency because the situation being what it is seems impossible. But I do feel a growing concern being out of the political arena."

"We should mention the possibility to Papa, Francis. Perhaps he'll have an idea or two."

He looked at her reflectively, thinking that indeed Colonel Tayloe's power in the county was the catalyst that could bring about his election if anything could. He also wondered vaguely if continued dependence on his father-in-law's wealth and position was going to bother him. He didn't think so, at least for the time being, and decided nothing would be accomplished by fretting over it.

Cate entered the room, bringing a cool punch and a note from Colonel Landon Carter. "Thank you, Cate," Francis said, opening the letter. "You are looking cheerful today."

"Yas-suh, Mistah Lee! I is indeed. De Lawd bin good to Cate. Yas-suh." She grinned, leaving them to their drinks.

"Colonel Landon has invited us to dine with him at Sabine Hall on Sunday next. Will we be able to attend?"

"That would be wonderful, darling. We're not often invited out alone. It seems people include us because they are inviting Mama and Papa."

"I'm not sure that's true. But you're right. It will be nice to go alone for a change. By the way, what is into Cate lately, that she bubbles so with all 'de Lawd's goodness'?"

Becky concentrated on the colored yarns in her lap. "There's to be another baby this winter."

"Well, it certainly does agree with her, I must say. Is it the same for all women, I wonder?"

191

It took her a while to reply. "I'm not sure. I'm most eager to find out, however ... for myself."

Francis laughed, shaking his head at her impatience, and returned to the *Gazette's* account of the assembly's actions.

But all the days of summer were not pleasant; some of them were beastly hot. One early August morning Becky sat alone in their sleeping chamber, Francis having gone to Menokin as usual. The weather, hot and humid, suggested a storm and he'd persuaded her to remain at home. Today there were decisions to be made about the fireplaces and that was better left to him anyway, she admitted. Restless and out of sorts, she gazed into the large gilt looking glass over her dressing table, examining her face, scrutinizing eyebrows, nose, shape of chin, and skin texture. It was attractive enough, she thought. Francis certainly commented on it frequently, as did her father. Why then, doesn't it please me to look at myself today, she wondered, applying a small smudge of coloring to each cheek.

She walked lazily to the window to stare into the courtyard. Cate was there in the distance, struggling with a load of clothes outside the laundry shed. It must be too hot in the laundry, with the wood burning to heat the water, she decided. She wondered if the energy required to haul the steaming buckets to the tub was worth it. There was no breeze. She watched as Cate made five or six trips and the tub was not yet full. Her pregnancy was beginning to show, she noticed, as Cate stretched to ease her back. A fullness showed. Not just in the abdomen where the baby grew, but especially in the breasts. They were filled out, swollen. The extra flesh was attractive. Becky moved her hands tentatively over her own body, wishing she could feel something unusual there. Cate turned to enter the building again. From this view another change was obvious, a spreading had occurred across the slave's waist and hips. The white apron didn't hide it.

"I'm not at all sure I'd like that part," Becky said aloud. She laughed at herself, wondering why these thoughts of babies kept plaguing her. There had always been babies in this house where she'd grown up, maybe that was the reason. Or was it that she felt guilty about how much she enjoyed the acts of love she shared with Francis? Did other women feel guilty over this pleasure? Was there a price to pay over being greedy about it? Or a feeling she owed something to her husband ... or to God? ... or did she simply want a babe of her own?

Sighing, she picked up the candle screen she was working on, now nearly completed. I refuse to be dispirited over such a silly thing as not having conceived a child in less than four months of marriage. Her hands felt sticky but she determined to complete a row or two of the needlepoint.

⟨∾⟩

At Menokin, Francis found that the heat and absence of any breeze at all had prompted activity to cease. Housewright Dobson, no doubt irritated at being caught half asleep in the shade of an enormous oak, struggled to his feet. "You, Abram!" he shouted to a large Negro lounging near a pile of roughly shaped brick, "get those lazy niggers to work! That mortar's wastin'." The stuff had dried too much already, it appeared to Francis.

The slave threw a sullen look in the direction of Dobson and stirred himself only slightly, then, catching sight of the master, thought better of any delay. With a shove, he directed a subordinate back to work. The meaning of the scene was obvious. "Mr. Dobson," Francis called, approaching slowly from where he tethered Cameron. "How are things going today? Any trouble? Problems? Sickness?" He gave the man every out he could think of. It was too damned hot to be disagreeable.

Dobson, having aroused quickly, answered honestly, "Only the heat, Mr. Lee, the friggin' heat is damnable today." He darted a glance at the man who paid his wages. "Bugs bitin', too." Relief swept his face when he saw there were to be no recriminations. Mr. Lee was a fair and understanding man after all.

While swatting at pesky flies, they discussed the chimneys. A fireplace was planned for every room, each to have the same size opening with the exception of the dining room which would boast a massive hearth suitable to the largest room in the house which measured twenty-two feet square, inside dimensions. All this Mr. Dobson repeated carefully to Francis. It meant that each chimney must support four fireplaces, two on each floor. Referring again to his drawings, Francis pointed out that the study to the left of the front entrance was very small. Perhaps they should follow the intent of the architect and limit the size of the hearth there, to approximately two feet in width. Would this not also help the draw on the large one backing up to it? Dobson, more concerned with remaining in the good graces of Mr. Lee than in arguing a point, hastily agreed. Satisfied they understood one another and having rapidly come to the conclusion this was no place to linger on such a miserable day, Francis left the work crew to the tedious flies and their own nasty tempers. He didn't expect to get much labor out of them in weather like this.

His presence would be of little or no help anyway, he told himself, settling on a log at the edge of the bay below his house where the landing to his plantation would be built. The mosquitoes were biting here but the flies hadn't followed him. At least he could dangle his feet in the cool water, he thought, pulling off his boots. Maybe even take a swim. He was in no particular hurry to return to Mount Airy. The heat was enough to make even conversation an effort. It was one of those days of summer one could only wish would end soon. He skimmed pebbles into the pond, thinking of Sunday and the visit to Sabine Hall. He was looking forward to it.

૯૭

"I awoke with a severe pain in my neck and down the upper portion of my shoulder," Carter moaned to Francis as soon as they were alone. "I have found it exceeding difficult to get a proper rest in this unbearable hot spell we are suffering. I can only attribute these pains to my restless nights and lack of sleep. It is nothing I've eaten, I'm sure."

Francis, familiar with the perennial complaints of his friend, took his usual complimentary approach. "You're looking fine despite your discomfort, Colonel. It fact I noticed at table you looked better than I've seen you in recent weeks. More vital, and in complete command of the entire body of us ... it was a fine meal and good company, by the way."

The two were in Landon Carter's study, the ladies having disappeared to the parlor, the other gentlemen to the card room immediately following the meal. Francis, not averse to a game of loo or whist by any means, accepted that in this case his host had no intention of allowing him that diversion today.

"Your consideration for me obviously far outshines your confidence in my abilities," Carter said, still whining. When he saw Francis looking puzzled, he continued, "A rumor has been brought to me that Colonel Tayloe is spreading word of your worth and sincerity, as well as your considerable experience of ten year's service in the House, in preparation to your name being placed as a delegate choice for our Richmond County voters next election."

The peevish note wasn't lost on Francis, although he didn't grasp immediately what Carter's point was, so he answered cautiously. "Well, Colonel, I hope you understand I have no desire to usurp the Carter seat Robert is eyeing. And I harbor no illusions I could do so even if I chose to try."

"Good God, man, I couldn't be more pleased than with the prospect of your defeating my wastrel son and dumping him on his spoiled ass! And as you know, I've decided not to submit my own name. I refuse to grovel at the mercy of the fickle freeholders of this county, who care more for how many times a man will treat them to rum than for his abilities. Such aversions don't seem to be a trait I have bred into my eldest son, however. But my point ... my point is that once again you have not come directly to me for help, when it would seem obvious I am the most logical choice! I'd expect such insensible tactics from my own sons, but not from you. I was under the impression we had reached a complete understanding where politics are concerned, when we spoke of such things at some length last year in the capital." He sat back, settled his ample bulk in the chair and waited for the other's rebuttal, which he was confident would be calculated to salve his wounded ego. He could always count on Frank Lee to boost his spirits.

Francis cleared his throat and took a long slow sip of his brandy, playing for time. It came to him he could lay the blame on the over-zealous nature of his wife. Silently begging her forgiveness for the lie, he began, "Well, first let me assure you most sincerely I'm distressed at having caused you disappointment, and I wish you to accept my apology for it. You see, I undoubtedly would have come first off to you, knowing your standing and power in the county. However, my dear Mrs. Lee in her desire to bring me out of a lethargy into which I seemed to have fallen, went to her papa seeking help. A natural enough action I think. There was nothing I could do but go along with whatever plans my father-in-law suggested after that." Francis peered intently at his host to see if this explanation was sufficient or if he should continue.

Carter grunted, deciding he was satisfied. He launched into a series of ploys and advices, which if laid end to end, Francis thought, would undoubtedly stretch all the way to the courthouse. And that was precisely what Carter intended they should do. He took the opportunity to point out the foolishness of his son in "kissing the backsides" of the freeholders in order to win votes, a disgusting display of bad taste, he grumbled. This conversation led, of course, to the vexing problems within his own family. "I have tried to talk to Robert about my assessment of

Governor Botetourt ... that I think he can force the British Ministry to see the error of overburdening the colonies with taxes, but discussing such serious matters with that reprobate Robert is a waste of time. He fidgets and jumps, bent only on hastening the interview so he may return to one of his sinful entertainments! I am absolutely convinced he will murder the genius of my grandson Landon by plying him with filthy diversions and directing him down the same evil paths. Why, the boy is but in his teens and already he is betting regularly on the horses and the cocks. It's an utter disgrace!"

"Perhaps the boy's mother could be of help?" Francis suggested lamely, for in truth he didn't know what to say.

"Winifred? That cow! She's too busy lounging in her bed until noon and stuffing sweets in her pouting red mouth the remainder of the day. A perfect Lady Fat, I call her in my journal!"

Francis couldn't restrain a smile. He was certain the colonel didn't limit his use of the unsavory name to his diary. That would explain the spiteful looks his daughter-in-law reserved for him. "Well, I was thinking that sometimes a mother has certain influence over a young boy in matters of discipline to duty. My own mother had ways of shaming us ruthlessly when she thought we weren't living up to the example set for us by our father ... she was very effective at it, but never unkind."

"Hannah Ludwell, your mother, was a fine and gracious woman, Frank, and a lady of gentle breeding and persuasion. Winifred Travers Beale's name should not be mentioned in the same breath. It's my cross to bear that the Beale blood has been brought into this house and flows through the veins of my grandchildren!"

Francis didn't mention that Carter's own third wife, by whom he had two daughters before her death, was a Beale—the way to harmony with this man was not to point out his shortcomings nor to verbalize his omissions. Having recognized Landon's genius and his brilliance, Francis had decided long ago to seek whatever benefits could be gained over the years from a peaceful relationship with the master of Sabine Hall. There was still much to learn from him and their friendship continued to flourish.

∽

When the Lees returned to Mount Airy, Becky elaborated on her impression of Mrs. Robert Wormeley Carter. "Poor Winifred. Francis, I do feel sorry for the dear soul. I've been thinking about her all the way home. I think she eats so much out of pure nervousness and unhappiness. Her father-in-law ridicules her un- mercifully, and her husband leaves her at every possible oppor- tunity to pursue his gambling and other pleasures ... not a few of which I can well imagine!" She adjusted the satin collar of her blue wrapper, wondering if Francis would notice it was new. She wondered also what she would do for a seamstress when they moved to Menokin. It wasn't likely they could afford to employ a slave girl full time with the task as did her mother. How would she even find one who was trained for that matter?

"Did she speak of these things in front of the other ladies?"

"Hmm? ... Oh, well, not exactly, but she did mention that Colonel Carter always comments on the number of times she asks for various platters of food to be passed. Once she attempted to turn the joke around, you know, do the same to him, and do you know what he had the gall to say? He said, down the length of the entire table, 'how rude is our Winifred today. Do you sup- pose, children, that she swallowed one of her chocolates whole and it has made a pain in her belly?' I don't know how she puts up with such insults from that crabby old man!"

"And so you have deduced she is miserably unhappy?"

"Yes. She said other things, darling. When we were alone for a time in the nursery, she confided to me that Robert comes very seldom to her chamber anymore. When he does, for a night or two, or sometimes a week, the result is always the same ... another child. She made it sound as if that was all he came for."

Having dismissed Cate and Ben, Francis blew out the candles and they climbed into bed. Becky knew that on such an evening with little breeze, the sheets would not long remain cool. She removed her new wrapper, thinking her husband quite unobservant after all. He hadn't noticed, and now it was too dark for him to see the nightdress that matched. Perhaps they weren't so fetching as she had hoped.

Francis sank into a comfortable position, hands behind his head. He told her of his conversation with Colonel Landon and confessed having used her skirts to hide behind when confronted with Carter's testiness. He wanted to be honest about it.

Becky surprised him by laughing. "You honor me by confiding to another man that I wield such power!"

He hadn't been worried about her reaction, but he was pleased that she understood. After all, he supposed, it was only half a lie. He stretched lazily. "Poor old Robert Wormeley," he chuckled, returning to the former subject. "Perhaps we're not giving him a fair viewing in the Carter family triangle. His father certainly expects a great deal from him. Corrects him like a child in public, heaps abuses, I am sure, just as often when the occasion doesn't warrant as when it does. His wife nags and eats, eats and nags, and he's more likely than not running from them both ... behaving reprehensibly out of sheer spite! He behaves quite civilly when I'm alone with him."

"He doesn't seem a bad sort actually. He's always been a perfect gentleman in my presence," Becky offered. "Perhaps you have a point."

Francis yawned. Drawing her close against him he ran a finger around her lips, sending delicious little shivers down her spine. After a moment he gently kissed her eyelids closed.

"No matter," he whispered. "We've had enough of the Carter family for one day. I think I shall ride to Nomini tomorrow and give my approval to the finishing preparations for the opening of our fulling mill. If it's not too hot, would you like to come with me? And Becky love ... your new wrapper is beautiful. I'm only jealous that for the past hour it's been closer to you than I've been."

She smiled a fine contentment into the dark as her arms closed around his neck. Why did she ever bother to doubt him?

Death is the Gate of Life

The unrelenting heat of August slipped gradually into an early September euphoria. Cooler temperatures also signaled the approach of the election, and Francis found himself impatient and out of sorts over the outcome's uncertainty. John Tayloe and Landon Carter had kept their promises, both having worked steadily on his behalf. Thus he supposed he at least had a chance. Yet voters, as Carter said, were fickle creatures and until a man walked up to the clerk and actually called his choice, there was no telling what matter of events might change his mind. As the time grew closer he knew more than ever that he wanted to win. He wanted to be part of the upcoming Virginia Assembly.

One day he wrote what was on his mind to his brothers in London. *"We in Virginia,"* he began, *"were happy to hear that Maryland and South Carolina have followed our example by signing nonimportation agreements against British goods. We feel it is the only way at present to fight the infamous Ministry. I am eagerly following the political scene in hopes I shall soon be involved in it once again. I am a candidate from the County of Richmond.*

"In order to keep myself occupied, as well as in hopes of earning some cash, I have entered into a partnership with Turberville at Nomini Fulling Mill, which is now open for the cleansing and preparation of cloth.

"I am sorry to have to inform you, but a terrible storm, a hurricane almost, destroyed a great deal of our tobacco crop in late August. Therefore only a very small ship will be needed next year. I must also inquire if you prefer to be paid for your service in tobacco, cash or bills? I do approve of your plan to send the ship in care of Colonel Phil." He stopped, chewing briefly on the end of the quill. *"I know he will be much*

flattered by the compliment. As for myself you may depend upon every service in my power, I hope from nobler motives than those of Colonel Phil. Do not spare me for fear of giving trouble, if I can be useful.

"*Although I remain occupied with the construction of my home, I have learned that when there is not enough business to engage the mind, it becomes quite irksome. I shall be pleased if elected for this very reason.*

"*I have as yet to hear from the trustees as to a date for the division of Ludwell's estate. Therefore you will know that neither Richard nor myself have done anything in that regard. I trust this letter will find you both in excellent health and good spirits. Mrs. Lee and I send you our best regards. Your affectionate brother, F. L. Lee.*"

Lighting the candle for his sealing wax, he wondered how long it would take to locate a reliable ship's captain making straightway for England with whom he could entrust the letter. He turned at the rustle of petticoats and found Becky watching him.

"I love to see you working at your desk. Soon you'll have accounts to keep for Menokin plantation and letters for the assembly, as well as those of Loudoun farm and your leased tracts. Then I'll be wishing I could have more of your time. Wait and see!"

"I'm not counting on the assembly, love. I could easily be defeated," he cautioned, glancing at the window. Black, vicious looking clouds were gathering down the river. "Another storm it looks like, coming in fast."

"Yes, I know. The wind was blowing so hard in the orchard, I could scarce pick any fruit. Leaves and branches flying everywhere. Here." She held out a firm perfectly round red apple. "And ... one for me," she said, perching on the arm of his chair before taking her first bite. "Darling, tomorrow Mama and I are going to see Mr. Ritchie. We're hoping to find some cloth suitable for Menokin's draperies. It will probably end with our having to send an order with Captain Dobbie, however, for I just know the merchant's store will have nothing suitable."

"Oh? Dobbie's ship is here?" Francis asked, thinking of his letter.

"Papa says it arrived this morning. It's too cloudy with the storm coming to see it ... but it's there." She peered in the direction of Hobbs' Hole. "Do you want to come with us across the river?"

He hedged. "Another section of the wall goes up and I should be at Menokin. But I'm sure you won't mind taking a letter to Dobbie that I've just written to William and Arthur."

"Of course we can deliver your letter, but I thought you might help me make a choice, of fabric, I mean." She'd already decided it would be easier with only herself and her mother to please.

"Whatever you choose will suit me just fine. I promised you, didn't I, that furnishing the house would be up to you?"

He was such a dear man. So agreeable. Becky jumped suddenly off the arm of the chair. "By all the saints," she cried, "here comes the rain! Catey, get Jacob, Ben, anybody ... and get these windows closed! Mama's furniture will be ruined. Hurry!" The rain lashed into the side of the building as Cate and Nan came running. "Francis, don't worry!" Becky yelled above the confusion. "They'll vote you in, I'm sure of it. How could they even consider anyone else?" She disappeared in search of Jacob and the house boys.

Francis shook his head. Gathering the papers on the desk against the wind, he finished the last of his apple. "Cate," he said, "that woman keeps a man busy. Just following her conversation is enough to wear me out."

"Yas-suh, Marse Frank. Sho 'nuff!" She was unaware that for the first time she had called him by the same affectionate name Ben and Berth used.

Francis, however, didn't miss it and was pleased. It appeared that Cate had accepted him, he chuckled to himself.

Rain teemed in sheets through the forests. It raged down hillsides and pummeled into the fields ready for harvest, beating the crops to the ground. The heavens opened, filling and overflowing every creek and pond. White-hot bolts of lightning staggered across the late afternoon sky and thunder rumbled through the countryside. When it was over, and it lasted less than an hour, the sun burst forth briefly. Casting a long reflection on the surging waters of the river Rappahannock, the huge crimson ball slipped out of sight over the edge of the world. That short glimpse of sunlight after the violent storm gave reassurance to both man and beast before the night fell. The storm, although nowhere near as destructive as the one Frances had written about to his brothers, nonetheless did considerable damage.

Mount Airy mill pond flooded, cutting off passage to the Menokin lands. By morning it had receded enough, although the pathway was damp and muddy, a quagmire after the procession passed. Francis led the way on horseback, Ben and the slaves chosen for the day's labor followed on foot or muleback, and a few rode in the creaking wooden cart loaded with supplies. They found everything at Menokin soaked. It took much longer than usual to get things organized. Mr. Dobson considered putting off the wall raising for another day due to the muddy, precarious footing inside the foundation. He would have followed his inclination had not the master urged him to proceed.

As work began Francis wandered off into the clearing where his first fields would be cultivated. Plodding through the mud he realized he hadn't yet chosen a site for the slave cabins. Giving it some serious thought, he knew it would be two or more years before the dependencies, smaller replicas of the great house, could be completed for the kitchen, laundry, office and chambers for house servants. Some arrangements should probably be made for Cate, at least, and Berth to sleep in the main house. He decided it was possible with the addition of a fireplace to house some of them in the cellar. He recalled having had the idea once before ... the day he'd been informed of Anne Aylett's death.

A decision must still be made where to site the quarter for the thirty slaves promised him as part of Becky's wedding dowry. He sauntered across the clearing where almost a year ago he'd imagined tobacco growing. A thick undergrowth kept his feet from sinking in the mire. It would take several plowings and careful hoeing to turn the earth to a proper depth. He thought it could easily be ready for seeding in the spring if they could get the labor from Mount Airy to Menokin, and that depended on his father-in-law. This field would be the start of turning his land to productivity. Then he'd experiment with rye, barley, oats, peas, and corn, as well as flax, timothy and of course, the staple, tobacco. Lost in reflection, he raised his head at the sound of a cry, turning in the direction of the house. As he did so, his name echoed across the clearing. It was Ben calling him. Francis broke into a run, compelled by the urgency he heard in the slave's voice.

He saw immediately there'd been an accident. The men were gathered together in fear and confusion. He didn't see Ben at first, and Dobson, at the edge of the work area, looked stricken speechless. The Negroes separated, standing aside for the master, and he saw the body on the ground knowing immediately it was serious.

Ben knelt beside the victim. "Oh, my God!" Francis exclaimed. "What happened? Who is it?" Then, recognizing the braided leather thong Isaac always wore around his left ankle, he knew the answer even as he spoke.

Tears streaming down his cheeks, Ben sobbed, "Isaac, Marse Frank." Francis was vaguely aware that an understanding had developed between the two slaves during the past year. It appeared the friendship was more that he'd imagined. "Please, Marse Frank, he'p me move him out o' de mud. We's got t' git him to de doctor."

Francis stooped beside the injured slave. The enormous beam across his body told the story. Apparently when it fell it had struck square in the chest knocking Isaac to the ground and pinning him. The middle of his body was crushed—surely a mortal blow. Blood gushed from the wound and dribbled from the corner of his mouth. His eyes were glazed and unfocused but with a supreme effort he managed to fasten them on Ben. "Cate," he wheezed, "take care ..." Then he slipped into merciful unconsciousness.

"I did dis, Marse Frank. Ain't nobody to blame but me," Ben moaned, as he cradled Isaac's head, trying futilely to stem the blood flowing through the bruised lips.

Telling Ben it was an accident, Francis turned to the men around him who were waiting to see what would happen. Under his direction the timber was lifted from Isaac's body, and he was placed on a stretcher of wood and some rags they found among the tools. Ben and another slave transported him to the cart. He groaned once as they set him down but otherwise gave no indication he was alive. Ben climbed in beside his friend for the trip to Mount Airy. Isaac died without opening his eyes before they reached the mill pond, his life's blood soaking red the bare planks of the work cart.

Francis was waiting for them at the barns. He saw immediately it was too late. "You'll have to tell Cate, Ben," he said as gently as he could.

Misery clouded the black countenance. "Marse Frank, don' ax me t' do dat. Miss Becky, she goin' have t' tell her." Ben's eyes were a sea of anguish. "I drop't de timber. I kilt him."

"But you couldn't help it. It was an accident," insisted Francis.

Guilt, raw and biting, flooded Ben's senses. He listened to his master and heard again Isaac's plea for him to watch after Cate. Me, his tormented mind hollered ... when I've lusted after dat gal since firs' I saw her. Oh, Isaac, don' die. I didn' mean it. Kin you hear me? It's Ben talkin' to you. Cate, she don' love nobody but you. Please ... don' die! At last he spoke aloud. "Cate ain't never goin' fo'give me for what I done today, Marse Frank. I can't tell her."

As Francis watched the bent head and sagging shoulders, he puzzled over a slave so genuinely distraught over the death of another, and one he'd known only a short time. He had never witnessed such a thing. Nor could he understand Ben's combined feelings of guilt and sorrow, when it was clearly an accident after all, but he accepted the fact that it was indeed a tragic problem to his servant, and let him go in silence.

Thus it fell to Francis to tell Cate of the day's tragedy. She stared as though uncomprehending for a moment then, uttering one piercing scream, ran to hide herself in her room over the nursery. There, on the straw mattress she had shared with Isaac and where they had conceived the baby she carried under her heart, she curled herself in a ball and remained unmoving. There was nothing to do but leave her alone with her grief.

Ben sent Zoey to wait on Miss Becky and dispatched Cris to station herself near Cate. Then he disappeared. Francis, knowing he'd return when ready, showed no worry as to his whereabouts, ignoring the concern of others, principally that of Colonel Tayloe. Ben had been for many years faithful to his master, and Francis trusted him to return when he'd driven whatever devil was tormenting him out of his soul.

The household settled into an uneasy quiet. After dark a mournful chanting began in the quarter. The slaves who had worked with Isaac in the stables initiated it and, soon joined by others who hadn't known him at all, the sad music continued well into the night.

For Ben the night stretched into endless darkness and some terror. He was alone, seated on the very timber that killed his friend, more frightened than he could remember being, yet bound to keep a lonely vigil. An atonement ... for Isaac.

It was not so much the dark that scared him as the demons of death that lurked in this place. Although it wasn't yet the time of year for wolves, he imagined he saw slanted evil eyes leering yellow at him from the shadows between the trees. A small furry creature scurried across his hand and he startled violently. His fear made him sweat. It rolled in huge drops down his neck and over his chest. Clothed in nothing but the britches he'd worn in the morning, the nighttime chill set him to shivering despite the sweat. The rustle of the bushes and the great horned owl's screech became terrifying omens as he waited through what seemed an interminable night. He didn't question his reason for remaining there. Somehow he just knew he owed this vigil to Isaac. The forest, full of the spirits of guilt and shame, love and jealousy, closed in around him. It wasn't until many hours had passed that he finally dozed fitfully. Sitting there on the huge beam, his head dropped and he slept.

At the first light of day, he found himself stiff and cold. He arose, daring to hope the painful weight had truly been lifted from his heart. It seemed it was gone. He didn't understand it and had no need to understand any more than that. He accepted happily that he couldn't have prevented the accident—to further atone for it, he would remain away from Cate. He wouldn't even look at her lovely oiled skin, nor her fruitful body grown rich with child. At least not for a very long time. Having reached these conclusions, Ben stretched, surveying the new day. His stomach screamed for food and he remembered he hadn't eaten since morning of the day before. Out of necessity, his thoughts turned easily to the physical demands of his body. For a moment longer he watched the first streaks of salmon-sunlight creep over the earth, marveling at the color for which he had no name. Then, putting an end to his vigil, he relieved himself against a mud bank, watching with interest as the steam rose, before heading at a trot for Mount Airy. Marse Frank would be awake soon and needing him, and there was a grave to be dug in the quarter.

If Ben expected Cate would react to his self-imposed penance, he was sadly disappointed. Ten days later she seemed not to have missed him. At least she gave no sign of it. He had been wont to spend evenings outside the dependency with Isaac. Leaning back on two legs of crude wooden stools against the side of the building, they had smoked and watched the moon come up. It had been that way all summer. Now ten days after the accident, Ben remained at loose ends every evening when seven or eight o'clock rolled around. And this in spite of the ten hours he spent daily in back-breaking labor at the Menokin house. For he'd taken it upon himself to appear every day at the construction site. Here, he slaved as none other, and through his own choice. His master did not interfere.

⚬

Mid-September arrived. Colonel Tayloe's people were busy bringing in what remained of the tobacco crop following the second storm, roof timbers were being raised at Menokin, and Becky and her mother had purchased a bolt of golden damask at Mr. Richie's Hobbs' Hole store. The wife of an Essex County planter, Ritchie told them, had changed her mind and he was more than happy to find another buyer. Lengths were measured and cut by seamstress Nan, following sketches Francis made for her. The rich looking draperies would grace the windows on Menokin's first floor.

On the prescribed day, September 15th, the freeholders of Richmond County turned out to cast their votes for delegates to the November assembly. Under the watchful eye of Sheriff Griffin, each man in turn approached the table where the county clerk sat waiting to record his choice. As the vote was called, the clerk would scratch his head importantly as he recalled to mind the spelling of the name and, while continuing to chew vigorously on his tobacco, set about writing the voter's name under that of the candidate of his choice. Four hundred and fifty-six freeholders, about average for a general election in the county, turned out. Such a get-together occasioned a celebration, and following the voting everyone stayed to partake of the beer, rum, and strong cider passed around the green. In fact most of the men spent the day in Richmond Courthouse and were more than a little tipsy by the time proceedings drew to a close. Colonel John Tayloe and his new son-in-law were no exception.

"What happened?" Becky called from the window. She shook her head as she watched them singing their way up from the stables. Jacob and Ben, following at a discreet distance, both smirked at the unsteady progress of their masters.

"What happened?" Francis repeated foolishly. "Why, we had a spot of rum, that's all!" He waved to his wife and hitched his cravat into place, aware it had slipped but it hadn't seemed important until he saw Becky.

"It's clear you had the rum, darling, but what happened at the polls? Who won?"

"Mr. Thomas Glascock didn't have a chance," Tayloe hooted.

Becky was delighted, it was more than she had dared to hope. Francis would be back in politics where he belonged. "I'm so glad! What was the count?"

"My dear daughter, your charming husband took the county quite by storm. He polled only five votes lesh than Robert Wormeley did, leaving Glascock wallowing in the dusht!" Tayloe roared gleefully at the slur of his own speech. He'd worked hard for the election of Becky's husband and felt he was due more than a little credit for the accomplishment. Swinging a proprietary arm over Frank's shoulder as they climbed the steps, he thought that here would be his voice in the House of Burgesses.

Francis looked behind him. "Where the hell are the lions?" he wanted to know, forgetting Tayloe.

"What's that, m'boy?"

Shrugging, Francis laughed, "A private joke, Sir. Just a bloody silly private joke!"

"It appears my charming husband will require someone to help him to bed after the strain of his victory," Becky called from the window, "Not to mention my equally inebriated father." She shook her head again at the foolish ways of men.

⌒

In the morning the Lees departed for a few days' visit at Chantilly. Francis couldn't wait to share his victory with his brother, and ignored his pounding head as they bounced along in the carriage bought the previous fall in Fredericksburg to carry his belongings from Loudoun County to Mount Airy; belongings that had included Ben, Berth, Zoey, and Cris.

Although they traveled the twenty-mile distance unannounced, such was the accepted custom, and they were met with warm greetings. Francis received hearty congratulations over the success of the election. Richard had, of course, been returned by the voters of Westmoreland and the brothers would once again complement each other's maneuverings in the House.

Francis was soon convinced this second marriage of Richard's was a fortunate happening after all. Mrs. Pinchard, for that is what everyone seemed to continue to call her, was a gentle lady, considerate and kind with the children. With the exception of Thomas, the eldest, they seemed to have easily accepted her new position in the household.

"Tom will come around in time," Richard Henry was saying. "Just a bit hesitant due to his age, I expect. To change the subject, Loudoun, has word reached you yet of the burning of Colonel Phil's tobacco warehouses at Stratford?"

"A fire at Stratford Landing? When? Was it destroyed?"

"Well, some tobacco and hay were salvaged, but the buildings are a loss. Phil plans to petition the assembly to rebuild."

"I'm not sure I approve of that. It won't be popular," Francis said.

A frown creased Richard's brow. "Phil has operated the landing and warehouses for public use, as well as his own, and therefore it seems right the colony should replace them. I'm not certain, however, it will be accepted by our county freeholders, but he's asked me to present the petition. Others do the same for their warehouse losses, you know."

"From the beginning, it's been a moneymaking venture with Philip, pure and simple. He's paid scant heed to the needs of the public, and they know it! Have you agreed to support his petition or just to present it?"

"I haven't said I'd support it in so many words, but I can see no other route open to me."

Francis resolved to press the question again later, after considering it further. "I'd like to ride over and see the damage for myself. Would you care to come tomorrow? We could go while the ladies are chatting or otherwise occupied. I'm sure Becky will want to share her plans for decorating and furnishing Menokin with Mrs. Pinchard. She thinks of little else these days."

"That's fine. I find my dear lady to be a good and faithful listener. She's brought a welcome companionship into my bereaved life."

"Then you are happy?"

"Very much so." Richard paused, his deep set serious eyes in the long aristocratic face boring into his brother. "She can't replace my first Anne ... I think she's accepted that, and we're compatible. Now ... my other news is that we have received another joint letter from William. Come, I'll let you read it for yourself."

The letter was brief. Francis scanned it quickly. It concerned the division of his wife's estate, and William's recent efforts to enroll other British merchants to join him in petitioning Parliament for a redress of the American grievances. "He seems to be having some success among the London merchants. I see he's asked for a copy of the Maryland and South Carolina nonimportation agreements. I recently wrote him of their action, but I gather you must have done so some time ago. Have you dispatched copies of the agreements yet?"

"No. Not yet. I'm sure by now he's received the newspapers in which they were printed," Richard answered.

"True ... true. By the way, R.H., this business over the division of the estate. I'm beginning to be annoyed over the constant nagging he puts forth," Francis remarked, impatient with the subject. "It's the sixth or seventh letter on the matter."

Poor Loudoun, his brother thought, smiling—I don't suppose he's considered the fact that his own fortune has come to him dished up on a silver platter through marriage—while William is having to do battle for his slice of the family pie! Aloud he said, "Our poor brother. It appears he's once again forced to fight for what is rightfully his. We shouldn't be too hard on him if he seems anxious about his situation."

It was a long time since Richard had referred to the twelve-year haggle with Philip over William's inheritance. Francis wondered if he was at last becoming put out with Colonel Phil's tightfistedness over the least farthing.

༄

The evenings at Chantilly were filled with pleasantries. Becky entertained on the harpsichord, the children sang and danced, and Richard's vintage wine flowed freely. Friends from the Washington's Pope's Creek Plantation joined them one night, and Philip and Elizabeth Lee with their two daughters, another. Becky thrived in the social excitement and promised she and Francis would soon welcome them all to Menokin. When the time for departure came, they were more than a little sad to see the visit come to an end.

"Perhaps we won't meet again until we arrive in Williamsburg," Francis said in parting. "Keep me informed on what you hear from Boston. Also any news you have of the Ministry's actions.

I understand that so far there's been no attempt on their part to enforce the ruling of trial in England."

"And I should hope there won't be! An outrageous law! Good to have you back with us, Loudoun ... in the Neck and in the Burgesses." Smiling at Becky, "You and your lovely lady are always welcome at Chantilly. Come again soon."

Becky turned to Francis, looking smug as they rumbled off. "See, darling, they make a lovely family. I told you we should have no concerns about Mr. Lee's remarriage. Everything's just fine."

Francis patted her hand. "Yes, love." His thoughts were on his brother Philip and the petition for reimbursement for the burned warehouses. He hoped he'd managed to dissuade Richard from presenting it; instinctively he knew it wasn't right. Westmoreland County freeholders would never support it. Indulging Philip in this matter would only lessen Richard's already precarious position in the House, he concluded, as he glanced at Becky to find her frowning at him. "Oh ... sorry, my love. My mind was on another matter," he apologized, vowing to give her the benefit of his full attention for the long ride home.

∽

In November, with plans for the journey to Williamsburg fully underway, Rebecca Tayloe decided abruptly that she would travel to Wye House in Maryland for the birth of her first grandchild instead of accompanying her husband to the assembly. It was further decided that Cate, nearing the term of her pregnancy, would also forego the trip. These arrangements left Becky in full control, with responsibility for management of the house on Nicholson Street as well as for that of her five sisters. It seemed a supreme challenge.

Her father sat on the Council daily and Francis was off to sessions of the House or committee meetings, leaving her to her first chores of housewifery. The experience afforded, besides hard work, a curious sense of satisfaction, she thought. Frequently she pretended it was her own house and her own children she tended.

It scarcely seemed possible that it was only a year and a half since the day she became reacquainted with Francis in the garden. She was gazing from the window at the stone bench where they had first rediscovered each other. A letter had arrived the day before that Elizabeth's baby was a little girl, but Becky didn't care to think about that just now. It was much more pleasant to remember the things she and Francis had whispered about and how she'd first noticed the teasing expression caused by his uneven eyebrows, as they sat side by side there on that bench.

The business before the assembly was exceedingly demanding. It was also lengthy, lasting from November 7th to December 21st, an unheard-of period of seven long weeks. Thus it was small wonder as the days passed that Francis paid scant attention to his wife's unusual periods of silence and her less than obvious signs of loss in spirit. He was too busy, and he attributed her behavior to the tremendous burden imposed upon her.

The problem in the House was that since Governor Botetourt had dissolved the May assembly after only nine days, they were overwhelmed with petitions, grievances, and regional county problems—everything had mushroomed. On the positive side, the dissolution had served to forge an unexpected link in the fragile chain of joint actions taken by opposing factions as regards their attitude toward the Crown's demands. For, as Richard Henry had reported with obvious satisfaction to Francis, the dismissed burgesses had promptly marched down the street and reconvened at the Raleigh Tavern. It was there they had approved the agreement banning import of certain British commodities. The document directed itself to all goods upon which a duty was levied, with the exception of paper, and also covered slaves and a long list of luxury items. It had clearly been a victory for Patrick Henry's team, and there was unity behind it this time.

Now, at the reassembled House, Botetourt opened the assembly with a speech in which he implied, again, that His Majesty's present administration had no intentions of laying further taxes for the sole purpose of raising a revenue. Soon, he promised, a proposal would be made in Parliament requesting repeal of duties on glass, paper, and paints. The liberals and moderates heard this and were, to varying degrees, dissatisfied that the duty on tea wasn't to be lifted also. The conservatives on the other hand rationalized that the action had been calculated to save face and allow the Ministry to maintain the upper hand, which was only proper.

So, once again, a vastly divided House raged and argued across the aisles of the Virginia Capitol. In the end the victory went to the group voting with Patrick Henry and Richard Henry Lee. That meant that the Nonimportation Agreement they prepared was not to be lifted until a positive action, not a verbal promise by the governor, was made by Britain. Botetourt seethed, as was expected.

In other business, Francis found himself appointed to several committees, including the powerful Privileges and Elections Committee, as well as that of Propositions and Grievances. The former addressed itself to the myriad complaints of fraud in elections; the testimony of witnesses was often tedious, although sometimes humorous enough to make up for it.

Such was the case of the freeholders of Halifax County against Nathaniel Terry. Mr. Terry, claiming honest election, was accused of having 'caned' the sheriff out of the courthouse when he attempted to close the polls before the bulk of Terry's promised votes had presented themselves. Besides a comic situation, the accused gentleman drew a great deal of attention by lodging noisy counter charges against his opponent, as well as against the sheriff. After hours of heated debate it was finally ruled that, having been fined and properly admonished for his bad temper, Nathaniel Terry could take his seat among the burgesses. His fellow delegate, Walter Coles, had himself pressed charges against Terry, yet had no choice but to accept the ruling.

There were, of course, the usual petitions by individuals seeking reimbursement for lost, injured, or incarcerated slaves. The deciding factor in these judgments seemed based more often on the man's reputation and popularity rather than on the merits of the case. If Francis occasionally wondered at the lack of justice in the system, he accepted it simply because it was the system and always had been so.

∽

Gray chilly evenings were spent in front of the fire in the comfortable parlor on Nicholson Street, when they weren't visiting, attending a ball, or enjoying a performance at the playhouse. Francis was proud of Becky's ability to preside over the tea table when they were joined by friends or relatives. He thought she handled it every bit as well as did her mother. Richard was often there, as was Landon Carter's son, Robert Wormeley. One evening Robert's cousin, the other Robert Carter, called on them with his lady. Leading members of the House conservative party also visited Colonel Tayloe with regularity; his political leanings were a reflection of their own and, from time to time, he was asked to do what he could to sway his son-in-law to assume a stance closer to the middle of the road. Tayloe was beginning to discover that his participation in getting Francis elected had not resulted in a feeling of obligation on Frank Lee's part. He had a mind of his own it seemed.

"Do you know what some are calling your friend Patrick Henry?" the colonel asked one evening when Francis had returned late following a meeting with friends at the tavern.

"No Sir, but I can well imagine it's not flattering. Was that Benjamin Harrison I saw riding away as I entered the street?" Reaching for his pipe, Francis nodded to Jacob to bring him some Madeira. He knew what was coming.

"They have actually affixed Henry with the label of 'radical.' And his followers along with him!" Tayloe paused to let the word sink in. "What say you to that, Frank?" He swallowed a healthy gulp of brandy and waited.

Always uncomfortable at having to defend himself and basically somewhat shy when it came to his political philosophy, Francis shifted in his chair. "As a matter of fact, Colonel," he began, taking time to draw on his pipe—the tobacco didn't want to take fire immediately, allowing time to put his words in order. "The term radical, I believe, has been around a long time. I seem to recall it was applied to Mr. Henry once before ... in the mid-sixties when he pushed through the opposition to stamp taxes ... and to that worthy Englishman John Locke before that. I grant you, it isn't used much. It seems to get dredged up when somebody wishes to damn an idea or hang a resolution out to dry. But it's certainly not new to the vocabulary. I fail to see that it's anything to get riled up about. By the by," he said, looking to the hall, "I haven't greeted my wife since I came in. Perhaps I should excuse myself to look for her."

The frown that hovered on John Tayloe's face slipped behind a smile at the subterfuge. "Becky? Oh, I suspect she's all right. She excused herself this evening after the meal. She said a headache, I think. Probably one of those female bad days, you know? I'm sure she'll join us soon."

"Well then, I have no need to worry," sighed her husband, daring to breathe easier at having accomplished a change of subject. He wondered if Becky might be coming down with something. She so rarely complained, it would be difficult to know if she were truly ill. Sitting back down he soon learned that Tayloe wasn't to be so easily put off.

"Being labeled a radical in these times in Virginia, means one can be assumed to be engaging in some form of disloyalty to the Crown, wouldn't you agree?"

Francis moaned audibly. "Sir, I must assure you that is not the intent of Mr. Henry's approach to government in this colony. Those who call him radical had no use for him in the first place. He has no purpose of abusing George III, nor of undermining our allegiance to him. He, and I also, merely feel that these American colonies should stand united, remaining free, as in the past, to make our own internal laws and to levy our own taxes ... while, of course, remaining under the benevolent eye of our generous and thoughtful monarch." He stopped then, pleased with his own eloquence.

"But while you espouse such a view, the actions for which Mr. Henry presses do nothing to encourage benevolence in King or Ministry! Rather the opposite. Continuing close alliance with Massachusetts can only bring us further troubles. Our entire way of life is being threatened to the core by these rumblings of Patrick Henry and your brother Richard. I sometimes wonder, Frank, were it not for Richard Henry, if you'd even be arguing these points with me right now."

Before Francis could reply, they were interrupted by Becky. Bending to kiss each in turn, she joined them, turning the talk to matters of the household and her sisters. Her father thought his discussion with his son-in-law had probably run its course anyway, while Francis knew they had reached an impasse, and welcomed Becky's arrival.

∾

In the days that followed, a number of petitions were presented to the assembly requesting reimbursement for tobacco losses, stolen from warehouses or destroyed by accident. Some, as that of Henry Sisson and John Eidson, inspectors at Cat Point Warehouse below Menokin, were approved. Most, however, were not because as the weeks wore on the mood of the assembly became less and less indulgent. Francis spoke to Becky of one of the cases in which he had a personal interest.

"Freeholders and merchants from Westmoreland County petitioned today against reconstruction of the tobacco warehouses at Colonel Phil's wharf," he told her, not knowing what her reaction might be.

Raising her head reluctantly from concentration over the housekeeping account book, she said, "It's my desire, Francis, to keep these records in as immaculate an order as my mother has always managed to do. Now," pausing to blow the ink dry before shutting the book, "what was that about the warehouses at Stratford?"

He was impressed by her attention to detail. He must make note to compliment her later on her exemplary care of the household records. But at the moment he wanted to tell her what he'd done. "A discussion was had in the house today on funding money for reestablishment of an inspection point at Stratford ... I supported those presenting the petition against doing that."

"Why ever did you do that, darling? Philip is your brother," she said, puzzled and troubled by his admission.

"I decided with the freeholders of the county that it would be too expensive. There are other inspection warehouses already in the area." He hoped for her approval. "Are you saying you disagree with my action?"

Becky finished cleaning her quill point and closed the inkwell carefully. "Would you have the same attitude if the brother involved had been Richard or Thomas?"

Francis stared at her, knowing that she thought he was wrong. "I don't know the answer to that question, Becky. I wasn't thinking of it in that context."

"Well, I think I'd have to understand your motive before I could give you a clear response. Was it a longtime animosity to

Colonel Phil or something somewhat more noble?" As soon as the words were out, she wished she could retract them.

Francis rose abruptly. It seemed an excellent time for a walk. "Thank you, Rebecca." He never called her that. "I wonder if you're aware how much I value your approval in these matters?" At the door, he turned back to her. "I think perhaps you are not," he announced stiffly.

When he was gone, the door closed loudly behind his wounded pride, she felt very much alone. It was with relief she greeted her father when he came to sit beside her.

"Well, my dear, and where has Frank gone? I thought I heard the door."

"Oh ... he's just out for a short while. A meeting at the Raleigh, I believe he said," she lied.

"Can't say that I mind. It's not often I have an opportunity to have the company of my lovely Becky all to myself these days."

"Papa," she said, deciding to ask his opinion about the Westmoreland petition. "Did you hear about the talk in the House today on reconstruction of the warehouses at Stratford Landing?"

"Well, I heard that money will probably not be funded, and that Frank supported that decision. Yes, I heard about that. He went against the wishes of Richard Henry to do so, I might add, to say nothing of Philip Lee's concerns in the matter."

"He did? Really? Defied Richard? Now why ... when he told me the story ... did he leave out that part I wonder?"

"I don't imagine he considered it important. Now what is this all about?"

"Nothing, Papa. Nothing worth repeating. I'll put it all to rights soon enough when Francis returns to his impetuous wife, who he is probably even now calling his 'shrewish Kate'!" Bubbling with laughter it came to her that for almost an hour she had forgotten her melancholy. It was a great relief. "That was most courageous of him, don't you agree, Papa? Yes, indeed, most courageous. I don't believe I've ever heard that he spoke out against Richard on an important matter before."

෧෨

Due to the length of the assembly term, it was well after Christmas before the family was reunited at Mount Airy. A great feast was prepared in joint celebration of the holiday past, the new year, and the new granddaughter. Roast duck and ham were prepared and served with winter greens, sweet yams, rice bread, caudled apples and claret wine. Everyone was merry and with such high spirits, the toasting was liberal.

"We welcome into our family the new little Anne Lloyd! She may not be with us this night, but she is in our hearts," announced the proud grandfather from head of table. "May her days be happy, and her face as fair as those of my own beautiful daughters." He drained his glass, winking at his wife as he did so. The Lord knew he was happy to have Rebe home. He had sorely missed her.

In the excitement no one noticed when Becky slipped away. It was her mother who called attention to her absence. "Where on earth is Becky? She was here a moment ago."

Francis, wanting to avoid a general exodus from the table, said, "She … Becky mentioned earlier, she was suffering from head-ache. Don't worry. Zoey has followed her and will tend to her needs."

An hour later, perplexed over what was really bothering his wife, yet not wishing to alarm anyone, Francis bid the family a good night and excused himself. Climbing the stairs, he pondered Becky's headaches. He had learned they didn't always mean the obvious. Sometimes her head didn't even hurt at all, he thought. Entering their chamber he found her apparently asleep. The curtains on the bed were drawn and, but for a flicker of firelight, the room was in darkness. Zoey was seated beside the hearth. Francis motioned her away and the door closed softly behind her.

Thinking he heard a sob, he lifted the bed curtain. Becky's face was in the pillow, her shoulders shaking.

"Say, what is this? Tears?" he whispered, willing some cheer into the words. He'd never seen her cry anything but tears of anger or frustration before. A curious lump came to his throat as her sadness invaded his mind, and he perceived the source of her anguish and felt helpless before it.

Oh, Francis," she sobbed, "hold me, just hold me. I'm so hateful and awful, no one will ever love me again!"

"Now, now," he soothed, "don't cry. Please, love, don't cry. I can't bear it. Tell me what you think you've done that's so terrible. I'm sure it's nothing ... nothing at all."

"The baby. Elizabeth's baby. I've wished her dead, or not born, so I could bring the first Tayloe grandchild into the world. I haven't even been able to rejoice with Mama and Papa. I've been outside their joy from the beginning ... and I can't bear to have Cate around me, all full of new life with her round belly and full breasts ... I told her to go away, I didn't need her."

He'd known before, or suspected, but now total understanding came to him. Her subtle withdrawal in past weeks. He'd passed it off to the burden of managing a household, when he'd bothered to consider it at all. For in truth, the politics in Williamsburg had occupied by far the greater portion of his thoughts. Remorse flooded him, bringing tears to his eyes and he drew her from the pillow, against his heart. At last, when he felt her sobbing stop, he told her, "Do you know what? Elizabeth, being your elder sister should be entitled to have the first grandchild. Now is that not logical? And here you are smudging up your lovely face with tears, all for naught. Next year, love, it will be our turn to present a grandchild to Mount Airy. Perhaps we might even surprise them with a son!"

Becky clutched at him thinking how foolish it all seemed now. "Do you really think so, darling? And will they be as pleased and excited as they are tonight?"

"I'm sure of it, but it will be the more likely to happen," he laughed, "if you'll allow this weary burgess to share your bed with you, my lady. For here is where it all begins."

∽

Following on the heels of the new year, another birth took place. Under the experienced hands of old Berth, Cate brought her second child into the world, coming just over a year since the death of her first. "Now, Cate, push!" ordered Berth from the foot of the birthing stool. "Harder! You goin' have t' do better'n dat. Dis baby is big. Come on, I sees his head. Clamp down on dat stick 'tween yo'r teeth an' push!" She had shooed Doc Ephrim from the room once and bodily shoved him out the second time. Cate didn't want him there. He wasn't needed, this was women's work, no man was required for this part.

Cate moaned between clenched teeth. Sweat poured from her body and trickled to the floor. She thought it would be easier this time, and she guessed it was, but were it not for the wood between her teeth, she wouldn't be able to keep from screaming. Why did Berth say he? She hadn't dared hope it might be a boy. Could it be a boy? Then the pain came again, closer this time to the one before. And harder. It pushed all other thought from her mind. There was nothing but the unbearable pain. Then abruptly, a small slimy creature slipped into Berth's hands in a flood of watery mucus and blood.

"Ain't he beauteous? He's a boy!" she shouted, loud enough for Ben to hear from the hall.

Cate collapsed, barely awake. Zoey helped her to lie down while Berth tended the child, cutting and knotting the cord. "Now watch t' see she bleeds clean, Zoey. Push her stomick if'n it don't come in a minit. Dis chile is sho' a strong lookin' boy! Um-mhmm." She finished washing the baby, dried him gently and wrapped him in a soft cloth before delivering the tiny bundle to his mother. He hadn't for a second stopped wailing since he took his first breath. Cate gathered the fruit of her womb to her breast. He was indeed beautiful, she thought, peeking into the blanket. She felt as she had the first time she'd seen Isaac. Another perfect man had come into her life. Knowing this, she shivered, having experienced how quickly one could lose what one had dared to love.

૭⌇

Some hours later Becky arrived to see the baby. She found Cate trying to teach the child to nurse, and watched in awe as Cate urged her enlarged nipple into the small mouth. The infant seemed not to know what was expected of him but experimented eagerly, and was soon sucking noisily. Cate pried her eyes reluctantly from her son to greet her mistress. "Look at Isaac's boy, Miss Becky. Jes' look at him. He's sucklin' like a li'l pig already!"

"He's beautiful, Catey. When you've finished feeding him, I shall look him over properly," Becky said, struggling to fight down the twinge of jealousy she felt watching the tiny black baby pull contentedly at his mother's breast.

"You kin see him now, Miss Becky," Cate offered, putting the infant away from her. "He won't git no milk at first anyway. It takes dem time t' bring it in." Tenderly, she unwrapped her son and laid him beside her.

The first thing Becky noticed was his color. He was not mulatto-cream like Cate nor shiny black like his African father. He was more a chocolate brown. His features weren't broad nor flat, they were precise and delicate. He moved his tiny frame with remarkable energy, pushing out his arms and legs with healthy thrusts. In a moment he began to cry, seeming to be expressing his frustration at having been forced to leave the warmth and comfort of his mother's body. His cry was strong and clear, a sign of a healthy baby, Becky decided, remembering the mewing wail of Cate's girl-child. "He's lovely, Cate. He really is," Becky whispered, cautiously wrapping the baby in his blanket again, which caused his unhappiness to cease immediately. She giggled. "He didn't like us staring at him, I guess! What will you name him?"

A look of alarm came over the face of the Negress. "Why Miss Becky, you knows your pappy names de black chillins when dey born. Don' play sech a trick on me."

"What would you like to call him?" Becky persisted.

Cate thought for only a minute. "If'n I could pick his name fo sho 'nuff, I'd take Samu'l 'cause its out de Holy Book. Jes' like Isaac. Yes'm, I'd take Samu'l. Dat's a fittin' name fo a strong boy."

"Then that shall be his name," Becky stated. "Goodnight, little Samuel. Sleep well, so your mother may rest."

"But, Miss Becky, Massa Tayloe ..."

"You leave Massa Tayloe to me. Don't worry."

When her mistress had gone, Cate once more unwrapped her son, examining him carefully, from top to bottom, marveling at his male beauty. Satisfied that he was perfect right down to the erect little penis, she bundled him snugly and gave him the other nipple. "Samu'l, Samu'l," she whispered sleepily, rolling the name on her tongue. "Isaac, if'n you kin hear me, I hopes you likes de name I done give your man-chile."

In the hall over the kitchen dependency, at the top of the steps, Becky was startled to see Ben hadn't moved since she'd passed him on her way into Cate's chamber. "What are you doing here, Ben?" she asked, as he stood to let her pass.

The slave gazed openly at her for a moment, letting the reason sift through his mind. He struggled with it, then answered warily, "I don' rightly think I kin explain it, Miss Becky." He was embarrassed, and also very relieved no one except Berth suspected his attachment to Cate.

His mistress shrugged and moved on down the passage. "Well, it's cold tonight and it's time to go to bed," she called over her shoulder.

Ben smiled and resumed his position on the second step where he could watch Cate's door and hear the sounds from within. Settling his buttocks into the worn circle on the step, he said, "Yas'm, Miss Becky."

A Quiet Time

Within a few days Francis settled again into the exhilarating, happy niche of his house building. When he pondered it, he was amazed at the eagerness he'd felt to set off for the assembly in the first place. He was beginning to understand that the greatest satisfaction of all was to be found in the coming home. A conviction was growing in him that he truly belonged to these fertile lands of Richmond County. The completion of Menokin would bind him irrevocably to this place. Political obligations might continue to call him away, perhaps even intrigue and entice him away, but when he had done with this duty, the call to home would always promise a sublime fulfillment.

Winter weather, however was hampering construction. The great stone blocks were slowly, painstakingly carted from the landing, but could only be mortared in place as temperature permitted. Tedious work and seemingly endless, he thought, but the result would be worth waiting for. One of the biggest thrills had come shortly after the death of the slave Isaac, when the finely proportioned hipped roof had begun to take shape. Francis felt his anticipation building daily, and often lingered on the site until dusk. He'd come to love the land and the house beyond all expectations, wondering how he'd ever considered remaining at Loudoun farm. He watched the giant sandstones hoisted into position to form foot-and-a-half thick walls, and admired the shape of the small but perfectly placed window openings, the rounded arch of the double doorway. Sometimes while he watched he dreamed of winter days he would spend in front of his study fire, of arranging his treasured collection of books, of musicals and entertainments, of dancing feet and the voices of children. He imagined the guests who would be invited there, and how Becky would touch every corner with her enchanting blend of grace and beauty. He conjured up the mouth-watering harvest of a summer orchard, the thrill of hunting and fishing his own lush acres, and the reward of prolific tobacco crops to make it all a reality. An integral part of every dream was his vision of the son he would one day teach to assume the responsibility of mastering the plantation.

Throughout 1770 Francis Lee was a man deeply involved in a dual love affair—with his passionate young wife and with the magnificent home he was bringing together block by stone block in which he would shelter his family. After he was gone, it would house his son's family, maybe even the children of his grandsons. It was an extraordinary dream, and richly satisfying.

In February of that year news arrived of an encounter between the King's troops and the local citizenry in a place called Golden Hill in the New York Colony. "It seems the New York Assembly ignored the will of the people when it voted to appropriate funds for the quartering of English soldiers. There's been a clash with the citizens," Francis related as he scanned the news.

"That isn't surprising, is it?" Becky answered. She allowed her hands to fall quiet on her needlework while she thought about what her husband had said. "Why should an American colony furnish money to house English troops anyway? I assume Parliament has demanded it, but why would a colonial government accept it? What did the New Yorkers do? Does it say?"

"First off, I've heard the assembly there is very loyal to the Crown, but it appears the citizenry have other ideas and took up arms, mostly clubs and rocks I imagine, and rioted under the leadership of a group calling themselves the Sons of Liberty. It was the arrest of one Alexander Mcdougall, who had authored a broadside critical of the assembly's decision to fund the troop quartering, that set them off. Soldiers used bayonets against the crowd and more than a few were wounded according to this account."

"Where will it all end?" Becky said, worried. "If only they'd repeal the taxes, then they'd have no need of soldiers from England in our colonies!"

"It's been promised that only the tax on tea will remain, as I've told you. But, Goddamn it, that's not acceptable. Forgive my language, love, but there's no other way of expressing it! And to forbid our expansion and development of the lands west of the mountains, is equally intolerable. Why, in '63 when some of us formed the Mississippi company, if we'd been permitted to carry out our plans, thousands of settlers would now be prospering on lands of their own and our settled boundaries would be greatly expanded. The purchasers would have been required to make payment in small amounts as they went along. An entire new society could have been established."

"And you and your brothers would all be the richer for it," Becky murmured quietly. She'd learned the background of the land scheme from her father.

His wife's objectivity continued to surprise him. He knew it was part and parcel of the charm she held for him, yet at times like this it tended to bring him up short and he hastened to explain, "Well ... of course that's true so far as it goes. Some of the Washingtons and Fitzhughs, as well as others, were in on the plan also," he defended himself. "The point being, that someone with the cash and the knowledge to carry the thing off had to organize it. There have been many such plans from time to time, but I think ours was set to be fair to all involved. We weren't seeking a proprietary as in the old days, but merely a grant to subdivide two-and-a-half million acres into individual plots ... for sale at easy payments, thus making it available to any freeholder."

"But England refused you the grant."

"Not only that. They continue to favor the French in every aspect of the territory. They even routed the American settlers already on those lands before our grant was requested!" It wasn't often that something aggravated him enough to set his blood to boiling, but this did it every time he reviewed the events. He got up to pace the room.

Becky ducked her head to hide her smile. She knew his irritation would cool quickly. His tempers came in short and infrequent bursts. But before he quit his pacing she saw him double suddenly, as if in pain and she dropped all thoughts of the Mississippi lands.

His face went pale and he clutched his hands to his stomach. "Dysentery. The damned bloody flux ... I'm not able to shake it," he moaned, returning to his chair.

"Have you taken the medicine Dr. Jones gave you?" Becky asked, coming to stand beside him. "My poor darling." She felt his forehead for fever but found no sign of it.

"Faithfully, my girl, faithfully. To no avail, obviously," he groaned as another of the convulsive pains swept his abdomen. Walter Jones was new at doctoring, but surely Edinburgh had taught him what there was to know about the flux. Francis wondered if something else could be the matter with him. He'd been feeling rotten for a few days.

"Perhaps you need a good rest. Why don't you lie down for the remainder of the day? Menokin will survive without your visit ... I'm sure of it," she couldn't refrain from adding slyly. She loved to tease him.

Despite his discomfort, he grinned. "Without my supervision the place would still be a rambling pile of planks and stones. And you know it, my love. But ... I suppose I need you to set me straight from time to time when I become puffed with my own importance." He stood to relieve his position, leaning on her arm. "Perhaps you're right. Dobson can manage for a day without me. A change will do me good, but not a day in bed. I think I'll ride to Sabine Hall. I've not had a good visit with Colonel Landon in several weeks. Besides, he has that amazing stock of medicinal remedies which may yield something more worthy than the emetic tartar and jalap Dr. Jones prescribed."

∽

While the evening was still early, before the damp of the February night waned cold enough to bring on a real chill, Francis returned to Mount Airy. He'd dined with the Carter family but gave special care to what foods he put in his stomach, avoiding the succulent pork and rich pudding. Nonetheless he was forced to stop once on the return ride. An unpleasant experience in the dark, squatting over a log on a frigid winter evening, he found.

He brought home a rhubarb preparation and some pills of mild soap, guaranteed to bring on the "gentle pukes" that Carter considered necessary to cure his malady. He also brought news of a christening to which they were invited at the end of March. Robert and Winifred's youngest was to be baptized.

"How are you feeling?" Becky asked in the morning when they awoke. "I didn't hear you get up in the night. Are you better?"

Francis stretched, moving his body tentatively. "I didn't take my soap pill or I'm sure you'd have heard me getting up! For one thing, or the other, if you know what I mean. But I do feel free of pain at the moment. Breakfast will tell I should think."

"Darling, do you know what Catey told me yesterday?" Becky asked as soon as she was assured he felt all right. "She says she won't come with us to live at Menokin ... that she's staying right here to wait on Mama!"

"What brought that on? I hope it's not because of me."

Becky shook her head, green eyes flashing. "Nothing like that. She simply says she can't live there and be forced to raise Samuel on the ground where Isaac spilled his blood. She says 'de

Lawd' told her not to go, that it would bring more bad luck! I haven't been able to do a thing with her, and if she won't go, then I won't go either!"

Francis couldn't take this very seriously. "Well since there's no possibility of our moving in before next year anyway, you both have plenty of time to change your minds," he laughed. "Looks to me as though we might do well to pray for a reverse message from the Lord, however."

"I wish you'd grasp the seriousness of the situation, Francis. If Cate doesn't have a change of heart then I shall have to order her to come. I refuse to be without Cate, do you understand? I could have her whipped for insubordination, and be well within my rights and good conscience!" she stormed.

He rubbed his eyes and pretended to whack his ear as though he hadn't heard her right. "That doesn't sound like the girl on Nicholson Street who argued for compassion toward the house slaves, love."

"Oh pooh, you know I don't mean it!" Bounding from bed, she hurried into her wrapper. The morning was frigid. "Now," she said, looking hard at him, "I think it's you who's trying to keep *me* in line, so all's fair I guess. But ... final word ... I will *not* be without her!" Then she was gone to locate the boy to rebuild the fire. Her husband shouldn't leave the warmth of their bed until the chamber was warmed.

The cold and fog and dampness of winter subsided at last as spring began to come in sporadic spurts to the pastoral lands of Richmond County. With the shift of seasons there were always colds, agues, fevers and other disorders. Scarcely a soul escaped one sort of suffering or another. All people of the Mount Airy plantation from youngest to eldest, black and white, were affected at some time during March through June; there were three deaths among the slaves.

Francis found he wasn't well enough to travel to Williamsburg for the start of the assembly on May 21st; the dysentery continued to plague him occasionally and that, along with a nasty cold, combined to keep him home. Recovering in time to attend the last several sessions, however, he was present in June when the burgesses signed the second Nonimportation Agreement against English goods. Although the Townshend Duties had been revised by Parliament under Lord North in April as promised, now covering tea only, the liberals were far from ready to let the issue die, as Francis had predicted. There was much discussion on the matter prior to the vote.

"But North has also allowed the Quartering Act to expire without renewal; the colonies no longer have to provide funds for housing British troops," argued Carter Braxton at an informal gathering in the Raleigh's Apollo Room. "That should pacify even the rabble of New York," he sneered.

"So," countered Patrick Henry, "they had no right to set their soldiers on American soil in the first place, yet there are troops in Boston and New York at this very moment!"

"The populace in those colonies has been brash and unruly. The laborers in Boston have provoked the clashes, asking for more trouble," Benjamin Harrison said, backing up Braxton.

"But only after the soldiers sought part-time work in that city, taking jobs away from the local boys and men. I have it from Sam Adams himself," persisted Henry.

"Well, I'm for allowing Virginia's ban on imports to expire, in view of British attempts to pacify us," sniffed Braxton. "I think it's time to cooperate and the other colonies will follow suit."

"No," Francis spoke up, entering the argument for the first time. "We made our bed. We said that *complete* repeal of the duties would be the prerequisite for dropping our sanctions against imports. And I think it would be a sign of weakness to go back on that pledge at this juncture. I would have to side with Patrick."

Ben Harrison, a staunch monarchist, having turned quickly from his brief fling at colonial patriotism during the Stamp Act crisis, expressed amazement at his colleague from Richmond County. "Mr. Lee, you are unreasonable, Sir! Surely you can see we'll only hurt ourselves by continuing to be stubborn and inflexible. These tactics won't endear us to our brothers across the sea. You have a new home to furnish, and I'm certain you require goods ... cloth, china, furniture and the like ... from Mother England? You also have a lovely young wife to clothe. Like the rest of them," he swept the room with a meaningful glance, "she is no doubt spoiled and quite accustomed to fine silks and dimity. Do you think she's ready to settle for homespun? These ladies of ours have a way of making our lives miserable when they don't get what they want. Right, Gentlemen?"

"Yes, Frank, what say you to that?" nagged Carter Braxton, with a broad grin. "Your lady will soon have exhausted her dowry, no matter how generous!"

Francis exhibited the control that made him so well liked by ignoring the jest. He and Richard had never cared for Braxton, but this wasn't the time to let personalities cloud his vision. "There are other countries from which to purchase. Mrs. Lee has ordered a bureau and two chairs from France. And there is fine American furniture to consider as well. As for cloth, Virginia planters are beginning to grow sizable amounts of their own flax and tend larger flocks of sheep. In a few years, we could be self-sufficient with the exception of the very finest goods and in time, I think, even that is possible. Mills are springing up in many counties even now."

"What are you suggesting? That we drop the tobacco that has made us all wealthy, and turn our lands into a pasturage for sheep?" Braxton continued to prod, as though looking for a fight.

"The tobacco isn't going to do us much good if we lose the British market," Francis remarked curtly. "Aside from all that, I stick by my original premise. We should renew the Agreement until *all* the conditions are met, including tea."

Now Thomas Jefferson spoke, taking sides. "I agree with Henry and Lee in this matter. We should continue the nonimportation until England repeals all the duties and withdraws all the troops."

"Well," countered Harrison with a fine arrogance, "it shall be decided on the floor of the House and not over the billiard table or the brandy glass, Gentlemen!"

Despite the eloquent arguments of Harrison, Braxton, Pendleton, Nelson, and the like, the liberal faction prevailed, retaining the most votes. The new Agreement was signed on the 22nd of June 1770, signaling that import of many English commodities would continue to be against the law in Virginia.

On a hot, sultry August evening, when summer had wrung the starch out of every living creature, Philip Lee hosted his annual get-together of the clan. The Lees gathered at Stratford for a fish feast and dance on the wharf at his landing on the Potomac River. Philip had concluded the place was good for nothing else, with the warehouses burned to the ground and not likely to be replaced anytime soon.

Heat had drawn the moisture from the wooded hillsides, leaving the earth parched and the the air feeling like steam rising from a great boiling kettle. Clouds of aimless little gnats swarmed in drifting patches, and mosquitoes hummed and buzzed hungrily in a never ending attack. It was all to be expected on an August day in the Neck of Virginia as the guests chattered and greeted one another, some having not been together since the last year's Stratford gathering.

"Just look at that river, Elizabeth," Becky commented lazily to her sister-in-law. "I swear to goodness it's not even making a single wiggle. It looks like the water is too hot to bother to change its tide." She giggled, enjoying her own joke.

Elizabeth Steptoe Lee, languishing in the center of the quilt on which they were sitting, dabbed at the exposed portion of her damp bosom with a lace handkerchief. "Phil hopes to begin the music as soon as the sun sets. Maybe we'll get a breeze by then." She watched the four Chantilly children and Thomas's four from Belleview dart up and down the hill with her own two daughters, Matilda and Flora, wondering where they got the energy in such weather. "Did you enjoy the fish, Becky? I thought the crabs and sheeps-head especially tasty this year."

"Oh yes, I agree, Elizabeth. Everything was delicious." Becky turned to smile at Francis, who sat beside her, and reached for his hand, a look of love passing between them.

Elizabeth, wondering why anyone wanted to touch another hot hand in this heat, said, "You two act as though you're still courting, what with all that hand holding. Here you've been married almost two years."

Becky smiled. "One year and a half," she corrected her hostess. "But I reckon that twenty years from now we'll still be the same, won't we, darling?"

"You know nothing's going to change us," he agreed. "You see the pickle I'm in, Elizabeth? This dear creature is quite deluded that I am totally under her spell! How can I disappoint her then? So I sit beside her, hold her hand from time to time, just to keep her confidence up." He tweaked Becky's nose. "Poor child."

It was a new experience, being teased in front of a sister-in-law. Becky decided her pride had probably needed deflating. It was a painless enough way he had accomplished it. "Isn't he a wit, Elizabeth? Such a wit!" She gave him a gentle shove. "Go to your brothers, darling. You can hold my hand anytime."

It was true. The four brothers hadn't been together since Francis and Becky's wedding. Thomas and his family could seldom arrange the trip from Stafford County up-river. Richard, Tom, and Francis watched as Philip inspected the barges moored to the wharf. Ship's lanterns were hung from the pilings and would soon light the dancing festivities. Philip called some instructions to the Negro fiddle players tuning their instruments on the sandy shore.

Finally the sun sank low on the river sending a brilliant trail across the deep green Potomac, painting the jagged Stratford Cliffs with crimson. The Maryland shores, invisible in the haze of midday heat, stood out clearly in the sun's last hurrah. A more peaceful sight could scarcely be imagined, thought Francis, drawing contentedly on his pipe. He thoroughly enjoyed a return to his boyhood haunts. Would the day ever come again, he wondered, when William and Arthur would join them? He sighed at the improbability of it, what with William established in business and Arthur soon to enter London's Middle Temple in pursuit of his law degree. Turning to Richard he spoke of another matter, a recent excitement at Mount Airy.

"I haven't had a chance to tell you of the killing of four of my father-in-law's horses. They were shot! Can you believe it? It happened a few days ago in the pasture that joins a field of our neighbor, Neale."

Richard was more than a little startled. "What? Shot, you say? Who would be responsible for such a low deed? Does Tayloe have any clues?"

"There is certain evidence pointing to Neale's overseer. The colonel has requested Colonel Landon, as county officer, to put the matter under immediate investigation. His thought is that if it can be proved the overseer is guilty, then he can sue Neale for trespass, thereby regaining the value of the animals."

"Why is Neale's man a suspect?" Thomas asked, joining the conversation.

"The principal reason is that a few weeks ago Mr. Neale threatened to shoot any Tayloe horses that wandered into his fields. If he kept his fences in better repair he'd have no such concern. But actually these horses were on Mount Airy land when killed." A mosquito landed on his hand and he slapped at it. "Damned critters!" he said, missing the insect. "I suppose in the end nothing will come of the investigation, and both sides will let the matter drop. There's been bad feeling there for some time I gather."

"Four blooded horses represent a good purse. But you're probably right, Frank. After the first anger wears off, one realizes the battle is seldom worth the cost. It could also be said that Tayloe should fence in his horses, for that matter," Thomas commented with his usual casualness. He was the most reserved and unhurried of the brothers, a lovable man, even more unruffled in the face of adversity than was Francis.

"One can only hope, dear brothers, that is not to be the way with our grievances against Mother England. We can't afford to let them drop when it becomes troublesome to pursue the cause of true liberty!" It never took Richard long to get to his favorite topic. "I have correspondence from Patrick regarding the canceled conference on Indian affairs that he traveled to New York to attend. He says the meeting was sabotaged by Ministry officials! And further, that the delegates from various colonies having never met before, except the few at the Stamp Tax Congress when Virginia wasn't represented, were poorly organized. They did little, if anything, to protest the futility of the trip, merely accepted the rebuff and returned home."

"Great Britain arranged the conference in the beginning, R.H., and therefore had the absolute right to cancel it!" Philip countered angrily. "I am of little patience with your hotheaded, whippersnapper of a friend, Patrick Henry!"

"Wait a minute," Thomas interjected. "The way I understand it, the conference was canceled because the New York governor feared the gathering of American colonials on any issue. After the rioting there over the issue of quartering soldiers, he was taking no more chances. Even though the Quartering Act has since been allowed to expire," he added.

"You can scarcely blame him for that. It's his duty to maintain peace and order in his colony," Philip snapped. It was a great trial to him that in family discussions of this sort his brothers were invariably banded together on the opposite side of the argument.

"At any rate, brothers, all was not lost," laughed Francis. "Patrick returned with a variety of interesting tidbits of information from the trip. Why, I understand that in New York he found they have Dutch churches, German Lutherans, a Presbyterian church for the Scots, a Catholic church for the Irish, and even the Jews have their own synagogue and cemetery. Apparently all live in harmony. It's enough to send Giberne to his knees for a week in consternation!" Francis felt no need to explain Lunenburg Parish's Isaac Giberne's prejudices, his reputation being wide spread.

Thomas smiled fondly at his younger brother. No doubt about it, Frank was the family peacemaker. "I hear rumors, Loudoun," using the affectionate name, "speaking of religion, that the Baptists have increased their numbers in the Neck. Our sister Hannah is, no doubt, rejoicing over this fact."

"I judge the rumor to be correct. Reverend Giberne has devoted several of his sermons in recent months to opposition of their tactics. He claims the basis of their gospel to be pure whimsy and overblown enthusiasm. But as you mention, Hannah is far from alone in her beliefs these days," Francis said.

Philip, glancing first to be certain his wife was out of hearing distance, said, "Elizabeth's mother is devoted to the Baptist cause also," he told them stiffly. "It is difficult to understand how one of good sensible family can be so persuaded."

What a burden it must be to the dogmatic Philip to suffer not only a sister, but a mother-in-law as well, won over to the bastard faith, thought Francis.

241

The ten children, ranging in age from three to twelve, suddenly hurtled upon the four men standing on the wharf. Having heard the fiddlers tuning up, they arrived pell-mell, pushing and laughing in their eagerness. The frivolity would start off with the country dances, the reels, they all loved so well. Down to the youngest they would participate with every ounce of vigor the humid evening would permit. Becky watched them, laughing at their antics. Little Hannah clung to Francis, tugging on the knees of his breeches, having made her selection of a partner.

"They so enjoy being together, all these little cousins," laughed Mrs. Pinchard, the newcomer among them. "I'm most anxious to contribute my share to the family numbers."

"When is your baby due?" Becky asked, already having observed it couldn't be too many months away.

"We look for our blessed event in December," answered Richard's wife. "Mary, you know, is also with child."

Becky watched as Mary Aylett Lee, Thomas's wife, spoke briefly with her children's governess. "How lovely for you both," she exclaimed somewhat wistfully. "How I long for the day when I'll be one of you new mothers. Wouldn't it be wonderful with three little ones close of an age?" The sigh that followed was a combination of yearning and perhaps a bit of lethargy brought on by the oppressive heat.

᷄

By December of 1770 the colonies of New York, Rhode Island, Pennsylvania, Massachusetts and South Carolina had dropped their sanctions against the import of British goods. Politically, Virginia continued to hold out. There were certain merchants who refused to cooperate, however, while others retaliated against the personal hardship imposed by their elected leaders by charging exorbitant prices for what goods they were able to smuggle.

There was a constant haggle going on, with charges of 'traitor' and 'radical' and 'scalawag' bandied about freely.

Looking out for their own interests, several of the Lees, the Carters, John Tayloe, and a few others gathered at Sabine Hall in January of the new year to hatch a scheme for opening a store of their own in the Northern Neck. When the afternoon ended spirits were high. Between them they had established a charter and bylaws for a general store to be subscribed to by "industrious planters" as Landon Carter put it. Their goal was to raise six-thousand pounds by subscription, allowing a vote to anyone who invested twenty or more pounds. The manager would be instructed to allow only those purchases which could be considered sufficient for each family's needs, thereby preventing hoarding. The jointly-owned store would be swift punishment for shopkeepers who refused to abide by the ban on goods from Great Britain.

Ten days later, an article advertising the proposed venture appeared in the Rind edition of the *Virginia Gazette*. Setting forth the restrictions and bylaws, it was ended with a note: *"Subscriptions towards establishing the above patriotic scheme, will be immediately opened under the patronage of the Honourable John Tayloe, Colonels Landon Carter, Richard Henry Lee, Francis Lightfoot Lee, Mr. Richard Parker, Mr. Samuel Hipkins, and many other well disposed Gentlemen of Richmond, Westmoreland, Northumberland, Lancaster, and the adjacent counties."*

What said gentlemen had not bargained for was the period of uneasiness and uncertainty pervading the colony in the months following the sudden death of Governor Botetourt in the October just past. By July, when the burgesses were next called to session by the council president, there being no governor yet appointed, sixty-three of their number failed to attend. Thus it was not a problem for the conservatives to gather strength among the moderates and vote out the Nonimportation Agreements. An undercurrent of tension prevailed, but soon life slipped back into the former pattern. Merchants were again free to purchase and sell supplies as they wished. Thus the plan for the Northern Neck 'patriotic' store was abandoned and soon forgotten.

Politically, it remained a quiet time on the surface of things. The Earl of Dunmore's appointment as the new Virginia governor came in September of '71, almost a year after the death of Botetourt and was greeted by Virginians with a notable lack of enthusiasm. Even the staunch loyalists among them couldn't deny Dunmore's limited show of manners, his crude ways in comparison to the elegant Botetourt.

Agitation against Great Britain did not die during these days, but it could be said to have dimmed, or perhaps gone under cover. Those remaining active behind the scenes included Richard Henry Lee and Patrick Henry, who continued an ongoing correspondence with Sam Adams and other north-easterners. Thus, although their public outcry assumed a latent posture, as might describe a hibernating bear—a beast resting while quietly gathering strength. There were those, however, who never doubted there would be renewed momentum and they would be ready when, at the first provocative whiff of infringement of colonial rights, the call came to leap into action once again.

Menokin House

The gray dawn was streaked with the first light of morning as an orange and red glow captured the eastern sky, reflecting into a south window at Menokin. Becky stirred sleepily. Her first thought was of the awakening day outside her window. It could only be beautiful, following as it did two days of rain, which was good for crops but bad for people, she mused, stretching lazily. When she reached for Francis she found his side of the bed empty. Where could he have gone so early? She missed him instantly. Early morning had become a special time of day since their move to Menokin House, no longer spoiled by noisy raids from the Tayloe sisters bent on discovering secrets behind closed doors. Now they enjoyed privacy, delicious privacy every morning. Today was the first time in the year they'd been in the house she remembered awakening to find herself alone. Curious, but not concerned, she decided to enjoy her solitude a bit longer. Letting her thoughts drift, she knew Cate would knock on the door soon with hot coffee. This was another early morning treat. Laced with fresh cow's milk and sugar, it was almost as satisfying as the English tea they denied themselves since the boycott began.

Thinking of Cate, she thought of Ben and then Samuel, and how they'd all come together to Menokin as a family. If it hadn't been for Ellie, she and Francis wouldn't have guessed how it happened as it did. It had been late June of 1771 when the final day for moving arrived. Until the very last minute, with wagons, carts, and the carriage loaded with furniture, bed linens, dishes, pots, kettles, utensils, food, candles, clothes, medicines, and a multitude of other necessities, Cate had stubbornly, steadfastly held to her decision. She refused to move to Menokin no matter what they did to her. Seating herself with Samuel, now grown to an alert toddler, in her one chair, she refused to budge. Sammy, huge black eyes darting in all directions, tipped his curly head from side to side as though trying to assess the situation. Zoey and Cris pleaded; Becky cajoled to the point of angry tears; finally old Berth begged Cate for the sake of her own hide, as well as theirs, to give in. All the while everyone waited outside thinking how foolish it was to put up with such nonsense, and yet no one had any idea what to do. Becky wouldn't leave without Cate, and Francis had no intention of threatening a whip, nor of going anywhere without his wife. Eventually Berth, too, gave up and, shrugging helplessly to Marse Frank, she took her place in the cart at the end of the procession.

"Dat gal needs a good lashin' to knock some sense upside her haid," Berth grumbled to anyone who wanted her opinion.

"No!" It was Ben who yelled, giving the old woman a look enough to shrivel. It brought snickers from the other blacks, who had begun quietly to make side bets on the fate of the recalcitrant Cate. What Ben did next drew loud guffaws from the slaves followed by a stern command to silence from the master.

"I'll be out in jes' a minit, Marse Frank. Cate, she goin' be wit me. If'n I has to drag her," Ben announced loud enough for all to hear. Striding across the courtyard he entered the dependency, slamming the door behind him. In the hall he passed Miss Ellie, but scarcely noticed her, so intent was he on his mission. He hadn't spoken to Cate since Isaac's death, but had kept a close watch over her every day. Now, he knew he must move fast or his nerve would fail. Drawing himself to his full height, which was considerable as he was proud to have descended from a tribe of tall men, he shoved open the door to Cate's tiny room, not bothering to close it behind him. He saw her eyes grow round with amazement and, recognizing a brief flicker of uncertainty there, pushed his advantage quickly.

Outside, Ellie pressed against the wall, listening, scarcely able to suppress her laughter.

"Pack yo' things, Cate. Dress Samu'l. We's leavin' fo' Menokin and you's comin' ... as my woman. It's time dat boy had a man to keer fo' him!" Petrified, unable to move, he waited.

Cate sat very still, her eyes never moving from his face. What Ben saw now was not hesitation. It was the look of a starving woman who, coming upon manna in the wilderness, needed a moment to deal with its promise. When he comprehended her thoughts, a grin began to spread at the corners of his wide mouth. He had won! His fierceness fell away, leaving him helpless, a sight that caused the little boy to giggle.

Cate knew Ben was a man of few words, that he meant every one he uttered. Like the night of Miss Becky's wedding. There had been no sense opposing him then, and there was no sense in doing it now, when it was very clear he'd made up his mind. In that instant it came to her that she'd been waiting for him, knowing he'd come eventually. What had taken him so long? Her eyes snapped, and seeing that grin take over his face she knew he read her mind. "You's got a pow'ful lot o' nerve, ol' man. But ... I likes a man wit nerve. We's comin', Ben." She pointed to Samuel's clothes folded neatly on the sagging bed and shoved the naked little body in Ben's direction. "Go to you new pa, Sammy. He's goin' dress you dis' mornin'."

Ben thought his heart would burst before he got the britches pulled over the firm brown bottom. It had been a long time since he'd dressed a child. His hands shook so he could barely manage the string that tied the neck of the small smock. When he emerged into the sunshine, Samuel astride his shoulders, he was a happy man. "Cate," he said with pride, "she's comin', Marse Frank. Start up de hosses ... we's all on our way to de new house, an' ol' Ben's got hisself a sassy new wife soons we kin find de preacher!"

Cate had sashayed out to the wagon, eyes flashing, daring anyone to make a snicker. And no one had. The way she strutted, you'd have thought she was the one who accomplished a miracle. Reaching for Ben's hand, she'd clambered up beside him, and pulled Samuel into her lap without a word. With the field hands jogging alongside and one of the young blacks Tayloe had given them driving the lead carriage, they set off.

It was in that way Ben, Cate, and Samuel became a family, but without Ellie's story, told amidst much hilarity, Becky and Francis would never have known the whole of it. The new family began life together in Menokin's snug cellar. It was the coolest place in summer except for the springhouse, and there was a fireplace to warm them in winter. Berth, Zoey, and Cris were lodged temporarily in the first cabin in the quarter with the cooks. Zoey usually slept in the upper hall in the great house, although sometimes her father or one of the others took her place as night servant to the master and mistress.

It still brought a smile to Becky's face to recall how it had all begun. Now, thinking again of her coffee, she wondered why Cate or Zoey hadn't brought it in, and decided it was high time to look for Francis. Pushing aside the muslin curtains they drew against mosquitoes, she rose to peer from the back window. She spotted him immediately. He was perched in the crook of a large branch of the beech tree that overhung the bower seemingly engrossed in something downhill. His brown hair, tied in a queue, gleamed golden in the morning sun just as it had on the day of their wedding when she had watched him from a window at Mount Airy.

"Halloo, Francis! Good morning, darling," she called.

Gazing up at the house, he found her face and waved. "Good day to you, sleepyhead! Say, what can you see from there?"

"You mean besides the man I love pretending to be a little boy on an adventure?"

"Yes," indulgently, to mask his impatience, "but what else do you see?" He'd wedged himself between branches as high as he could climb in order to get a better view of the hillside leading back up to the house.

"Well ... I see trees and birds, Sammy playing by the steps," she nodded to the child who had looked up upon hearing his name, "and I see the sun and ...

"Violets, Becky," he interrupted. "Do you see any violets?"

"Oh, yes, I do see some, there by the path."

"It's July, my love! Remember when we first went to the bower and ... well, among other memories, there were violets? That was mid-summer also. I think there are several varieties here, and I've decided to find other types also, plant them in various locations so you'll have violets as much of the year as possible. If woods violets bloom in summer as well as the dogtooth variety in spring, think what I should be able to do by cross-pollinating them with some cultured varieties!"

Her face felt warm, for she blushed at his mention of the first time they had lain in the bower. Oh my dearest love, you are such a joyful man and so thoughtful, she whispered to herself. Aloud she said, "Thank you, thank you, a thousand times thank you! And now, shall I come down to you or you come up to me?"

"You come out to me, and I'll show you where I intend to plant star-of-bethlehem over your terraces to complement the spring violets and jonquils."

As weeks multiplied into months, eventually passing into years, the gardens at Menokin grew in size and splendor. Francis created a fruitful paradise in the wilderness. He came to regard the strong branches of the beech tree as an excellent vantage point from which to survey his domain. From there he laid out the rose garden, decided where to plant the persian lilacs and the jasmin and thought about his fruit tree orchard, which in time came to produce not only peaches, but apples, mulberry trees, plums, wild cherries, persimmons, dates, and his favorite, figs. Paths were developed and laid with crushed oyster shells, and the whole took on the gracious character of a small but elegant country manor house.

The interior of the house was also skillfully completed over a period of time. The progress depended as well upon availability of cash as it did upon the procurement of skilled labor. The staircase rose immediately to the left of the main entry. Four spindle posts on each step were turned at an angle rather than placed square, thus imparting a unique touch to an otherwise ordinary stairway. The wall going up was richly paneled to about chest height. Paneling was also used on the wall below the bannister as well as on the sloped ceiling under the steps, after the turn at the small landing. Much care was given to finishing the dining room and its mantel, for this was to be the grandest room in the house. Above the lower mantel which was carved with a floral design confined to circles and set off by a narrow dentil, a paneled overmantle was designed which rose to the ceiling. Here, carved dentil work was again used to adorn the ceiling moldings. All in all, it was very pleasing and quite grand, Becky thought, each time she surveyed the finished effect. She decided on a deep grey-blue color for the plastered walls above the lower section, which was paneled to the chair rail. The blue was lovely with the golden damask draperies Nan had sewn.

For the parlors and her husband's study she chose a softer shade of the same blue. But in their sleeping chamber she had the walls painted pale green. Windows in all the downstairs rooms were hung with the yellow damask over inside paneled shutters. While in many Virginia homes outside shutters were popular, Menokin, following the Paladian design of Mount Airy, had heavy stone trim around the windows. As this style didn't lend itself to shutters, Francis determined they should be used inside the deepset windows. Here they could be folded back against the recesses when not in use, and the window ornamented by draperies.

On the second floor, with some subtle urging from Francis, Becky decided upon heavy linen flax from a local Virginia loom. Her compromise was that the curtains should be trimmed with an imported braid and tied back fashionably with gold tassels.

Actually, she was only mildly disappointed in the use of a common homespun. And Francis said it was patriotic, saving money as well.

The Lees had everything to provide them with domestic bliss and tranquility. With one exception. At the close of 1772, after three and a half years of supreme compatibility in every sense of the word, and a year and a half in their own house, Becky had not conceived the child they both so yearned to have. They rarely spoke of it anymore, but their family circle was incomplete and they both felt it to be so.

As for the rest of the family, on both sides they went right on populating the fertile plantation lands. Richard Henry's daughter Anne, was born in late 1770, and Thomas's daughter Lucinda, shortly thereafter. In 1771 Becky's sister Elizabeth gave birth to her second child, also a girl, and named her Rebecca. In September of '71 little short of a miracle had occurred.

"Becky? Becky, your mother has delivered of a son!" hollered Francis, throwing his reins to a slave boy as he jumped from his horse.

When she heard his call, she was in the middle of instructing Eve and Milly, the cooks, on how to prepare a recipe of apple-butter she had copied from a Boston newspaper. Emerging from the temporary wooden structure they were using for a kitchen, she wiped her hands on her apron and pushed her hair back from her damp brow. "Here I am, Francis. Did you call?"

Distracted by his wife's disheveled appearance, Francis was momentarily put off from his mission. "You have butter or something on your nose. What are you doing in the kitchen on such a warm afternoon?"

"I'm showing Eve how to make apple-butter. At least I'm trying. We were just finishing up. If we got it right I know it will be delicious."

"Is it not possible to *tell* her how to do it, rather than show her? Really, Becky, sometimes I think you carry things too far."

She shrugged. "I felt like stirring it myself. What a prig you are sometimes! Now what was your news?"

"Well ... you seem to have enjoyed yourself," he responded and, placing an arm around her shoulders, led her toward the house. "I have just come from Mount Airy. You have a brother!"

"A boy? I don't believe it! I just don't believe it. Why Papa must be ecstatic. Mama's fine, I suppose? She usually is after she delivers. It's only the last weeks before the birth that are hard on her."

Francis nodded yes to everything. She looked so happy at the news, he decided not to tell her that her mother had actually given birth to twin boys, one a healthy baby, while the other died shortly after being born. She would learn the sad news soon enough. He didn't want to spoil her joy at having a brother at last.

"Could you have my horse saddled while I change my clothes? I want to ride over to see my baby brother. Oh, darling, isn't it just wonderful? Papa finally has his son!"

Leaving her at the door, he turned to do her bidding. Remembering something, he called over his shoulder, "His name is John. John Tayloe III. As if you couldn't guess!"

Young John had passed his first birthday, was the apple of his father's eye, and a cherished favorite of his sister Becky. She rode over several times a week to play with him. Often she sat by his cradle, rocking it gently and singing to him. When he grew older, she spent hours teaching him to walk. He accomplished this feat, with her patient encouragement, before he turned a year old.

"You and Francis should really have a baby of your own, Becky," her mother advised quietly, coming upon the two in the orangery one day.

"I know, Mama. I know. It hasn't ... well, it isn't because we haven't wanted one, you know." She lowered her head, but the movement wasn't quick enough to prevent the older woman from seeing her daughter's eyes fill with tears.

"Becky, why Becky, you're crying. My dear child, I had no intention of making you cry. That will do no good, no good at all." She pushed an unruly strand of Becky's soft curls back into place. "Perhaps one of our good doctors could be of some assistance. There might be some chance there, I suppose."

"Oh pooh, Mama, what do they know? They don't even prescribe the right medicines half the time when we have the disorders." She dabbed at her eyes. "Don't worry. One day I shall bring a child to Francis and to Menokin. I just have to. I love him so much, it has to happen, Mama. In the meantime, I shall enjoy to the fullest the love of our precious Johnny." Gathering the fat little boy hungrily to her heart, she pressed her lips to one rosy cheek. "He's such a lovely robust baby, isn't he?"

It would be a gala celebration that snowy December day in 1772, the first formal entertainment Francis and Becky had planned—a joyful spirit of holiday pervaded Menokin House. At the top of the list of those invited were the Tayloes, for indeed the party was partially in appreciation to them because without the generosity of Becky's father and mother, there would not even be a house on the Menokin land in which to celebrate. Also on the guest list were the Carter family from Sabine Hall with their children, Philip and Elizabeth Lee, Robert and Frances Carter of Nomini, Becky's sister Ellie and her new husband Ralph Wormeley, Reverend Isaac Giberne and his lady, Martha and George Turberville from Peckatone, the elder Turbervilles as well, Hannah Corbin and Richard Hall with their children, and of course Richard Henry's Chantilly family. Thomas, too, had been invited but due to the distance and the uncertainty of the December weather, that family was not expected.

"If everyone comes, with as many children as there are, we most surely will be sitting on one another's laps!" Becky laughed as the serious planning got underway. "Why, from Sabine Hall alone three entire families will be here."

"It ought to warm the house up a bit, love. The Lord knows we could tolerate some of that." It had been an early winter and a challenge to keep the fires filled with wood.

For several weeks the household had been preparing for the big evening. Berth, with Zoey and Cris at her command, had given every inch of the house a thorough going over. The few pieces of precious silver shone and the furniture was buffed to a mellow glow. Even the windows gleamed. Cate, Samuel at her side, had found things to launder in every cupboard. She'd also done a fair job of altering Becky's wedding dress for the occasion. Rebecca Tayloe attributed her daughter's weight loss to a "growing-out" of baby fat—there was no denying the dress was too big before Cate set to work on it—and Becky thought her body did seem to be slimming down, maturing, as her mother said.

Standing before the oval looking glass she examined herself critically. At the second turn she paused to pinch some color into her cheeks. "Well," she said, as if not quite certain she approved of what she saw. "Do I look all right, darling?"

"You could not possibly look more lovely! Not even Aphrodite in all her glory could begin to compare. On our wedding eve, your beauty didn't surpass the way you look today," Francis assured her. He watched as she dabbed the jasmine scent he loved behind her ears and onto her wrists.

"Oh pooh, Aphrodite! And on our wedding night, you were too tipsy to even notice. Are you sure I look all right? I'm so nervous. You'd think we were expecting a company of royalty instead of people we've known all our lives. I'm that nervous."

He ignored the remark about being tipsy; he wasn't ready to laugh at himself over that yet. "Your nerves will settle as soon as everyone is here. It's just that you're excited. Perfectly natural. And you do look beautiful, love. I mean it."

She knew everything was ready. The sideboard was piled with summer's tenderly hoarded and preserved fruits, and sweets of every description. There were brandied peaches and cherries, a sugar gingerbread, plum cakes, and a rich fruit cake; while vegetables, sweetbreads and oyster pie, roast pork, ham, venison and lamb steamed in the kitchen. The guests had been invited for two o'clock and, together, they went downstairs to wait.

The wheels of the elegant carriage from Nomini Hall, crunching on the crusty snow as it rounded the drive, alerted them to the first arrivals. Mrs. Carter and the young ladies clambered down, and soon the boys and Councilor Carter rode up behind. The girls giggled, trying to keep their party skirts out of the snow and their fancy shoes dry. They were soon in the house hugging and curtseying to their host and hostess. Next to pull up to the steps were Colonel and Mrs. Tayloe, with Anne, Polly, Kitty, Sally and little John. "My brood is shrinking with three daughters married now, but we're still a coach full," laughed John Tayloe as he stamped the snow from his boots and planted a kiss on the forehead of his favorite daughter.

Soon the house was filled, chatter and laughter resounded throughout. Under Ben's direction, the fire in every room was kept blazing and candles were lit in the windows at dusk to encourage the guests to each corner of the house. It wasn't long before several of the Sabine Hall Carters organized a card game in the small front parlor, much to the chagrin of Colonel Landon.

"By God, Frank," he mumbled as he followed his host to the relative quiet of the study, "Robert the gangster feels it necessary to humiliate me once again by including young Landon in that game! The next thing you'll see will be Isaac Giberne, our morally depraved pastor, right there in the middle of it. Together, son and priest, they put me on the rack and turn the screws. It's more than a man can bear, to be forced to witness such depravity amongst one's own."

"You're wrong about one thing, Sir. The next one to join them will be my brother Philip, for a rousing card game with some betting on the side is dear to his heart also. At the moment, Colonel, Reverend Giberne is deeply engrossed in the musical concert. Several of the young ladies brought guitars and violins and Becky has a spinet. A gift from her father last year. They are gathered in the back parlor. Listen. That's a lovely melody for the Christmas season I think. A carol of peace on earth to all men. A most worthy sentiment, and one guaranteed to help a man look more kindly on those petty grievances within the family."

"Humph! Nonetheless, Giberne will soon overindulge himself on your good punch and decide one of the young ladies is to his liking! That's where my young grandson belongs. In with the young ladies, instead of drinking and gambling. Frank," he lowered his voice to a confidential tone, "regardless of your attempt to cheer me by pointing out the virtues of the carols, I must tell you that my days are becoming more miserable than ever. Robert has convinced the overseers that I'm a crazy old man, incapable of directing my own plantations any longer." He reached for Francis' arm, his fingers clutching at the fabric of his coat. "Tell me, do you think you might find an opportunity to speak with him about it? Perhaps a word from you on my behalf would be of some benefit. Robert respects you greatly."

Richard Henry and John Tayloe entered the room at that moment, sparing Francis the need to respond to the pathetic and embarrassing request. As much as he might privately sympathize with Carter, he wanted no part of another family's squabble.

"Well, Richard, your friends in Massachusetts are at it again I see. The London papers are full of the report on Boston's newly formed correspondence committee," Tayloe was saying

A serious man, Richard wasn't given to casual response when he considered the matter crucial. It was not in his nature to avoid conflict or open argument. "Sir," he said, "I am sure you are aware it's become necessary to pursue such methods in order to reach all the colonies with the seriousness of the English threat to carry off American citizens to stand trial in London! Such attacks on the liberty of our fellow colonials cannot be allowed. Indeed, such attacks on the liberties of any Englishman should not be tolerated by freedom loving men. I'm assuming you still continue to call yourself an Englishman?" His spare face and prominent nose had reddened somewhat due to his agitation and to the wine he'd consumed.

"Those particular Americans you refer to, Richard, are none other than common criminals. They boarded and burned a British vessel and they deserve to be punished!" Landon Carter's feelings on the matter were closely aligned with those of John Tayloe. In this case, he was referring to the Rhode Islanders who set fire to an English customs schooner off their coastline. "The Gaspée ran aground and they injured the captain and destroyed the vessel! You can't let them go unpunished!"

"But they should be tried in our own courts," Francis said firmly. "In an *American* court, Gentlemen. Americans shouldn't be carried to England for trial. It is wrong."

"Here or there, I really doubt that it's important enough to stir up the embers again. Parliament is attempting these days to understand our predicament. After all, they've imposed no new taxes, and we all know they're at least listening to us now," retorted Carter.

"Well then, what say you to the announcement that the Massachusetts governor and judges are all to be paid by the Crown from now on?" Richard was far from ready to abandon the subject.

"Hmm," Carter allowed as he dropped into a chair by the fire. He was always cold lately it seemed. "I think that is not particularly good news actually." He was beginning to feel his age these days, and wondered briefly if maybe Robert was right.

"Not very good news!" Richard repeated, growing emotional, his face redder than ever. "An American governor drawing his salary from the Crown will cripple all power of that assembly!"

John Tayloe launched upon the old conservative viewpoint which cautioned against over reacting to affairs in other colonies that did not need to concern Virginia. In a moment Francis excused himself, not relishing a political debate with his father-in-law. Richard would have to haggle on his own with the two old men. Besides, it was preying on his mind to check on Becky's state of nerves.

His concerns were unfounded. From the moment her family arrived and she presented baby John with his Christmas toy, she lost whatever qualms she'd harbored earlier. It was an intricate wooden wagon she gave him, carved in the slave quarter. It boasted clever movable wheels which immediately fascinated the child. Becky carried him off to the small chamber upstairs where she set Samuel, now three, to entertaining him. The small black boy raised eyes huge with wonder to the shimmering, rustling, silken gown his mistress was wearing, then finally to her face. He was clearly overwhelmed by the excitement, but at last he spoke.

"Come play, Mastah John. Ah's got blocks. You like dem?" he asked, offering one to the newcomer.

Becky left them, secure in the knowledge that Sammy would come for her or for Cate, if there were need. Downstairs, however, she changed her mind and sent Cris to watch over them, before stopping to greet Martha Turberville, Hannah Corbin's daughter and Francis's niece.

"Your house is nice, Becky. Small, but proper."

"Why thank you, Martha. I forgot until this moment that you haven't been here before, have you? Honestly, I must confess, we do love it." Martha's reference to size wasn't lost on Becky.

"How fortunate. Of course you know, George Richard and I are quite accustomed to the elaborate spaciousness of Peckatone."

Becky willed herself to be polite. "I suppose you are. It's all in what makes one feel most comfortable, I expect. For instance, take Mount Airy, now Francis and I would simply rattle in a place that size. We prefer the easy intimacy that we have here," she announced in as lofty a manner as she could summon.

"Well, of course you do, or you wouldn't have built it, would you? And of course you have no children and that does make a difference." Married the same year as the Lees, the Turbervilles now had a young son.

It was an unnecessary remark and a mean one. Becky knew that Martha was aware she had drawn blood. "No, no we haven't been so blessed. Not yet." Her eyes never dropped from the arrogant face of her guest as she sought to change the subject. "I haven't seen your mother arrive. They are coming, don't you suppose? Francis always looks forward to seeing his sister."

Martha glanced nonchalantly into the gilt looking glass over the dining buffet. She pursed her lips and, feigning some slight arrangement of her lavishly powdered hair, turned back to Becky. "I should think they will not come, Becky. Since they've moved to Woodberry, Mother doesn't attend many social gatherings. She's far too busy with all that Baptist foolishness. Actually, I'm quite surprised you bothered to ask them."

It was after midnight when the last team of horses disappeared into the night, and an hour later before all the house guests were settled and quiet. A three-quarter winter moon shone silver across the frosty fields penetrating the thick forest with patches of eerie light. The carriages didn't have far to travel with their well bundled and inebriated passengers, for those not remaining at Menokin would be put up at nearby Sabine Hall and Mount Airy. The howl of a wolf echoed above the distant fields as the household prepared for sleep. Becky, the last to retire, climbed the stairs slowly, savoring a lingering satisfaction that, in spite of Martha Turberville, it had been a most successful entertainment. She stopped at the north window upstairs to listen as a great horned owl, somewhere in the direction of the springhouse, hooted to its mate. Shivering at the lonely cries of the two predators, she jumped at a rustle behind her. The servant girl, Zoey, had been dozing but at the approach of her mistress, she struggled to her feet.

"Go to sleep, child," Becky whispered. "It's late. Master Francis is already in bed I'm sure, and we shan't need you any more today."

The slave returned gratefully to her curled up position on the thin pallet, securing the blanket tightly around herself. "Good night, Miss Becky," she mumbled drowsily.

Snuffing the last candle in the frosted window brought the moonlight indoors, until Becky drew the shutters against the night. "Zoey, don't forget first thing in the morning it's warm milk for Colonel Richard. Oh, and tell Berth that Milly is to prepare porridge for the children's breakfast." She paused, trying to think of everything that needed doing first thing. "Oh, and one thing more. Tell Cate to check with Mrs. Pinchard early on, to see if there's anything special she requires for the baby. And be sure Ben rounds up several of those lazy boys to tend the fires properly in the morning. I will brook no criticism on that count from our guests." With this, and shaking her head at the sleepy "yas'm" from Zoey, she hurried into the warmer privacy of her sleeping chamber, where a fire still burned in the grate. When she found Francis propped up in bed, waiting, she launched immediately into the conversation with Martha Turberville.

While she rambled, Francis watched as she undressed and brushed out her hair. It was one of the things he liked best about the day. To watch his wife prepare herself for bed at the end of it. He was happy she rarely asked Cate to help her with the task anymore. "Martha's father spoiled her abominably before he died. I'm convinced of it. It couldn't have been Hannah who made her the way she is," he explained when she finished telling him what happened. "And I suppose she resented the appearance of Dr. Hall into her mother's life. To say nothing of the children who came later."

"But her attitude toward her mother, regardless of all that, is quite unforgivable," whispered Becky, aware suddenly that her voice mustn't carry to the guests in the other chambers.

"That is, no doubt, one reason Hannah didn't come today, don't you imagine?" he asked, mimicking her whisper.

"Well, if being mistress of drafty old Peckatone means so much to Martha that she rejoices in turning her mother out so she can run it alone ... I say let her rot in it!"

"Forget Martha, love. Come to bed. It's been a long day and I need you by my side before I can rest properly."

Slipping in next to him, she thrilled to the warmth and comfort that greeted her, realizing at that moment just how tired she really was. "It was a lovely party, darling, and if I had the choice, I would take Menokin over Peckatone any day." Then sliding her arm tentatively across his chest, "but only if you promise always to be here with me."

"You had my promise before you asked. Do you know how much I need you? Really need you?" He knew she didn't because he couldn't begin to fathom it himself.

Closer now to the plantation house, the wolf's ghostly call trailed into the crystal night. Safe, in the snug haven of bed and togetherness, their arms tightened around each other.

"I do cherish you, Becky. Nothing will ever change that."

She squirmed happily, melting into the familiar mold of his body, falling asleep even before the lonely wolf howled again.

The Bear Growls

"Are we to be captive Englishmen on our native soil? Gentlemen, I say to you, we have no choice but to support our friends in Boston! It's the only road open to us. And for the moment the proper action to take, as I see it, is to make certain that this assembly establishes our own committee of correspondence. It's imperative we have active communication between all the colonies if we're to break the back of the evil Parliament!" So spoke Patrick Henry to four of his confidants on the eve of the March 1773 Assembly of Burgesses. The American bear was indeed emerging from hibernation. Aroused by the burning of the Gaspée off the Rhode Island coast, followed by a serious threat to haul the perpetrators to trial in England, the sleeping giant rolled over and stretched. It tested the air, warily at first, but quickly gained confidence. When the Massachusetts governor and judges proclaimed that henceforth their salaries would come directly from the Crown, the bear growled and, in Virginia, bared its teeth.

Five angry men gathered around the large oak table in a private room of the Raleigh Tavern, half-full mugs of ale or rum before them. Henry searched the faces of his compatriots, staring first at the solemn, hawk-nosed Richard Henry Lee, then the self assured Tom Jefferson, the pensive eyes of Frank Lee and, finally at his friend Dabney Carr. What he saw there gave him courage. It was unanimity of purpose that he gleaned from the joint expression of those four faces.

"Dear friends, I propose we put our heads together and write a resolution that the assembly will not be able to turn down," he offered.

Richard, however, was miffed. "It's not as though this is a new idea, Sir! I've been corresponding for years with patriots in the other colonies as well as in England."

Patrick Henry's impatience showed. "I'm aware of that. And so have I, we all know that. But we haven't been doing it officially, not under the auspices of the House," he hastened to point out. "You see, this way we'll be saying to the Ministry as well as to the world that Virginia supports her northern neighbors in their struggle against oppressions ... that we recognize the urgency of corresponding with them, and with others who see the danger in allowing any American liberties to be threatened!"

Richard Henry was silent, aware of the difference, but not quite ready to admit it.

Pride played an enormous role in his brother's psyche, and Francis knew it better than the rest of them. "It will make an important contribution to the cause of liberty, R.H. If the Virginia Assembly goes on record as supporting an inter-colonial correspondence, and then appoints a committee to carry it out, it will deal Parliament a great blow," he said. "It's a certainty as well, that what you've accomplished in the past was a first step to these ends."

"Well," interjected Jefferson, now quite at ease in the group, "I, of course, am for it. But the main problem, as I see it, will be to word the resolution so it will pass. We have to tread lightly on the toes of the loyalists and conservatives amongst us. I think you'll all agree to that."

"Therein lies the danger of all this, Gentlemen. Should we fail to convince them, it will mean we drive another nail in the division between our members. I, for one, don't think if we decide to present a resolution to formally set up such a committee, that we can afford to take a chance on failure!" Richard had overcome his bout with hurt feelings and was ready to contribute.

Patrick spoke again. "Richard, if you and Tom can put the ideas in proper language as we toss them out, as well as I trust you are both able, how can we fail? We'll get Dabney to present it to the House. He has fewer enemies amongst the conservatives. And we'll soon show Sam Adams that Virginia is behind him!"

The resolution they wrote that night was indeed passed by the House of Burgesses, and with no amendment. Their further proposal that the first order of correspondence be to call for a meeting of representatives from each colony at some central place, was also accepted. Governor Dunmore was ill pleased with the actions although this time they did not catch him by surprise. Prior to calling the assembly, and hoping to divert it from just such a resolution, the governor had prepared a lengthy diatribe designed to capture their attentions. It condemned the use of certain counterfeit currency which was in circulation in the colony. When the burgesses arrived in Williamsburg he took a further step. He ordered several men, including one member of the House itself, arrested and thrown in jail for perpetrating the spread of the sham money. Those accused were denied the customary examination by a magistrate, and were simply locked in the public gaol.

But the tactic had the reverse effect of what Dunmore had planned. In a brilliant countermove Patrick Henry adopted this affront to colonial liberty—this jailing without the preliminary appearance before a magistrate—as his second noble cause. When he spoke to his fellow delegates he branded it as the vile deed of an English governor insensitive to the rights of freemen. In response, the burgesses named Henry chairman of a committee to present a protest to Governor Dunmore. It was precisely what Patrick had hoped for. He said, in part:

" ... The duty we owe our constituents obliges us, My Lord, to be as attentive to the safety of the innocent, as we are desirous of punishing the guilty; and we apprehend that a doubtful construction and various execution of Criminal Law, does greatly endanger the safety of innocent men."

Thus Dunmore was subjected to a stiff dose of the flowery barb that packed a powerful sting and for which the burgesses of Virginia were renowned. While the lawmakers in no way defended the possible criminal action of their fellow official, they were adamant he should be served with proper English justice, which meant proper legal action. Already frustrated by the formation of the Correspondence Committee, poor Dunmore now angrily dismissed the assembly, proroguing it barely ten days after it opened its business.

∽

"There's no telling what it will come to," Francis said, recounting the matter to his wife on the return journey to Richmond County. "For the first time, Becky, I'm concerned with how far we'll be allowed to move, demanding our liberties, before the King refuses to put up with it. If Arthur is to be believed, he writes that many Englishmen feel that we echo their own cry for liberty as well, when we protest unfair treatment. I'm sure that's so, and yet ... " sighing he gazed unseeing at the sprouting wheat fields they passed, "somehow at this moment, I feel we stand terribly alone."

She searched his face, seeking every shred of his meaning. It was true then. He'd never expressed worry over the colony's political stance, or was it a kind of supreme fear she detected underlying his words? She reached for his hand beneath the shawl that wrapped their knees against the mid-March chill, saying nothing.

"It puts a mighty burden on a man, love. A mighty burden indeed. I must confess, I'm not a bit unhappy that the assembly was dissolved. Who knows what might have happened had we persisted in our present mood? I'd much prefer, I think, to tend my crops than to struggle with the unbelievably complicated maneuverings of government. I don't deny it."

Kissing him lightly on the cheek, she said, "Don't forget your people and your flocks, my dear man. They need tending, too.

Whenever you become too embroiled in the political pot, all you have to do to raise your spirits, is to remember Menokin. Isn't it wonderful? I'm convinced after four years of truly knowing you, that is where your love runs deepest. Am I right?"

"You know, Becky, I suppose you're closer to the truth in your analysis of me than you can know. But you've left out the one thing I cherish most ... you! Without you, the rest would be nothing."

Thus Francis was diverted from commiserating over concerns of his country to matters closer to home. That meant struggling with the mixed joys and frustrations of being master of a growing plantation in troubled economic times. Aware suddenly that the carriage seemed unnecessarily crowded, he fixed his gaze on the seat opposite. "Cate," he said, moving his eyes to a spot above the slave's impassive face, "Cate, that Sam of yours is growing fast, and a fine boy he is, too. You know, I think it's time we untied him from his mother's apron strings and sent him out to the quarter with the other children." He ignored the slight movement as Cate drew her arm closer around her son. "Beginning tomorrow, you put him out there during the day with one of the older women, perhaps old Winny, to take charge of him. In the evening, he may come to the house."

Cate said not a word, but at this order from the master, fear entered her heart and found expression in her eyes. Francis preferred not to notice. To Becky he explained, "There's no reason why we had to bring him on this trip. The carriage is crowded enough what with Zoey and Cate in here. The horses have too much weight to pull as it is, without a boy who could just as well have remained at Menokin."

"Marse Frank ... he ain't heavy," Cate said quietly.

A look from her mistress silenced her, commanding her to wait until later. Becky perceived that her husband, having voiced the decision, had already turned his thoughts to the countryside of Essex County. It would be wise to let the matter drop for the present.

૭∿୬

Two days later, Becky waited until Francis departed for Richmond Courthouse, then called Cate to her chamber. "Cate, I want you to find Samuel and bring him to me."

"Marse Frank, he say Sammy ain't to be in de great house daytimes no more," Cate said, fidgeting with her large apron. "B'sides, he's right, Marse Frank is. If'n Sammy ain't goin' be a house nigger, den he goin' have t' learn to fight his way in de quarter best's he kin. He mights well git started."

"Fight? What do you mean?"

"Dey beat him yistahday," Cate announced dramatically.

"Beat him? Who beat him? What on earth are you talking about, girl?"

"Venus's boy an' dat big bully, Winny's George. Dey both older 'n bigger."

"Well. I don't understand why they'd pick on a sweet child like Samuel." There were things Becky had spent a lifetime not wanting to know about.

"Cuz he's mine. House nigras ain't welcome in de quarter. Y'all know dat, Miss Becky. We gits special priv-a-liges an' all, bein' in de great house. Deys jealous."

"Pooh. Don't they understand we couldn't afford for them all to have extra food and better clothing? The idea is ridiculous!"

Cate felt a tightness in her throat. She couldn't think of anything to say. It wasn't possible that Miss Becky didn't know exactly what she meant. She waited.

"No ... no, I don't suppose they do understand ... any of it. Well, anyway, you do as I say this minute before I change my mind. Bring Samuel to me."

"What you goin' do to him, Miss Becky? You not mad, is you?" Was it possible her mistress had found out Sammy had only been spending half of the prescribed time in the quarter?

"Mad? Gracious no. What would I be mad about? I just want to talk to him before Master Francis returns."

Cate ran as though her life depended on it to Winny's cabin. The yard was filled with slave children playing, swinging sticks at each other. Soon when Marse Frank's seeds started sprouting, they'd have plenty enough to fill their time in the fields working with their parents but, for now, there was little for them to do except play in the muddy yard. Samuel was not among them. Entering the cabin, Cate found Winny stirring a pot over the fire. Sammy was hunched in the corner counting his fingers. Winny nodded at Cate's entrance, her wrinkled face impassive and, pointing to the boy, she turned back to her kettle.

"Why you not outside wit de others?" Cate asked her son.

He shrugged his shoulders and rose to meet her. She saw he'd been crying again and gathered him in her arms, then held him off to look at him. "Samu'l, Miss Becky she done axed fo you. She goin' talk to you, son. Be polite now an' don' fo'git yo'r manners. Heah me now?" Taking a corner of her apron she moistened it with spit and wiped at the streaks on his cheeks. "An' hol' yo' haid up high when we walks pas' dem ugly nigra chillins in de yard!"

With her hand on the door, ready to slam it, Cate turned around. Winny was watching her. "Thanks fo' keepin' him away from George an' Hector dis mornin'," Cate said slowly. Winny nodded as the door rattled shut on its hinges.

At the great house Cate pushed the child ahead of her up the steps, urging him to hurry. The knot of pain she'd carried in her heart since that fateful moment in the carriage was beginning to dissolve, although she couldn't have said why since she had no idea what Miss Becky wanted to say to Sammy. Somehow, she thought, it was bound to improve his recent fate.

Becky sat in the window seat reading her scripture lesson, but quickly closed the book when the boy entered. "That will be all, Cate," she said, waiting for her maid to leave. "Come sit here next to me, Samuel." Looking at him, she was shocked at the ugly cut on his left brow, which had caused the eye to be swollen almost shut. And his lips were puffy and bruised. Her heart went out to the child, so incapable of defending himself, so unaware there had been any need to learn to do that. But she knew sympathy wasn't the right course, the intent wasn't to make a sissy out of him after all. Not when the plan was that one day he'd grow to fill Ben's shoes and keep the house slaves in line. To be good at that he must learn to be strong and wise. Forcing herself, she asked casually, "Sammy, how old are you now?"

He hadn't expected this question, thinking she'd ask him about his bruises. He raised four fingers slowly.

"Can you say four?"

"Four. I's four."

"That's right. But you should say, 'I am four, Miss Becky.' It's polite to use someone's name when you speak to them."

"Yas-ma'm, Miz Becky," he said, ducking his head, ashamed of having forgotten what he'd been taught. He was very glad his mammy wasn't there to hear it.

"Don't worry, you just forgot, but you'll remember next time. I know you will. Now ... I want you to tell me if you've had a good time in the quarter playing with the other children?"

The little boy wagged his head, tears welling in the ebony eyes. Determined, he dashed them away, but remained silent.

"Say it," she urged gently. "You can tell me."

"No-ma'm, Miz Becky. Dey's mean."

"Well then, do you think you might rather be in here, in the great house all day if we can find something for you to do?"

"Oh, yas, Miz Becky. Deed I would."

His face would have been answer enough, she thought. "You will have to work."

"Work?"

"Why yes, we'll have to find some jobs you can do. So Master Frank will think you're worthy. Do you think you could carry wood? Help Berth polish the furniture? Do you think you could do that?"

"Yas-mam, an' I could do all dat. An' I could he'p Mammy polish shoes an' boots, an' ... an' watch de fire under de wash kett'l ... an' ..."

"My goodness! All that. Could you really? Well, I'll bet Ben would show you how to lay out Master Frank's clothes for him each day, too."

Too excited to remain seated, Samuel began to hop up and down while continuing to list all the household tasks he could think of, in the grand game he was to be permitted to play. He counted on his fingers and Becky was surprised to find when he reached ten, he kept going until he became confused at sixteen. Puzzled, he started over again at one.

"Oh, that's fine, Sammy. Just fine! Wonderful, wonderful, as Master Frank would say!" she laughed. "So it's settled between us. You are my new house-boy. I'll tell Master Frank all about it tonight."

"He likes me?" the child asked doubtfully.

"Why, of course he likes you. He just didn't realize you were old enough and smart enough to help in the house, so he sent you out to play. But I'm going to explain it all to him."

"You tell him dat I's four? An' dat I kin count my fingers so I won' fo'git all de jobs he goin' give me?"

"I'll tell him, Sammy. I promise. Just as soon as he comes home."

"I's goin' tell Mammy I's a real house-boy now!" Forgetting his manners, his bruises, everything except his pressing need to share the astonishing turn of events with his mother, he left his mistress staring at the space his lithe brown body had occupied a second before he disappeared.

Becky forgave him his rude departure, thinking there was plenty of time to work on his manners another day. Pleased with herself, she began rehearsing how she would explain all this to Francis. He'd never denied her a wish before and she didn't expect him to do so in this case. Still, she knew it was important to handle him carefully in order to assure success. It was a lesson she'd learned at a tender age from dealing with her father—men accepted an idea ever so much more readily if permitted to believe that they had originated it.

ᓚ

With the arrival of summer the plantation flourished. Francis took great pride in his spring wheat crop. Others in the county had also been successful in raising this basic food, but they all agreed there would be a problem marketing it.

"There are no ships putting in here, on which we can consign our wheat," he wrote his brother William in September. *"Take my word for it, we grow some of the best wheat in Virginia here on this river. As you are acquainted with the merchants concerned in the grain trade, you would do us a great piece of service if you would arrange a business here. We presently are forced to ship to Baltimore for want of a market locally. This means we must pass on this added cost of shipment when we finally sell.*

"On another subject, as you instructed, we have placed an advertisement in the Gazette *offering for sale your tenements in Williamsburg. For your sake, it disturbs me the estate settlement did not work out as you wished and you have the burden of the disposition of these three houses. We have worded the advertisement so that if the tenements should not be sold in the meantime, they shall be offered at Public Sale on Friday the 29th of October. I shall make every effort to be there on that date if necessary.*

"I am having difficulty placing my tobacco for shipment also. There are a number here, including myself, who would prefer to ship to you, but we do not know what arrangements you have made. Are you sending a

ship? Colonel Carter is becoming more annoyed with his London contact and I think would be happy to make a change. I would suggest again that you write to him.

"We are now faced with Parliament's new Tea Act. What with the tax removed at that end, but reinforced at our ports, you can well imagine our distress. Further, it is to the last pound consigned to a select group of merchants and not open for purchase by any other. There will be serious trouble over this."

Becky found him, hunched over his table, making the copy of his letter in the same fine, elegant penmanship as the original. If the letter should be lost in passage he'd have the main points of what he had written. "You're working too long over your papers in this heat. Why don't you stop and come for a walk with me? The sun is setting and it's much cooler outside."

He held out his arms to her. When she came, he drew her into his lap. "William's going to lose many consignees, Becky, if he doesn't inform me what shipping arrangements he's made. We have tobacco ready to ship now, and the new crop will soon be harvested."

"Is that what you're worried about today? Why yesterday, it was the tea on its way to Boston, New York and Philadelphia! What will furrow your brow tomorrow?"

"Poking fun at me, are you? Humph! Well ... I *am* concerned about what will happen when all that tea arrives in our ports. As the East India Company has been allowed to consign it to certain merchants of their choice, all friendly to the Crown of course, and allowed to ship it without any export duty, an honest merchant will be priced right out of the market. They'll not even be able to sell what they have on hand at any sort of a profit. I was just telling William, there will be trouble over it. I'm positive of that."

"What do you think should be done?"

"The best thing would be to close the ports and forbid the tea being unloaded. To turn the ships and send them back to

England still loaded with their damned bloody tea. That would show them just how serious we are!"

"Is that possible?"

"I truly doubt it. The situation is too complex. I fail to see how any of our colonial assemblies are united enough to accomplish such a feat ... but I'd feel much better about the whole thing if I could get our Menokin tobacco and wheat safely on its way to the British market before all hell gives way and we're caught in the middle. And that's why I'm writing to William."

Her skirts felt stuck to her thighs, and she shifted in his lap. "Can you tell me more about it while we walk? It's frightfully hot to sit this way, darling."

"You are persistent, aren't you? Very well then. We shall walk. My letter can be finished in the morning as well as now I suppose."

"It's so lovely at Menokin this time of year, Francis. I simply can't express it in words, that's how much I cherish it." She sighed as they left the house. The steps leading to the rose garden were high, and from the top occasional glimpses of the river could be seen through the trees after the leaves had fallen, but on this day all they saw was the lush forest that surrounded their house. Voices and the twang of a fiddle drifted up from the quarter, and the smell of frying fish was on the still air as they made their way hand in hand through the orchard toward the creek. Early evening was a peaceful time on the plantation. The daytime birds had ceased their chirp and chatter for the most part, and it was too early to hear the chuck-wills-widow trill his repetitious call, or the night chorus of cicadas in the marshes. Becky stopped to pull some apples off a tree and they ate them as they descended the hill. When they reached the creek, without discussing it, they sat to remove their shoes and dabble their feet in the cool spring water.

"My," Becky said, leaning back against the mossy hill, "this is just about the most perfect spot on a hot evening, don't you agree?"

"Looks as though someone else thinks so, too," Francis laughed, pointing downstream where a small brown body cavorted in the shallows. Samuel spotted them at almost the same moment. Startled, he scrambled up the bank and reached for his clothes.

"Sam, did you remember to give my boots a good shine when I got back from court today?" Francis called gruffly. The child nodded vigorously, clutching his breeches in front of his naked torso. "Well then, go for your swim. It's too hot to do much else, boy." The child flashed them a wide grin, still embarrassed.

A look passed between husband and wife. While Samuel's newly appointed post in the household had been agreed to by Francis, he'd approved it on a trial basis only. The look Becky caught in her husband's eyes told her he was probably ready to give final approval to the arrangement. Francis felt her surmising his thoughts and said, "I must caution you, my love, you are not to spoil him. I know your fondness for children. Just remember, he is black and he is a slave. You won't help his lot by allowing him to become soft or too dependent on your favors."

She nodded, not taking the warning too seriously. "Of course I won't spoil him. But thank goodness the threat of that dreadful quarter isn't hanging over his head any longer." She squeezed his hand. "I appreciate what you've done, and I love you for it."

Looking at her out of the corner of his eye, he had to smile. "Well, Mrs. Lee, I suggest you wipe that smug expression off your pretty face, or perhaps I shall be forced to show you how refreshing this water can be when sampled above the ankles!"

"You wouldn't dare," she shrieked.

"Oh, wouldn't I? We shall see about that." In a flash he jumped down the bank. Standing knee deep in the cold water, he grabbed for her feet, pulling her in with him. He cotton skirts hung limply, growing heavy as they soaked up the water.

"I declare, Francis Lee, you certainly have a way about you," she giggled. "I've been hoping for just such a cooling off all day!"

Clinging together they slipped on the creek bottom, laughing and tickling each other, until they went down splashing. "Now we've done it!" he said. "Might as well enjoy it." He kissed her neck and behind her ear, searching for the jasmine. "I was always curious what it would be like to make love in the water!"

"Francis! Don't forget Samuel."

"Gone, Becky. I saw him head downstream. Nothing can save you now, love." Slipping the sodden dress off her shoulders, he fumbled with her undergarments. His cool wet hands were on her bare skin.

"I surrender, darling. Just don't drown me." Then his mouth closed on her own and she stopped thinking of anything else.

In late November, with a strong wind behind him kicking up the dust, Francis rode into the county hub of Richmond Courthouse to find the streets already crowded. John Tayloe's Yorick was scheduled to race Dr. Flood's Gift. Many, blacks as well as white servants and freeholders, had arrived before him. He'd covered the four miles down dusty Menokin Road at an exhilarating rate of speed. Both horse and rider were in a lather and in need of a cool drink. He led Cameron to the public trough, nodding to the familiar faces he passed. While the animal sucked long gulps of water, Francis searched the crowd for a friend with whom he might share a nip of his rum flask. He didn't spot anyone immediately and turned to the task of dusting off his gray breeches and gold buttoned waistcoat. Looking up, he found Hudson Muse also watering his horse. Muse was a local small farmer of some repute with a number of business interests in the community. At sight of him Francis paused, wondering if he should press again for the debt owed by Muse to brother William. Muse had ordered supplies and household items on credit from England, but had yet to ship a large enough or worthy enough load of tobacco to pay for the order. Francis had it on good authority that Muse had, in the meantime, shipped with other merchants. Muse spoke before he'd made up his mind whether to mention the debt.

"Why, if it isn't Colonel Lee, himself, come to enjoy the horse race," Muse greeted him, while taking special pleasure in watching the gentleman from Menokin trying to shake the grime of the road from his ruffled cuffs and linen shirtfront. His eyes crinkled in a smile that was not altogether friendly. Muse had never been able to overlook the fact that his own family was several steps down on the social ladder from the local gentry. It galled him every time he thought about it.

Today wasn't the first time Francis had felt a prickle of irritation as he faced the cocky Muse. They'd been pitted against each other in the '71 election and Muse had almost unseated him. More recently, the frustrating circumstances surrounding broken contracts with William's shipping interest did nothing to further his esteem for the fellow, making him reach the conclusion Muse was a ne'er-do-well, not to be trusted. "Good morning to you, Mr. Muse," he said, mustering up a cheerful smile and tipping his tricorn. "It promises to be an exciting race today. Yorick, I'm told, is in excellent form. Where have you put your purse? On Yorick or Flood's Gift?" He decided to go through the courtesies before mentioning the matter of the debt.

"I've not yet placed my bet. I find myself a wee short of ready cash, you see ... thought I'd squeeze what I could out of some of those what owe me, before the race starts."

Listening, Francis decided it was one way of saying there was no use in reminding him, on this day, of his past-due debts. "In that case, Mr. Muse, I won't press you for the funds you owe a member of my family, but I suggest you do your best to hurry. With your collections, as well as your repayment arrangements. I understand the purse is to be 500 pounds and there should be countless profitable side wagers." Francis pulled Cameron's head from the trough, tipped his hat for the second time and moved off. He'd spotted the gentlemen from Nomini way and was anxious for a word with his friends John Turberville and Councilman Carter. He'd deal with Hudson Muse another day.

Muse stared as Colonel Lee became one with the milling crowd. Mr. High-and-Mighty Lee, always hounding me for money, he raged. You'll get your comeuppance one day! Glancing around he found he had an audience clustered about the water trough. Ten or twelve men, tenants and servants mostly, lounging near the scene had witnessed the encounter and were obviously interested. Muse, seeing he had their attention, carefully ejected a long stream of brown tobacco juice between his teeth into the dust where a moment before had stood Francis Lee. The men responded with loud guffaws and knee slapping, loving nothing better than an act of artful chicanery or a good horse laugh at the expense of one of the landed gents. There was little doubt in any of their minds that Hudson Muse, a man of the people, had won this round. And it had not cost him a farthing.

"That's tellin' 'im, Hudson. Him with his fancy dooded up arse!"

"'I understand the purse is to be five hundred pounds, Mr. Muse,' says he, as if we didn't know it!" mimicked another.

"Shit! What does 500 pounds mean to the likes of him anyway?"

"Hold it a minute," interjected James West, a newcomer to the county. "I've been told on good authority that Mr. Lee is not a bad sort. Treats those workin' for him fair-like."

Reluctantly, a few of the others having had their little joke, nodded their heads affirmatively. "No worse than the rest of them gents, I s'pose. Better'n some."

Joining the group along with John Selfe, an overseer for Landon Carter, West explained, "I'm to meet Colonel Lee tomorrow. He's lookin' for an overseer and I plan on seekin' the job."

"Don't let them bastards fool you none! Most of them'd give their eye teeth to work at Menokin. Francis Lee has the reputation for bein' an honest man. Hard workin' hisself, I understand, when he's not off politikin'. Got a good lookin' wife, too. Now she's the one what won't put up with no foolishness, if you want my opinion! Got the last overseer fired I heard, just because he was sleepin' around with the wenches." He turned to West, trying to size him up by peering into the brilliant blue eyes. "That's not your fancy by no chance, is it?"

"Well, don't reckon so. Least ways not since you warn me. I need that job bad ... times bein' what they are, you know. Why, up north a fellow told me they'd be conscriptin' for the army soon. I sure don't cotton to no soldierin'!"

Up the road a way, near the clerk's office, his two friends John Turberville and Councilor Robert Carter from Nomini stood talking to a young man Francis didn't recognize.

Carter greeted him, shaking his hand, before making an introduction. "Mr. Fithian, please meet my dear friend, Colonel Frank Lee of Menokin. The colonel's father-in-law has one of the horses in today's race." Turning to Francis, "Young Fithian here is a Princeton scholar studying for the ministry. I've just hired him as tutor at Nomini Hall. I trust he'll be skilled at keeping those young ones of mine in line ... as well as teaching them a love for the classics and mathematics."

Francis held out his hand to the pale young stranger. "How do you do, Mr. Fithian? Welcome to Virginia. The land of plenty, we say. What do you think of us so far? Do we meet your expectations?"

"Well Sir, I've been made to feel most welcome at Nomini Hall if that is what you mean. As to Virginia as a whole ... well ... I must confess, at the moment I'm quite homesick. I trust that will pass in time," he finished, embarrassed, and thinking he was glad he hadn't mentioned he was finding southern customs to be shockingly unrestrained and unlike any he had known. The climate also, he suspected, was unhealthy as he'd been warned, and wouldn't agree with him.

The horse race proved an event of great excitement. When the young tutor, witness to the frivolous ways of the south, sat at his desk later that evening, he took up his quill to record the event in his journal. *"... The horses started promptly at five minutes after three. The Course was one mile in circumference. They performed the first round in two minutes, third in two minutes and a half, Yorick came out the fifth time round about 40 rods before Gift. They were both, when the riders dismounted, very lame. They run five miles, and carried 180 pounds."*

The extravagant purse of 500 pounds shocked Philip Fithian greatly. He was dismayed that men would bet so carelessly on a single race. It seemed to him also that the violent strain on the animals must surely be an act of unreasoned men.

അ

The following day Francis received James West in his study. The two men shook hands, sizing each other up. Francis saw West as a lean man, of average height, with an open expression. He liked that. His former overseer had been nervous in his presence, always shifting his eyes, but this man met his gaze straight on. West was muscular, especially in the upper portion of his body. Francis returned to the chair behind his desk, motioning West to a seat opposite. "I understand you're from up around Baltimore way?" At West's nod, he continued, "Well, are you pleased with what you find on this side of the Potomac?"

"Sir, if you have any concern that I might up and leave, I can set your mind at rest. I've been in the county 'most a year now. Met and married a nice girl, a Barrett, do you know the family?" Francis indicated he didn't. "Well, anyway, we'll be havin' a young'un soon, and we're stayin' right here. That's why it's important for me to latch on to some kind of steady work. I been doin' odd jobs mostly, as they come along."

"Have you had experience as an overseer before?"

"No. But helpin' one, sort of an assistant you might say. On a tobacca plantation in Maryland. Before that I worked the docks in Baltimore, and I started out shearin' sheep up in Penn country."

That, decided Francis, explained the muscled shoulders and chest. Shearing sheep built muscle. It might be a bad sign that the man had shifted jobs so often but there was probably an explanation for it. "Do you have any credentials, a recommendation from a former employer or anything?"

"I got a letter here, from the master in Maryland." He fumbled inside his smock, producing a well creased, considerably soiled paper.

Francis studied it carefully, wondering if West could read. That was important. There were crop books and daily journals to keep, receipts to give and bills to pay. It was almost necessary the burden be shared with the overseer. That was a shortcoming of Grimes at Loudoun farm, but with those lands mostly rented to tenants now, it was less of a problem. The rents were annual and so far Francis had managed to tend to that matter in person. He decided not to ask James West directly if he could read and write, asking instead, "What was your master's Christian name?"

"Why it says real clear there on the paper, Sir. William John Murray." West looked perplexed.

"No. No, it has only the initials," Francis insisted.

"I read it myself, Sir. It says clear as day, John William Murray, Esquire. Read it again, Sir."

It was enough. It answered the question ... James West was lettered, at least to some extent. Francis completed the charade, unfolding the paper again. "Oh, yes. Sorry, Mr. West. Foolish of me. Just overlooked it. Well, Mr. Murray certainly speaks highly of your work. He also says a man could look forward to an honest relationship with you. But he didn't say why you left his employ?" The eyebrow quirked.

West fidgeted, looking uncomfortable for the first time. "I don't suppose it would do no good to muck about or lie to you. Might as well tell you straight out. Sir, Mr. Murray had three daughters. Good lookin' sassy girls, all of 'em. One kept hangin' around the stables. That's where I worked mostly. I swear ...." West raised his hand, palm out, blue eyes inscrutable. "I tried to put an end to it, but she was a stubborn one, kept comin' back. Wouldn't pay no mind when I told her that her daddy wouldn't like it when he found out where she was. One day we went a mite too far and well ... if you know what I mean ... Sir, I swear I could tell in a hurry it weren't the first time for her neither. That's when I decided I mights well enjoy it cause she kept comin' back for more. I never did find out who told her daddy, but the first thing I knowed, a couple of weeks later he calls me in. Offers me a fort-night's pay an' this letter. Says he's sorry about the whole thing, but I have t' leave within the hour. I guess he must of knowed it were her doin' in the beginnin' or he wouldn't of been so consider-ate about it." West shrugged, breaking into an innocent grin. "It was clear, I reckon, Mr. Murray had other plans for his daughter than the son of a sheep-man."

"I see." Francis had been weighing West's merits against his demerits while the man was talking and had made up his mind to give him a chance. He desperately needed an overseer and he needed him now. "Well, then. It looks as though we can both take advantage of what the other has to offer, Mr. West. Shall we get down to business regarding salary and so on? Then we'll make a tour of the plantation so you can see just what your duties will encompass."

Several hours later, in front of the small steep-roofed house where the overseer's family would live, they discussed the first big problem they would face together.

"My brother, a London merchant, has sent a ship to load at Hobbs' Hole. It's just newly arrived, the *Eliza*. Now, in the ab-sence of knowing that he was going to do this, I had placed my tobacco with other ships. I had advised others to do the same. It's a ticklish situation and I'll be in a pickle if we can't arrange, by whatever means possible, to transfer some hogsheads from other ships into the hold of the *Eliza*. I'd like you to walk the docks ... learn what you can from the captains of ships not yet ready to sail, bargain with them or whatever ... and I'll visit Essex Courthouse to see what else I can work out. I'm absolutely obligated, through good will to my brother, to see the *Eliza* sails from here with a full cargo, and as soon as possible. Understood?"

"Yes Sir, I understand. Do we go tomorrow?"

"Well, tomorrow or soon thereafter," Francis said, surprised at West's eagerness. He was highly pleased with the man so far, with the exception of the story about the girl in Maryland, and wondered just how much of that he should believe. West certainly didn't look like a Romeo, except perhaps for those compelling blue eyes. "Make yourself at home, Mr. West. Get your wife settled. The house should be comfortable enough. Four rooms, and solid built. After you've moved your things in, come to see me, and we'll make arrangements to take the ferry to Hobbs' Hole for our visit to the *Eliza*. Later in December, I may try to get to Williamsburg. A sale of some family property scheduled in October didn't take place, and we've arranged to try again. It's a busy month for me, and I may have to leave you in charge quite soon. By the way, Ben is the name of my man-servant. He's been with me since I was a boy, we more or less grew up together. You'll find him at the house or around the stable. Introduce yourself. He'll fix you up with a cart you may borrow to transfer your belongings." Francis moved to close the interview, but not before he thought to add, "Ben is a slave in a million. It will go well if you treat him with respect."

He started across the field toward Menokin House, then turned back remembering his promise to Becky. "Oh, just one more thing, Mr. West. We have a good relationship with our slaves here, and try always to treat them with fairness. What they do when they aren't in the fields or otherwise working, is their own business, so long as it doesn't threaten the prosperity or safety of the plantation. They're allowed their family life as they see fit. I won't separate families unless absolutely necessary, and anyone who makes trouble will have a hearing before being punished ... and I don't believe in trying to improve the strain by mixing it with white blood. Do I make myself perfectly clear?"

West had been expecting something like this. "Yes, no way I could mistake your meanin', Sir. Might I ask if the field hands are treated the same as the house niggers?"

"The house servants have some privileges, of course. But they know their place and they don't cross the line. You can leave the house Negroes to Ben and to me, however, and what they do should be of no concern to you. But, I strongly suggest you keep in mind what I said regarding the mixture of white and black blood. That is if you wish your duty here to be of any duration."

James West could see that he meant it, and held out his hand. "You have my word, Sir, I will stay away from the black wenches."

Francis and Richard had known for several years that their clever brother Arthur had been authoring sometimes critical, even scathing, articles directed to select members of the British establishment. These appeared in London papers, and were frequently reprinted in Williamsburg's *Virginia Gazette*, all under the pen name of Junius Americanus. Depending on the circumstances, the author lauded or attacked the man he addressed, in the name of English liberty for all, including the American colonists. In September 1773, someone bent on exposing the skillful Junius, no doubt in hopes of stamping out his growing literary career by dealing his anonymity a mortal blow, published the following in the *Gazette*: *"Doctor Lee was some time since appointed Agent by*

the Honorable House, in case of the Death or other incapacity of Doctor Franklin. Doctor Lee is generally supposed to be the writer of Junius Americanus, whose pieces have often been reprinted in some of the papers here."

When they met after the new year, Richard Henry and Francis were anxious to discuss the consequences of Arthur's identity having been revealed in such a way.

"If you ask me, he has to change his pen name if he wants to remain anonymous and continue his pursuit of those he chooses to vilify. There've been vague public hints in the past, but this is the ultimate exposé," Richard chuckled. The brothers were sharing a cup of warm grog in front of Chantilly's blazing fire.

"You could say he's been 'defrocked' or stripped of his cover! It's really quite amusing, isn't it? But, seriously, it may not be so simple to change his pen name and get away with it. Arthur's style is unique. I'm certain readers have come to recognize the peculiar style of his biting attack." Every time he thought of his two brothers in England, Francis was saddened, and wished so much they could be there to talk to in person. "How long is it, R.H., since we've had the pleasure of Arthur and William's company? Can it really be five years?" He shook his head wishing it wasn't so. "I miss them mightily."

"I also, Loudoun. So much has happened since they left. With the relations between England and America becoming more strained daily, however, I wouldn't be surprised to see at least William and his family on their way home. It seems impossible to imagine that Americans could be made to feel very welcome there now. Arthur, I think, might escape to Paris."

"Maybe. What you say is true, yet both write of the Englanders who are in sympathy with our cause, and both have formed many close friendships. Of course, my correspondence from them is all prior to these latest disturbances. American brashness may have cooled the general attitude of the people of Britain toward the colonies."

"I assume you're referring to the tea? I thought so. Well, I can't get over it. It's really more than we could have hoped for. In New York, Philadelphia and Charleston, too! ... patriots have forced every merchant waiting for his consigned tea from East India to resign his commission. It's quite unbelievable, isn't it? I wonder what Patrick and Jefferson are saying about it."

"And in Boston," Francis added, "where the resignations couldn't be forced, Sam Adams wouldn't allow the duties to be paid as ordered, he just forced the whole damned shipment to be dumped into the harbor! I read there were some 342 chests of tea destroyed. We're actually getting somewhere, aren't we?"

"Do you realize what all this means? These thirteen colonies have, with a united action, turned a confrontation into a victory. The corresponding committees are working! I'm going to continue to press for a meeting of a joint colonial congress where we can send representatives to talk out our grievances and share suggestions for solutions. Right now, while feelings are high is the time to do it!"

They sat in silence for a few minutes, each thinking, knowing it was the same all over America. Brother was talking to brother, friend to friend, and neighbor to neighbor. The Bear was on the offensive now. In small groups from Maine to Georgia the movement was beginning to gain momentum. It wouldn't be long now before an incredible roar would echo around the world. Francis spoke first. "And we're, some of us at least, a big part of it, aren't we? Do you honestly think, Richard, that there is enough support among our assemblymen to urge a resolution for a joint congress?"

"I believe more of them are reaching that conclusion. As always, it takes time to convince the more stubborn. There's a certain amount of fear, which you no doubt have noticed, that such a step will carry things too far. Some, while on the one hand not wanting to submit to the British stranglehold, on the other hand are afraid we'll forfeit our old standard of values. There's concern over how we'll run our plantations if we're forced to give up the slave market. If England retaliates by cutting off our trade, this could happen."

Francis studied his brother intently. "For years I've heard you hint at disapproval of the import of slaves from Africa. Apparently, you have some idea that we could do better otherwise and, therefore, loss of the slave trade doesn't matter to you."

"Frank ... " he began, then spotting his wife on the staircase, motioned to her to wait. "You must understand my reasons. Surely you've heard of fields and tobacco lands to the north of us, smaller than ours that produce larger crops. Now I don't for one minute believe their soil is more rich than the fertile lands of Virginia. I believe it's because they use white indentured labor, not slave labor, as was formerly done in our great-grandfather's time."

"Then is it your opinion that it's because they are *white* ... that the lands are more productive?" It was a loaded question, but a subject that sometimes came up in the southern colonies.

"I think you know that I'm not certain, although I've given it a great deal of thought over the years. It's true the indentured are more industrious ... perhaps the black is inferior as many claim ... but I'm inclined to think that simple motivation is at the root of the difference. A man who has something to work toward must certainly be more willing to put forth an effort than one who faces an ongoing cheerless existence. That seems like common sense to me."

"Well, that's exactly how I've felt for some time. Now take the Negro. As an example, how about Ben, who I would trust with my life. I think we must allow our slaves to have a family life, something to look forward to at the end of the day. I insist on it, at Menokin as I did at Loudoun farm, even before I'd given the matter much serious consideration. I guess some would say it's the reason Becky's Cate is spoiled beyond reason! By the way, I've engaged a new overseer. Seems a hard working fellow so far, and appears to accept my rules when it comes to the slaves, whether he agrees with me or not. At any rate I think we are agreed it doesn't make any difference if they are white or black. A servant is a servant is a servant. It is how you treat them that makes the difference."

"You'd better not let our friend Landon Carter hear you say that. The very notion that between black and white there is no inherent difference would raise all his hackles. And I believe the older he gets, the more hackles he has to raise!"

"I've actually argued the matter with him on more than one occasion. To no avail, I might add. And Brother Phil would also take a dim view of our philosophy, I'm sure," Francis added.

"As would a number of our other planter friends no doubt. They'd say you have fallen under the spell ... the spell of radicalism!"

"Or liberalism?"

"How about whiggism?"

"How about liberal whiggish radicalism?" said Francis thinking, as always, how much he enjoyed a good chat with his brother.

The men laughed heartily. Suddenly Richard remembered his wife, who had been waiting patiently for his attention. He apologized when he realized how long he'd ignored her presence. "Forgive me, my dear. It was rude of me to ask you to wait. Come, join us. I merely wished to finish our conversation before the thoughts escaped me. Am I forgiven?" He reached for her hand.

"You are looking lovely today, dear sister," Francis complimented. "The birth of a new child seems to enhance your beauty." He stood to kiss her cheek and include her in their circle around the fireplace. He had come to accept Mrs. Pinchard for herself, ceasing to make comparisons to the former Anne.

"How you do flatter, Mr. Lee. I can't believe what you say, but must confess I love to hear it nonetheless. The baby is exactly why I came downstairs, to ask if you would like to see her."

"Why, of course I do. It was a prime reason for my visit." He moved to follow her.

"Oh no, you stay right there by the fire with Richard and continue your conversation. I'll fetch our little love and return in a few minutes. She's awake and it's a good time to give her some attention."

"Six children you've fathered now, Richard. That's quite a record. And the way young Thomas is growing, it won't be long before you'll have to start thinking of how you'll react to being a grandfather!"

Richard laughed again. "The boy is not quite sixteen, Loudoun! By the way, he and Ludwell are settled and doing well in school, so William reports. I suppose, should our brother decide to return to America, that would be the end of English schooling for my sons. I couldn't permit them to remain in an unfriendly country without their uncle to look after them. In all seriousness, being a grandfather is one of the few features of old age I think will be rewarding. It should make up for life's disappointments as well as its aches and pains, I hope."

"Yes, yes ... I'm sure it will." A feeling of longing swept over Francis as he wondered if he would ever be able to look forward to the same reward. He was familiar with the worry now as it came to him from time to time. He hoped it didn't show in his face. Noting Richard's inquisitive gaze, however, he saw that it did. "Sorry, R.H., I don't usually allow myself the luxury of self pity or foolish depression ... over things I cannot change."

"It's the only flaw in your personal happiness, is it not?"

"The only one. Absolutely the only one. Otherwise, Becky and I are far happier together than ... well, than any two people have the right to expect in this world. It frightens me sometimes, we are so content with one another. I admitted to myself one day that we are truly one; one thought, one feeling, one love, one person. Neither of us could exist for long without our other half. I wonder how many married couples can say the same?" He lapsed into silence, not wishing to say more.

Richard, looking at his brother, listened to the words, understood what was meant, but was uncomfortable with the depth of passion he saw in Francis's eyes. For once he was speechless.

"Ah," smiled Francis, "here comes little Henrietta." He reached out his arms to take the small bundle his sister-in-law offered him.

"We're going to call her Harriot, I think. Even though her christian name be Henrietta," she explained.

"Well now, isn't she a beauty? And her hands, so tiny and perfect. It always amazes me how they arrive with all their little parts in perfect working order." Francis looked up, laughing self-consciously. The small fingers had closed around his thumb. "I guess if everything wasn't working it would be a matter for concern, wouldn't it?"

Anne Lee smiled at her brother-in-law. "Yes, indeed, Francis, it would that. I'm so sorry your sweet wife wasn't able to be here to see her. Becky does love a baby, I've noticed."

"She was sorry also. It happened that with her sister Anne married now and gone for several months, Lady Tayloe has been feeling lonesome for her older daughters. Becky, being the nearest at hand, felt this was an opportunity to spend a few days at Mount Airy. Did I mention that Mrs. Tayloe is expecting another child this year herself? She's not been feeling well on that score, I might add." He was rocking the baby gently in his arms as he spoke, never taking his eyes off the miniature features. She turned her little mouth in a bow of contentment at the pleasant sensation and he chuckled softly.

"I'm sorry to hear Mrs. Tayloe hasn't been well," Richard said. "It's a bad time of year. My gout has been acting up, too. I've had several attacks this winter. And speaking of sickness, someone brought word to Westmoreland Courthouse yesterday, of slaves over your way being hit by what they called the putrid yellow fever."

"Yes, I think two have died. They are also calling it jail fever, as it apparently was brought in by a convict ship out of Liverpool. Colonel Carter said it was on one of his plantations, but he doesn't allow the blacks to mingle between plantations, so it shouldn't spread. He's a strange man in many ways, isn't he? With all his belittlement of the Negro as an inferior race, he's always out there with his medicines, helping to nurse them back to health at the first sign of any sickness."

"Oh, come now, Frank. They are valuable! That's surely his motive. I have no doubt," scoffed his brother.

"Perhaps ... yet there's no denying the man's experimental mind. He has an overwhelming desire to learn new things, improve the treatments and refine the medicines, whatever his other motives," Francis defended.

Returning the following day to Menokin, he found Becky frantic with fear. "The fever! It's here ... at Menokin! Venus's Charles, and two children are down with it." Her eyes reflected better than her words the terror she felt. "Francis, they say it spreads as rapidly as the smallpox and is every bit as deadly!"

"How long have you known?" he asked, forcing a calmness into his voice he was far from feeling.

"Two days. We've not been able to get a doctor to come. Mr. West assured me he tried. He left yesterday, to take his wife to her father's for safety. Where are you going?" Her voice rose to a further pitch of fear as he put his hand on the door.

"To the quarter."

"Francis, please don't go," she pleaded. "Send someone else. You won't be able to help them anyway. Don't go out there!"

"They'll expect it, Becky. I must go. Just sit here by the window and watch for me," he said firmly, guiding her to a chair. "I'll be back soon, and I promise to be very careful."

Becky watched him cross the curved drive, pass the kitchen house, and disappear out of sight. "Oh dear sweet merciful Jesus," she whispered, "if you have ever listened to me, hear me now. Keep him safe and don't let him breathe that foul fever!"

He wasn't gone long. He strode quickly to the house with a determination beyond his usual manner, beckoned his wife, while calling loudly to Cate to follow him to their chamber upstairs. He went immediately to the hearth where he tossed his linen handkerchief on the flames. Tongues of orange and yellow licked the edges of the fabric, then consumed it hungrily, leaving only a shriveled unrecognizable heap of ash. Francis watched in silence until nothing remained of his handkerchief then, crossing to the wash stand, he reached for the bar of soap. He lathered his hands thoroughly and proceeded to scrub them methodically.

"Francis, whatever are you doing?" Becky asked hysterically.

"I want to impress you both with the importance of the orders I am about to give you. One of the pickaninnies is dead. From what I was told he was a sickly child anyway, probably had no stamina to withstand the high fever. I've ordered his body wrapped and removed. They are to bury him within the hour. Now ... we might not lose anyone else if you will do as I say. All clothing and bedding allowed in contact with those stricken, is to be burned."

"But Marse Frank, I kin scrub it clean," Cate said quietly. "No needs to burn it."

"No, Cate! A few years ago we were warned that no amount of scrubbing was good enough with the smallpox, and I think it's not good enough with this putrid fever. We'll burn all clothing! Secondly, anyone suspected of having the disease, white or black, is to be put in Old Winny's cabin. She has agreed to nurse them as she suffered the pox some years ago and survived. No one else is to enter that place without my permission. Is that clear?"

The two women nodded. They had never seen him take so firm a stance when issuing an order. It left them tongue-tied, in awe of the master they thought they'd come to know so well.

"When the ill recover, they're to be scrubbed with lye soap over every inch of their body before being allowed out with the others. I have instructed Winny and she understands. I'll also speak to West as soon as he returns. Now ... I want you to see that these instructions are spread to all the house servants and throughout the quarter. Immediately. I'm going to ride straight-away to Colonel Carter's to see what medicinal remedies he's using on his slaves, and also attempt to find out who was foolish enough to cause the fever to be brought here in the first place. It's not necessarily one of those who are sick, you know," he finished, drying his hands. He saw they were gathering confidence from his words, and hoped that soon the impact of his directions would cause him to feel better about the crisis also.

Tears swam in Becky's eyes. Blinking, she blurted, "I'm glad you're home." It was feeble gratitude, she knew, and added, "I'm proud of you, darling. I am so proud of you."

"Proud?" he asked, remembering he'd not even kissed her since his return. He slipped an arm around her waist and marched her down the steps. "You, Sam," he said, spotting a small foot in the cellar doorway, "Get upstairs to your mother. She has something to tell you."

"Why should you be proud of me, Mrs. Lee?" he asked, turning back to his wife.

"Because, Mr. Lee, some men I think, take the title of master for granted, without knowing the many responsibilities it entails. I've just learned that my husband isn't one of those. It makes me feel very safe." Her green eyes shown with happiness, all signs of fear having disappeared.

"I'll return before dark," he promised, kissing her warmly. He was elated with her answer.

Two weeks later it seemed fairly certain the fever had run its course. Several other Menokin people had contracted the illness, but there were no more deaths, and life began to return to normal. Old Winny, with the aid of Landon Carter's concoctions, had made a satisfactory nurse. Francis gave up his search to find the person whose carelessness had threatened his plantation. He was reasonably convinced his new overseer was the guilty culprit, but since he couldn't prove it, decided that the scare and his own treatment of it had probably been lesson enough for James West. The man was doing a good job, especially handling the public side of the business. It was more than Francis had hoped for when he hired the fellow, what with the difficulties of procuring goods for the *Eliza* thrown immediately upon his shoulders. It had taken some doing, that. Leaning back in his chair and placing his hands behind his head, Francis surveyed the sanctum of his study, thinking how very comfortable it really was. Pouring himself a second glass of Madeira, his thoughts returned to the *Eliza*.

It had taken a good portion of the winter, but she was finally loaded and on her way. With West's fancy talking they had managed to get over 300 hogsheads from the large planters by prevailing upon the Potomac gentry to ship their early crops out of the Rappahannock. Of course this would mean he and others in Richmond County would have to send their spring shipments out of the Potomac landing, but at least the *Eliza* had sailed with a full cargo. The venture should be more profitable than the ship Philip had put together the year before, with that cheating devil Captain Roman in charge. West had also rounded up a number of hogsheads from the small farmers, who sometimes had as few as one or two barrels a season, but whose business nonetheless, was generally profitable—with a few exceptions—Hudson Muse and his nefarious schemes being a prime example. The nerve of the fellow, suggesting that any tobacco he could manage to get to William ahead of the *Eliza's* arrival in London should be considered for an extra interest payment in his behalf. Thinking this, Francis spoke aloud, remembering their most recent unpleasant confrontation: "...and when I hesitated, saying this would have to be carefully studied by William ...the scoundrel had the gall to inform me that times being slippery at best, Mr. William had better comply with his offer! Damn his hide!"

Hearing his master's voice, Ben roused himself. "You call me, Marse Frank? Somethin' I kin git you now?" he called sleepily from the hall, hoping he wouldn't be called on to move.

"What? ... oh, Ben. No. Just thinking out loud I guess."

Relieved, Ben resumed his doze. He wished Marse Frank would go upstairs so he could go to bed, knowing Cate was waiting for him.

Then there were the Trents, Francis thought, continuing his review of recent happenings. Deeper in debt by far than Muse, and more difficult to corner, too. Well, something would have to be worked out on that score. Maybe at the Merchant's Meeting in Williamsburg he'd have a chance to confront them, squeeze from them a promise for at least partial payment. Returning to the minute book spread before him, he completed the day's entries, listing the continued repair of fences destroyed by wind, and work on the road leading to where the mill pond would be dammed. He must remember to question West in the morning regarding the progress of the plowing. It was past time to put in the corn. This fever business had set everything behind.

Swallowing the last of his wine, he stretched, snuffed the candles, then felt his way to the stairs. "Good night, Ben. Light my way upstairs, if you will. Then you may go." Bone tired, he wondered that he'd worked so late. It was long after midnight when he slipped wearily under the quilt next to his sleeping wife, hoping he wouldn't disturb her.

"I'm not asleep yet," she murmured, reaching for him.

"Oh, I was sure you would be, it's very late." He took her in his arms, loving the smell of her freshly washed hair. Even that smelled like jasmine. Then he recalled that she'd ordered the soap to be scented with it this year. "I hope it's not due to my having worked so late? That you're awake."

"No, not really. Now that the excitement concerning the fever is over I'm finding time and inclination to think on my visit to Mount Airy while you were at Chantilly. I really had a lovely time, darling."

"Did you now? Well, it's too bad you had to come home to such a crisis." Rolling away from her, he stretched lazily, yawning and ready for sleep.

Becky wasn't tired. "There were lots of things I enjoyed of course. Visiting with Mama and Papa and having little John to cuddle. But the funniest thing was that foolish Bob Carter, from Nomini you know? He's the one who's about sixteen? Well, he came with his older brother Ben, and their new tutor, Philip Fithian. Bob is simply head over heels about Polly! And he was so obvious about it, following her around like a puppy dog for two days. Polly kept trying to pretend she didn't care in the least, but there was no doubt she craved the attention. Francis, are you listening to me?" She had detected the beginnings of a snore.

"What ... what? Oh ... yes, of course I'm listening," he mumbled, rousing himself. "Young Bob Carter was trying to find a way to entice Polly behind the barn or into the orangery."

"Well, that's not exactly what I said. Yet it's close enough, I guess. Anyway, we had this perfectly divine evening, with fiddle music, singing and dancing. Every single person present was in the best possible frame of mind. All jolly and happy, and no one, absolutely no one brought up that tiresome subject of politics to spoil the fun. It was a relief for a change, I can tell you that. Well, Mr. Fithian, you know how shy he is, he just joined right in the merrymaking. He dances passably well I might add, for a man from the north. That is, once he could be coaxed onto the floor."

He was wide awake now. "Did you dance?"

"Why Francis Lee, I thought you'd never ask! I do believe I detect a hint of the green-eyed monster in your tone."

"Of course I'm not jealous," he responded, hoping he didn't sound foolish. "Why should I be? Yet, I've heard it rumored that Mr. Fithian is quite a ladies' man." He was sitting up in bed now. "Becky? I don't have cause to be jealous, do I?"

She burst into gales of laughter. It seemed she'd carried the teasing far enough. "Have you ever seen an elephant fly?"

"I've never seen an elephant do anything. Answer my question. Did you dance?"

"Yes, silly, I danced! Just because I'm a stuffy old married lady doesn't mean I must forgo all the pleasures, does it? But to set your mind at ease, Philip Fithian spent the entire evening waiting on Miss Garrot, Johnny's new governess. He paid but scant attention to any of the married ladies present. I danced with Papa, with Robert Wormeley ..."

"Oh, the Sabine Hall Carters were there, too?"

"Some of them. I told you it was a festive evening. And I danced with Mr. Ritchie from Hobbs' Hole, and let me see ... I think that's all."

The darkness hid his smile. No threat was posed by that trio. "Well, I'm most delighted you had an enjoyable visit, my love."

"One thing more, Francis, before you sleep. While I was home, Papa sat me down and read his Will to me. At first I didn't want to listen, but he kept saying it was important for me to know. Of course he's leaving the Mount Airy plantation and the majority of his estate to Mama and then to little John ... how he does worship that child. Anyway, did you know he has named you, along with his other sons-in-law and several others, an executor of the estate?"

"Yes, he told me last year when he was preparing the Will."

"But you haven't seen the document?"

"No, he didn't offer, and I didn't ask."

"Well, he's willed us Menokin, the land and the house. The entire thousand acre tract is to be mine, in place of the two thousand pounds he's leaving to each of my sisters. In addition, if the dependencies aren't completed by the time of his death, they are to be finished with money from the estate."

Again he was wide awake, up on his elbow, listening with interest. "I'm happy to hear that, Becky. I find it more than generous. With the price of tobacco falling again, and the difficulties with shipping, we probably wouldn't be able to afford to complete those outbuildings even halfway as grandly as originally planned, if ever." He folded his hands behind his head, thinking. "I'm certain they'll be finished before he dies though. Your papa is still very hale and hearty."

"I know. I just thought you'd be interested to know he was willing us Menokin, for our very own." She hesitated, arranging the next sentence in her mind. "Papa ... has planned that if I ... we don't have any children ... that following our deaths, Menokin will return to the Tayloe family."

"You mean it wouldn't go to my appointed next of kin, presumably a Lee?"

"No, it wouldn't. I take that to be his intention."

"I see," he said, more rankled than he cared to admit. He decided it was wise to keep his irritation to himself for the time being, however. "I'm not sure that's of any great concern. One day soon we shall surprise him with an heir of our own, love!"

"Mmm. It's what I pray for every day. You know that, darling. But ... tonight I've talked so long I'm too tired to do anything about it. I can see you are, too." Kissing him lightly, she turned over and snuggled into the quilt.

Now that she has thoroughly awakened and aroused me, he thought, *she is tired! Unfathomable woman, thy name is Rebecca.* Aloud he said, "Good night, Becky. Sleep well." For more than an hour he remained awake, thinking about all she had said. Before finally dozing off, he became sure in his own mind that it was important to him to keep Menokin House in the Lee family. What else could one leave behind, especially if one had no sons to carry on the name?

Williamsburg to Philadelphia

Becky sat on a bench in the newly planted boxwood maze, legs stretched out, ankles crossed, and hands at rest in her lap. It was a superb spot, she thought, at the crossing of two garden paths. The born-again joy of new life and fresh beginnings was everywhere—an ancient drama repeated every spring. The fruit trees nodded in spectacular blossom; intriguing scents drifted from every corner of the garden. She had tried to concentrate on her scripture lesson but the psalms were no match for the natural beauty surrounding her. Finches and bluebirds flitted from branch to branch. The robins flew up and down constantly, pecking for worms in the damp earth, cocking their perky caps as they listened for a telltale sound. They all ignored her, even the skittish squirrels raced daringly close to her feet in pursuit of one another. The hillside was vibrant with color—tiny white star-of-Bethlehem interspersed with purple violets and yellow jonquils, forming a lush carpet between the trees. It was marvelous how it all came back to glory after the cold hard winter.

The thud of hoofbeats intruded on her serenity, and in a few minutes Francis strode into view around the corner of the house, but he wasn't alone. Happy to have a guest, she hurried to meet them.

"Look who I ran into over Richmond Courthouse way," Francis called.

"Richard! What a surprise! Come, both of you. Sit with me in the garden. It's a paradise today, you'll see. Call Milly, darling, to bring refreshments."

When they were settled for a while sipping on cool ciders, and Richard had passed on his news from Westmoreland and home, the conversation took the direction it always took when the brothers were together. "I trust we'll not bore you, my dear, if we speak about the most recent outrages proposed by Parliament?" Richard had held off as long as he could; his own wife would have long since been drawn away by some demand of the children. He felt vaguely disconcerted by Becky's continued presence—equally uneasy about including her in the conversation or ignoring her. He fixed on the latter, although he was hazy as to why. Perhaps impatience.

Francis always found his brother's awkwardness with women amusing. "Becky reads the papers, you know." He winked at her. "She might even be capable of understanding as much as any of us do, I dare say. What do you think, love?"

Becky smiled gratefully at her husband. It was clear she wasn't ready to leave the garden, whether it was expected of her or not. Richard nodded, anxious to talk in any case. "It appears Lord North's hatchet men are determined to punish Boston for her sins. And what more evil and effective way than to close her ports to shipping?"

"I've heard," Francis said, "that they promise to allow the port to reopen as soon as Massachusetts pays for the tea lost in the harbor!" He waited for Richard's guffaw.

"Unthinkable! Impossible!"

Becky, having been encouraged by Francis, spoke up. "Well, you can be certain Samuel Adams will have none of that, from what I understand of it," she offered, ignoring Richard's expression, thinking it was time he learned she was not a silly flibbertigibbet. "I'm positive he wouldn't allow one shilling to be paid for that tea!"

Richard cleared his throat. "That's what we're led to believe, my dear Becky, but the situation is far more complicated than a mere port blockade. And Sam Adams isn't the only voice in

Boston. These new Parliamentary Acts provide protection for Crown officials in their collection of revenues, or in criminal actions taken against Americans in putting down riots or other forms of protest we may indulge in. And these senior officials, including the governor, can all be appointed by the Crown and not by the elected assembly. So, you see, they have us by the tail or, should I say the throat?"

Francis shook his head. "If other officials in addition to the governor were to be appointed by the Crown, that would, in the case of the Bay Colony, essentially annul the Massachusetts charter!"

"That's absolutely correct. And who is to say Virginia is not next in the demon minds of the Ministry leaders? There's also a plan afoot to provide a civil government for Quebec which would extend her boundaries to include the western lands of the Ohio and Mississippi Rivers."

"Richard, what of the claims many Virginians have on those lands, like ourselves? Surely, England can't propose to ignore our claims?"

"That's precisely what I think they intend to do ... and the claims of Massachusetts and Connecticut also. Ignore them, as though they never existed."

"How certain is it these bills will pass the Parliament? Right now they're just threats. How are they being labeled?"

Richard shook his head. "It's my opinion there's little doubt they'll become law. I'm told that in England they're being referred to as 'Coercive Acts,' but I say we shall call them *outrageous Acts*! Another tidbit is that they propose to reinstate the Quartering Act as part of this package. However, this time British troops may be housed in occupied dwellings, as well as taverns or public buildings! That means wherever they damned well choose to put them! Begging your pardon, Becky."

She laughed, appreciating his show of manners. She'd long since come to expect the Lee men to be gentlemen, and they rarely let her down. "More cider, Richard?" she responded, hoping he was beginning to feel at ease with her.

"Perhaps a bit more. It's very refreshing. Your garden's coming along nicely, by the way. Every time I visit there seems more to enchant the eye." He would have liked to tell her he felt the same about her—each time they met he was more attracted to the easy way she had about her, her open warmth and graciousness, but he had no idea how to say that. He turned again to his brother, "Now Frank, have you had any word in your area as to when our own Crown-appointed governor might decide to convene the assembly?" When Francis shook his head, Richard continued, "Neither have we in Westmoreland. But I trust it won't be too long from now. We should be ready with some plans for action."

"I'm willing to help in any way I can. What do you have in mind?"

Becky decided it was time to allow them their privacy. "If you'll excuse me, I have some chores to attend. Don't sit out here so long you get chilled. You know how easily you pick up a cold, darling. Ben will have the fires lit for the evening soon. We're happy to have you with us, Richard. You'll stay the night?" she asked out of courtesy, knowing he was planning on it.

"Of course. I'd be delighted. Don't arrange anything special. I prefer to be as one of the family. I hope you think of me that way, my dear."

∽

As it turned out, Richard Henry remained several days at Menokin, a victim of a severe gout attack. Immobile in bed, he suffered painfully. The brothers conversed constantly about the new British threats to American liberty. Landon Carter, hearing of the turn of events at his neighbor's, sent his slave Nassau, who performed two small operations which relieved the inflamed areas of Richard's leg. Nassau, well trained by Carter, accomplished the feat as he did everything else for the white man—when he hadn't been drinking, Nassau was an extremely able, if somewhat haughty, servant.

∾

When they met again in early May in Williamsburg, the brothers found the entire assembled body of burgesses to have virtually but one subject on their collective mind. They had gathered not to do the governor's bidding nor to accomplish the business of the colony, but to determine the matter of how to retaliate against the Coercive Acts—namely the Boston Port Bill, the revised Quartering Act, the Quebec Act, and the act affecting governmental powers in the Massachusetts Bay Colony. For the most part these measures were set to go into effect on June 1, 1774, barely three weeks away. When word reached the Assembly that General Gage had arrived in Boston to replace former Governor Hutchinson and to close the Boston port, it was time to stop talking and take action. Under the leadership of Thomas Jefferson, Patrick Henry, Francis Lightfoot and Richard Henry Lee, and a few others, they passed a series of resolutions setting aside June 1st as a Solemn Day of Prayer and Fast. Governor Dunmore flew into an immediate rage, ordering the assemblymen home. Only later were they to learn that other colonies had taken the same action, and also been dissolved by angry governors. Not one piece of colonial legislation did they accomplish.

Ignoring the consequences, the burgesses gathered during the next days at Raleigh Tavern, assembled together as a revolutionary body—not as the House of Burgesses of the British Colony of Virginia in America. Before leaving the city they endorsed a resolution calling for an annual General Congress of all the thirteen American colonies. Further, they agreed to another meeting of their own dissolved assembly in early August, and that the news of their actions be sent immediately to their sister colonies by the Correspondence Committee.

Francis, returning from the last of the meetings, was in a very somber frame of mind. "I have just signed my name, and though I was fourth from the last of eighty-some delegates to do so, I have signed the first document that is likely to be labeled as treason. We are guilty of irrevocable opposition to the King's laws. The magnitude of our actions is appalling! And the magnificent British constitution, which we all mightily believe in, sadly will not save us now. And yet it was the only way ... I won't apologize for my actions and I would do it all over again," he announced to Becky.

"Then there is no turning back?"

"None whatsoever, we have crossed our Rubicon. Our hope lies in a joint Congress where we must seek means and methods to a peaceful path, if such be even possible, to a reconciliation of our differences with England. If the joint Congress fails to do that, then all will be lost, and frightening as it may seem to you, love, I must warn you that likely will mean our very heads!"

❦

John Tayloe, thoroughly steeped in the English tradition, was finding great difficulty in accepting the assembly's brash actions. If the truth be known, he sympathized to a considerable degree with the governor's enraged decision to send them packing. He found it impossible to believe that a small group of zealous, young, hot-headed progressives could so sway the minds of the more staid members that they would brazenly defy, indeed flaunt disobedience in Dunmore's face. He had no particular objection, he told himself, to the day of prayer and fast. But he felt the wording of the resolution proclaiming it had left George III's poor Governor Dunmore no choice but to express the strongest possible disapproval. And that meant to dissolve the assembly for insubordination. He was especially disturbed at his own son-in-law's participation in all this. On a pleasant Sunday in June he ushered Francis into the library at Mount Airy proposing to confront him with his actions. By unspoken agreement in the past, the two had managed to avoid discussion of political areas in which they suspected they'd discover sharp differences. Recognizing that he was about to wade into one of these off-limit areas, the colonel set the scene by first offering a healthy cup of brandy to his guest.

"Well, Frank. Here's to your good health! Fine meal we've just finished. I enjoyed those oysters. And my cherries are delicious this year, if I may say so. Scarcely a blemish despite the frost in late April."

"No doubt about it, Sir. The cherries at Menokin are also at their peak. Becky has several new methods for preserving them, so we're going to experiment. We've had to turn all children out to cherry picking while the weeds grow rampant in the corn field!"

"Do you make the cherry brandy?"

"I think I'll try it this year. My peach brandy was most successful, if you recall. Actually this is the first time our cherry trees have born enough fruit to allow for any big plans."

Tayloe strolled behind his desk, a move to bolster his authority figure. Clearing his throat, he took a sip of brandy as he fiddled with an account book.

Francis suspecting what was coming, decided to steer away from serious conversation as long as possible. "I expect the ladies enjoyed the meal as well, they've all retired to nap for an hour. Lady Tayloe looks well, Sir, following the birth of little Jane. I complimented her on her usual remarkable recovery." He sniffed his brandy, rolling it in the cup. From the colonel's expression, viewed over the rim, he guessed the man was about to embark on his planned course.

"Yes, yes ... that remarkable woman is, at her age, better able to bear the discomforts of child bearing than many a younger one. Her own daughters included. And now Frank, if you have no objection, or even if you do, I think we must discuss a very serious matter. I can't put off any longer mentioning to you that I'm more than a little distressed with your actions as regards recent civil disturbances."

"Civil disturbance? Sir, you surely can't name a day of prayer and abstinence a civil disobedience?"

Tayloe scowled. "No, I do not. Only the method by which it was proclaimed. And the spreading of the word through this county, for which you are quite responsible, was calculated to arouse the freeholders and yes, even the tenants, to a fevered pitch. The proposal to send supplies to relieve the peasants of Boston is on every damned tongue!"

"I wish you could accept the necessity for us to share the burden of Boston's blockaded port. Suppose for a moment, that it were Virginia who suffered a blockade ... perhaps on this very river? What then?" Francis paced to the window, staring beyond the fields to where the Rappahannock, continuing its course, flowed to the Chesapeake Bay and hence to the open ocean.

"That would be our problem and I trust if it came to that, we should well deserve our fate! These colonies owe everything to Great Britain. Why, we draw our very breath from England's culture, her intellectualism, her laws, her religious faith, and King George's benevolence! Under her generous propriety we've been permitted and encouraged to amass our fortunes. We educate our sons in her universities. We'd have no doctors, no capable lawyers in these colonies were it not for England! Would you throw all this over to support a passel of hot heads to the north to whom we owe nothing?"

Francis's respect for his father-in-law was already somewhat tempered by a nagging concern over the provisions of Tayloe's last will and testament as revealed to Becky. He now threw aside the cloak of caution. "Colonel, I ask you by manner of reply, would you have us sit idly by, while an evil and wicked Parliament imposes one injustice after another upon our homeland? Forces us to submit to the quartering of troops in our very homes, usurps the western lands we have laid claim to, forbids us a free market? All the while attempting to tax us out of existence?" Spurred by his own enthusiasm, he went on, "There are some, Sir, at this very moment, who call themselves Americans, rather than Virginians, Pennsylvanians, or whatever. Men like Sam Adams, Gladsden of South Carolina, probably John Dickinson of Philadelphia, and our own Patrick Henry. These are fearless men ... men determined to stand against the tyranny of Britain! I'm sorry it distresses you, but I'm proud to count myself among the number who will fight to the last political breath to convince the King he has been misguided in his treatment of the American colonies!" Heart pounding, Francis drank deeply of the strong liquor, taking fierce pleasure from the stark burning sensation he felt as it went down. He awaited the other's response, praying the brandy would strengthen his resolve not to back down from his position, nor to waver in the least.

"Well, it appears you're not prepared to so much as converse sensibly on the possible consequences of your actions," Tayloe spit out angrily. "Have you considered that in your recent assembly, no concern was given to the matters of routine government in our own colony? Laws have expired, criminals await punishment, problems compound, and not one bloody thing was done about any of it! All the talk was of the problems of Massachusetts. We must look to our own concerns before we can look to those of others," he declared, voice rising. "This democratic nonsense, this burning passion for liberty you espouse, by availing yourself of the opportunity to include the lower classes in your protest fastings and so on, will accomplish nothing but to create unrest. Last week, that effigy burning of Lord North in Richmond Courthouse was despicable! How can you expect to control the base nature of the common wretches if on the one hand, you arouse them while, on the other, you completely ignore the passage of the very laws of government by which it's possible to regulate their lives? Answer me that, if you can! What you and your fellow radicals are suggesting smacks of the vilest sedition imaginable!"

Tayloe's face was purple—for a heavyset man, the cords in his neck were astonishingly visible. Francis knew the brandy was working on both of them. It occurred to him the situation did have its humorous aspects, one of them being the reference to Lord North's recent Richmond County demise. "You know, there are times, Sir, when you surely remind me of Colonel Landon. It's amazing, the similarity." He decided it wasn't the time to express Patrick's thoughts on the methods of keeping the people stirred up with urgency over the cause of liberty. Although he would have relished shocking Tayloe with that. That "base" nature, as he so aptly put it, was undoubtedly more inclined to action over an effigy hanging than it was over a tea boycott or a fancy petition of protest to the King! That was a fact well proven in recent days.

John Tayloe decided to calm himself. "I believe I shall accept that as a compliment, my dear boy, knowing your fondness for Carter. Don't bother to explain on what basis you note the similarity. A few things are perhaps better left unsaid between relatives."

Francis held out his cup—his host refilled it and then his own. "Perhaps this entire discussion would have been better left unspoken between us. It has gotten us nowhere," he said kindly. "Before we leave it, however, may I say one thing more? In preference to answering your previous question, that is."

"What was my previous question?" When Tayloe looked perplexed, Francis laughed, greatly relieved at the return to normalcy between them. "Well, now we have both forgot! At any rate, I must confess that I do have a concern over the necessity of shipping our crops as quickly as possible this year. There could be further blockades, or even further associations forbidding export to Britain. My brother William has a ship in Potomac right now. We're trying to load her as quickly as possible. Might I suggest that you consign as much ready tobacco to her hold as you have on hand? It would be to your advantage."

Shrewd, thought Tayloe. Very shrewd. He admitted grudgingly to a deep admiration of his son-in-law's astute business sense. "Well, I suppose you think you can badger me into accepting any terms at all, merely by pressuring me with this fear of immediacy?" he asked, only half joking.

Francis coughed, wishing so many didn't question William's fairness. "I think you'll find the terms are the best you can obtain anywhere in these troubled days, Sir. William's services are quite admired. Your order for supplies, excepting those on the boycott list, of course, will be filled satisfactorily and promptly returned on the next crossing. I urge you to look on the deal favorably."

Tayloe, smelling an opportunity for a possible bargain after all, said, "I'll tell you what. In return for my consideration of William Lee's ship, you must agree to behave reasonably sensibly in the next assembly. I think, under the urging of the Council, that Dunmore will call for new elections soon."

"I agree with you on the necessity of attending to our expiring laws. I don't argue that point." Would Tayloe accept this as enough of a concession?

"Then I have your promise to do whatever is in your power to bring the House back into a more normal posture? To put aside this revolutionary foolishness and stop pestering our King with these wild resolutions?"

"That will depend entirely on Dunmore I should say. But assuming that he has learned a lesson, I should be able to comply with your wishes," Francis hedged. He was most anxious to bring this entire conversation to an end.

"Then I shall consider loading my hogsheads on Mr. Lee's ship in Potomac," Colonel Tayloe stated, knowing full well he would probably ship out of Hobbs' Hole as planned.

❧

By evening that day the glow of brandy had worn off and Francis found himself more irritated than ever at his father-in-law. It seemed impossible that in the entirety of their afternoon time together they'd not once touched on the inter-colonial Congress which was virtually a certainty—and one that would come about within a very few months. Nor had they mentioned the August convention planned by the dissolved burgesses. Whether or not Dunmore called another assembly, matters would be taken up by a revolutionary convention of the elected lawmakers at their own convening. John Tayloe, apparently refusing to admit that affairs of state had reached this stage, talked as though the burgesses would meet, make laws, and carry them to the governor's council for approval as before. And bow to the royal governor with a thank you!

Francis fumed. The danger behind all this, he decided on the way home to Menokin, lay in the fact that many others, friends and people he respected, felt exactly as did Tayloe. Naming them in his head, Nomini Hall had been ordered by its master not to participate in the June 1st fast day; Landon Carter continued to express worry over the drastic measures which further separated the colonies from the good graces of George III; certainly Benjamin Harrison, while supporting the necessity for a joint congress, was actually far more closely aligned with the philosophy of the wealthy planters than with the radical departures of Patrick Henry! Even considering these few who came to mind so quickly, he knew in his heart they represented majority thought among upper-class Virginians. Recognizing this and facing it squarely, Francis was forced to wonder what in the name of heaven he was doing on the other side of the fence? Was it due in total to the influence of his brothers? With the exception of Philip, they all stood staunchly for a firm opposition to English domination.

Or, aside from his family, was there something within himself that forced him to choose the dangerous course on which he'd embarked? If so, how could he know if he was choosing the path to his own destruction as the colonel had suggested? Would it be the end of their happy, plentiful, comfortable lives?

Frustrated and deeply troubled, he turned at the end of the day to his wife for solace. But not in the usual way. He didn't even try to explain to her what was preying on his mind, or to share his fears and uncertainty. He had engaged in more than enough conversation for one day.

A storm, blowing up suddenly soon after their arrival home, thundered and crashed across the summer sky. Jagged bolts of lightning pierced the dark chamber with vivid flashes of brightness as desperately needed rain flooded the dusty fields. The fury of the storm matched his mood and he allowed the sight and sound and smell of it to feed his desire. Once in bed, he gave himself freely to nature's primitive urge as he never had before, making fierce and passionate love to Becky. She cried out once, whether in ecstasy or pain, he neither knew nor cared. It was enough that she perceived his need and matched it with her own.

When he'd exhausted himself she continued to hold him tightly to her breast, stroking his hair and crooning a low sound that comforted and soothed him. It seemed to her that he'd never needed her more—had any feeling ever filled her with such joy?

A fortunate man indeed to be able to vent his emotions in such a mutual and totally rewarding act of love, Francis closed his eyes and fell instantly into a deep sleep.

ॐ

During the weeks that followed, Francis continued having doubts. Serious ones. Yet he didn't change one whit in his posture toward Great Britain. Nor did he contribute a single word in any attempt to motivate his fellow legislators to a return to what John Tayloe considered rational colonial legislation. On the other hand, neither did Tayloe place a single hogshead of tobacco on William Lee's Potomac ship. The two men moved into an uneasy truce, each deciding separately that prudence was the better side of the coin. True to Tayloe's prediction, elections were called; Governor Dunmore set August 11th as the date of Assembly. Just as true to their own plan, the elected assemblymen convened at Raleigh Tavern on the first day of August. The year was 1774.

Becky chose not to accompany Francis on this trip, blaming her decision on the scorching heat and unusual drought. The roads were deplorable at best, she told him, and they'd be near to impassable with this year's dust. This was only part of her reason, however. For some days prior to Francis's departure she hadn't felt particularly well. A sort of colic, causing a painful dysentery was prevalent in the county, as was an eruptive fever called the swine pox. The seed ticks had caused everyone to suffer more festering sores than ever before, and a great many persons were ill with a severe ague. Becky didn't claim the specific symptoms of any of these, yet she knew something was wrong. She simply couldn't muster enough strength for the journey. All her husband's energies these days seemed involved with the worsening state of colonial affairs, and she hesitated to burden him further by telling of her indisposition when he was in such a constant turmoil over the state of government. His pre-occupation with getting tobacco loaded and off to England before ports were closed, as well as attendance at frequent political meetings in both Richmond and Westmoreland Counties, had kept him away from home a good deal. When he was at Menokin, he was always engrossed in thought or letter writing. Since the night of the storm they had shared few intimate moments. It hadn't been difficult to hide her lassitude, if that's all it was.

"I'll bring you the news from Williamsburg, including a report on the latest fashions. And a surprise. A surprise from one of the shops," he promised, swinging a leg over Cameron. "Steady boy, ho … this old man, despite his graying muzzle, will carry me safely there and home again with a fine gift for you!" He patted the horse fondly, not ready to admit he'd have to turn him out to pasture in a few years.

Becky smiled, waving and trying to look happy. "That's nice, darling. I'll be waiting." She watched him settle in the saddle, listening to the familiar creak of the leather. She saw Ben was ready, mounted with the pack horse behind; he bid goodbye to Samuel, shooing him out of the roadway. The child had absolutely no fear of animals, she thought, shaking her head as Sam offered a handful of grass to Ben's old nag. "I almost wish I were going with you now. Seeing you leave is making me lonesome already," she told Francis.

"I've been so busy I've not been much company lately. I'll make it up to you when I get home, love. Look after yourself now. Don't stay too long in the hot sun and, whatever you do, take care West doesn't badger you with questions. I've given him directions aplenty. He should have no trouble keeping things going. The big tasks are to finish getting up the wheat, gather in the fodder and keep the weeds down everywhere. And pray for rain," he laughed, saluting her. Why, he wondered for a moment, did she look so forlorn standing there, twisting the folds of her blue calico skirt? "Are you sure you'll be all right, Becky?"

"I'll be just fine. We'll all be fine, won't we, Sammy? Don't worry. When should I expect your return? We haven't even talked about that."

"If all goes well, you can look for me within the fortnight. We'll elect our delegates to the Congress, lay out the course for them to follow, and that should be the whole of it. Unless Dunmore actually allows us to convene as the assembly after that. If Richard has his way, the instructions for the Philadelphia delegates will be part and parcel of the Association drawn up by him in June, and presently making its round of the counties. I'll be helping with that."

In the relative cool of early morning he galloped down the road and out of her sight—exuberant and eager to meet with his fellows, riding high on the tide of his own growing enthusiasm for a cause he would soon cease to question at all. At the crossroad above Mount Airy, by prearrangement, he joined Robert Wormeley Carter. Setting their horses at an easy gait, they rode to the ferry that would carry them across the Rappahannock to Essex County on the first leg of their journey to the Virginia capital.

Shortly after noon, dusty and hot from the road, the travelers decided to stop at a wayside ordinary to eat and get relief from the midday sun. The fare was simple—coarse-grained bread, pungent yellow goat cheese, and eggs—and the beer was a welcome treat to their parched throats. They ate in silence for the most part. When they finished, Francis leaned back in his chair and unbuttoned his vest, thinking there was no one here he had to impress. "What say you, Robert, do you think this damned drought will ruin all chance for a decent crop?" He signaled the proprietor for a light to his pipe and was soon blowing smoke rings into fragile circles, feeling more relaxed than he had in days, despite knowing that what happened during the next week could change all of their lives forever.

"If this convention approves a resolution to prohibit the shipping of our tobacco to London, it shan't matter a tinker's damn whether or no our crops dry up!" his friend responded, indulging himself in a pleasant belch. Robert had consumed a large quantity of dark country beer.

"True ... except that the ban on export will be directed only to England as it is our only market at present ... but given time, we could develop arrangements with other European countries. My brother William is very much for the ban. He says the merchants will raise such a ruckus in protest over the loss of tobacco to sell that Parliament will be forced to give in to our demands! It could be the lever we need."

"What an optimist you are, Frank! We won't develop any other arrangements, as you say, with the British navy blocking our ports. We're probably courting economic disaster to even consider blocking our own export to London. I know Richard intends to stand firm behind an export ban, hoping it will force them to end the blockade of Boston's harbor, but do you actually think such a ploy can possibly succeed?"

"Perhaps," Francis answered, "but who can promise what will be forthcoming from such an irrational Parliament, Robert? We can't, at any cost however, back down from the forward thrust of our present position. Having stirred the small freeholders to support our actions to look to the liberties of their own government, we must continue to show them leadership by positive action. We can't afford to lose their support."

"You know it's this involvement of the lower classes that disturbs my father. He's never recovered from the fact that I debased myself by seeking the votes of the common man in order to take his seat in the House!"

Francis nodded. "I'm aware of that. He feels the voters to be generally ungrateful souls who have ceased to cast their votes in unquestioned and unsolicited support of those who would most graciously protect their best interests ...."

"By that he refers, of course, to himself," Robert interrupted. "I do believe he considers himself the county's most benevolent benefactor! But that's only so long as the lowly don't pass too often within his sight nor deafen his ears with their unseemly prattle!"

They both chuckled, knowing there was much truth in those words. "And yet, my friend, he stands strongly on the need to remain firm against the injustices forced upon us by England's Parliament, and is quite enraged over the threats to usurp our claims to the western lands by putting them in the hands of a French Canada! He told me last week that he believed the colonies should have as little commerce as possible with Britain until a complete redress of all our grievances takes place."

"My father and I find few enough things on which to agree. Fortunately, that's one of them. He's become petty, impossible to please in his old age ... I gave up trying a long time ago. I'm not proud of it, Frank, but it's the God's truth."

Francis sensed a side of Robert he'd not been aware of and it made him think more highly of the man. "To me Landon Carter will always be a dear and trusted friend, no matter what temper he shows. He has a mind that is a rarity among the men I have known." He hoped Robert would understand he didn't meant it as a chastisement, but simply as an acknowledgment of the respect he felt for his father.

"There are subjects more pleasant to me than the idiosyncrasy of my father's mind. How about Tayloe? He hasn't come around in his opinion of our previous assembly's actions, I'll wager!"

"No, and I'm afraid he's not likely to change his mind. He agrees the British Acts against us are wrong and unjust, but still feels we should proceed sensibly through the means provided us by our governor and his council, instead of risking our entire establishment. His position reflects the council view as well as that of some of our own members, you know. It's the varying degrees to which each is willing to compromise or bargain that will ultimately decide our course, I think."

Robert, thinking suddenly of the horse races and the tavern gaming tables, shoved back his chair. "Well, have we rested long enough? If we push, we could arrive by late tomorrow evening. Come, Frank, let's be off!" Snapping his fingers at the innkeeper, he called loudly for their horses and servants to be alerted, and tossed some coins on the table before striding from the room.

An unkind thought crossed Francis's mind. *With your lord-of-the-manner attitude you are not unlike your father in some ways after all, my friend.* Chuckling to himself, he nodded to the hovering proprietor and his timid wife, handed them his portion of the bill, and followed Robert into the steamy sunshine. They would ride until after dark tonight.

⌒⌒

Arriving in the capital at dusk the following evening, Francis spotted a familiar drab parson's suit ahead of them on Gloucester Street, and urged his horse forward. In his hurry to join Patrick Henry he left Robert, Ben, and Carter's two waiting men in a cloud of dust. After a brief greeting they agreed to meet at the tavern within the hour. It would give him time to change his clothes and settle things on Nicholson Street.

A short time later the two men shook hands eagerly. After the separation since early summer and considering all that was happening, they would talk far into the night. Of that Francis was certain, hoping selfishly no one would disturb them, because many of the delegates wouldn't arrive until the morrow—the first meeting called for the day after. He wanted to have some time alone with Patrick and other intimate friends. It was not to his liking to converse on serious matters in a large group; the larger the number, the more inhibited he became. Not so with the recalcitrant Mr. Henry, however. The larger the gathering, the more eloquent he seemed to become, Francis thought, not for the first time admitting envy of Patrick's ability to captivate an audience.

"Good to see you, old friend. How is your family since last we met?" Francis inquired when the two had settled in the usual corner of the Raleigh.

"Mrs. Henry is ... ah, reasonably well. As well as can be expected, I suppose. And Mrs. Lee? Your lovely bride? She didn't accompany you this time?" His piercing dark eyes scanned the room like a hawk, taking in everyone present.

"Hardly a bride any longer! We've been married five years now, Patrick. Although I must honestly admit, more like yesterday is what it seems," Francis confessed, smiling broadly.

"She remained at Menokin ... heat and dusty roads, she said. I'll miss her tender attentions."

As time went on, the tavern rooms became crowded; greetings and signs of camaraderie echoed from every corner. Many, as Robert Carter, contented themselves at cards or tried their luck at the billiard table. Most, however, simply took their leisure with conversations and a brimming mug. A full moon, rising blood-orange on the horizon in the early evening had, as the hours progressed, ascended above the tree tops and turned to brilliant white. Eventually the gentlemen, revived but tired from their journeys, began to bid farewells and head for their homes, rented tenements, or boarding houses. Most had departed when Patrick Henry turned to Francis in confidence. He spoke of an incident that occurred to him earlier in the day as he'd approached Williamsburg: a servant of Jefferson's hailed him on the road, saying that Mr. Jefferson had been forced to turn back due to illness.

"I thanked him for the information and expressed my condolences, but wondered why the news had been passed to me. As I was about to resume my journey into town, the slave produced a packet saying it contained a pamphlet written by Jefferson for presentation to the convention. His instructions were to request me to give it my immediate attention and to present it to the delegates in the absence of the author." Pausing briefly, he turned his hawk eyes on Francis, who waited, suspecting the story hadn't come to an end. In a moment Henry continued, "I've read the document, Frank. In fact, shortly after Tom's servant rode out of sight, I stopped to look it over, curious as the devil to see what it contained." He hesitated a second time.

"Well? What does it say?" Francis asked.

"It's a treatise on the rights of British America. He states that when a colonial assembly is forcibly dissolved, as was ours, then all power reverts to the people, who may then use it in any way they think proper."

"My God ... those are strong words. Am I right in assuming you agree with this wording? I guess you should be mightily flattered Tom acknowledges your gift of oratory by entrusting it to your care. You will, of course, read it to our convention?"

"I should like you to read it tonight. Then tomorrow let me have your opinion," Henry answered, handing him a small parcel wrapped in brown paper.

They parted shortly thereafter, each going his separate way to lodgings. Francis headed for Nicholson Street where he knew Ben would have prepared his room. Finding the house lonely, he wandered about for a while, wishing Richard had arrived. He settled finally in Colonel Tayloe's study where he sat to address himself to Thomas Jefferson's *Summary View of the Rights of British America.* The text was defiant, arrogant even, yet its learned statements of grievances and historical precedents were extremely well put. It proclaimed that George III had no right to land a single armed man on American shores; that those already here were subject to colonial law. One paragraph particularly fascinated Francis. In order to absorb the full impact of its meaning, he read it aloud, not once but twice: *Let those flatter who fear; it is not an American art. To give praise where it is not due might be well from the venal, but would ill beseem those who are asserting the rights of human nature.*

It was a direct slap at the time honored traditions of the Virginia House of Burgesses—and a call to that body to alert itself to the new order of things.

❦

By the following afternoon Francis began to suspect Patrick might be avoiding him. When he'd returned the treatise there was no time to talk, and after that no convenient moment seemed to present itself. The hours passed, and it turned out that Jefferson's pamphlet was apparently not to be read by Patrick Henry. It was circulated freely amongst them, however, and Francis saw that quite a few admired Tom's scholarly tone. In the end it was not adopted as a resolution for the simple reason that the strongest reactions, as vocalized in a dramatic fashion by Harrison and Braxton, labeled it as too rash, too *revolutionary*, and their voices won out.

A day later Francis met Patrick alone for the first time since the evening of their arrival, and he asked about the decision not to read the Jefferson treatise. "Why, if I may inquire, didn't you present it as Thomas requested? Had you done so, I feel certain it would have received approval."

"Did you then, think it so worthy, Frank?"

"Yes. Yes, I did. Why didn't you give it your acceptance by reading it?" Francis persisted. The shrewd side of his mind was working feverishly as he gleaned a hint of annoyance in his friend's eyes.

"I reached the decision it wasn't my duty to publicly advance the thoughts of another, most particularly ideas of such a radical nature," Patrick responded.

"I see." Francis scrutinized the familiar craggy face, the expression on which suddenly appeared very vain. "Then you didn't agree with Jefferson's philosophy after all?"

"I agreed with it, my friend. I simply found it too seditious for the present state of mind of our delegates. They haven't yet reached the necessary point of acceptance. But mark my words, they will soon enough. We'll be at war with Britain within the year!"

Francis felt extremely irritated. "And do you, my patriotic friend, consort with Athene to bring you such wisdom, or do you come by it naturally?" He went away convinced that Patrick had acted solely out of vanity—it must be his intent to enflame the colony with words of his own choosing—not those of Thomas Jefferson. So be it, he finally decided. Was it not perhaps this very quality that made a true statesman? But considerations of this sort tended to remind him of his own inadequacies and he never pondered them overly long.

It was not until several days had passed that the full impact of Patrick's last words to him burned in his brain. *At war with Britain within the year?* Could it be true? Is this, then, where we're heading? Impossible! It was madness, pure madness, to contemplate such a thing!

Meanwhile, Richard was having his own troubles. Following the pattern established between the two brothers, he called upon Francis to plunge immediately into the fight to secure votes— Richard wanted to be one of the Virginia delegates to Philadelphia. Recognizing his popularity among his fellow planters was an on-again, off-again proposition, he knew that although they admired his oratory, his ability to turn a fancy phrase, a great many of them were not able to forget, nor forgive, his unprecedented disclosure of the indiscretions of Treasurer Robinson so long ago. It had been a direct attack on one of their own. Thus, he felt it necessary to form a plan, with the aid of Francis and Patrick Henry to enroll the sympathies of a few whom they knew would vote with them. These would, in turn, be urged to approach others of their own friends seeking assurances of votes for Richard and Patrick as delegates to the Congress. The Lee brothers were by no means the only members of the convention scurrying behind the scenes in an attempt to secure votes. Harrison, an absolute dunderhead so far as Francis was concerned, was not only pushing hard for his own election, he was arguing *against* the election of Lee or Henry as well. Big Ben Harrison knew how to play a dirty game. The morning of the vote, Richard and Francis assessed the chances of Richard's being elected.

"I find Washington, Bland, Pendleton and Mason to be safely in your corner. And of course, Robert Wormeley. Now that the word is out that we'll send seven men, I think we can count positively on you to be one of them." Francis forced as much enthusiasm as possible into his voice, knowing how much this meant to his brother. In his heart he harbored grave doubt, however.

Richard's close alliance with Patrick, the radical in their group, didn't further his cause among the old family planters. "If only we had Dabney here to espouse your case. It's still hard to believe he's no longer with us." They all missed the staunch reassuring support of Dabney Carr.

"A sudden death like that ... and for so young a man, is truly a tragedy," Richard agreed, as he continued to glance over the resolutions he'd written. He'd read and reread them several times this morning. The brothers, both enjoying the hospitality of Tayloe's house, had arisen early to allow time to finalize plans for the day's meeting. It was a big day. Not only was the vote on delegates to take place, but final decisions would also be made on the resolution that would form their instructions. Richard Lee had worked long and arduously on the proposals he would present, and felt that nothing other than an absolute halt to the entire trade with Britain would be effective—import and export. He urged a program of supplies to beleaguered Boston, and an immediate alert to danger by every possible means, of every man, woman, and child in the colony. The peril that lay off their very shoreline must be made public knowledge.

Francis couldn't ever recall seeing his brother more agitated and nervous. The skin across the handsome cheekbones was stretched taut as a drum; the eyes burned in their deep sockets with a fire of intensity. None could deny this man had tuned every fiber of his being to the cause. Perhaps that, more than anything he said or did, would convince his fellows to take heed, thought Francis, as they left the house.

"We should walk, R.H. It's not too hot this morning and the exercise will relax you." Francis started down the steps, hat in hand.

"It will take longer!" Then, glancing over his shoulder, Richard pleaded, "The horses are saddled."

Francis continued on. Without turning he said, "Come. The distance is short. You'll feel better for the walk."

Shortly they arrived at the Raleigh. The delegates were gathering by twos and threes, the clerks hurrying inside to get settled first, to be ready. Putting his hand on Richard's arm, Francis spoke quietly. "Whatever is decided today, console yourself with the fact that you have put your heart and soul into it. God knows you've tried. And that's all any man who loves his country can do. If you lose, you must accept it gracefully, and go on from there."

"What God knows, and I do not, my dear Loudoun, is how we two ever came to be brothers! How in the name of heaven can you stand there acting so bloody calm?"

"Because there is jolly well nothing to be gained by being otherwise, and much to be lost," Francis said. For a rare moment, he felt the elder of the two.

The interchange took only a minute, but apparently it was enough. A quietude that he couldn't explain settled over Richard when he was called upon to read and enlarge upon his lengthy resolution. He urged unity and personal sacrifice upon his fellow Virginians in order to secure for themselves a freedom and liberty to which they were entitled by birthright under the English constitution. He was eloquent, he was provocative, he was stimulating and he was irresistible. He exuded the very essence of confidence.

Catching sight of the worried frown on Benjamin Harrison's face, the virile, chubby countenance drawn into frustrated lines, Francis knew they had won.

There was a compromise, as expected, on the export ban. It was to take effect in August a year away, if Britain did not in the meantime adjust American grievances. But import of all English products, including slaves, was to cease on November first. Richard, arguing for immediacy on both issues, lost on the former to the plea for moderation brought forth by Randolph and Harrison. But he was satisfied enough.

Late in the afternoon the convention voted to send Peyton Randolph, their honored speaker, along with Richard Henry Lee,

George Washington, Patrick Henry, Richard Bland, Benjamin Harrison, and Edmund Pendleton to represent the Virginia Colony at the first Colonial Congress, to be convened in Philadelphia in September. It wasn't by any means a totally compatible group, but their differences for the time being hovered out of sight, below a thin surface of unanimity.

Observing the unified face put on by the delegates, Governor Dunmore, to no one's surprise, prorogued the assembly to a date in November. The action was scarcely noted nor barely remarked upon; routine legislation would go begging once more. By the tenth day of August Francis, exhausted but satisfied, was on his way home.

A Bitter Pill

Becky had watched her husband disappear down the long, flat road between the fields. The sound of hoofbeats on dry, packed earth echoed the dull throb of her heart. He'd passed from sight, growing smaller and smaller until he was a mere speck on the horizon. Yet she remained, watching nothing, for several minutes. It probably might have been wiser to tell him the truth about why she stayed home. Or would it? At any rate, right now she must organize the chores for the day or nothing would be done. There was the soap to be made; Berth's task. Milly should be set to gathering, sorting, and hanging the herbs to dry—anise, pennyroyal, marjoram, sage, tarragon, savory, hyssop, fennel, angelica and basil—all were ready to cut, only this year there must be a way devised to label them. The sharp tang of dried basil had ruined last summer's apple jelly when Milly had mistaken the crushed leaf for sweet angelica. There was the possibility she'd done it on purpose, of course. Nonetheless, this year they'd be marked. Peaches also had to be gathered and the kitchen garden needed a thorough grubbing out. The weeds never minded the drought it seemed. Becky set about putting everyone to work.

An hour later, leaving them to their labors, she wandered down the hillside taking a circuitous route so as to conceal her true destination. A few minutes later she darted quickly inside the leafy haven of the bower. Here, alone, she could sort out and face what had been troubling her. A few late blooming white violets caught her attention, and she wondered if Francis had planted them here, but even such favorites as these couldn't command her interest for long. Secure in her aloneness, she dropped with abandon to the soft earth, burying her face in the sweet smelling wild things that thrived there. Protected from the direct rays of the hot sun, there was a delicious feel of damp and cool that could be found nowhere else on the parched plantation.

Becky wasn't certain when the idea had come to her that she might be carrying a child. It had been at least a week on her mind, she knew that. Once having decided not to tell Francis until she was sure, it had burned in her heart like a flame, until she felt as though she might burst with the very possibility of it. It wouldn't be fair to tell him when he'd waited patiently, hopefully, for word that he'd have a son—not unless it was a certainty. How cruel, she thought, if it turned out to be a false alarm. And she wasn't at all sure. Raising to a seated position, she began to examine herself, searching for a telltale sign somewhere. The only encouragement she discovered was a tenderness in her breasts, and she'd felt that before at her time of the month. They felt much fuller, however, than normal. Did that mean anything? She'd been sick to her stomach several times a week ago, but not since then. That could have been a meat or fish that didn't agree with her. Despondent, she lay back on the grass, curling on her side, hands under her cheek. More than anything in the world, she wanted to please Francis. And it seemed so long as she remained childless she wouldn't please him forever. Remembering the passionate abandon they'd shared the night of the storm, she thought that if ever one were going to conceive, such a night would be the occasion upon which it would happen. Could it be then ... that very night was at the root of her feeling she might be with child? If she was, then why did she continue to feel so dreadful? Every bone ached, her back hurt and she was weary, depressed. The joy she should have known wasn't there; it remained overshadowed by the fear that her prayer would once again go unanswered.

Content to be alone, she remained in the bower into the afternoon, eventually sleeping for more than an hour. When she awakened she felt sticky-hot. Not a breeze stirred and the heat was oppressive. She made her way slowly up the hill feeling more dispirited than when she'd left the house, and in a worse mood. So engrossed in her worries was she that it took several minutes for her to realize that Samuel was yelling from the direction of the barns. Soon she heard other voices, excited shouts, then raucous laughter.

The slave child had been set to weeding; it was hot and he'd tired after several hours. His father and the master had ridden away, his mistress was nowhere in sight and, when he saw his mother disappear into the house, Samuel had meandered to the goat pen, his favorite spot. Here he could sit on the gate, dangle his legs aimlessly while he watched the animals butt each other and do all the other things animals do that children find fascinating. Almost five, Samuel was curious about many things, and he learned more answers here than he could ever hope to pry from his mother or Ben. Besides, he didn't really know exactly what it was he wanted to ask.

In spite of the heat the goats were even more spirited than usual. He'd brought them some salsify and comfrey stalks from Berth's patch of greens, but the big goats were getting it all. When he jumped inside the pen to feed one of the little kids, a large billy goat came at him head down, shoving him into the rail fence. In his hurry to escape the butting horns, he opened the gate, but tripped on his way out, losing hold of the latch and the wooden gate swung wide. One after another the goats frisked past. Horrified, Samuel tried to throw his weight against the gate in order to close and latch it, but recent bouts with summer dysentery had sapped much of his normal strength. Helpless, he was forced back into the fence, as every last one of the goats ran free, making straightaway for Berth's kitchen garden.

He hollered as loud as he could, and several of the older slaves came running. James West strode out of the barn, annoyed at the disturbance. It was then the boy realized he was in serious trouble. But everyone ignored him for the moment as they began trying to round up the goats, laughing at the week's biggest diversion. There were five grown animals and four young kids in all, and together they routed and snorted their way through the cabbages and squash, heading all the while for the tall leafy sprigs of comfrey, determined to get their share of the hairy greens. Samuel stood behind the gate, his mouth agape, staring at the overseer whom he greatly feared.

Becky came upon the scene, scowling at the trampled vegetables as she passed. She marched straight to James West for an explanation.

"I've just this minute determined that the boy Samuel," he said, jabbing an accusing finger in the direction of the by now tremulous child, "stupidly allowed the animals to escape, your Ladyship!"

Becky's face turned scarlet. "Please refrain from calling me by that ridiculous title, Mr. West! A simple Mrs. Lee will do. Now, what is going on?" Why was it Francis's overseers always irritated her? "Samuel, come here this instant," she commanded, not waiting for an answer from West. When he stood in a woeful state before her, she lowered her voice, remembering how dangerous it was to let the slaves see their mistress reacting out of anger. "Sam, did you do this? Let the goats out?"

He nodded his head. "Yas-ma'm, Miss Becky. I din' mean t' have dis happ'n," he told her solemnly. He couldn't say it but he'd have given up anything, even his supper, not to have made Miss Becky mad at him. His devotion to her since the day she rescued him from old Winny's cabin was absolute.

"I see. Well, that was a very foolish thing to do. It has caused a great deal of damage and made a shambles out of the garden. It disturbs me very much. You must be punished for your carelessness." Turning back to the overseer she ordered, loud enough so everyone could hear, "Samuel is to be taken to the fields tomorrow and for the next week, and made to grub weeds with the others. He's to be treated the same as everyone else. Do you understand?"

"Yes-mam, Mrs. Lee!"

If there was an overemphasis on her name, she preferred not to notice it in her anxiety to leave the place. Suffering suddenly from an excruciating headache, she raised her skirts and picked her way as quickly as possible away from the smells and sights of the barnyard.

Cate approached her later, explaining that Sammy had been sick, and pleaded that his punishment be something other than working all day in the broiling sun with the field crew. Becky refused to budge. "I'll hear no more about it. He deserves to be punished and I've made up my mind. The boy had no business in the goat pen to begin with. Now leave me. I'm dreadfully tired, Cate ... and not feeling at all well. I wish only to rest."

∽

It was two nights later when it happened. Awakening, Becky was first aware of the summer chorus of frogs and noisy cicadas along the creek bank. The night voices always soothed her, but tonight the sound seemed deafening and annoying. She felt unbearably hot and wide awake. After a while she called Zoey to light a candle, then told her to leave. Pushing aside the gauzy bed netting, she threw back the bed sheet thinking to sit by the window. Not until she stood did she see the blood—awful, sticky dark blood that could mean only one thing—there would be no baby.

It had all been a figment of imagination. A cruel trick played on her by one of nature's occasional mistimings and her own foolish fantasies stemming from an especial night of love. In the frightening unreal world of darkness she tended first to herself, washing and changing her gown, before calling Zoey back to remove the soiled linens and remake the bed. In a daze she crawled back into bed, sobbing out her grief until the gray of dawn was in the sky. Zoey heeded her training and, although she recognized the sounds of grief from within the chamber, she remained in the hall ready to answer if she was called again.

By daybreak, Becky found the strength of acceptance which was a part of her nature. "There will be other times," she whispered. "We must believe, my dearest love, there will be another time."

∽

It was late afternoon, nearing four o'clock when she noticed the wind blowing up. The trees began to sway under a fury of hot gusty air. Rain clouds wouldn't be far behind. She had made progress in easing her disappointment during the day by setting herself to accomplish various tasks, and was just finishing a letter to her sister Elizabeth Lloyd, congratulating her on the birth of a third daughter when she heard Berth call from the hall.

"Come! Miss Becky, you's got to come. It's Samu'l!" Berth, up in years now, usually crept around, taking her time getting anywhere. But she fairly flew down the steps and headed toward the barns. Turning once, she made sure her mistress followed, then went straight to the shed where the field hands kept their tools. A few slaves, vaguely curious, lounged about waiting to see what the mistress would do about the boy stretched, limp and still, on the ground. Most, however, went about their evening chores uncaring, anxious to be finished.

"What happened?" was all Becky could trust herself to say, she was that frightened at sight of Cate's son. Guilt swept over her as she realized this was probably her fault for sending the child to the fields when she'd known he was already unwell.

"I guess the sun got to him or somethin'," James West spoke up from the corner of the shed. At all cost he wanted to avoid another tongue lashing in front of the blacks, and he continued carefully, "Don't look too serious to me, Mrs. Lee. I was just goin' to send him to Winny's cabin to be nursed for a day, when your old one here," pointing to Berth, "came along and insisted on disturbin' you."

"You were right to come for me, Berth," Becky assured her. Kneeling beside Samuel, she felt his forehead. Her hand came away hot, unbelievably hot. "Why he's burning up with fever. That's not from the sun! We must get him immediately to Sabine Hall. Colonel Landon will know what to do ... or else he'll send for a doctor."

By now huge black clouds were moving fast across the river turning the bright afternoon to twilight in seconds, and the wind began to whip the dust in the yard into circles. James West glanced around him thinking it was no time to set out through the forest in face of such a threat. "It's a terrible storm brewin', Mrs. Lee. I'll take him first thing in the mornin'. Meantime we'll do what we can for him here. Or maybe in a few hours, we could send for Doc Ephrim from Mount Airy."

Becky looked again at Samuel. He might not make it through the night with that fever. She rose slowly, the wind twisting her skirts around her legs as she shielded her eyes from the billowing dust with one hand. Her other fist was clenched at her side. She thought about it later and still couldn't determine what prompted her to act as she did—genuine concern for the slave, her own guilt, or scorn for the overseer's unmanly caution—but in an instant she made up her mind. "Mr. West, harness up the post-chaise with my mare immediately. Berth, get Sam out of this wind until the chaise is ready." She glared at West until he moved reluctantly toward the stable. "We're not going to Mount Airy. I intend to do the very best I can for Samuel, and that means Sabine Hall. Where is Cate?" she asked suddenly.

"Gone on a errand to Moun' Airy, Miss Becky. She done took some sewin' to Nan. Left 'bout a hour ago," Berth answered.

"Tell her when she returns that Sammy will be in the hands of Colonel Carter and Nassau, Berth. She will trust Nassau. Now, run to the house for a blanket and bring me my light cloak. And don't forget my mask. Hurry!"

When the horse and two-seated vehicle were led round, West followed slowly, garnering nerve for his next battle with the mistress. He glowered at her from under the kerchief he'd tied around his head to keep the sweat from running in his eyes when he was in the fields. He fully expected to be ordered, against his wishes, to transport the boy. The wind was howling now, the pines bent nearly double, and everything not tied down was blowing around the barn yard.

Becky fastened the hooded cloak about herself and adjusted the mask over her face. She looked back at the overseer, seeing curiosity in his eyes. "I would thank you kindly to assist me up," she ordered firmly.

"What?" he exclaimed. "You can't go by yourself. Colonel Lee, he'd have my hide if he knew I let you go off in this wind! That chaise could be blown right off the road and down one of them deep ravines." He could see that she meant to go. She intended to take the chaise alone. "Mrs. Lee, please, I beg you. I'll take the boy, if you insist he go today!"

"Your generous concern for my safety and Samuel's health comes a bit late, Mr. West. Now are you going to help me into this carriage or am I going to have to use this?" She reached toward the horse whip propped in the chaise footrest, knowing her words to be an empty threat. The movement had the desired affect on the overseer, however. "Well, I'm relieved to see you've decided to obey my orders," she snapped. "Now place the child here beside me and tuck the blanket securely around him. It will aid in propping him against me."

Settling herself, she clucked all the while to the frightened Lilliput. Her way with horses would have to stand her in good stead on the six mile ride. The wind made the mare skittish and she snorted, rolling her eyes and tossing her mane so that the boy holding her head almost lost his grip. "Now, all of you," with a bravado she didn't feel, Becky addressed the group of servants clustered there, "get inside the buildings and close things up before the storm hits. Tell Cate she's not to worry. I'll see to it that Samuel is safe, and we'll return as soon as we can. You may release the harness now," she directed the boy. The freed mare pawed the ground, reared once, and then feeling a light touch of the whip on her back, took off with a jerk. The chaise lurched forward, bumping over the rutted barnyard path and through the gate.

"Damned if that don't beat all," muttered James West, now totally convinced he'd never be able to fathom Rebecca Lee no matter how long he worked at Menokin. She had one hell of a spirit. Too bad she was so stuck on the master. "Get on with it!" he shouted suddenly to the slaves gawking after the chaise. "You heard the missus! Finish your chores. Come on. Move! And you, Berth, see that I get double my usual ration of beer tonight!" The experience had shaken him more than he cared to admit.

Becky could feel the heat of Samuel's body through the blanket and her cloak. She was certain it was one of the highest fevers she'd ever witnessed. He spoke only twice, the first time to explain that he really hadn't meant to let the goats out.

"I know, Sam," was all she answered, her attention concentrated on holding the mare steady against the gusts of wind that were causing the chaise to sway perilously from side to side. The only hope, she knew, was to reach Sabine Hall before the rain hit. A deluge of water would quickly turn the sandy roadbed into a sea of mud. They had to cross the mill pond and get on relatively flat ground behind Mount Airy before it rained. She'd chosen the back way through the forest knowing it to be faster, but now wondered at the wisdom of her choice. Perhaps they should have gone around through Richmond Courthouse where the roads were more traveled. The Lord is with us, she sighed thankfully as they passed Mount Airy road and headed for Sabine Hall's Fork quarter. There was a brief glimpse of the river from the top of the hill when they crossed the spot where Francis and Robert Carter had met a few days earlier.

"I got mo' weeds den anybody," Samuel ventured weakly. He thought about telling Miss Becky that two of the boys had threatened to set the goats loose again and blame him if he didn't grub their share as well as his own, but decided he couldn't get all the words together. Besides that would only get someone else in trouble. Unlike his mother, Sam had never developed a dislike for the slaves in the quarter, except for George and Hector, who had beat him up. Even at his tender age he'd come to realize his life was better than those who lived in the cabins, and felt sorry for them. "Mammy'd be proud o' me, Miss Becky. I work't hard," was all he could manage to tell her of his experience in the field.

At long last they arrived at the Carters' front entrance. It was almost dark now, and the rain began in earnest. It pelted the chaise roof as a bolt of lightning streaked the southern sky. Becky called, then screamed for someone to come. Thinking she couldn't manage to rein in the terrified mare for one more minute, she was about to give up and let the horse take them around to the stables, when Nassau and a young black boy appeared in the doorway. Within minutes they were safely inside and Becky, nearing exhaustion, told why they had come.

Landon Carter led the way through the house to the room where he stored his amazing medicinal repertoire. There he examined the weak and failing Samuel, who was by then only semiconscious. "It is indeed fortunate you were able to bring him to me, Rebecca. I don't believe with this fever he'd have survived the night." Motioning to Nassau he called for twenty-four grains of Pulvis Bazilicus, which the slave procured immediately from among the hundreds of small bottles and containers that lined the shelves. "Now Nassau, set out some Ipecacuana, as we may prescribe it later. What do you think, my man, has the boy a case of worms, far advanced?"

"He has the twitchin' belly, suh, an' a pulse irregulah," answered the slave with the same curious accent Becky had observed before. She imagined it to be a relic of his childhood in the French West Indies, although she knew the colonel had owned him since he was very young.

"The very symptoms that would lead to supposition that worms work their evil within, hey what?" Carter asked, obviously enjoying the challenge of diagnosis. "Do you think we should bleed him?"

"It could cause no harm, Colon'l, suh," the slave responded, probing cautiously at Samuel's exposed belly.

Remembering they had an audience, Carter glanced at Becky and, seeing she had turned a chalky white at the mention of bloodletting, said, "Come, dear child, you do not wish to observe such mundane operations. We'll send you up to visit Winifred. There perhaps, you can prevail upon her to share with you a drop or two of her precious claret. I think it would help you to recover from your hazardous journey." Whereupon, not waiting for a reply, he summoned a slave to escort her upstairs to Winifred's chambers.

Becky found Carter's daughter-in-law in a sorry state, her face puffy from crying, with eyes swollen to half their normal size. Winifred Carter made no attempt, however, to disguise her state as her maid ushered Becky into the room. "Please forgive me, my dear. I'm sorely depressed this evening, having suffered through a most humiliating meal earlier, with the entire family present to witness my father-in-law's biting criticism of me. He was even more cruel than usual, if that's possible."

Becky wished Winifred wouldn't try to explain. Having been through so much herself in the past few days, she didn't feel she had any strength left to sympathize. "I'm sorry to intrude on you, Winifred," she said kindly. "Perhaps another time would be more suitable." She explained briefly about Samuel being the reason for her visit. "I can certainly wait downstairs until the colonel is finished treating him."

"Please stay. Sit with me and share a glass of wine. I find it can be quite cheering, unless one consumes too much at one time, at which point the exact reverse takes place. I'm afraid that's what has happened to me tonight," she said, pouring her guest a glass.

"Thank you. I'll be happy to sit with you a while." Thinking to raise Winifred's spirits, she said, "Soon our dear husbands will be home, and our cares will vanish. I've missed Francis dreadfully."

"You are so fortunate, Becky. Do you know how fortunate you are? Your husband worships you, adores you, hangs on your every word. He'll return eagerly to your arms. See how you dream of his homecoming?" Her tears returned but she plunged doggedly on, seemingly bent on a macabre form of self-torture, she poured out her tale of lonely existence. Shut in her elaborate apartment, frequently for days at a time, she said, she'd see no one other than her children and her maid. Not that she was forbidden the house, but merely that each time she ventured out she was made to feel more miserable than when she remained alone. And so she ate more, craving sweets, and had learned to drink the tempting red wine to flavor her loneliness.

"But Robert? ... surely ..." Becky began, close to tears herself.

"I told you once that Robert rarely visits me unless he notices the youngest is no longer a baby. And when he has me with child again, he leaves. For months on end we share no more than a few words. He uses me, as a farmer sends the bull to breed the cows. I've even heard the old man remarking on it with great relish when he entertains his friends at my expense."

This was too much for her guest to take in silence. "Surely Colonel Landon is not speaking of you, dear Winifred. He could not be that cruel, he who can so gently nurse a sick slave! Perhaps he refers to some joke about cattle in his pens," she finished lamely.

Winifred shrugged. "It doesn't matter any more. So long as Landon Carter is alive, I shall remain a prisoner in this house ... you know, Becky, Robert and I used to love one another once."

"Of course you did."

"No, I mean we really did. If he hadn't brought me here to live, but built our own house as you did Menokin, then maybe we'd have some love left ...." Her voice trailed off leaving the sentence unfinished.

"He's the eldest son. He'll inherit Sabine Hall. Why would he have wanted another house?"

"Oh, I know his reasons. Yet sometimes I dream of how it was when he used to come to me, bringing me news of his day. He was always eager to share himself with me. It hardly seems possible he used to be that person." Lost in thought, she fondled her wine glass, watching the liquid through a haze of tears until, in a quick movement, she drained it. "Whatever the reason, a man can be tempted to stray, Becky. Keep a careful watch that it doesn't happen to your marriage. Sometimes ... I think there's no reason to go on."

Hearing this and realizing how deep was Winifred's despair, Becky also knew, by comparison, her own problems were as nothing for she had Francis and his unquestioned love and devotion. What else did there really have to be? She felt defeated when it came to offering Winifred a scrap of hope to cheer her tattered soul. As though an unseen voice bid her look, she spied a Bible on the table. Picking it up, she opened it without thinking to her favorite psalm. "The Lord is my Shepherd," she read in her melodic voice. "I shall not want ..." When she finished the verse, Winifred's face looked more calm and her eyelids drooped until they were nearly closed. Becky continued, "The earth is the Lord's and the fullness thereof; the world, and all they that dwell therein. For he hath founded it upon the seas; and hath prepared it upon the rivers." For an hour she read, and when she grew tired, she returned to where she had begun. "... surely goodness and mercy shall follow me all the days of my life, and I will dwell in the house of the Lord forever."

She thought Winifred had fallen asleep but when she closed the book and rose to leave, the woman said, "Amen," in a calm tone, and her eyes were free of tears. "Thank you, dear friend. You'll come back to visit me, won't you?"

Becky promised to return in a week or so. "Goodnight, Winifred. Please rest now. You'll feel better tomorrow." She hurried downstairs where she learned that Samuel was doing better, the fever had subsided, and he'd fallen into an untroubled sleep. The storm had passed, having brought little rain after its fierce and ominous portent. Becky was anxious to be on her way home.

The child, explained Carter, should remain where he was for a few days, and of course Becky was more than welcome to stay the night. Wishing for the comfort of her own bed, as well as being eager to assure Cate that Samuel would be all right, she declined the invitation. But there was the problem of how to get home now that darkness had fallen.

"I shall send Nassau to deliver you. He can tie his own horse to the rear of the chaise and return in the morning. It won't hurt him to bed down in your barn for one night. You won't be uneasy traveling alone with him, will you, my dear?" Carter inquired.

"Not so long as you say I'll be safe," she answered without hesitation.

"Well, I say it is very safe. So long as the scoundrel hasn't been at the rum bottle. And I have done a fair job of keeping it hidden lately!" He chuckled in one of his rare moments of joviality. "Now you tell that wandering husband of yours that he owes me a visit as soon as he's back in Richmond. I shall have all the news from him. I'm sure I will get but a smattering from Robert! And most especially you must pass on to Frank that the eighteenth coming up is my birthday celebration, and I shall expect both of you here for the day."

So it was decided. Amidst thank you's and varied last minute additions to Samuel's diagnosis and assurances of his imminent recovery, they set off. As they made their way through the night an exceptional thing occurred. It came about most likely because of the dark and the intimacy of the small chaise, but it also sprang from the events of the evening. After they traveled in silence for a mile or more, Becky asked a question.

"How did you know, Nassau, what bottle to hand Colonel Landon when he asked you for the medicine?"

"Ah don't undahstand the question, Madame Lee, if you please," he responded after a pause.

Unlike others who used the title, he put the emphasis on the second syllable of madam—definitely French, Becky thought. "There are hundreds of bottles, all labeled. How did you know which ones he meant?"

They rode along for another few minutes. Nassau concentrated hard on guiding the mare. The wheels of the light chaise were slipping dangerously on the wet road. "Ah read the words," he said, so quietly she wasn't sure she had really heard him.

The enormity of his confession didn't dawn on her for another several minutes, at which point she asked, "How does the colonel think you select the bottles?"

"He teached me dey place on the shelf, but ah learned the lettahs," he confessed proudly. "Ah know every one, an' kin write them as well."

"So Colonel Carter doesn't know you can read ... is that what you're saying?" They both knew it was against the law for slaves to learn reading and writing.

"He knows, he jus' make out he don' know," Nassau said, laughing softly.

As they reached the Menokin gate she turned to look at him. "Nassau, why have you trusted me with your secret?"

In the darkness he shrugged, uncertain how to answer. Just before he knew they would no longer be alone, he said, "You brought the little black one through the storm."

Then Cate and Berth and the Wests were running out, and everyone was talking and asking questions at once. Many times Becky was to remember, however, the ride in the dark from Sabine Hall to Menokin, and the conversation with the black West Indies slave who sometimes drank too much rum and taught himself to read by studying the complicated English and Latin words on Colonel Landon's elaborate assortment of medicine bottles.

Fife and Drum

Her arms were around him almost before his feet touched the ground. She clung as though never to let go. Francis was overwhelmed. "Say, what's all this?" he stammered. "I've not been away so long as all that, love, that you should smother me before I've dismounted!" Despite the protest, the welcome pleased him. "Is anything the matter? Have you been all right?"

"Everything ... and nothing. Oh, not really much. I did miss you so, darling." Forgetting Ben's presence she placed his hand over her heart so he could know the pounding there. Ben, intrigued with the show of affection, chuckled as he led the horses away, just loud enough for his master to know he'd observed the caress. Francis reddened, but didn't remove his hand. He'd missed this unpredictable girl who was his wife, and could barely wait to get her in the house where they could be alone.

It was seven o'clock, almost dusk. As soon as they reached their chamber he presented her with the delicate filigreed gold locket he'd bought her. They spent two quiet hours upstairs before deciding to dress and have supper in the study. "I adore the locket, darling," Becky told him again after they'd eaten. Then she told him about the incident involving Samuel, including the punishment that she'd ordered after he allowed the goats to escape, as well as the trip to Sabine Hall. The episode continued to prey on his mind later, as he made a pretense of going through his papers. Some mail had arrived and there were accounts to post. He found it difficult to concentrate, however, and turning from his desk he said, "I don't understand whatever possessed you to go alone in the storm."

"You mean to Sabine Hall with Sam?"

"What else could I mean?" He peered at her, wondering what she wasn't telling him. "Why didn't you send West? I pay him to obey orders, you know."

"Well, I told him it was urgent, but he didn't want to go. He said it could wait till morning when the storm passed. So, I did it myself, that's all. Had I not, Colonel Landon even agreed with me, the boy might have died."

Francis decided to speak to the overseer about it. He couldn't imagine him allowing Becky to take the chaise alone on stormy roads. "The other thing that bothers me is that you're becoming unreasonably attached to Samuel. Do you remember what I told you when I agreed he could be trained for the house?"

"Yes." Dear God, don't let him ask me what put me in the mood to punish Sam so severely. I can't tell him. He doesn't need to know about that day.

"Well, it appears you haven't thought about what I said, even though you say you remember it. He's a slave, my love, and will never be anything else. He's not for one minute worth risking your life for. And you did risk your life and, I might add, young Sam's as well."

"I know." Becky stabbed the needle furiously at her tapestry. "Francis, let's don't fuss over it any longer. Can't you understand it was just something I had to do, darling?"

"I suppose," he admitted, although grudgingly. For a while he fell silent, returning to his papers.

Becky, for some reason, began to remember the conversation with Winifred Carter. Was it possible that Robert's disinterest in his wife was something that happened in most marriages after a few years? Francis certainly seemed occupied elsewhere these days. He always had something on his mind, and it was unusual for him to criticize her actions as he had just done. He truly seemed put out with her this evening. Maybe he'd enjoyed the days away from her. She couldn't recall that he'd wasted any time urging her to accompany him either. When he rode away she'd counted on being able to surprise him upon his return with the news that they would have a son early in the new year. How long could he continue to have interest in her if she couldn't bear him a child? What did men do with themselves when they were away from their wives? What did they talk about? The questions chased each other in circles, as horses on a racetrack. Was Winifred right when she said they bragged about personal matters, about their ... conquests? Did Francis ever tell about ... ? It was at that point her needlepoint fell unheeded in her lap and she sat up straight, staring at the back of his head.

"Joe Grimes, darling, your overseer at Loudoun farm? You rarely mention him anymore. Is he doing well there, on your land?"

Perplexed, he nodded. "Well enough, I suppose. Considering my rare visits to hound him. Why do you ask?"

"Oh, no reason really, just something Winifred said the other evening made me think of him." She straightened the tapestry, pulling at the wrinkles her stitches had made. "He's married, didn't you say? With children?"

Francis set down his quill, giving her his full attention. "I don't believe I've ever said, Becky, one way or the other. Yes, he is married. Has been for some time."

"To Martha?"

Astonishment blazed across his face. "How do you know her name?" He felt a flush crawling upwards from his neck.

She scrutinized him steadily, allowing no quarter. "Cate told me. A long time ago. Before we moved to Menokin."

"Cate?" he croaked, trying desperately to connect the pieces of this conversation.

Seeing his heightened color her heart softened, and she added, "I know all about her, Francis. The slaves have a way of telling you things they think you should know."

"And Berth told Cate and Cate told you?"

345

"Something like that. Further, it hasn't mattered a whit to me in all this time since I heard it."

"And yet you want to ask me something, don't you? What is it, Becky, that bothers you enough that you should bring it up tonight?" he managed, appalled that they should be discussing such a thing.

She cleared her throat. Long ago she'd promised herself she would never bring up the matter, but maybe it was time. "Did you love her?"

"No," he answered honestly enough.

"Then why?" She knew the answer. If it wasn't love, it was the other.

He sighed, fumbling for an explanation. "Because ... I suppose I'm no different from other men ... I saw an opportunity. It didn't seem wrong at the time ... we ... needed each other, I suppose," he finished lamely.

Becky searched his face for assurance that such would never happen again, but he couldn't know her fears. "I can understand that, darling." She returned to the work in her lap, jabbing the needle with the blue thread in and out, in and out until the yarn was gone. For a while the only sound in the room was the scratch of Francis's quill and the ticking of the mantle clock. Finally Becky found the nerve to break the silence again.

"Francis, the thing you needed her for. Am I ... I mean, do I ... give you as much pleasure?"

He covered the distance between the desk and her chair in two strides. On his knees, head buried in the warmth of her lap, he answered brokenly, "My dear Becky. More. Much, much more. Why do you even need to ask such a thing?"

Her tears splashed salt on his lips when he raised his face to meet her eyes. With a finger she wiped his wet mouth. "I promise never to mention it again, darling. I guess I just had to know." She thought her heart would burst with the pure joy of loving him that night. It had never been better.

∾

There was uneasiness, an uncertainty about the future, in the county that fall of 1774. You could hear it, see it on the faces, breathe it in the air. It hovered, a pall over everyone's thoughts, like the weight of a sticky-hot summer thunderstorm an hour before it hit. Francis and Robert Carter took to the roads talking up the American Colonial Congress, promising that the rascally Parliament would soon be dealt a blow it would not forget. Subtly, without raising any hackles, they also kept an eye open for anyone not anxious to sign the non-importation pact. November wasn't long off and, after all, those who attended the county meeting at Richmond Courthouse had agreed they would abide by the August convention's decision against imports. In Westmoreland they had drawn an even stiffer agreement, at the urging of Richard, of course.

Landon Carter stood well enough behind the plan, although these days he rarely allowed such things to interrupt his planting, nor his preoccupation with the illnesses of all and sundry on his plantations. "I tell you, Frank," he raved one day as they left Mount Airy together, "that boy's stomach was swelled up as round as a cow's belly before she drops her calf!"

"Mmm." Francis listened with one ear. He'd left Becky to visit with her mother and baby Jane, and was thinking about getting his fields plowed, wondering if there would be any market for tobacco in the spring. "It's almost time, Colonel, to set out the barley and winter wheat. I've thought to start the seeding, but the fields are like dust."

Carter sat his saddle, thinking that more and more, even his friends paid no attention to him. He was used to it at home but this was too much. "My sense of propriety compels me to call your attention to the fact you've changed the subject in the middle of my narrative!"

Francis, hearing the testiness in his voice, apologized quickly. "Sorry!" He knew the old man was more out of sorts than usual. His teeth were rotten, and he'd asked Brockenbrough to pull them. Not a pleasant prospect, but apparently a necessary one.

Carter grunted. "Well, that's better. As I was saying, the stomach was mightily swollen. I determined upon examination that it was caused by a blockage at the head of the bladder, so did his sweat smell like urine! Do you know what I prescribed?"

"No, no indeed. I don't dare hazard a guess."

"Thirty coffee berries boiled in a quart of water with a little lime, until the whole should turn green. That should open the passage for his urine if anything will!" Pleased with himself, he set his face in a smile, awaiting approval. Francis rarely disappointed him at such times.

"Amazing, Sir. That you should think of such a thing! Most clever indeed. It was your own experiment then, not from one of your medical books?" When Carter assented happily, Francis knew it was safe to return to what was on his mind. "Well now. About the crops. Have you set your barley yet?"

"Soon. We've cleaned the well these last two days, and plowed the turnip field. I thought to wait for rain before seeding."

"Cleaned the well, you say? We've been mending fences waiting for the rain, but I'll wager my well needs cleaning, too. Did you find much debris?"

Carter let out a roar. "You can't imagine the trash! Two plows, two pairs of handcuffs, all hopelessly rusted, rocks, bottles ... a shoe, buckets of mud! Things that have been missing for months suddenly appeared. It's obvious whenever one of the slaves receives a whipping, and that not nearly so often as he needs it, he gets even by throwing a piece of my property in the well. From now on I shall set a guard to it ... yet, it's hard to know who to trust for the job." His lips tightened and the cleft in his chin grew deeper. "The water is low, Frank, in the well. A bare four feet I think, and formerly thirty. We must all pray with our dear

Reverend that the drought be broken. The wells run dry and our crops are scorched in the fields."

"I think we should better pray, Colonel, if I may suggest it, for the success of the Congress. For if we're forced to carry out our threat of shipping no tobacco to England a year from now, it will be a sorry state of affairs indeed."

"That, my boy, will never be necessary. Parliament will be dissuaded from her vengeful stranglehold on us long before that time. Our dear King will become once more convinced of our loyalty. He'll loosen the noose around the neck of Boston, and we shall all return to our former blessed state. It's my ardent prediction."

Francis couldn't hide his skepticism. "We mean business, you know. It's not an idle threat we make. We'll shed blood before we knuckle under any further."

Carter looked at him as though he'd not quite understood what was said, yet had no desire to have it repeated. Fortunately, he wasn't required to comment because at that moment they reached the crossroad where they must part. "I will look for you on the eighteenth. My birthday celebration. Sixty-four years I shall be. And a pain for every year! Goodbye, my friend."

"Adieu, Colonel. The eighteenth, then. But we'll see you at church tomorrow, I hope. Then we'll learn whether Reverend Giberne addresses his prayers to the political state of affairs, the shriveling crops, or both!"

However, there was no sermon at Lunenburg Church on Sunday, due to the illness of Isaac Giberne. He recovered, comfortably enough, at Sabine Hall, playing cards for a week. The games, of course, agitated his host as much as they pleased Robert and young Landon. It so happened during that time that the rains came at last, thus Carter's disgruntlement with the mood of his household was appeased.

೦೪

Richard was in Philadelphia until the end of October. He returned weary but elated, for the most part, over what had transpired and journeyed to Menokin to see his brother even before returning home. The two talked until after midnight; in the morning Francis dispatched Ben to round up as many freeholders as he could, to pass the word they would all meet at Richmond Courthouse the following day to hear what Colonel Richard had to tell about the Congress. At the appointed hour, about forty were assembled. Robert Carter of Nomini, Richard Corbin of King and Queen County, Archibald Ritchie from Hobbs' Hole and John Tayloe were among those who listened, grumbled, and went away more than ever convinced that Richard Henry Lee was a hothead who would hasten the Armageddon of the colonies.

They met on the green. Richard stood above them, on the courthouse steps. His good hand was tucked in the front of his coat—he'd found it effective to use the deformed one, which he wrapped in a black kerchief, to gesticulate for emphasis. The old injury resulted from a hunting accident and, although it no longer pained him, he was repulsed by the disfigurement and preferred to keep it covered. Now, he waved his hand, calling for attention. They'd agreed Francis would introduce him to start things off.

"Gentlemen ... my brother is just returned from Carpenter's Hall in Philadelphia where representatives of each of our thirteen colonies were meeting since early September!" he called out. "He tells me they're to meet again next May, and he has much to share with us of what they accomplished. That's why I summoned you here today. Colonel Lee, tell our Richmond friends of the first meeting of the American Congress!"

Richard, while eyeballing the crowd for possible enemies, cleared his throat before beginning. "We were fifty-six strong, and a more dedicated and spirited body I have never seen! It was inevitable, of course, that we should come to some divisions among ourselves and indeed, that's the first thing that happened. We split into two basic factions. One, led by the Bostonians,

Carolinians, and ourselves; the other by New York's Jay and Duane, Pennsylvania's Galloway, and Read from Delaware. This group, which I shall refer to only as the moderates, although Galloway himself named them the Loyalists, wished to do nothing but petition the British. This Galloway was against supporting the Resolves from Suffolk which will aid Boston, against the appointment of our own Peyton Randolph as president, against Thomson as secretary, and against Carpenter Hall as our meeting place. Indeed I believe the man would be against eating and sleeping if you put it to him in the form of a resolution!" There was laughter from his audience. "Why, he introduced a disastrous plan proposing a union of England and the Colonies that would allow total regulation of our trade by the British. And so smooth was he, so seductive in his argument, it was defeated by a mere vote of one!"

"One vote?" someone called out.

"Well, one colony. We voted by colonies, not individual delegates, you see."

John Tayloe had maneuvered himself gradually forward in the crowd, and now stood near the front, but off to one side where his voice could be clearly heard by all. "It is your contention then, that no hope for a reconciliation exists, Colonel Lee?" The question dropped like a rock into Lee's enthusiastic opening presentation. Almost instantly, the mood of the men wavered expectantly. As a body, they sensed a confrontation.

Richard was too wise, however, to allow an argument with Tayloe in front of the county freeholders. "No, Colonel Tayloe. It's my contention, as you put it, that we are a separate realm of England's great empire, Sir, and while we have an allegiance to our King, which no man here would deny, we owe nothing to his Parliament. Nothing to Townshend or North or their abominable taxes or acts of domination over our own governments. Mr. Galloway, on the other hand, would continue to allow them great power over us."

"You agree with Thomas Jefferson then, the honorable burgess from Albemarle, that we should respect the authority of the Crown?" probed Landon Carter, thinking to stress the positive in the case, thereby aiding the speaker.

Richard glanced at Francis, wondering if he had shared Jefferson's latest treatise with Carter, and received a slight affirmative nod in return.

"I do indeed, Sir. I do indeed. Be aware, however, I also stand with those who find a Tory to be among the lowliest of creatures. A spider, a toad," he spat the word, "a snake even, could not be more despicable in the realm of things." Richard was unaware he had used the very words of his new friend, John Adams, to describe the traitor. "A man who does not stand with his countrymen in their hour of need, is against them, Sir! And while most among us at the Congress spoke out with generous and noble sentiments in favor of supporting Boston, when the rumor reached us that General Gage had attacked, Mr. Galloway was not so disposed."

"Tell us what happened there, in Boston?"

"Yes, what really happened?"

"We heard a mighty lot of rumors!"

Richard was annoyed over this second interruption of his narrative, yet he explained patiently that Gage had merely stolen the provincial powder at Cambridge and had not bombarded the city as was first reported. It had been enough, nonetheless, to stir things up in the Congress and had no doubt moved a few of the moderates into the radical camp. Galloway had hinted to someone that he suspected Sam Adams of plotting the entire rumor to gain sympathy for Massachusetts. This sort of gossip had lowered everyone's opinion of Galloway even further, Richard assured them. Then, anxious to tell of his own contributions, he moved on. "Shortly upon convening, Gentlemen, we were appointed to committees. Mine was charged with the task of stating our rights, grievances, and means of redress. Our biggest bone of contention, aside from Joseph Galloway himself, was the matter of what powers should be alloted to Parliament. I set the tone of the discussion by telling them I thought our rights are built on a fourfold foundation; that is, on the law of nature first, on the British Constitution, on our Colonial Charters, and on immemorial usage. This was favorably accepted by most, and strongly supported by John Adams and Gladsden of South Carolina. The Navigation Act imposed upon us is a capital violation of all four, and I pointed to this as a primary example. I was asked to write a comprehensive memorial to the people of England stating our position and to present it to the Congress. I did so ... and ...." He barely hesitated, but it was long enough to allow a question.

"And was your fine memorial accepted by those gentlemen, Colonel Lee?" Archibald Ritchie from Essex County had never forgiven Lee for the humiliating public pressure which had prevented him from paying the stamp tax and clearing the shipment in the hold of his merchant vessel. Nine years had passed, but he remembered it clearly every time he saw the spare figure of Richard Henry Lee. Ritchie leaned against a tree, thumbs tucked in his pocket flaps, a half-smile flickering on his face as he observed Lee's color rise.

"No, they did not as a matter of fact, Mr. Ritchie. They accepted a similar one the following day from Mr. Jay of New York."

There followed an uncertain silence. "That, I should think, was no disgrace," Francis spoke up in his brother's behalf.

"No," the murmurs went around. "No disgrace." They nodded their heads, agreeing with one another.

Richard threw his brother a grateful look and continued. "But we did approve a Continental Association which I can happily say is virtually identical to one I drew up for Westmoreland County, and to the Association entered into by the Virginia Convention in August last. It provides for non-import and non-export, and non-consumption of all English luxury products, as well as a cessation of the slave trade ... all in due time, as we felt to be appropriate."

"What in thunderation is to happen to our tobacco crop which can't be shipped for a year after it's cut down?" It was John Tayloe again.

"That's right!" came another voice from the rear of the group. "And how about slaves? That hurts the south, too! New England, your Boston friends, get off scot-free ... they don't grow tobacco and they ain't got t' have slaves to grow it!"

Richard thought the last outburst was from Hudson Muse, but he wasn't sure. "Now, now, Gentlemen. We debated all these things, long and hard. Compromises had to be made. It's recognized that certain areas will suffer more by embargoes, but there's nothing to be done about it. We're confident, as a body, that these measures will bring England to her senses in short order and none will suffer overly long."

Ritchie was not ready to let up. "I was just thinking ... of money actually. You know," he smiled at those standing near him, "a merchant does have to think of his livelihood. You mentioned we're not to import or use any of England's luxury items. By this I take it we're to put a luxury in a different class than a necessity? Well, it appears t' me that tobacco is as much of a luxury as any I can think of. We can't hurt 'em by withholding it. Why not sell it to 'em, let 'em have it, and take their money?"

"Yes, why not take their silver? Hell, we need it bad enough!"

Damn the man! Richard thought. "Mr. Ritchie, I appreciate your question. And I do agree, tobacco is a luxury. The lack of it will merely deprive England of pleasure and not of sustenance. But don't forget, the British merchants are a powerful group as, of course, are our American merchants such as yourself, and they will scream for it. That means they'll agitate in the Parliament. I have firsthand reports of this from my brother, William Lee. And surely, if you will use your common sense, Sir, you will see that the other colonies, exporters of rice, cotton, whale oil, wheat and so on, would not agree to a continuance of Virginia's trade while their own is curtailed."

Richard decided he had said enough. There were some things you couldn't explain to a dunderhead. It was time to wind it up. "I cannot answer all your questions, my friends, but I can tell you this: at the first violent act committed by England against America, or any attempt to reinforce General Gage, the entire continent will be up in arms from Maine to Georgia! We left Philadelphia determined and united. We will not seek war with our mother country, but if it comes to that, we shall meet it bravely."

"War?"

"Is there chance of war?"

"Why, I heerd the milishy's already activated in Massachusetts!"

"We goin' t' have a Virginia army, Colonel Lee?"

"I expect we are indeed, Mr. Barker," Richard answered, happy that at least *all* the men didn't appear to be following in Ritchie's footsteps. Perhaps he'd overcharged too many of them too often.

"If our militia's called," yelled John Allgood, "then I'm goin' to be the fifer! Yessir, I'll take my fife and lead the troop. I'll play one o' them patriotic tunes, and march right down Richmond Road, and all the boys'll line up behind me, too!" He screwed up his face, pursed his lips and danced off tooting on a make-believe flute.

No Foolish Flattery

Boston's port remained closed during the months that followed. Despite the efforts of Lord Chatham and his Whig following on behalf of the beleaguered city, the British Parliament declared Massachusetts to be in open rebellion, and passed a bill barring them from the north Atlantic fishing waters and forbidding their trade with anyone but England herself. Later, when the Lords learned of the Continental Association entered into by the American Congress, they extended the new act to cover New Jersey, Pennsylvania, Maryland, South Carolina, and Virginia.

The northern colonies prepared for war; in Virginia, Patrick Henry predicted the outbreak of hostilities momentarily, shouting a call of defiance to the convention gathered in St. John's Church in Richmond City. *"Give me liberty or give me death!"* his fiery words echoed throughout the colony, and it was this voice that finally drowned out the Virginia conservatives, forcing them to either side with Governor Dunmore or to be silent.

Life was generally acknowledged to be in a state of chaos politically speaking, and on the home front as well. Francis was spending all his time trying to arrange for as much export of tobacco as possible before the embargo went into effect. William wrote of changes in plans, ships, and captains constantly. Everything, it seemed, was topsy-turvy. Then one day came word of Philip Lee's sudden death at Stratford Plantation. Francis felt instantly numb, waiting to feel something more, but he did not. His own brother had died, yet he was void of all emotion. It worried him; finally it worried him enough to talk about it.

"I don't feel the least sense of loss, Becky," he confessed. "I can think of only one thing, and I know you can't guess what it is ... that Stratford will have no master. Father's beloved home has no master." Weeks later, when he learned that Elizabeth Lee's third child was born a son and she'd named him Philip after his father, but that the child had died within a few days, he realized there was nothing to do but to accept things as they were. Then soon he was too busy again, with the shipping arrangements, to even think about it.

It was William's plan to send the ship *Adventure* to the mouth of the Rappahannock where Francis was to meet it and direct whether it should load that river or the Potomac first. He spent every day in the countryside signing up hogsheads—if the ship couldn't hold all that he procured, he or Richard were to charter space in a second vessel as well. To complicate matters further, the *Adventure's* incoming cargo was going to include more than fifty servants. The ship's captain, John Brown, having one-third interest in them was to handle their sale, but Francis must direct him in which river to best accomplish this. Convicts had recently been offered for sale in both rivers and the choice required some careful observation. There was little time, William warned, as the British meant to close the ports any day. Francis had picked up a new letter at Hobbs' Hole just yesterday.

"I tell you, Becky, it makes my head swim with all that's going on these days. William's so distraught he's written letters with five different sets of instructions! A good bit of news is that he's been elected to a post of alderman in a most respected London district, and is working for our cause along with Lord Chatham and the merchant interests ... he goes on to say that among the servants to be sold is a decent, well-behaved schoolmaster who knows Greek and Latin. William wants him to be offered first to our sister, Hannah. He ends by telling me that he's returning John Turberville's boy on the *Adventure* because the lad is so dreadfully undisciplined! That leaves me with the task of delivering the little scoundrel to his father I suppose."

"Well, you might arrange with Mr. Turberville to meet the ship himself and save yourself the trouble. You'll manage it all somehow, darling, you always do. By the by, why doesn't Richard send for his sons? I should think with the threat of war hanging over our heads he'd be anxious to have Thomas and Ludwell come home as soon as possible." The boys had been at St. Bees School in London for some time.

Francis quirked his eyebrow. "Richard is too busy perhaps, to think of the danger to his own family ... although that's probably unfair of me to think such. I suspect he feels they're safe enough, with William watching over them. Did I tell you Ludwell was sponsor for William's little son?"

"Yes, dear, you read me the letter all about how William and Hannah Phillipa have named their sweet baby 'the little patriot,' and that they're sending me some silk worm eggs to experiment with, which is very thoughtful of them."

"Then I'm sure I must also have mentioned the rhubarb and cantaloupe musk melon seeds. That reminds me, I must speak to West about locating a new pasture for the sheep to graze, and then I'm off to see Hudson Muse, Hipkins, and Gordon regarding the debts they owe to our brother William."

Becky thought again how preoccupied he was these days with William's problems, as well as his own. "How can melon seed remind you of all that?" she laughed.

∽

Suddenly corn and tobacco were beginning to poke their green shoots above the earth's surface as another beautiful spring in Virginia emerged; it was almost enough to make one forget world problems. That is until the day word from Massachusetts told of four thousand militia who had chased the British troops from Lexington and Concord back into Charlestown outside of Boston, and there laid siege to General Gage's redcoats. The Massachusetts Provincial Congress sent an urgent appeal to every colony to raise their militia regiments and send help; they also authorized General Benedict Arnold to march north, where he was to cross the Canadian border and capture British forts. Ethan Allen, with a force of militia from Vermont was not far behind. The battle had truly begun.

In June, surprising everyone, Governor Dunmore stoked up his nerve and called the Virginia Assembly to session. A year had passed since he'd dissolved it in his fit of frustration and, in the meantime, he had kept himself occupied with the Indians on the western frontier. This is not to say he wasn't following events in the colony's revolutionary conventions and the treasonous intercolonial get-togethers in Philadelphia. Indignant and desperate, he now urged the burgesses once more to a course of moderation.

"Whatever you do, Loudoun," Richard wrote from Philadelphia when he heard of it, *"make sure the assembly supports our Congress. One of Parliament's chief arguments has been that our provincial conventions are not colonial government, and we must prove to them that Congress also has the approval of the elected Assemblies."* Richard cautioned against the use of superfluous flattery in any document to come out of the assembly. It seemed the southerners had been sharply criticized for this practice by their northern friends. He said, *"If it is necessary to compliment the governor at all, a few words regarding soldiery on his Indian expedition should be sufficient."* He closed by asking Francis to make it known in the assembly that the Tory leaders in New York were overthrown and that colony's delegates had now assumed a thoroughly patriotic pose. Pennsylvania's Galloway had also disappeared and that removed yet another thorn to unanimity.

Francis felt Dunmore's calling of the assembly to be nothing more than a farce and decided he wouldn't bother to make the trip, but Richard's letter got him thinking it over again. When he learned shortly thereafter that Tom Jefferson had thought it important enough to leave the Congress in order to be present, he thought perhaps he'd been wrong in his judgment, and made up his mind to attend after all. It remained to be seen, however, just what they could accomplish.

❦

A group of the burgesses, many now referring to themselves as elected lawmakers or representatives to the colony's governing body, approached the powder magazine in Williamsburg. They included Francis and his cousin Carter Braxton, and they went as appointees of the House Speaker to investigate rumors that Dunmore had ordered the colonial powder removed. The magazine was located in a field across from the courthouse. As they approached, Braxton fretted over the task.

"It seems impossible to believe Dunmore refused to give us the key to the magazine. It's too hot to be out here on this errand when there's probably nothing for us to find."

"That, I say, would be the entire point. There's nothing to find because the magazine will be locked and it's empty, and we've been sent together to bear witness to that fact," Francis responded.

"Well, we don't know for certain it's empty, do we? Why would he lock it if he knows it's empty, Frank?"

"No doubt to confound the issue, my dear fellow. Why else? Why doesn't he make it easy for us by giving us the key?"

Braxton looked hurt. "Perhaps because we insult him by our suspicions."

"Poppycock! Our sources are accurate enough, Carter. It is locked and it's empty. Would you care to wager?"

His cousin shook his head. "I rarely win a bet," he confided.

Although they took turns rattling and shaking the door, it refused to budge. From a small window high on the east wall they were able to peer inside. The room was bare. For months, more than twenty kegs of powder had been stored in the magazine; now they were gone. Things went from bad to worse after they all returned with the same story. Confronted by the burgesses with their discovery, Dunmore threatened to free slaves and burn the Capitol if any attempt was made to retrieve the powder. Then he fled to his schooner on the York River and begged all loyal burgesses to attend him there. Instead, they sat as a group with Jefferson as he drafted the document which would effectively bury Lord North's February conciliatory proclamation. His Majesty's government in Virginia had come to an end, although some were not ready, even yet, to admit it.

It took Congress a month to agree to legalize the militia troops, name them the Continental Army, and appoint George Washington as commander-in-chief. The uniform that Washington had worn every day to Congress suddenly took on new meaning. In Pennsylvania, Maryland, and Virginia rifle companies were being raised to aid the northern colonies. In Richmond County John Allgood polished up his fife and almost mastered *Fish and Tea*.

"The Congress have appointed Washington as General of the Army, Becky. My letter from Richard tells me the British have moved on Bunker Hill and Breed's Hill and burned Charlestown, and that idiot Dunmore offers to free any slaves who will join his forces! And what are we in the country to do? Here we are, faced with farmers who must bring in their crops before they'll even consider going north to fight a war most of them can't begin to understand ... and the Archibald Ritchies of our counties threaten to make a fortune out of everyone else's misfortune!"

"Mr. Ritchie is a friend of Papa's," Becky reminded him.

"I know, and that is what worries me most about it, I suppose."

"What do you mean?"

"Colonel Landon is for making a case out of it. Ritchie is buying up everything in sight, hoarding it for speculation later. There's little doubt this will affect not only Essex County consumers but Richmond County as well. The colonel suggested we turn him over to the Essex County Committee of Safety."

"What did you say to that?"

""Well, it is my sentiment, my dear, that although it's scandalous, we'd be better off to mind our own business. Mr. Ritchie is breaking no law but a moral one, to my way of thinking."

Becky couldn't help but wonder if Francis's opinion was influenced by her father, but decided not to ask. It certainly seemed a middle road for him to take.

∽

When the Virginia lawmakers called their own meeting the next month, they named themselves the Provincial Convention, but Francis was not among them. Ben was ill and his master, having no heart to travel alone, remained at Menokin. At least, that's the explanation Francis was giving. The truth, far more serious, was that he feared to start a panic on the plantation and in the county if it was known that his man-servant was desperately ill with the smallpox. Somewhere, somehow, Ben had been exposed to the disease—he lay sweating and groaning in the Menokin cellar, covered with sores, his face swollen beyond recognition. Francis felt compelled to supervise his care and had told no one what he knew to be the matter. Twice a day he went outside to descend the narrow stairway to the cellar, only at the last minute placing the protective mask over his face. Dr. Jones, sworn to secrecy, had given him some powder and a poultice to be applied to the festering sores. Cate, nursing her husband, didn't suspect the truth of

Ben's ailment either, nor had Francis shared a word of his worst fears even with Becky.

The stench was overpowering in the stuffy room, and he was thankful for the mask. "Well, Ben, how are you feeling this morning?" he asked halfway through the second week. He'd been asking the same question every day.

"Gawd, Marse Frank, I itches somethin' fierce."

"You itch?"

"Yas-suh, Marse Frank, I does indeed."

"He bin scratchin' and tossin' fit t' be tied since you bin here yisterday evenin'!" Cate said from a dark corner.

"That's great news, Ben. Wonderful news! That's exactly what Dr. Jones says you do when you're going to get well. Thank God!"

"What you mean, Marse Frank?" Cate whispered. "Did you think he ain't goin' git well?"

"I wasn't sure, Cate. I just wasn't sure. You see, Ben has the smallpox, and many people don't survive it. Just to be on the safe side, however, I don't want you talking about this to anyone, not even Miss Becky, until we're completely sure of his recovery. Do you understand?"

After hearing her assurance that she would remain silent, he left. Upstairs again, in the fresh air, he gulped two deep breaths as he stuffed the mask in his pocket. Relief that Ben would recover made him a little giddy. He found Becky in the garden gathering roses, the early morning dew still on the petals.

"Becky, we must pray that no one else comes down with it. We've all been exposed one way or the other. But I think now that Ben will live. No, I'm sure of it! He's itching."

"Live? Itching? Whatever is that all about? You didn't tell me he was seriously ill. What's the matter with him?" She turned from the flowers when he didn't answer immediately and saw the hesitation in his eyes. "Francis?"

It was almost a whisper when he told her. He hadn't meant to, the words seemed to have sprung from his mouth of their own accord. "Smallpox. Ben has ... the ... smallpox."

She stood very still, her eyes growing wide, green pools of mute fear which provoked an instant thudding in his own heart. It was the very reason he hadn't told her before. Talking about it would have made it even more fearful.

༄

While Francis argued county politics with Landon Carter and was kept busy worrying about his sick slave and whether the pox would spread to others, the Provincial Convention approved Patrick Henry's appointment as commander-in-chief of Virginia Military Forces over some strenuous objections; and elected Richard Bland, Benjamin Harrison, Thomas Jefferson, Richard Henry Lee, Thomas Nelson, Peyton Randolph, and George Wythe to the Second Continental Congress. Upon the decline of Bland and a motion by George Mason, they elected his replacement. Robert Carter, hair flying in the wind, coat rumpled from travel, pounded up the Menokin road bearing the news.

"My God, Frank, where in hell are you?" he shouted, barely past the row of trees which delineated the house from the quarter. "You've been elected to the Congress! The session meets in September, the fifth. A fortnight away!"

༄

The night was warm. Cicadas screeched from the marsh and Becky thought she could hear a bullfrog trying to out-croak them. But mostly she was thinking of how excited Francis was; his body fairly quivered with every word he spoke, and just about every word was about his election to the Congress. He'd been chattering on steadily since Robert left, until a few minutes ago. Had he fallen asleep? It hardly seemed possible so quickly, and she wanted to talk to him. "Darling?"

"Umm? Beautiful night isn't it, love? And by God, I'm going to the Congress of American Colonies in Philadelphia! Me! Can you believe it? I always wanted to see Philadelphia. Did I ever tell you? I can't believe it! I simply cannot believe it."

"I can. I'm not in the least surprised they chose you. I told you that a hundred times this evening. Besides, it all seems very real to me ... the part about your leaving especially. And the short time you have to make all your arrangements. Two weeks, Robert said. Sooner than two weeks and you must be on your way."

He sat up, heart stopping in mid-beat. "Oh, good Lord, it means leaving you!" He reached for her, pulling her against him. "I am so selfish ... I haven't so much as given that part a thought. I can't do it, then. I can't go. Not and leave you here alone. They'll have to find someone else. I'll have to turn it down. Becky? ... I ... will just have to turn it down."

It was a gloomy pronouncement if she'd ever heard one. Holding him close, her fingers kneaded the back of his neck, soothing him. Rocking back and forth, holding his head tight against her breast, she said, "You won't have to, darling. You don't have to turn it down, or leave me either ... because I plan on going with you."

Francis couldn't believe what he was hearing. "What? How? Do you know how far away it is? The country is at war! The roads will undoubtedly be dangerous. How on earth can I take you with me?"

Her hands had moved to his shoulders, massaging tensions away. "I don't know yet. We have to figure out a plan. In the morning, we'll make a plan." She kissed the top of his head where the first gray mingled with brown. Without an argument or any coaxing, she knew she had won. He'd accepted what she'd known for hours. They would be miserable apart. "I love you. I love you very much indeed, and I'm going with you to Philadelphia. But right now, Mr. Congressman, we're going to do something else." Pressing against him, she allowed desire to erase all other considerations.

∽

They learned of a public coach from Baltimore to Philadelphia, but discarded the idea when arrangements for the first part of the journey became cumbersome. Francis toyed with the idea of asking John Tayloe if they could borrow his large coach and six to get to Baltimore but, as relations between them continued to be strained due to politics, he decided against it. That left their own much smaller carriage and four, the post-chaise, which was certainly not suitable for any distance, and an assortment of ox-carts and farm wagons to consider. Ben, Cate, and Samuel would, of course, accompany them. The other house slaves, including Berth and Ben's daughters, Zoey and Cris, would remain under the direction of James West and the supervision of Tayloe. They would have to close the house. In a week they made their choices and were as ready as they would ever be.

Ben, although still recovering, was almost his old self. From the driver's seat of the carriage, he checked the trunks on top one last time to be sure they were secure. Then, with a signal from his master, he clucked to the team, which included Becky's mare, and the journey began amidst the sounds of creaking harness, rattling doors and the clip-clop of hoofs. They made the turn out of the circular drive into the lane with Francis riding Cameron in the lead.

Francis wondered if he would ever see old Berth again. The old woman had shriveled during the past year; now she stood apart from the others, near the foundation of the new kitchen house. He thought her wrinkled face was tear streaked as she mouthed a toothless farewell. Berth had been a good and loyal servant and he would miss her quiet humor. He bowed slightly from the waist, and tipped his hat, watching her beam. The slaves who were not in the fields lined the roadway. White teeth flashed in black faces as they waved and shouted the caravan off. Francis tipped his hat to them also as he passed.

Becky, Cate and Samuel crowded onto the rear seat of the carriage. Across from them were piled boxes, cases, satchels and Francis's folding writing table, all tied securely in place. Another trunk was fastened precariously to the rear of the coach. Once out of the drive, Francis rode behind to keep an eye on it for the first mile, but the dust was impossible and at the corner where his property joined the road, he caught up and leaned in the window. Becky had her face buried in a handkerchief blowing her nose. "Can you still see the chimneys?" she sniffed.

"No love, they are long out of sight."

She looked behind her as though she hoped he might be mistaken. Neatly furrowed winter wheat fields, as yet unseeded, lined the narrow lane where dust raised by their passing had already settled back into the ruts. Tears blurred her vision.

"Don't look back, Becky. We're on our way to help our country win the war! When we've done our part, we'll return. God grant that it'll be soon. Menokin will wait for us." His face felt flushed and he felt warm. He hoped it was from emotion.

Becky was too wrapped in her own thoughts to even notice the bright splotches on his cheeks. "Oh darling, I am happy to be going. It's just that I do so love this place and ... I thought never to have to leave it."

"You're not sorry to be coming?"

"No. Not sorry. Only a little bit sad."

෴

At Annapolis Francis made arrangements for crossing the Chesapeake by ferry. They would travel up Maryland's eastern shore following the Elk River. He learned that the passage for his vehicle, family, and five horses would cost him a scandalous twenty shillings. He felt too weak to argue. He'd known he was sick before they crossed the Potomac the day before. Trying desperately to ignore the warning signals his body was giving him, he barely made it back to the carriage before he fainted. It fell to Ben to find them a lodging. He managed to get Francis into the carriage where they propped him, half-conscious. The slave recognized the signs—his master had the smallpox.

Ben knocked on the door of a small inn on a side street. Becky had directed him to it after the first place they stopped had refused to take them because a member of the party was ill. "Tell them he has a recurring ague and merely needs a rest. And Ben, tell them he's a member of the American Congress from Virginia!" Becky refused to admit to herself that Francis might have the dreaded pox. The woman in the doorway hesitated. Reluctance was written all over her plump features as clearly as the letters on her wooden signboard. She moved her eyes over Ben's belted homespun smock and his baggy trousers. In Richmond County Francis had never felt it necessary to outfit his servant in a fancy livery. Becky could see that in the city such extravagance would be an asset.

"Congress, you say? I heard they was meetin' again." She wagged her head. "But I don't know. Take a sick man in there, I'm liable to expose my whole family to somethin' awful. I run a clean establishment. A good clean establishment. The cookin's included in the price. He willin' to pay for that?"

Ben nodded. "Marse Frank'll pay what he need, to make sure his Lady is comfut'ble." He sized the woman up, a trick he'd mastered while continuing to smile, so as never to appear rude, and decided the money was going to be important. "An, might be, if'n he be pleased, he pay some extry," he drawled, in what he hoped was a casual tone. From his pocket he pulled out the pound note Becky had given him, turning it over several times.

He didn't miss the look of greed that crossed her face. Suddenly her family's health was forgotten.

"Well, in that case ...." Thus they moved into the third floor of the inn where they had two rooms. Ben had to make do in the barn with Samuel, while Cate remained in the house to help Becky nurse Francis. He broke out in sores almost immediately, but there were not nearly so many as Ben had suffered. It was four days before he returned to consciousness, at which point he felt as though a demon had dropped a red hot poker down his throat and left it to sizzle his innards. Only then did he realize Becky lay in the lumpy bed next to him and that her face was swollen and flushed with fever.

"How bad is she, Cate?" The fear that gripped him was so intense he thought for a moment he might throw up.

Cate stood over them waving a large fan slowly, back and forth, back and forth. The flies in the stuffy room were drawn to the festering sores and the soiled bed linen. She didn't dare ask for clean linen too often or the innkeeper would become suspicious. So she'd been cleaning up the best she could, and fanning the flies away. "Not too bad, Marse Frank. Not near as bad as Ben was. An' you ... she's not dat bad neither." She swatted at a large fly with the fan. "Dere's one dat won't bite Miss Becky no mo'! Marse Frank? You got de itches yet?"

But he was asleep again, dreaming they were on the road. The journey was overland now, to Chester, a half day south of Philadelphia. There was then the Schuylkill River to cross and that meant another ferry. He thought the ferry master wasn't going to take them because they were disfigured with smallpox. But he threatened to have the fellow's license revoked by the Pennsylvania legislature when he got to the Congress, and they were finally allowed to clatter on board. He slept and woke fitfully for several more days, frequently dreaming he was being chewed to pieces by bed lice, until one morning he opened his eyes to find it was the sores itching him. He was on the mend. He had survived and, looking around, when he saw Becky sitting in a chair smiling at him, he knew he was no longer dreaming.

On the sixth of September, over a fortnight after leaving Menokin, they were able to continue the journey to Philadelphia. While Francis had dreamed of the stubborn ferry master, Becky dwelt constantly on the promise of clean beds, good food, and the loving faces of Alice Lee Shippen's family. "If it weren't for the hospitality of your dear sister which I know awaits us, I should burst into tears this very minute, darling," she told him as they finally left Annapolis. Like a prayer, she repeated it over and over during the last days of the miserable, hot, dusty ride. In her weakened condition and despite the mask she wore for protection, the unrelenting dust which caked her throat and burned her eyes, and the constant jolting of the carriage were almost unbearable.

PART III
THE CONTINENTAL CONGRESS
1776 – 1779

"Our late King and his Parliament having declared us Rebels and Enemies, confiscated our property as far as they were likely to lay hands on it; have effectually decided for us whether or no we shou'd be independent .... Is it not prudent therefore to fit our minds to the state that is inevitable?"

Letter, F. L. Lee to Landon Carter
Philadelphia, March 19, 1776

Common Sense

The city was large by colonial standards. With a population of twenty to thirty thousand, depending on whom you asked, it continued to swell daily with newcomers flocking to do business with the Congress. It was noisy and bustling. The streets remained clogged from the crack of dawn until after midnight, reeling with the constant bump and clatter of humanity and horseflesh, carts and carriages, while a raucous chorus of voices raised in shout and song, curse and greeting, continued all the while. At Shippen House on Fourth Street if the wind was right, the sounds from the busiest wharfs in America four blocks away could be heard. Also, if the wind was right, the rank smells of fish and seaweed wafted into the third floor chamber. The noises and the smells were what impressed Becky from the beginning.

"I can't get over it, darling," she remarked, early on the fourth day in Philadelphia, holding up the hem of her long skirt to better view it in light of the window. "They empty the chamber pots into the streets! No wonder it smells so dreadful, worse than Menokin's barnyard." Sniffing, she discovered the odor clung to the hem of her brown challis dress where it must have trailed in the street when she accompanied Alice Shippen to market, and decided to put it in the pile for Cate to launder. Virginia dust or red clay would seem a blessing after this filth.

Francis only half-way heard her. He was nervous, and couldn't remember a time in his life feeling this way except when Colonel Phil had dragged him to Loudoun County to sign his name as an incorporator of the town of Leesburg. It was important now, as then, that he make a good first impression. His credentials were to be presented today. The two previous meetings having been dismissed for lack of a quorum, he was relieved his days of sickness in Annapolis hadn't made him tardy for the opening. It was now the thirteenth of September and today President Hancock would take the chair to open the business. He debated which buckles to use on his breeches. "Should I wear these with the gilt design or the plain ones, Becky?"

"The plain, I should think. To show you're not a frivolous man. Francis, did you hear what I said about the disgusting odors?"

"Oh, yes ... sorry. My mind's on the business of the day and not on observations of the city. Well, they simply have no other spot to dump them, I guess. The chamber pots. It's always like that in cities I've been told."

"I'm thankful we have fields and gardens where such things can be disposed of properly." He really wasn't paying any attention to her. "Are you that worried about today, darling?"

A tap on the door interrupted. Becky opened it to admit Ben who, smiling proudly, held up a spotless, unwrinkled, brushed beige waistcoat for inspection. Each brass button gleamed as brilliantly as a newly minted sovereign.

"How in the name of heaven did you do it, Ben? That coat looked wretched when it came out of the trunk." Becky rejoiced constantly that Cate and Ben were with them; never had she appreciated them more. They were a prodigious touch of home in a strange land.

"Cate, she got a secret o' two, Miss Becky," Ben bragged. "She says we has t' make Marse Frank ready fo de gen'lemens, an' dat means he goin' look better den dey do!"

Francis laughed. "There, you see? Wonder why I'm nervous? It must be all this fussing over me. Do you suppose all congressmen get such attention?" He remembered well the night Becky had first called him by the impressive sounding name—there was definitely a promise to the ring of it.

Without warning the door burst open to reveal a pink-cheeked cherub face. "Uncle Frank! Aunt Becky! Mama says to come quickly. A Pennsylvania troop is marching down the street. They'll soon be outside the house. Some are dressed in fine uniforms and they're marching to the drums!" Nancy Shippen was twelve but there were times when her bright eyed innocence bespoke a younger child. She was a lovely girl with a dazzling smile, but dreadfully spoiled by both her father and her mother. Tommy stood behind her, peering into the room. Two years her junior and painfully shy, her brother hung back. He grinned at his uncle who was caught awkwardly in his underclothes. Nancy ran to grab her aunt's hand and pulled her from the room.

"It looks as though I'm going to see the soldiers, darling! Come when you're ready," Becky called, blowing him a kiss. She noticed he was only half dressed; the flush on his face evidence he was embarrassed at the intrusion of his niece, but Nancy gave no sign of having witnessed anything unusual.

Life in Philadelphia had begun.

∾

Committee work started at seven-thirty every day except Sunday. At nine or ten the delegates assembled in the State House to begin their regular sessions, and they worked steadily until around four, when they dispersed exhausted, for dinner. Committees frequently met again in the evening. They were long days, but there was still time for socializing. At least, they all found time for it somehow. The new City Tavern drew the delegates as bees to the honeycomb, just as the Raleigh in Williamsburg had done, Francis observed. It was the place to gather when the business was over, the place where deals were struck, promises made, and the next day's plans were hatched.

There was another place for some, however. More often than not the Virginians and the Bostonians could be found in Alice

Shippen's parlor on Fourth Street those winter evenings of 1775. They shared intimate late suppers, card games almost every evening, and rehashed the day's business. If some regular visitors were tied up with work or called back to committee meetings, there were always others to take their places. In addition to the Lees there gathered the Virginians—Peyton Randolph, Ben Harrison, Tom Jefferson, the Wythes, and the Nelsons—as well as John Adams, Robert Paine, John Hancock and many prominent Philadelphians, associates of Dr. William Shippen. John Dickinson visited with Francis occasionally during the early weeks, when Adams was elsewhere. It was no secret. Adams and Dickinson, having had a serious falling-out, no longer spoke to one another; Francis thought the reason stemmed from Dickinson's underlying desire to continue to make overtures of reconciliation with England.

To Becky's way of thinking, these evenings were the principal saving grace of their new existence. She was unaccustomed to having Francis gone from breakfast until evening, and sorely missed plantation life when he would be in and out at least ten times a day. There were none of her old housekeeping tasks to occupy her—no gardens and flower beds to tend; no soap to make; no jams, vinegar, lard, cheese, butter, candle-making; no curing of meat to concern her; no preserving of vegetables, herbs or fruit; no wine distilling; and no weaving of cloth which they had begun in recent years with cloth from the fulling mill. All the things that had heretofore filled her days were no more. She missed the frequent visits to Mount Airy, the games with little John and baby Jane, who were growing up without her, and tried to think of them only once in a while, for it made her much too melancholy. When she thought about it, she even missed the afternoons spent with Winifred Carter. An hour with Winifred could be counted on to make her count her own blessings, if nothing else. Virginia seemed as remote as Paris, Vienna, or the Orient.

Dr. William Shippen's house was a large brick structure wedged between two smaller homes, and boasted five floors. From the entry one could go up a few steps to the comfortably furnished parlor and dining room or, down to the English-style basement where the servants lived. Alice Shippen was one of the few Philadelphians who kept Negro house slaves. Room had been made for not only Ben, Cate, and Samuel, but also for Richard Henry's Lucas. Due to the above ground windows in the basement there was more light and it wasn't damp and moldy as Menokin's cellar sometimes was. But Cate, as well as her mistress, missed the familiar. Whether better or worse, she didn't bother to analyze; she merely dreamed of the day they could pack up and head back down the long road to Richmond County. In Philadelphia people were kind enough, but they stared at blacks, and some of them asked outlandish questions of the southern slaves.

Samuel, not quite six, noticed the difference, too. "What do free mean, Miss Becky?" he asked one day. He was busy with his morning task of checking the pots and filling water basins.

Becky frowned, pausing in mid-sentence of the letter she was writing to her mother. "Where on earth did you hear that, Sam?" She supposed the boy had been hanging around the neighbor's white servant children again. She'd observed he'd also lost his baby talk from his contact with them.

"I hears it mos' every day when I goes to de ribber." His mistress had a mighty scowl on her face and he wondered if it was a mistake to ask her. He'd already asked his mammy, and she'd merely scolded him for not eating his fritter cakes and told him he was too young to understand, and it could only get him in a peck of trouble talking like that. Hush, she'd said, and eat.

"The river?"

"Yas'm, Miss Becky. Mammy says I kin go dere when I's done my chores."

Cate was obviously getting some new ideas in the northern climate it seemed. Becky decided it would bear watching. "What do they say? The men at the river?"

"Dey's men dere tellin' de black mens what to do. Dey ax me, do I want t' come 'n be a 'prentice. Dey says den I kin be free. Dat I kin be a cabin-boy, a *free* cabin-boy." He moved to the window preparing to dump the wash basin Francis had used for his shaving.

"Sam, stop! Don't do that," Becky commanded sharply.

"Miz Shippen's boy do it dis way," Samuel said, looking defensive.

"I don't care who does it. You'll do as you've been taught at home. Carry it down to the yard."

"Yas-ma'm." He set the heavy china basin near the door, knowing that it was three flights down.

"What do you answer the men at the wharf, Sam?"

"I says thank you an' dat I's jes' visitin' ... an' dat my mammy is waitin' fo' me to come back." Dumping the chamber pot into a large bucket, he placed that next to the basin. The pot, he shoved back under the bed.

"After we finish talking, you can take the bucket and the basin to the yard, Sam, and then please take the chamber pot to the yard also and scrub it out. Mrs. Shippen says there is plenty of water." When he nodded that he understood, she continued. "I guess it's all right for you to go to the river, but you shouldn't talk to the men. Some of them are very evil, and would think nothing of whisking you off to sea, taking you away from your mammy and pappy, and you'd never see them again. Stay away from the ships, Sam. I've heard of bad men doing wretched things to little boys." She saw his eyes grow big and decided a good fright would constitute the most lasting impression. "Things like cutting off a finger or a toe, or burning a brand on your arm or leg." It wasn't a lie. It was true they sometimes pressed runaways into service on the ships, threatening them with death or a return to their masters if they didn't do as they were told. "Do you understand?"

The slave child nodded his head, having already decided not to tell her he'd been invited onto one of the merchant ships by a real cabin-boy—a white boy of about ten who wore a fine blue uniform with big brass buttons, had a bed of his very own that he called a bunk near the kitchen, which was called the galley. It had been a very exciting experience, unlike anything that had ever happened to him. "Yas-ma'm, Miss Becky." He guessed his mistress wasn't going to tell him what free meant either. He couldn't ask her again and, smiling, he picked up the bucket to make his first trip down the stairs.

The next day Samuel sought out Ben in the stable as he was rubbing down the master's big gelding. "Ol' Cam'ron, he got some years on him, Sam," Ben said in greeting. Handing him a rag he pointed to the dusty saddle lopped over a partition. "I kin use some help, son, 'less you got other chores?"

Samuel sent an answering smile to the only father he'd ever known. "Some gray in your hair, Pappy, jes' like Cam'ron," The boy dusted the saddle, then went for water and the soap they used to wash the leather. When he was finished he would rub oil into it and polish it with a soft clean rag to protect the leather from cracking. He was proud of all the man-jobs he could do. "I want to ax you somethin'," he said finally, broaching the subject that preyed on his mind, the reason he'd entered the stable in the first place. "What do it mean to be free, Pappy? What do it really mean?"

Ben was cleaning the horse's left rear hoof; Cameron's leg bent and propped on his knee, he was scraping out the dung between the hoof's boney wall and the tender frog. At the question he dropped the animal's foot, sat back on his haunches and stared at the boy. About to speak, his eyes grew misty. What happened next was incomprehensible to Samuel. Two huge, perfectly formed tears rolled from the corners of Ben's eyes. They tracked slowly through the fine dust on his cheeks to splash, after what seemed an eternity, onto the worn homespun of his black winter breeches. Without awareness that he had crossed the space between them, Samuel threw his arms around the big man and buried his face in Ben's neck. "Oh, Pappy," he cried. He didn't understand any of it, only knew it was a word nobody wanted to explain, and now it had made Ben sad enough to cry. Powerless to stop the sobs that tore at his chest, he simply clung there, sobbing out his questions wordlessly into the familiar smell of Ben's neck. It was an experience neither of them ever forgot. And never again did Samuel ask anyone what it meant to be free.

◦～◦

The Congress struggled daily with the impossible task of maintaining the Continental Army. A rag-tag army at best, it was half Continental, half militia; some on the Continental dollar, some paid by the provincial conventions if they were paid at all; some in uniform and most not, but all suffering the same hardships and uncertainty. General Washington, encamped at Cambridge outside of Boston, besieged Congress with his problems of desertions, enlistments about to expire, lack of food, clothing, shoes, and most especially his lack of powder. By what miraculous means could he be expected to rout the British from Boston if he had no powder with which to load his guns? Finally, at Washington's repeated request, a Congressional committee was dispatched to Cambridge to confer with him. Something must be worked out. These were the circumstances surrounding them all when Becky decided to approach John Adams one evening.

"Well, I declare, Mr. Adams," she smiled at the pudgy delegate from Massachusetts, "you gentlemen in the Congress certainly do think kindly of our Virginians! Naming Mr. Washington General of the Army, Mr. Randolph as first president of Congress, and now choosing Mr. Benjamin Harrison to the committee to confer with the General regarding his many needs. It gives us great satisfaction to know there's such confidence in the abilities of our Virginians."

John Adams blinked. The owl-like eyes opened and closed rapidly several times as he fumbled for words, finding it a struggle to understand these southern women. They made pointed comments about matters political, yet dressed them in sugar-coated frills as though they asked a man if he preferred one lump or two in his tea! Did she understand the courtesies and tradeoffs they must make in the various appointments, and wish for some reason merely to tease him, or was she totally oblivious to his reasons for flattering the southerners? He darted another glance at her. She was a beautiful woman. Richard's brother had chosen well. But was she also intelligent? He hadn't yet made up his mind. "Why, yes, Madam. We're sending Mr. Harrison, along with Dr. Franklin and Mr. Lynch to talk to the general." Adams readjusted his ample posterior in Alice Shippen's fashionable imported chair, sighing as he did so, and wondered what his dear Abigail would think of Francis Lee's young wife. He didn't think they would have much in common.

Determined to ignore the strain he seemed to feel in her company, Becky decided although it was not easy to relax with Mr. Adams, she would keep the conversation going. He usually managed, rather curiously, to dominate any room in which he was present. It had kept her constantly on her guard. "And I understand it was you, in the beginning, who suggested Mr. Washington for the post of commander, in spite of the fact that your own colony's Mr. Hancock and others desired the honor. Richard, my husband's brother, has also told us that your cousin favored Washington." She blushed, flustering under his scrutiny but, not waiting for an answer, continued, "By the by, we never see your cousin Samuel here at Shippen House. You must bring him with you one evening."

"Sam Adams," he explained, "is not a social man. He's known for his insatiable capacity for work. Other than that, to the best of my observation, he merely eats and sleeps as necessity dictates."

It was Becky's turn to blink. She found it difficult to visualize a man much less social than the stuffy, round, grim-faced and balding John Adams. She'd heard so much about him from Francis and Richard before she met him that she'd expected to feel quite comfortable with him. Now she discovered that after several encounters he still fidgeted painfully if she so much as flirted the least tiny bit. It was unnerving. Within a short time she excused herself and made her way to the familiar side of one of the Virginia gentlemen. They, at least, knew how to put a lady at ease.

Another evening, having consciously rehearsed her words, Becky broached another subject she'd heard discussed within the family circle. "Mr. Adams, I wonder if it's crossed your mind to consider our able Dr. Shippen for a post in the continental hospital? I've heard it rumored that Dr. Church will be replaced as director-general shortly. In my humble opinion I feel Dr. Shippen to be a very capable physician." Benjamin Church was found to have been a Tory; Francis had told her in no uncertain terms how disgraceful it was that the army's senior surgeon turned out to be "another case of the enemy stalking among us."

"I, too, have heard the same." John Adams glanced to assure himself Shippen was out of hearing. He knew Dr. John Morgan was being considered favorably for the post of chief of hospitals. "Dr. Shippen is, unfortunately, labeled as a bit too radical by some." He lowered his voice even further before confiding, "The Pennsylvania moderates refer to him as the 'Radical Whig' in a most unflattering manner. I assure you, however, Madam, I shall take your suggestion into careful consideration. The differences between the moderates and Shippen's faction seem as much founded on religion, Presbyterian versus Quaker, as anything," he added almost to himself.

"Why, thank you kindly, Sir. I certainly think we all owe the doctor a great deal for his most generous hospitality, don't you?" Her gesture encompassed the tea table, the game of whist being enjoyed by four gentlemen, including Francis, and the relaxed faces of the room in general. "It would seem the more appropriate to me if someone other than one of Dr. Shippen's own brothers-in-law should recommend him. That is the only reason I brought it up." She tilted her head, eyeing him; he seemed more receptive tonight, less uncomfortable with her presence. "I do so wish, Mr. Adams, that your wife might some day join us in Philadelphia. Surely you could locate a suitable lodging? We would all love to meet your Abigail."

He nodded, his mind still on the hospital. "And she'd be more than delighted to meet my new friends from the other colonies ... umm ... states." Adams had begun to interject the bold concept of colonies turned states at every opportunity. It was necessary to get people accustomed to it gradually, he told himself, so they would accept it proudly when the time came.

"Then perhaps you should send for her. Francis and I have wondered why she's not here with you now."

The Bostonian looked at her as though she might as well have inquired why he didn't climb a mountain in India. "Why, Mrs. Lee? Primarily because of the children. We have four, you know. Nab, John, Charley and Tommy. Their proper place is with their mother ... and with their other relatives on our farm in Braintree. I firmly believe in family stability. I don't find it logical to disrupt an entire family's routine." He remembered the years in Boston when all the while Abigail yearned to take the children home to the country. "Children demand a personal discipline from a man. He must relinquish his own selfish desires." He hadn't intended it to sound like a lecture but he was afraid it must have, as Mrs. Lee looked distressed.

"Of course. I do understand. I come from a large family my-self. I should not have questioned your reasons. It's simply that

I never think of the complications children might cause, not having any of my own. It's not that we haven't wanted them," she hastened to add. "We would even be willing to agree to a separation if need be, as you have done, difficult as that must be. Yes, we would indeed." Her voice trailed off as, for a moment, she watched her husband, thinking they'd now been married almost seven years. "I have so prayed to give him a son," she whispered.

John Adams gave Becky Lee his complete attention. If he'd not been looking at her he might have missed her last sentence; there was an anguish in her eyes he would be hard-put to describe. Impulsively, he reached out his hand, placing it over hers. "My dear, perhaps one day the Lord may yet answer your prayer. Until then, take my word for it, you are much too beautiful to let sorrow rule your life."

It was the beginning of a fruitful friendship. But never again did the two come quite so close to a complete understanding of what was in the other's heart.

It took Francis some time to become reacquainted with his sister. They'd not been together in sixteen years and he found little of the sparkling fun-filled girl he remembered. He suspected she no doubt recognized just as many changes in him. Alice had donned the garb of a matron—in spirit as well as outer garments—in her stiff high necked frocks and her strict religious convictions, she was no longer a girl. It wasn't unusual, he soon discovered, for her to praise the Lord in mid-sentence, no matter the subject at hand, a habit he found disconcerting although her family was obviously accustomed to it. Judging by the eagerness she exhibited for any tidbit of news from Westmoreland, particularly anything to do with Stratford, Francis concluded that Richard must have spent little time with her during the previous congressional session. But he was wrong. Comparing notes with his brother, he learned that Alice asked for the same stories to be repeated five or six times. So her brothers chuckled and obliged her, knowing even as they talked that their tales of Virginia were already out of date.

∽

No sooner had Benjamin Franklin, Ben Harrison, and Mr. Lynch returned from General Washington's camp than their recommendations were approved. Congress agreed to increase the force around Boston to over twenty thousand troops—almost as many soldiers to brave the perils of smallpox, starvation, nakedness, imprisonment, and death as there were citizens in Philadelphia. Horrified by the committee's report of slovenliness and ungentlemanly pursuits of many of the officers, the delegates set about to revitalize the Articles of War. They decided to raise officer pay in the hopes of attracting a more select group. Soon another committee was dispatched to confer with General Schuyler in Ticonderoga, having been instructed to urge Schuyler, again, to press the Canadians to call their own provincial convention and send delegates to the Congress. The war news, when it got through, was in bits and pieces, so it was a month after the fact when word reached Philadelphia that General Montgomery had taken Montreal. So desperate were they for good news that most congressmen rejoiced totally, thinking that their troubles in Canada were over. Later, however, with the return of the committee sent to meet with Schuyler came the devastating news of naked, starving troops faced with a freezing Canadian winter. Schuyler had returned home due to ill health, leaving the army to General Montgomery. At Montreal, they said, Montgomery's men had deserted in droves leaving him with fewer than three hundred soldiers, and those ragged few, cold and hungry. Congress listened but showed little reaction, it being truthfully more than they could absorb. Most found it scarcely possible to imagine such absolute horror in an event taking place hundreds of miles away. They referred the matter to another committee, once again directing that the general, now Montgomery, should invite the Canadians to join them in the Congress.

Montgomery, wishing only to have his resignation approved, so as to escape a situation he now recognized as hopeless, linked his wretched little force with Benedict Arnold's troops outside of Quebec City. The committee had been informed Colonel Arnold's men were in no better condition. It clearly was Arnold's sheer force of will that had managed to march them through the ungodly wilderness to their present position, but even that could not sustain them much longer. The joint attack Montgomery and Arnold mounted on the French city was fated for dismal failure. Montgomery didn't need to request release a second time; he spilled his life's blood in the assault on Quebec. Arnold, wounded, was carried from the battlefield, the Americans having suffered a bitterly crushing defeat.

ഇ

It was late one evening in early winter. Snow had fallen steadily since mid-afternoon; streets, rooftops, trees and window ledges lay heavy with it. For a brief time the city appeared clean. At the corner of Fourth and Spruce the lamp threw a circle of pristine sparkle on virgin ground. The streets were deserted. Those few sots who lingered in the taverns clustered around wood burning fireplaces for warmth and companionship, continuing to nurse their tankards. It was a quiet night in Philadelphia. Even the whores remained out of sight. Perhaps they were all occupied, Francis mused, peering through the bumpy window pane. A night like this made a man think of a warm bed earlier than usual. He knew Becky awaited him in their chamber, might even have drifted off to sleep by now, but he had something on his mind. The guests had some time ago departed, the family gone to bed, and now only he and Richard remained in the strangely quiet parlor. He summoned a sleepy servant to add wood and stoke the fire's dying embers. When the slave had finished, Francis turned to serious conversation.

"Adams sounded me out tonight ... on a permanent independence from the Crown. He says it's time we took another look at Franklin's pamphlet on confederation and perpetual union."

Richard nodded. "He's been making the rounds, I think, talking to each of us in turn, in order to drum up support. It's much on his mind." Richard re-lit his pipe with a wood stick from the fire and the sweet smell of Virginia tobacco filled the room. "What did you answer him?"

"I told him I was of the understanding Jefferson highly approved of the concept, although it's obvious others are still unable to conceive of such a thing."

"No, Loudoun. That's not what I'm asking you. I want to know what you told him regarding your own convictions on total independence."

"I said I thought there was no other course open to us, as George III has so summarily declared us in open rebellion and refused to negotiate on our terms of reconciliation." His voice was hard, leaving no room for doubt.

"I would be careful of what I say to others if I were you."

"You're a fine one to talk!" Francis laughed. "I'm always being accused of being too cautious. To Adams, you mean?"

"To anyone. Very few are ready to consider total independence as an alternative. It could still go either way, you know. We're not winning these military battles. Our old friend Dickinson pulls in his horns daily."

Francis thought about the man he had so recently admired. "John Dickinson. The fellow who boldly attacked Great Britain in the early days! Inspired us with his avid patriotism. Urged us to unite through correspondence. Remember? He was one of the first men you corresponded with. And now he pussyfoots around like an old woman! It's no wonder Adams will have nothing to do with him any longer."

"How right you are," said Richard. "The word independence sticks in his craw like a barb. But he's not the only one who can't seem to spit it out! Why do you suppose Harrison and ... what's that idiot's name from North Carolina? ... Hooper ... won't support the concept of a new government in each colony? It's a step toward the fearful state of independence. Or should I say a further step, a final step? They can't be Tories, yet will not allow themselves to be patriots! They straddle the fence waiting for a miracle that will never come."

"But if we don't all form those state governments ... states ... not colonies, as our friend John keeps pushing us to think of ourselves, this Congress has no meaning, no powers, no entity at all. It's simply a totally unsubstantiated body. Yet we manufacture money, appoint generals, and even talk of a navy! How in hell can we consider the formation of an American navy when we're not able to supply, nor control for that matter, the rabble of an army we've already raised? The problem as I see it, is that we have no means of governing our colonies, states if you will, and no central control over all. Except perhaps in some northern colonies where they've managed to organize. Virginia is in total chaos and indecision according to Colonel Landon and John Tayloe, with some of her strongest voices, and wisest, right here in Philadelphia!"

"That's one of the reasons I shall request a leave of absence in a couple of weeks. Virginia must be urged and guided to set a government."

"When is the baby due at Chantilly?" Francis smiled, thinking it wasn't difficult to read his brother's mind.

"Soon. Any day now and, of course, that's my other reason for wanting to go home," he explained. "Which reminds me, speaking of wives, did you know Becky called for you over an hour ago?"

"Yes, yes. I'll go up soon. Poor dear. She spends a great deal of her time these days waiting for me and worrying about my health. Says I don't get enough rest or relaxation. Who among us does? She'll have a glass of warm milk ready, with a few drops of one of Carter's concoctions to make me sleep, I have no doubt."

"I fear your Becky is quite homesick for Richmond County."

Francis nodded. "She doesn't have enough to do here. You don't think there's any chance of a recess at Christmas, do you?"

"I doubt it. What do you think? I see only work ahead and Congress can hardly close its doors while the army starves in winter camps."

"Becky will be disappointed. I think she's set her hopes on going home for Christmas," Francis said slowly, pouring himself another glass of his brother-in-law's ruby port before returning to their former subject. "Regarding the government at home, R.H., with the word we had from Thomas concerning Dunmore's takeover of Norfolk and the raising of a Negro regiment, I should think every last one of our planters would be ready and willing to abandon the Tory cause immediately! By the way, I'm delighted about Thomas having been elected to the convention in Williamsburg. He'll keep us better informed as to what's going on. It's good to have him back in politics."

Richard looked thoughtful. "I'm happy for his election also, Loudoun, but our brother Tom doesn't have the strength to be as forceful a leader as we might wish."

That brought a frown to Francis's face. "We can't, all of us, be as eloquent in public as you are," he blurted.

"What kind of a comment is that?" Richard asked, clearly irritated. "I do what I have to. And at the moment I feel my presence is needed at home. They can't allow Dunmore to run rampant! The only way to fight him is to organize the government so he can be fought off with a unified effort. And we need a strong voice to motivate that organization."

Sometimes, Francis fumed, Richard was insufferable. He acted as though he was the only one able to accomplish anything. "Well, I have twice begged Robert Carter to take my own suggestions to the convention floor! I advised they should send a sufficient force of militia to drive that demon Dunmore back to his ships and out to sea. We should burn all his proclamations, publicly, and fine anyone caught distributing the abominable things. I haven't wanted to burden Patrick since we learned of his wife's death and now that he has the added responsibility of the militia." Forgetting his huff, he went on, "Old Landon, I'm afraid, is through with active politics for good. He prefers now to remain at home and haggle from the sidelines. So that's why I wrote to Robert. A lesser man, to be sure, in my estimation, yet I think trustworthy. I've also written to them both that the navy is under consideration because I wanted their reactions."

"I'm still opposed to the formation of a navy," Richard said. "It's utterly ridiculous to suppose we can effect such a thing. The south has no ships, bottoms, brigantines, schooners, or anything that floats and is suitable for an armed vessel. Our trade has all been done in British ships, while the New Englanders have built their own ships for trade. We have no ship builders. All the vessels would be raised in the north ...."

"And undoubtedly protect primarily northern ports and fill northern pockets. Umm. I thought of that, too. Nonetheless, I suspect we'll soon have a navy, and you and I will both support it. You know, in the beginning, Adams himself referred to coping with Britain on the seas as pure Quixotism. Yet now he pushes for it."

"That man is a genius at knowing when to turn his cards. He plays us each against the other with skill and dexterity, confident that in the end we must unite or perish in slavery. Yes, Frank, I'll support the vote on the navy when it comes up next week. But some of our southerners won't. You may be sure of that. I haven't spoken out publicly against it, you know. Which reminds me,

I want you to promise me something. Keep a watch over your words regarding independence while I'm away. Listen and wait. We must learn prudence from John Adams ... and ..." this said more reluctantly, "from Jefferson, too, in this game we play. I believe it's crucial that we not set off an alarm prematurely."

"Agreed. Besides, there should be some word from Arthur soon." Arthur Lee had been appointed by Congress to sound out the countries of Europe on the American position, in essence he was sent as a spy to learn what he could and report back to the Congress. "If he learns there's possible support from European powers, it will shed a new light on our position, don't you think? For myself, I think we can't consider any alternative to total slavery other than separation from the oppressor, whether we have help or not."

"We can't do it without help, Frank. France and Spain will never agree to aid us unless we break completely with England. And we can't do *that* until we indoctrinate our own members to accept independence as a solution! But we'll certainly not solve the dilemma tonight. It's after midnight. I heard the watchman cry the hour. He must be having a cold time of it in the snow. Come, let's go to bed. Becky may have locked the door against you by this time," Richard teased.

"That, my dear brother, is one thing in this world I can assure you with absolute certainty will never happen," Francis bragged. He stretched lazily and, for the time being, gave up his worries, thinking his country would have to wait until morning.

∽

The Continental Navy became a reality before Christmas. It also promised to be lucrative to certain New England interests as predicted. Samuel Ward, for instance, Rhode Island delegate and a ship builder in private life, fought hard for the birth of the fledgling navy. He wrote his brother on the eve of the vote that he hoped for a contract to build two of the ships. It didn't pay to waste time in these matters, he reasoned, once the Congress was decided.

Also in December, Lord Dunmore, Virginia's outcast royal governor, was defeated by a force of Virginians and Carolinians at Great Bridge. He evacuated Norfolk, but later reoccupied it before leaving behind him the second time, a burned, partially destroyed city. In his ships he moved to threaten Virginia's rivers. Landon Carter wrote Francis that the militia was stationed in Richmond Courthouse in the event of attack, but that the officers spent most of their time drinking and playing cards. Francis wondered if it was the same in other counties or if Carter might be exaggerating about such happenings.

Anne Pinchard Lee gave birth to their third child, a girl, whom they named Sarah, a month before her husband's arrival. Richard remained in Virginia, not returning to the Congress until March. Before his return a small pamphlet called *Common Sense* was off the press. Its words spread like a forest fire through the thirteen colonies. It was January of the new year—1776. Francis tossed his cape at the coat hook in the entry and missed. Hoping Ben would spot it before Alice did, he took the stairs two at a time.

"Becky, where are you? Listen to this. You've got to listen to this!" He burst into the room in such a dither he failed to notice her startled expression. Seated near the window, she held a book in her lap. Samuel scuttled through the door as Francis entered.

"Aftanoon, Marse Frank," he mumbled, as he hurried past.

"What's gotten into him?" Francis asked, kissing her warmly on the lips. "Umm. You taste good. You always taste so good to me," he whispered against her hair. "And smell so good … like jasmine." But in a moment he was seating himself businesslike at her feet.

Becky smiled the smile she saved only for him, and moved the book from her lap to behind her. "Who, Sam? Oh, nothing.

I suspect he was afraid you might think of a task for him. What on earth are you so exited about, darling?"

"This," he said, slapping a little booklet from one hand to the other. "Someone has put into print the words that just might be able to reach the fence-sitters in Congress, and in every colony! He's written things Adams has said for months, only more daringly. And more down to earth, so even the unlettered can understand it. He points the finger right at the Crown. Lays the blame at the feet of the *Royal Brute*. He actually calls him that! Can you imagine?" She shook her head. "He makes his appeal to the common man. Anyone who reads or hears it must rally behind the cause of freedom as he describes it." Thumbing at random, he said, "Here, just listen to this: *No man was a warmer wisher for a reconciliation than myself, before the fatal nineteenth of April, 1775, but the moment the event of that day was made known, I rejected the hardened, sullen-tempered Pharoah of England for ever; and disdain the wretch, that with the pretended title of Father of his People can unfeelingly hear of their slaughter, and composedly sleep with their blood upon his soul. He refers, of course, to the day at Lexington,"* Francis concluded.

For over an hour he read to her. She watched his expression, absorbing the intensity of his excitement. When he'd satisfied himself, having read the pamphlet aloud twice, he leaned back, resting his head against her knee and for a time was quiet.

"Becky," he said finally. "It's inevitable. America will declare her independence. I feel it in my bones. The King, having labeled us rebels of the worst order, has effectually decided for us whether or no we should break the ties. This fiery little book by an unknown Englander named Thomas Paine is what we needed."

She ran her fingers through his hair, knowing he wasn't expecting a reply; he wasn't finished thinking aloud. He needed her in strange ways these days. More often than not their conversations were completely one-sided. When she felt slighted she didn't let him know it.

"But should we fail, should Britain defeat us, every last one of us in Congress, as well as every general and colonel ... can expect to be hung from the gallows as a traitor. For it is indeed a treasonous act we be about."

She slipped off the chair and into his arms. "If you are to be strung from the gibbet, darling, there's no time to lose, is there?" she said, knowing he still needed her in the old ways as well.

Richard's return to Philadelphia was short-lived. He was there a bare three months before he was off again for Virginia. This time, although the colony had formed a government, they were squabbling over the confederation, and Patrick Henry called for his friend's help; at Chantilly, Anne was ill; a third reason for his departure was rumored, but Francis prayed there was no truth in it. It was being whispered among a few jealous and contemptible men that Richard Henry Lee, in anticipation of the fact he wouldn't be asked to write the Declaration, was leaving the city in a fit of petulance. Francis didn't believe it for a moment. For Richard, who had displayed the utmost patriotism by presenting his dramatic resolution for independence; nobly laid it on the table of Congress along with his own colony's Declaration of Independence, such egocentrism would surely be unthinkable, wouldn't it?

The morning Richard had presented his motion, in Francis's opinion, his brother was purely magnificent. If ever he'd earned his old nickname of Cicero, it was that day. A hush had come over the room when he rose to be recognized by the Chair. Many guessed what he was about to say, some feared what it would be and prayed it wouldn't be what they'd heard, and others cheered silently in their hearts, but no one was really surprised.

"Resolved: That these United Colonies are, and of right ought to be," his voice rang out, *"free and independent States, that they are absolved*

from all allegiance to the British Crown, and that all political connection between them and the State of Great Britain is, and ought to be, totally dissolved." The black wrapped hand gracefully punctuated each bold phrase, as he went on to call for a plan to form foreign alliances and an immediate plan of confederation. His voice exploded into the room and sparked a fuse. John Adams rose to second the motion, and all hell broke loose. The sergeant-at-arms pounded again and again for order.

"You are all madmen!" yelled Edward Rutledge of South Carolina, glaring at the Virginians and the Bostonians.

Benjamin Harrison and Carter Braxton squirmed in their seats. They had allowed the Lees, Wythe, and Jefferson to out-talk them, and were now sorry for it. Harrison sank even lower in his chair, his face turning purple. This was too much. He'd been right. Sensible voices, moderate men were not going to buy this treasonous motion of Lee's. Damn Patrick Henry! Damn Tom Jefferson! And damn that bloody bastard Richard Henry Lee! Virginia had now placed herself forever in the camp of the traitors! Harrison supposed he'd always known it would be so, since his first days in Congress, but it made the acceptance of his capitulation to the power of those strong voices no easier.

At the end of the day, the conservatives won a postponement of the question until July 1st. But just in the event it should pass at that time, "Let us be prepared!" shouted John Adams, and five delegates were appointed to prepare a "declaration to the effect of the said resolution." Those named were Thomas Jefferson, John Adams, Benjamin Franklin, Roger Sherman, and Robert Livingston. Richard Henry Lee left for Virginia two days hence, his reasons known only to himself.

The Declaration of Independence as prepared by Thomas Jefferson was approved by vote of Congress a few days later on July 4th. The next step was to send it to each colony for approval—the signing was finally completed in August—both Francis and Richard affixed their signatures for the new state of Virginia.

Market Street

Alice Shippen was by nature preoccupied, frequently not raising her eyes from whatever the task before her for hours at a time. Religion had entered her life, as it did her sister Hannah's, and in Alice's case, it altered her personality. Any vestige of frivolity was gone, lost during the gradual transformation from youth to middle age. Over time her focus had turned inward, to her soul. It was likely that her quest for grace had been hastened by the painful periods of loss following the deaths of several babies. Yet she never spoke of these tragedies. Seemingly satisfied with the companionship of her family, she would have preferred to remain socially invisible, but her husband's temperament didn't permit this option; she had to content herself with maintaining a reticent dignity in the face of constant company and frequent house guests.

Alice had so perfected quietude that Becky was astonished one morning when her sister-in-law, while arranging fresh roses in a vase, began to question her on a personal matter. It seemed somehow out of character for the prim, withdrawn Alice. "What is the matter, child? You seem depressed. Is it the heat?" she asked. "I believe you've lost weight since your arrival and your coloring is positively ashen this morning."

"Just a little melancholia, I suppose, Alice. I can't shake it. I seem to be engulfed in a stubborn web of melancholy. Maybe it's a little worse today due to this fearsome heat." It was inept, but she could do no better. "I'm sorry you noticed it. I'll try to cheer up a bit."

"Did you say ... a web?"

Becky felt foolish. "I know it sounds like an affectation, but I do feel captured by a horrible depression. It seems I never see

Francis long enough to try to explain it. When he's here, he's too tired to listen ... or there are so many others around. I just don't know what's the matter with me."

"These are difficult times for all of us, my dear. I expect you're longing for your home, your family, and the old ways." Alice turned to a servant, directing that fish be purchased for the evening meal. "See if you can get two large trout, Bessie. No, best make that three. I expect the doctor will want to entertain some of his cronies this evening. Just ask them to put it on the doctor's bill. He's very pleased with his appointment as chief surgeon to the Flying Camp, Becky," she confided, dismissing the cook with a wave of her hand. "He'll serve gladly, and without pay." General Washington had set the stage for this practice.

A smile flickered briefly in Becky's eyes. "We all thought he'd be happy to accept the commission. Does he know yet when he'll have to leave for Bethlehem?"

"Not exactly, but as he's been directed by Congress to make that his headquarters, I should imagine it won't be long."

"Then, for a change, I'll have the task of consoling you, instead of the other way round. You'll be lonely without him, even though you have two of your brothers here with you." Becky couldn't imagine she'd be up to consoling anyone in her present mood but thought it a proper thing to say.

Alice shifted a tightly curled pink rosebud to the left side of the Chinese export vase. Stepping back, she studied the affect. "Is it balanced? Yes. I suppose I shall," she answered slowly, "miss him. But I'll have the children to occupy my days, and my Bible group meetings. Praise God for His goodness in allowing me that. I do wish you'd come with me to the meetings, dear. It could be such a help to you."

Becky twisted the dimity fabric of her skirt between two fingers, thinking about how best to respond, as she had no desire to attend the peculiar prayer meetings in Alice's Presbyterian Church. Deciding to sidestep the issue, she said, "Alice?"

"Yes?"

"Are we in the way here?"

"Why, of course you're not in the least ...."

"Well, I know we must be. We're a dreadful bother to you, and we don't mean to be. I'm sorry we've all descended on you ... why, we've imposed on you for almost a twelvemonth. I've tried to talk to Francis about it but, as I said before, he has his mind on so many other things. I thought after the Declaration was out of the way he'd slow down a bit, but he's busier than ever. Between the struggle over wording the Confederation and fussing over the war problems, Congress meets constantly. Francis says it's utter foolishness to be bickering over government to such a degree when it's urgent to unite immediately, in order to be victorious in battle." She hesitated, having gotten off her subject. "And while he worries about all that, I fret about our imposition on you and your family."

"If you want my opinion, child, although you've not asked for it, I believe the root of the problem is that you don't have enough to occupy you, and you miss your family. I think I shall speak to that husband of yours about it."

"Mother, Mother, can we go out to Quid Vis today and see Grandpapa?" It was Tommy. He halted, momentarily chagrined, seeing that he'd interrupted but didn't bother to apologize. "Can we, Mother?" he chirped again. The Shippens' country home, where his grandfather lived, was about twenty miles away in Mt. Peace.

"Yes," Nancy mimicked, mincing through the doorway with her newest style of walking. "Will you take us? Can we leave this very hour?"

Becky suppressed a smile. Ever since Nancy had sprouted her bosoms she walked as though she had a stick up her back, taking dainty steps whenever she remembered to do so. It reminded her of her sister Annie a few years back.

"It would be lovely in the country. I know it would, and cool. Please, Mama," Nancy begged.

"Children ... my dears, we have plans to go tomorrow so your father may bid farewell to everyone. But not today. I've just ordered fresh trout for dinner and raspberry shrub. Papa will expect us to be home. He'll have guests."

"Oh," Nancy pouted. "You never let us do anything anymore. We used to spend the entire summer at Quid Vis. Stupid old war! It interferes with everything!"

"That will be enough, young lady. I shall forbid you the shrub if you continue in that tone. Now run along and practice your music. You have a lesson this afternoon. The Lord doesn't reward laziness or petulance."

Nancy made a splendid grimace behind her mother's back. Until that moment she had conveniently forgotten the lesson. "Well, I'm old enough to express an opinion. And I say it's a stupid war. Even Uncle Frank says the poor army can't possibly win because we don't send them enough food or powder for their muskets!"

It was an awkward moment. Alice stabbed the remaining roses into the arrangement.

Becky intervened. "Yes, dear, your uncle did say something like that as I recall. But he never gave you the idea he considered the war to be anything but justified, and very necessary despite all the hardships. He'd be distressed to hear you talk this way."

"Well ... you know what I mean, Aunt Becky." Nancy half-smiled, showing even white teeth and a more pleasant expression on her reckless little face.

"Mother?" Tommy persisted, ignoring the rebuke to his sister. "Why can't we go to Quid Vis right now? Grandpapa promised to show me how to load his musket next time we're there. And besides, I'm dreadfully bored."

He was a beautiful child, Becky thought, even when he pouted. Although he lacked the bright eyes and jaunty peevishness of Nancy, yet in his little boy fashion, he was every bit as beautiful.

A most handsome boy. Wondering what little John looked like now, she remembered the letter from Virginia. "Come, children! I have a letter from my own mama I'll share with you. She tells about the lovely wedding of my sister Polly to our cousin, Mann Page. There was music playing half the night, a horse race to entertain the guests, and a grand feast. Papa does know how to put on a wedding! She wrote of the exciting celebration in Williamsburg also, when the Declaration was read. Muskets fired and the cannon sounded, thirteen times."

"For the thirteen colonies?"

"Mm-hmm. Only from now on we shall call them states, not colonies. And then the militia marched up and down in front of the governor's palace. It's such a lovely place, Williamsburg," she said. "But the old governor isn't there anymore. They've thrown him out on his royal arse, as your uncle says. Later, Mama says in the letter, after dark, there were bonfires and a torchlight procession and many toasts were drunk to the health of our glorious United States of America. And to our new Governor Patrick Henry." What must her father think of all that? "You remember Mr. Henry when he was here, don't you? I'm sure you met him, he's a close acquaintance of Uncle Richard's."

"Let's get the letter! I want to hear you read it." Tommy, grabbing his aunt's hand, pulled her along having forgotten all about Quid Vis.

Nancy hung back. When they were gone, she threw her arms around her mother's warm plumpness. "I'm sorry, Mama. For being so ugly. I don't know what made me do it."

"I do, dear." Alice patted her daughter's shoulder. "You are forgiven. It's difficult to grow up during a war. It's difficult to grow up in the best of worlds for that matter. But this is a time that makes us all edgy. I was just saying that to your Aunt Becky."

"I am growing up, aren't I, Mama? Uncle Frank said he noticed I was. I do so love Uncle Frank! He's exactly the kind of man I want to marry. Uncle Richard's nice, too, but he's not sweet like Uncle Frank."

Alice smiled. "The girls have always admired your Uncle Frank, Nancy. You're not alone in that observation. Now run along. Aunt Becky wants to share her letter with you. And I promise we shall visit Grandfather Shippen tomorrow, weather permitting. The berries should be ripe. We'll take Aunt Becky with us. The countryside will remind her of our precious Virginia."

"I hope so, Mama. She's been looking dreadfully sad, hasn't she?"

೧౦

More than an hour had passed since the children went upstairs with Becky when Alice heard the door slam. She supposed it was Bessie returned with the fish. She was reading her scripture, having opened the book at random, but glanced up at the noise from the hall to see her brother. "Frank! Whatever in the world are you doing home so early? Becky won't believe our good fortune." He looked tired but there was an excitement about him; the twinkle in his eyes overrode his weariness.

"I'm happy to catch you first, dear sister. I want to surprise Becky, but I fear I may burst if I can't tell someone soon! I've just finished signing the papers to lease a house for us. I've known about the possibility for several weeks but didn't want to say anything until I was certain we could get it. It belongs to a relative of Mr. Dickinson, a known Tory who's fled the city leaving the house in the care of another cousin."

"How wonderful! Where is it?"

"On Market Street. Not far from the State House. It's fairly large, with three floors. We'll lease it furnished, of course."

"Dear Frank. You get better as you grow older, if that is possible. You must be the world's sweetest, kindest, most thoughtful and perceptive husband. I was planning on talking to you about Becky's despondency but, here you are, already having done something about it. It will make her very happy. It will also make her feel useful again, when she has a house to keep for you. How nice."

He beamed, moving to her side. "Come with us. We'll round up the children and all have a look at it. I've not been able to get inside myself yet. But I now have the key. We should be ready to move in a few days." Bending over his sister, his lips brushed the top of her head. "Will you miss me?" he asked.

"Of course I'll miss you both. But it's not as though you'll be very far away ... Loudoun." It was the closest she could come to an endearment. For a moment she recalled how, as children, she had adored him ... not always in a strictly sisterly way. She blushed, but thankfully he was too excited to notice. When he'd gone upstairs to get the others, she sat for a moment thinking that perhaps this was just what they had all needed—a little separation in their togetherness would be good for all of them. She glanced back at the Bible in her lap, open to Peter, chapter four. She read: *"But the end of all things is at hand: be ye therefore sober, and watch unto prayer. And above all things have fervent charity among yourselves, for charity shall cover the multitude of sins. Use hospitality one to the other without grudging. As every man hath received the gift, even so minister the same to one another, as good stewards of the manifold grace of God."*

Alice gazed upward, toward the ceiling. "I have been charitable and hospitable, have I not, Lord? It has only been a small burden, for I do love my dear brothers." She wasn't surprised that the scripture seemed to apply. She'd found that, even taken at random, most words of the Lord's book applied to whatever the situation at hand. This knowledge had long been one of her sustaining comforts.

∽

Shortly after the move to Market Street, Francis and Becky planned an entertainment. They borrowed Alice's punch bowl and Francis mixed John Tayloe's recipe for brandy punch as nearly as he could recall it. After a cup or two, no one would know the difference anyway. They invited friends, acquaintances, and relatives—Mr. Hancock was included and Samuel Chase from Maryland; John Adams, Caesar Rodney from Delaware, the Shippens, Dr. Franklin, and the new delegates from Jersey—more than thirty guests. It was a homogeneous get-together crossing the lines of politics and position.

"Isn't it wonderful to be able to make up our very own guest list?" Becky raved, at the height of preparation. She danced from room to room, adding last minute touches.

"My God, love, it's nothing short of a marvel to see you happy again. Why didn't I think of this a long time ago?" He felt younger than he had in months. "It's worth every penny it will cost, and all the bother to boot!"

❦

Later, much later, when the guests had departed and the house was again quiet and private, the only sound to penetrate the walls was the watchman calling it was after two o'clock. His voice trailed down Market Street and disappeared around the corner.

"Francis," she said, "I do believe you're beginning to like it."

"Like what?" He pulled the shirt over his head. Ben and Cate were cleaning up the first floor. He was glad they were occupied as he had no intention of calling for help this evening. He wanted his wife all to himself.

"Politics. The give and take, the thrill of thinking you might be doing something really important. The challenge of all those different minds."

"Politics? Liking it?" he said, his back to her.

"Well, you know. You didn't used to be stimulated by it, not like you are now. I think you felt as though you had to join in, or remain an outsider." When he turned, his eyebrow was down and the lines had deepened across his forehead. She hoped her words hadn't disturbed him, but she'd observed something tonight, or rather felt it, and she had to tell him. "Richard wasn't here this evening. We had all those important people ... talking, eating, drinking, dancing, having a marvelous time, and Richard wasn't here to help carry it off. And, you know what? We didn't need him. They like you for yourself, darling. They appreciate what you can do. More important, I saw tonight that you like *them*! It's not necessary for you to be thought of as Richard Henry Lee's younger brother all the time. Anyway," she didn't care how foolish he thought her, she was bound to say every word of it, "I am so proud to be Mrs. Francis Lightfoot Lee, I'm about to burst!" She wrapped her arms around him, having said all there was to say.

"My love, my dearest love. I'm glad you are yourself again." He kissed her in the hollow of her neck just above the collar bone. "Bless this house for making it possible. Bless us all in this crazy uncertain world we live in."

❧

In the morning they had coffee in the small chamber off the dining room and marveled again at their good fortune. "I can't believe they would leave even the books behind."

"I rather think they were frightened. Not knowing how hard we might crack down on Tory sympathizers. And, after all, the house is right under the nose of the Congress, barely two blocks away."

Becky laughed. "Maybe they should have stayed. Congress would probably not have remembered to notice them. I've heard you say yourself that the august body is more than a little myopic!" Pouring him a half cup more, she added a lump of sugar and a healthy splash of cream.

"I know you're in a hurry, darling, but I'm reminded of one more thing that happened last evening. Mr. Jefferson, in a moment's private conversation, gave me the definite impression he wouldn't be disinclined to renting a room from us. At first I assumed he was merely flirting, but he brought it up twice in that round-about way of his. I do believe he was serious."

"Oh, Becky, I trust you didn't make him any promises. He'll probably be gone from Congress for some time anyway, his wife being very ill, you know. At any rate, I wrote to Richard a fortnight ago giving him his choice of rooms when he returns. So I don't wish to go back on that." He had drunk too much punch last night and his head felt abominable, his stomach worse; the thought of Jefferson, as well as his brother, in his home every day brought on a devilish uneasiness.

A swift glance told her she'd heard him right. Richard was to live with them. It had been too good to be true, having him all to herself after the year of sharing him with a host of relatives. "Oh," she said finally. "You hadn't told me. No, I didn't encourage Mr. Jefferson ... nor would I anyone." There were too many things to do today to worry about it. She wouldn't let it matter. "I love you, darling, and it's nine o'clock. You're late for your committee meeting."

❧

Life in the new house was a joy. Becky thrived on new challenges daily. She began to make friends among the congressmen's wives, those few who had accompanied their husbands. She was also teaching Samuel to read. The day Francis had burst into the room with Thomas Paine's *Common Sense* pamphlet was the day they had begun. She wasn't sure just why she'd taken this step, nor why she continued to keep it a secret from her husband, but a secret it remained. Had the idea seeded itself the night Landon Carter's slave Nassau drove her home after the storm? Perhaps. One thing she knew for certain, had she children of her own, she wouldn't have embarked on the project. By the time they finished the fourth lesson, she became so entranced with the speed at which Samuel absorbed letters and words that she gave up trying to analyze her reasons or to consider the consequences of it. In the beginning, not knowing what to expect, it had come as something of a surprise that Negro children had the same ability and desire to learn as white children did. Sam soaked up the letters and each new word like a dry sponge; he took immense pride in getting everything right, making no mistakes. They soon reached the point where both student and teacher looked forward eagerly to the time each day when they'd pore over the dog-eared copy of *Robinson Crusoe*. Becky had borrowed it and Milton's *Paradise Lost* from the Shippen's library. Having not read Milton herself, she hoped Sam could learn new words from it even if he didn't understand a single thing. Now, of course, there was the library in the house to choose from. It being quite extensive, she hoped to find a book or two more suitable for children.

~

It promised to be another hot day. Through the open windows from the direction of the public square Becky heard the thump of a drum, occasionally the high pitched notes of a fife, all familiar sounds these days. A militia unit was straggling through its daily paces, probably preparing for departure to New York any day. From what Francis told her she knew there was no encouraging war news since March, when the great guns captured in that colony at Ticonderoga were hauled all the way to Boston, enabling Washington's Continental Army to at last drive the enemy from that city. The Canadian scene remained gloomy. Smallpox, famine, and five foot snows wasted Arnold's force until it lay huddled in shreds; yet the prevailing voices in Congress refused to abandon the place and Washington had been forced to part with ten regiments to aid Arnold's humiliated troops outside Quebec. This, in face of mounting fears over the defense of New York, caused a flurry of effort to raise new militia. But Washington didn't want militia. He wanted a fighting force—trained, armed, and dedicated enough to sign up for three years. What he got was more like a weak cup of tea squeezed from the left over dregs.

Becky watched from the second floor as the men she'd heard drilling at a distance now moved down Market Street. Above the music there rattled the clatter and clank of pots and kettles. Each man carried his belongings tied about his waist. One of the soldiers, a large simple looking fellow, called to a bystander that they were from Maryland, newly conscripted, and on their way to New York. Catching sight of Becky, he let out a lewd whistle. From the safety of her window, she waved to him thinking how morals changed in wartime. Or maybe it was that things had been different in Virginia.

Francis had said all regiments had been warned to skirt Philadelphia because of the smallpox scare—yet here they were—it was a fact, more orders were broken than followed in this pitiful army. Everyone knew it. She noticed that only the officers had uniforms. The rest wore a mismatched assortment of country smocks, dirty leggings, leather vests, and baggy breeches. They all looked unkempt. It made one wonder where so many rough looking men had been found, and a number of them were limping. It was as though their shoes had holes in the bottoms or pinched their feet. Or were they not accustomed to wearing footgear? She puzzled, knowing they were but three or four days march from home. How would they ever make it all the way to New York?

At that moment she became aware of the lack of muskets. Not more than ten or twelve had muskets. The rest, of all things, marched along with large wooden clubs over their shoulders! Was that to cheer their own spirits or in hopes it would fool the populace? Despite their tatterdemalion air they looked sprightly enough as they tramped through the early morning haze headed for the Delaware. She said a prayer wishing them well, as the last ragged marcher disappeared from view. Today was a big day. In a few hours Ben would take her to visit the cabinetmaker's shop. She had inquired of everyone for the very best of artisans. Sifting through the suggestions, she'd settled finally on Mr. William Hauck, who operated the Three Trees.

It took only a few minutes to reach Hauck's shop, which fronted on Pear Street where a large paned window looked out at the world. A signboard carved with the branches of three spreading trees swung above the door. Through the glass Becky could see several Windsor chairs displayed, but nothing else. She'd been assured the man was an expert at desks and tables, and hoped she hadn't been misled, for it was her plan to purchase for Francis the finest desk she could afford. There was one in Dr. Shippen's library she admired greatly but she supposed something so elaborate was out of the question.

Mr. Hauck impressed her immediately by welcoming her as though she were a valued customer, and graciously ushering her through his shop and out of hearing of the workmen. Once in his office, he offered her a cool fruit drink. "Now, Madam, what may I do for you today?" He was large of build, ruddy complected, with an honest air about him. "My very humble establishment is at your disposal." There was the touch of a German accent.

It seemed impossible that Mr. Hauck felt the least bit *humble* about his business. His pride stuck out like a ripe plum on a pear tree. She giggled a little at the thought, deciding she must be more nervous than she thought over the venture. "You're very kind, Sir. What I'm hoping to do is to place a commission with you to build a desk for my husband's birthday in October. I've been told you're a most accomplished craftsman. Your reputation for fine furniture is excellent. I only hope I'm not too late in discussing it with you, but I've only recently come upon the idea. You see, we've leased a house and there is no desk in it. Mr. Lee, my husband, being a member of the Congress, has frequent need of one. We're here from Virginia and therefore don't have our furnishings with us."

Hauck jabbed at the thick mass of his unruly blond hair. "A member of the Congress, hmm? From as far away as Virginia? My, my. I pray your good husband is paying close attention to the needs of our army. I have two sons in New York. They are with General Washington in the regiment of Colonel Samuel Miles. Good boys, they are. Good patriotic boys. Peter, he's the youngest, and his mama tried to talk him into waiting a year, but he wanted to go with Karl. They left more than a month ago. We ..." He stopped, sheepish, sucking in his breath. "Accept my apologies! Here, you come to purchase from me a desk, and I go on like some sentimental old papa over my boys. I did not mean to bore you with personal matters. So, you are here to order a desk," he repeated. "Well, let's see what we have to offer you." He reached easily to a high shelf wherein stood four or five volumes, selecting a shabby book.

"Oh, Mr. Hauck," Becky exclaimed, liking him more every minute, "be assured that I think it perfectly natural for you to talk about your sons. I'm happy to hear of our brave young men who serve the cause of liberty!" A picture of the ragamuffin crew she'd just witnessed flashed through her mind. What would it be like to lead such an unlikely troop into battle?

William Hauck twinkled with delight. "Ja," he grinned, "I am going to like doing business with you, Madam! Colonel Miles, the regimental commander, gave them each a company. Can you imagine that, for boys so young?" he asked, as he thumbed through Chippendale's Cabinetmaker's Directory. "What we can do concerning the desk, is this: I will show you the most popular patterns. You may browse through the book yourself if you wish. Then we will adapt to suit you, the one you select. For example, do you prefer a desk-on-frame such as this lovely Queen Anne style, or perhaps here ... a heavier version, still graceful mind you, but on legs. Or ..." he turned the pages with familiarity, "do you think Mr. Lee would be more comfortable with this slant top desk with the advantages of full drawer space, as in a secretary?"

Never dreaming there could be so many choices, Becky looked confused. "I ... well, I don't know. I do know he's very partial to walnut. He does prefer it to even the curly maple or imported mahogany."

"American black walnut?"

"I'm not sure. What other kind is there?"

"Well, for years we have imported walnut from England. It's only since they have begun asking for *our* black walnut, that we have taken a second look at it ourselves. It has become very popular in recent years. There is also cherry to consider. Wild cherry wood can be fashioned into a beautiful piece of furniture, and I believe we have some on hand."

She nodded, thinking again that Francis had frequently commented on the other. "Do you have the black walnut available?"

"Certainly. It is what we use most often since the hostilities."

"That is what I'd prefer, Mr. Hauck. Mr. Lee will be happiest with an American wood rather than an imported one."

"Good. A wise choice, my dear Mrs. Lee. Now, shall we look again at the styles?" He handed her his precious book, intending to return to work. At the door he removed a large leather apron from a peg and hung his coat in its place. "I will leave you to arrive at a selection in peace."

It took her more than an hour. When he checked on her for the third time, she pointed to a well-turned secretary with serpentine front, and typical ball and claw feet. It had a slant top and three full drawers across the front. The interior was plain, which she hoped would hold the cost down. There were small drawers, of course, and cubby holes, but no ornamentation inside. "Do you think you could put a small shell design here, in the center, inside? I think Mr. Lee would be pleased with that as he appreciates intricate workmanship."

So it was decided. It took another half hour to select the hardware and iron out the details of cost. At twenty-five pounds, it would come to just about seventy dollars. She knew it was high, but with inflation as it was, everything was expensive these days. The cabinetmaker promised completion in eight weeks; he would put two men to work on it immediately. There was time after all—Francis's birthday wasn't until the fourteenth of October when he would be forty-two years old.

A letter arrived one day from Mount Airy. Francis scanned it without comment, then seemed to forget it. Becky read it so many times she committed the words to memory. *"Your father is not able to accept the seat to which he was elected in the new state legislature,"* her mother wrote. *"He stresses his health to be the reason, but there are other considerations as you may well imagine."* How she wished she didn't know what those other reasons were. Her father couldn't bring himself to accept the new order of things, nor face a public service under Governor Patrick Henry! Did that mean Papa was a Tory? Did everyone know how he felt? Did he discuss it with Landon Carter, Isaac Giberne, Dr. Jones or others? What was the mood of the county? Why had they elected Hudson Muse and Charles McCarty to the convention in May instead of Francis and Robert Carter? Of course, that no longer mattered for Francis, now that there was a new government; it was only the principle of the insult that galled. But had the insult been brought on in part by her father's refusal to speak out in the patriotic cause or, worse yet, had he spoken out *against* it? A hundred such questions troubled her, as frustrating as the buzzing flies that bit and chewed in the early fall heat. She slapped one off her arm, but it was too late. A large welt began to appear as she waited for the inevitable itching to begin. Before long she made up her mind. The only thing to do was to ignore her father's philosophies—and the fly bites—as there was precious little she could do about either.

෨෭

The Congress wallowed in a quagmire over the Articles of Confederation. The Marylanders went so far as to leave in a huff over the taxation article, although for politeness they covered their exit with the excuse of attending a state convention. Thomas Jefferson agitated daily to go home but hung on, waiting impatiently for Richard Lee or George Wythe to return. Without another Virginian, Francis and Thomas Nelson would be left alone and would have no vote. Harrison and Braxton had departed in early August. Other delegations had similar problems. Representation was spread thinner than it had ever been.

The army's bitter defeat on Long Island came as another crushing blow to Congressional spirits. One and all, they felt the noose tightening. From New York, Britain's Lord Howe took the opportunity to press for a conference with a committee of the Congress although, he cautioned, he would meet with them as private gentlemen, and not as representatives of a governmental body. The meeting was a waste of time, a fiasco, in spite of Howe's obviously friendly overtures toward the Americans. At one point John Adams bristled irritably at the British lord's proposals, announcing he would answer to almost any name dubbed on him, with the exception of that of Englishman! When this committee returned and presented their negative report, the Congress addressed itself once more to the stubborn problem of confederation.

Despite the Long Island defeat, the campaign in New York continued, with Washington maneuvering his generals hither and yon, but always Howe's superior British force breathed down their collective neck. Francis and Becky were to have a firsthand account of the bloody Long Island battle and its aftermath. They would hear the story from the lips of young Peter Hauck, returned home with war injuries.

Peter was twenty years old in 1776. He was blond as was his father and his grandfather before him, who was the immigrant to the new world from the streets of Hamburg. He inherited a goodly height from his sturdy father but, unlike him, Peter was of a slender build. At the age of fifteen, it had been decided Peter should be apprenticed to a house builder, a prosperous man and a member of the successful Carpenter's Guild. His brother Karl, three years his senior, would remain in their father's cabinet shop, where he worked along side a journeyman, an apprentice boy, and five laborers, two of whom were free blacks. William Hauck insisted that Karl learn the trade from the bottom up so as to prepare himself to be master of the business. The Haucks lived in a tiny house off the alley behind the cabinet shop. Mrs. Hauck, a typical German housewife, kept the place immaculate; the flower pots were removed and the doorsill and window sills scrubbed daily, rain or shine. Growing up, the brothers learned prudence and economy from both parents. William Hauck considered Benjamin Franklin's *Poor Richard* barely a notch below the Holy Scriptures. He taught his sons the true meaning of the word independence, long before it came on the national scene. Mr. Hauck was, from the outset, a staunch American patriot. For obvious reasons he had long opposed the import of English products over colonial manufacture. William and Gertrude Hauck raised their sons in the only faith they knew, that of Philadelphia's German Lutheran Church, training Karl and Peter in the virtues of charity by contributing regularly to the Deutsche Gesellschaft, which aided the city's elderly poor and sick. When the war started, it followed as naturally as spring follows the snows that the Hauck boys—proud, independent, and patriotic—would be among the first to march away to fight their young country's battles. Setting off, they were cocky, determined to return as heroes so their parents would be proud of them. Karl was destined not to return at all, while Peter came home, not as a hero, but bitter and evasive, positive he would never go into battle again no matter the cause.

Becky had no knowledge of most of these things the afternoon she met William Hauck's youngest son. The picture he presented, however, as he supervised the delivery of the new desk, was not at all what she would have expected. She was excited, watching the two Negroes unload the desk from the cart, but also curious wondering who the young man was in the somber black coat directing them. It occurred to her he might be one of the Hauck boys as she noticed his coloring, and something about the face was very similar to Mr. Hauck's. But why was he here, in Philadelphia? There was a meanness about him as he spoke to the men, unlike the father's description of his sons, and he carried his right arm across the front of his body, hand wedged to his side. Could he be in pain? If so, it might explain why he spoke to his helpers in such a gruff, even rude, manner when they didn't appear to be doing anything to deserve such abuse.

She decided to be cheerful. "You must surely be Karl or Peter," she greeted him, holding out her hand. "Your father has spoken of you frequently." She'd made it a habit to stop at the shop weekly to check on the progress of the desk.

He stared through her, uncomprehending. Blinking, he seemed to remember that of course she would have met his father. "Yes. I am Peter. My brother is dead." The tone of his voice was as cold as his eyes, and he moved brusquely to pass her, apparently not wishing to converse further.

Becky stepped back allowing him to enter. Dead? How could it be? That would explain his eyes, staring at the world through windows of pain. "I'm so sorry, Captain Hauck, to hear about your brother. So very sorry. I had no idea. I saw your father just last week, and he was so happy and proud of you both, knowing you'd conducted yourselves bravely in the face of the enemy at New York. He mentioned you had both been wounded, but ..."

"Suffice it to say, Madam, that my father wasn't informed of Karl's unnecessary death until four days ago when I returned from the ... uh ... so-called hospital. And now, if you'll be so kind, I am in a hurry. Where would you like my men to place the desk?"

Unnecessary death? What did he mean? "Captain Hauck, I ..." but something in his frosty stare silenced her. "The desk is to go in the small room behind the parlor, please." Continuing to study Peter as he instructed the men, she thought of a clock spring—wound so tightly it can't tick. That's what he was. She shivered, there must be something she could say to help him. But how could anyone bring even a hint of a smile to that taut mouth, those lifeless hazel eyes?

When the piece of furniture was in place Becky exclaimed over it, genuinely thrilled with its beauty. It was everything she'd imagined. For a moment she forgot the desperate young man leaning in the doorway behind her. What a joy this desk was going to be for Francis. He didn't have an inkling of the surprise he would have this evening, and she was quite sure he'd even forgotten it was his birthday tomorrow.

"Wait until they polish it."

"What?" His words brought her back to the present. Looking at him again, she saw how handsome Peter really was. His father hadn't exaggerated that one whit.

"I said, don't praise it until they rub on the final coat of oil. That will remove the fingerprints their carelessness has caused."

"But Captain Hauck, they couldn't have lifted it without touching it," she smiled, fixing him with her green-eyed gaze.

Peter shrugged, avoiding her eyes, knowing she was right. "They didn't have to maul it, however."

Becky ignored that. "I know what we shall do. Your father has always been exceptionally kind to me when I called at his shop. He's given me a cool drink each time I've been there, encouraged me to stay, even though I must have interrupted his work. Let me repay his hospitality by offering you a little wine.

Madeira perhaps? It's my husband's favorite." She walked resolutely into the parlor, at the same time calling for Cate. As she hoped, there was nothing for Peter to do but follow. The Negroes finished their work and went outside to wait, no doubt happy for a while at least that Captain Hauck was otherwise engaged.

For an hour Becky and Peter talked. Not about anything in particular. Just talk. Peter was guarded, reserved at first, but she thought before he left that he seemed more relaxed. The wine had been a good idea. He skirted any mention of his soldiering or his wound, other than to mention it was the reason he was home, and he didn't refer even once to his brother Karl. Becky was wise enough not to press him. He finally smiled when he left and, thanking her, promised to return one evening when he would find Francis at home.

૭∿૭

It soon became clear that Francis didn't understand about the Haucks. At least not in the beginning. In the first place, he was very late arriving home. Becky heard the city cryer call that it was past nine o'clock just before she heard his step on the porch. It seemed she'd waited for days, instead of hours, to tell him about Peter. She rushed to open the door.

"I've been waiting and waiting for you! I want to tell you about Peter Hauck. His poor brother was killed at Long Island." She began to pour out everything she knew about the family as she guided Francis into the parlor, and kept on talking, as she urged him into a chair. "The boy is simply devastated over the death of his brother, darling. He can't even discuss it. There must be something we can do. Something that might help him revert to the sweet and loving boy he must have been before."

Francis had not said a word. He'd listened because he had no choice. Bone weary after a twelve-hour day, he heard his wife's voice but she was making no sense. "Who in the name of sweet

419

heaven are you talking about, Becky? I am tired. Exhausted. Sick to death of everything. Yes, and even hungry, in case that should surprise you. I would dearly love a little peace, if you could arrange it, and something to eat."

"Oh, darling. I'm wretched not to have given you a chance to catch your breath. But I'm terribly upset about this young man. I've never met a soldier face to face before. He was wounded. A musket ball ripped through his side!"

"What do you mean, you've never met a soldier before? You know General Washington quite well, do you not?"

Becky gave him a trifling glance. He really did appear haggard. When he lost his sweet disposition, she always knew he was tired or coming down with something. "Yes, of course, but that's quite different. He's not a *real* soldier, engaging in combat with the enemy. But Peter ... "

"My God, Becky! Do you know what you sound like? I'm not in the mood for riddles. Tell me ... is this mysterious Peter a lover you've taken in my absence?" It was mean or a poor attempt at humor, he knew. He didn't know what made him say it, but he was in such a foul mood he actually enjoyed seeing her eyes fill with tears and felt no remorse.

"Francis," she sniffed. "You have no call to speak to me like that." She dabbed furiously at her eyes knowing she shouldn't have had the second glass of Madeira while waiting for him. It made her teary and far too emotional.

Francis stared at his wife. He felt like heading right back out the door and returning to the City Tavern. His last committee meeting had been held there, in a back room; there, at least, he could be assured of another glass of wine, some hot food, and fairly sensible companionship. "All right. I apologize for asking you if you've taken a lover. A lot of women do, you know. Especially when their husbands are forced, in this case by circumstances quite beyond my control, to work around the clock."

"Francis!"

"Well, what the hell am I to think? I walk in the door and run into a tirade of nonsense about a tall, blond, twenty-year-old German. A handsome lad and a brave soldier, I think you called him, who has for some unexplained reason spent a good portion of the afternoon with my wife! In my house! Drinking my wine! Now, damn it, what is going on? Is something wrong with me that I feel this urgent need to uncover ... who the hell is Peter Hauck?"

His voice had risen to an alarming pitch. It triggered a memory of the date—his birthday eve. It wasn't right that he should be so aggravated on his birthday. "Oh, darling!" She dismissed their entire conversation. It was so irrelevant. Grabbing his arm, she pushed him ahead of her. She pushed him all the way across the parlor and into the room she was turning into a study for him. "There. See what I've almost forgotten to show you. Happy Birthday, Francis. Happy Birthday!"

In a daze, he stood in silence, his mouth open. Soon he was caught by her excitement and the elegance of the piece. He dropped to his knees in front of the desk, running his fingers over the smooth dark surface. "She's beautiful. Just beautiful," he marveled, as though speaking of a new ship or a new horse. He slowly glided each drawer toward him, closing it carefully before trying the next, then examined the hardware and the intricate serpentine curves of the front. At last he stood and opened the slant-top. "Oh Becky, the design is perfect. The shell is the same as on Dr. Shippen's desk, is it not? So rich," he said, feeling each curve with his finger tips.

Becky watched him, delighted with herself for having thought of the idea. She could tell he more than liked it.

"I'm really pleased. I don't remember being so pleased with a gift since my father gave me my first pair of boots when I was ten! Do you know, I forgot it was my birthday tomorrow? Completely forgot." A puzzled look came over his face. "But where ... is it new? It looks new. Wherever did you get it? Who made it?"

Becky went to him. Putting her arms around his waist, she pressed her body into the familiar curve. Before she had a chance to answer, she felt the hardness of him growing against her stomach. "Mr. Hauck, darling. I tried to tell you before."

They laughed all the way upstairs. Francis forgot he was hungry and thirsty and tired. Right then all he wanted was his wife.

"Richard will surely be home soon, don't forget," Becky whispered when they reached the landing. "And Cate will have supper ready."

He took her by the hand. "You shouldn't worry so much. This is my house and it's my birthday, and I plan to do what I want to do. And right now, I intend to celebrate by making love to my beautiful wife, if she can forgive me my vile outburst of temper."

Peter

Peter Hauck stood at the window. Ignoring the draperies, he allowed his shoulder to press against the sash. The first snow was on the ground, the air frigid. Frost glistened in an arc on the lower panes. Before dawn, ice crystals would blot out any view of the street if the fire wasn't kept burning. Behind him, Peter was aware his host was poking at the logs; he sensed sparks flying as new wood caused the flame to sputter, blaze anew. Peter thought it was good to know that a man raised on slavery consented to do occasional tasks for himself. It was one of the things that drew him to Francis Lee. That, and the fact he was a member of the Congress, as well as a relative of the army hospital's Dr. William Shippen. What better combination to help him execute his plan? In the beginning, he'd had no actual plan because then he knew only hatred; an all-pervasive bitter desire to retaliate. It had rendered him virtually incapable of drawing breath without bringing up the taste of bile. As the weeks passed, however, the utter senselessness of permitting such violent desires to burn up his insides brought him to the realization that he must take logical action if he wished to vindicate Karl, save others in the future, and free himself. Only by taking affirmative action against the monster who dared call himself *doctor* could he ever hope to retain his own sanity. It was only then the obsession became a plan, the goal of which was to bring about the downfall of the butcher of Long Island.

Then, unexpectedly one evening, he'd observed the Lees, recognizing them only when he was afforded a close view of Mrs. Lee's face. They were riding in an impressive carriage with the

Shippen arms painted on the door. Knowing that Dr. Shippen was very senior in the army's medical hierarchy, the pieces of his plan began to fall into place that very night. It was a simple matter to strike up an acquaintance. First off, Mrs. Lee had invited him to return to meet her husband, had she not? And secondly, the opportunity presented itself because there was the chair to deliver, for Mr. Lee's desk. It came as a surprise to Peter that he and Francis Lee hit it off right from the start, and he was invited to return again for a meal and conversation. He soon came to admire Mr. Lee's quiet reasoning and firm commitment to the American cause. There was plenty of gossip in the city that certain others of the Congress didn't share the same degree of dedication. Peter had witnessed more than a few of them boasting and bragging, expounding like fools in the taverns after they'd sloshed down sufficient quantities of spirits to loosen their tongues. What did such men know of warfare? The chilling sight of blood and guts strewn over a field of battle? The searing pain of frozen feet and fingers? The misery of icy rain that could pelt eyes, ears, and run down a man's neck until he feared he'd drown before dawn? Worst of all, were the sounds of war—no one could imagine the sounds unless he'd actually heard them—the trumpet's bloodcurdling peal to attack, minutes before enemy horsemen pounded into the heart of a foot unit; the deafening throb in a man's own throat, scarcely less intense than the thudding hoofbeats, as he crouched, helpless, waiting to be hacked to pieces by the slashing swords; swords that whistled as they ripped and tore into flesh and bone. The mighty sword could wring more inhuman screams from men than any cannon ball. The swordsman, a cruelly personal enemy, came supremely close in order to inflict his severing blows. For a foot soldier, there was no escape. Screams and panic, blood and terror—unbidden, the awful scene closed in on Peter again as he leaned against the window in Francis Lee's parlor and stared into the night. Dear God, when? When will I stop remembering? "Will I never stop hearing it?" he exploded into the peaceful room. Pressing both fists hard against his temples, he felt external pain challenge inward horror.

Hauck wheeled blindly, groping for a chair. His companion, uncommonly startled, set down the poker thinking how dispassionate Peter had been a moment before, how coolly proper. "What ... ?" he began, but the anguish in the boy's eyes brought him up short; had he ever witnessed such mental torment? But he saw something else that frightened him. Snapping his fingers, Francis signaled Ben to bring brandy. Peter slumped motionless, staring glassy-eyed into the fire. His body began to twitch spasmodically.

"Drink this," Francis commanded, holding the cup under his nose. "Do you hear me, Peter? Drink it!" Thank God Becky had excused herself early this evening, he thought, his mind racing for ways to handle the situation.

In a daze Peter accepted the cup but didn't raise it to his lips. Tears welled in his eyes. He allowed them to splash unashamedly onto the stuff of his waistcoat where they left telltale wet blotches. He'd not shed a tear since Karl's death and, now that he did, he was only vaguely aware that the wracking sobs he heard, were his own.

Francis laid a firm hand on the thin shoulder sensing somehow what a father must feel the first time his son suffers a pain so enormous that it is forever beyond the father's ability to rectify it. Tenderly he raised the cup to Peter's mouth, holding it until he forced the boy to drain it.

The fiery liquid drew a gasp from Peter, jerking him back to the present. "I'm sorry," he mumbled. "My apologies, Colonel Lee. I don't know what came over me." He shuddered, feeling a cold far greater than that of the room, and dashed a hand over his wet cheeks.

"Memories, Peter. Whether good or bad, they return to haunt us. We must learn to live with them. I'm afraid you'll have yours with you a long time. Maybe forever. I've wondered from time to time if you wished to talk about what happened out there on Long Island. What is eating at you?" He searched the haunted eyes. "You'll find me a loyal listener, and perhaps the time is appropriate."

Recognizing the gesture as something he'd been waiting for without even knowing it, Peter accepted another cup of brandy as Francis poured one for himself before sitting down. After a few minutes he was able to allow his heart to guide his lips, as he began to spill the poison from his soul.

"They came on us during the night. We didn't suspect a thing. We'd had a report earlier that all was quiet, and the white spots of their tents were visible in the valley. So we assumed they were asleep in camp. That assumption was to cost us the battle. Colonel Miles had ordered a patrol on the pass, but for some reason he didn't feel it necessary after dark and he called in the pickets. The first warning we had that something was afoot was just before dawn. At that time we were told General Stirling had ordered up two more regiments because there'd been some firing from the enemy in the direction of Brooklyn. Our unit was way out on the left of Stirling's main force, but I think they hit us all at the same time. Their plan, someone told me later, was to cut Stirling off from Bedford Town and from the other American forces.

"It was cleverly planned and the battalions of our regiment were separated almost immediately, but Karl and I were both in the group with Miles. It was hopeless from the start. The Hessians are bestial savage fighters. They screamed gutter obscenities as they ran their swords through our men ... they were all over us in minutes. Their favorite trick was to back a man against a tree and run him through ... pinning him to the tree. It was like a game they played, shouting back and forth, yelling out their body count. Unfortunately, I could understand them because my parents spoke German to us, and for the first time in my life I was ashamed of my ancestry. I wouldn't have believed any man but

426

the unchristian savage could be so inhumane, had I not witnessed it." Peter paused, took a gulp of his brandy, then continued:

"Karl moved his company cleverly around to the right, trying always to remain as much out of sight as possible. I followed his example and my men were able to use their muskets from behind the trees to put an end to a number of the enemy. We kept it up as long as we could, moving from tree to tree, waiting for them to come close enough for us to strike, but a foot soldier is no match for a cavalryman, even in a wooded area." Peter stared at the fire, wagging his head slowly. "Finally, Miles sent the order down the line to make a run for it. It had become clear we'd all be slaughtered if we continued the slow withdrawal tactic. Only a few of us got away. I never saw Miles again, and many were killed or captured. I have no idea what happened to them. But Karl and I, with about fifteen others managed, I don't know how, to reach Stirling's main force. We offered our services to Colonel Atlee's Pennsylvanians. We felt we'd rather fight there than with complete strangers from Maryland or Delaware. Not that we had much choice. As Karl joked later, so long as they weren't Yorkers we didn't care, but we just lucked upon some of our own."

At this mention of his brother, Peter stopped, clearing his throat. The brandy had done its job, however, and he didn't break down again. It was time he spilled the story that had been bottled up in him for too long. He'd told his parents no more than the barest essentials, wishing to spare them as much pain as possible. Tonight, he knew, staring openly at Francis Lee, he would tell it all. Continuing, he picked up the thread of his narrative:

"Try to imagine yourself with a group of utterly panicked men, routed from their positions by a force so superior they cannot even begin to comprehend how many there are against them. The redcoats stretched for miles, in every direction it seemed. They'd been on the move all night to get into position to attack us. So we escape the Hessian's green, only to run smack into the British cavalry. If anything, that was worse. Those swords swinging and slicing from everywhere until there were bloody arms and legs and heads littering the field, and all the screams and cries of the terrified and the wounded became one enormous roar that never ended! There was no order to our retreat, believe me. We were simply a hunted, floundering rabble, with each man taking to his heels, knowing that the only shred of hope was to make it to the Brooklyn forts.

"For hours I didn't see Karl. Or anyone. I got separated. Completely alone, I crawled on my belly, elbowed my way through what seemed like unending cornfield. I could hear fighting everywhere around me. But I had no weapon by that time, my musket having been snatched by an Englander on the scramble down the heights. I remember thinking my first objective should be to find another musket. But, truly, I didn't want to find it too quickly or I'd have to direct my thoughts to a further objective, and I wasn't sure I could manage that. Can you possibly understand? I finally spotted the end of the cornfield ahead but there were shouts and shooting from all sides, so I had no idea where was enemy or where was friend. Then I saw this poor devil on his stomach ... one of ours, I knew, by his buckskin shirt. I inched my way up to him, terrified of making movement or sound that would call attention to my position. When I rolled him over he was still warm, but very dead. I saw he had no face ... none at all. Just a big bloody hole. A mass of oozing pulp. He might have been my closest friend and I wouldn't have recognized him. Do you know what I did? I threw up, right there, my face pressed to the earth in my own vomit. Some time later, when I was able, I slid his musket from under him and stood up. Then I was running, headed for the road before I fully grasped my own foolishness. But I no longer cared. All I wanted was to get the hell out of there ... to put as much distance between me and that poor bloody bastard as I could. I would have made it, too. Except I heard a voice call my name, and I hesitated, changing direction. It was just enough, those few seconds delay, to cause me to take the ball in my side. I remember hearing the crack and the pain came, but I kept on running toward the voice. It was Karl who'd called me. He grabbed me as I pitched into the grass. I saw his face before I passed out. I remember wondering if I looked as woebegone as he did.

"It was after dark before we were able to make it along the side of the road until we finally staggered into the Brooklyn fort. I'd lost a lot of blood, been unconscious some of the time, but realized there were others with us. When I was lucid I could hobble along. When I wasn't, someone half-carried me. It was night before I even knew about Karl's leg wound. When he fell it was the first time I knew something was wrong. He told me he'd taken the slash of a sword in the upper thigh. Later we discovered it hadn't hit the main muscles, and that was how he was able to force himself to keep going.

"The next two days were a black nightmare. There was no food except rotted pork, no shelter, and it pelted rain continually. We lay in the trenches, wedged in like sheep at a shearing. The wounded were packed together, waiting for the surgeons to get to them. They took the most serious cases first. Karl's leg had stiffened badly but we had pushed the skin together and, so long as he didn't move, the dried blood held the wound closed. Mine was just a surface wound although it bled like a crazy thing because there was no skin left where the musket ball had taken the chunk out. Anyway, they never got around to doing anything for either of us. Then we learned that the sick and wounded were to be removed to a hospital quarters in New York, that we'd be ferried across the following morning.

"It turned out our entire army, what was left of it, escaped right from under Howe's nose! General Washington ordered them all out. The boats plied back and forth all night. I scarcely remember the trip. Someone said the tide had shifted. I guess they were right because the crossing was very treacherous. Karl began losing blood again from all the bumping around, but he never complained once until we were crawling out of the boat and someone stumbled into him. Then he yelled, calling him an ugly pisspot ... that was Karl's favorite expression when he was angry. It used to make Papa laugh. There wasn't anything funny about that day however! The hospital was a barn of a building. They shuffled us all in there and lined us up on the floor, row on row. The stench was unbelievable. I'll never forget it ... a combination of urine, feces, vomit, sweat, rotting flesh, and fresh blood ... everything offensive you can think of is what it smelled like. The weather for August was chill, thank God, or it would have been far worse. I couldn't see where they put Karl but I prayed they'd take him soon. I knew by now his leg was probably infected and needed attention fast.

"There was a large table in the center of the room where the doctors worked. When they saw how many of us there were, they called for more tables and set them up together. I think there might have been five surgeons. Although it would be more truthful to call them butchers! They hacked and sawed and chopped all day and through the night, until there were piles of arms and legs and entrails under their tables. The only thing they bothered to carry out were the dead, when they noticed them. Screams and curses filled the place and I felt as though I might as well be back on the battlefield with the cavalrymen slicing us to ribbons. Sometime shortly past noon they sawed off Karl's leg, almost to the groin. Afterward I heard him scream my name and I crawled from pallet to pallet until I found him. There was nothing I could do except hold him. He called me Mama once. He bled to death before dark ... the pitch they poured on the stump couldn't stem the blood."

"My God, dear merciful God," Francis muttered, but Peter didn't even hear him. His tale, at last unleashed, continued to pour out.

"The next day I learned through the grape vine that the surgeon who'd made the decision to take my brother's leg had been drunk. The story went around that he was so incompetent that when faced with all those two and three-day-old powder and sabre wounds, all he knew to do was amputate. And in order to lace himself with courage he drank a bottle of rum before he even entered the place. Half the amputations weren't remotely necessary is what they said. It didn't take me long before I decided what I must do. I don't know what I expected to accomplish, but I went to him as soon as I learned where he was lodged. I had to see him alone, to confront him. Of course, he denied the whole thing. Said he'd have me court martialed for insubordination. I soon realized he didn't know my brother from the rest ... after all, hundreds had come under his knife. How could he remember one tall Pennsylvanian with an injured thigh? But to ease my own anger, I stupidly forced some meaningless confession out of the wretch. Fortunately, he was drunk enough even then, so he probably forgot the incident by the next day!

"I left there positive that Karl would have lived and recovered had he been allowed to keep his leg. I don't remember much about the following days. I was so consumed with hatred I considered killing the man. Then, within the week I heard that one of the other fine upstanding doctors, although by this time I had ceased to think of them as anything but executioners, was selling little pieces of paper that declared the bearer to be unfit for military service. That's how I managed to come home, and why I'm still here. It cost me ten shillings, although I learned some went for only sixpence. Had it not been for that, I would've deserted before I faced the idiotic, useless, unscrupulous, degrading senselessness of the battlefield again! What's the point? You fight your ass off, do everything you're told. Conduct yourself with outward bravery, when inside you're a mass of jelly, and what happens? Dear Sweet Jesus! Some drunken sot of a surgeon hacks your leg off and lets you bleed to death as reward for all your trouble!" Peter heaved a brokenhearted sigh, and slid, silent and exhausted, even lower in the chair.

Francis was deeply moved. Again he thought of the father-son relationship; he'd grown immoderately fond of Peter over the past weeks. "Give me the name of the man!" he said angrily. "I'll arrange to speak with Dr. Shippen about him immediately."

Peter felt faint, incredibly weary. All he could think of was the marvelous sense of relief that had come over him, a warm gratefulness that someone had lightened his burden by sharing his grief. He almost forgot what had been his plan all along—to persuade Colonel Lee to set Dr. Shippen on the heels of the murderer. At the moment it no longer seemed of prime importance but he told Francis the name. "Thank you, Colonel. I appreciate your kindness. Whatever you can do to have this evil man, who calls himself doctor, removed will put me forever in your debt."

❧

"It seems the only news we hear is bad news these days, darling. Have you nothing cheerful to tell of your day?" Becky hoped Francis wouldn't fall asleep at his desk again tonight. Ever since he'd heard Peter's story, she thought he was driven to work harder than ever. On everything. Right now she knew he was bent over his papers trying to cope with the problems his overseer was having at Menokin. It might as well have been a million miles away in another age, for all the progress he seemed to be making. "Are we making a profit these days?" she asked, when he didn't answer her first question.

There was a squeaky sound as Francis stirred his quill point in the inkwell. "I suppose so. As much as can be expected anyway." He glanced at her, trying to remember if he'd told her the Virginia Legislature had cut his salary from forty-five to thirty shillings a day. "But do you realize, I don't even know if we harvested a winter wheat crop this season and, if so, where it might have been sold? I should like very much to go home, put things to order and then return to my duties here. We must earn the maximum possible on the plantation with prices going up. More than ever, it's important to produce for sale. I'm sure your father is doing his best ... and yet ... I do worry about it."

"And what about a rest, my good man? That you dearly could stand. It's a wonder you're not more sickly than you are, with as little sleep as you're able to snatch."

"I am subject to occasional colds, love, but I'm hardly what you'd call sickly." He thought what a comfort it was to have a wife like Becky. He enjoyed being fussed over; she always worried about him, even when it wasn't strictly necessary. He'd decided a long time ago that he couldn't bear it in Philadelphia if he had to come home to an empty room every night as did many of the delegates. Of course, there were a few who hired other arrangements. But all they could buy was a warm body, if that. No conversation. No tenderness. No love. Not even what he'd found with Martha Tutt. In most cases he suspected it was something far less. "Becky, do you know how grateful I am that you would spend these years with me? Away from everything you've known and loved?" He scraped his new chair back and crossed the room to sit at her feet where he could watch as she worked her needles back and forth. Alice had taught her to knit and she was making him a scarf. Fingering the soft gray wool reminded him of the fulling mill and he wondered if it was still going; he hadn't heard for months. The nubby texture of the yarn was pleasing and he knew it would be comfortable protection against the wind. "You're always doing something for me."

Becky lived for moments like these. It was so seldom he took the time to just sit and talk, admire whatever she was doing or wearing, as he used to do. "Well, I love you. That's why I'm here in this place so unlike our Virginia home, and it's also why I do things for you." She lost a stitch and had to concentrate while she fished in the row below for it. "Sister Alice mentioned yesterday that she thinks by now your brother Arthur is meeting with

Silas Deane and Dr. Franklin in Paris to work on the treaties with foreign powers. Have you heard anything?"

"Nothing I haven't already told you. I doubt Alice knows anything more either. Did she say she got it from Arthur himself?"

"Well, no. But she knows some of Mr. Deane's relatives I think. I'm not sure, but you know how she is. Sometimes she's very positive about things ... doesn't take time to explain, just expects you to believe what she says is fact."

"We had all best pray those three commissioners are successful in obtaining help from somewhere. With Arnold's makeshift navy destroyed on Lake Champlain and Washington fleeing from New York, there is no good news, to answer the question you asked a while ago. We suffer defeat after defeat. And always the enlistments run out and our forces dwindle. It's the same old story in every dispatch. Some say Howe is bent on taking Philadelphia this winter." He hadn't meant to tell her tonight of the scare talk but, perhaps, it was just as well to plant the idea now. It wouldn't be fair for her to hear it from someone else.

"Howe in Philadelphia? Oh, pooh. Surely General Washington wouldn't allow that. Why, this is our capital!" She wasn't nearly so frightened, as incredulous. "I've heard, Francis, that Generals Putnam and Mifflin are come here to defend us."

"Then, my love, someone has already spoken to you of the danger. I'd thought to discuss it with you first."

"You know how rumors fly. I don't take most of them seriously, as with this. I don't for one minute believe the British can overrun Philadelphia! Do you?" Her eyes fixed on him, waiting.

Francis thought of all the weak-kneed voices in Congress. He suspected some were even now planning their escape. "Well, I told you Peter's story of their tremendous numbers, and you know our own weaknesses. There are some who've begun rumbling against Washington again, saying he should be replaced if we're to have any chance of defending ourselves. But I'll tell you this ... if I didn't have you here to be concerned about, I'd never vote to flee!"

She continued to look him straight in the eye. "Francis Lee, don't you ever be worried that I can't take care of myself. I'm not for one instant afraid of some silly soldiers in red coats! And don't you ever, ever let my presence affect your voting!"

"What a feisty little girl you are. But I'd have you no other way." To himself he wondered if her reaction to the war's encroachment would be the same if she'd heard Peter's tale herself. "Becky, by the way, I do have a bit of good news. I stopped by the shop today to talk with Peter on my way home. He's decided to join up with another Pennsylvania regiment after all. Some unit under Mifflin's command, I believe."

His tone of voice told her he was pleased. "I'm glad he made that choice, darling. I'm sure it's the right one. But it makes me sad, also. I wish he didn't have to fight again. He's become a dear friend to both of us, hasn't he?"

"I'm almost as fond of him as I would be of my own son," Francis answered.

She gazed at him, saying nothing.

❧

By mid-December it became obvious Congress wasn't able to function with any reasonable sense of order. With the city fast turning into an armed camp and jittery delegates growing more nervous daily, a decision was made to remove to Baltimore. Government would be resumed in that city on the twentieth. In the house on Market Street the Lees had very little time to prepare for departure because Becky had refused to believe it would be necessary until the last moment.

With everyone rushing around, they were finally ready. Peter insisted on accompanying them as far as Chester, fearing Tory agitators, or possible trouble from deserters from both armies who hung around the city's outskirts. From Chester Town he'd return to join the forces assigned to defend the city. Now that he had determined to rejoin the army he seemed almost eager to get on with it; perhaps he'd known it was what he would elect to do from the very time he gave ten shillings for an ill-gotten ticket to freedom, but had needed something or someone to reveal to him what was in his own heart. Unwittingly, Francis Lee had supplied the leaven that moved him.

It seemed incredible to Becky that the enemy could actually be close enough to force them out. Making a final round through the shuttered house, she realized there was already an abandoned air about it. The sound of Ben's hammer echoed through the deserted rooms as he pounded boards over the front windows. The door would be nailed shut when they were all out; even though it would never deter the British Army, it might prevent Tory looting. Becky gave Sam a push to hurry him along, calling to Cate not to forget the jug with water. "Mr. Francis says we mustn't travel without water." Actually it was Peter who had put the notion in Francis's head, insisting they pack their own food and water. It was foolhardy to rely on what they might find along the way, he cautioned. In wartime, it is all for one, but seldom does the reverse of the adage appear to be true, Peter had stated solemnly, not from the maturity of his years, but from his experience.

They set out before dawn, heading for the open road before the city was awake. In the east a weak December sun cracked the somber sky by the time they reached the Schuylkill. The Carriage bumped and jogged along the rutted road, a treacherous morass which froze by night and thawed by day. The passage of thousands of troops and the ravages of winter had speckled it with scores of potholes. Raw was the only word for the damp, depressing morning, made worse for Becky because she couldn't shake the image of rats deserting a sinking ship which had planted itself in her mind when Francis told her it was time to pack. Huddling under a blanket, she wondered how Francis and Peter were faring on horseback, and if the British were within the city even now. The women in the carriage shared the iron foot warmer. At least temporarily it lulled them into thinking they weren't going to freeze. Becky prayed it wouldn't snow before they reached Baltimore.

Ben's "Hoa!" and the screech of the traces reached their ears at the same time. The carriage lurched to an uneven stop. Sam was up on top with Ben, his childish voice babbling into the sudden stillness. Ben told him to hush as Becky and Cate peered through the dingy window. What they saw was enough to alert the two women instantly to the awful reality of war.

A man, dressed in the frayed remnants of what had once been a British uniform, straddled a body on the ground. He wasn't more than thirty feet from the roadbed and seemed unaware he had an audience. Becky and Cate watched in horror as he rammed his body ever faster between the spread legs on the ground beneath him. Becky could see a small bare foot and one knobby knee—he was violating a child! A scream bubbled in her throat, an involuntary sound over which she had no control. But before she let it go, Cate's hand was tight across her mouth, fingers digging into flesh. The crack of a musket pierced the air. The rutting soldier, for Becky could think of nothing but an animal, lurched once, then fell forward, smothering his victim. A circle of crimson grew ever wider in the back of the frayed jacket.

"Did you have to do it that way?" Francis appeared stunned, but jumped quickly from his horse.

"What else?" shrugged Peter. "This is war. It's them or us. I told you that."

Within seconds an untidy country woman and two grubby urchins appeared from nowhere and began tugging at the body. Peter nudged the woman aside and, grabbing the man by his feet, yanked him off the girl. The head of the dead soldier bumped on the frozen ground, the arms falling limply in a scarecrow pose.

"My God! She can't be more than ten," Francis moaned under his breath. At first he feared the child was dead, so still she lay, her eyelids blue and shuttered against the world.

"Nine years," the mother said, kneeling beside her ravished daughter. The girl's entire body had a bluish cast, whether from fright, or the cold, who could tell? There was blood between the spindly legs. The woman restored modesty with a quick jerk on the homespun skirt. "I don't need no help. Leastways not from the likes of you. That was the third one," she mumbled, more to herself than to the three men, none of whom had moved. "I couldn't do nothin' agin three, could I? Not without exposin' my others. The first two got through with her quick-like and slunk off. She'd stopped screamin' by the time this 'un got to her. I see'd what you did, an' I thank you for it, but I don't need no help from the likes of you." She jabbed her finger at the dead man and thrust her chin at Peter's uniform. It became clear she considered all soldiers to be of the same mettle.

Peter wondered, after what had happened, who could blame her? "There's no point in arguing. She means it, poor biddy." He turned away, nodding to Ben that they would move on.

"But the body. Shouldn't we bury it or something?" Francis couldn't believe this was happening and that they would just leave the dead man where he lay.

"What's the or something? They don't bury ours. Any further delay will only get us in trouble, endanger Mrs. Lee. We've done all we can for these miserable souls. You heard that addled creature. The vultures will take care of him soon enough." Peter spat his contempt onto the uncaring earth.

Francis stood, watching, before remembering his wife—Becky had seen the rape as well as the killing—stumbling in his hurry, he returned to the carriage. As he reached the door, it burst open and Cate fell against him in her haste to get out. She doubled over, her body heaving as she gagged, retching into the weeds.

Becky sat sphinx-like, her reflexes turned to stone. First I will explain to him about Cate, she told her voice. "Cate was raped ... she was near the same age, do you remember I told you ... yet, today, she knew better than to scream or get sick until it was over. And I didn't. By screaming I was about to alert that beast, had Catey not prevented me." She groped for his hand. "I'm sorry, darling. You were right to be anxious about getting out of Philadelphia. Away from the war. You were right. Now, I'm very much afraid."

He squeezed her hands, loving her. "I'm the one who's sorry. But how could I have shielded you? I'd do anything to erase the sight from your mind if it was in my power. Oh, God, I can't do anything. Let it be a lesson to us both."

❦

That evening they bid goodbye to Peter with heavy hearts. "I don't know how to thank you," Francis began, referring to the morning's incident. "Without your quick thinking we might have had a real fight on our hands." Uncomfortable with farewells, he wished they could be gotten past somehow, without all the words and sadness.

Peter searched the older man's face, amazed at how much the Virginian had come to mean to him. "Francis," he said. He, too, felt awkward standing there in the chilly room above the tavern where the Lees would spend the night. "I hope you don't mind that I call you by your Christian name, my friend, it is I who am grateful to you. For whether you know it or not, your calm understanding has kept me from destroying everything that was dear to me. My home, my parents, my hopes for the future. I was ready to sacrifice it all. Throw it over. To bitterness, to anger, to hatred and revenge. I would have desecrated my brother's memory. I owe you ... everything."

Francis studied the tips of his boots. This youth certainly knew how to touch a chord in him. "Peter, I only listened. That is all I did, nothing else." The young man's frankness deeply moved him, leaving him at a loss for words; there were few who attempted to speak such thoughts aloud. "Any friend would have listened," he added lamely.

"But that's my point. Only a *true* friend would listen to such a tale ... and understand it. And ... well, thank you, Sir, from my heart. Most sincerely, thank you." Peter reached for Francis's hand, clasping it between his own two strong ones. "Until we meet again."

"Until we meet again, Peter. I'll keep in touch with your whereabouts through your father. As soon as we return to Philadelphia I shall look him up." His eyes misted, but not before he saw that Peter's had, also.

Becky, watching the interchange between them, felt overwhelmed by an alarming premonition they would never see Peter Hauck again in this life. It was only with extreme effort she erased the fear in her eyes before Peter turned to her to bid farewell.

Baltimore

They put twenty-five to thirty miles a day behind them; in bone chilling dampness, through blowing snow and rain turned to sleet, over the foreboding roads of a strange and unfriendly countryside, they fled before the imagined threat of an enemy unseen. In the Lee's small carriage and four, the retreat became everything frightening and disagreeable that Becky could imagine. Suffering the fickle Pennsylvania and Maryland winter astride a horse, Francis found it even worse. Except for what Becky termed the "swaying stomach" which she insisted came upon a carriage passenger after a few hours of bounce and jostle, she didn't debate the point.

The third day out, the lead mare developed a limp; not noticeable at first, the condition worsened steadily. Lilliput, behind her in harness, grew visibly irritated by the uneven pace, nipping at the rump ahead of her until it became obvious they had to stop. A cursory examination told Francis a sharp piece of rock had lodged under the left forehoof. It was wedged so deeply he feared it might be necessary to trade the animal, as she was certain to continue limping even after the stone was removed, if it was possible to even remove it.

Shivering against a biting wind, Ben also studied the developing situation. As expected, his master eventually turned to him. Wordlessly, Ben demanded full attention, then raised a finger to poke at his head under the old beaver top-hat Francis had recently acquired for him. Several minutes passed. Francis waited impatiently for the slave to speak, knowing if he pushed Ben now, he might just as well count on looking for a fresh horse.

Eventually a smile curved Ben's mouth; how comforting to know a man well enough to be able to anticipate what was to happen. He guessed it didn't often happen that way—not between black and white. But he'd learned a long time ago, without a doubt, that given time and the inclination, Ben could probably put the entire worrisome incident to rights. So he allowed the slave to take his sweet time, which could be considerable.

"It's pressin 'gainst de frog," Ben announced. "Wedg'd 'tween de bar an' de frog. Dat's all, Marse Frank. Gimme 'bout a hour an' I'll have dis ol' hoss ready to run. I'll have t' unhitch her. Got t' git her off by herse'f t' work on her."

The Negro was as good as his word. He pried the stone loose, not without a certain amount of difficulty, and examined the damage. It took him some time to locate the root he needed, and the moss. The secret was one he'd learned from old Doc Ephrim at Mount Airy, and Ben had no intention of sharing it with his master. It wasn't long until he'd pounded the stringy fibre to a pulp, and worked it into the winter moss. The juice would deaden the pain in the injured frog before the moss worked loose. Packing the hoof carefully, he talked the mare out of her skittishness the entire time, knowing she'd forget the discomfort soon enough. When he'd finished, he walked her around for a few minutes before returning to the carriage. "We's ready t' roll, suh," Ben declared with a fine display of pride.

ᕦᕤ

With no further troubles, late on the fifth day they crested a rise to spot a cluster of dark buildings huddled on the shore of the Patapsco River. Francis decided instantly that Baltimore looked every bit as dreary as he remembered it from a visit many years before. "I'll take the lead, Ben," he shouted. Spurring Cameron and leaning forward in the saddle, he strained to overtake the team. Sensing the end of the day the horses began putting on speed. They, too, had spotted the settlement which meant oats and fresh hay. Pelting down the final mile, mouths foaming, eyes rolling wildly, tails and manes whipped by the wind, they were as unprepared for the mist turned downpour that greeted them near the city outskirts as were the humans. Francis became alarmed at the treacherous condition of the muddy road and motioned Ben to pull the carriage to the high side where the ruts weren't so deep. It had obviously been raining for hours here, the streets were nothing but intersecting branches of swirling streams. Forced to proceed at a plodding walk, the horses soon found even that was difficult going.

Francis hadn't the foggiest idea of where to go and saw not a soul to ask. At the first tavern he reined in, dismounted and went inside. He was gone only a few minutes. Becky watched him return, crossing the street in the fading light, head bent against the angle of the rain.

"An uncouth bunch if ever I saw one. Not in the least helpful," he called to her above the wind. "We have to go on." She opened the door several inches in order to understand him and rain ran down her arm, collecting in a puddle in the wool of her skirt. Absentmindedly, he dabbed at the water with a damp glove. "It seems some of the Congress has found lodgings down the way. To the left, the keeper said, at the sign of the apothecary. I'm hoping to locate Richard. He promised to see what he could arrange for us. Keep your chin up awhile longer. Are you dreadfully tired? I am."

How downcast he did look. And miserable. "I'm delighted to hear, at least, that we're in the wrong end of town! It's got to be less sinister wherever we're headed. I could do with a bowl of hot broth and a good sleep, if that's what you mean about being tired."

"I'll do the best I can. love, to see you have both, and as soon as possible." Slamming the door, he felt the carriage shake under the force of his hand.

A splash of water hit Becky's face as he did so, but she scarcely noticed it as she watched him wade through the mud. Bless those well-stitched boots. If Baltimore's winter continued like this he'd soon be forced to purchase a second pair. The street was little short of an impassable bog from what she could see. No better than the trail to Menokin had been that first winter; quite an appalling state of affairs for a metropolis, she thought.

Ben's whip flicked into the near darkness. Inside the carriage they felt the tug as the animals leaned into the traces and they began to inch forward, mud sucking at the wheels. Becky peered out at several houses with drawn blinds, thinking the graceless gray bulk of them did nothing to welcome strangers. Baltimore appeared anything but promising. The consequences of their flight from Philadelphia began to evidence themselves. Somehow they'd have to swallow disappointment and make the best of whatever happened. The first thing to pray for was that Francis wouldn't catch another cold. He'd barely recovered from the last one; the danger came when he took a chill, so probably there was no avoiding it. Still, as a precaution, once they found lodging, she'd lace him with brandy and apply a hot poultice to clear his chest. Then, realizing the carriage had ceased to move, she thought perhaps they were arrived at their destination.

Ben shouted at the horses. "Git up, you lazy good fo' nothin' critters!" His whip cracked the air again and again, demanding the team to step out.

Hearing this, Becky looked to Cate, her son asleep against her shoulder. "No such luck, Cate, I hoped we'd found our lodging. But I fear that's not why we're stopped."

"Don't soun' good, Miss Becky. Ben's havin' a heap o' trouble, an' we ain't moved one bit. De wheels might's well be square as roun' fo' all de rollin' we's done."

Becky laughed. "What would I ever do without you, Catey? You can always bring a smile, no matter what." Outside it was so black, even the street had disappeared from view.

"She's stuck for sure, Ben!" they heard Francis yell. "The right rear wheel is stuck clear to the axle in this damned muck. I'll watch. Give it one more try."

It was to no avail. Whatever they did only drove the wheels deeper. It took three hours for Francis to locate his brother, borrow another chaise to move Becky and their belongings to the room Richard had let for them. He finally managed to have the empty carriage pried out of the mud sometime close to midnight. Rain poured without pity the entire time. Returning at last to Bolton's rooming house, soaked to the skin and spattered almost beyond recognition, he found himself in surprisingly good spirits. He suspected it was because he was too bloody tired to feel anything, but maybe it was partly due to the high compliment Peter had paid him that he hadn't stopped thinking about all day.

He found Becky alone. Cate had fed the fire to a blaze, then taken Samuel with her to bargain with the proprietress for a hot supper for them all. Francis, surveying the room, hung his dripping cape on a peg he spotted in a chink of the chimney. He peeled his coat off, forcing a grin as he studied his sodden boots.

"Here, let me help you, darling." Then, taking a second look, "Where's Ben?" she asked uncertainly.

"With the horses. He'll be a while I'm afraid. Mrs. Bolton has given Ben and Cate a place to sleep in the back of the house." He braced himself while Becky tugged at the boot, ignoring the mud as best she could.

"When we get you out of these wet things, you'll feel ever so much better," she promised. "You'll see. A roof over our heads, a warm fire, and dry clothes work wonders, I've found. They've never seemed quite so dear as they do tonight."

"I hope so, love. What a night! What a wretched journey, worth nothing but forgetting." With a groan he lifted the other foot. Becky raised a hand to brush her hair back, smudging her nose, and he laughed. "Well, Mrs. Lee, tell me, how do you think you'll enjoy life in the incredibly unlikely city of Baltimore?"

Her eyes hinted mischief. She knew so long as he was there it would never be a hopeless place. "I should think I prefer to wait a day or so before I respond, Mr. Lee. At the moment I'm too immersed in the grime of it to make a judgment." Leaning his boots near the hearth, she held out two mud-caked hands for inspection. "Just look at me, darling."

Seeing her, so disheveled, yet her eyes sparkling with love for him, he was touched once again by her goodness. "We're safe and together. After what's happened in the last few weeks, I hope it's enough for you in these perilous times. It's all I have to offer, love." He kissed the one clean spot left in the palm of her hand and drew her into his lap. When Cate returned with a steaming chowder and fresh bread and jam, she found them asleep in the chair.

The newcomers to Baltimore grumbled constantly; it is hard to say whether the mud or the exorbitant prices occasioned the most debate as the Congress settled into the new routine. Some of the delegations fell short of their required numbers and were forced to sacrifice their vote. More than a few among them had succumbed to the call of home rather than face a lonely miserable Christmas in Maryland. The change, however, seemed to have accomplished *some* good—Sam Adams said it appeared they were at last proceeding with a much needed new vigor, despite the grumbles. Of course there were serious complainers, like William Hooper, who fretted that every decision was made without proper understanding or sufficient study; he was heard muttering frequently about the ignoramuses amongst his fellow officials, a category which undoubtedly included not only Sam Adams, but Richard Henry Lee as well.

Within days the Congress reached a decision to establish separate Boards of War, Treasury, Admiralty, and Commerce, whose members would be appointed from outside its own body. Shortly after that, they agreed that General Washington should be confirmed with supreme powers over his army, these to continue for a six month period. The first days in Baltimore were as action-packed as any the young government had known. It kept them from dwelling too heavily on the dismal military scene, and they all but forgot their regional feuds over the Confederation.

On the day before Christmas, Francis was handed a letter from Virginia. In the corner, neatly inscribed, was the name of Becky's new brother-in-law, Mann Page. This particular day dragged in a seemingly endless series of non-accomplishments, it seemed to Francis, until he was finally on his way home with the exciting news. He gave Cameron his head, allowing him to pick his way through the muddy streets, directing him only at the cross roads. His Christmas gift to Becky, an elegant blue velvet cape he had ordered made before they left Philadelphia, he'd considered the best possible of surprises—until this morning's news from Mann which he knew would please her far more than any gift of clothing. Riding home, he pondered how proud he was of Becky. She had cheerfully survived the journey, accepted the unfortunate change in their home life, rarely complaining, and during the first week in Baltimore had ventured into the public rooms of the lodging house to become acquainted with Mrs. Bolton, the proprietress. He saw that they seemed to enjoy each other's company, sharing an hour or so each afternoon while they sewed or talked together. Mrs. Bolton, a rather dumpy-looking widow in her fifties, had taken an instant liking to the young Virginia housewife it seemed; having two grown daughters of her own, Becky explained, who both lived at a distance, she was lonely. So was Becky.

"How else can a poor widow expect to find her next day's bread if she doesn't earn it by the sweat of her brow?" he heard the landlady ask as he entered the hall. Francis had been subjected to the plight of widows through the example of his sister Hannah; there did seem an inequity in the way society treated them.

"But your daughters. Surely they can help?" Becky could think of no more to say. It was Christmas Eve and she was feeling very homesick.

Her companion cleared her throat. "Well, they send a pittance now and then. Nothing regular, mind you. Whatever they can afford, I suspect, but it would never be enough to sustain me. I hope you'll never have to find out for yourself, dear Mrs. Lee, but the world does little fretting over the plight of women left on their own! The powers that be are always quick enough to claim the taxes, however. At any rate, it's a godsend to me to have you here for these weeks. My humble lodging has never been so full for so many days running. Nor have I had such charming guests, I might add."

Francis had paused in the hall to hear the conversation. It was more than likely the dear, sweet woman had increased her rates considerably, he thought, upon learning of the dire need of such desperate men as himself requiring immediate lodgings. Strangers to the city were indeed at the mercy of local entrepreneurs; although he hadn't mentioned it to Becky, he had no reason to believe the motherly, overweight Mrs. Bolton was any different in that respect from the others.

"Excuse me, ladies," he said from the doorway, giving them his disarming smile. "Something has come up. Rather a family matter, if you'll excuse us, Madam." To Becky he said, "Come, my love. Upstairs. I have something to show you."

Winking at Lydia Bolton, and waving the letter mysteriously, he started up the staircase. "I've no doubt Mrs. Lee will be back directly, to share her good news, Mrs. Bolton."

Becky crossed the room quickly, tugging at his sleeve as soon as she caught up. "What is it?"

"You'll see."

"What's it about? Will I like it, for it's surely a surprise, isn't it?"

"Oh, most definitely."

"Then tell me! You are so exasperating at times! You can see how I'm fairly trembling with anticipation."

Opening the door to their chamber, he drew her inside, closing it behind them. "First, my love, your Christmas gift from me." On the way home, he'd planned exactly how he'd go about it. From under the bed he pulled a parcel, carefully wrapped and tied, slowly undoing the twine that held it.

Becky was frantic with excitement. "Oh, I wonder what it is. Whatever in the world is it? I promise I haven't touched the package since you told me not to," she assured him. The letter slipped her mind as she concentrated on his slow, deliberate opening of the brown wrapping.

"Close your eyes, Becky. Very tight, and don't peek." When she obeyed him, he shook out the cloak, frowning at the creases made by folding. It was truly a beautiful piece of cloth, of good enough quality to shake off wrinkles he hoped. He'd been so fortunate the seamstress had it, and it had cost him dear. Stepping behind her, he dropped it over her shoulders, adjusting the folds.

"May I open now?" She was already fingering the nap.

"Not yet. Not quite yet." He maneuvered her in a circle, noting with satisfaction that the cape fell nearly to the hem of her skirt. Perfect. Then, opening her hand he pressed the letter in it. "There. Now when you open, you'll see what I have got you for Christmas ... and then you will read that your sister Polly is any day to arrive in this very city! Mann is elected to the Congress!"

Her eyes flew open. She took in the new cloak in an instant; the news took longer to absorb. "Polly? Here? I can't believe it! Oh, it's too lovely. When? Oh, darling." Bursting into tears, she flung herself into his waiting arms.

Francis was crushed. "It's too much. What have I done? I should never have presented you with both surprises at once!" He smoothed her hair, hugging her, crooning as to a child.

"Oh, no. It's not too much. It's only that I'm so happy. I've been moping around all day, wishing we were in Richmond

County, but now I feel ever so much better. To think I shall have my own dear Polly here, and you have given me such a lovely gift! Oh, darling. It's a perfect Christmas. Our blessed Lord and all his saints are smiling on me this day! I am so very happy."

He wondered if she knew how much she sometimes sounded like Alice Shippen, but he was amused and pleased by her gratitude. "I love you, Rebecca Lee. When you are happy, I am happy. Where are you going?" he asked as she had her hand on the doorknob.

"To tell Mrs. Bolton the news and show her my cape, of course!"

☙

Before the ringing in of the new year there was another cause for celebration. "A victory at last!" Francis shouted, bursting into Richard's room without a by-your-leave. He found his brother with both legs propped up, nursing his gout.

Richard beckoned him in. "Where? What have you heard?"

"Washington, my dear brother. Our heretofore unaccomplished general has finally earned the acclaim of the Congress! He marched upon the Hessian encampment at Trenton and routed the whole damned lot of Rall's regiments. He's taken over nine hundred prisoners!"

"My God! What good news, Loudoun! What arms have they captured? Any cannon?" Leaning forward, Richard impatiently grasped his bad leg with both hands. Lifting it to the floor, he grunted a little with the pain. "Hand me my boots, will you? I must read the dispatches."

"But can you wear your boots? Over that foot, swollen as it is?"

"I am bloody well going to suffer it."

Uncertain how bad his brother's leg had become, Francis was relieved he could walk tonight. The bad days seemed to come in spurts, more frequently this winter than ever before. "I thought the news would cheer you, R.H., but never expected it to cure you! Captured battle flags, the spoils of war, have arrived from the camp. Washington's account is restrained as usual, but there are several eyewitnesses in town spreading their versions. It's all quite a legitimate reason to celebrate, I should think." Sobering, he felt compelled to add his apprehensions. "Of course there is still the problem of the enlistments which are soon to expire. We'll have no army if Washington isn't allowed to pay an extra bounty to those who agree to stay on. Something must be done immediately to grant him the money."

"What do you suggest?" Richard tested his weight, wincing as he limped gingerly across the room. "Whenever I want that bastard Lucas, he's never around," he grumbled, after the fashion of a man who is not well.

"I don't know. Where will the dollars come from?"

Richard sighed, shoving his arm into his coat. "We'll print them, I suppose, as before."

"That's exactly why we're in this pickle right now. We can't continue to simply print money, for God's sake, whenever we need it."

"I know. I know. But what else? I keep harping on it. Until we have the support of France, what other choices have we?"

Several evenings later Francis watched as Lucas helped his master from the saddle. Richard's gout was barely improved, yet he'd insisted on going out. In addition, he noted, his brother was more than a little tipsy. They had consumed port at Nelson's lodging before turning to rum at the tavern, where many toasts had been made to His Excellency's glorious victory, for that is how they were referring to Washington now. When a courier had arrived with the general's latest dispatch it had been reason enough to break out another jug of rum; for drunk on the nectar of victory at Trenton, or swept by their leader's fervent plea, or both, whole regiments of weary soldiers had actually signed on for another month of hell! It seemed incredible to Francis that men, hungry, exhausted, battle weary and, yes, even barefoot, would agree to such a thing. It made him feel very humble. His part was so insignificant by comparison. He wondered if Peter had been there, at the battle of Trenton? Shivering in the cold night air, he swayed slightly, fumbling out for support. He was aware he lurched into Richard in the darkness.

"Hey, what'sa matter? You drunk, Loudoun?"

Francis chuckled in spite of himself, happy to escape from thoughts of Peter Hauck floundering in snow and mud. "I don't think so, but I have a brother who most certainly is."

"Who me? Surely you jesht, old chap." Richard felt very relaxed which was, for him, a superbly peculiar diversion. His feet didn't even hurt.

'I've no doubt you are hopelessly inebriated. You slurred, Sir!" Francis stated indignantly.

"I didn't!"

"Oh, but you did. You slurred."

Laughing, their arms around each other, the brothers wobbled up the walk, leaving Lucas to the care of the horses. The house was dark except for the friendly candle in a second floor window announcing that Becky was probably awake.

"Do you suppose Mrs. Bolton could arrange to accommodate another Mrs. Lee, Frank?" Richard queried suddenly, halting to stare at the candle's illumination.

Francis could scarcely believe his ears—Richard, who didn't believe it possible to mix business and pleasure. "Anne?" When his brother nodded, he said, "I'll never understand you. You've maintained all along that dragging a wife into these circumstances could only compound the worry."

"I'm damned lonely, Loudoun. I've not slept well for weeks. I think I shall send for her. What do you think?"

"Fine. Fine! Becky will be beside herself. With the Pages coming, and now Anne, it will be a regular family reunion. But what about the children?"

Richard hiccuped. "Well, I don't know. She'll work something out. What wives are for, ishn't it? Smooth things out for a man, make his life bearable, warm his bed when he returns from the abominations of government, or whatever?"

Some wives manage much more than that, Francis told himself, leaning his weight against Mrs. Bolton's front door until the latch clicked. Some wives are the true jewels of the universe. Worth risking everything for, and then some. He ached with a sudden poignant desire for the feel of Becky's arms around him. But then, when did he not?

What with General Washington's triumph, the arrival of loved ones expected, and Becky waiting for him upstairs, it seemed 1777 would be riding in on a high wave indeed. He tipped his battered tricorn to the new year as he ascended the sagging steps of the Baltimore rooming house behind Richard's clumpy limp.

'Tis Vain to Sow the Field

It was a pleasant, almost warm day In February. Becky and Polly decided on a walk to the tobacconist where Becky planned to buy pipe tobacco for Francis. "It seems ridiculous that at home we plant row after row of the stuff, and yet here we're forced to buy it, doesn't it?"

"Hmm? Oh ... the tobacco?" Polly asked, more interested in a group of children playing kick ball in the dreary roadway.

Becky went on: "Unless someone who is coming this way happens to think of us, or once or twice when Francis arranged for a special shipment, why, he's had to buy it. And as you can see, the price of everything in Baltimore is quite outrageous." Becky inclined her head to the shopkeeper, maintaining a formal aloofness, as she wondered how much he'd raised the price, knowing she was one of the Congress wives. It served him right if he'd heard every word she'd said to Polly about high prices. "Scheming merchant," she mumbled under her breath as they left.

Moving on down the street, the children's high pitched banter behind them, Polly spoke. "I wish we'd known how things were with you. Mann and I would happily have brought you whatever you needed, Becky. Not that we had an inch of room in the carriage!" she laughed, "but we'd have squeezed ... for you and Frank." Polly took a long, penetrating glance at her older sister. "You look just marvelous. All the hardships seem to have agreed with you. I love your cape, Becky. It's splendid. We've seen nothing like that in the county for years! So modern and stylish." Glancing down at her own brown woolen wrap, serviceable and plain, she nudged her sister, forcing her further off the road. "It's too muddy here, where the carts and horses have gone. It's not a very nice place to walk really, is it?"

"No. I guess it isn't. But I'm happy to be able to walk it with you anyway. Polly, there's not a thing wrong with your clothes. To tell the truth, they remind me so much of home, I can hardly stand it!" It occurred to Becky at that moment her new blue cape was probably taking on the shade of the Baltimore dirt, while Polly's practical brown one resisted soiling.

"Well, you just don't know how it is, that's all. We can't order any of the fabrics we used to get, nothing fancy at all, nothing fine or elegant, nothing ...." Polly's voice faded into silence; her mouth in a pout.

"Nothing ... *English?*" Becky supplied, smirking.

"Oh." Polly tossed her head. "I suppose that's what I do mean at that. And don't say it! I know I shouldn't complain. It's the very least one can do for the cause, or so I've been told often enough. But honestly ... wearing homespun, and dresses made out of any old thing one can scrounge up, I declare Becky, is not my idea of how a lady ought to dress! Anyway," she added, skipping to keep up with her sister's determined pace, "I'm delighted to see that in your part of the world, at least, things don't seem quite so depressed or you wouldn't have that gorgeous new cape, now would you?"

Becky wasn't amused, but seeing no reason to apologize for her precious velvet cloak, she decided to make allowance for Polly's youth. "I do think Francis went to a great deal of trouble and expense to arrange for this. It took a bit of doing just to locate a seamstress who had the fabric. How strange you should refer to this place as 'my part of the world.' I don't think of it as being very different anymore ... although I suppose I did at first," she finished, drawing her brows together.

"Why, Becky, you know it's different! God knows, I never would have dreamed of coming here, had it not been for your presence. Of course, Pennsylvania is better, I guess," she suggested doubtfully. "There must be many shops in Philadelphia. Frank told me it was a bustling, progressive place. Do you like it there?" But she wasn't really waiting for a reply; Philadelphia was an uncertain prospect, Baltimore was now. "Let's have tea when we get back to Mrs. Bolton's. Just the two of us! We could stop at that baker's shop you told me about, buy some biscuits or something."

"Don't you think we should ask Mrs. Pinchard, Anne, to join us? It would be rude, I think, not to, Polly." Richard Henry's wife had arrived late in January in answer to her husband's summons, leaving all her children in the care of Chantilly's governess. "She's very lonely without her little ones, poor thing."

"It's selfish of me, I know, but I hoped we might just sit and gossip a bit about Richmond County, Papa and Mama, my new home at Mannsfield, or Menokin, or whatever comes to mind. Like we used to do before the war took you away. I've things I want to tell you about and, well, you know ... private things."

Becky huddled into her cape, drawing the hood tighter around her face. The wind was picking up, she noticed. It was colder than when they set out; a winter sun could never be depended upon. "What you want to tell me about, Polly ... could it be that you and Mann are going to have a baby?"

Polly stopped, a startled expression on her rosy face. "How did you know? I didn't think anyone could tell yet! I wasn't going to tell you until ... well, until the time was right and I thought you'd want to hear it. I didn't want to upset you or anything," she finished nervously.

"For heaven's sake, Polly, why would it upset me to hear such lovely news?"

Polly was uncertain. "Oh, you know. Mama said not to go bragging or carrying on about it. That's all."

Becky dispelled her sister's fears with a smile and a hug. It really didn't bother her anymore, this talk of babies. She'd become used to other people having them when she didn't. She'd also learned to cherish her precious time alone with Francis. "I'm not sure I'd even want a baby now, Polly. It would mean sharing Francis, and I don't see him enough as it is anymore, to want to share him with anyone!"

"Oh, Becky, I'm so happy you're taking it this way. Mama worries about you. It's not the same with Annie. She's married three years and doesn't have any, but neither she nor anyone else seems the least bit concerned about it. Anne is too busy bustling up and down the river visiting, to care if she *ever* has any!"

"Here we are at the baker's shop," Becky announced, taking Polly's arm. A tiny bell over the door tinkled their entrance, and the pungent scent of gingerbread welcomed them. "He makes a little cookie out of French chocolate, when he can get it, that's delicious. Shall we see if he has some of those? And tomorrow, Polly, I think I shall write to Mama and tell her not to worry about me anymore. I'm the happiest wife in the world, no exceptions. Isn't this a perfectly marvelous place?" she asked, pointing to some miniature cakes decorated with pale pink icing.

But on the way home, she brought the subject up again. "I'm really pleased for you, Polly ... that you are with child. I hope you understand that. We'll have to take good care of you, all of us, so you can present Mann, and the Congress of course, with a healthy little patriot." She kept her head lowered to hide the tears, unbidden, she felt stinging her eyelids.

Polly's arm went around Becky's shoulder. Licking the fingers of her other hand, she said, "These are yummy, Becky! You were right. Do you think it's safe for me to eat them? Oh, I'm sure it is," she laughed. "I've decided we should ask Mrs. Pinchard to share our tea after all. We don't want her to feel left out, do we? Do we have any tea, by the way, or must we have some wretched substitute?"

"It's so good to have you here, Polly! I can't tell you how good it is. I have some lovely mint leaves I've been saving for just such an occasion," Becky assured her. "They make a fine brew."

～

The enemy didn't occupy Philadelphia after all; the three members of Congress who remained there to handle the business of the new country wrote daily of the brashness of the Tories in the city. General Washington claimed he couldn't prevent it if the British did decide to attack Philadelphia, so for the time being the Congress had little choice but to stick it out in muddy, backward Baltimore, plagued to death by the distance and the prices. The victories at Trenton and later at Princeton would soon cease to elate anyone, as concern mounted over the deterioration of General Washington's army camped for the winter near Morristown in New Jersey. Smallpox and hunger ran rampant through the camp; desertions multiplied. It was ordered that every soldier be inoculated, thus for weeks at a time large numbers were ill. For some amazing reason, however, the general's soldiers were able to effectively harass and hamper the attempts of Howe's much larger force to obtain forage for themselves and their horses; camped in the New Brunswick hills, the British supply lines remained at the mercy of the Continentals. Under the circumstances, the Americans had to content themselves with making it difficult for their enemy to obtain food—a puny victory—when what they wanted was to drive him from their shores.

It was evening and the family group had gathered around the dining table. "The disgrace is that the general can't drive them out of the Jersies altogether!" Richard exploded as he entered the room. He took his seat at the head of table, his glare menacing each of the company before him, before reaching for his Madeira. "It's a pill I can't swallow that we must allow our enemy to winter peacefully on a hillside in the heartland of America!"

Anne Pinchard Lee sought her husband's hand under the table, a sweet but firm expression on her face. "You're late, my dear. I'm sorry we didn't wait for you. But Richard," she reminded him, "you promised we wouldn't discuss politics tonight. That it was to be a celebration before Polly and Mann must be inoculated tomorrow. Please. Mrs. Bolton has made special arrangements to allow us private dining this evening."

Richard felt irrevocably out of sorts. He wondered what on earth they should possibly have to talk about if the state of the country was excluded, but out of courtesy he raised his glass. "To be sure, dear Anne. I did indeed make a promise. Well, then. May I propose a toast ... to the safety of our general, the increase of his forces, and the improvement of our hospitals! Now, if it please you, I shall remain silent."

Francis frowned at his brother. "Technically speaking, that could be called a military toast, Anne, not a political one," he said, hoping to lighten the mood brought on by his brother's arrival.

"I should like to propose a toast also, if I may," Becky began, as soon as they had all sipped. "To a speedy and safe recovery, for Polly and our dear brother-in-law, from the smallpox serum."

"Hear, hear," called Francis. "May they suffer but mildly from the inoculation!" All glasses were raised once more.

"I wish Dr. Shippen were here to administer the serum himself," Polly admitted. Neither she nor Mann were anxious to submit to inoculation, but it had been so strongly suggested by the good doctor they dared not ignore the warning.

"It's not the receiving the injection that is the uncomfortable part, dear sister," Francis assured her. "It is later, your reaction to it. Right, Becky? Of course, our cases were far worse than anything that will happen to you, as I understand it. We had the disease itself, pure and simple, no inoculation." The words barely out of his mouth, Francis seemed to have forgotten Anne's warning to Richard. Turning to his brother he blurted, "With Morgan relieved of command of hospitals, and Shippen in as director-general, we should soon see some improvements in the treatment of the sick and injured. My guess is that many soldiers will probably survive to fight again, who formerly might have perished. Morgan's folly and inefficiency, I hope, is removed forever."

Becky knew he was thinking of Karl Hauck and the surgeon who amputated his leg. "Has Dr. Shippen been formally appointed then?"

"Only on a temporary basis, to fill the place of Dr. Morgan. But we're moving toward a permanent appointment to the job," Richard answered quickly. "Rush is against it, of course."

"With the three of us pulling for him, Dr. Shippen can hardly lose, I think," Mann Page added. "Poor fellows, it was bad enough when they had you two lined up on an issue. Now we shall be the formidable three!"

"Tell me about Dr. Rush, Richard." Becky leaned her elbows on the table, leveling her gaze at her brother-in-law, who had yet to begin his meal. "I know he's a prominent physician in Philadelphia, as is Dr. Shippen. Why should he be against our kinsman's appointment?"

Anne's sigh was audible, but it passed unnoticed. It seemed no one cared about her plans for the evening, not even Becky, who obviously had been weaned on the political back and forth every evening, had come to expect it and seemed even to enjoy it.

Richard made Becky a mock salute. "Dear Rebecca, it's always a pleasure to have you at table. A man need not harbor fear of boring you with his conversation. No intention to slight the other ladies present, to be sure." He smiled congenially at his wife before continuing, "You'll allow me to answer the lady's question, will you not? It goes back to the time, my dear, when Benjamin Rush and William Shippen were both founders of the Medical College in Philadelphia ... but I'm sure you already know that much. At any rate, over the years there have no doubt been the usual feuds and fusses as I understand it. And Rush has long been an intimate friend of Dr. Morgan. But aside from that, I just wonder if our able Dr. Rush does not have a secret yearning to drop his place in Congress and take over the hospitals himself? What do you think, Loudoun? Any chance that might be why he's taken such an avid interest in new appointments? He took it upon himself to follow in the army's footsteps during the campaign at Princeton, even treating wounded officers. To be sure, he searched out those of sufficient rank. I had several letters from him concerning his treatment of General Mercer, you know. And then the poor fellow died." Richard made a clicking noise with his tongue which while not exactly unkind, was certainly not sympathetic. "Rush has been quick to point out that a British surgeon got to Mercer first, of course."

Francis watched his brother carefully. Richard was in a nasty mood, there was no denying it. Something must have happened before he arrived home. "If Benjamin Rush expects to get an appointment to military hospitals, he'd better cease his snide and frequent criticisms of our general. He's become very careless to whom he points out Washington's lack of military finesse and his inability to make meaningful decisions." Was he heaping fuel on Richard's already blazing fire, he wondered? He hadn't thought of it that way until he'd spoken his piece.

"There are times," Richard said, choosing his words carefully, "when such ... ah, criticism of the general may not be totally ... unwarranted, Frank."

A pregnant silence followed; everyone seemed concentrated on the empty dinner plates. No one looked at Richard. He, however, apparently oblivious or uncaring that he had shocked them went on, "As I said earlier, it's disgraceful Washington's not found it in his power to drive them out of the Jersey hills. Every day he tarries, they gain strength. Our own deserters are helping to fill the British ranks. They're being offered four pounds to join, that is if they come equipped with a musket. I have it on good authority."

"Then you fault Washington?" Mann asked finally. "John Adams says we venerate him far too highly, that it was wrong to endow him with the superior powers, even if it is for only six months ... but John Adams is not a Virginian. He owes no loyalty on that score. I suppose some would say that gives him the ability to see the whole more clearly."

Becky looked puzzled. Francis explained, "You'll remember, love, I told you that we voted in December to give General Washington supreme control over all military forces for six months, including the hospitals, in the hope it would alleviate some of the confusion caused by conflicting instructions from various generals and the Board of War."

"The general must manage under crippling handicaps. We all know that." Richard paused to sip his fresh glass of Madeira; it did a great deal toward easing the pain in his legs and, tonight, in his heart as well. "No," he told them slowly, "I don't fault our general *personally*." But everyone remembered what he'd said a few minutes before.

Mrs. Bolton appeared in the doorway. "More pudding, Mrs. Lee?" she inquired, addressing Becky.

Becky, engrossed in the conversation, jumped at the voice behind her. "Oh, no ... thank you. I think we are quite finished. All except Colonel Richard who joined us after we'd been served. Perhaps you could dish him up a warm plate of your excellent stew." Looking at Anne, she said, "Actually, ladies, I think it's time for us to retire to the parlor and leave the gentlemen to their pipes, don't you?" She knew the talk would continue for hours and Anne looked in no frame of mind to to put up with it although, she herself, would have preferred to stay and listen.

"Of all the poppycock, Becky," Anne said, as soon as they were out of earshot. "You play right into their selfish hands. This was supposed to have been a happy family evening where we talked about home, children, music ... anything but war and politics. I am quite disappointed."

"Yes, it's your fault, Becky Tayloe. You go right along, play their little game by asking questions every time the talk slows down! You're changed from the way I remember you. What happened to your gaiety? You used to love to flirt and sing, play music and dance after supper. Oh, how I'd love to dance the reel again! Don't you ever do those things anymore?" Polly was clearly on Anne Pinchard's side of this argument.

Becky waited until they were settled by the fire before she responded to their frustration. "Permit me to explain myself at least, whether you accept it graciously or not is up to you, but you have to realize that things aren't the same as they used to be. There is a war. A *war*! I don't think you grasp the enormity of what we're about. People are dying, in states all over this country, to bring about a freedom we're just beginning to imagine."

"Not in Virginia, and things are not really changed there, either. Except for the blasted shortages!" Polly fumed.

Becky glared at her sister, losing patience. "Have you heard a word I said? Perhaps the lack of interest in Virginia is one of the reasons we're not *winning*. Francis said it was certainly so in Pennsylvania, although now that we've left those lackaday Whigs to their own miserable devices, we hear many of them have come to their senses. The Tories are making life risky for them in the absence of the Congress. Perhaps Virginia needs an awakening also," she said, thinking of her father.

Polly and Anne exchanged glances. "Is there nothing else that interests you these days?" Anne asked, speaking for both of them.

"The independence of America and my family's part in it, since you force me to state the obvious, is uppermost in my thoughts. My husband, as do yours, lives and breathes it. I consider it the very least I can do, to support him in his efforts!" When her companions didn't respond, she sensed their combined surprise and incredulity from the expressions on their faces. It provoked her to jar them further. Keeping her voice low, she started at the beginning, retelling Peter's story of the slaughter on the heights of Long Island. She left nothing out, as Francis had repeated it to her. She told of Peter's recent letter after the battle of Trenton; he'd been with General Mifflin's Pennsylvania militia near the bridge, and once again in heavy fighting. She told of the butchery in the hospitals, of the starvation of the soldiers, of bloody feet and frozen limbs. And she told of the rape they witnessed on the way to Baltimore. "The girl was only nine years old. And that Briton was the third animal who forced himself on her poor, frail little body ... that baby child. Her mother was so accustomed to such horror, she barely reacted. Deserters roam the countrysides after every battle, men half-crazed with fear and hunger, looting, burning, raping ... what else can I say?" She brushed her hair back from her forehead and dashed a finger at her eyes where tears threatened.

Becky knew she was flushed and unnerved, but she wasn't finished yet. "If you don't understand now why I encourage our men, you never will, for I have no more to tell. Their wisdom, their decisions mean the difference between our ultimate freedom ... or a return to British tyranny ... and the deaths of every member of our congressional body. Francis is frightened by the lethargy of the Virginia assembly. He's written to everyone he knows that Virginia must put aside all other considerations except active preparation for war. The way he put it in a letter to Landon Carter the other evening was that *'it was utterly in vain to sow the field, unless it was fenced against the spoiler.'* I think that's exactly how he wrote it, word for word. Virginia must arm to defend herself, and she must take positive action to regulate her own currency to save herself from economic disaster!"

"Oh, Becky," Polly wailed.

"Where on earth have you learned all these things?" Anne moaned.

"And why?" her sister asked. "It is all gentlemen's business when it gets right down to it, isn't it?"

⌒⌒

It was much later when Francis fumbled his way into the bed chamber. He had lit his way up the stairs, but snuffed the lamp before opening the door where he stood while his eyes adjusted to the dark. He knew he was a bit tight; the Madeira for some reason had gone to his head this evening. Perhaps he'd allowed himself to become overly keyed up at the things Richard said. Moving slowly, he felt his way to the straight-backed chair near the smoldering fire, and began to undress. He found his nightshirt folded there, waiting for him. Samuel never forgot; the child had been well trained by Ben to treat a gentleman's clothing with careful respect. This was some consolation in a topsy-turvy world, he thought, letting himself down gently on the edge of the bed. He had to struggle with the boots. They had been on his feet too long and were damp inside. Becky stirred behind him. He hadn't meant to disturb her, although he would have liked to hold her for the warmth and comfort it gave him, but he had no energy left to make love or even talk. Tomorrow he'd share with her the disturbing news from Richard's letter. He felt completely drained, as though a mysterious force superior to his own intellect had sucked out all his bodily fluids. Her voice, when she spoke, startled him considerably.

"Hello, darling. I've been waiting for you. I was so tired, but I've been stretched out here, thinking and waiting. What time is it?"

"You haven't been asleep? Why, it's after two o'clock, love. I should have come up long ago except Richard wouldn't stop talking."

"And for my part, with the ladies, I was the one who talked too much. I told them all about Peter, and the war. Francis, when I looked at them and saw those blank faces, half-interested eyes, I even told them about the Redcoat soldier who raped the little girl. I just couldn't stop once I got started. They believed me, but I know they both find me a far different person from the one they knew in Richmond County. Can I possibly be so changed that my own sister thinks me strange?"

Francis dropped his breeches from under the nightshirt, jerked off his stockings and rolled in beside her. She moved immediately into his arms where, bodies pressed together, they sought reality in an otherwise unreal world. "If you've done any changing, love, it can only be for the better. It's true that every day that passes, you mean more to me than you did even one day before. I don't tell you that often enough, do I, hmm?" He twirled the curl on the side of her cheek around one finger, remembering a long ago time in the Tayloe house on Nicholson Street when first he'd touched her hair. Such promise it had held for him. "Some day I'll make it all up to you. We'll return to Menokin and you'll have your garden, your lovely flowers. God grant they are caring for it in our absence but, if not, then we shall plant it all again. And the house ... the house will awaken to your touch when you walk through the door. Everything will come alive, the furniture will shine, the flowers bloom, the birds sing and the wind whisper in the pines. And every servant will smile to see you walking there again. In the evenings we can wander down the hill to the creek, or maybe stroll the road to the ends of the fields. We might even visit the bower one day. Wait and see! As for me, well, I'll devote my time to experimenting with new crops, raising a good crop of grain, and maybe enlarge the milk herd and build a bigger sheep pasture."

"It sounds like a dream, darling. All our friends will come to visit on Sundays after church. I'll serve delicious Sunday suppers, and maybe they'll become famous in the county, like Mama's. Even Colonel Landon will have to pay me a compliment now and again, I'll wager. Oh, and Francis, little John and baby Jane can come from Mount Airy to stay with us sometimes, and I'll teach them to read. I love teaching ..." She had never told him about Sam learning to read. "I just love teaching children anything.

They are so receptive and eager to learn. Did I tell you Polly is expecting? We haven't had a moment to ourselves since she told me. Late August or early September she thinks. She's so excited about it. Like a child herself."

Francis tightened his arms around her. Polly and Anne were right about her changing in some ways. She'd abandoned the desperate yearning for her own baby and now seemed ready to share in the joy of others. And there was no doubt about it, she had matured remarkably in the year and a half they'd been away from home. "That is wonderful ... wonderful. God, I am tired. I am so tired I could sleep for a week, but tomorrow I must be up early again. There's to be a vote on whether or not we should postpone our return back to Philadelphia."

"So if it's defeated, we'll be going back soon? That's good news!"

"Not really. For us, maybe, but not for the Congress. It means another interruption of work, a reason for those looking for an excuse to take a leave, to do so. I'm not for moving back right now."

"Sometimes I don't understand you at all! But if you have to get up early," she sighed, perplexed, "It's best we get to sleep." Kissing him lightly, she moved away.

Very soon he could tell by her even breathing she had dozed off. Becky always slept the immediate and contented sleep of an innocent, he smiled to himself, as well she deserved. But he was wide awake now, his mind churning, unable to join her in slumber. What Richard had said about the move threatened against him in the Virginia Legislature was uppermost in his thoughts. It seemed incredible that such a thing could actually be possible, happening even now. Richard—who had devoted his entire life to his country, who now lived for no other reason than to further the cause of freedom in America—how could anyone threaten to blacken the name of such a man with scandal? It never ceased to alarm Francis that political protagonists seemed destined to suffer under an eminent sort of explicit jealousy of one another. But, he raged, what right had anyone to question Richard's motives? No more honorable nor devoted man ever walked the face of the continent. Yet the letter from Joseph Blackwell, and he'd seen it with his own eyes, had said that two prominent citizens were Richard's mortal enemies and warned him they intended to publish Richard's letter to one of his tenants in the *Gazette*. They accused him of using his power to deflate the value of paper money, and then refusing to accept it in payment of rent. The damned truth was, Richard had written to some tenants asking that rent be paid in gold, silver, or tobacco. But he had every right to do that, in view of changing times and slipping valuation. Was a man expected to give up his home, his health, his comforts, and then toss his means of livelihood on the pyre of sacrifice to the public good as well? It wasn't Richard's fault the money they printed was losing in value almost daily! "My God, what do they want of us?" Francis shouted aloud, forgetting about the sleeping household.

"Hmm?" Becky mumbled, startled out of dreams. Turning, she moved toward him, burying her face in the warmth of his nightshirt.

He tingled to the pointed tips of her breasts as the fullness pressed against him. Without conscious thought, he abandoned his concern over the threat to Richard's integrity, abandoned everything except joyful anticipation of the soft eager response of her body under his hands. As weary as he was, he knew he must have her tonight. Becky seemed to predict his desire almost before he did, and within a moment had slipped out of her gown to give herself to his caresses. It was a long time since they had made love and her passion peaked as quickly as did his. It was over in a few minutes. "You still smell like jasmine. It makes me so happy," he murmured into her hair. "You must never change that, love." Holding her lightly so he might continue to pleasure in the curve of her bare thigh within the crook of his body, Francis fell into a contented sleep.

∽

During the next days there were violent debates over the issue of returning to Philadelphia. Washington was quite clear in his dispatches; he could not defend that city if the enemy pressed an attack. Militia regiments, he said, were needed from every state if they were to be expected to hold the army together; and he did not need any more foreign officers, he cautioned. It was not the first time he had sent them the same news. The fight over the removal from Baltimore erupted into a heated argument as to whether or not a state had the right to put off the debate until another time. After a wasted day of fierce wrangling, it became clear that the Congress, as a body, had a case of nervous jitters. Business was damnably difficult at their present distance and it was also damnably uncomfortable. To this they'd all agreed. But they were now arguing over moot points merely for the sake of argument. Finally, in the second day, the vote went for adjournment; they were to reconvene four days hence in Philadelphia. In the interim, once again, government would virtually cease to function.

Within an hour, Richard made his decision to head for Westmoreland County to return Anne to her children. Polly, being quite ill from her inoculation and combined with her pregnancy, would be unable to travel for some time; the Pages had no choice but to temporarily remain behind. For Becky and Francis it meant another hurried packing up and another cold, miserable trip through a winter countryside. This time Becky didn't care. Her excitement knew no bounds, returning to Philadelphia would be almost like going home. They'd have a house again and their own belongings. Briefly, she considered remaining in Baltimore to nurse Polly, but no sooner had the thought occurred to her, than she discarded it. Francis must not go alone. So far they'd managed to remain together every step of the way and so long as she had a breath left, that was not going to change.

Then, at the last minute, peeved at the decision made by Congress and knowing a quorum wouldn't be gathered in Philadelphia for some time no matter what the plan, Francis decided they should stay another week in Baltimore so Becky could be with Polly. He had just been named as Chairman of the Whole but, without enough members present to form a committee, he could hardly be needed for a while. Or so he rationalized.

As it turned out Francis and Mann Page didn't take their seats in Congress until early April, more than a month after the vote to adjourn. Richard was back with them a few days later. Within the week, William Shippen was given his permanent appointment to the post of Director-General of the hospitals; if Benjamin Rush must be named Surgeon-General in the Middle States to accomplish this goal, Richard decided, then so be it.

On another front, Arthur Lee had been in Spain for two months. Although Congress had intended Benjamin Franklin for this assignment, the three commissioners to France—Franklin, Silas Deane, and Lee—had decided among themselves that Arthur should be the one to go to Spain; the powerful Secret Committee of Congress rectified the mix-up by authorizing Doctor Lee to negotiate with the Spanish Court for money and munitions, a feat he was never able to accomplish. Richard Henry, a member of the Secret Committee, now turned his sights on the appointment of his brother William as commercial agent to Berlin and Vienna. Within weeks, the deed was done. Meanwhile at home, brother Thomas continued to serve in the Virginia Legislature. The family, it seemed, had an iron grip on the direction the new country would take.

At the same time, however, the plot to depose the haughty, indefatigable Richard, stewed and bubbled over the flame his enemies had kindled in the hearts of the tenant farmers on his estates in Virginia. Near the end of May word reached the brothers in Philadelphia that while Francis had been re-elected to his congressional seat, Richard had not.

"Harrison," wrote Thomas, *"is beside himself with unmasked glee. He runs up and down the roads telling everyone he meets of your infamous treatment of the poor tenants. He has spread the story far and wide. I should not be surprised if a vote passes to call you home in the middle of your term, to account for your conduct. I did all in my power, yet it was not enough. You were not elected."*

∽

Francis soon realized he was taking his brother's defeat very personally. He couldn't help imagining that the blow had been leveled at the entire family. Seldom had he felt so low; but the last thing he wanted was to let Richard sense his dismay. Frowning, and without a word, he turned his horse over to Ben and headed for the house. With luck, he could have a quiet hour alone to put his thoughts in order before Richard returned from City Tavern. But no sooner was he seated than his brother arrived.

"They're going to have enough votes to reinstate General Schuyler as commander of the Northern Army, damn it!" Richard pronounced, flinging himself into a chair and propping his bad foot on a stool.

Francis was dumbfounded. While the disgrace of his own defeat must weigh heavily on his heart, Richard continued to throw himself into the squabbles of government as though nothing had happened. It was the attitude of a supreme patriot or, he pondered grimly, that of a madman! Best to play along for the time being, he decided quickly. "Oh? It doesn't surprise me. The New York delegates, Duer in particular, have been hawking Schuyler's merits for days. But how do you know for certain?"

"Henry Laurens, the new South Carolina delegate who, by the way, is very impressive ... an extremely intelligent gentleman, confided in me they have the South Carolina vote. If they carry Maryland, and it appears they will, that's all they need. But Schuyler is an ass! From every quarter I've had the same report.

Tales of his neglect of the command are rife. He's always some-where else when the going gets rough."

"Yes, I met Laurens this morning, and he seemed like a good addition to our overburdened group. But, back to Schuyler. Who's primarily responsible for those tales, Richard? Gates, that's who! General Horatio Gates. The little general with the big ambition. It's quite clear to me, Gates wants the Northern Department for himself. Hence, he flits here and there, spreading his gossip about poor Schuyler."

"Poor Schuyler?" Richard's head snapped alert, reminded of something. "Are you trying to tell me, Loudoun, that the same theory could explain Harrison's malicious attacks on my character in Williamsburg? He desires the senior Virginia seat in Congress, *my* seat?"

"Perhaps. It might be a valid comparison at that ... although we know Big Ben isn't at the root of the rumors." They had stumbled into the Virginia problem before Francis had expected. "Before we tackle that subject, R.H., I think it only fair to tell you that Mann and I have talked it over, and we find nothing conclusive in the charges directed at Philip Schuyler. We're not going to vote against him and that means, as we are at the moment only three delegates, Virginia's vote will be cast as yea. I'm sorry, but I thought you'd want to know ahead of time that we'll not be voting with you."

Richard felt as though he'd been struck. His gaunt features assumed an even more pinched look than usual as he leveled a withering gaze at his younger brother. "You bastards! Since when have you taken to conspiring behind my back? Don't you realize how it will make me look? Duer, Duane, Rush ... they'll all mark me for a fool! This, of all times, I expected you to follow me. I've gone as far in my support of Gates as I have in my damnation of Schuyler. You know that. Why are you taking this attitude?"

"Would you rather we voted against our conscience?" Francis asked quietly, his eyes hard.

For a long minute Richard stared at him. Suddenly the anger seemed to drain from him and he slumped in the chair. "My God, Frank," he moaned, "I guess this thing at home has gotten to me more than I care to admit. It has forced my reason, blurred my vision. My personal frustration at the blow I've suffered makes me strike out at those I love most. Forgive me."

Francis experienced a pain like a knife in his chest. He'd never witnessed Richard in a humble pose and the idea terrified him. "What are you going to do?" he asked unevenly, voice cracking.

"Do?"

"About the election? You lost it because of lies circulated about you. You have to defend yourself, prove that the charges against you are false."

"Why must I?" Richard gazed into the small picket-fenced yard behind the house. Cate was clapping her hands to drive some chickens back into the pen. Wings flapped and feathers flew, but the wench won out. "They must have escaped ... the chickens ... I ... am tired, Loudoun. I am so damnably tired. I crave nothing more than an extended rest at Chantilly in the company of my dear wife and children. The Legislature has done me a favor of sorts by voting me out."

"Then why, may I ask, were you so bloody busy today, beating the bushes for votes to defeat Schuyler, if you're so bloody sick of the whole mess?"

"Because if I'm to be booted out, my dear brother, then the country shall know I went out still fighting for what I perceive to be right. I refuse to slink quietly out of town like a Tory in the night. But I'll be ready, when the time comes and seeing no other choice, to capitulate. If my usefulness is at an end, then so be it," he finished petulantly.

"Oh?" Francis knew he was being called upon. It was why he'd desired time to himself before confronting Richard. He weighed his brother's words, trying to place a value on them. Richard's next move was in his hands; that much was clear. He was expected to suggest something ... some plan ... a course of action. With a flash of intuition it came to him what they must do. Eagerly he paced the room, the movement relieving his tension, the pieces beginning to drop into place. As an opening wedge, he favored Richard with a disarming smile. "Your country and your state need you more than they ever have. What is more, you know it! So, admit it. Capitulation is tantamount to a confession. Now listen ... I have a plan. The reputation of our family is at stake here, and we must all rally round. Here is what we'll do. The first step is for you to write a full account of the entire rent business to Patrick Henry. As governor, he's in a position to see that truth is spread where it will do the most good. Besides, he's always been friendly to you. Patrick can be counted on to take your side against the Harrison and Braxton faction."

"You mean explain to Patrick that I instituted the plan for my tenants to pay in tobacco and so on, long before the first paper money was even printed?"

"Exactly! You've got to prove that at no time was it your intention to encourage the depreciation of the paper currency by refusing to accept it as lawful payment. Remind him that certain tenants in Loudoun County petitioned the assembly *themselves*, to be able to pay their *own* rents in produce. Remember? It was when the non-export association was to take effect and they feared there'd be no market for their tobacco."

Richard nodded, a trace of hope touching his eyes. "Go on," he urged. "Step two?"

"All right. So far, so good. Get off a few more letters, besides the one to Henry, directed to the most judicious places. Allow time for their arrival, then get yourself down to Virginia, straight to Williamsburg. Demand a hearing. Press the fact that malicious damage has been dealt your character, without your side of the story being heard. It seems to me, with a little luck, not only will you be fully exonerated, but that such a course of action will lead to your reinstatement as a delegate to Congress. If not the coming session, then the next."

"And if it doesn't work?"

"Then, my dear Richard, Mann and I will both resign in indignant protest to such ill treatment, and they'll really find themselves in a pickle!"

"You would do that? Resign your seat in Congress? For me?"

"I would indeed," Francis promised loftily. "Ben," he laughed, "Ben, get your lazy hide in here and serve Colonel Richard a glass! We propose to drink a toast to the sovereign state of Virginia and her temporarily misguided legislature!"

Ben's surprised face appeared in the doorway. "Things mus' be lookin' up, Marse Frank! I ain't seen you wit' a smile on yo' face in two days."

"They are indeed, Ben. Everything is going to be fine, just fine."

Ben scurried for the hall. If he was quick about it, he had just enough time to be the first to tell Miss Becky the good news before he fetched the wine.

Virginia had elected John Harvis, Joseph Jones, Francis Lightfoot Lee, Benjamin Harrison, and George Mason to that next session of Congress, leaving out Mann Page as well as Richard Henry Lee. But time still remained in the present session which didn't expire until August 1777. When Richard left for home in June he carried a letter in his pocket addressed to the Honorable George Wythe, Speaker of the House of Delegates. It contained the resignations of both Francis and Mann Page from Congress, ammunition to be held in reserve. He never had to use it. Within a week, he found himself vindicated by the upper and lower houses of the legislature, publicly thanked for his services and, two days later, he was voted a delegate to the Congress in the place of George Mason, who had declined the honor. The entire matter went exactly according to plan, he reported to Francis upon his triumphant return to Philadelphia in August.

During Richard's absence, neither Congress nor the country had remained dormant. In mid-July devastating news of the retreat from Ticonderoga began to filter in. Francis mused that Richard would certainly label it predictable. Most members, now thoroughly disenchanted with General Schuyler for allowing the English "Gentleman Johnny" Burgoyne to take the fort without so much as a shot being fired, were in favor of immediate recall of Schuyler for investigation. Those who defended him, however, principally Schuyler's fellow New Yorkers, blamed the fiasco on the failure of the eastern states to send their quota of troops to the northern defenses. It was a sticky argument, loaded with factions.

"It looks as though I made a bad decision, backing Schuyler over General Gates," Francis told Becky one August evening. "I should have listened to Richard on that one, I'm afraid."

"Who'll replace General Schuyler in the north?" she asked, delighted to have his attention. With Polly and Mann gone from the house, it was empty. She missed their company more than she'd thought possible.

"Oh, there was little debate on that. Gates was voted the assignment today, eleven to one."

"Then Richard will come back to find himself on the right side of the issue for a change. That should please him." She guessed she missed even Richard these days.

"Umm," he nodded. "As for me, well I can't pinpoint it, but I'm still uneasy about Horatio Gates. However, at the moment, he seems to be the only choice."

∽

The flurry over Ticonderoga and the influx of foreign mercenaries come to aid the American cause was overshadowed by uncertainty surrounding the whereabouts of Britain's Lord Howe and his 18,000 troops. During the summer they had departed New Jersey and moved into New York, but there were later reports that Howe had put to sea and was sailing southward, causing great speculation over his destination. At one point his ships were sighted off the Virginia capes, then again were reported in the Chesapeake Bay. It wasn't until one hot, miserable day late in August that word reached Philadelphia that Lord Howe was heading, following a round-about route, to that very city. Meanwhile it was said Washington moved his troops through the countryside like a wraith, jockeying for position in face of Howe's advance, his piecemeal army foraging so it could eat. Still plagued by other problems that had haunted him from the beginning—green militia and a host of "prima-donna" generals, both domestic and foreign—Washington knew that as often as not his orders were twisted to suit the purposes of those who passed them on. There was also growing rivalry between American officers and the French and German volunteers, many of whom could not speak understandable English. Promotions and commands were hotly, bitterly contested.

Receiving dispatches almost daily from General Washington describing the sorry state of his forces, Congress once again began preparations to evacuate. Stacks of books and official documents were stuffed hurriedly into chests and headed down the road on their way, this time to Lancaster, Pennsylvania, which was to be the next seat of government.

"We aren't going to panic and run like the rest of this foolish city," Francis told his wife. "We're going to wait until there's no alternative, and then proceed calmly."

A loud clatter at the doorway early on the morning of September 19th aroused the Lee household from sleep. They heard muffled voices, and then Ben bounding the steps two at a time. It was the British, he panted, eyes rolling until they showed only the whites behind the sputtering candle he held in his shaking hands. General Washington couldn't hold them. On the march, they would be at the city outskirts any minute. Ben's terror communicated itself to his master and mistress. In the dark of night anything, and indeed everything, seemed possible.

With the first rays of light, Francis held stubbornly to his plan; they would remain calm about their removal. It was a flight nonetheless. Becky remarked that somehow it seemed more final than the last departure as she watched anxiously when Francis emptied the contents of his desk into the large portmanteau. The desk had become a favorite piece of furniture and she intended to see it one day in the Menokin study, but for now they would have to leave it to fate once more.

"Don't worry," he said, bustling about, "it will be here when we get back."

"Will it?" Did he really believe what he was saying? More likely it was his way of trying to assure her the world was not really falling apart.

Leaving him, she hurried upstairs to direct Cate with the clothing. "I think we should pack everything, Cate. There's no telling how long we'll be away. And don't forget the Jesuit bark for Master Francis. It's stored in the hall cupboard. When you're ready to fetch it, I'll give you the key." A precious and scarce commodity thought to cure many illnesses, the bark had been sent from Europe by William, and she wasn't about to leave it behind.

"Yas-ma'm. As hard as dat be t' come by, we won't fo'git it," Cate said with a shiver. "And I's not fo'gitin' Sam's book, Miss Becky, neither." As panicked as her mistress, she revealed for the first time that she knew Sam had learned to read. "Do dey shoot de famlies of de congressmens if dey ketches dem?" she asked quickly.

"No!" came the adamant reply. Then, "I don't know. Hush, Catey, just hush. You're frightening me."

Reaching the upper hall an hour later Francis heard a very strange thing. The voices of his wife and her maid were joined in a hymn to the Almighty. *"Oh God, our help in ages past,"* they sang, *"Our hope for years to come ..."*

"Our shelter from the stormy blast, and our eternal home," he added his clear tenor to their shaky sopranos.

"Francis! I am so *frightened,*" Becky cried. "I've never been so frightened." The sound of his voice had withered her last shreds of courage.

"I know. I know," he whispered, feeling his own heart pounding. And I also, he thought, if only you knew.

∽

They traveled northeast, by way of Reading, so as best to avoid the British Army to the southwest. Alice Shippen followed them, headed for Virginia and her sister Hannah Corbin, everyone thankful Nancy and Tommy were safely back in their boarding schools. It was that much less to worry about. Mail addressed to the Board of War caught up with Francis in Reading and, as a member of that committee, he found time that second evening to dash off some hurried correspondence. Soon they would be safely arrived in Lancaster, Becky comforted herself as she fell asleep, leaving both Francis and his sister to their letter writing.

After several days in the new city, everyone began to settle down. The town wasn't elaborate but things could have been worse. Then, without warning, two days later Francis returned to announce that the Congress, what there was of it at the moment, had voted to move on. The decision was made to put the Schuykill River between the American governing body and General Howe's redcoats.

"What?" Becky cried.

"We're moving on. To York Town. Get Cate ... it's time to pack up again," he ordered as gently as he could.

"Dear saints in heaven," she wailed, bursting into tears. "Where *is* York, Francis? I've never even heard of it!"

Congress in Exile

General Horatio Gates had claimed an astounding victory in New York at Saratoga. Dashing Johnny Burgoyne, cunning even in defeat, surrendered his entire army to the triumphant American commander, but managed to extract a peace agreement out of Gates which was shockingly favorable to the British. All prisoners, quartered temporarily in New York, were to be returned to England as soon as possible; in addition, British officers were guaranteed preferential treatment by the foolishly benign Gates, whose success, some thought, had all too obviously gone to his head. No one denied, however, he was riding a high wave.

Meanwhile, Britain's Lord Howe sat tight in the American capital enjoying the conspicuous favors of a married lady, his redcoats languishing happily with him in that hotbed of Toryism. A short distance away, General Washington's army huddled helplessly, engrossed in the pressing matter of staying alive—the titular military commanders of both countries were thus overshadowed by the drama being played out by Gates and Burgoyne. At the same time Congress listened and waited, alternately rejoicing and despairing as the country floundered in deep, uncharted seas. It was a wintry, uncertain November in the year 1777.

The Lees had been in York Town over a month, Becky realized, gazing into the dismal street below. She watched as a bent old man sloshed through the wet snow, struggling under an enormous load of firewood. The stuff, splintered kindling from what she could see, poked jaggedly from the large bundle on his back. It was a poor town, York, full of poor people. And the old man appeared worse off than most. He'd probably been abroad since dawn scavenging the woodlands in search of fallen branches and wood small enough to carry home, so that he might keep from freezing for another evening. Becky drew her shawl closer about her shoulders, crossing her arms over her chest for warmth. It was bitterly cold and a sleet-gray sky held no promise for change.

Besides being poor, the people in York were inhospitable; or did it just seem so because they were resentful of the danger imposed on their community by the presence of the Congress? It was impossible to obtain decent food, even if one had the money to afford it. Richard sent Lucas into the fields daily to hunt for pigeon, complaining there wasn't the cash to do otherwise. It was true; the prices were even higher than they'd been the previous winter in Baltimore, and the currency worth far less. How long must they suffer the outrage caused by Lord Howe's occupation of Philadelphia? For the first time since the early days in Shippen House, Becky wished desperately to go home to Menokin. Not for a visit or by herself but with her husband, to stay. She yearned for life as they'd known it before the war. More than two long years had passed since their departure, and what had gone before seemed more and more like a dream in some long-ago previous lifetime.

Richard had been home twice, and so had most other delegates for that matter. With Mann Page out of Congress, Anne Pinchard months ago returned to Chantilly, Alice Shippen on a prolonged visit to Virginia, and Nancy and Tommy away at school, Becky felt very much a stranger in a strange land—alone and lonely, with a husband too preoccupied to notice—or so it seemed. The rooms they leased on Beaver Street were plain, equipped with rudimentary furnishings. The third floor in a private home, it was at least clean. The sloped eaves of the roof added a dubious charm, she supposed, and from two small dormers in the sitting room one could see the street below. There was a crude stone fireplace, and that was something to be thankful for. Some congressmen, she'd heard, were not nearly so fortunate. A small sparse room across the hall, containing a lumpy bed and one chest of drawers, served as their sleeping chamber, where their trunks lined the wall under the single window. An identical room on the other side of a large fireless chimney, served as Richard's chamber. The chimney had hearths on the first and second floors, but not the third; the only heat in the bed chambers came through warmth accumulated in the stones from the fires below.

Becky was ever grateful they had Ben, Cate, and old Lucas to look out for them. There was little doubt that certain persons among the sanctimonious northerners were wishing now that they could avail themselves of precisely such arrangements. Discretion, of course, would prevent them admitting it. Quarters for the slaves were a problem, but the Lees were finally allowed a clapboard lean-to attached to the stable and formerly occupied by goats. Only Samuel was permitted to sleep on a pallet in the crowded sitting room. Cate grumbled incessantly, but then who didn't?

Becky moved aimlessly around the room. She blew dust off a pewter candlestick on the mantle, straightened Francis's papers and sealing wax on the table, and stopped to stare at the blue stockings she was knitting him. She had completed one, the second lay crumpled in the chair where she'd left it the previous evening. Straining her eyes in the poor light for a long time, she'd finally given up about midnight, leaving Francis still hunched over his paperwork. She knew he was working too hard, barely sleeping five or six hours a night, attending endless committee meetings in addition to the regular sessions, and then poring over his notes when he arrived home. They were once again hard at the Confederation which would bind them together as states. Every evening she prayed he'd come with the news that they'd finally voted it finished.

The attendance, Francis reported, was thinner than ever. It was amazing how the threat of another frigid winter in miserable accommodations had caused all types of suddenly urgent matters to press upon so many delegates, beckoning them homeward! Yesterday they'd been down to a mere twenty-two members. Even John and Samuel Adams had found sufficient cause to return to Boston. Some whispers had been gotten about that with Hancock's resignation from the presidency, Frank Lee would be chosen to replace him. For a fleeting moment Becky exalted over the prestige and prominence such a position would afford them. Then she'd paused to contemplate the man who was her husband: the gentle, lovable, lighthearted, yet sublimely serious man who was Francis Lee. A quiet man he was, shy and unselfish, rarely boastful, inarticulate sometimes in public but a brilliant peacemaker in private circumstances, and always a favorite with the ladies.

"I couldn't do it, Becky," he'd told her, as though he felt a need to apologize "I'm not a leader. It would destroy my usefulness altogether." She'd recognized the truth in what he said. They were the words of a man mortified at the very contemplation of such an honor.

Richard and Francis agreed between themselves to promote the election of Henry Laurens. The South Carolinian, only three months a member of Congress, had immediately earned the admiration of his fellow delegates as a man of intelligence and prudence; a friendship had developed with the Adamses and James Lovell of Massachusetts, and thence with the Lees. Laurens, a prominent merchant in Charleston before the revolution, found he had much in common with the Virginians, but he didn't publicly or privately cast his lot with anyone, being an astute man above all else. Socially, he enjoyed the Lee brothers but, neither before nor after his election as president of the Congress, did he always take their side.

Becky picked up her knitting, and counted the stitches she must bind off for the heel. Within a moment the needles were clicking busily and she'd forgotten the Congress. Cate had a pot of soup simmering over the fire. When she came to check on it, if

Ben hadn't brought more wood in, she'd tell Cate to remind him. The landlady had forbidden them to cook in the room so for the most part, Cate struggled over an open fire outside the household kitchen, but stews and soups, she smuggled upstairs. It smelled like winter greens and leeks again tonight. It was Ben's day to hunt and if he'd been lucky, they might even have rabbit for supper. It was a fact, they were all sick of pigeon. The sound of boots on the sagging steps demanded her attention, causing her to lose count on the decrease stitches.

"Darling," she exclaimed, jumping up when the door opened. "I never expected you home so early. How wonderful. You're not sick or anything? Oh, but you're wet. Come, here to the fire."

He threw his cloak over a chair, reaching for her hands. "No, I'm not sick, and I'm wet because it's begun to rain. And ... I'm early because the day's business is finished. The child is born! After two years of haggling, Congress has at last brought forth a *Confederation of the States*! It's not perfect, mind you, far from it, but it's as perfect as our wisdoms and tempers have allowed us to make it." His eyes were shining circles of excitement ringed by gray fatigue. "Laurens is the one who thought of calling it a child," he admitted grudgingly. "Terribly clever, don't you think, considering all the birthing pains we've suffered through?"

"My, yes. Very clever indeed. Oh, I'm so happy for all of you. Although I confess I was afraid it would never be possible with all the differences ... in manufacture, commerce, religion, even personal habits and sentiments ... and of course, our slaves. It's truly a miracle to have come to some agreement."

He was leaning over the kettle to get a better whiff of the soup. "To tell the truth, there is so much bickering and backbiting connected with everything we do, it is an honest miracle for sure. As Richard says, we must each yield a little to the others, and that's exactly what we've done. Richard, by the way, has been named to write the circular letter that is to accompany the articles when they're sent to the states for ratifications. He should be here soon. We're anxious to discuss the formation of the new Board of War before it comes on the floor ... there's talk of making it all military. Probably Lovell, Peters, and myself would then act in some sort of an advisory capacity. I have mixed feelings about it, but God knows we haven't been able to accomplish what we should the way it is now."

"Francis Lee! Here the Congress have barely finished one thing and you're already engrossed in the next!" She felt the sting of hot tears and ducked her head so he wouldn't know. "I'd hoped we might play backgammon this evening or go for a carriage ride together."

"A carriage ride? In this weather? The streets are icing up already and it's just three o'clock." But the quiver in her voice was obvious; he heard it and didn't doubt its meaning. "Come, love, and sit with me until Richard arrives. I need your hand a thousand times more than you need mine. I promise before two days have passed, you'll have your backgammon game. And I shall beat you this time, wench," he teased. "You can depend upon it."

Appeased, as well as intrigued by what he had called her, she drew her chair close to his and leaned her head against him. "I'm sorry, darling. I'm just a jealous old witch. It's only that sometimes I do feel left out, and would you know a secret? I hate York Town! It's a beastly, dreadful place, crawling with scandalous people."

"That's no secret," he laughed. "Those sentiments and far worse are sounded loud and clear by each and every member of Congress almost every day. Were it not for the Golden Plough and its ready supply of rum toddy, it's doubtful we'd have even the few members that we do." A twinkle replaced the zealous energy in his tired eyes. "But while the most of them have their tavern, and a few of them seek out the local ladies of doubtful virtue to entertain them, I have you. A far better bargain I have drawn, you may be sure!"

Becky blinked with mock innocence. "What do I lack that those painted night ladies can offer?" Forgetting they weren't alone, could never be alone while sharing these cramped quarters with his brother, she hiked her skirts above her knees, pirouetted, and danced a provocative jig around the table.

"Very little."

"Boldness, my man?" she suggested, blowing kisses and bobbing just beyond his reach.

"Oh, never that!" He grabbed for her swaying hips but captured only a fistful of blue linen cloth.

"Let's go to bed, Francis."

"What?"

"You heard me. I said ... let's go to bed."

"If that's not bold, I never heard bold. I wouldn't dare turn down such a wanton request, for fear of incurring my lady's wrath, heaven forbid. Madam, you're about to lose whatever virtues you claim to possess!" He cornered her near the window.

"Darling," she giggled, "you always could chase my blues away. I promise you this will be infinitely more satisfying than a stuffy old backgammon game."

Without warning the door creaked, revealing Richard's austere face. "Well," he said, one eyebrow arched in a classic question mark.

∾

In later years Francis was never certain at what point the prickly barb of gossip and innuendo ceased rolling off his outer shell and began to penetrate his complacency. One thing was fact—the winter of '77 would forever remain a landmark in the process of his political education. He asked himself what lay at the root of his uneasiness, his mounting discontent with the way things were? Was it the letters from Arthur telling of misconduct on the part of the American Commissioners to Paris, his now increasing enmity toward Silas Deane? Or was it more personal, this blight on his peace of mind? Could it relate to the constant feud in Congress over the Board of War, which reflected, however indirectly, on the actions of the present board, including himself? And there was now open gossip over the chronic inability of Washington to manage his army, and this criticism bothered him, too. Perhaps all of these and more burdened his heavy heart. During the weeks before Christmas he found it exceedingly necessary to steal time to himself, to be alone, to think, to allow his mind to bring an order to all that was happening. He took to riding in the countryside on fair afternoons, between committee meetings, or whenever he could make the time.

One such afternoon Francis trotted down West Market Street heading for Penn Common, a bivouac area for militia, located just outside town. He'd finished a reasonably decent meal at the Golden Plough with James Lovell and Henry Laurens, and hoped the excuse he had made for his leave taking was accepted by the president and Lovell. It was true, he really did have to call at the shoemaker's before he closed. For the third time it was necessary to have the toes of his boots stitched and the soles repaired. The man wasn't an expert craftsman, but he did a fair job. And new boots were too costly unless there was no other choice.

Francis passed Penn Common—empty barracks and cold campfires for the present. Then it was rolling farm country he rode through. Large stone barns and sheds for storing grain dotted the landscape. The pastoral scene was comfort of itself. Although the crops and architecture weren't the same as in Virginia, they made him yearn passionately for Menokin. He'd been away too long. John Tayloe was getting on in age, and in ill health from all accounts. There was no telling how long James West could hold the place together without Tayloe's direct supervision. And if the draft were forced, West might likely be called to serve, would surely be called. Things were no more certain on the lands in Loudoun County. Most of the Horsepen Tract had been leased; Joe Grimes still saw to what rents were collected, but he knew much of his acreage lay fallow at a time when he needed all the money he could get.

These considerations, however, where not what was on his mind for long, not for more than a few minutes at a time. It was the world of Congress that he must cope with daily, not the world of plantation and produce. As he rode through the farmlands of York, Pennsylvania, on this particular afternoon, he fretted over General Washington and his pitiful forces at Valley Forge. Those in Congress who supported General Gates, pushing for his appointment as president of a reconstituted Board of War, and that was damned near everybody he had to admit, were indirectly crucifying Washington. Some, not so indirectly, at that. There were polite cover-up reasons given for actions taken, of course, such as the two thousand dollars dispatched immediately to Gates upon his request—whereas the money requested by Commander-in-Chief Washington the very same week was declared "not available" at the moment. The appointment of General Conway to Washington's staff was bound to cause friction—everyone knew Washington couldn't abide the man—but Conway, being a protégé of Horatio Gates, would be appointed regardless of other considerations. Right or wrong, Congress was pushing Washington to the wall or, at the very least, allowing it to happen. The victory at Saratoga made Gates an important man. There was no denying it, Gates was a viable force to be reckoned with. Ambitious and demanding, his reward would be the Board of War, a grand plum for a grand hero if this continued on the same course. And poor Washington had been long without a victory. As Francis pondered, he noted it was getting late. The sun was a huge red ball, horizon high; time to turn back. But he wondered, reining Cameron into a turn-about, wasn't the crux of the problem that the army was incredibly poorly supplied and virtually untrained? Word had filtered in that His Excellency's troops were to winter on a desolate hillside outside Philadelphia, where they'd been coerced by an irate Pennsylvania Legislature demanding protection. It was near an old iron-making village called Valley Forge. Things could only get worse there, as that same legislature was apparently unwilling to carry its share of the burden of feeding and clothing the troops! It was a vicious circle. Rumors were rife. They bounced and ricocheted from one end of the little town to the other with no regard for who might be hurt in the barrage. There were broad hints of a conspiracy against Washington. Could it be true? Someone had told him it was rumored R.H. Lee was involved in it. That had to be poppycock! ... yet Richard pursued friendships with Gates, Conway, and others of Washington's least likely supporters. My God, Francis thought, there are evil men abroad these days, but certainly my brother isn't one of them. They work their wickedness within our circles in such insidious manner that one can't point a finger at them! What and where was the answer?

As he rode through the darkening evening, Francis wished fervently that Richard hadn't chosen this time to return to Virginia. But there was no changing it now. His brother had obtained a leave of absence and would be off in two days. Sighing, he knew he would have to once again brave troubled days alone.

೦ೖಿ

Becky had paper before her, pen in hand, and feet propped off the drafty floor on a footstool. In a further attempt to stay warm she'd wrapped herself in an old woolen robe. Trying to write a letter to her parents, she was finding it difficult to put the right words to paper. It would hardly do to tell them she was miserable. Yet it was the plain truth. All she could think of was that she wished desperately for Francis to get home. It seemed she spent her life in this dreary room by herself. When she heard the stairway creak, her heart quickened as the doorway opened.

"Oh. Richard." She knew her disappointment must be obvious.

Richard covered the distance from door to table quickly for one with lame feet. Laying a hand gently on her shoulder, he brushed the top of her head with his lips. It was a generous show of affection for him, surprising them both. "Dear child," he said, backing off to remove his cloak, "the note of passionate delight I detect in your greeting quite overwhelms me." Curiously crestfallen, he tried to make a joke of it but, watching her face, he wasn't sure she understood. "I deduce from the undisguised longing in your lovely green eyes that my brother isn't yet home?"

Becky couldn't help laughing. "I'm sorry, Richard. Of course I'm happy to see you. It's merely that I've been waiting for Francis for what seems like hours, and I thought hearing your steps that he was here at last. Do you know where he is?"

"No. A report came to me that he dined with Mr. Lovell and the president around two o'clock, then promptly disappeared."

"There's no reason to worry is there? I mean he couldn't be in any danger?"

Richard smiled, noting how pleasing it was when a woman evidenced true worry for her husband's whereabouts; too frequently, the element of jealousy lurked behind concern, but it was not so with Becky. "Nothing to worry about I'm sure. Unless he's taken a fall. And that's highly unlikely, for our Loudoun is both an accomplished rider and a sensible one."

Seeing Richard was struggling with his boots, she unwrapped her own feet and moved to help him. "Give me your foot and I'll pull it off for you. Francis says I've become an expert at this." Taking hold of the heel of the boot she wiggled, pulling carefully until it began to slide. She knew his swollen feet couldn't stand much pressure and she was very gentle. In a minute, slowly, painlessly, the boot eased off. Dropping it with a thud, she turned to the other one. It occurred to her that right now might be the time to talk to Richard about something that had been troubling her. She wedged his heel between her knees and began work on the second boot. "Richard, have you noticed anything different about Francis lately?" Letting the boot fall, she reached for the footstool she'd been using and, to his utter amazement, she lifted his feet, one at a time, placing each on the stool before tucking the old shawl around them. "There, now you'll feel better." Hands on hips, she surveyed her accomplishment.

Richard stared at his sister-in-law. She was grown to a beautiful woman. He'd thought of her as young and frivolous for so long, had carelessly flattered her from time to time when she seemed to pick up the thread of some conversation or other, but most often had considered her merely a pretty child Frank had cleverly chosen to play with. He realized she was waiting for him to speak. "You're a beautiful woman, Rebecca," he said, repeating his thoughts aloud. Her expression told him that was not at all what she'd been expecting.

"Did you hear a word I said?" Becky stammered. Uncomfortable, and not knowing why, she moved across the room, peering out the window. Seeing it turning dark, she bent to get a light from the fire and lit the candle on the table. Richard's silence continued to fill the room, but she felt certain it must be her own mood that made the moment so strange. Perhaps if she repeated the question, it would ease the tension. "I was just wondering if you had noticed Francis seeming under a strain lately? Well ... almost despondent at times."

Richard felt better than he had all day. His feet were warming, and for a brief time no enormous decisions pressed on him. He wasn't inclined to concentrate on what she deemed his brother's peculiar behavior, but sensing a tenseness about Becky, a flush to her high cheek bones, he pushed himself to answer. "Yes, since you ask, I suppose I have noticed he seems to be under some pressure. His position on the war board is very demanding and frequently pains him. In addition, it has become tenuous."

"It bothers him? That he may not be on the new board?"

Richard nodded. "It's fairly likely the board will soon be composed of military gentlemen, or those outside the Congress. It has long been contemplated. General Gates has been suggested to head it. Actually, it's quite certain to happen that way."

"Yes, Francis told me. He's not particularly fond of General Gates."

"I know that, we've discussed it at length. But there's open discontent with His Excellency these days," Richard confided, clearing his throat as he referred to Washington. "And General Gates has recently commanded a great victory. We must move with the times as they happen."

Becky wasn't convinced. "I don't think it's the Board of War that's responsible for Francis's dilemma, and most certainly it's not the only issue." It was so difficult to know what one should say to Richard. There was the risk of making it sound as though Francis were weak, and that was the last thing she believed or wanted to imply, but there were matters that had to be aired. "May I tell you something? In confidence? I think it's possible that Francis is distraught over the hints of scandal that are touching the family ... and others." She stopped, watching his eyes.

My God, Richard thought, she is truly beautiful. Where have I been that I haven't noticed? The light in slanted green eyes was pure fire. He found it necessary to clear his throat again before he could speak. "Yes," he said, "the family. Well. My problems with the tenant rents seem to be controlled at the moment, and I'm leaving shortly as you know for Virginia where I'll put the entire matter to rights once and for all."

"That," Becky said quietly, "is only part of the problem. I don't know how to say this, Richard, except straight out. You must forgive me if I'm blunt. You heap too much on his shoulders. You leave him alone too frequently to defend you. These scrapes, these intrigues, none of them are of his making. The maneuvers to get Dr. Shippen assigned to the head of hospitals, Arthur's discontents in France, the bargaining to push William into the commercial position in Nantes, your own squabbles over the rents ... each of these concerns has forced Francis to take a defensive position. Then off you go, leaving him to battle it alone. I think it was happening that way long before I entered the picture. Since you were young boys maybe. He's a kind man, a gentle man, a man full of joy and compassion. He is *not* a fighter. I have it from his own mouth."

"Yes," Richard murmured, disturbed by her frankness. "Loudoun is gentle. The most sensitive of us all. Whenever we bickered as children, he always suffered until he managed to make the peace. He never wanted to hurt anyone ... yes, he is like that." He passed his hand over his eyes as though he thought to see more clearly. "But I need that quality from him."

Becky decided if she didn't say it now, there would never be another chance. "You *use* him," she blurted. "He adores you, and you use him."

Richard's immediate reaction was anger. But he recognized an element of truth in her outburst. Besides, she was so lovely in this pose, how could he condemn her? "Becky, you know I love Frank. I couldn't be what I am, without him. It's a fact. I could ..."

"I know," she interrupted. "That's what I'm trying to tell you! He follows you, he supports you, he does what you ask, but there comes a time, when it's too much. I think he's on the verge of having had his fill of public scorn. He can't cope with it like some others can." She knew she was becoming too excited. A warning within told her she'd gone far enough, but she couldn't stop. It was like the night in Baltimore when she'd talked to Polly and Anne Pinchard. "He's not sleeping well. He dreams, dreams that awaken him. They're so bad he's not even able to tell me about them. But I know. I've heard him call Peter's name."

"Peter?"

"Peter Hauck. You know, the son of the cabinetmaker in Philadelphia? Peter is with Mifflin's militia, or was. Who knows now? With the army moving into that terrible camp at Valley ... whatever it's called, I suppose he's there, but who knows? He may even be dead. Francis sees Peter in a special way, his own lost youth, or the son he's never had, or his younger brother who's spent most of his life halfway around the world. Anyway, he symbolizes something dear to Francis. Every soldier who goes hungry or is unclothed or isn't given a weapon ... well, to him, it's Peter."

"He dreams about him?" Richard was searching for the connection.

Becky supplied it. "Yes. Almost every night since we came to York. It's a matter of tremendous concern to him. It's simply too much to have all the other worries as well. It's ruining him."

Richard didn't know what to say. The impact of having recognized her infinite charms, combined with what she'd told him about his brother, left him feeling depleted and curiously inadequate—it was not a familiar pose for him. "I understand what you've said, Becky, and I promise you I'll keep it in mind. Perhaps, as you say, I do occasionally take advantage of Frank's easy nature." He saw her face brighten with each word. Clearly, she'd been fearful of discussing the matter with him. "Between us, we have only to take better care of him." He was absolutely inspired to please her tonight, he could see that.

"Oh, yes! Between us. He does need care, Richard. I've always known that. It's partly why I love him so much, I think." She clasped his hands between her own for a moment. "Now ... we shall not speak of it further. I feel ever so much better, having unburdened my worries. I'll pour you some wine. Francis will surely be home soon. I must find Ben to stoke the fire and see to it that Cate starts the supper."

"All I can say is, Frank had better get here quickly if he knows what's good for him, or he could find his lovely wife in a compromised situation!" Richard chuckled as he watched her slip gracefully into her cloak, preparing to fetch the servants. The nasty fight brewing in Congress over whether they should consult Washington with appointments to the new Board of War seemed to have vanished into thin air. "Have I told you, my dear Rebecca, that you look perfectly ravishing this evening?"

"Oh my, how you do carry on," Becky laughed, shaking her head at him. "Whatever is into you today?"

It was a certainty he told himself sadly when she'd left the room, that he must be growing old. There hadn't been so much as a glimmer in her eyes to indicate she took him the least bit seriously. If she were married to anyone except my dear brother, I believe I might have to prove to her she had something to be concerned about, he mused, thinking again of those haunting green eyes, that mass of delicious auburn hair. God, he did miss his wife lately. The thought that in a few days he would be at Chantilly was comforting.

Within a few minutes he scooted his chair to the table. Reaching for the paper Becky hadn't used, he began to scratch out plans for recalling Silas Deane from Paris. It wasn't only the turmoil the fool had caused by sending those scores of foreign officers with promises of commissions in their hands to plague the Congress there was also Arthur's continued correspondence about the man—in every letter there were more indications of Deane's dishonesty, of his misuse of the public trust to benefit himself. The man must be recalled to answer for his actions. If in so doing, it removed him from Arthur's hair, so much the better. It was the last thing he must accomplish before departing for Virginia, he decided. Deane would be ordered home by the the Secret Committee of Congress.

◦◦

Moonlight flooded the tiny chamber. Through the small panes pale light poked into every corner, enabling Becky to identify even the flowers on the faded wallpaper. She'd been awake for hours. When the clock on the second floor landing struck one, two, and then four, she knew she must have dozed briefly. Beside her Francis, too, slept fitfully. She knew he was beside himself with worry over the worsening state of the army. At Valley Forge, General Washington's men were freezing, dying of starvation and the ever-present smallpox. Two letters just received from the general had prompted Congress to appoint another special committee to do something about it. Francis had been named chairman.

"What am I to do?" he'd moaned to her earlier in the evening. "They're eating only fire-cakes for supper." When she'd nodded he asked, "Do you know what a fire-cake is?"

"No, but I know it must be dreadful."

"It's a watered down paste of flour, baked on hot stones, if you can imagine surviving on such a diet! And that was the extent of their Christmas feast. Soon, they'll not even have any flour left!" Francis was like a man possessed. She'd never known him to be so enmeshed, nor so helpless. The problem could be solved in several months' time, but that would be too late. The army would be dying and dead in days if relief were not immediate, he told her. And Congress had no jurisdiction over the individual states. It was an impossible situation.

By moonlight, Becky studied her husband's profile. He was dreaming, every few seconds his body twitched convulsively. He tried to speak, to answer some mysterious figure in a murky exchange she couldn't share with him. His words were eerie, indistinguishable in sleep, slurred garble in the night. Only the tone, the pitch of his voice, conveyed the desperate urgency he was feeling. Not knowing whether to awaken him, she waited, shivering in the warm bed. And when a single scream—Peter!— was torn from him, she knew in an instant where he was and of what stuff his dreams were made. Francis jerked upward, eyes open. Half awake, he turned, unseeing. "Peter?" This time it was only a whisper. Then his eyes focused and he realized he was dreaming.

He hoped Becky wouldn't start talking. He couldn't explain his fears, not now. For the first time in their life together, he thought she couldn't possibly understand his burden. Reaching for her hand, he sank into the pillow, resting his cheek in the hollow of her palm. Within a short time he felt himself drifting back into the night. The dream would come again. He tried to shut it out but knew he couldn't win. It lurked, on the other side of consciousness, waiting to draw him into the abject misery and deprivation of the camp ... we're marching again, someone called. He gathered up the pitiful remnants of his belongings—the tin cup and battered plate that for three days had remained empty, the half-full powder horn, the ragged blanket, his musket—and fell into line. By fastening his eyes on the back of the man ahead of him he found it possible to stumble along, one pace at a time. To lose sight of the sad figure plodding in front could mean death alone in the wilderness or capture by an enemy patrol. On and on they slogged. He had to concentrate on every step he took in order to keep his feet moving, he was that weak. For miles, a long straggling line, they headed somewhere ... but where? No one bothered to tell a militia man the destination, maybe they weren't supposed to know it. A soldier didn't need to understand, only to obey orders ... march when told ... sleep when told ... eat when told ... fire when told ... and die when told. No questions. Silence your belly when it began the now familiar churning that meant hunger. He was amazed at the savage pain he felt at the mere thought of food. Was there any left in the country? Were there other people somewhere, somehow, still eating? It's starting to snow, someone mumbled behind him. Oh, God. Snow. He looked up, saw the wet flakes falling, getting thicker until they frosted his shirt, matted his hair, stung his eyes. And yet on they went, trudging, bumping, dragging along. Stumble, but get up again. Always get up again or be trampled by those in the rear. The ground was white now, he saw. Or was it? Staring at the footprints ahead, he recoiled in horror. Red stains tracked the path. He knew without looking at his own feet that they too, were blood soaked in the worn-out boots. Something else penetrated his mind. The dream was moving to its conclusion. He was familiar with it now, he'd been here before and knew what was going to happen. Again, he floundered, helpless to turn the tide, to change the ending. This time, when the man ahead of him pitched headlong into the snow, he raced to catch him, break his fall. Please God, let me save him this time! Maybe he'd hit his head before. Or let it be someone else when I turn him over. Petrified, he clutched the fallen soldier. Then, as before, exactly as before, he stared into the sightless, sunken eyes of Peter Hauck. An emaciated skeleton of a Peter. Why? Why? Don't die, Peter. Don't die. I'll get you some food. Somehow ... somewhere ... even if I have to steal it ....

Francis knew he was crying. Tears of outrage streamed down his cheeks and he did nothing to stop them. He woke to find Becky crooning to him. "Oh, God," was all he could say. "Oh, God!"

"It's only a dream, darling. A dream. You're all right."

"I dreamt that Peter ..." but he couldn't finish.

"Oh Francis, the Lord never meant us to suffer another man's hell for him. I'm sure of it."

He saw her face clearly in the moonlight. Every precious detail of it called out to him. Had he actually doubted her ability to know his heart? To help him? Of what use dreams? What use indeed, unless they could be made to serve a purpose? It took him only a minute to formulate the plan. What was it he said to Peter in the dream? That he would steal food if necessary? Maybe he'd had it in the back of his mind all along.

"You're right, of course. Becky, by God, you're right! And I'm going to do the only thing left open to me. It will be frowned upon, or worse. I might be condemned for it, but I'm going to do it and to see that it works! In the name of Congress and the Board of War, of which I am no longer a voting member, I'm going to order the governors of Pennsylvania and Maryland to feed our starving army! And following that I'm not going to wait for their responses. I'm going to begin by openly stealing what there is in the neighborhood of the camp. Polite request has accomplished less than nothing. There's no more time for milk-and-water drivel!" Vaulting from bed, he headed for the door.

Soon he was hard at work. She heard the bustle of his activity from the adjacent room, saw the candle light square off the doorway with a yellow crack. The clock struck six. But Becky was no longer counting, she was asleep, a peaceful smile on her face after a long night.

"This committee regrets the necessity they are under of sending officers with parties to collect such cattle, hogs, flour and grain as the Army shall need. The crisis is too alarming to admit of the business being postponed on any consideration," he wrote to His Excellency President Wharton, Governor of Pennsylvania. *"The government of this state will be obliged to give orders for the taking, conveying, and driving all cattle, hogs, pork, flour and grain fit for their consumption to the Army. Certificates will be given to the owners, expressing as nearly as possible the weight and quality of what is taken and agreeing to pay for it at such prices as shall be settled by the Convention of Committees from the several states who are to meet at New Haven the 15th of January next."*

It took him over three hours to complete the two letters, the second to the Maryland governor to whom he explained that all the states would be contacted but that the ones closest to hand must send help immediately. With a great sense of accomplishment he slowly relinquished his pen. Had men in good conscience, laboring under the guise of sanity ever undertaken such a hopeless task as faced America? He couldn't imagine any situation worse than the one they faced. Starvation and sickness threatened to defeat them even if the British did not, he sighed. Sometimes he abhorred his part in creating the monster of Independence.

At other times he knew he would do the same again. But now, for a while at least, he was satisfied he'd done his best to see that the army wouldn't be forced to disperse, to dissolve as Washington had threatened, nor yet to starve. The letters he'd just written would provide stop-gap relief. Francis recognized it as the boldest action he had taken since arriving at the Congress.

Deed of Gift

The Americans at Valley Forge didn't perish that winter, nor was General Washington forced to disperse his troops as he'd feared would be necessary. Once Francis Lee's bold plan was expanded to other states and activated, and the militiamen had sustenance in their bellies, they responded if not brilliantly, at least cogently, to the teachings of an aggressive, egotistic foreigner who appeared in their midst. Allowing no time for wound licking, the Baron von Steuben strode the drill field, shouting obscenities in broken English at their collective clumsiness as he bombarded his way into their hearts. By spring he'd not only saved Washington's army from boredom and subsequent mass desertion, he'd molded it into the closest imitation of a Prussian fighting force (which is not to imply a great deal of similarity) that anyone could have achieved against such insurmountable odds. It was true that hundreds died as a result of malnutrition or disease but, thanks to the Baron, those who survived the winter could for the first time be called soldiers.

Francis, still in York Town, wondered from time to time just how much his own actions at that crucial period had contributed to the salvation of the Continental Army; for besides his plan to feed them, he'd been instrumental in the decision to assign von Steuben to Valley Forge. Upon hearing by word of mouth that Peter Hauck was indeed at the camp and had been moved up to Mifflin's staff, he sent off a letter promptly. Peter's reply informed them that twice he'd been able to smuggle his way into Philadelphia to visit his parents, where he'd witnessed considerable destruction, but probably nothing that couldn't be mended.

The most shocking bit of news he reported was the way the American Tories had opened their arms and the doors of the city to the British. That scourge of the first Congress, Joseph Galloway, was serving General Howe as his chief of intelligence, as well as acting as mayor of the occupied city! Peter also gave Francis a shock when he wrote that some members of the Shippen family, relatives of Doctor William, were said to be among the worst traitors. Near the end of the letter he mentioned a young lady he'd met, who lived near the village of Valley Forge—he was giving serious thought to proposing marriage after the war was over and wanted to know if Francis would stand up for him. With Karl gone, he said, there was no one he admired more. The request pleased Francis beyond measure.

As the weeks of the new year progressed, however, no matter how much satisfaction he felt for having done his best as regarded Washington's Continentals, Francis faced new problems over decisions being made by the Board of War. A conglomerate of the old and new boards met in joint session frequently, an exercise he found disturbing. One plan they drew up was to send an immediate expedition into Canada. General Gates proposed to place Washington's favorite, the Marquis de Lafayette in command with General Conway as second in command. The young Frenchman, upon being summoned to York to confer on the matter and, under questioning by the joint war boards, refused to accept Conway, and made certain other stipulations which weren't at all pleasing to Gates. While Francis hesitated to speak out against the plan itself—with all the others apparently on the side of Gates, whose brain-child it was—he did support Lafayette's demands.

Gates, apparently choosing to ignore the prerequisites of the Marquis, planned a gala banquet to provide himself the opportunity to convince Congress of the rightness of the expedition and the magnificent cooperation they were receiving from Layfayette, who had actually threatened to return to France immediately taking other French officers with him, if he wasn't given his way.

Preparations for the banquet created quite a stir in the little town of York. In the leased rooms on Beaver Street, Cate spent two days teasing the wrinkles out of her mistress's fine silk dress and sprucing up the master's old velvet waistcoat.

One of the few wives present, Becky was the belle of the ball, swirled from partner to partner in the yards of green silk in which she had been married. She danced until her feet throbbed and her knees threatened to buckle. The square stone house rented by General Gates was the scene of much frivolity and toasting that January evening. The Lees bubbled over with tidbits and gossip to tell each other on the way home.

"Did you ever hear so many grand toasts?" Becky sighed.

Francis shook his head. "But did you notice, not a single one was made to our general?"

"Why, yes, there was. I heard the Marquis propose a splendid toast to General Washington."

"That's my point, Becky. No one else made one. Not until Lafayette forced them to raise their glasses, did anyone drink to His Excellency."

"Do you think it was on purpose, or that a toast to him was merely overlooked in the excitement of the evening?"

"I think, yes, it was *purposely* overlooked. It was the intent of Gates all along to ignore Washington. I told you, he wants him out of there and he'll stoop to any means to accomplish his ends. It's clear to me now, Gates only wants Lafayette to take this command to make it impossible for Washington to protest the expedition! It was a bold action tonight on the part of the Frenchman. By toasting Washington he showed us all very clearly where his sentiments lie."

"Well, perhaps that will put an end to it then," she suggested.

"Perhaps," he answered, not believing it for a minute.

"President Laurens told me that, personally, he's not in favor of the Canadian expedition." Becky enjoyed repeating bits of

507

information gleaned at parties, and since arriving in York this was her first opportunity.

"I would be more in favor of the expedition myself had we consulted with Washington to begin with. But, there again, you see some of the maneuvering that's going on."

When they arrived home Becky settled on the edge of the bed while Cate took her hair down and began to brush it. "You looks happy dis evenin' Miss Becky," she said. "Did you have a good time? You and Marse Frank?"

"Oh indeed we did, Cate. It was spectacular. Candlelight and music, and all the gentlemen forgetting to be stuffy ... dancing and toasting." Did she sound like Polly? "Almost like home, I declare. Wasn't it just grand, Francis?" she asked as he entered the room.

He was overcome with tenderness at sight of her shining face. "Wonderful ... just wonderful," he agreed, not wishing to spoil her excitement.

"Oh, darling! I haven't heard you say that in ever so long."

"Well, I've not seen you so radiant in ever so long." He sat beside her, watching Cate's strong hands pull the brush through the silky softness. "I have a surprise for you, love," he announced abruptly. "We're going home."

"For good?" she cried.

"No, Becky, not for good. But for a nice long visit. I decided this evening it was time we took a rest from this place. I think we shall go in May, or June perhaps. I have to request a leave of absence, but I'll have to wait until after Richard returns before we can leave."

"Well, thank goodness for that. I certainly wouldn't want you to leave permanently, before the job was done, Francis Lee."

Cate hooted. "You said yistahday, Miss Becky, dat you'd do anythin' in dis world to get out o' dis place and never come back!"

Becky scowled at her. "Pooh. That was yesterday. And besides, you knew I didn't mean it."

"Of course you didn't mean it, love," Francis agreed. He gathered her in his arms, remembering how beautiful and delicate she'd looked dancing the minuet. He was happy he'd decided it was time to take her home where she could dance and sing and forget the troubles for a while.

Cate went right on brushing the long auburn hair, grinning. She wouldn't mind a trip home herself. Not one bit. She and Ben could have their own room again, the privacy of their bed, without having to sneak around until they were sure old Lucas and Sammy were out of the way. Even with Lucas gone to Virginia these past weeks, she still didn't like York. Hallelujah! She could hardly wait to break the news to Ben.

∽

Francis was true to his word. With the rest of Congress making preparations to return to Philadelphia following the great news of the British withdrawal, summer found the Lees returned to Menokin House for a well deserved rest. Some things were sadly in need of attention, and there had been a few changes. Old Berth was gone, having died quietly in her sleep a month before their arrival, and a Mr. Jeremiah Sutton had replaced James West as overseer. Mann Page and John Tayloe together had hired him. The south forty was cleared and seeded in Indian corn, fodder for the animals; there were now ten milk cows, several hogs, and a much larger herd of sheep grazed on the hillside. Tayloe had managed well, Francis was pleased to see. The plantation as a whole had mellowed—no longer looked spanking new—and the kitchen and office buildings stood completed. But otherwise, it was as they had left it and they rejoiced daily in being home.

What caused them alarm was the change in Becky's father. He was ill and aging fast. His memory frequently lapsed in the middle of a conversation and he was often in such pain as to confine him to bed. Landon Carter was no better off; a constant complainer, his case seemed the more keenly pathetic of the two. Francis's brother Thomas had passed away in April after a bout with rheumatic fever, and Francis could see the same fate was soon in store for his two old friends. He was thankful for the opportunity to visit with them both. Having sorely missed her family, Becky spent every moment she could at Mount Airy. One day in September, she arrived in mid-morning to find her father had a visitor.

"Becky, my dear, I want to introduce you to one of our brave doctors from the Continental Army, Dr. Maximilian Richter. Dr. Richter has served in many campaigns, treating our wounded soldiers." John Tayloe smiled approval at his guest. "The doctor is on his way southward to served the military in Georgia."

Becky curtsied politely, and held out her hand. "Good morning, Dr. Richter. Perhaps you've met our kinsman, Dr. Shippen. He's my husband's brother-in-law. A talented and dedicated man ... it's a sad fact however, and very unfair, that his enemies have cast criticisms at his management capabilities from time to time."

The visitor blinked several times before he spoke. "Most unfortunate, my dear Mrs. Lee. It is Mrs. Lee, isn't it?"

His warm moist hand left Becky feeling unexpectedly wary, and she didn't miss the fact that he hadn't acknowledged whether he knew William Shippen, who would have been his commanding officer as Director-General of Hospitals. "Yes, I'm Mrs. Lee. My husband, Francis, is a member of the Congress. We're home on a leave of absence this summer. And ..." she smiled indulgently at her father, "very happy to be here with my dear parents."

"To be sure," Dr. Richter said.

"I'll leave you now, if you don't mind, Papa. "I want to visit Mama and take little John and Jane to the orangery. Perhaps I shall see you later, Doctor."

Nodding absentmindedly to Jacob in the great hall, she was feeling limp, parched from the heat, like a plant left too long untended in a sunny window. Meeting Dr. Richter had been vaguely disturbing, although she didn't know why. What was he doing here anyway? A northerner on his way to join the army in Georgia? It didn't sound right. She'd remember to ask Francis about it. Finding her mother seated at her dressing table having her hair done, her spirits took a notch upward. "Mama," she called, with a burst of enthusiasm. "You look simply beautiful with your hair combed that way." Kissing her cheek, she settled to watch.

"I've worn it this way for ever so long, dear. But thank you. It's so good to have you home. How did you find your father? And did you meet that military surgeon who's passing through?"

Becky frowned. "Is that what he's doing? Passing through? Papa didn't explain why he was here at Mount Airy."

"Well, he was sent here, he says, by our Dr. Jones, who thought since Dr. Richter was in the vicinity, he might have some fresh ideas on Papa's condition."

"And does he?"

"He only arrived last evening. He gave Papa something to help the pain, but that's all."

"Umm."

"How is Francis this morning, dear? Is his cold better?"

"He's quite fine, Mama. Much better in fact. They're bringing in a flax crop, and his only wish this morning was to supervise. It's so exciting for him, being back here, seeing his plantation at work. We've both missed the farm. Especially Francis."

Rebecca waved to the maid, dismissing her. "You truly adore that man, don't you? And it's clear he worships you. That's been evident from the beginning."

"The beginning?"

"One would surely think, Becky," she began, reaching for her daughter's hand, "that with so much affection between you, well ... it would seem there would be a child by this time."

Becky's mouth hardened into a firm line. This was a topic she no longer wished to consider, not wanting to reopen the wound that had almost healed. "We've been married almost ten years, Mama," she said quietly. "There will never be a child. We have accepted that." She moved to leave, knowing it the only sure way to end the discussion. "I'll be back. I want to play with John and Janie before they take their naps."

"Wait, Becky. There's something I must tell you. Your father has, well … he has prevailed upon Dr. Richter, who has experience in these matters, to give you a brief examination. Had you not come by, we planned to send for you this afternoon."

"What?" Becky felt stricken. "There's nothing wrong with me."

"Dear, your father is getting up in years. We must humor him. It's very important to him that you have an heir. He'd like to be certain there's not some simple reason you do not conceive."

Becky's face was ashen. "Mama, I am not a cow, to be prodded and poked. Nor am I a slave to be handled and examined when I don't supply my quota of increase. And most certainly, I will not, under any circumstances, submit to an examination by that … damp, ugly little stranger!"

"That is partly the point, child. As he's not familiar to us, it will be less embarrassing for all concerned. He's assured Papa he will be … circumspect. So you have no worry on that count." Rebecca had seldom found herself in a more awkward situation. John had insisted against her wishes that she prepare Becky for this. There was to be no refusal. He was convinced there was some simple problem, that could be made right as soon as it was discovered. He had become quite obsessed with the idea that Becky and Francis must provide an heir to Menokin.

Becky felt tears forming and angrily blinked them back. "I am not going to submit to such an invasion of my privacy! And there is *no problem*!" She threw herself on the bed, remembering how it had felt long ago to be a child and forced to obey a command against her will.

Half an hour later, her mother's pleading having dissolved in tears of frustration, Becky finally gave in. She agreed to undressing and, shortly thereafter, with her mother and two slaves to sustain her, Dr. Maximilian Richter was ushered into the chamber.

Issuing a few curt orders to the servants, the doctor began his examination. Becky caught a stale whiff of spirits when he leaned over the bed. She went rigid, her face turned as far into the pillow as she could manage, eyes clamped shut, her fists clenched under the sheet. As the bed clothes were raised to reveal her lower anatomy to what she imagined as the lusting gaze of the doctor, she felt the nipples on her breasts go tight. Everything inside her cried out with shame as, suddenly, she remembered the little girl on the roadside in their flight from Philadelphia and knew how that frightened child must have felt. Remaining silent, she didn't protest nor flinch as his sweaty fingers probed between her legs. Even when they entered her body and his other hand prodded her stomach, she refused to wince. When he was finished and the sheet drawn over her, relief came like a cool wave. But her face continued to burn fiery red.

"Now, Mrs. Lee," he said, kindly enough, "I know you're happy to have that much completed. You were very brave." It was what he said to every patient no matter the ailment because he'd learned it seemed to please them. With her, it was as he'd guessed; the birth canal was very small, immaturely formed, not remotely large enough for the head of an infant to pass through. The woman was not built for child bearing and she was fortunate that she'd been spared the agony of undergoing it because it quite likely would have killed her. Beautiful body though. Soft white skin and exquisitely pointed breasts. He decided at that moment that he'd talk to her alone, ask her some questions before pronouncing to her father that his grandchildren would have to be produced in his other daughters' wombs, not this one. If he played it right, he reasoned, he should collect a handsome fee and be on his way by mid-afternoon. Or, perhaps, he shouldn't be so hasty, leave them with a shred of hope—he could give Mrs. Lee some harmless medicine to take, as he already planned to do with the old colonel. Then he might linger to enjoy a few more meals. His funds were running dangerously low. "You may dress now and when you're ready I'll return, and perhaps we can have a few moments to discuss the situation. We shall have a short private talk and then we'll be finished. I think you'd rather face me after you've had a chance to regain your composure."

By the time Becky had dressed and assured her mother that she was capable of facing the man alone, just for a short talk as he'd mentioned, she found she had indeed composed herself. "I apologize for my fright. It's merely that I was un-aware this examination was to take place and I had no time to prepare myself for it." A small flame of hope had begun to flicker in her heart. Was it just possible he might be able to help them? He was smiling at her, waiting for her to continue. "I ... we have very much wanted a child, Dr. Richter. Can you help us?" Now she wanted to cooperate, thinking there might be a small chance he knew some way, and how wonderful that would be.

"Well now, Mrs. Lee, as I indicated when I suggested I speak with you alone, I have a few ... um ... delicate questions that might shed some light. Try to relax and answer as best you can." He settled in a chair as close to her as the furniture placement allowed—four feet of space separated them. Thinking what a beauty she was and what a pleasure it would be to watch her color rise, he began. "Now, to begin with, you love your husband. And he loves you, is that correct?"

Becky nodded, wondering what was coming next.

"And you have been married a number of years, nine or ten? Always sharing the same bed?"

Her reply was again a silent nod, but her cheeks were beginning to feel hot as before.

"And to your knowledge has he ever been a man with interests elsewhere than at home? In other words, is he promiscuous?"

Becky's head was bent and she didn't look up. "Oh, no never!" The feeling of panic returned.

"Well, that's good news, good news indeed. He spends his nights at home and warms himself in your bed I presume?" Becky's dismay would have been heightened had she looked at the doctor's eyes just then; they were fastened on the base of her throat. There he could watch the pulsating throb of heartbeat in the V formed by the sinews, and still enjoy the slight cleft indicating the rounded bosom below, such soft white skin above the printed dimity of her gown. And poor Mr. Lee couldn't breed her! Well, now. "Since you're not new to the married state and therefore not innocent in that sense, please answer me something else. When he makes love to you, how do you feel? I mean, what does it do to you inside?"

At his words Becky's hands flew to her face. She remained frozen, unable to draw breath, let alone speak.

He pursued. "Perhaps my question isn't clear. When your husband loves you, does he touch you, caress you?" His voice was rising now, his pulse quickening.

"Yes," she whispered from behind her hands.

"And do you like it when he does this to you?"

Again she whimpered affirmatively, feeling like a wooden doll unable to take any action on her own."

"Do you respond to him? Do you open your heart and your lovely body to him, and come to meet him with passion when he ... enters?"

"Yes, yes, yes!" she screamed. "Leave me alone!" Losing all control, she burst into tears.

The doctor had lied to Tayloe. He'd had few women patients, but had delighted in the experience each time. It gave him a

feeling of power he was incapable of achieving in a personal relationship. This time he'd worked himself into such a state he'd
almost forgotten the awkward circumstances surrounding his reason for being in this place. He'd never met Walter Jones, the
local physician, only knew his name and county of origin through
military rolls. It wouldn't do to make a mistake now. His life
depended on keeping his head. Having escaped after the court
martial through a series of harrowing events, he knew they might
still pursue him. With an effort, he forced himself to walk to the
window. When he'd regained control of himself, he turned back
to the young woman. She had straightened in her chair and was
glaring hatred at him. Briefly, he considered the font of inner
strength he discerned in her pose and decided to be honest with
her regarding her condition.

"My dear Mrs. Lee, I regret I must be the one to inform you
that if your marriage is one of wedded bliss as you indicate, then
based upon my examination I think there is very little chance that
after ten years you will ever bear a child. Furthermore, your body
is small, delicate, not made for child bearing. It is quite possible
you would not survive giving birth." It had never been his plan to
tell her all this—it was the fury in those incredible green eyes that
had drawn it from him—and the same that made him continue.
"Your father is thinking of deeding you the lands on which you
and your husband have built your house, but he's worried about
who will inherit the plantation ... Menokin, isn't it called ... upon
your deaths."

Following what had just transpired, Becky found it difficult
to concentrate on what the man was saying, but she heard the last
clearly. "I don't believe you," she gasped. "Papa wouldn't have
confided such things to you, a total stranger!"

Dr. Richter sensed immediately he was digging his hole ever
deeper. It could only spell trouble for him if she went directly to
her father. The old man had been quite under the debilitating af-
fects of laudanum prescribed for his pain, when he'd rambled on

about plans to deed the property the previous evening. Richter knew he must pacify her, then clear out fast. "My dear, there are many women who never have children and yet lead very happy and fruitful lives. I trust and hope it may be so with you." Moving to the doorway, he felt almost benevolent. "Goodbye, Mrs. Lee. If we ever meet again, may it be under more pleasant circumstances for both of us."

Becky was out of the house even before the doctor's hurried departure. Meeting Jacob in the dependency hall she asked him to bring the chaise around immediately. As he hurried to the stable he wondered what had happened to make Miss Becky so angry. The only thing she remembered later about the ride home was taking the turn at the bottom of the mill pond going so fast she barely avoided tipping over. Her first action upon arriving at Menokin was to write a note to her father. *"My dear Father,"* she wrote, *"It is with regret that I inform you I shall never be able to forgive you for forcing me to submit to such an outrage. Respectfully, your daughter Rebecca."* Then she paced the house, impatient for Francis to return from the fields. When she'd poured out her story, omitting only the most agonizing details, she told him of the note she had written.

"Don't send it, Becky," he advised.

"I've already done so. Cate is probably on her way back even now. I'm sure he has it in hand at this very moment."

"It will break his heart. You know he never intended to hurt you."

"I don't care. He *did* hurt me, and he deserves worse than a silly angry note!"

"He couldn't have known what the doctor was like, or he wouldn't have asked him to see you at all. Can't you at least try to see it from his point of view?"

"Well if he didn't know the man why would he choose to subject his daughter to such an examination by a complete stranger?"

Francis was frowning now, thinking she certainly had a point. It occurred to him they should stop the fellow, call him to account before he left the county. Of course! That should have been his first consideration! If he was a quack as Becky seemed to think, he might have given Tayloe some harmful medicine. There was no telling. "Becky, what did you say the doctor's name was? I'm going after him, it's for certain he can't have got across the river yet."

"I didn't say. But if it matters, which I doubt, it was Richter, Maximilian Richter. I'm not likely to forget it, nor his filthy damp fingers!"

Francis dropped his pipe. It clattered to the floor but he didn't stoop to pick it up. "My God," was all he said, and then he was gone. The horse was still saddled, tied to the post. For once he was thankful for the laxity of his slaves. He had never mounted an animal in such a hurry.

In all the months since Peter Hauck had told him the story of his brother's death Francis had kept the name of the attending surgeon in his mind; even Shippen had seemed unable to track the man down, records were sketchy at best, he'd said and doctors came and went. But there could only be one Maximilian Richter who was a doctor! Francis tore down the lane leading to Mount Airy at top speed, his horse lathered and breathing foam. But he was too late. The stable slave told him the visitor had left in a mighty hurry several hours before. The butcher-surgeon, now tormentor of women, was undoubtedly across the Rappahannock by now.

In the morning one of the Mount Airy people brought a story of the drowning to Menokin. The doctor who had been a guest at the plantation had been drinking heavily before he boarded the ferry and apparently had toppled overboard while crossing the river. No one was able to save him because his body was not spotted in time, and his cries for help were heard too late. It was an ugly accident, the ferry captain had reported upon his return.

"Thank God," Francis announced to Becky when he brought her the news. "In the mood I was in yesterday I might have shot him, had I caught up with him." He hadn't told her who the doctor was, only that he'd known of him in the past. Now, he decided, there was no point in saying more. Justice had been served on two accounts. "Now come, we'll go speak with your father."

"No."

"Becky, you must make up with him. He's a sick man grieving over having hurt you. The doctor is dead, it doesn't matter any longer."

"You don't understand, Francis. It's not the wretched doctor I blame. It's Papa."

❧

Two weeks later John Tayloe felt well enough to do something he'd planned to do all along. He drew up a deed of gift by which he transferred the ownership of Menokin Plantation to his daughter and her heirs; should her husband outlive her, he was to have the estate for his lifetime. Thus did the colonel assure the lands and house would remain the property of the Tayloe family.

"You see what he's doing, don't you?" Becky asked Francis when the document was carried to Menokin for their reading of it.

"Yes, I do. He seems determined this plantation should not leave his family."

"That's not what I mean. He's trying to make up with me for the anguish he caused. But it's not going to work. I can't forgive him."

Francis knelt before her, taking her hands in his. "You're wrong, love. He needs to know you care about him, before we go away again. Don't you see that? You've always been his favorite. Even after little John, you are *still* his special child. You have to forgive him." He could see she was listening to him. "There is one thing that disturbs me about the deed," he continued. "And you can help me, if you will. If you relinquish your right of dower, then we'll be free to name our own heir. I should like to put Menokin in trust for Richard and his sons. I truly don't think your father will mind."

"Richard?" she asked dumbly.

"I've given it a great deal of thought, Becky. Richard has two sons by Anne Aylett. I've always been exceedingly fond of them both. Only one will benefit from Richard's will, and that is Thomas. I would very much like Ludwell to have Menokin eventually."

"I ... well ..." She thought that if nothing else, it would help her get even with her father for his high-handedness. "All right. We'll do it. I agree with you. Menokin should belong to the Lees. It has *your* heart and soul in it, not Papa's."

"But you must promise me that you'll explain it to him before any papers are drawn. Promise?"

She nodded vaguely, no longer listening. This would make it clear to her father that he'd had no right to subject her to such humiliation, she reasoned. Francis's reasons aside, it would be her way of proving her point.

Court day came in early October, and they were ready for it. When they arrived, although he wasn't required to be present, John Tayloe was inside the courthouse. The colonel, enjoying a respite from his pain, was seated with an old friend on a bench in the front row. His shoulders sagged and his head was near-white. For a moment Becky quivered, then raising her chin she reached for Francis's arm and proceeded into the bustling courtroom. They took seats on a second row bench on the opposite side. Francis tried to get Tayloe's attention but then the gavel sounded and there was no time. Three other cases were heard first: Mr. Thornton's inventory and the appraisement of his estate; Glascock's inspectors were ordered to sell an outstanding tobacco transfer; and finally William Stonum's account of his guardianship of two orphans was admitted to record. Becky kept her eyes fastened on a small window in line with—but above—her father's head. The minutes dragged as separate eternities until the call was given for Tayloe's Deed of Gift to Lee. Becky's hand shook when she took the pen to sign; she never once let her father know she was aware of his presence. Then it was over and they sat down.

The clerk read the next item on the docket—Lee's Deed of Trust to Lee—at which point John Tayloe's head snapped around, an agony of disbelief blazing across his face.

Somehow Becky managed to get through it, although a hundred times during the reading she wanted to call out that she'd changed her mind. But she'd already signed away her right of dower to her husband; that had been accomplished an hour before the court convened. So it didn't matter what she did now, she reminded herself, it would be too late anyway. When finally the deed was recorded and she turned around, the front bench was empty. "He's gone," she whispered. "Darling, Papa has left."

"You *did* tell him what we planned to do?" Oh, my God, he moaned silently. I should have asked her before. I'm to blame.

Terrified, she shook her head. "No." I wanted to hurt him, her heart screamed ... and I did.

Francis grabbed her hand and with her in tow, he strode quickly through the crowded room, glancing neither right nor left. Once outside, he paused to survey the yard. But Becky had already spotted what she was looking for. She flew down the steps, across the dusty yard and into the open arms of her father. "Papa. Papa," she cried, kissing and hugging him. "I am so sorry. I have been wicked. I shouldn't have done it without telling you! I promised Francis to ask you about it."

Tayloe didn't try to depend on his voice. Heart throbbing, he merely clutched the lovely child he thought he'd lost forever because of his own faulty and callous judgement. He patted her, he petted her, he crooned to her. His baby girl. His green-eyed love.

"Do you forgive me? Can you ever forgive me for signing it away without telling you?" She was trembling, her voice coming in jerks.

The colonel cleared his throat, relief spreading in waves through his body. "It doesn't matter, sweetheart. What matters is you ... here ... forgiving me for the pain and distress I caused you."

There was a handsome hickory tree in the yard, planted about the same time the courthouse had been built. Francis leaned there under the spreading branches, arms folded across his chest, a contented smile on his face. He was remembering the horse race when Yorick was pitted against Gift when he'd stood on this very spot trying to make up his mind. Like that race, he wouldn't have wanted to place any bets on today's outcome. Had he suspected Becky's angry deceit, he'd not have dared. But in both cases, had he played his hunch, he would have won. "Wonderful, wonderful," he said to no one. Now, he could begin to plan for the return journey to Philadelphia, probably they should leave before October passed. He'd remained away from the Congress four months already.

What Damn'd Dirty Business

Before Francis had taken his leave from Congress, he had participated in the momentous decision to ratify the treaties with France. America now stood formally allied with her old enemy, who for almost a century had armed the Indians and led them in bloody attacks against the western settlements. This so-called French Alliance was the culmination of months of negotiations between the three American commissioners in Paris and the French Court; Benjamin Franklin, Silas Deane, and Arthur Lee had found little on which to agree amongst themselves, yet amidst the charges and counter charges they flung at one another with Arthur playing odd-man-out, they had miraculously come to terms with the French government. The agreement they sent to Congress was in two parts—the first provided for amity and commerce, while the second pledged that both agreed to fight until American independence from the British was won. Despite varying degrees of opposition from some quarters, the treaties were considered by most to be the only possible ticket to salvation for the struggling new nation.

The Congress was in the highest spirits it had known since the early days. There was not only the alliance with France to elate them, but the return to Philadelphia as well; the British and their Tory friends had decamped to New York on orders from London immediately following the news of France having entered the war. Steadied by the promise of money and arms and the savoir-faire the Congress was counting on their new ally to provide, the delegates bravely scoffed at a British overture to peace. Upon his return, Francis soon learned, however, that many segments

523

of government remained in varying stages of confusion, despite these very hopeful developments.

Richard had departed three days prior to his arrival. The brothers met briefly on the Maryland road, just long enough for Richard to pass on a bare outline of the factions now forming over the fate of Silas Deane, but he touched only vaguely on the Lees' involvement in the making of a crisis. The first real clues Francis had concerning the shocking muddle of Mr. Deane, who had arrived in America as summoned, came from Henry Laurens.

"I have a note here from President Laurens," he told Becky, opening the folded message he'd been given upon reporting in. "He invites me to visit him at my earliest convenience. Something about Mr. Dean's homecoming."

Silas Deane, recalled from his post at Paris primarily through the efforts of Richard and his political chums, had presented himself in the capitol accompanied by the new French Minister to America, Monsieur Conrad Alexandre Gérard, with whom it was believed Deane had established a close acquaintanceship on the long voyage. Their arrival had sparked a great caterwaul on and off the congressional floor, Richard had told him during their short time together on the road.

"I trust there's not some new problem to plague you? I mean ... well, surely, the president is eager to fill you in on what has transpired during our five months in Virginia. Why don't you call on him this evening? I won't mind. I have much to do here to get things back in order." Apparently the owners of the house, returning during the occupation, had stripped the place of everything they could carry with them before fleeing in the wake of the British forces. Becky thought it a rewarding mark of Christian character, however, that they'd not claimed one thing that didn't belong to them personally. Including the desk. Dusty, and more than a little scratched and ink blotched, it stood exactly where the Lees had left it.

"I think I'll do that, love, if you're certain you won't mind. I'll call on Mr. Laurens tonight."

Francis walked the short distance, seeking exercise. It was snowing, early this year for it was still November. The flakes were like large white magic swirling about him, lending an air of promise to the somber streets, and a feeling of hope surged through him for a moment. At the same time he sensed he was about to be thrust into the position of defending the family honor once again. That grim realization stayed with him for the rest of the way as he hurried his footsteps, no longer intrigued by the snow.

Henry Laurens lazed before a roaring fire. Like Richard, the Carolinian suffered from gout; his feet were elevated on a non-descript wooden footstool as close to the blaze as was possible without singeing them. The scent of blistered varnish was in the room. "Ah, Frank. Good to see you. Forgive me if I don't stand up, will you? We've missed your sage wisdom these months past," he confessed honestly. "I trust you found things well at home?"

"As well as could be expected, Sir. Some family illness and of course our business suffers in our absence ... the same is true in your case, I imagine. But how have you been?" Francis brushed the remnants of the blustery weather from his waistcoat. Lauren's relaxed pose was reassuring—it encouraged him to shed the bulk of his apprehension with the cloak he handed to the houseboy.

"Oh, things go along and come along. As you know ...." Laurens gazed into the fire as though searching for something. "Nothing like a good crackling blaze to coax a man to leisure, is there? Sit down, sit down, Frank. My servant will bring us some wine in a few minutes ... if there's anything left in my larder worth drinking," he chuckled. "Wine is becoming difficult to come by these days. Even for a merchant. And between the British and the Tories they did a fine job of stripping the city of anything useful!"

"The trade agreements with the French should ease the wine shortage, Mr. President," Francis suggested tentatively, taking a seat opposite his host in a curiously loose-bottomed chair, designed either for comfort or well worn, he couldn't tell. He began to relax.

"Umm. One would hope for such a result. But, it's foolish to indulge in premature speculation in my opinion."

"You doubt the rewards of the alliance?" Francis asked.

"No. Oh, no, I have faith enough in the intent."

"Then what?"

"Well, I think the precise wording of the treaty lacks any divine finality, which Mr. Deane would have us believe it does. The truth of the matter is, as your brother Arthur Lee so ably pointed out, that probably two of the articles in the commerce treaty will actually hamper our future world trade. Lately it appears our meddling with these interpretations threatens to weaken the framework of the whole, however. Monsieur Gérard has placed himself awkwardly in the middle of our squabbles and the matter, as so often happens, has degenerated into personalities."

"Oh? I'm sorry to hear that." Francis felt a familiar tingle up his spine.

"The blunt fact is ... well, a sentiment was repeated to me the other day. I think you should hear it. As it was told me, it went something like this: *'the storm increases and Deane, who has rendered the most essential services, stands as one accused. The only solution appears to be that some one of the tall Congressional trees must be torn up by the roots.'* Does that make any sense to you Frank?"

Francis sipped the claret the houseboy had brought him. He used the savoring of it to delay an immediate response to what he saw now as the ugly fruition of his recent premonition. The bouquet fell far short of that of his favorite, Madeira, but seemed nonetheless congenial on a cold winter's evening. He prayed it would ease his angst. "The author of that sentiment refers, of course, to my brother Richard?" The question was scarcely necessary.

"Yes, I would think so."

"Of course. Otherwise you wouldn't bother to present it to me in such an elaborate fashion." Taking another swallow of wine he felt anger bubble—not toward his companion—but at the unnamed assailant who conspired against Richard. "Who said it, Henry? Who is against us?"

"A New Yorker. That's all I feel free to say. It was told to me in confidence, more as a warning than for any other reason."

"Duer? Jemmy Duane?"

The president shook his head. "No, neither of them. I would really rather not be specific."

"Well, I'm thankful it's not one of them at least. After working with Duer so closely on the war board lo these many months, I'd be appalled if he could strike so unconscionable a blow."

"Actually," Laurens said, changing his mind abruptly, "don't be misled. Duer is probably in on it, but it came out in a conversation I had with Jay. He had it in a letter from Governor Morris in August."

"I see," Francis said sadly. "The entire New York contingent. But why the death-wish for Richard? Unless ... could it have anything to do with the affair at Nantes when my brother William was sent to settle the public accounts of the deceased American commercial agent, the Morris kinsman? The man was a drunkard, a reprobate as I understand it. William would hardly have been the epitome of tact if he uncovered irregularities, which I understand he did. I can assure you of that."

Laurens stared hard at him. Burrowing in search of an answer he narrowed his eyes, wishing he could penetrate the inner shell of the man sitting opposite him. "Your brother Arthur has been called many things, including less than diplomatic upon occasion. Deane, and Dr. Franklin as well, say he's totally lacking in candor, unfit to negotiate with foreign powers. Coming from the old doctor ... the man who has taken the Parisians by storm, tickled their fancy with one clever *bon mot* after another ... I am forced to give heed to this criticism." It was meant as a challenge, he supposed. Was he being too hard on poor Frank?

Francis nodded and, watching the flames burst behind a new log, he pondered what had prompted the words. "I've heard that, Henry. I've heard that." The servant was attentive, alert enough to have refilled their glasses. "Arthur is a brilliant man, I think, an enigmatic genius in his own way. He's astute and far reaching in all his considerations. I wish you could know him. But, perhaps, he's arrogant as well, even demanding at times, much as Richard is. Brilliant men often suffer from arrogance, I've found, and perhaps they don't even recognize it in themselves. They're always a step ahead of the rest of the world, impatient with those who drag their intellectual feet. And Dr. Franklin is an old man, brilliant in his own way, laboring under his own brand of self-righteousness, and inclined to be petty." He knew it might be dangerous to criticize Franklin. "Perhaps Deane never allowed the other two a chance to understand each other. But ... I'm straying from the subject. Why do you think Morris has hatched this cabal to supplant Richard?"

"And Arthur," Henry Laurens added. "I think there has developed a clearly obvious conspiracy to remove them both from the public arena. Let me tell you of another incident. There was an Englander here about a month or so ago. A Dr. Berkenhout. Did Richard write you of him? Well, the doctor created quite a stir here in Philadelphia, ended up in jail, accused of being a British spy sent to infiltrate the Congress. It became known Berkenhout had more than a passing acquaintance with Arthur Lee from university days in Edinburgh ... a friendship kept alive over the years through an active correspondence, apparently some of it on a political level. The fellow used Richard's name to earn himself a pass through the lines of our army. You should have heard the Deane faction howl over that one! They were absolutely certain they'd stumbled upon a supreme weapon with which to unseat two Lees in one unequivocal coup d'état."

"But they failed because they had no real evidence of wrong-doing on the part of either of my brothers." Richard had told him that much, passing the matter off lightly when they'd met on the Maryland road; he'd barely mentioned Berkenhout in fact.

"It ... blew over, as most of these nasty little flurries do. The English doctor was sent packing, and Richard vindicated. Richard swore he'd never laid eyes on the man before, knew nothing about him, and I had no reason to doubt his word."

"It's the truth. But another log has been tossed on Richard's funeral pyre nonetheless," Francis observed.

"If you wish to look at it that way, but it's one of the scourges each of us must be prepared to face when we take the oath of office, Frank. An outspoken man like Richard is infinitely more susceptible to envy and malice than most. And, as you will soon learn, Silas Deane is very vocal in his condemnation of Arthur. The more rumors Deane puts about, the more determined Richard has become to press charges of corruption and abuse of public funds against him, none of which can be proved at this point by a single shred of solid evidence! Richard has only Arthur's word to go on. And that is from letters a half year old."

"How do *you* feel about it?" Francis felt compelled to ask.

"Distressed. Confused. To be perfectly honest with you, I plain don't know. It's the reason I asked you here to talk ... to pick your brain in private regarding your family, your brothers. I'm seeking anything that will help me rise above the gossip and innuendo that pervades the matter, so that I may form a fair opinion of Mr. Deane. Damn'd if I've been able to accomplish it thus far!"

"Where does Lovell stand now?" Francis asked. James Lovell, a Massachusetts delegate, was closely allied with Richard's views in most cases. Lovell had tried unsuccessfully for an earlier recall of Deane himself.

"Staunchly in favor of sacrificing Deane to the cause of justice."

"Sam Adams?"

"Sam's a wily old codger, but he's backing Richard a hundred percent. I value his opinion, though he can be an expert at twisting the facts to suit his particular purpose. Such as recently when, from the floor, he stated that Deane had never been vested with any political powers whatsoever. That is simply not true."

"What powers would you say we gave to him?" Francis pressed, raising his eyebrow.

"It's difficult to define exactly. And that's undoubtedly where part of the problem lies. But Deane was definitely sent frequent and explicit instructions from the Secret Committee for actions he was to take in the French Court."

"I don't believe I would term that to be the 'conferring of political powers' on the man, Henry."

Laurens shrugged. "It's a fine line. I do freely admit he was never given authority to hire those countless foreign officers, promising them the glories of command and rank."

"I should hope not!" Francis allowed a laugh, realizing as he did so it was the first time in nearly two hours anything had struck him as the least bit humorous. "I'm reminded of an incident involving the Marquis, De Kalb the German, and whoever else arrived in that group. There were about twenty of them as I recall. It was before you were elected ... Lovell, assigned the task due to his fluency in French, ordered them in no uncertain terms to look for the next ship back across the Atlantic. He could claim no plume for diplomacy on that one! He didn't even invite them into the building, but met them on the steps outside. Lafayette, as Lovell himself informed us, flew into a childish fury, almost challenging him to a duel on the spot! The poor boy's ego was sorely damaged, I was told ... he would no doubt have sailed within the month had he not immediately thereafter attached himself so satisfactorily to His Excellency's broad receptive epaulets! And, of course, now with the dismal failure of Gate's misbegotten Canadian expedition, there's another bitter pill for our French boy-wonder. How I wish I'd evidenced the strength of my convictions by opposing that fatal plan! But then ... I've always been heavy on the hindsight, Henry. I wouldn't know myself were I to become suddenly bold about expressing my occasional clairvoyance."

"Nor would you be the same without your charming reticence," Laurens chuckled. "It's good to have you back, Frank! I've missed your wit ... and your honesty. It's a lonely chair I occupy. How lonely, no one can ever really know unless he has sat in it."

"That's probably the only thing you share in common with your predecessor, Sir ... the physical use of the chair."

"You don't like Hancock, do you?"

Francis demurred. "There are few men I don't like," he admitted, "only some that I am more fond of than others. Our friend Sam had plenty to say on the subject of John Hancock."

"Ah, the Adams viewpoint. The Lees and the Adamses. Tell me, since we're being candid, do the Adams and the Lees always stick together, Frank?"

"I would have to say, not always, but probably most of the time for a good many years now. At least up to now we owe each other no favors that I'm aware of."

"In other words, what is given is repaid from both sides in full, *n'est-ce pas?*" Laurens tipped his glass and drained the few drops remaining. "Well, we haven't solved anything, but I have enjoyed the evening immensely. I hope you have."

"Definitely," Francis agreed, rising. "I must be going home. Mrs. Lee will wonder into what diversion I have strayed."

"Mrs. Lee knows better than to contemplate anything unsavory ... from either of us. But it is late. Before you go, there is one point on which we haven't touched. Monsieur Gérard, the French Minister. You've not had time to meet him, have you? I can tell you he's thrown our little society into quite a tizzy."

Francis shook his head. Richard had written of being impressed by Gérard at first meeting. But a later letter had revealed second thoughts. "Richard indicated Monsieur Gérard, while inordinately charming, was overly friendly with Silas Deane," he offered. "I suppose that could be said to have colored my opinion without my ever having met the man."

"It's a fact that was to be expected. After all, Gérard and Deane have known each other for some time and made the crossing together, with all the opportunities for intimacy that implies."

"That arrangement, I surmise, was a clever maneuver on the part of Deane. He surely could have sailed on any number of vessels, yet he waited for the one that was to carry the minister." Francis eased himself back into the chair as he tried to remember if it was Arthur or William who had put that viewpoint in his head.

Henry Laurens sucked at his pipe which had gone out, but made no move to re-light it. "There is another point I wish to make. As you are aware, we're in the sticky throes of determining the course of our finance. There are accusations that certain of our decisions lean to the benefit of the eastern states, to the detriment of Virginia, the Carolinas, and Georgia. It is gossiped by the Deane camp, and some of your fellow Virginians, Harvey and Griffen to name names, that Richard Henry Lee has prostituted his voting on the finances in order to gain the support of his northeastern friends against Mr. Deane."

"Poppycock," Francis murmured. "I can't for a minute believe there is any truth to that."

"Well, I don't propose to judge it, I'm only repeating what I've heard. And I think you should be prepared for the beehive you'll be walking into. Griffin has insinuated that according to Gérard, there is no one but Deane capable of satisfactorily completing the French treaty. Further, that Richard intends to sacrifice Deane for the political advancement of his own brothers ... meaning

William and Arthur. You know William was refused by the Court of Berlin, and Arthur by Spain, do you not?"

"Yes, I've had word of that. But, would it not have been true of any American in both cases under the present circumstances?"

"Perhaps. However, you see, the faction won't let us have it that way. Even now they are questioning the patriotism of your brothers. Witness the incident over Dr. Berkenhout."

Francis gripped the arms of his chair until his knuckles turned white. "There are no more dedicated patriots to ever draw breath than my brothers. And none more able nor trustworthy."

"You are absolutely certain of that?" Laurens asked quietly. "You harbor not the slightest doubt? It's not merely family loyalty that directs your tongue?"

"Do you doubt me, Sir?"

"No. I'm seeking your rock-bottom gut opinion, minus the trappings of brotherly love."

"Well, you shall have it, Mr. President. I am without the least reservation in what I say. If Arthur states that Mr. Deane has lined his pockets with public money, than I say we had bloody well better investigate his accounts to uncover in what manner and to what extent the scoundrel has cheated us!"

"Those accounts, I've learned, aren't available to us at the moment, Deane having overlooked the importance of bringing them with him from France."

Francis scoffed. "You see, he has much to hide, as Arthur says."

"Without the accounts we have no evidence. And Gérard seems bent on making Deane out a hero, intimating that it's due to Deane's efforts alone that the French fleet under d'Estaing is here to defend our shores. As I've said, there is a vicious plot afoot to defame the Lees and to promote Mr. Silas Deane, and it crosses international boundary lines. It appears to me, without a doubt, that our new French minister is in on it."

"What am I to do?" Francis wondered aloud, more to himself than to Laurens.

"Watch. Wait, for the time being, and keep your ears open. Write to your brothers in Europe to send facts. Complaints, suspicions, uneasiness are one thing, but only facts can bring this matter to a head."

The fire had dwindled. Embers glowed in the darkened room. Somehow, Francis pondered, the blaze had contributed materially to their conversation; kept it warm in an aura of comradery. "It was a good fire," he said, feeling inadequate because what he really wanted to do was to thank Henry Laurens for his friendship.

"Yes. Didn't I mention upon your arrival that a pleasant hearth fosters ease? ... in this case, good will, I might add."

"Yes indeed, you did at that, Henry."

"Have another swig of claret before you brave the snow, Frank. It will do us both good to have a bit more."

Francis held out his glass and the boy tipped the decanter, scarlet liquid sparkled to the brim. "Thank you, Henry. The wine is good, also. Thank you," he said again.

Laurens recognized his guest wasn't referring to the warm fire and the drink alone. "Yes, but I think it's perhaps I who should thank you. You've helped me to make up my mind on an issue that has hitherto confounded me."

The two men exchanged glances and continued to sit comfortably sipping wine and meditating on the fire. A new log was blazing now.

∽

Within a few days Francis learned that Deane's appearance before the delegates in August had touched off a near riot on the congressional floor. Everyone who told the story agreed that Deane had subjected them to an ordeal, while they in turn had harangued him. Thereafter he'd been dismissed and asked to submit his testimony in writing. Deane was now charging, three months later, that he was not being permitted to present said testimony. From what he could glean, Francis decided there was no truth to that at all—the fact was that Congress was so bogged down in the financial matters that threatened to sink the American ship, there simply was no time for Mr. Deane at the moment. There was little doubt, however, that the members dreaded another outburst from the pro and con Deane men among their group, but Francis couldn't see that they were intentionally putting it off.

When it burst upon them, the explosion came from an unexpected quarter. On December 5th, Silas Deane, impatient and totally frustrated by a Congress cold to his personal anguish, published an account in the *Pennsylvania Packet*. It was a far cry from the accounting of the actions of the three commissioners in Paris he'd been requested to prepare. It was an open assault, pure and simple, on the Lees.

"My God, I don't believe this," Francis raged to Becky. "It's not possible that a man can spread such lies ... lies ... in the public papers! He's come right out and accused Arthur of giving away state secrets to the British while in Berlin, saying he accomplished no other business, that Arthur's acquaintance with various 'patrons' in England plus his undisguised hatred and expression of contempt for the French nation in general, led him to this traitorous path!"

Becky could think of nothing to say to this nightmare which had suddenly appeared in the black and white of newsprint to defame one of her husband's brothers.

"There's more! He says Arthur has carried on a criminal, mind you, a *criminal* correspondence with that Dr. Berken-whatsits and others, on matters of political importance ... that he sent the doctor here to extract matters of secret from the Congress, through Richard, and further, that Arthur gave great cause for disgust to the Court of Spain, and on and on." Tossing the paper angrily onto a table, he began pacing the room. "Well, the leopard has shown his spots at last ... the first thing I must do is write a rebuttal. Those attacked, Arthur and Richard, aren't here to defend themselves. Mr. Silas Deane can't be allowed to get away with such slander!"

Two hours later Francis stared at the second complete draft of his counterattack. He'd been through all Arthur's letters and some of Richard's, searching for ammunition. He read slowly through what he had written; it contained nothing to make him proud of himself. Rather, it made him feel reduced in stature and reeking of meanness, worse than he imagined Deane himself to be. It wasn't his style. There was nothing to do but to start all over. Begin again. Take a different tack. He shredded the paper into little pieces and picked up a clean sheet.

When he'd finished the third time, he sat with an entirely different article in his hands. This one he could be pleased to have printed under his own signature. In it he asked for justice to be served the characters who suffered injury in Mr. Deane's recent attack, calling for full investigation of the insinuations, innuendoes, and assertions. He asked that the propriety of such a publication as Deane's be judged by the real friends of the independency of America. *"I do most sincerely wish you to be on your guard,"* he read aloud. *"Trust not accusations, hear both sides, and judge from well attested facts."*

The day following the appearance of this piece in the *Packet*, Henry Laurens resigned his chair as president of the Congress, explaining to Francis privately that although he'd considered doing such for some time, he did it now as a direct protest to the attack against the Lees. Deane's publication, he said, was a pernicious and unprovoked libel, and he could do far more to counteract it seated as a delegate than he could from the president's chair. Francis felt bewildered, saddened, yet grateful over the action of his friend. He knew this was a debt he could never repay.

When New York's John Jay was elected to replace Laurens, it became clear that sentiment was running in favor of Deane, but

the battle seemed destined to be fought in the press and the parlors and taverns of Philadelphia, for Congress continued to avoid
definitive action regarding Mr. Deane. They neither cleared him
nor charged him—as though by ignoring him they hoped the
trouble would evaporate. Just before Christmas, however, Silas
Deane presented written narratives of his transactions and accusations as had earlier been requested by Congress.

"The first was the most pompous and bloated thing I've ever
heard!" Francis reported when he got home. "And the only charges
he made against Arthur were that he is suspicious, jealous, con-
frontational to everybody he has business with, and possessed of
a violent hatred for the French. Of William, he calls him mean,
and accused him of going shares with the commercial agents he
has appointed. The Congress sat there as a body, sucking it up
like nectar and ambrosia, the party that backs Deane murmuring
that as they are moderate, they wouldn't dream of injuring anyone. Yet they have some of their own men ready and alerted to fill
the appointments, should Arthur and William be called home!"

༄

By the end of February when Richard returned to the city, no
action had yet been taken regarding Silas Deane's status. John
Adams had long since replaced him in Paris, and it seemed no
one wished to press the matter further. The attacks on Richard stepped up following his return, however, and soon thereafter
charges against the Lees' brother-in-law, Dr. Shippen, gathered
renewed momentum. It wasn't difficult to foresee that sentiments
would be split straight down party lines on these issues also.

Richard brought details from home of Landon Carter's
December death. That, as well as family persecution, preyed on
Francis's mind; there would be no more letters from his favorite
correspondent giving them news of home. He had trouble believing the old man was really gone, grieving sorely over the one he'd

always thought of as the lion of Richmond County. He pondered long on the futile time Landon had wasted on the behavior of his sons and grandsons—none of whom, in Francis's opinion, were capable of striking a pose to halfway match the old master of Sabine Hall. Robert Wormeley in his ambivalence had never succeeded in dethroning the feisty patriarch although he'd pecked away at it from time to time. The grand old man had died, consumed perhaps by the agony of his own frustrations over an imperfect world as much as by his physical ailments, leaving a vast fortune to the son he believed, to the bitter end, had accomplished nothing so royally well in life as he had the job of disappointing the father who sired him. Francis couldn't reconcile the irony of any of it; life was nothing so much as it was unfair and unjust. He thought that he must be sinking daily into ever deeper depression and, try as he might, he knew no way to rise above it. Each day became a collection of hours through which he hastily stumbled in an anxiety for them to end. The nights, shadowy limbos of broken sleep and fretful dreams, were repetitions of daylight's inevitable public intrusion into personal privacy.

As days turned into weeks, then months, and regardless of whatever personal afflictions there were, work in the Congress went on; talks had begun on the conditions to be included in a future peace treaty with England; the fishing rights question had been labeled a New England issue and a grueling session of heated discussion over the inclusion of American rights to fish the North Atlantic went on for several hours. Those southerners, like Richard and Francis Lee and Henry Laurens, who supported it, had come under fire from their compatriots and the New Yorkers, who seemed to have solidified their forces since the Deane matter surfaced.

The day's debate had done nothing to improve Francis's mood. When shortly thereafter, and quite unexpectedly, he met face to face with Silas Deane on Market Street, he was unprepared. Deane made an obvious scurry to avoid speaking, and the remnants of

Francis's composure crumpled. Not anger, but an awful sadness came over him. "I am no leper, Sir, that you need avoid me on the public street," he said, placing himself in Deane's path.

For the briefest second Deane's eyes flickered an amiable response then, apparently thinking better of it, he drew his portly frame stiffly erect as he fastened his gaze on something to the right and above Francis's head. "Good day, Sir. I don't believe we have the least item of consequence to say to one another."

There was a grim finality to the haughty words that wasn't lost on Francis. "I had hoped, naively perhaps, that we might exchange a civil good afternoon. That's all."

Deane shrugged. "In view of present circumstances, I see no reason ..."

Francis didn't wait for him to finish. "I have no desire to start an argument, Mr. Deane, merely to wish you a good day rather than to pass you in silence. Adieu, Sir."

❦

It was later that same evening that his spirits sank to their lowest ebb. He met Richard at the door. "It's all right, Ben," he called. "It's my brother. I'll let him in. I've been waiting for him."

"I am resigning," Francis announced bluntly as soon as Richard was inside. "Tomorrow. This week. Immediately."

"Resigning?" The implication was that it was an unknown word in a foreign language. Richard threw an arm about Francis's shoulder as they entered the parlor, feeling the tenseness there and, he thought, the merest hint of withdrawal from his touch.

"Hello, Richard," Becky greeted him. Her cheeks were tear stained. "He means it, you know."

"I see. Well." Richard sputtered a laugh, a nervous chortle he didn't intend. "I don't suppose there's any need to question what brought this on, is there?"

Francis's expression was bitter. "Don't be callous. And don't be ingratiating with me. You know perfectly well what the reasons are. I'm sick to death of the entire damned dirty business of politics! All of it, and all the men who make it so. They have lambasted us, undercut us, harpooned us. When we were down, they cut out our hearts and sliced them to ribbons. And now ... united in the glory of victory over the infamous Lees, they prepare to trample what is left into the proverbial dust!"

He coughed, leaving Becky to wonder if his cold was returning. She couldn't bear to think of anything hurting him further, even a cold.

"Well," he continued when he'd cleared his throat, "I'll not allow them the satisfaction of that final travesty upon my sacred honor. I am going home ... where I have always belonged." Breaking with emotion, he stood before his brother, pleading, "R.H., I beg you to come with me. They'll kill you in the end. I know it. Please. Come home."

Richard's voice was flat, uninspired. "I can't. And you can't. We must stay and fight it out. Even if, in the end, Congress shall vindicate Deane and condemn Arthur. We mustn't let them defeat us. We're in the right. Loudoun, don't give up. Not yet."

Francis turned from him in anger. "You're a fool! A God-damned bloody fool. You've given your heart and soul for the cause of liberty, and what has it got you? Nothing. Absolutely nothing. It's time to give it up. Politics ... it stinks with all the rotten, putrid stench of human excrement! I can't bear it any longer." He turned from them, moving blindly to the hall. When he looked back, there were tears in his eyes. "Richard, I ... have no more to give." Removing his cape from the hook and flinging it about his shoulders, he disappeared into the night, the door slamming a resounding amen.

Becky looked stricken. "I am so sorry, Richard. So very sorry. I don't know what to do for him, or for you. I'm sorry."

"There's nothing to do. It was inevitable." Sighing, Richard heaved himself into a chair. "I'll sit with you for an hour, if you don't mind. I am ungodly tired this evening, Becky. Could you just put up with me for a while?"

She sat woodenly, hands clenched in her lap, on the threshold of tears again. "What should I do?" she asked him again.

"Love him," said Richard, closing his eyes and leaning back in the winged chair. "Just love him."

∞

When Francis returned several hours later, he found his wife in their bed chamber and sensed immediately she'd been waiting for him. "I feel somewhat better," he said, discovering he still had a smile left. "I shouldn't have exploded at Richard."

"No, but he understood." There was a faint smell of spirits and tobacco smoke about him and she supposed he'd been at the City Tavern. Had she asked, she would have learned he spent the evening with William Hauck in the stuffy office behind the Three Trees cabinet shop. But she didn't inquire, because it wasn't important where he'd been—only that he'd returned safely.

Francis dropped onto the bed and began tugging at his boots. "Why, Becky? Why does it have to be this way? We've given our time, our fortunes, our peace of mind, and even our health for something we believe in. Every one of us. Five brothers, six if you count Philip. And every last one of us has come under attack for it. Richard accused of the rent fraud and intriguing with Berkenhout, Arthur of dealing with the British and hating the French and spying, William of taking bribes from the agents, me of forming an unholy alliance with the northeasterners on the finances and the fishery rights ... and there's no truth in any of it. It's a pack of scandalous lies. What makes a man put up with such a lack of appreciation for so many years? Why have we stuck out our necks to serve the public good, only to have our heads chopped off before the moment of achievement? Why?"

Reaching for his hand, she squeezed it hard enough to command his full attention. "Why? I'll tell you why, Francis. Because you all are sons of Thomas Lee ... that is why. It's that simple. And if he were alive today, he'd burst with pride over the accomplishments of each and every one of you! As do I." She thought the creases in his forehead eased a bit, but she wasn't sure. She began to rub his back, afraid she might cry again if she continued to look at him. "I love you," she said, her voice cracking. "I love you, darling, and no matter what happens, I always will." In the morning she would direct Ben and Cate to begin the packing, for even when his pain faded, she knew he wouldn't change his mind. Their life in Philadelphia had run its course, it was over. They were going home to Menokin.

PART IV
HOMECOMING
1780 – 1797

"My Dear Brother, I can readily conceive, and it is with very great concern, the distressed situation you must be in; and it gives me pain when I reflect how little it is in my power to assist you ... I am so very little in the world and find it so impossible to get anybody to do any business for me ...the world seems crazy, and we old people must scuffle with it, as well as we can, for our few days of existance."

Letter, F. L. Lee to William Lee at Green Spring
Menokin, April 30, 1795

Out of the Ashes

The leave-taking was devastating; the coming home even worse, in every sense of the word. Yet nothing Francis or Becky could have done would have made any difference, nor prepared them for it. A week prior to their departure from Philadelphia Richard, giving no warning of his decision, submitted his own resignation from Congress. His health was failing, he'd be destitute without Francis at his side—this was the essence of his explanation to Becky. He avoided his brother, however, until the last day when the two close companions spent an hour in quiet conversation. It seemed inconceivable but Richard had word of a new crisis about to strike the family. Congress had voted to slash Dr. Shippen's request for a hospital budget in half—it was clearly an attempt to force the doctor's resignation, Richard thought. The drive was spearheaded by the Deane supporters but didn't strictly follow party lines; even their faithful friend Henry Laurens had voted against Shippen's budget request; voting no on the half measure as well, which called first for sufficient inquiry into the conduct of the director-general. Shippen was accused of selling great quantities of geese, chickens, ducks, and other hospital stores to his own advantage, and of wasting gallons of wine on persons other than the sick for whom it had been provided, Richard told him.

"So now Laurens, too, has abandoned us," Francis said sadly. Would Lovell be next? Sam Adams? It was more than he could cope with in his state of mind, and he changed the subject quickly. He couldn't imagine how he would adjust to life in Richmond County, he complained, without his old friend Landon Carter to

545

commiserate with. It was almost more than a man could be expected to bear, he confided.

Richard didn't linger long in his brother's company, the meeting was too painful and he had things to move out of the house, he said. They bid each other a tearful farewell vowing to meet up soon in Virginia. *"Tristis eris si solus eris,"* were his parting words to Francis. "Don't remain by yourself too long, Loudoun, make new friends."

Returning home, the Lees retraced the footsteps of their first journey northward, stopping over in Annapolis. While there, awaiting some repairs on the carriage, word reached them of the death of John Tayloe at Mount Airy. Thunderstruck, they clung to the sanity of daily routine, and rolled into Richmond Courthouse five days after the old colonel had been laid to rest in the burial ground near Old House.

Throughout that spring and summer of 1779 Francis and Becky remained close to home. The house and the land seemed curiously aware of their need to be welcomed and, embittered and saddened, they allowed the refuge of Menokin to heal their wounds. They didn't lack for things to do—perhaps that is what saved them—the blessed activity. Some of the buildings demanded repair, fences needed mending, sheep and cattle were bred, meat was smoked for winter, new crops were planted, the harvest was brought in, and two new drying sheds were built for tobacco.

Becky discovered all over again the amazing culinary delights that could be produced and preserved from a fresh garden and orchard. Although they'd brought back lamps from the north and now burned oil in the evenings, she still saw to it that plenty of candles were dipped for use on long winter evenings. The herb garden had become completely overgrown and she pressed Zoey and Cris to clear it out and begin again. When they showed a marked lack of interest in the project, she put them to work making soap and sachets for the drawers and saw to it they were taught to weave, leaving the garden work to others.

The task of cultivating herbs was turned over to Samuel, now ten and eager as well as capable. He would cheerfully do anything in order to keep his distance from the other Menokin slaves. If he'd been uncomfortable with them as a toddler, he was a hundred times more so now. Sam was a loner; his life in the streets of northern cities had made him different. He entertained himself secretly with year-old *Gazettes* and other papers the master discarded, rather than spend time with the other children. With the exception of his mother, Miss Becky was the only person who knew he could read. But his mistress didn't know that he was also teaching himself to write—an accomplishment he wasn't certain she would approve of, although he could see quite clearly that writing was a natural outgrowth of reading— yet Miss Becky had never suggested it. Sam had learned during his ten years that as a black slave, he got along better by avoiding the appearance of having too many new ideas. Thus, he kept silent, and his precious supply of paper, ink, and quill remained his secret.

By the time fall painted the countryside with color, the Lees were ready to venture into the community to begin reestablishing relationships with friends and relatives. Hannah Corbin had lost her Dr. Hall and was anxious for company; at Stratford, Philip's widow Elizabeth had remarried and once again opened her house to entertainments. Colonel Phil's daughter, Matilda, had grown to be an exceptional beauty, much sought after, and recently had attracted the romantic attentions of her cousin Henry Lee of the Continental Army. At Chantilly, Anne Pinchard and Richard had a new baby son, Cassius, their fourth born. Closer to home, Becky's sister Kitty was being courted by young Landon Carter, Robert's eldest. Winifred Carter had emerged from her shell since the death of her father-in-law and frequently invited Becky and Francis to dine at Sabine Hall. Kitty and Landon were soon to be married and there were many parties. One by one, Francis and Becky began to appreciate the many reasons it was good to be home.

While the Deane matter continued to rage in Philadelphia, the fight over the fisheries still sputtered angrily on the floor of Congress and, first William Lee, then Arthur were relieved of their diplomatic posts in Europe in a compromise maneuver between the Deaneites and the Adams-Lee Radicals, a new term dubbed on the old junto. Francis spent his days seeking peace within himself, through the peace he found in his surroundings. One nippy November morning he was up early, tramping along the edge of an open field, his gun held loosely at his side. Three lone geese tracked across a bleak skyline. Necks laid straight-out, wings flapping in rhythm, they were moving southward. He followed them until they disappeared behind the pines. Somehow, with just the three of them coming into view like that, he didn't feel like raising his gun to his shoulder. Down below in the marsh he could hear the honking of the rest of the flock. How sweet the sound, and how satisfying it was to be home. To be free. Let the geese be free this time, too. He wouldn't shoot one today. Government and armies and political squabbles seemed a blessed distance away. Even the lies of Silas Deane were far enough removed so the anguish they'd etched on his heart was almost obliterated.

He turned for home knowing it was time to give his answer to those who'd put their faith in him by giving him their vote even when he hadn't sought it; his name had been put up for senator, and he'd won without campaigning. It salved his ego, but that was all. The aroma of sausage frying tempted him as he passed the cookhouse. He was hungry.

"I've made up my mind," he told Becky as he entered the house. "I'll write the letter today. It wouldn't be fair to you, to myself, nor the state legislature, to accept the post as senator from this district. Perhaps next time, but I'm not ready for it yet."

Becky nodded. "I'm not surprised, darling."

"Do you approve?" The slight motion she made with her shoulders told him that perhaps she was disappointed. Well, if so, he couldn't help it.

"It's not my decision to make," she answered evasively. "A man must act as his conscience dictates. Whatever is right for you, I will agree with. I always have, I think, haven't I?" Kissing him lightly she left to order the serving of his breakfast.

∽

A year later, however, Francis did not turn down the request to serve, when once again he was elected senator to represent the district of Lancaster, Northumberland, and Richmond Counties in the Virginia State Legislature. October 1780 found him making preparations to leave. The general assembly under newly elected Governor Thomas Jefferson, was moving its location from Williamsburg to Richmond City, up river on the James. Seeking safety from a British threat to the lower rivers, the assembly would probably be in session a month to six weeks. Richard Henry, too, was newly elected to serve, not to the senate, but to the house of representatives.

Despite the somberness of a parting with her husband, Becky rejoiced seeing the two comrades checking their saddlebags and preparing to depart. "It seems just like old times," she ventured, handing them each a small sack of the precious Jesuit bark from the dwindling supply William had once again sent before leaving Brussels. Richard looked happier than she had seen him in an age. And Francis? Well, she thought, he looked pleased to be going with Richard. "Tighten your scarf, darling. The wind is chilly and you mustn't take cold."

Francis kissed her soundly. "I'll miss you, love. I wish you were coming with us."

"That's all been decided. You don't even know where you'll be staying in Richmond City, and I'll be just fine here alone. Especially with Ben to look after everything." Francis was taking Samuel with him. The boy, astride an old horse laden with satchels and supplies, looked as though he might be setting off to discover the Orient. His attempt at nonchalance was a miserable failure, but only Cate was paying attention to her son's excitement.

I'll miss you sorely nonetheless," Francis said, wondering if she had any idea how much he meant it, "and I'll write often, I promise."

"I'll see to that," Richard chimed in. "I won't keep him out so late he's too tired to write."

"Take care, my dears," she called as they rode away.

Rebecca Tayloe was not a person to be easily disturbed by events. She had always managed to keep problems firmly in perspective while maintaining a calm exterior. When she arrived at Menokin a few weeks later, however, it was clear she'd abandoned all pretext of orderly thought. Pushing Cate aside, she strode pell-mell through the hall calling for her daughter. She was closely followed by fifteen-year-old Sally, who had John and Jane in tow; two slaves were behind them. "Becky? Becky, for heaven's sake, where are you?"

"Miss Becky," Cate began for the second time, "she down to ...."

"Listen to me, girl ... this is no time for chatter! Now, where in the name of the blessed saints is she?"

"I's bein tryin' t' tell y'all, Miz Tayloe, she in the cellar wit Ben. Shall I git her?"

Rebecca Tayloe glowered, taking a menacing step forward. Cate didn't hesitate. Sailing out the door and rounding the corner of the house, she raced down the steps, colliding smack into her mistress at the bottom. The wine decanter slipped from Becky's hands, the top of it smashing on the bottom step, wine and glass splattering in all directions.

"Oh, Cate! Now see what you've done. And that's my favorite decanter! How could you be so careless?"

"It's your Mama, Miss Becky. She up dere fit t' be tied cause you not dere t' talk to. Hurry!" Cate scurried back up the steps, pausing at the top she peered past her mistress into the darkness below. "Ben, stop standin' dere gawkin', ol' man. Clean up dat mess and den git youse'f up here! Dey's trouble."

At sight of Becky, her mother collapsed in the nearest chair.

"Get some smelling salts, Sally. Ask Cate," Becky directed, before rushing to her mother's side where she knelt and began slapping her wrists gently.

"It's all right, Becky. I haven't fainted." But Rebecca Tayloe's voice wavered. "Although I'm about to, if you don't tell me what we're to do."

"For goodness sake, Mama, you're not making any sense. What are you talking about?"

"The British. That's what I'm talking about. They're sailing up our river, straight up the Rappahannock!"

Becky recalled the panic she'd suffered in Philadelphia when the British were advancing, but then Francis had been there to lean upon. Now there was no one. "Stay calm, Mama. We must stay calm or we shan't be able to make any plans," she pleaded, her heart racing. Where could they go? What should they do?

"They're burning and looting! Raiding all the big houses and taking prisoners, too, I'll wager."

"What about the slaves? What are they doing with the slaves?" If they were being turned loose on the countryside that could be a far worse peril than the soldiers themselves.

"I ... don't know." Rebecca hadn't considered this angle. Her eyes grew large and her hand flew to her heart.

"Oh, Mama. I didn't mean to give you even more of a fright. Please. I'll think of something. John," she smiled, turning to her little brother. "John darling, you're going to have to be the man of the house. Now go downstairs. Tell Ben to forget about the broken glass. We'll tend to that later. Tell him to lock the wine cellar carefully, and to bring me the key. Then go outside and see if you can find Mr. Sutton. He might be around the stables or maybe at the drying sheds. Tell him I must see him immediately. Can you remember all that?"

John screwed up his nine-year-old face and puffed out his chest importantly. "Consider it done," he boasted, heading to the cellar steps. Jane scuttled after him.

"Not you, Janie! You stay with Mama. Come, Sally. You can help me pack a few things."

"Pack?" Sally asked, stumbling in her hurry to keep up.

"What else?" Becky called over her shoulder. "If the British Army is landing here in Richmond County at any moment, we surely can't sit here and wait for them to ravish us!"

"But where can we go? Where will we be safe?"

"I don't know. But by the time I've decided what to pack, I expect I shall think of where we'll go."

They fled to Stratford Plantation. Once there, they remained for over a fortnight, until further reports convinced them that the scare had been a foolishly exaggerated report. A letter from Francis was delivered to Becky at Stratford. "He says we needn't have fled, Mama. That those British privateers would never come so far up the river as Hobbs' Hole. He does say there were two houses actually burned though," she added, reading further. "And he may be home by Christmas as the assembly is doing very little. How wonderful!"

"Well, you can blame our panic on me," her mother said. "I was the one who decided we should leave, not you."

"I'm afraid I was too frightened to have managed anything at all. At least you kept calm and held us together, dear."

Becky was still reading her letter. "He goes on to say that if Mr. Sutton doesn't do my bidding when we return home, that I should feel free to dismiss him. I wrote Francis that Mr. Sutton wasn't seeing to it there was enough wood to keep the fireplaces going."

"When Francis is away, Jeremiah Sutton is to do what you tell him. You'll never run a plantation unless you're firm. Why do you put up with that, Becky?"

"Oh, he had some excuse about using the carts to bring in the corn for fodder. Sometimes I have the feeling he goes out of his way to avoid me so I won't give him any new orders."

"If you want my opinion, you should wait until Francis returns if you're thinking of letting him go. It's better than not having anyone, isn't it?"

"Umm. Francis suggests here, should I dismiss him, you might loan me Charles until we can make some other arrangement," Becky suggested.

"Charles? I see. Well, there's little doubt Charles is to be trusted and can be relied upon to do what's right. But he's no good at managing anything ... except horses." Charles MacIntosh had been a derelict wanderer twenty years before, moving from place to place, doing odd jobs up and down the river in return for a jug of rum or a hot meal. Leading a flea-bitten old mule, who staggered pitifully under the weight of the quack medicines and iron pots MacIntosh offered for sale, the peddler had limped his way into the Mount Airy stable yard one morning. Probably in his mid-thirties at the time, he was ill, infested with lice and suffering from malnutrition. John Tayloe agreed to allow him to stay until he was recovered. MacIntosh, who appeared lacking in every social grace, was born of a union between an Indian squaw, said to have descended from the ancient tribe of Rappahannocks, and a fiery-tempered Scotsman. He was more at home in a stable than in any house, and animals responded to him as they did to no other human. Albeit ragged and disreputable, Charles could salve a pulled muscle, assist in the delivery of a stubborn colt, and sweet-talk a sick horse into recovery better than any man John Tayloe had ever met. When MacIntosh rubbed his stubbled red whiskers against a mare's muzzle, she became as agreeable as a bride on her wedding day—hence Tayloe never got around to asking him to leave Mount Airy. "Charles isn't capable of replacing an overseer, Becky. I wonder that Francis should have suggested it."

Becky decided she'd been wrong to mention it. Her mother adored Charles. So long as he didn't come near the Great House.

"Still ... I suppose I *could* part with him. But only to help you on a temporary basis, mind you. You'd have to remember to keep the wine cellar locked up tight. He still has a fatal weakness. Your father never cured him of that!"

Francis didn't arrive home in time for Christmas after all, but he rode in soon after the new year commenced. He reported the British under the traitorous Benedict Arnold were even now ravishing and burning Richmond City. The fact that Arnold was wed to Peggy, a Shippen cousin, turned the event into a personal disaster as well. The war seemed to be following them, he complained. He didn't know where the general assembly would meet in the spring; with things so uncertain they'd have to wait and see. "How is everything here?" he got around to asking in time.

"I had to let Jeremiah Sutton go, Francis. He was just impossible. When we returned from Stratford, he hadn't accomplished a single task except to get the slaves all stirred up. I left Ben to watch the house and Mr. Sutton filled his head with wild ideas, telling him that if British soldiers came, he would be set free! Imagine it. Ben wouldn't know what to do, left to his own measures. Why ... none of them would, would they?"

"No, I don't suppose they would. But you can be assured they'd all be off quick enough if given half an opportunity. Even Ben, I think, although the thought pains me. How is he now, by the way, still suffering under delusions of freedom?"

"He hasn't said much. Just like always." But she'd noticed there were changes in Ben that had nothing to do with Jeremiah Sutton. He'd aged rapidly since the return from Pennsylvania. His hair was almost white now, his mind wandered, and he went around humming what she took to be bits of Baptist spirituals under his breath. His eyes were sad as he moved about his chores as though he saw something others didn't see. But she'd let Francis discover that for himself. "Mama sent Charles over, like you suggested. She wants him back though."

"Well, it looks as though I must begin a search for a new overseer. We can't operate without one for long. I'll put the word about in the county tomorrow."

"I'm sorry you had to come home to a problem, darling. I guess I'm not good with overseers, am I?"

"I'm home again, Becky. That's all that matters. The rest will take care of itself. Coming home is always something of a miracle to me." He didn't say it, but it was here his world was anchored, but no matter *where* home was, she was always the center of it.

Times were changing and it seemed life was no longer so simple as it had once been. The war raged in Virginia that year and into the next as well. The state militia took many of the younger men who would have worked a plantation, and many of the older ones, too. Those who were left weren't so eager to labor long days in return for a house and food for their families. They wanted more— they wanted cash—and cash was a commodity very difficult if not impossible to come by. Francis recognized the signs of unrest and knew that no matter what happened after the peace treaty was affected, their lives on the plantation would never be the same as they had been before the revolution. During the year following the dismissal of Sutton he tried, for varying periods of time, no less than five overseers before finally taking Jeremiah Sutton back. The man made a shaky peace with Becky, promising to spread no more rumors and to keep his nose to the grindstone. It was a poor bargain and she wasn't happy with it, but there were no choices.

〜◦

Spring 1781 found the Virginia general assembly meeting in Charlottesville, near Governor Jefferson's Monticello plantation. They weren't long in session before a warning came that the British General Cornwallis had dispatched a cavalry force intent on their capture. Once again by the first glimmer of daylight, Francis found himself fleeing with his government for his life. They reconvened at a church in Staunton on the other side of the Blue Ridge Mountains, but little business was accomplished. Several of the delegates were actually captured, putting a pall over the proceedings that no one seemed able to shake.

In the fall when the general assembly met once again, the Lee brothers welcomed back into the fold one of their long lost siblings. Arthur Lee, who had returned to vindicate himself in Congress the year before, had been elected to represent Prince William County in the Virginia House. Francis and Richard muddled through that session in a kind of euphoria, boasting about and hawking their younger brother's great accomplishments in Europe. Bargaining and trading off compromises until, by the time the session was concluded, they managed to get Arthur elected to the next term of Congress. Who else, they argued, could be better qualified to aid in hammering out a proper peace treaty? But in the course of events and not in their power to stop, Benjamin Harrison also won an election—he was chosen to be the next governor of the state of Virginia. When the vote was tallied, Francis felt a knot growing in the pit of his stomach. It wouldn't leave him, growing more bothersome daily. It plagued him all the way home to Menokin.

He turned into the rutted road that led across his farmlands to the house. Stark and winter-neat, the fields paved his route with welcome. As he drew closer he looked past the barns and out-buildings to the huge chimneys on his roof; like staunch guardians they were etched against the cold gray sky. No matter the weather, the sight never failed to raise his spirits, and it was no different today. But something was wrong. He sensed it immediately. Where was everybody? He turned to Samuel, riding with him. "What do you think, Sam? It seems too quiet."

Sam was already dismounted, heading for the barn. "I'll check, Marse Frank. Somethin's not right. Dat's for sure." He disappeared into the nearest shed, but was out in a moment, coming on a run. "It's Ben," he cried, his face twisted in pain. "He died last night in his bed. He died ...." Sam didn't wait to help his master off his horse. There was only one thing on his mind—Cate—his mother.

"What?" Francis called after him in a broken voice. Not Ben. Surely there was some mistake. "What happened, Sam?" he repeated, feeling the pain in his stomach renew its attack.

For just a moment the boy hesitated, the thin shoulders tightening. Without turning to look at the man who owned him, he called in a clear voice, "It's Ben. My daddy ... is gone free."

Although totally unrelated, Ben's death shook Francis enough to shift his indecision into a positive course. He'd never be able to operate successfully in the assembly with Harrison as governor. Maybe Richard could forgive that man the damage he'd done their characters in the past, but Francis could never overlook it. He'd be miserable serving under Harrison. Hence, he would be ineffective. It was as plain as that.

"With Arthur back, Richard doesn't need me anymore," he rationalized a few days later to Becky. "Arthur's young, he's got energy and he's eager. Just the tonic the doctor ordered."

"And you've decided you're needed here. Am I right?"

Reaching for the cup of his homemade apple brandy, he said, "That's exactly what I've decided. With Ben gone and Sutton limping along in his inimitable way, this place needs me more than does the senate." Having said it, he let his mind wander. Ben had known he was going to die; he'd often joked that when Cameron went, his own time would soon be up. The old horse had died nine or ten weeks before ... strange. How had Ben known? Is there a warning about such things, he wondered, losing interest in the assembly immediately. God, he truly missed that black man!

"Or the Congress?" Becky asked, watching his face.

"Hmm? ... oh. The Congress? Funny you should mention that. I have no thoughts of trying to return to the Congress," he told her, drawing his eyebrow down.

Walking to the window, she stood watching Samuel struggle under a load of firewood big enough to stagger a grown man. "I've thought from time to time you might consider it. There will be a country to run when the war is over. Old enmities can be forgotten, if we allow it, you know." Perhaps after he got over the shock of Ben's death, she thought, and Harrison could be out of office in a year.

"No, love. Come sit by me and hear what I have to say. I am finished with politics. This time for good. I've devoted almost twenty-five years to public service. It's time to give it up while I still have the energy needed to make things run here. This county needs me ... as county lieutenant, justice, or wherever I can be useful. The church needs me. Lunenburg Church is decaying and falling apart. I should become active on the vestry in these, my later years. Can you understand what I'm saying?"

"Of course I understand. And I suppose you're right. It's for certain that Menokin needs you." Still, she thought, he'll change his mind. Like always. Some crisis will come along. Richard will call for him, and he'll answer. She knew him better than he did himself. It was also the first time she freely admitted to herself that there were things about their life in Congress that she actually missed.

Portia and Cornelia

Gradually life for the Lees evolved into the pleasant pattern of days gone by, days before the revolution and the war had turned everything upside down. It was a pattern that neither of them spoke about changing anymore. From time to time Becky wondered why she'd ever thought Francis would desire the challenge of public life again. Menokin was his challenge, these things were his meat. The peace treaty with England having been signed in September past, the fledgling country now stood on wobbly legs, but it remained standing. Let Richard struggle with his new task as president of the Congress, living in his fancy New York house; and Arthur do battle with the Morrises over the federal treasury if that kept him happy; even William, although in constant ill health and losing his sight to cataracts, after serving a term in the state legislature was now active in the plans to organize the Protestant Episcopal Church of the United States. Meanwhile, Francis remained content to return to the simplicity of the soil.

In spite of his constant attentions, however, Menokin was not able to show a profit—times were depressed as the new nation rocked precariously in a search for stability—but neither did Menokin fail, as had some other Virginia plantations. Hard work and perseverance on the part of the master saw to that. In addition, along with Mann Page, Thomas Lomax, Ralph Wormeley, and Landon Carter, husbands of Becky's sisters, Francis saw to it that Mount Airy's head stayed above water as well. Yes, he thought, returning one day from Naylor's Hole on the river, despite the waverings of a new government they were living in reasonably good times. He'd gone for the post and been rewarded to find several letters waiting for him.

"Letter from William," he called as he entered. "One from Peter Hauck, too. Here, you open one, and I will the other." He handed her the letter from Pennsylvania. They were quiet for a few minutes, reading.

"Peter's fine, darling, he tells all about his lovely children. The eldest is now three, and they named the new baby Karl. No surprise there. How about William? Have his daughters arrived at Green Spring yet?" William's wife's death on the eve of departure from Belgium to join her husband and young son in America had been a terrible and unexpected shock to them all. Poor William had been trying to make arrangements to have his daughters sent over to him ever since.

Francis sat with his mouth ajar, staggered by the impact of what was written on the paper in his hands. "They're coming here ... William ... he's bringing them *here*. Within the month I should say," he blurted.

"Wonderful!" she exclaimed. "We shall have a nice long visit with William's little family, and get to know them at last."

"No, not for a holiday, Becky ... to *live* ... with us. He's bringing them here to live. He wants you to raise his daughters, here at Menokin."

"Oh my ... oh my goodness," she stammered. "Do you suppose they speak English? I mean, they've been raised in France, Brussels, Germany ... everywhere except Virginia. What if they can't speak English? How old are they now? Oh, Francis, whatever will I do with two little girls? I shan't know how to act ... or anything," she wailed, terrified at the prospect.

It was as he had expected, after he'd collected his wits. When she adjusted to the idea, Becky flew around the house like a mother hen, making ready for her new charges. Nothing would do but a complete rejuvenation of the large bed chamber; paint, draperies, bed linens, everything. Francis winced under the expense, but held his silence. Becky raided Mount Airy's nursery for toys, dolls, games, any sort of plaything. She wore herself out in the preparations, so that by the day the carriage arrived delivering the Misses Portia and Cornelia, accompanied by their father, she was in a state of nervous fatigue. Her greatest concern was that the little girls be pleased with the room prepared for them. "Oh, merci, Madame," Portia said politely, dipping in a practiced curtsy. "It is very kind, what you have done for us."

"Oui, Madame, merci!" Cornelia parroted, her curls bobbing. "We will try very hard to be worthy of your kindness." Wandering into the room the child bent to examine some of the toys. Her glance fell upon a doll Cate had fashioned for them out of corn cobs, dressed in a gay cotton skirt and a printed bandana. "Voyez! Portia," she giggled, "look at the strange little dolly." She turned the thing over, wrinkling her button nose with distaste as she examined the back.

"Hush, sister! You will hurt Madame's feelings. Things are different here than on the Continent ... we must get use to ... simple ways." The nine-year-old voice carried distinctly to Becky who stood anxiously in the doorway, as Portia intended that it should.

"No, dear, don't reprimand your sister for speaking her thoughts. In order to understand one another, we should always be honest. You mustn't worry if all the toys don't please you. Just play with the ones you like. And please, won't you call me Aunt Becky? Madame is so ... *formal*." Becky felt a shiver of uneasiness as she turned from the room knowing two pairs of eyes bored into her retreating back. It was going to take a while to get used to William's strange little daughters, she could see that. Although they did speak perfect English, they were curiously foreign.

"Oui, Tante," came two voices in unison.

During the second week Portia approached her aunt asking when they might plan a trip to the village. She explained they were used to taking daily walks in the city with Mamma; visiting the bakery or the pet shop where the little monkeys mimicked children who peered into the cages at them. Cornelia adored the colorful birds from the islands while, she herself, was intrigued with the striped snakes.

"We have no city close by, child," Becky told her, wondering that anyone would take an interest in snakes. "Only a very small town with a courthouse, a church, and a few merchants' stores. But perhaps when I've finished my household tasks this morning, we might take a ride over to Sabine Hall. You and Cornelia will enjoy the children there." Becky was almost certain Portia had known there was no city in the neighborhood, but it was unkind to be suspicious and she pushed the thought from her mind.

"Thank you, Tante. I think Cornelia and I would prefer to remain here." Portia trailed her fingers over the keys on the spinet piano, stringing discordant notes into the room. "But, of course, we will not mind if you wish to go. We are quite used to being alone ... since Mamma was taken from us," she ended matter-of-factly before skipping from the room.

"It's simply not natural," Becky told Francis later. "That child speaks of her mother's death as though she's describing what she ate for breakfast ... or the snakes in the pet shop! She has a hard little shell around her. It's almost as if she's daring me to try and crack it."

"I wonder if it's because she misses her father or, perhaps resents that he left them here at all? Maybe she's unhappy here."

"She's hardly been here long enough to feel that way. No, it seems to me it's more than homesickness. I think she's covering up a hurt over something in the past and by staying aloof she's not pressured to share her thoughts. She certainly appears to have no inclination to share them with me at any rate."

"What about Cornelia? She seems open enough. She brought me my pipe when I came in today, then demanded a kiss before she'd let me have it."

"She's the same with me. Unless Portia is present and then she clams up. Cornelia is much under Portia's influence, but being only six she strives to please everyone. She's a lovely, sweet child

... but what am I to do with her sister? I've tried everything. Soon we'll have to begin lessons, and already I anticipate she'll resist anything I suggest."

After thinking for a minute Francis said, "How about inquiring of your mother if the girls could join the lessons under Jane's tutor several days a week? That would take some of the burden off your shoulders." It seemed a sad irony that Becky, who had always prayed for a child, now had two of them to care for and yet felt sadly unequal to the task. Perhaps it was true that Portia was unreasonably difficult; it worried him greatly.

"Why, that's a splendid idea, darling. Why didn't I think of it? That would leave me free to concentrate on the simple and more enjoyable instructions such as music, dancing, maybe even needlework. You know, I couldn't get Portia to even take an interest in backgammon this morning! She's bound and determined to shun any suggestion I make."

Francis remained puzzled. The more he heard, the more he wondered. "Well then, by all means, speak to your mother. I'm certain things will improve for all of us in time and we'll soon become a happy family. It's what we've always wanted, love. A family."

∽

As the days and weeks multiplied into months, there seemed no visible change in Portia's attitude. If anything, she became increasingly withdrawn. She attended lessons with her sisters three mornings a week at Mount Airy, but refused to be drawn into conversation about what she'd learned. Ignoring all overtures her aunt made at companionship, she sneered openly at signs of affection. Portia seemed fond of her uncle in a detached sort of way, but continued to merely tolerate Becky. The only person in her new world to whom she became in the least devoted, with the exception of her sister, was the old half-breed, Charles MacIntosh.

She escaped the tutor at every opportunity to make her way to the Mount Airy stables. There, with the black boy Sam on one side of him, and Portia Lee in her sophisticated Paris frock perched on the other, Charles would regale them with spine tingling tales of the early days when the Indians had roamed the forests. He knew the names of all the old villages—of Cawwuntoll, Poyektank, Matchopick, and Winsack which had stood almost where Old House sat decaying today. He told them of the magnificent chiefs—of Bright Eagle, Singing Rock, and Cross Bow; of how they taught their sons to hunt by running fleetly through the forest on silent feet to send their arrows whistling straight to the heart of their prey. Again and again, Portia wanted to hear of how they sent the spirits of their loved ones to the happiest of all hunting grounds, the place the white man called Heaven. She sat entranced, never tiring of the repetitious stories. Actually, now that MacIntosh discovered his audience had doubled, Sam having heard the stories many times, he became uniquely inspired. Memories of what his Indian mother had taught him mingled splendidly with vivid episodes of imagination. He now fancied himself a storyteller of the highest order, and he strove constantly to outdo himself, to the utter delight of the two children.

Portia and Sam, whose job it was to deliver and return the two Lee daughters to and from Mount Airy for lessons, never spoke of what Charles told them as they crowded close together on the seat of the chaise, bumping along on the return to Menokin. That would mean sharing their excitement with Cornelia, who preferred after instruction to read her French lesson to Cousin Jane anyway, or to play by herself in the orangery. By an unspoken pact Portia and Sam were agreed, their superb new knowledge was the more delicious when kept secret.

The hour she could spend with Charles MacIntosh was the only reason Portia agreed to attend the lessons at Mount Airy without putting up an argument. She knew more and far better French than did the tutor, she boasted to Aunt Becky often enough, and was bored to death with numbers. Becky, ignorant of the time the girl stole with the half-breed, was grateful Portia consented to the arrangement at all. Had she not, they would have been forced to admit defeat, she supposed, and send her back to her father at Green Spring. It was a grim alternative.

∽

The girls had been at Menokin for almost a year before Becky stumbled upon the first clue to unraveling Portia's hostility. They'd just struggled through a particularly trying lesson on the spinet. Becky felt drained, exhausted by what could only be termed an ordeal. Portia's fingers clumped like sticks on the keys and today she'd exhibited even less talent than usual. "Well, dear," Becky said, wishing for the hundredth time she could like the child, even a little, "that should be enough for one day. Why don't you practice a bit longer, so you can play the piece for Uncle Frank after supper this evening? He'd like that." She smiled tightly, ignoring Portia's pout. "I have some things to attend to for table setting," she finished, rising.

"Tante, why must I always play my pieces for Uncle Frank? He probably doesn't want to hear them at all, and it's not as though he's my *father*."

Portia had a way of turning every suggestion into a confrontation. Becky stopped, sensing that whatever she replied at this moment might be important. "No," she began slowly, marshaling her thoughts, "and your uncle would never wish to replace your father in your affections. But I should think you might be pleased to play for him ... as a trial. Why not consider it a practice for when your father comes to visit?" She watched the scowl fade as her niece absorbed the idea. Dear Lord, she prayed, for once let me have said the right thing.

"When is my father coming?" Portia asked eagerly. She wanted desperately to share her Indian tales with him; it was a dream she'd had several times. She'd mentioned the idea to Sam only yesterday, trying to sound casual. He hadn't seemed impressed but had agreed it might be a good thing to share with a father.

"Why, I don't know exactly. but I expect it won't be too long. I know he misses you both very much."

"Maybe he doesn't ... he has our brother with him." Portia was counting on the fact that her brother, William, didn't know a thing about Indians.

"Yes, but that's not the same as a daughter, Portia. My own papa used to tell me how special daughters were to a father."

"Do you know why Father sent us here?" Portia asked abruptly then, not waiting for an answer, she answered herself. "Because he's dying. He is going blind and he's dying. He didn't want us to see him suffer after ...." The brittle voice broke, fading away.

In an instant Becky was at her side, but fate prevented any closer contact—Cate burst into the room, interrupting what might have been their first honest words to each other—for Portia was surely reaching out.

"Miss Becky! Dey done sent fo' y'all at Moun' Airy. It's your mama, Miz Tayloe. She's not well ... turned very sick, they says."

Three days later it was over. Rebecca Tayloe, after a brief illness, was gone. Becky consoled herself with the brevity of the illness and the fact there had been very little pain. "Mama's at peace. I'm going to keep telling myself she's with Papa," she whispered to Francis, pressing her face into the solid comfort of his shoulder. He'd arrived, with Portia and Cornelia bundled into the carriage beside him, to begin arrangements for the burial. The road had been dangerously icy and it was a cold January; he worried about how they would manage to dig the grave. Becky had already sent for the reverend, and her sisters and their families. The mourners would gather to pay last respects to the mistress of Mount Airy.

"Poor, poor Mama," sniffed Polly, as they waited to file into the parlor to kneel by the coffin four days later. "Maria," she cried to her daughter, "hush. We must be quiet." Maria continued to chase after her cousins, ignoring her mother. She was an only child and seemed unable to contain herself in the excitement of family get-togethers.

"Becky says she didn't suffer," Ellie said, an arm about Polly.

"It was so sudden," Anne whispered. "We were here for Christmas and she was fine. Just fine." Anne's third child was due any time. Swollen and uncomfortable, she leaned awkwardly on her husband's arm.

"She wasn't fine, Annie! I noticed long before that she seemed to be failing. So did Becky." It was Kitty who spoke.

"You-all see her more often. That's why you noticed the change and we didn't. Oh, poor, poor Mama," Polly wailed again. She dabbed at her teary eyes with a lace-edged handkerchief she'd crumpled into a sodden ball.

Becky and Francis stood at the end of the line, Portia and Cornelia silent between them. Cornelia looked as though she'd like to join the other children but Francis had her firmly by the hand. Portia's face remained inscrutable as always. If only Elizabeth were here, Becky thought, they'd all be present for Mama's viewing. Mama would have liked that. But Becky knew well the hazards and impossibility of a journey from Maryland on such short notice and in the dead of winter. Her mind returned to the incident with Portia a few days before. Glancing down at the erect little body, the prim expression on the childish features, her heart went out to the lonely girl. Could they have spanned the barrier that separated them, had Cate's message not interrupted? Such a moment might never come again. Portia had retreated into her former aloofness as though nothing had transpired between them. Pushing worries about her niece temporarily from her mind,

Becky began silently to pray for the soul of her mother. But very soon an uncertain squeeze from a small moist hand caused her to look down again.

Portia's face was ashen-gray. Perspiration stood in droplets on her upper lip and her forehead, and her eyes were starting to roll upward in the sockets. Becky tried to hold her, but Portia slipped into an unconscious heap on the floor. Francis moved quickly, gathering up the the limp little body in his arms, he rushed her out of sight into the library. "I'll stay with her. You take Cornelia and go back with the family," he told Becky, trying to revive Portia who was mumbling as though in delirium.

"No," Becky said firmly. "I'll stay. I think I'm beginning to see what is haunting her. Please, darling, ... leave me alone with her."

When he'd left the room, Portia showed signs of recovery. Becky wiped her forehead with the cool cloth a servant had brought, and caressed the soft curls back from her damp brow.

"That feels like Mamma," Portia murmured, eyes fluttering with the tears she had almost spilled the week before.

"Yes. Your mother loved you very much. I know you loved her."

"They took her away."

"God took her, dear. He took her to heaven to live with his angels."

Portia sat bolt upright, pushing Becky's hand away. "No! That's not true! They told me she was going to God in heaven, but it was a lie. They put her in a box." Portia began to shake. Huge wracking sobs tore through her thin chest. When she could, she continued haltingly. "They closed the box ... I saw them ... I tried and tried to make them understand they must open it ... and let her out, but no one listened to me. They took the box ... with Mamma inside and put it in the ground. *Oublier je ne peux*," she whispered frantically, lapsing into French. "That's how I know they lied to us. They wouldn't let her out to go with the angels, but they kept *saying* that was where she had gone." She leaned forward, grasping her aunt with incredible strength. "You mustn't let them do that to your mamma, Tante Becky. I saw the box! They have already put her in the same kind of box as Mama. You must make them leave it open ... until the angels come to get her. Don't let them put it in the ground!" Her eyes were round black coals, swimming in tears, drowning in fear.

"Oh, Portia. My poor darling child." Becky folded the little girl to her heart, holding her tightly. She soothed and whispered, and then she hummed until the sobs subsided. Miraculously, tears streaming down her own cheeks, she struggled, but found words to explain death and resurrection to the tormented child.

When Francis returned, he found them curled together in John Tayloe's large wing chair close to the fire, sound asleep. Portia's dark curls were pressed snugly against Becky's breast and someone had covered them with a woolen shawl.

"I have lost a mother," Becky confided later, in the quietude of their bed, "but today the Lord has at last blessed me with a daughter."

"Two daughters," he reminded, pulling her into his arms. "Don't forget our precious little Cornie."

"*Cornie?* Since when do you call her that?" Becky laughed.

"Since the two of us had a heart to heart and decided that was a fitting name for a sweet little vixon," he joked, making it up.

"So ... while I've been wrestling over my problems with Portia, you've been making up to Cornie, hmm?"

"Who says you're the only one to be blessed by the charms of a child?" he teased. "We're in this together for better or worse. How does it feel to be a parent, Mrs. Lee?"

"Wonderful," she whispered, "just wonderful, Colonel Lee." Tracing her fingers from his lips down the middle of his body, she began to make love to him. "Let's dedicate this night to a celebration in honor of Mama and Papa's reunion," she said after a while. His face was inscrutable in the darkness, but she thought he chuckled.

"Maybe at this very moment they're celebrating, too, love," he said into the pulse beat of her throat, never breaking the rhythm of his caress.

"What a perfectly rewarding thought," she purred. "I'm going to count on it."

Samuel

As usual in Virginia's Northern Neck, balmy weather flitted in and out during the weeks between winter and springtime, taunting daily with the promise of better things to come. The drastic temperature changes, Francis noted, bore a marked similarity to his frequent changes of heart regarding the 1787 political scene, up one day and down the next. Until now he'd been true to his pledge to remain out of state or federal government and had no regrets about that. During recent months, however, he found himself more and more agitated over the fate of the federal Constitution. A convention of the states had prepared the document, the Congress ratified it, and it was now being considered by the various state governments. Word had gotten around that Virginia might not ratify; it was at this point Francis became deeply concerned. After considerable vacillation at the outset, he was now convinced that this constitution, as written, and at this time, should be put into effect as quickly as possible. If it failed to be approved by the states, he reasoned, the country stood to lose all it had gained by the years of struggle against British domination. He believed there must be a strong central government else the union they had formed would dissolve in chaos. This constitution while not perfect would provide for strength—with a senate, a house of representatives, and a president who would have powers over all—a president who would not be merely elected by Congress, but a *President of the United States of America elected by the people.* What had persuaded him, beyond a doubt of the rightness of it, was to recall that miserable winter at Valley Forge. While the army starved, Congress had stood helplessly by, empowered with no controls over the individual states that would allow them to order the troops to be fed. He'd never forget those early morning hours during which he'd penned his illegal letters to the Maryland and Pennsylvania governors. The new constitution would make it unnecessary for a legislator to make such drastic and dangerous decisions; it would untie the hands of Congress by providing it with substance and a power over the states which would be absolutely necessary were the union to survive.

Although he'd not been a member of the Virginia Legislature for six years, Francis still had many friends there. As he searched his heart for what action to take, he flattered himself that his voice surely would be listened to by some of them. But there was one man above all others he hoped to convince—Richard—for his brother had left the side of their friend John Adams in this great issue. Bolstered by Arthur, he'd joined forces with their old compatriots Patrick Henry and George Mason, who were engaged in the serious business of opposing the ratification. Their chief argument was that no government should have a constitution without a bill of rights attached to it. Somehow, Francis decided, he had to make them see that a bill of rights could be accomplished in future days, by attaching amendments to the original. The immediate step as he saw it now was to protect the present momentum going for the union; eight states had already ratified. A way must be found to refute Patrick's arguments that the document favored the north, and would lead to the abolishment of slavery and hence the downfall of the south. He had to try.

Once he made up his mind to go to Richmond City where the State Ratification Convention was meeting, it didn't take him long to prepare for the journey. It seemed also a fitting time for Portia and Cornelia to visit their father. Francis borrowed the old carriage from Mount Airy, his own no longer in good enough condition for a journey of this length. He planned to drop the girls at Green Spring near Jamestown, which was out of his way, but would allow him to avail himself of whatever thoughts

William might have concerning the constitution. Young John Tayloe was at school in England, Sally and Jane now resided at Menokin since their mother's death, so no one would miss the Mount Airy carriage. It seemed an appropriate plan and he was anxious to be on his way.

More than once as he bustled about seeing to the packing of his papers and clothing, Becky smiled to herself thinking how right she'd been after all; once politics got into a man's blood, nothing short of the grave could destroy his taste for it. Suppressing the "I told you so" on the tip of her tongue, she knew it wouldn't surprise her if he returned saying he planned to run for some office next election.

It was typical of Francis, at the height of his preparations, to think of Jane. Becky's youngest sister was fourteen, only three years older than Portia and would undoubtedly enjoy the trip to Jamestown. An infant during the years of her father's illness, Jane hadn't known the gaity and excitement of the old seasons in Williamsburg. The journey would be an education for her, Francis told Becky. Perhaps William would return with them to the Northern Neck for a visit, he suggested at the last minute.

Becky nodded, her thoughts on settling the children in the carriage. "Be careful, Francis," she cautioned him for the tenth time. "See to it they don't get overly tired, and keep the windows closed when you can, the dust can be devastating. Make sure they eat properly, Cornie will be ill if she eats too many sweets." She was going to miss the children terribly. Hugging each in turn, she fought to hold back the tears. They'd think her a foolish old woman to cry when they were so happy to be going on a holiday.

"Take good care of Matchopick," Portia reminded. She and Jane leaned from the carriage, waving, the ribbons on their bonnets tossed by the breeze.

"And Délicat, too, Tante Becky," Cornelia called, shoving for a place at the window. Matchopick and Délicat were two lively balls of gray fur Francis had brought home to his nieces. Portia, quite predictably, named hers after one of Charles MacIntosh's Indian towns, but Cornelia surprised them. She pronounced her kitten's name in the proper French, a hard sound on the first syllable. It came out sounding like "daily-cat" which everyone found very amusing. Cornelia reveled in having chosen a far more clever name than had her sister.

Becky and Sally watched as a dust cloud gradually billowed up behind the carriage when the team gathered speed on the straightaway of the farm road. "Well, they're off at last," Sally sighed, relieved to see Becky wasn't going to cry after all. She didn't remember Becky crying frequently when they were growing up. Polly, yes, but not Becky. Yet as the years passed, it seemed Becky was more apt to let tears flow over things that weren't even very important. Perhaps it was her age; after all, she *was* thirty-six. "They'll have a marvelous time, I know they will. It was very considerate of Frank to include Janie in the journey. He's the most thoughtful man, Becky. Did you suspect how kind he was before you decided on him?"

"Of course!" Becky answered jauntily, her mind flashing back to how grand it had felt to be sixteen in Williamsburg, and to be squired by the debonair Francis Lee wearing his dashing velvet waistcoat. She didn't think it was his kindness she had on her mind then ... and yet ... "His eyes were the softest I'd ever seen," she remembered aloud, "and he thought that life was wonderful ... just wonderful. To tell the truth he hasn't changed much since then, Sally."

"If I ever get married, which is beginning to look doubtful at my advanced age of twenty-three, I hope to find a duplicate copy of your Frank."

"Of course you'll be married! The right man will come along one day. You'll see. As Mama once told me, he'll probably be somebody you already know."

"Maybe ... oh well," she sighed again, turning toward the house. "Come on. We have the entire day, at least six hours of good light to work on my quilt."

"The quilt? I've completely forgotten it in the flurry of getting everyone ready to travel! Let's see, have we completed the green leaves in the center square yet? I can't remember. Sam," she called, catching sight of him. "Sam, Miss Sally and I will be up in her chamber if you need us. I'd like to have water brought up for the tub so we can bathe later. And then see about getting the meat and vegetables the cooks will need for supper. Cate knows the menu. Oh, and no need to ring the prayer bell until Master Francis and the young ladies return. Miss Sally and I will arrange our own time."

"Yes-ma'm, Miss Becky," Sam answered. He didn't wait to see if she had more to say, but made his way quickly down the hillside to the well. He was feeling out of sorts because he'd been left at Menokin. With Ben gone, Marse Frank had trained two other boys to help drive the carriage and wait on the house—Sam understood the need for that, but it was a bitter pill that Pompey had been chosen to go on the trip. Pompey was no good with the horses. And he didn't know his way around Richmond City like Sam did, having been there before when Marse Frank was a senator. Pompey would probably get lost, or run the team too hard without a rest. It just didn't seem fair, Sam thought, as he began to fill the buckets, lowering them into the well. The fact that his master entrusted him above the others with the care of Miss Becky was little consolation.

Samuel would begin his nineteenth year in January, less than half a year away. Physically he possessed the strength and size of a man; his mind had matured far beyond that of the average slave, but his sexual experience hadn't advanced much beyond the point of that which he could learn from his own body. Given these factors, it was easy to explain why he frequently found himself angry and bewildered, frustrated to the point of belligerence at times. It was a devilish thing to have to admit to himself that he craved companionship after all the years of feeling self-sufficient. But the truth was, he was unbearably lonely. He didn't have much in common with Pompey or Zeke, the new house boys and, though he loved his mother and would do anything for her, she seemed increasingly similar to the other slaves.

It wasn't that he craved the white man's world, he'd remind himself, it was merely that he felt no empathy with the white man's black slaves. With his own eyes he'd seen black men living another life—in Philadelphia, on the docks and in the shops of Baltimore, and on the farms in Pennsylvania. There were Negroes who knew trades, built furniture or the great ships that sailed the oceans; there were even blacks who worked in Philadelphia's printing shops. And that is where his mind kept returning. Those men weren't slaves, they were free men who worked for a wage. He'd laugh bitterly at himself when he entertained these ridiculous notions. Who do you think you are? he'd ask himself. You are Samuel, son of the mulatto Cate and the black African Isaac; Samuel, slave of Menokin Plantation, Richmond County, Virginia. You can never be apprenticed to the editor of a newspaper! Forget these foolish dreams. Look around you. Find yourself a handsome wench with rounded hips and shiny pointed breasts, one who is docile and unthinking, one who doesn't ask questions about the newspapers and books you sneak into the cabin to read by candlelight until after midnight. Or maybe she should be smart, eager to learn to read and write also. Sometimes he thought that would be the best thing because then they could discuss the books and papers he pored over every chance he got.

The fantasies about having someone of his own to sleep with could set his heart to racing, but hard as he tried, Sam was never able to picture what their relationship would be when the morning came. What would they say to each other—he and that unknown black girl? The only female he'd ever really talked to, besides Miss Becky and his mother, was not any of the things he told himself to look for in a wife. She was still a child and she wasn't black. He and Miss Portia would sit sometimes, when no one was around, elaborating on the Indian tales of their half-breed friend. Most of the time she spoke openly to him; only occasionally did she seem to remember who she was, and who he was. Then they'd grow uncomfortable, their talk become stilted. Sam knew that every time he lingered one minute alone in the company of Miss Portia, he ran the risk of a serious lashing, yet it was worth the danger to be able to share thoughts on something other than chores or daily problems. Marse Frank would never understand his interest in Miss Portia went no further than their joint fascination with the ancient Indian lore. He expected the girl herself would soon be finding herself too old for such conversations anyway. Then he'd be even more lonely than he was now.

Taking a deep breath, Sam began the trek up the hill, a wooden bucket sloshing-full of chilly spring water balanced evenly on either end of the yoke across his strong shoulders. "Goddamn!" he muttered, venting his anger on the empty garden, "I wish't I was ridin' dat carriage on my way to Richmon' City!"

༄

By late afternoon the temperature was hot enough to make a man sweat, even if he wasn't working too hard. Sam, after carrying out Miss Becky's instructions, had taken it upon himself to polish the dining room furniture and sweep the back steps to help out his mother. Then he decided to head to the barn.

Taking his time, he curried a team of work horses that hadn't been needed in the field that morning. As he brushed, he sang to himself, relieving his tension and trying to improve his humor. Deciding he'd done enough, he stretched out in some clean smelling hay, hands behind his head, and chomped on a piece of straw.

Maybe he should be thankful he wasn't sitting on top of that old carriage jogging along on that bumpy road. It'd be mighty hot up there right now, he imagined, thinking of Pompey all sweaty and covered with grime, his eyes swollen almost shut with skeeter bites and dust. By the time he heard the hands returning from the fields, Sam had decided he was just as glad to be where he was for the time being. It was Philadelphia he dreamed about anyway, not Richmond City. Swinging himself off the hay by means of a frayed halter left hanging on a post, he was back at work on the horses, humming, when Jeremiah Sutton entered the barn. Sam grinned at him, having learned a long time ago it was a wise idea to stay on the friendly side of an overseer. Even so, Sutton wasn't always predictable.

The white man grunted, as he sloshed water on his face and arms from a trough. "Didn't expect to find you here. Thought you'd be up at the house." He wiped his hands on his breeches, then ran them through his stringy hair. "But long's yo're starin' at me so hard I might's well tell you. I'm goin' into town. Be back b'fore mornin'. If you know what's good for you, you'll keep your damn mouth shut, Sam. The missus don't have t'know I'm gone. Understand?"

Sam nodded, wondering who an old man like Sutton would find to entertain himself with until dawn. Some toothless doxy, more than likely he guessed, grinning again. Doxy. He'd learned the word in Philadelphia. It seemed appropriate for the likes of Jeremiah Sutton; it wasn't only black slaves who'd earned Sam's scorn. "The blacks in the quarter's goin' be drinkin' tonight," he warned the overseer. "Always do, first night after Marse Frank leaves. Might be trouble."

"Leave that to me. I'll deal quick enough with any damage they do. All they ever do when they get drunk is to bust each other's heads anyway." He studied Samuel intently. "You never join them, do you?" Then, swinging a saddle over one of the horses Sam had groomed, and motioning the slave to get a bridle, he said, "You're a strange one, nigger, you know that? A real misfit is how I see it."

◦⌇◦

Sam was restless. He'd been in bed over an hour, unable to sleep. Sounds of music and raucous laughter drifted from the quarter through an open window in the room he shared with Pompey and Zeke over the master's office in the dependency. Through the other window he heard occasional murmurs and twitters that told him Miss Becky and Miss Sally were still sitting in the garden. It was a foolish thing for them to be doing, alone and well after dark. Thinking he heard a rustling closer to hand, he crossed to the window. He knew it was his job to see to Miss Becky's safety, and his sense of duty prompted him to rise and begin to pull his pants on. The moon lit up the open spaces but the buildings and huge trees cast long shadows and he didn't see any movement. Just then, the unmistakable sound of a hiccup reached his ears. There was someone out there on the grounds, between where he stood and where Miss Becky sat with her sister. Probably Cate or Zoey, maybe Zeke. But he couldn't take chances.

Silently he descended the stairs, slid through the doorway and, hugging the wall, made it to the corner of the building without hearing anything other than the fiddles in the quarter. The music picked up tempo, and he knew they were dancing. Some of them would already be drunk on the corn liquor they always managed to sneak in from somewhere. He knew Marse Frank allowed them a certain amount of it, so long as they only brought it out on holidays or special occasions. But this was no holiday. Sam flattened himself against the wall peering in the direction of the garden bench. Miss Becky laughed again. And then he heard the sound that had made him get out of bed in the first place, only this time it was very close. Someone—and now he knew it wasn't Cate, or any woman—was watching his mistress in the garden. He felt rather than saw that whoever it was, couldn't be more than ten feet from where he was. Hearing a whisper, followed by a grunt, he figured instantly there were at least two of them. His heart began to pump blood and his palms were clammy. As soon as he stepped away from the wall, he knew he'd be exposed by moonlight. Whoever was there would see him before he could hope to spot them. There was only one thing to do. Keeping his arms relaxed, ready to swing out if he had to, Sam strode boldly into the open. He didn't break stride nor look behind him until he was a few feet from his mistress.

"Sam!" she gasped. "You frightened me, coming up like that in the dark. We were just sitting here enjoying the fiddle music."

"Miss Becky ... you an' Miss Sally got t'come wit me. Now! To the house." His voice was low, urgent. He prayed they wouldn't argue, still not knowing who or what he might be up against. Or even if it was anything at all to worry about.

"What's the matter with you, Sam? We'll do no such thing," Sally snapped, turning obstinate at being ordered about by a servant.

But Becky knew Sam well. Instinctively, she was prepared to do his bidding. A bond had developed between the two over the years; they understood and respected each other, although they'd never spoken of it. "Sally, come! We'll do what Sam says. He can explain it later."

He hurried them to the house, almost pushing them toward the steps. Sally caught her dress on the thorns of a rose bush and stopped, exasperated, to free herself. "Hurry!" Sam whispered, and then he was bundling them through the door. Over his shoulder, he glimpsed two men move out of the shadow of the office dependency. They were black and he was sure they were very drunk, but he couldn't tell who they were.

Cate sat nodding in a chair in the hall. She'd been waiting for her mistress to come in to bed. Except for a candle that flickered on the table beside her, Sam saw the house was in darkness. "Good," he said, taking charge. "Blow out the candle, Mammy, an' bolt the back door. Quick." He slammed the bolt in the front door and moved catlike into the parlor where he could view the garden. The men were no longer in sight. If the women would stop their infernal chatter, he might be able to hear something.

"For heavens sake, Becky, what are we doing this for? Sam acts as though he's gone crazy." Sally giggled nervously, squeezing her sister's hand. She'd always found Sam peculiar, but Becky favored him above the others for some reason.

"Hush. Sam, tell me what's out there that we should be afraid of," Becky prodded him.

"Two men," he answered. "Dey was watchin' you. Dey's black."

"What are you going to do?" she asked, trusting him. Thank God, Francis hadn't left them here alone with Zeke or Pompey.

"Mammy," Sam said, turning to Cate as soon as she returned, "take Miss Becky and Miss Sally upstairs. Lock yo'sefs in the back chamber. I's goin' lead 'em away from the house if I can. Bolt the door after me." And he was gone, leaving them quaking in the dark house.

Sam had never been so scared in his life. It was mainly the element of the unknown that terrified him. If only he knew who he was up against but, whoever it was, he couldn't let them see he was afraid. As loudly as he could, he stomped down the steps, taking the path leading to the rose garden. They were sure to hear him if they didn't see him. Above the pounding of his heart he detected what he took to be a chuckle.

"Over here, white man's black boy," came a sing-song voice to the left of him. He whipped to face it. "Look at him," came the voice again. "Come t' save de white ladies fum de big black niggers! Ain't he de brave one?"

At that moment he recognized the voice. It was George, the son of old Winny, and Sam could bet his life the other one would be Hector, the worst wheeler-dealer in the quarter. Together they caused more trouble among the slaves than any ten others. He'd heard Marse Frank threaten to sell them more than once. George was an enormous hulk of a man, dumb and mean tempered. His sidekick, scrawny and shifty-eyed, would give his own sister away if he thought it would please George. Physically, Sam knew he was no match for the two of them. Could he reason with them? He didn't think so. They'd hated his guts since childhood. Quickly, he decided his only hope was to goad them into chasing him. He knew he could outrun them, especially in their drunken conditions. And he'd be leading them away from the house.

"We wasn' goin' do nuthin' to de ladies, Sambo. Ain't no need for y'all gittin' all het up, now is dere?" That was Hector. He was always brave when George was with him. And George was always with him; their relationship had become a lewd joke among the other Negroes.

"Wot sh'd we do wit' him, Hector? Want t' teach him a lessin he won' fo'git?"

"What you say, George, is what we's goin' do. I's wit' you all de way."

The two men had gradually moved closer to where Sam had planted himself and now, a bare fifteen or twenty paces separated them. He could almost see the whites of their eyes, smell the whisky on their breath. It was time to move and he pushed his legs to action. In a flash he was away and down the hill. He didn't pause until he reached the bottom, and then only to make certain the two were lumbering after him. Running again, doubling back along the creek line so he wouldn't lose his way, he paced himself. He heard them thrashing behind him, and hoped his lead still held. On and on he went, driven by terror of what they could do to him if they caught him alone, this far from any hope of assistance. But he was running out of breath and short stabs of pain had begun to shoot through his chest forcing him to slow to almost a walk. Finally, leaning against a tree, he gulped for air. It was a few moments before he realized there was only silence behind him in the forest. His fears began anew. What if they'd turned around? Gone back to the house. Crazed by drink, the bully in George could have sent him back to terrorize the women he knew were now alone and unprotected! He'd heard of slaves who massacred their owners in cold blood. And Cate was there, just as likely a victim as the others.

Sam began to retrace his footsteps. Covering ground as fast as possible, despite the feeling his lungs might burst, he followed the stream back in the direction he'd just come from. He was amazed, horrified, at how far he'd run and was tiring fast. On the brink of abandoning all caution and logic, he allowed the night to overcome him with desperation. He was the one who thrashed and stumbled his way now, until—stopping short, he was aghast at what confronted him. Sam found himself face to face with Hector, who was panting and heaving like a wild thing. The weasel eyes were crazed with pain and anger. The little man came at Sam using his hands like claws set to gouge and maim. Sam had been in few fights since he was a child when Hector and others used to gang up on him, but he knew how to use his fists. He also knew that in any fight with the puny Hector, he might strike a crucial blow. So instead of swinging, he grabbed his assailant by the wrists pinning his arms to his sides.

"What's the matter wit' you, Hector? You gone mad?" Sam asked, gasping, hoping against hope that George wasn't about to jump him from behind.

"Toad! Nigger! Son-of-a-bitch! You kilt him! My George is *daid*," Hector wailed, trying frantically to disengage himself from Sam's iron grip.

It took Sam several minutes to calm him enough so Hector agreed to lead the way to where he'd left George. A cursory examination revealed that the big man was indeed dead. Sam's hand came away from the large head with his fingers sticky with blood. George's head had struck a sharp rock protruding from the hillside. He must have slipped in the dark, but Sam didn't wait to ask any questions. Leaving the stricken Hector moaning to himself, he headed for the house.

"I'll git you fo dis, Sambo!" the little man screamed after him.

It took him over an hour to decide he needed to talk to someone about what had happened. When George's body was discovered, and Hector would see to that, there'd be hell to pay. It was one thing for blacks to have a drunken fight, but a killing was something else. And Sam harbored no doubt that Hector would holler "murder" loud and clear. The punishment for a black accused of murder was swift and final. Leaving his room, he padded silently up the steps to Menokin House. His hand on the door, he remembered he'd told Cate to bolt it, so he went instead to tap on the cellar window of her room. He thought he heard something inside, and called to her quietly so as not to alarm her. "It's me, Samu'l. Open the door!"

After she let him in, he followed her back to the cellar where Cate lit a stubby candle. The wick sputtered stubbornly, finally taking flame to disclose Sam's disheveled appearance. He hadn't realized until he saw his mother staring at him that his smock was torn. His bare feet were caked with mud from the creek bed; his hands still bore traces of dried blood. In a stream of sentences strung together by urgency, he spilled the story. When he finished, they sat quietly while Cate considered the situation.

"You thinkin' what I's thinkin'?" he asked her finally, unable to remain silent any longer.

"Miss Becky?"

Sam nodded, gratified he didn't have to explain it.

"No time t' waste," Cate whispered. She'd grown heavy with the years and breathed hard after the two flights of stairs. "I'll git her up. Den you come tell her wot happ'nd," she told him. Cate had not yet permitted herself to consider that she might be going to lose her precious son.

∽

Several hours after daylight Becky stood on the back porch. She was thinking it was almost as though she'd expected something like this to happen, or had she wanted it to happen? She imagined the river down there, although with the trees leafing out, it would be impossible to get even a glimpse of Rappahannock Creek. The sky was clear and the sun would soon be above the tree line, promising a beautiful day. She tried to estimate how far Sam would have gotten by now, leaving as he did three hours before dawn. She'd sent him to the ferry above Stratford on the Potomac knowing he might be recognized on the Rappahannock. Had she always known she would one day set him free? Uncertain, she turned back to the house. Some hot tea would sooth her nerves while she waited for Sally to wake up. However, the brew tasted acrid and she couldn't drink it. Instead, she nibbled on a biscuit, trying to ignore Cate's red-rimmed, puffy eyes.

She'd managed to find a well used pair of boots that were only slightly too small, and gave Sam an old shirt and seldom worn jacket of Francis's. While he was changing she'd penned a hastily worded paper for him, stating: *I, Rebecca Tayloe Lee, owner of the slave Samuel by virtue of the will of my deceased father, the Honorable John Tayloe Esquire of Mount Airy Plantation, Richmond County, Virginia, hereby grant to the said Samuel Lee his freedom from this day forward.* Was it enough? Would it be binding? The worst they could do to him if he was challenged would be to send him back. The letter would serve at the very least to identify him and where he was from. She knew it wasn't strictly legal, not being witnessed nor recorded, but it was the best she'd been able to do. Then a troubling thought came to her—she had taught the boy Sam to read, put ideas in his head, made him so different from the other slaves that he couldn't accept them as his equals. Knowing this and, further, that by the time he was fourteen or fifteen

Sam no longer belonged at Menokin, why had she waited until a crisis forced her to release him? On the other hand, why hadn't she simply told him to stay where he was until Master Francis came home to help them decide what to do? The dead slave belonged to them and Sam belonged to them; therefore no law could touch him without the master's request. Why had they all panicked?

Somewhere in the midst of recriminations and self-doubt, Becky decided to conceal her part in Sam's escape. Only Cate knew the truth, and she wouldn't dare to reveal anything without her mistress's knowledge. From the tiny seed of learning she had secretly planted in an eager childish mind, there now emerged a much larger and more dangerous deception. Trembling over her part in it, she rehearsed her story several times before Sally appeared for breakfast.

Francis was home for several hours before he missed Sam. He came in bubbling with the excitement of the convention. Whether through his efforts or not, Richard had acquiesced, agreeing not to launch an all-out campaign against ratification of the constitution. "Patrick raved at great length about Jefferson's mistrust of the document," he explained, "only to be countered by the sage calm of Mr. Madison, who assured the gentlemen that in recent weeks Jefferson had written from abroad of his confident approval and his sincere hope that ratification would be most speedily effected! He even produced the letter, which forced poor Patrick to admit defeat."

That it had been a show of the most exhilarating sort, and that being in harmony with the proponents of the winning side had put him in high spirits, was obvious. "Any desire to go back?" Becky teased, anxious to talk about anything that would put off the time when she must reveal Sam's disappearance.

"None at all," he stated flatly, remembering he'd not told her about the children and that she hadn't asked. "William and the girls will be here in a few days. My brother will stay for a while, I think, if we encourage him. He's much discouraged with the condition of his various properties, including the house at Green Spring, which I saw for myself is in a sadly dilapidated state. I'm sure he'll welcome the comforts we can offer him. As to a return to politics, I think my enjoyment of the scene these days is limited strictly to observing the antics of others! I have no desire to subject myself to those tortures again. By the by," he questioned, eyes searching the corners of the room, "the kittens are all right, I suppose? Portia and Cornie fretted over them the entire way to Jamestown."

Becky nodded, giving him a weak smile. If only it was merely the fate of two cats she had on her conscience. She'd decided to be as casual as possible concerning Sam's escape, allowing Francis to see she wasn't overly disturbed by it. It would give him the idea she'd accepted the fact the slave was gone, and preferred to do nothing about hunting him down.

It was after he'd gone upstairs, found his satchel and portmanteau on the floor of the chamber, not unpacked, that he began to wonder. "Sam?" he called into the hall. Then, "Cate? Cate, get Sam up here to unpack for me." But Cate had made herself scarce at Becky's suggestion when they'd heard the carriage approaching.

"Frank?" came Sally's clear voice. "Didn't you know? Samuel ran away. Hasn't Becky told you? It's curious she hasn't mentioned it yet."

"Yes, it is," Francis agreed, taking Sally's hand and leading her down the steps with him. "I can't believe it. When did it happen?" Sam? Run away? It wasn't possible. The boy was as loyal as ever Ben had been and surely wouldn't have gone off leaving the women alone.

"Well, it was the night two of the Negroes were drunk and Sam thought they were going to attack us, I suppose. He rushed us into the house and then pursued them. There was a fight, and apparently Sam killed one of them. Or so the other one has said. Mr. Sutton has been in a perfect rage ever since. He's locked up the one called Hector, and put word out in the county that there'll be a reward for information leading to the return of Samuel."

"What has Becky done about it?"

Sally avoided his eyes. She had her own suspicions but she wasn't going to pass them on, not directly at least. "Well," she answered, trying to be vague, "not a terrible lot. Oh ... she's talked to Mr. Sutton ... told him to wait to list any reward until you returned. Actually, Frank," she blurted, "Becky doesn't seem surprised that it happened and I don't think she's anxious to have the slave hunted down. But that is only my own opinion. She told Cate to train Zeke to wait on table."

"So ... Sally," Becky announced from the parlor door, "it seems you've told Francis the whole sad story of our escapade." Her voice was strained, hollow sounding in spite of the smile she gave them. "It was an ordeal, I can tell you that, darling. Sam was most diligent about protecting us, as Sally says, but when the accident occurred, he panicked ... and ran. I say we should let him go." She couldn't look at him, didn't want to see that quirked eyebrow.

"No," he said, suddenly annoyed with her. "By God, the loss of one slave is enough in these hard times. I can't afford to suffer the loss of two. I shall put a notice in the *Gazette* and send Sutton around the county this very afternoon. How many days has he been gone?"

"About a fortnight," Becky answered meekly. It wasn't going at all the way she'd planned. Francis never got angry with her, but now his eyes were flashing.

"More like three weeks," Sally corrected. "Yes, I think it's definitely that long. In fact, it was the day after you left." She watched her sister, waiting for her to speak.

Francis marched across the hall and into his study, closing the door deliberately behind him.

"Are you going to tell him?" Sally whispered.

"Tell him what?" Green eyes widened, professing innocence.

"The truth about Sam."

"I've told him all there is to tell."

"Becky, I know there's more. I've heard you and Cate talking. I'm not blind and neither is Frank."

Becky turned on her heel without a word and left the house.

❧

Sally was right. Francis, too, began to suspect there was more to the matter. The evening was singularly strained, both Becky and Sally remaining quiet and aloof from each other and from him; they spoke at supper but only the necessary platitudes. He desperately wanted to share the details of the Richmond convention with them, but surmised his words were unlikely to register on preoccupied minds. Sighing, he contented himself with the New York newspapers that had arrived in his absence.

At last the hours passed and he was alone with his wife. Becky eased onto the bed keeping her back to him. He reached for her, needing her, wanting her after the separation. Her movement was slight, but he sensed rejection. "What's the matter?" he asked, allowing his fingers to glory in the softness of her just-brushed hair.

"Nothing." She shifted her weight, moving again, ever so slightly away from him.

"We've been together too long, love, for me not to know when something is wrong. You're not going to make me figure it out for myself ... now are you?"

"It's nothing I can tell you about, Francis."

"Why? Don't you trust me to understand?"

"I don't know."

"You don't know? Surely you can't mean that."

"I don't know what I mean. I just don't know!"

"Is it that bad then?" he asked softly, taking her face in his hands and forcing her to look at him. "Does it concern Sam? Tell me."

For a full minute she sat petrified. Then, "Yes," she cried. "Yes. Yes." Her arms went around him, clinging. "I ... set him free ... told him where to go ... gave him clothes, a paper ... he didn't run away." She started to sob.

"Why couldn't you tell me before?" he demanded, more hurt than he would have believed possible that she'd purposely lied to him.

Becky didn't answer right away. "That's not all. I taught him to read. Years ago. I made him different. Sam can read as well as I can! Don't you see? I *had* to set him free. I didn't think you would understand, darling. I trusted you. I just didn't think you'd understand. I don't understand it myself!"

Outraged, he rolled away from her. "I see," he mumbled into his pillow. "Goodnight, Becky."

It took several quiet days by himself for Francis to get over the blow she had dealt his ego. When he'd sorted it all out for the hundredth time, put the pieces back together, he realized he loved her more for what she'd done, than had she done nothing at all. It was one of the myriad facets of the fascination she had always held for him. Out of the quagmire of his hurt feelings, he extracted another revelation—he recognized that deep within the core of his being he'd always known his wife desired his participation in public affairs far more than he himself did. Yet, strangely enough, it was the very phenomenal independence of Becky's nature, as illustrated by her freeing of the slave, that had rendered him less able to exert himself in any direction away from her. He hoped he had not been a disappointment to her in that respect. It was a certainty, he never would have learned the meaning of love without her. Nor would he have lived at all, he admitted to himself.

He found her in the garden, among the roses. She held out a perfect pink rosebud for his inspection, early morning sunshine glinting off drops of dew on the curled petals.

"I'm not angry," he said. "I love you."

"I know," she smiled, handing him the rose.

Debt to Nature

"It looks like Adams will be our next president," Francis called into the empty hallway upon his return from Richmond Courthouse. He traveled back and forth these days in an open buggy he'd purchased from young Landon Carter. The slave Zeke drove it for him, and there was ample room for Portia or Cornelia to accompany them. He rarely traveled any great distance now, and seldom by himself. Riding his own horse was still a pleasure, but he attempted it with less and less frequency. Occasionally he'd mount up, take a turn around the fields for an hour, but his back always suffered for it. Saddle jounce, he supposed, too hard on his sixty-two-year-old bones.

"Did you hear me, Becky? John Adams, they say, will keep the Federalists in power for four more years! Wagers are that he'll defeat Jefferson ... not sure how I feel about that." He still thought of Jefferson as "young Tom," and was vague about his movements in recent years, although it was obvious his old acquaintance had gathered quite a national political following and, after all, he was a Virginian.

"I'm coming, darling." She was upstairs. "Mr. Adams, you say? How nice. I approved of Mr. Adams, after I got to know him a bit ... although we didn't have much to say to one another as I recall. I never understood what you and Richard saw in him to cause you to admire him quite so fervently as you did. He wasn't particularly polished, did you think?"

"A brilliant and determined man, John was. He didn't really need polish, any more than Patrick did in his day. And we did admire them both, didn't we? John was firm, strict as I recall, in his political philosophy, and always caustic in his judgment of those who weren't. Few Virginians knew how to appreciate his qualities, did they? I wonder with the passage of all these years if they will even now? There's still a certain amount of opposition feeling to the constitution and its affect on southern interests. But, you know, I've never changed my mind ... I'd still be for it if the vote were today."

Becky wiped her hands on her apron. She'd heard all this before. From the bottom step she leaned over the railing to plant a kiss on his mouth. "I was helping Zoey clean that old wardrobe ... the one the girls used to keep their toys and treasures in? You'd be amazed at what we uncovered. One of them actually stashed away a box of bird feathers, the skin of a water moccasin, and a packet of dead beetles!"

"That had to be Cornie," Francis laughed. "Portia would never stoop to such a mundane pastime as beetle collecting. Did you find any arrowheads?" he asked. "*That* would be Portia's idea of treasure."

She nodded. "Some of those, too. Come," she said, taking his arm. "Let's sit together over a cup of tea. It would do us both good. You know, Francis, I believe I'll tease the girls by telling them I've put Portia's beetles on her night table and thrown out all those useless arrowheads of Cornie's. That should start a lively conversation at supper! They're over at Mount Airy, playing with John's babies I suppose, but I expect them home soon. Jane invited them to Blandfield for the weekend, and Mr. Beverley is sending a carriage to pick them up." Like her sister Kitty, who had married a grandson of Landon Carter, Jane had also married a grandson of a wealthy planter, Robert Beverley; the Beverley family's plantation boasted an enormous mansion house located across the river in Essex County; it was here Portia and Cornelia would spend Saturday and Sunday.

Francis brought up the subject of the presidency again as soon as they settled with their tea. "Funny," he began, spacing his words, "I always expected ... that somehow ... once the war was over and that ugly Deane to-do forgotten ... and the confederation established, that Richard might one day become president. Do you suppose, had he not opposed the constitution, that he might have been?"

"He was, after all, president of the Congress for a time," she pacified him, knowing what a blow Richard's death had been to Francis, and his brother hadn't lived long enough to succeed Washington anyway, so how could he have been elected president of the United States?

"That's not the same. That was more like being chairman of the whole, which even I held briefly. It didn't give the powers to a man that the constitution gives to a president elected by the people. It seemed to me that Richard had the perfect stature, and certainly the background for the role. Arthur had a better mind, perhaps, but neither the bearing nor the temperament. But Richard, I thought, would have made an excellent president of these United States."

Arthur, too, was gone. And William, just over a year ago, totally blind at the end, had passed away. And Hannah dead. Only Alice still lived. Becky's heart went out to her husband, knowing how he missed them, but especially Richard. Yet, he had happy memories of each of them, and talked about them frequently. He never brooded and she was thankful for that. "And you, my man, would you have made an excellent governor of Virginia? Since we're in the land of make-believe today."

"Oh, that's pure whimsy. You know it."

"You'd have made a just and honorable one, my dear," she insisted.

"Perhaps. But I'd have resented every minute of my private life that I had to give up ... and the time I couldn't spend with you. It would have taken me away from you. If I've not learned much about myself over the years, I've at least learned that.

Besides, I've told you more than once, I wasn't cut out to be a leader of men."

Looking at him, Becky thought that he wouldn't have had to give her up. Why had she never been able to make him understand that? Yet he was right in some ways; their life wouldn't have been the same. "How about Ludwell?" she asked, changing the subject to Richard's second son. "I think you have your sights set on seeing him as governor one day. How long has he been in the General Assembly now?"

Francis didn't hesitate; he followed his nephew's career avidly. "He was in the House for three years you know, and now he's serving his fifth term in the Senate. I tell you, Becky, that boy is going places!"

"He's hardly a boy, darling. Why, he must be almost forty years old ... a fact I can scarcely believe."

"Time has a way of leaving us behind, love. But Ludwell is now and always has been my favorite nephew. The fact that he's Richard's second son, plus being a fine young man, is why I've been so determined to leave my estate to him."

"I wish I could be more fond of Flora." Ludwell had married his cousin, Philip Lee's youngest daughter.

A hint of the old boyish smile flickered on Francis's face. "There's a lot of Colonel Phil in that girl! I don't wonder at your dilemma."

Ignoring that, she went on, "You know, darling, have you considered the fact that Ludwell and Flora up there in Alexandria have their own home now? They might not want Menokin. Maybe they wouldn't even wish to be bothered with it. It's getting old, a bit run-down. The roof needs repair and the window frames need painting again. It suits us, but what would they want with it?"

It occurred to him she might be chiding him for his laxness in fixing the place up. It wasn't that he didn't want to, or hadn't thought about it. He'd never worried Becky with money problems in the past and didn't want to start now but, if truth be told, they were damned short of cash. He'd sold one of his lots in Alexandria last year to tide them over, but now he was in another tight spot. The years of tobacco production had taken their toll on the fields. He didn't have the slaves, the implements of modern husbandry, or the energy needed to clear great quantities of forest for new croplands. What was it young John Tayloe had said to him a couple of years back? "Keep up with the times, Frank," he'd warned, one Sunday at a family dinner. "Tobacco is no longer the money crop. Cotton. That's the coming thing. You'll be lost in the shuffle if you don't put as many acres as you can clear into cotton." John's tone had seemed somewhat patronizing, Francis remembered thinking at the time, yet maybe he should have listened. But it wasn't easy to keep up. Things were constantly changing. Next year it would be something else. And the taxes would go up again. One could always count on the damn'd taxes going up.

"Francis?" Becky asked, shaking his arm. "Are you listening to me?"

"Hmm? Oh, yes indeed, love. I am that. Just thinking on what you said about Menokin, that's all. Well," he stood up, stretching, "I guess I'll mosey back to the stable. I told Pompey to see what he could do with that buggy wheel. It's come loose again ... I surely miss Ben when it comes to things like that. I'll just wander out to check on him before I call the family to prayers."

"Don't forget," she reminded, "when you finish the psalm, it's Portia's turn to read the lesson."

Francis nodded vaguely. He was no longer listening. There was another thing about Menokin that had been preying on his mind—the distance from town. Oh, he remembered well enough, in the beginning, that had been the charm of it. But they no longer had a carriage, only the buggy and the old post-chaise, and they were down to three horses. Not counting the two work animals, of course. He realized he could purchase a good animal or two from young John at a reasonable price, but John had that off-handed way of making him feel curiously inadequate lately. His brother-in-law was also frequently in Alexandria, hard to catch up with. John had business interests, banking, and horse racing to occupy his time. He was always busy. Francis took him to be a young man of enormous goals, not the least of which was money. John was also a clever opportunist. While still in his twenties, he'd made his name known throughout the state and on the national scene as well—in politics, in business and, in a limited way, in a military capacity. All this did nothing toward making the new master of Mount Airy any easier to deal with in Richmond County, Francis grumbled to himself, wondering why he should fret about it anyway.

What he had seriously started to think about, was how far away from a doctor they lived; from the company of friends and relatives. They had fewer visitors every year. Everything was changing—no one even called Hobbs' Hole by its familiar name anymore—now they called it Tappahannock. He'd never get used to that. Something else nagged at his mind. He wished very much to send Portia and Cornelia to a suitable school for young ladies. It was the thing to do nowadays. But expenses at a boarding school were prohibitive; he'd actually made inquiry and been told there were some highly recommended schools in Alexandria. And that was where his thoughts kept straying. To Alexandria. If they moved there, the girls could live at home and go to school. Would he consider the sale of Menokin? Could he? He wasn't at all certain, but he knew there were many reasons why he should analyze the prospect, long and hard. Becky. She was the most important reason of all. It wouldn't be too long before she could be a widow. A defenseless and attractive widow. How long could she manage by herself out here in the loneliness of Menokin? Who would care if she couldn't manage? Her brother John? Young Landon Carter? They were of another generation, and he didn't think they would overly concern themselves with the plight of a bereaved widow, even a relative.

∽

Indecision continued to plague him during the months that followed. The girls were growing up, fast becoming attractive young ladies. Why, Portia was as old as Becky had been when he wed her. They needed the companionship and gaiety of other young people. Social life in the Neck no longer was what it had been before the war, nor even during the years directly following it. One couldn't rely on the social contacts of the Anglican church either. Lunenburg Parish Church had stood locked and empty for two years, the vestry unable to obtain a minister. Some of their former parishioners had long since joined the Baptists, but Francis had never considered that as an option. Now, he'd heard, The Reverend George Young had been hired. It was agreed he would preach one out of three Sundays at Farnham Parish, the other two at Upper and Lower Lunenburg. But whether he could revitalize the church, breathe life into it again, remained to be seen.

One morning Francis told Zeke to harness up the horse; they would be going the twelve miles to Nomini Hall. There he visited with some of Councillor Carter's family, before making his way to the Turberville home. In each place he passed the word that he was considering selling out, moving to Alexandria. Next he rode to the courthouse where he spread the message to a few other friends. All expressed shock at the idea, telling him it was a drastic mistake, but they promised to pass on the information to anyone looking for an acreage with a medium sized mansion house, brick dependencies, and multiple outbuildings. Then he told Zeke to take him home.

He couldn't look at the chimneys etched against the skyline as the buggy bumped down the road that had become more rutted than ever. He guessed it was the first time he'd ever failed to do so, from the very first day they were erected. He didn't say a word to Becky about his afternoon. It wasn't his intention to deceive her, he told himself—but quite likely nothing would come of the scheme anyway. There seemed no need for unnecessary alarm.

⤫

It was a brilliant day in June a few weeks later when a visitor arrived at Menokin, his name was John James Maund. He explained he was married to Harriet, one of the Carter daughters from Nomini, and was looking to buy a home. Francis thought he remembered meeting him on another occasion, and asked how his wife was doing—he did remember little Harriet, recalling that her lively nature had made him think of Becky as a child. Mr. Maund, being a young man of the law, wasted no time in getting right to the business at hand, and asked the colonel to call him James. Large homes in good condition were not easy to come by, he said, and he preferred not to go to the trouble and expense of building. The two men made an extensive tour of the house before retiring to the study, where Francis offered his guest a glass of wine. He was feeling in need of one himself. Mr. Maund expressed his satisfaction with the house saying he was especially pleased with the gardens. Francis promised that Jeremiah Sutton would conduct him on a further tour of the outbuildings, meadows, fields, and pastures when they finished their chat. Yes, he said in answer to Maund's question, they would consider selling some of the furniture with the house. They would take the house servants, and whatever pieces of furniture Mrs. Lee selected, with them to Alexandria. The field slaves and, of course, the farm equipment would stay. Yes, he assured Maund, the plantation was around one thousand acres more or less. No, it hadn't been recently surveyed. How soon did he think they would be ready to move? Well, if there appeared no problems connected with the sale, he supposed they could make it in three months or so. Francis explained his plans to build a town home on a lot he owned in

Alexandria within a short time. In the meantime they could stay with his nephew, Ludwell Lee, or lease a home.

They discussed price. Did 3,000 pounds sound too far out of the realm of reality? Well, no, James Maund answered, that could be a starting point for negotiation. He'd talk the situation over with his wife, suggested Colonel Lee do the same, and he'd return in a few days. Directing the prospective buyer in the direction of the stables, where he'd already sent word to Sutton to expect him, he closed the door, returned to his study and sat down in front of his desk, his Philadelphia desk. Breathing a sigh of relief that Becky, Sally, and the girls had fortunately chosen this day to visit at Sabine Hall, he looked around the room which had served him well. Then, turning, he glanced across the hall to the small parlor, where late afternoon sun cast a glow over the Persian carpet, a wedding gift from Landon Carter. He'd always liked that room although they never used it much. Somehow they preferred to gather around the table in the dining room ... or in the back parlor where Sally or Becky could play for them on the spinet. He cleared his throat. Well. If he intended to see about letting a house in Alexandria, he had some letters to write. But the first thing he had to do was to break the news to Becky. He'd do so the minute she came in, he vowed.

Some time later, after James Maund had left the property, he heard the crunch of buggy wheels on oyster shell, the clop of the horse's hooves, and then the excited chatter of women's voices—his family was home. Cornelia and Portia rushed past his door first, arms laden. "Just some dresses Aunt Kitty gave me," Cornie called. "We're the same size. Portia borrowed a book and some sheet music." And an assortment of other things he supposed, shaking his head. He'd learned the females in families were constantly trading back and forth, seeming always to take great joy in the process.

Becky's face appeared in the doorway. "Hello, darling. How are you? We've had a lovely day. Kitty gave me the plumpest goose-down pillow for my blue chair, and Landon sent you over his new recipe for peach brandy, says it's much better than the stuff his grandfather used to make. I hope you don't mind, but I promised him some of your raspberry wine when it's ready." She stopped, looking at him for the first time. "Whatever is the matter, Francis? You look positively stricken! Did you miss us? Is something wrong?"

There was nowhere to hide. He had to tell her ... now. "Becky, there is something serious I must talk to you about. Do you have a minute?" He hoped his face didn't look as pinched as it felt.

"Of course I have time. It sounds important. Just let me put these things down and speak to Cate about supper. The girls are starved. Sally's stopped off to see what Cook is about. Chances are she's not even put the potatoes on to boil! I'll only be a few minutes, darling. Then we shall have our little talk if you wish."

Francis sat for a long time after the sound of her skirts rustled down the hall. He folded his hands and placed them on the desk, waiting. He didn't feel like doing anything else. He merely sat there. After a while Cornelia and Portia convinced him some fresh air was what he needed. They thought he looked pale, they said. The three of them took a walk in the garden and he heard all about the twenty spring lambs in the meadow on Sabine's fork quarter. After supper, Becky seemed to have forgotten he had something to tell her. When she didn't ask about it, he never got around to bringing it up himself.

∿

Several days passed. Before he knew it, James Maund was back. This time he was accompanied by Harriet, his wife, and carried a portfolio stuffed with important looking papers. Becky, having no idea of the purpose of their visit, welcomed them and ushered them into the parlor, offering tea. She was happy to have visitors and, if perplexed as to the reason for their unexpected arrival, she didn't show it. Francis remarked how much Harriet Lucy resembled her mother and decided he wasn't feeling very well, all in the same instant.

"Oh, James, I just know we're going to love it here." Harriet Maund said.

Becky's eyes opened wide. "Sugar? Milk?" she murmured politely, as she poured, and before anyone else could speak. "Did you say, my dear, that you're going to love it here?" she repeated distinctly, as she passed each one a cup. Her gaze moved slowly around the room until it came to rest on her husband's anguished features.

"Becky," Francis began. Damn, he thought, how in God's name did I ever allow this to happen?

"It's all right, darling. Mrs. Maund was just saying how much she likes our house. It always pleases me to hear that someone appreciates what we have done with it."

Her eyes crinkled at the corners but Francis couldn't tell what kind of an expression it was; he'd never seen it before. "Becky, you don't understand ..." he tried again. If he could only have a moment alone with her ....

"Would you care for a sweet, Mr. Maund? My sister has made them herself. She's an excellent baker, you know. Our cooks can't compare to Sally when it comes to candies." Becky smiled at Sally, who was beginning to sense a crisis brewing.

"Did you know Colonel Lee has offered to sell us the plantation for 3,000 pounds?" James Maund interjected, unwilling to allow the game to continue He couldn't fathom the man's not having told his wife of their meeting—it was utterly absurd if he hadn't—it made for a very strained situation indeed. Perhaps the colonel was getting old, forgetful. Whatever the reason, there was no sense beating around the bush about it, and he decided to get right to the point. "He has indicated you could probably be ready to move in three months or thereabouts." Pausing, he took a loud slurp of his tea, avoiding her eyes.

Harriet Maund was embarrassed, thinking her husband sounded almost defiant and she wished he hadn't said that. The spoon rattled against the china cup as she stirred busily at the sugar in the bottom. Her heart was really set on the house. She had always loved it, since visiting with her parents long ago.

Becky smiled sweetly at Francis, then fastened her attention on their guests. Her back was very straight and her eyes held absolutely steady. "I see," she said. "Well. You saw the gardens as you came in? They are terraced. Did you notice? All the products of Colonel Lee's skill. He works out there every morning of his life. He prunes, and he grafts, and he cross-pollinates. Why, he spends half the day in that garden. It's the joy of his retirement. Of course, he has help ... Zeke works out there with him. And Pompey sometimes. But he does a great deal of it himself. He always has. Why, a number of years ago, before we went away to the Congress, he cultivated a dozen varieties of violets for me! Those violets have multiplied until they bloom on every corner of our hillside almost all year long. They're my favorite flower. And then each day when he's finished his chores, we have our noon day meal. The whole family together, right across the hall ... our nieces, my sister, and ourselves. More often than not, Colonel Lee brings us some flowers for the table, or maybe a basket of peaches, sometimes figs or berries—whatever is in season. It's a rare day that he comes empty handed from his garden. When we bow our heads for grace I've never failed to hear him offer his thanks for the blessings our Savior has bestowed upon this house."

Her voice grew soft, losing its edge, becoming almost dream-like. "After we've eaten and exchanged our plans for the afternoon, if he's feeling well, Colonel Lee will have Zeke drive him around the fields in the buggy to see what's going on and what may need to be done. He stops, talks to the hands, asks if they have any problems, gives them encouragement. I know this ... because I frequently ride along with him. I think that's what makes a place run, don't you? When the master has a great deal of love for it, then through his caring and appreciation of the land, every person who lives there, right down to the lowliest field Negro, learns and benefits through his love and example. That's how it is here at Menokin. You know, Mr. Maund, I just can't imagine this place without Colonel Lee's hand in it." Becky raised her napkin to her face, sniffing ever so slightly. "Would you care for more tea, Mrs. Maund ... Harriet, dear? All this talking has made me dreadfully neglectful as a hostess. Please do forgive me."

She filled one cup, then set the teapot down with a clatter. "I declare, I don't know what's come over me. It must be this unseasonable heat we're having. Sally, would you mind pouring? I'm feeling rather poorly all of a sudden." Excusing herself, she fled to the safety of the bed chamber she'd shared with Francis for twenty-five years.

෨෬

"It wasn't a very good idea, I guess, was it, love?" Francis asked her later.

"It was a terrible idea, darling. What did you tell them?"

"Nothing, yet."

"You mean they still think we're going to sell Menokin to them?"

"I suppose they do. But don't worry. I'm to meet James at the courthouse day after tomorrow. He insisted we take our time. I'll tell him then that I've ... *we've* changed our minds."

"Are you sure?"

"I'm sure. When you were telling them about our garden ... well ... ah, all of a sudden I realized how unbearable mornings would be were I not to spend them in the garden. I hadn't thought of it precisely that way until you mentioned it. I was only thinking of you and the girls. I'm most grateful to you for telling them what it means to me."

"I wasn't talking to them, Francis. I was talking to you."

"So you were," he chuckled, having known all along that she'd been up to her old tricks and, once again, she had manipulated him and was feeling pleased with herself for it.

☙

All night long thick and murky fog worried up and down the Rappahannock. It swallowed the ferry tied up to Naylor's wharf as it played back and forth, crossing to the opposite shore where it dropped a shroud over the small dories and the half-dozen or so merchant vessels bobbing at anchor on a low tide. It blew ghostly breath into the marshes and along every branch and creek line. Franicis awoke to find a dense, impenetrable blanket had literally captured Menokin House; the stuff had laid siege to even the tallest trees. From his window he couldn't see the tops of the pines nor was he able to distinguish the eaves of the office or the kitchen house. It looked an excellent day to stay inside, he decided, and work on his account books. He'd let the postings pile up—it was time to put himself to task.

About three o'clock he stopped to have afternoon tea with Becky. She encouraged this quiet hour each day to be shared by just the two of them. His eyes felt strained. He was rubbing them when she entered, followed by Cate with the tea caddy.

"You look tired, darling. Why don't you put the crop book away for today? It will keep."

He shrugged. "A little cold seems to be bothering me. Nothing serious. My throat was sore when I woke up, but it's better now." When they'd finished their tea, he told her he wanted to work an hour or so longer. Becky scolded his stubbornness but left him to his books. The light was abominable on such a dreary day; he decided that was probably why his eyes were bothering him. But before many minutes passed, he became aware he was truly not feeling well, that he must have a fever. The ache he'd noticed in his chest earlier wasn't caused by sitting in the chair too long.

Soon he found himself tucked snugly in bed. Cate hovered in the background and Becky didn't leave his side. Portia, Cornelia, and Sally flitted in and out, chattering and bringing him things to drink and read. Pompey was dispatched in the morning to fetch the new doctor from Richmond Courthouse.

ლ

Francis remained ill through the Christmas season, and into the new year. It was hard to believe it was 1797, so close to the turn of a new century. He found himself wondering if it could possibly bring about as many changes as this one had; it didn't seem likely. A day or so later he became aware he was seriously ill. Becky had caught his cold but, after a few days, was up and caring for him again; Portia went to bed for two days, but soon recovered under the doctor's care. Only he, after almost a month, was not getting any better. The weaker he became, the longer the faces that popped in and out of his chamber. One day he decided he'd have to put on a cheerful pose no matter how wretched he felt. He owed it to them, and he'd begin with Becky.

"Read to me a while, love. Would you mind?" He willed himself to feel like smiling.

Becky sat in the chair nearest the fire, a shawl wrapped around herself. The prolonged cold weather had penetrated the think walls—the house was frigid—everyone said it was the worst winter they could remember. She was working on woolen scarfs for the girls and had hoped to finish them for Christmas, but with Francis's illness there hadn't been time. "I wouldn't mind in the least," she assured him, putting aside the knitting. "I'll get the book Ludwell brought you. I'll be back in a minute."

Once out of his sight, Becky moved more slowly. The pain in her chest was definitely worse today. She no longer doubted its warning. Where was Cate? She glanced behind her, half expecting to see her maid. If Cate suspected she was sick again, she'd refuse to permit her to nurse Francis, and it was obvious he needed her more than ever. He didn't seem to be improving at all, not even since the fever broke. Becky reached for the book of Shakespeare's *Sonnets* on the study shelf. A sheet of paper tucked between the pages of another book caught her attention. Pulling it out, she had to smile. It was the flowery little poem Nancy Shippen had written her favorite uncle. "Why that must have been fifteen years ago," she mused aloud.

"Do you remember the verses Nancy wrote for you shortly after her marriage, darling?" she asked when she returned upstairs. "I came across it just now."

Francis grinned, feeling embarrassed all over again. "How could I forget? They're the most trumped up bit of foolish prattle anyone ever astounded me with! Do you have it there?"

"Yes. Shall I read it?"

"If you wish," he answered, flushing slightly not wanting to admit how much he'd enjoyed Nancy's flattery.

"Thou sweetest of all the Lee race," Becky read, "that ever adorned our shore,

O with us do fix thine abode and leave Philadelphia no more.

Thy temper's as soft as the dove's when she warbles aloft in the air,

And thy converse enchantingly sweet when engaged in discourse with the fair.

But when learning engrosses thy thought, then thy genius shines brighter and best,

And shows that thou surely will be an adornment to all in the West."

She read on, to the end, right down to "But one clear and bright, perfect day."

Francis had his eyebrow quirked in the old way. "Marvelous!" he exclaimed. "I'm so glad she put in that part about my genius shining through. I wonder whatever prompted Nancy to compose such words of praise to her old uncle?"

"Maybe her own unhappiness ... that marriage to Mr. Livingston was a disaster from the beginning. Perhaps in desperation she was striking out in any direction to bring back moments of past joy. And she did adore you, Francis." Becky folded the poem, setting it under the candlestick on the night table. "As do Cornie and Portia."

Francis was quiet, remembering Shippen House and Philadelphia. They were good memories. He always thought of his sister Alice as she was in those days—such a patient and gracious hostess, she was. How good she'd been to all of them, and how their comings and goings must have exasperated her! It pained him deeply to think of things as they were today for the Shippens—Nancy, miserable and separated from her husband and little daughter; Alice, withdrawn and silent, a recluse; the doctor, living alone for the most part, still arrogant in the old way from all accounts—and Shippen House sold to pay his debts. Only Tom led any semblance of a normal life, and he wasn't in good health. Thomas Lee Shippen, married with two youngsters. How times had changed for all of them. "Isn't it curious, we all start out with the same chances for happiness, yet some of us get the lion's share while others, not enough to gratify a mouse." he said sadly.

"Lion's share of what?" Becky asked.

"Love. You knew what I meant, wench."

"Yes," she admitted, eyes twinkling.

"Then why did you ask?"

"I wanted to hear you say it, darling. I like the way you say *love*. And I'll wager most people would mean wealth or fame if they spoke of chances for happiness."

"Not us, love," he smiled. Was he feeling a little better, he wondered? "You look like love to me, Becky. All our life together I've called you that, but I never stopped to think how very much you look the part."

"Only to you, darling, only to you. To everyone else I am simply a wrinkled old woman with white creeping into her hair."

"Poppycock!" It seeming impossible, but the short effort at conversation had exhausted him. "Read to me now, before the light is gone. I think I should like to lie here and listen to your voice." Closing his eyes, he felt his body go limp.

She began on the first page. They both enjoyed Shakespeare. The sonnets of themselves were melodious—her reading made them more so. The words seemed to fill the room. They penetrated every fiber of his being. "Her voice was ever soft, gentle, and low, an excellent thing in woman." His mind heard and repeated. Over and over the words turned, tumbling and twisting in his thoughts, until magnified by repetition, they absorbed the fabric of his soul. After a while he could no longer concentrate on the meaning. It seemed enough to have the sound surround him. Then a peculiar thing happened. He felt himself becoming one with her voice and filling the room with light and sound. He thought it the most beautiful experience he'd ever had—all that brilliance and loveliness, and the two of them merging together as one with it.

Becky saw that he was asleep. His breathing was shallow, but it sounded measured and peaceful. Two bright fever spots marked his cheeks again. She read on, afraid to stop for fear of disturbing him. Eventually she grew tired, her throat dry and, letting the book drop in her lap, she closed her eyes. She'd just rest a while until the room grew dark. Then Cate would come to feed Francis. She prayed he'd be able to eat tonight. He was grown so thin these past weeks.

An hour passed. Becky's eyelids fluttered. She opened them to find a quilt tucked around her legs and the comforting bulk of Cate, spooning broth into Francis, greeted her awakening.

"Well," he smiled between swallows. "My lady awakes."

"Umm." Becky stretched, stood up and leaned over the bed.

Francis touched her cheek. "Just a minute, Cate." He held off the spoon, wanting to tell Becky of the experience he'd had while she was reading. "It was amazing, nothing short of ... well ... wonderful. Like ..." would she think him foolish? "making love."

Appreciation shone in her tired eyes. "Perhaps we did," she suggested. "Do you suppose?"

He laughed. She hadn't heard him laugh in days. "More broth, Cate. I have a feeling I'm going to need my strength," he teased.

"You heard the master, Cate. He wants to eat. I'm so glad. Darling, while you're occupied, I'll check on the girls."

"Dey in de dinin' room, Miss Becky. Havin' supper. Dey all went on a sleigh ride dis aftahnoon an' come home hungry as young fillies, as your ol' papa would o' said!"

Becky barely made it through the door before another pain gripped her. She descended the stairs by sheer force of will, holding the railing and trying to ignore the tightness in her chest. By the time she reached the bottom, she had it under control. She found Sally, with Portia and Cornelia, whispering around the dining table. "Francis is awake, girls. You needn't whisper. He's eating. Did you have a good time? Cate said you took the sleigh."

They scurried to make a place for her, heaping food on her plate. Becky protested. She really didn't feel very hungry, but seeing their concern she ate to satisfy them. She even let Sally talk her into going straight to bed after supper. She was so tired. So very tired. Sally promised to sit with Francis, and to wake her if his fever went higher.

"You get a good rest, and don't worry about me," Francis told her when she came to kiss him goodnight.

"Goodnight, darling. I'll be so happy when this awful winter is over. I can't remember when it's been so cold, can you? Some days, I swear, it seems we'll never see the flowers again."

He blew her a kiss.

☙

"Cate! Cate, where are you? I've been calling you. Where are you?" His voice was crusty, cantankerous.

Cate sighed, stepping closer to the bed. "I's right here, Marse Frank. An' I sent Zeke fo' de doctor jes' like you tol' me."

For a moment he was confused; his eyes became unfocused. "There's no need to bother the doctor, Cate. Becky's taking good care of me. You know that. Would you ask her when she's finished her knitting if she'd read to me a while?"

The slave stared down at him, her eyes filled with pain. "I done tol' you, Marse Frank, Miss Becky, she done ... pass't on. Two days ago. She ain't never waked up in de mornin'."

Francis returned Cate's stare. Cate had aged, he thought, so that she'd taken to babbling like Old Berth used to do. "Just do as I've said. Get Miss Becky, or I'll have to find her myself," he told her again.

Cate nodded, tears streaming down her cheeks. In the hall she met Portia and gathered the girl to her bosom. "He don' want t' b'lieve it. He jes' don' want t' b'lieve it," she sobbed.

"I know. I know. But he'll have to, Cate. We must all try to stay calm. Tell him again if he asks. Just keep telling him, as gently as you can. But stay calm. He'll have to accept eventually that Tante Becky is gone." Portia's eyes were swollen from crying also, although at the moment they were dry. She really didn't know what to do about Uncle Frank. He seemed to linger a little longer each day in some other world. "The doctor should be here soon, if he can get through the snow. He'll be able to help Master Francis and ... tell us how to arrange for my aunt's burial," Portia said in a tight little voice.

☙

It was late, after midnight, but Francis had no idea what time it was, only that it was dark outside. Someone had told him it was snowing ... and something else ... but he couldn't remember what it was now. The house was quiet so everyone must be asleep. Then he thought he heard a rustle in the hall. Was it Becky? Was she calling him? Struggling, he pulled himself up, managing to get his legs over the side of the bed. Then he heard it again. Someone was calling his name. He wobbled to the door and pulled it open. His knees felt like jelly but he made it to the stairs. Then he saw her ... at almost the same moment he became aware of the familiar scent of jasmine ... he saw her. She waved her hand, beckoning him down. It made him feel the same way it had years ago when she'd summoned him to the garden bench on Nicholson Street—speechless and superbly vulnerable. She'd opened the door to paradise that time, why not again? Yet he hesitated, remembering his illness and that he felt very weak.

"Don't worry, darling. It's wonderful out there. Come, I've found some violets blooming in the snow."

He could restrain himself no longer and summoned his strength. "My God, Becky, you still look beautiful in that green dress. Where have you hidden it all these years? I've not seen it since that ball General Gates threw during the war to thwart Washington and Lafayette."

She smiled, that mischievous grin she knew could turn his heart over. "And to think I almost chose the pink one for this occasion. I declare, Francis Lee, you always were one to flatter a girl, no matter what!"

In the morning Cate found his bed empty. The hollow worn by his body over the years wasn't even warm to the touch. Apprehensive, she shivered, thinking there was finality in the cold bed. In a while, after searching the house, she found his tracks down the back steps. Tightening her shawl around her shoulders, she followed the frozen footsteps down the hillside in the direction of the bower, remembering that a long time ago Marse Frank and Miss Becky used to go there on lazy summer afternoons ... it seemed a *very* long time ago and a far distance as she plodded through the snow.

Suddenly, there he was. He was sitting very still, propped against a tree trunk, a small clump of violets clutched in one hand. His face hinted at the old smile but she knew before she touched him that he couldn't see her. Where in the name of the blessed Lord Jesus had the violets come from? Then, slowly, and without questioning how or why, it came to her.

"Lawsy me. Lawsy me, Marse Frank, you done found Miss Becky jes' like you said. I know you done gone wit Miss Becky fo' sure." At the same time her heart was struck with joy, an awful feeling of desolation came over the slave and, lifting her arms in supplication, a wail escaped her lips. "Lawd, Lawd, what's t' b'come of ol' Cate now? Tell me dat, Lawd. Whatever in de world's ol' Cate goin' do now?"

In a moment the answer came, bounding on the frigid air. "Yoo-hoo! Cate! Where's our breakfast? It's freezing in the house, and the fires have all gone out!" It was Miss Cornelia. "There's no wood!"

How quick the younguns recover, she thought, and come right back to the world at hand. "I's comin', Miss Cornie, I's comin'." She had to hurry. It would never do for them to know about Marse Frank until she got him fixed all proper-like in his bed. That'd keep her busy for a while, Pompey could help. And then tomorrow, or maybe next week even, Sammy'd come to see his old mammy. Was it possible? Whether it was or not, she'd dream about it anyway. Why he might even take her away with him to Philadelphy! If she prayed hard enough.

"Lawsy me," she mumbled, gasping a little after the steep climb up the hill. "It's jes' bout time ol' Cate got a taste o' dat freedom place where Miss Becky done sent Samu'l. Yep, ever'thin's goin' work out jes' fine, Lawd, long's you keep pointin' de way!"

" ... *My poor uncle Frank has paid his last debt to nature, following Mrs. Lee who went a few days before him. I have no doubt but her constant attendance upon him is said to have occasioned the illness which proved fatal to her ... Love to all friends, my dear Mother, last of the Stratford Lees in particular.*"

Letter, Thomas Lee Shippen to his parents
Williamsburg, Jan. 25, 1797

After Notes

At some point in my research I determined that 1768 was the plot's obvious stepping-off point— while Francis Lee courted sixteen-year-old Becky Tayloe to the altar—the Massachusetts legislature was courting her twelve sister-colonies to revolt against British rule. I occasionally found it helpful to take some liberties with historical facts in the opening and as the novel progressed.

For example, neither Richard Henry Lee or Landon Carter are known to have been present in Williamsburg during that March 1768 burgess assembly. Richard's presence in the first chapter, however, enabled me to develop the tenacious relationship between Francis and this older brother in an appropriate setting at a vital time, both politically and personally. For similar reasons the reader is also introduced at this time to Landon Carter, the crusty old lion of Richmond County. A great deal of Francis Lee's extant correspondence is with this uneven tempered, but oddly likable egoist, this revered friend who exerted an enduring influence over him.

The dreaded smallpox disease, rampant in early colonial life, was particularly prevalent during the revolution, both in the military camps as well as throughout the civilian population. I came across some information indicating that the Lees were inoculated against smallpox by Dr. Shippen upon their arrival in Philadelphia. Unlike the vaccination of today, this meant they would have actually suffered a mild case of the disease in order to prevent a life threatening case later. Other accounts suggested they both had mild cases of the disease prior to their arrival in that city. Finding this confusing, I chose my own way to deal with the issue, which may or may not be what actually happened, but it suited my story line.

When the Lees traveled back and forth through Maryland, one has to wonder if they stayed with Becky's sister Elizabeth, Mrs. Edward

Lloyd IV, at Wey House. It seems quite likely that was the case, but a cursory search in Lee and Tayloe family letters around that period revealed no mention of such stop-overs. I decided not to pursue the idea, and allowed my imagination to take over during the times they were in both Annapolis and Baltimore.

I believe that many of those already familiar with the lives of Francis and Becky Lee have wondered, as I have, about their not having had children. It certainly seems to have been of concern to John Tayloe, Becky's father, who didn't want to leave the property to the couple unless they produced an heir. Perhaps there were miscarriages, or it's possible one of them was sterile. Once these "unknowns" began to germinate in my mind, I decided to allow Dr. Richter, the "butcher-surgeon of Long Island" to play the bad guy once again. It also provided an opportunity to elaborate on the real interchange between the Lee and Tayloe families over John Tayloe's will, by following up Becky's fictional encounter with said doctor with the ensuing scene at the courthouse with her father.

For those who care about history, you may be curious about what actually happened in the latter days of the Lees' lives at Menokin. Portia and Cornelia did come to live with them after their mother died (correspondence from William to brother Francis confirms this), as did Becky's sisters, Sally and Jane, when *their* mother died. And Francis *did* almost sell Menokin. In the *William and Mary College Quarterly*, Vol. 20, (I) p. 277, I found a 1796 letter of John James Maund to R. Carter of Nomini, his father-in-law. Maund wrote the following: ". . . *Col. Lee of Menokin moves to Alexandria in two months. I have purchased him out, and shall remove there this fall. I am detained in completing the payment and negotiating the value of the crops, stocks, etc. And now that I shall have all good houses and a well-improved plantation, I do believe I am fixed for the remainder of my life, unless the education of my children should make my removal to a town necessary at a future day. Mrs. Lee says that Col. Lee is exchanging ease for trouble, and I believe she judges right. She has cast every impediment in the way and perhaps even yet she may succeed, and that he may wish to relinquish his bargain. Of this I am certain that a town life will be a misery to Col. Lee ....*" Thus we know that Francis did, indeed, contemplate a move to Alexandria and later, for reasons known only to him, had a change of heart. It seems most likely that Maund was right and Becky changed his mind.

After the deaths of both the Lees in January 1797, Francis's last will and testament, in his own handwriting and dated December 30, 1795, was presented to the court in Richmond County by his nephew and named executor, Ludwell Lee, on February 6, 1797; Mr. Lee was then granted a certificate for obtaining a probate. Later that year, on July 3, 1797, executor Ludwell Lee presented to the court an inventory and appraisement of the Menokin estate totaling £11,165. Then things become interesting. John Tayloe III was no doubt aware of his father's wishes that the property itself return to Tayloe ownership as it was contiguous with their own holdings. Due to the Lees having died within a few days of each other, the settlement of the estate apparently became more complicated, but it appears some deals might have been made. Recorded in the deed books of Richmond County one learns that one-half of the estate passed to Ludwell Lee, while the other half transferred to Becky's siblings—all eight of them—meaning they each inherited 1/16th of the approximate 1,100 acres *"together with all and singular the houses, Dove houses, Barns, Buildings, Stables, yards, Gardens, orchards, lands, Tenements, Meadows, Pastures, Feedings, Commons, Woods, under Woods, Ways, Waters, Watercourses, Fishings, Privaleges, profits, easements . . ."* etc. That made it more than a little complex!

Here's what happened. Ludwell Lee, who was awarded half of the estate (meaning land and structure), sold his half to Henry Lee for £1,000 on January 12, 1799. If, in addition to half of the estate, Ludwell inherited "slaves, cattle, and various possessions," as historian Paul C. Nagel (*The Lees of Virginia,* 1990) suggests, then the selling price sounds fair enough. What happened next? Well, Henry Lee then sold Lee's half to Vincent Redman for £1,100 on February 11, 1799; and Redman sold it to John Tayloe III for £1,100 pounds on February 13, two days later! These deeds of sale were all recorded on April 1, 1799. As to the remaining half of Francis and Becky's Menokin House and estate, well, that took a little longer.

Now that he had Ludwell Lee's half as well as his own 1/16th, John Tayloe had to convince each of his seven sisters (*and* their spouses) to part with their shares. Eventually they all did just that, each selling for

£125, between 1799 and 1800; however the last deed was not recorded in the order books until December 6, 1802. Thus, John Tayloe III came to own the entire Menokin tract, despite Francis Lee's desire that it be his legacy to Richard Henry's second son, Ludwell.

Strangely enough, in 1823, a few years before his death, Tayloe sold the property to one William Boughton—all 1,106 and a quarter acres of it, "with the exception of the Menokin mill and land on the outside of the south enclosure of Menokin," for $4,000. From the executors of Tayloe's estate Boughton later acquired the mill and remainder of the original lands given to Francis and Becky Lee. These transfers of the Menokin property are recorded in the deed books of Richmond County, Virginia. The property continued to change hands a number of times before finally coming under the care of the Menokin Foundation in 1995, as mentioned in the *Author's Note* of this book.

As for Francis and Becky, although originally buried elsewhere, they now rest in the Tayloe cemetery at Mount Airy along with other members of this large family. The cemetery is maintained by Tayloe descendants, and members of the family continue to reside in the beautiful old mansion, Mount Airy, high above the Rappahannock River, built by John II, father of Becky and father-in-law of Francis Lee.

Suzanne Hadfield Semsch

Acknowledgements

In the mid-1970s when I first began this project, there were many people who helped and encouraged me. Some of them are no longer living, and the others may not even remember what they said or did that kept me going in the quest to learn more about Menokin House. I thank them one and all, beginning with the first person I asked to read a draft chapter—Paula Robertson—although her comments and criticism were devastating at the time, they set me on the straight and narrow and brought me down off the mountain of excitement I had climbed and helped me to begin again. Other Northern Neck friends and acquaintances who contributed to my knowledge and desire to learn more about Menokin, were Sophie and Tom Bass for their encouragement and for sharing their knowledge and love for Stratford Hall and the Lee family; Virginia Harris, who arranged with the Omohundro family for permission to visit the site; Marty Taylor, who has helped me in more ways than she can know, especially for reminding me early this year that I had a story worth telling; Mildred and John Boddie at Twiford, who inspired and shared ideas; Dabney and Harriett Wellford at Sabine Hall; Gwynne Tayloe, who walked me down the hill at Mount Airy to see Francis and Becky Lee's gravesites; Pat Pateman and Marty Stanton, my dear friends, who listened to more than they ever wanted to hear about Francis Lightfoot Lee; my son Michael, who ventured into the pitch-dark basement, no flashlight, to discover the wine cellar and later sketch what he had felt with his hands, well enough, so that the Colonial Williamsburg Foundation was able to identify what it was he had found; and to St. Margaret's School where, as director of publications, I learned to limit the adverbs and drop the adjectives. I also want to thank my editor, Laurie Curtin, who has not only been prompt and accurate, but knew how to cheer me up and keep me going when I was discouraged. She is also exceedingly patient and pays amazing attention to detail—thank you, Laurie, for everything. Although he didn't live to see the Menokin story in print, I would be remiss if I didn't acknowledge my husband Philip, who suffered through all those months when I was glued to my KayPro and reference books. He provided understanding, assistance, and guidance throughout my research efforts, never failing to show an interest in reading new chapters as they were completed. He was also the one who convinced me I needed to keep very careful notes so I could create a bibliography—I'm glad I listened. As the novel neared final edit this year, I asked my daughter Kathleen Townsend to read it. History isn't one of her favorites, so I was surprised and pleased when she not only enjoyed it, but said she didn't want it to end, and actually put off reading the last chapter for two days. Thanks to my son-in-law, Norris, who pointed me in the right direction for some of the cover copy, especially the author bio. I thank my entire family (too many to name) for their interest, encouragement, and enthusiasm—you are the best.

Bibliography

THE LEES OF MENOKIN

PRINTED SOURCES

Alexander, Frederick Warren. *Stratford Hall and the Lees Connected with its History.* Oak Grove, VA, 1912.

Armes, Ethel. *Stratford Hall—The Great House of the Lees.* Garrett & Massie, Inc., Richmond, VA, 1936.

Armes, Ethel. *Stratford on the Potomac.* Wm. Alexander Jr. Chapter, United Daughters of Confederacy, Greenwich, CT, 1928.

Armes, Ethel, compiler and editor. *Nancy Shippen—Her Journal Book.* J.B. Lippencott, Philadelphia, 1935.

Bailey, Thomas A. *A Diplomatic History of the American People.* F.S. Crofts & Co., 1946.

Beverley, Robert. *The History and Present State of Virginia.* Edited by Louis B. Morton. Reprint Dominion Books, Charlottesville, VA, 1968.

Ballagh, James Curtis, editor. *The Letters of Richard Henry Lee* (2 volumes). NY, 1912.

Blanton, Wyndham. *Medicine in Virginia in the Eighteenth Century.* Garrett & Massie, Richmond, VA, 1931.

Boatner, Mark M. *Landmarks of the American Revolution.* Hawthorn Books, Inc., NY, 1975.

Bodine, A. Aubrey. *Chesapeake Bay and Tidewater.* Bodine & Associates, Inc., Baltimore, MD, 1967.

Burnett, Edmund Cody. *The Continental Congress.* MacMillan Co., 1941.

Burt, Nathaniel. *First Families—The Making of an American Aristocracy.* Little, Brown and Co., 1970.

Busch, Noel F. *Winter Quarters.* Liveright, NY, 1974.

Campbell, Charles. *History of the Colony and Ancient Dominion of Virginia.* J.B. Lippencott, 1860; reprint: The Reprint Co., Spartanburg, SC, 1965.

Chandler, J.A.C. and Thames, T.B. *Colonial Virginia.* Times-Dispatch Co., Richmond, VA, 1907.

Chitwood, Oliver Perry. *Richard Henry Lee—Statesman of the Revolution.* WVA University Foundation, 1967.

Claiborne, John Herbert. *The Old Virginia Doctor.* Petersburg, VA, 1895.

Commager, Henry Steele and Morris, Richard B., editors. *The Spirit of 'Seventy-Six—The story of the American Revolution as told by participants.* Harper and Row, 1958; reprint 1975.

Davis, Burke. *George Washington and the American Revolution.* Random House, Inc., NY, 1975.

Davis, Richard Beale. *Literature and Society in Early Virginia, 1608-1840.* Louisiana State Univ. Press, Baton Rouge, 1973.

Dowdey, Clifford. *The Golden Age.* Little, Brown and Co., 1970.

Dowdey, Clifford. *The Great Plantation.* Bonanza Books, div. of Crown Pub. Co., by arrangement with Holt, Rinehart & Winston, Inc., 1957.

Earle, Alice Morse. *Home Life in Colonial Days.* MacMillan Co., 1898; reprint 1960.

Eubank, H. Ragland. *Historic Northern Neck of Virginia.* Whittet & Shepperson, Richmond, VA, 1934.

Farish, Hunter Dickinson, editor. *Journal and Letters of Philip Vickers Fithian.* University of VA Press, 1957; reprint Dominion Books, 1968.

Farrar, Emmie Ferguson and Hines, Emilee. *Old Virginia Houses—The Northern Peninsulas.* Hastings House, NY, 1972.

Ferris, Robert G., series editor. *Signers of the Declaration.* U.S. Government Printing Office, 1973.

Fiske, John. *Old Virginia and Her Neighbors* (2 volumes). Houghton, Mifflin Co., 1897 and 1900.

Fitzpatrick, John C., editor. *Diaries of George Washington* (volume II). Riverside Press, Cambridge, MA, 1925.

Foner, Eric. *Tom Paine and Revolutionary America.* Oxford Univ. Press, NY, 1976.

Ford, W.C., editor. *Letters of Joseph Jones of Virginia, 1777-1787.* Arno Press, Inc., 1889; reprint 1971.

Freeman, Douglas Southall. *George Washington* (volumes I and II). Charles Scribner's Sons, 1948.

Garrison, Webb. *Sidelights on the American Revolution.* Abingdon Press, Nashville-New York, 1974.

Greene, Jack P., editor. *The Diary of Landon Carter—1752-1778* (2 volumes). University of VA Press, 1965.

Griffith, Lucille. *Virginia House of Burgesses—1750-1774.* Colonial Press, Northport, AL, 1963.

Hardy, Stella Pickett. *Colonial Families of the Southern States of America.* Genealogical Pub. Co., NY, 1911.

Hendrick, Burton J. *Lees of Virginia.* Cornwall Press, NY, 1935.

Kelley, Joseph J. Jr. *Life and Times in Colonial Philadelphia.* The Stackpole Co., Harrisburg, PA, 1973.

Klein, Randolph Shipley. *Portrait of an Early American Family.* University of PA Press, 1975.

Lancaster, Robert A. *Historic Virginia Homes and Churches.* J.B. Lippencott, 1915.

Langdon, William Chauncy. *Everyday Things in American Life.* Charles Scribner's Sons, NY, 1937.

Lee, Cazenove Gardner Jr. *Lee Chronicle.* Compiled and edited by Dorothy Mills Parker, NY Univ. Press, 1957.

Lee, Edmund Jennings. *Lee of Virginia, Part I, 1642-1892.* Pub. 1895; reprint Baltimore, MD, 1974; Genealogical Pub. Co., Inc., 1983.

Lengyel, Cornel. *Four Days in July.* Doubleday & Co., Inc., Garden City, NY, 1958.

Lomax, Edward Lloyd. *Genealogy of the Virginia Family of Lomax.* Rand, McNally & Co., Chicago, 1913.

Malone, Dumas. *Jefferson The Virginian.* Little, Brown and Co., Boston, 1948.

Mead, Edward C. *Genealogical History of the Lee Family.* 1871.

Meade, Robert Douthat. *Patrick Henry—Patriot in the Making* (volume I). J.B. Lippencott Co., Philadelphia & NY, 1957; reprint 1969.

Morton, Lewis. *Robert Carter of Nomini Hall.* Dominion Books, University of VA Press, reprint 1969.

Nagle, Paul C. *The Lees of Virginia.* Oxford University Press, 1990.

Parrington, Vernon L. *Main Currents in American Thought—The Colonial Mind 1620-1800* (volume I, pp. 183-197). Harcourt, Brace, and World, Inc., 1927.

Randolph, Mary. *The Virginia Housewife or Methodical Cook.* E.H. Butler & Co., Philadelphia, 1860.

Ryland, E. L., editor. *Richmond County, Virginia.* Richmond County Bicentennial Committee, Whittet & Shepperson, Richmond, VA, 1976.

Sack, Albert. *Fine Points of Furniture—Early American.* Crown Publishers, 1950.

Sanderson, John. *Biographies of the Signers of the Declaration of Independence.* Robert T. Conrad, revisor and editor. William Brotherhood, Philadelphia, 1865.

Scheel, Eugene M. *The Guide to Loudoun.* Loudoun County Chamber of Commerce, 1975.

Schriftgiesser, Karl. *Families.* Howell, Soskin, NY, 1940.

Stanard, Mary Newton. *Colonial Virginia—Its People and Customs.* J.B. Lippencott, 1917.

Tayloe, W. Randolph. *The Tayloes of Virginia.* Berryville, VA, 1965.

Tower, Charlemagne Jr. *Marquis de Lafayette in the American Revolution.* Books for Libraries Press, Freeport, NY, 1894; reprint 1971.

Tunis, Edwin. *Colonial Craftsmen and the Beginnings of American Industry.* World Publishing-Times Mirror, NY, 1972.

Umbreit, Kenneth. *Founding Fathers.* Harper and Row, 1941, reissue Kennikat Press, NY, 1969.

Van Schreeven, William J., compiler. Scribner, Robert L., editor. *Revolutionary Virginia—The Road to Independence* (volume I). University of VA Press, 1973.

Wallace, David D. *The Life of Henry Laurens.* G.P. Putnam's Sons, 1915; reprint Russell & Russell, 1967.

Ward, Harry M. and Greer, Harold E. Jr. *Richmond During the Revolution.* University of VA Press, 1977.

Ward, Harry M. *Duty, Honor or Country—General George Weedon and The American Revolution.* The American Philosophical Society, 1979.

Warner, Sam Bass Jr. *The Private City* (pp. 3-45). University of PA Press, 1968.

Waterman, Thomas Tileston. *The Mansions of Virginia 1706-1776.* University of NC Press, Van Rees Press, NY, 1945.

Whitney, Janet. *Abigail Adams.* Little, Brown and Co., 1947.

Williams, Harrison. *Legends of Loudoun.* Garrett & Massie, Richmond, VA, 1938.

Wright, Louis B. *The First Gentlemen of Virginia.* Dominion Books, Charlottesville, VA, reprint 1970.

Wright, T.R.B. *Westmoreland County, Virginia 1653-1912.* Whittet & Shepperson, Richmond, VA, 1912.

NEWSPAPERS (selected readings 1768-1800)

Virginia Gazette and General Advertiser. Richmond, VA.

Republican Citizen. Fredericksburg, VA.

The Virginia Herald and Falmouth Advertiser. Fredericksburg, VA.

Virginia Gazette. Published by Purdie & Dixon, Williamsburg, VA; ibid, published by Rind, Williamsburg, VA; ibid, published by Pinckney, Williamsburg, VA.

MAGAZINES AND PERIODICALS (selected articles)
The Virginia Magazine of History and Biography.
The Annals of the American Academy of Political and Social Science.
The Northern Neck of Virginia Historical Magazine.
William and Mary Quarterly.
Tylers Quarterly Historical and Genealogical Magazine.

BOOKLETS and PAMPHLETS
Cometti, Elizabeth. *Social Life in Virginia During the War for Independence.* Virginia Independence Bicentennial Commission, 1978.

Dill, Alonzo T. and Cheek, Mary Tyler. *A Visit to Stratford and The Story of the Lees.* John D. Lucas Printing Co., Baltimore, MD, 1976.

Dill, Alonzo T. *William Lee—Militia Diplomat.* Virginia Independence Bicentennial Commission, 1976.

Dill, Alonzo T. *Francis Lightfoot Lee—The Incomparable Signer.* Virginia Independence Bicentennial Commission, 1976.

Dill, Alonzo T. *Carter Braxton—Last Virginia Signer.* Virginia Independence Bicentennial Commission, 1976.

Lee, Lucinda. *Journal of a Young Lady of Virginia, 1787.* Whittet & Shepperson, Richmond, VA, 1976.

_____ *Legacy from the Past.* The Colonial Williamsburg Foundation, Williamsburg, VA, reprint 1975.

Matthews, John Carter. *Richard Henry Lee.* Virginia Independence Bicentennial Commission, 1978.

Rutland, Robert A. *George Mason and the War for Independence.* Virginia Independence Bicentennial Commission, 1976.

Riggs, A. R. *The Nine Lives of Arthur Lee—Virginia Patriot.* Virginia Independence Bicentennial Commission, 1976.

Shepherd, Catharine. *A Colonial Belle's Message or My Lady's Toilette Table* (from an 1811 handmade book). C.H. Graves, Philadelphia, 1911.

Selby, John E. *A Chronology of Virginia and the War of Independence 1763-1783.* University of VA Press, 1973.

Templeman, Eleanor Lee. *Virginia Homes of the Lees.* 1975.

_____ *The Lees of Virginia.* Published by the Society of the Lees of Virginia, 1967.

MANUSCRIPTS

Lee Family Papers—1638-1867 (Sect. 112). Virginia Historical Society, Richmond, VA.

Lee, William, Letterbook 1769-1772 (Sect. 113). Virginia Historical Society, Richmond, VA.

Tayloe Family Papers (Sect. 6, 19, 27, 42, 45, and 49, including architectural drawing of Menokin, ca. 1770, Sect. 23). Virginia Historical Society, Richmond, VA.

Lee Transcripts. Lee Family Papers, (6 volumes). Virginia Historical Society, Richmond, VA

Lee Family Papers (microfilm rolls 3-8). Alderman Library, University of VA, Charlottesville, VA.

Lee, Francis Lightfoot, letters of (collection on microfilm). New York Public Library.

Lee, Francis Lightfoot, misc. letters of. Pennsylvania Historical Society.

Shippen Family Papers (collection 1031). Manuscript Div., Library of Congress.

REFERENCE VOLUMES

Hening's Statutes—Being a collection of all the laws of Virginia.

Virginia Colonial Register. Compiled by William G. and Mary Newton Stanard. Joel Munsell's Sons, Albany, NY, 1902.

Journals of the House of Burgesses, 1766-1774. Edited by John Pendleton Kennedy. Richmond, VA, 1906.

The National Cyclopaedia of American Biography (volume V). J.T. White & Co., NY, 1894.

Appleton's Cyclopaedia of American Biography (volume III, D). Appleton & Co., NY, 1887.

Bible Records. Virginia Historical Society.

Encyclopedia of American History. Edited by Richard B. Morris and Henry Steele Commager. Harper and Row, 1970.

Letters of Members of the Continental Congress (Volumes I, II, III, IV, and V) edited by Edmund C. Burnett. Lord Baltimore Press, Baltimore, MD, 1921.

Dictionary of American Biography. Dumas Malone. Charles Scribner's Sons, NY, 1936.

The Registers of North Farnham Parish 1663-1814 and *Lunenburg Parish 1783-1800.* Compiled and published by George H. S. King, Fredericksburg, VA.

Richmond County Deed, Order, and Will Books. Warsaw, VA.

Loudoun County Deed Books. Virginia State Library, Richmond, VA.

About the Author

Suzanne Hadfield Semsch's lifelong interest in writing and literature and her insatiable curiosity inspired her to explore history and complete her debut novel, *The Lees of Menokin*. Raised in a military family and married to a career army officer, she has traveled extensively and lived in Europe and thirteen of the United States. More than half her life, however, has been spent in Virginia. Today, she resides in Charlottesville and considers herself a "Virginian by choice." She  has been writing both personally and professionally for many years, and is currently at work on her next project, a multi-generational saga of an American military family. She may be contacted at suzanne.semsch@gmail.com.

11517848R20410

Made in the USA
Charleston, SC
02 March 2012